Clash

The Arinthian Line: Book Four

SEVER BRONNY

This book is a work of fiction. Names, characters, places and incidents either are the product of the author's imagination or are used fictitiously, and any similarity to actual persons, living or deceased, establishments of any kind, events, or locales is entirely coincidental.

Library and Archives Canada Cataloguing in Publication

Bronny, Sever, 1979-, author
Clash / Sever Bronny.

(The Arinthian line ; bk. 4)

Issued in print and electronic formats.

ISBN 978-0-9937676-6-1 (paperback).—
ISBN 978-0-9937676-7-8 (ebook)

I. Title.

PS8603.R652C53 2016 C813'.6

C2016-901333-2
C2016-901334-0

Version 1.1

Map and cover by author using creative commons and commercial licensing. "Clash" cover font by Steve Deffeyes, deffeyes.com. For information about permission to reproduce certain portions of this work, please contact the author at severbronny@gmail.com or via **www.severbronny.com**

Omnio incipus equa
liberatus corsisi mei

MIDDLE OF NOWHERE

Augum Stone raised his sun-bronzed arm just in time. The powerful jet of water smashed into a hard black lightning shield that had not been there a moment before, pushing him back a step. The shield disappeared from his forearm as soon as the attack was over.

"Your first one was stronger," he said.

Leera Jones raised a sharply arched brow and gave a competitive grin. "The one that knocked you on your butt?"

His eyes narrowed playfully as he paced around her on the rickety wooden platform, initialed by warlocks from ages past. "My turn again. Ready?"

"You have to stop warning me. How am I supposed to learn to sense an attack?"

"Don't want to hurt you."

She waved dismissively. "I can take it. Besides, Mrs. Stone can heal me."

"Is that so?"

"Uh huh."

"She's a thousand leagues away."

Leera smirked. "She's just on the other side of that." She thumbed at the Orb of Orion, resting neatly in their picnic basket amongst bananas, oranges, bread, salted beef, and a skin of water. Mrs. Stone was now tuned to the ancient artifact, allowing her to perform all manner of spells through it.

Augum expelled a long breath while pacing the platform barefoot, contemplating his next move. He kept catching satisfying glimpses of the wavering horizon. Here they were, the only objects amongst an entire blue ocean, practicing spellcraft on a secret Trainer once used by the Academy of Arcane Arts, now abandoned since the Legion took control of the famous institution. In a way, the orb made him feel closer than ever to the institution he would have liked to attend, for it had been gifted to the academy a thousand years ago upon its opening. Not to mention Mrs. Stone had been its headmistress for thirty-five years. How he wished things were different. How he wished they weren't in so much danger.

He placed his hand between his eyes and the hot sun. It was so quiet and peaceful here, so far away from everything—the melting snow, his father, the war.

"Suppose we get stuck here?" he asked. "Then what?"

"Then you better learn how to fish—" Three watery rings instantly flared around her arm as she smacked her palms together. "Annihilo!"

The jet of water caught him unaware, slamming into his chest and easily shoving him off the platform. He heard her giggle as he plummeted to the ocean below, stomach in his throat, soon feeling the hard slap of water on his back.

The salty coolness was refreshing, and he took his time swimming to the ladder.

Her arms were crossed as he stepped back onto the platform. "Was that one strong enough?"

He said nothing, making a show of wringing the water out of his loose lace-up shirt.

"It was a weak shot at least," she added.

True—Augum saw her jet of water smash through a plank board once.

Leera adjusted her pale blouse and wrinkled her nose mischievously. "You're cute and kind of handsome when you're wet."

"Kind of?" Augum surrendered a crooked smile, noting how the sun glinted off the small smattering of freckles on her slightly tanned face, how her raven hair, falling loosely just past her chin, reflected the rays. Thanks to careful nurturing at the Okeke home, the harrowing ordeal in Bahbell had left no physical traces, except for perhaps the slightest hollow shadow in their cheeks.

They were slowly gaining on the prime of their youth. She was a little taller now, as was he. His voice had deepened slightly whereas hers had sweetened, but still maintained its raucous edge. Much to his embarrassment (and her amusement), his occasionally cracked, as if brittle. Both were filling out in places that would make them man and woman. He felt leaner, stronger, sharper. She was more expressive, moodier, and ever cuter.

But the trio had grown together in more ways than one since first meeting in Sparrow's Perch, becoming tight friends … and much more in the case of himself and Leera. The last month of grueling training in the 4th degree, along with their other spells, had hardened them physically and mentally, giving them more confidence. In that time, Mrs. Stone tested them on the 3rd degree, which they passed, earning their third stripe.

Leera had this way of staring unwaveringly at him that made his stomach dance. He did not know if he wanted to push her off the platform or kiss her. He probably would have already kissed her, except the last thing they needed was Mrs. Stone finding out about them. Nana had enough to worry her, especially with his father now possessing five of the seven scions. She was teleporting around Sithesia trying to evade the Legion, while helping Tiberra with the war and training the trio.

"Let's switch to Fear," he said. He needed to stay focused, something he found difficult of late whenever their eyes met.

Her lips pressed in a pout. "Can't we eat already? I'm starved."

"Soon." He raised his arm and pointed his palm at her, focusing on channeling the appropriate arcane energies. Three lightning rings unconsciously crackled to life around his arm while Mrs. Stone's detailed instructions on how to correctly perform the spell echoed through his mind.

"You're taking too long," Leera said. "Could have knocked you off twice already."

"I'm not as good with it as you are yet."

She raised her arm and narrowed her eyes. "Dreadus terrablus."

An anxious feeling swept over Augum like a wave. He felt the prickle of sweat on his forehead. Suddenly the platform seemed very high and he had to sit down. The feeling soon passed though, unlike the time Vion Rames had cast the spell on him—he would never forget that terrifying moment when he thought he had peed himself in front of the girls, not to mention the imagined horrors he had seen.

She bit her lip. "Still weak, isn't it?"

"Made me dizzy at least." He stood up and shook off the tension. "Nana did say there are three stages to these mind altercation spells—"

"—alteration," Leera corrected.

"Whatever. Anyway, there are three stages—the learning stage, the proficiency stage, and the mastery stage."

"I get it, we suck at first, like everything to do with arcanery. You sound like Bridget."

His eyes flicked to the orb. "I'm trying to take this seriously. You should too."

That mischievous look returned. She ran her fingers through her hair and started taking a step back at a time.

"Careful or you're going to—"

"—to what?" Leera's last step was purposefully off the platform and she disappeared. There was a splash a moment later.

Augum strode to the edge. "We should be training!"

"I needed to cool down!" she called from below, treading water. "Get in!"

He grimaced but took a few steps back. "Uh, just going for a quick dip, Nana," he said to the pumpkin-sized Orb of Orion, then ran and jumped off, tucking his legs in before slamming into the water. When he surfaced, Leera swam up to him.

"Wish we could spend a whole day alone here," she said, dark eyes fixed on him.

"You know I want to. We've got to train though." He had never felt more comfortable with anyone, but she was his first girlfriend and he still felt like he was a fumbling fool, a toddler in the ways of women. They had snuck whatever alone time they could since getting back to Milham, yet it never seemed enough.

"You worry too much," Leera said, and swam nearer, until they were smiling at each other nose-to-nose.

Suddenly there was a THWOMP sound above and the two of them hurriedly broke apart. They glanced up to see Mrs. Stone peek over the edge of the platform, an unimpressed look on her ancient face, staff firmly in hand.

Augum and Leera timidly swam back to the ladder and climbed, lining up before her.

"Uh, hi, Nana," Augum said, dripping water. "We were just taking a quick swim."

"Indeed." Mrs. Stone smoothed her opalescent robe. She was stooping, and her face looked more lined than ever. "How goes your work with Reflect?"

"All right I guess," Augum lied, ashamed they hadn't been practicing the rare 6th degree off-the-books spell she had taken great pains to teach them. The spell paired with a prismatic crystal specially carved by an expert arcaneologist, which each of the trio possessed. They had come across the raw crystals deep in the caverns under Bahbell. The problem was the spell was extremely difficult. As much detailed training as they had received, they had yet to successfully cast it even once. It was all about the angle with which one held the crystal, the thoughts of the caster, the timing of the trigger word, and blah, blah, blah. As far as Augum and Leera were concerned, it would only waste precious moments in battle, especially as the spell was sun-tuned, meaning it could only be successfully cast once a day.

"Dramask has fallen," Mrs. Stone said. "King Bimal Pradeep has been put to death. Tiberra is now in Lividius' hands."

Augum had been expecting this piece of news. "What about Erika?" Erika Scarson, that vicious woman who had kept them imprisoned in Evergray tower, and who herself was imprisoned in Tiberra, was probably already free. He pictured her—stupid noisy earrings dangling—joining her nephew and Augum's nemesis, Robin Scarson. Thinking about Mya's murderer was enough to make him shift uncomfortably. He recalled punching Robin's stupid, evil face. That was a good moment. The idiot deserved a worse fate though.

"I would think your main concern would be about the unfortunate citizens of Tiberra, who now must suffer Legion rule."

Augum dropped his eyes. "Of course. Sorry, Nana."

She stared at him for an uncomfortable moment. "You need not worry about Ms. Scarson suddenly showing up. As soon as she arrived in Milham, I ensured she would not have the orientation knowledge necessary to allow her to teleport back."

Augum and Leera breathed a sigh of relief.

Mrs. Stone turned a tired gaze to the flat horizon. "I am afraid there is more. Lividius has found the sixth scion."

Augum and Leera exchanged a dark look. This was something they had feared. Lividius "Sparkstone" Stone, the Lord of the Legion—*and Augum's father*—would now devote all his energies to finding that last scion, the one embedded in Mrs. Stone's staff, the Arinthian scion. Ever since that witch from Ley, Magua, helped him forge a special divining rod that could seek the scions out, his father had been finding them rapidly. And now it was only a matter of time until he found Mrs. Stone.

"He found them so quickly," Leera whispered. "I thought we would have more time."

"As did I," Mrs. Stone said. "As did I …"

"What do we do now, Nana?"

Mrs. Stone turned back to them, raising her chin. The ancient lines in her face were deep and full of weariness. "I have failed to learn how the Agonex works."

Great, more bad news. Augum envisioned the heavy bronze disk with its depictions of skulls and runes. Somehow it was supposed to control Occulus' old army, an army equipped with Dreadnought weapons and armor, an army waiting 1500 years for the call to battle. Except Nana had not figured out a way to control it.

The disk had been one of two triumphs at Bahbell—the other being the destruction of the recipe that would have allowed his father to finish building an ancient arcane gate, a gate that would have simultaneously provided access to the Leyan plane while unleashing the monstrosities of Hell. To a former farm boy, it all still sounded ludicrous and far-fetched.

Mrs. Stone left the staff to arcanely stand on its own and began pacing around the platform, hands behind her back, shoulders heavy as if carrying a great burden. Augum observed thirty-five years of being Headmistress of the Academy of Arcane Arts in his great-grandmother's ambling gait. She was the only living master, and a kingdom's entire hopes rested on those shoulders.

"It has been impossible for me to get into or near the ancient library in Antioc without being pursued by the Legion," she began wearily, "yet I believe there is information about the Agonex there, information that may allow us to control Occulus' army."

"But Mrs. Stone," Leera said, "don't you think Sparkstone would have stripped the army of its weapons and armor by now? It's been over a month."

"I do not. He would consider it a triumph to control the same army the great Occulus created. Not to mention it would be impractical." She circled them once before coming to a stop to face them. "I was rather hoping not to ask this of you, but under the circumstances, I have little choice."

Uh oh. "Ask us what, Nana?"

"I would like you to find your way into the library and uncover what you can about the Agonex."

Augum and Leera gaped.

"The annual Antioc Classic is to be held soon, giving you a perfect opportunity to blend in."

"The warlock tournament?" Leera asked incredulously.

"You will disguise yourselves as *non-participating* knowledge-seeking necrophytes."

Leera's shoulders fell.

"I want only the three of you to go. But you are to be as proficient with the 4th degree as possible."

"We'll do it, Nana. Whatever it takes." Augum wanted to say it sounded fun, but he knew that would not go over well. It was a serious matter. And what was a warlock tournament like? Maybe they'd get a chance to watch some of it …

"I am glad to hear of your resolve—" Mrs. Stone stopped to cough and wheeze. She summoned her staff to her and leaned on it.

Leera took a step forward. "Are you all right, Mrs. Stone?"

Mrs. Stone dabbed at her lips with a cloth. "Worry not of me."

"Is it Cron, Nana?" Augum asked delicately, sharing a worried look with Leera. Annocronomus Tempusari, otherwise known as Cron, was a legendary and ancient spell that allowed the caster to travel back in time a very brief period—only moments, in fact. It was the most powerful battle spell the trio had heard of. Mrs. Stone had been trying to learn it in order to teach it to them. She believed it was the trio's destiny to face the Lord of the Legion armed with the spell. The problem was she refused to speak of her progress. Every time she returned to them, she seemed to age a little bit more, a highly dangerous side effect of the spell. How much more aging could she take? Sure, the scion was obviously helping to keep her alive, but this couldn't possibly go on much longer, especially considering she was being chased by the Legion.

"Mrs. Stone, is there anyone else who can learn the spell on your behalf and teach it to us?" Leera asked.

Mrs. Stone gave a derisive grunt, cloth pressed to her mouth. "Mercy, child, such a spell cannot be trusted to any other warlock in this grave time." She kept her eyes closed as she spoke, but put the cloth away. "Do not fear Cron is beyond my strength, for conviction alone shall see me through. I have dreamed of mastering such a spell for a long, long time. And mastery … mastery always has a price. Yes, it may be the end of me, but we must all make sacrifices. Your time, I dare say, will come. When I am ready, you will learn the spell, for one of my challenges is making it palatable for you." She wagged a finger. "But not before. Not before …"

She straightened a little. "In the meantime, you must keep training, and you must train harder than you have ever trained before." Her brows furrowed hawk-like. "You *must* apply yourselves. Do you understand?"

"Yes, Mrs. Stone," Augum and Leera chorused, swallowing.

Mrs. Stone glanced at the flat and distant ocean horizon, whispering, "For time is most precious, most precious indeed …" Then she turned back to them, clearing her throat. "Mr. Harvus is expecting you back in Milham when you finish here."

Augum and Leera groaned simultaneously. Both hated training with Harvus, who had the sense of humor of a bullfrog. He looked like one too—a pale, sickly bullfrog with a blonde hairpiece once probably belonging to some unfortunate minstrel. Mrs. Stone had hired the warlock before they departed for Bahbell to train Haylee and Jengo. The man constantly got on the trio's nerves with his particular ways and constant nagging, but because Mrs. Stone ordered it, they had to do as he asked. And the more time Mrs. Stone spent away, the worse the man seemed to become. Maybe they could find a way to train on their own tonight …

"Can't you come and train us again, Mrs. Stone?" Leera whined. "Mr. Harvus is just so … annoying."

"And his breath stinks like rot," Augum added. More like sewage.

"You are perfectly aware that it is dangerous for me to remain in one place for too long. And I will not place

Milham in any more danger than necessary. Mr. Harvus is more than adequate for the job. I will not suffer another word on the matter. You shall obey him as you do me, is that understood?"

"Yes, Mrs. Stone," Augum and Leera chorused blandly.

"And you will practice the Reflect spell until you have it mastered."

"Yes, Mrs. Stone."

Mrs. Stone shook her head, muttering, "Merciful spirits give me patience."

Augum had the impression she would have lambasted them for not working hard enough with the spell—if she hadn't been so tired.

"Bridget, Haylee and Jengo have already begun today's lesson with Mr. Harvus. You are to have your lunch and join them. Inform me when you are ready to return."

"Yes, Mrs. Stone."

She frowned before teleporting away with a THWOMP.

Leera slumped down beside the basket and fished out a banana. "You'd think Harvus would be more worried about his city falling to the Legion."

Augum scoffed as he sat beside her. The stumpy Tiberran hardly cared about trivial things like family, or being a good citizen. All he cared about was money and looking clean—the man utterly despised dirt.

"Still can't believe he had us wash the outside of the cabin," Augum said, recalling two tendays back when Harvus suddenly declared the entire facade of the Okeke home contaminated because a bird had pooped on it.

"And he didn't even lift a finger to help," Leera added. "Sat on his rump picking at those stupid white cotton gloves of his." She squeezed her hands together, strangling thin air.

"Not true, he did point out all the spots you missed. Helped a lot."

Leera smirked. "I swear that one day I'm going to steal that awful hairpiece of his and dump it into a washbasin of filthy water. And I *know* I'm not the only one who thinks it looks like a horse's—"

"Then you better make sure you're leagues away when he finds out." There were two things Harvus could not stand—dirt, and anyone drawing attention to his hairpiece. But complaining about Harvus to Mrs. Stone did little, for she had apparently taken up the position that he was good for them somehow, though Augum thought it might be the eat-your-vegetables kind of good. In any case, Augum, Leera, Haylee and Jengo certainly made a sport of griping about the man.

Bridget was Harvus' favorite, probably because she was the only one never to talk back to him, though she did crack up when Leera told her what she thought of his hairpiece. Nonetheless, Bridget had promptly declared that a truly awful thing to say and made Leera promise never to repeat it within earshot, a promise Leera crept around with winks or sly grins every time she noticed Harvus carefully adjusting his hairpiece. It never ceased to draw a smile from Augum, who occasionally had to suffer a silencing look from Bridget for encouraging Leera's rebelliousness.

Leera shoved a banana at him. "Eat it. It's not like you get to have one often." She watched him dully peel back the skin. "You have that worried look on your face again."

"What look?"

"This look." She made an overly serious face.

"That bad, huh?"

"I know what you're thinking, and Mrs. Stone'll be fine. She's always fine."

"Not always." He recalled the time Nana had pushed her arcane boundaries almost to the point of death, falling prey to arcane fever. Now she was obviously struggling with a spell that might be the death of her—one she expected them to learn, and they were only 3rd degree! They couldn't even nail Reflect, a 6th degree spell. Cron was what … at least 10th, probably higher. For whatever reason, Nana refused to share even that little detail about the spell.

Leera sighed, finished her banana and tossed the peel into the water. "I know, all of Sithesia is about to burn, and here we are having a banana in the middle of the ocean. I get it, I do. But you know what?"

"What?" he said, catching a witty look in her eyes.

"It doesn't matter, because that was a great birthday you had."

"It was, wasn't it?"

"You wearing it?"

"'Course I'm wearing it." He reached down his shirt and pulled out a thin chain on which hung several tiny medallions, each commissioned by a friend.

"Means a lot to me," he said, examining each of the medallions while finishing his banana. The one from Mr. Goss and Leland depicted a warlock with a lit palm. Jengo and Mr. Okeke's showed three stripes, in honor of Augum achieving his 3rd degree. Haylee and Chaska's showed a flock of harpies and a mountain, commemorating their battle with the creatures in the Muranians. Mrs. Stone's depicted a book, while Bridget and Leera's had three interlocking hands symbolizing the strength of their friendship.

Leera eyed the banana. "Yeah, looks it too."

"What, I can be hungry!"

She playfully stabbed his chest with each word. "It. Never. Comes. Off."

"You know it won't. I'll be buried with it."

Her head bobbed in a satisfied way. "I personally liked the cake the most."

"You mean the towering monolith?"

"It was supposed to look like Evergray Tower!"

"More like one of the Spikes," he muttered.

"Hey, I spent ages on it!" She punched his shoulder.

He raised a brow at her. "You know I was jesting."

"I know. I wanted to punch you anyway. All right, fine, if it wasn't the food, what did you like most—the games? The singing? Jengo accidentally lighting his robe on fire and screaming that he'd been attacked by a warlock?"

"You know what I liked most."

"I have a sneaking suspicion I do."

He glanced furtively at the orb, wishing they were alone so he could repeat that moment. He thought of it often, when they both happened to be outside the Okeke cabin and she suddenly yanked him behind a nearby tree, giving him a tender birthday kiss.

"But seriously, you've got to stop worrying so much. She's the legendary Anna Atticus Stone. She'll be fine."

That instantly brought his worries crashing back. "Then why does she look so worried?" He stood up and began pacing, tucking the necklace away. "My father has six scions, Leera, *six*." He whipped the banana peel into the ocean. "Now that Tiberra is his, guess what he's going to devote all his time to?"

She squinted against the sun. "You're going to say something obvious, aren't you?"

"He's going to hunt for Nana, and that's *all*. He wants that seventh scion. He wants the family heirloom, and he's not going to stop until he gets it."

Leera made an impatient noise. "That's why we're training so hard."

Augum felt his blood rising. "We're only 3rd degree! What, you think we're going to defeat my father, the Lord of the Legion—a 20th degree warlock—all by ourselves? Are you crazy? This *whole plan* is crazy. And learning some stupid Reflect spell isn't going to make a spit of difference."

Leera stood. "What's gotten into you?"

The anguished look on her face made him flush with shame. What *had* gotten into him? He slumped on the edge of the platform and began putting on his turnshoes. "I guess I'm just worried—I'm worried for Nana, I'm worried we'll get everyone around us killed, I'm worried about you and Bridget, and I'm—" He stopped short of voicing his greatest recent fear—Cron. The aging thing. How will it affect them?

She placed a hand on his shoulder, giving it a light squeeze. "And you worry too much, especially recently. You only just turned fifteen, not even a man yet."

"Not even a man yet. *Exactly*. Thanks for reminding me." He shrugged her hand away, immediately regretting it.

"Aug, really, you can be so … ugh." She roughly put on her turnshoes and snatched the basket, leaning into the orb. "Ready, Mrs. Stone."

Augum paced over and rested his palm beside hers on the orb. He tried giving her an apologetic look but she would not meet his gaze. A moment later, he felt his body yank.

MR. HARVUS

Back at the Okeke home in Milham, Augum took a seat by the fire to dry his clothes and calm his stomach. Teleporting felt like being stretched on a torture rack—he always feared he would pop into existence torn limb from limb.

"How did it go?" Mr. Goss absently asked from the table, pushing round spectacles up his nose.

Leera shrugged. "Tedious," and slumped on the floor beside Augum, still refusing to meet his gaze.

"Has Mrs. Stone told you about Dramask?" Mr. Goss pressed.

"Yes, it's awful, isn't it?" While she and Mr. Goss bantered about the news, Augum glanced through the window. The snow had almost completely melted away. He could hear the trickle of water, the chirp of birds, and the distant singing of rowdy miners having a drink. The sun was only an hour or so from setting, telling him wherever the Trainer platform was had to be very far away indeed.

His mind kept going over what he had said. Why had he been rude to Leera? What had gotten into him? He'd noticed he'd been running short of patience lately, which was affecting his concentration, and therefore his training. Was it the pressure? Was it his relationship with Leera, his inexperience, his clumsiness? Or was it something else, something he did not understand yet?

Leera casually punched him on the shoulder when referring to him in a story to Mr. Goss, a gesture Augum translated as, *I forgive you but you're still a jerk.* He smiled apologetically at her. She gave a wry smile back and continued conversing with Mr. Goss. She was so understanding, so forgiving. It warmed his heart.

Augum was trying to absorb the peace of the fire when the door swung open and in zoomed Jengo Okeke, a very tall ebony-skinned Sierran boy with short, curly black hair, wearing a burgundy apprentice robe under a coat too warm for the weather. He began speaking in a rapid and nervous manner while flinging off his muddy boots.

"Have you heard? Dramask has fallen, we're done for—"

"Yes, we heard, Jengo," Leera said patiently.

"Harvus told us in the forest." Jengo floated over to the table and slumped down beside Mr. Goss. "How long do you think we have? A month? A day?" His eyes zipped about as his voice dropped to a whisper. "Or do you think we're down to hours?"

"Maybe you should take your coat off," Leera said.

"Coat … right." He scrambled to take it off at the table, then seemed to realize he should do it standing up.

"How's Haylee doing?" Augum asked. She had been training with them, but her leg was inhibiting her concentration. She had broken it during a life-and-death struggle facing harpies on a high mountain ridge.

Unfortunately for her, even with the help of a healer, it hadn't healed correctly, and so she walked around with a pronounced limp.

Jengo finally managed to fight the coat off and hung it up by the door. "Frustrated as always. She hates that cane."

"Pretty sure that's not all she hates," Leera muttered, referring to the fact Haylee was not getting along with Harvus at all, not to mention Ms. Singh. Harvus constantly made comments about Chaska, somehow taking Haylee's courtship with him personally. Luckily, after moving in to the Singh household, Haylee had found a bosom buddy in Priya. Priya, engaged to be married to Jengo, enjoyed snickering with Haylee about boys and their daft ways, which only gave more ammo to the wretchedly particular Ms. Singh, who already resented having a "pasty and crippled Solian" living under her roof, although perhaps not as much as she hated seeing her precious daughter frolicking about with "that gangly Sierran demon", Jengo.

The door opened and in strode Bridget Burns wearing a royal blue robe tied at the waist with a golden rope, her long cinnamon hair swinging in a tight ponytail. Leland Goss clung to her hand, his face one giant scar from being melted by Sparkstone's lightning. The boy was blind and mute but managed to crack a grin which dimpled his one good cheek.

"Hello everyone," Bridget said with a tired smile as she led Leland to his father.

Just as Jengo closed the door, a stubby gloved hand snuck through, jamming itself between the frame and door. "If you please," said a stout man with the perfunctory and bland expression of a teacher long tired of his profession. His potbelly was so large he appeared to be with child. He wore an immaculate cream-colored robe fringed with silver. A ridiculous blonde hairpiece sat perched on his head like a sad bird of prey. Augum once made the mistake of asking Mr. Harvus about it, only to suffer "detention", which out in the woods apparently meant digging a latrine hole.

"Sorry, Mr. Harvus, didn't see you there," Jengo said. He turned to Bridget. "Where's Haylee?"

Bridget rubbed the tiredness from her hazel eyes. "Snuck off to Priya's, I presume." She hadn't been sleeping too well lately, and it showed. Her face was tighter than usual, eyes puffy. Her pert nose was still red from a cold she had recently gotten over, and there were stray hairs poking out from her ponytail.

"Wonder why," Leera muttered sarcastically to Augum. Haylee avoided being in the same room with Harvus at all costs. If he hadn't been the only mentor around, she would have long ago stopped taking his stupid lessons, lessons paid for by Mrs. Stone.

"But none of that matters anymore because we'll all be dead soon," Jengo said in mock cheer. "Have you heard what the Legion are doing to Sierrans? They cook us alive."

"That's the Occi," Leera said, referring to the undead cannibals the trio encountered back at Bahbell, "and they do that to everyone."

Augum refrained from saying what he, Bridget and Leera surely had to be thinking—the Legion might not eat people, but they do *burn* them alive.

"Hello, Leopold, how did the lessons go?" Mr. Goss asked with a dimpled smile, placing his son on his knee.

Mr. Harvus' lips pressed into a parchment-thin line. "Splendidly, Mr. Goss," he replied without a trace of sincerity. Augum knew the man hated being addressed by his first name, always preferring to keep things "proper" and "civilized".

"Jengo, place your boots together, young man," Harvus said, gloved hands folded together. "It dishonors your father's home."

"Yes, Mr. Harvus, sorry Mr. Harvus." Jengo haphazardly rearranged his boots and scampered out of the stubby man's way.

Mr. Harvus made a tut-tut sound with his teeth and opened his palm. The boots arcanely arranged themselves into neatness. He then proceeded to do the same to everyone else's boots. After finishing, he gave the lightest adjustment to his hairpiece. Leera immediately winked at Augum, who had to look away to avoid cracking up.

"I am sorry to hear about your hometown, Leopold," Mr. Goss continued. "Most tragic news."

Harvus smoothed his robe underneath his legs as he took a seat in one of the rustic armchairs. "If you will forgive me, Mr. Goss, I have always found that city to be a rotten, stinking hovel infested by rats. I can only thank the Unnameables that it is not, nor ever was, my hometown."

"Oh, I see. But surely you have family—"

Harvus got up, dusted off the chair, and sat down again. "I have no one, Mr. Goss. My family perished in the necrotic plague. I grew up desperately poor and had to work very hard for everything."

"I am sorry to hear that, Leopold."

"Life is struggle and hard work."

After a thoughtful silence, Augum's curiosity got the best of him. "So if you're not from Dramask, Mr. Harvus, then where are you from?"

Harvus' eyes took in Augum's wet attire in one practiced movement of displeasure. "My dear boy, why are you soaked? Get changed immediately."

"But I'm fine by the fire, Mr. Harvus, it was just the ocean Trainer again—"

"You will get changed, Augum Stone." His voice was deadly soft.

If Harvus had not been an accomplished warlock, Augum would have told him to stuff it. Instead, he yanked his new robe off the chair and strode into Jengo's room, closing the door. He could not believe Mrs. Stone put so much stock in the man.

"He lacks a proper father figure, it is plain as day," Augum heard Harvus say through the door. "Now, to answer the uncouth young man's question, I am from Canterra, the cleanest and most civilized kingdom in Sithesia. In Canterra, savages are slaves, women know their place, and men are genteel bastions of honor."

" 'Women know their place'?" Leera said. "What does that mean?"

"That means, young lady, that women know the Unnameables put them on Sithesia for three reasons—to keep a clean house, to entertain, and to serve their men."

"The Canterrans have different beliefs than us Solians, Leera," Bridget said, coming to Mr. Harvus' defense as usual.

Leera made a disgusted noise. "Does Mrs. Stone know you're Canterran?"

"You shall refer to me as *Mr. Harvus.* And the venerable Mrs. Stone had not inquired on the matter of my birth before my employment. Prudently, she did not see it as relevant, and nor do I."

"Why did you get kicked out of that kingdom then, *Mr. Harvus*?"

"*Leera—*" Bridget said in scandalized tones.

Augum suppressed a laugh while getting dressed, wishing he could see the look on Harvus' face.

"Mind your tongue, young Leera Jones. And I was not 'kicked out' as you say, I was forced to leave, a marked difference. You see, Canterrans unfortunately perceive warlocks as ... heretical witches. It is one of a thankfully small handful of failings in Canterran class and culture."

Augum finished changing into his new royal blue robe, signifying he had attained his 3rd degree, and returned to the living room. Mr. Harvus inspected him from head to toe and gave the slightest nod of approval.

"Now hang them up properly, young man," Harvus said.

Out of spite, Augum took his time fiddling with his wet clothes by the fire.

"Dear me, Leopold," Mr. Goss said, returning to the topic at hand. "How did you become a warlock in a kingdom so unforgiving with arcanery?"

"Well, they do have an ancient academy, but it is in disrepair and underfunded. Nor is attendance encouraged." Harvus crossed one leg over the other and placed his hands on his knee. "But that is aside the point. I survived Canterra with great risk, sacrifice and secrecy. I scraped and scavenged and begged for every copper I could to pay for a mentor, a mentor who proved harsh and bitter and angry." He stared distantly as if seeing painful memories come alive, before blinking rapidly and continuing. "Regardless, I managed to finish my training, vowing to never be poor again."

"Is it really that dangerous to be a warlock in Canterra?" Bridget asked.

"I assure you it is, my dear. My mentor ended up getting betrayed to a gang of witch hunters just after I finished my studies with him, forcing me to flee." He cleared his throat lightly, quickly adding, "but otherwise it is the finest kingdom in Sithesia. Unlike Tiberra, with its rowdy, disheveled and dirty people."

"But Tiberra is a very different culture from Canterra, Leopold," Mr. Goss rebutted. "Tiberrans are naturally loud and messy and colorful, with great big hearts that fill the size of a room."

"Then perhaps they should use those hearts to hire street cleaners. I find them simply disgusting." His eyes flicked to Leera, as if she reminded him of those streets. "Young lady, are you sitting on that filthy floor wet as an autumn dog?"

"Fine, I'll get changed," Leera said. She snatched her new blue robe before striding to Jengo's room.

Augum gave her a *You got into trouble too* expression as she passed, recalling how Leera once tried standing up to Mr. Harvus only to be run over by a barrage of phrases like, "What an absurd and immature thing to say!" and "You will regret speaking to me in such a manner, young lady." Mr. Harvus then proceeded to have Leera, a nearly fifteen-year-old girl and almost a lady, stand in a corner with soap arcanely stuck in her mouth. The man managed to make even Mrs. Stone look lenient.

"Bridget did very well today," Harvus went on. "She reduced Jengo to a puddle of confusion and fear in back-to-back castings." He gazed fondly at Bridget as if she were his very own daughter.

"Jengo did very well too, Mr. Harvus," Bridget said.

Harvus barely attempted a smile. "I am sure he did."

The door opened and in walked Kwabe Okeke, Jengo's father, wearing a gold and scarlet tunic. "Greetings, everyone," he said with a slight Sierran accent, flashing a tired but genuine smile that disappeared the moment he laid eyes on Mr. Harvus. It was no secret Mr. Okeke did not like Harvus, though he would never outright say so.

"You're home early, Father," Jengo said, standing to take his father's coat, a practice he had begun since his father consented to Jengo marrying Priya.

Mr. Okeke's thick brows gathered with worry. "I closed the mine early. The news of Dramask hit the men hard."

"Can we afford that, Father?"

"There are more important things than money, Son. Some of the men have family in Dramask and departed immediately. None of them believed the city would fall."

"Well you certainly tried warning them, Father. I told them the place would burn to the ground. In fact, I forecasted it three tendays ago."

"You also said Antioc would get swallowed up by a giant earthquake," Leera added dryly, returning to the room wearing her new robe, "and that Blackhaven would get annihilated by a comet, and—"

"Yes but this is different—"

"Because you finally guessed right?"

Jengo sighed. "I should see how Haylee, Priya, and her mother are doing. They must be in an awful state at the news." He put on his boots and coat before leaving.

Bridget pursed her lips at Leera.

Leera shrugged. "I'll apologize later. Anyway, too bad you're scared of heights, Bridge, the platform has a heck of a view."

"I'm sure it's the *view* you were looking at the entire time."

"Oh, I almost forgot, Bridge—" Augum quickly interrupted as Leera turned a bright shade of pink. "Nana has a big quest for us."

Bridget took a seat at the table. Mr. Goss gently handed her Leland, as he often did, perhaps enjoying seeing him being so loved. She placed him on her lap with a cooing smile. The blind boy had a tight hold on the Agonex, which looked giant in his tiny hands. He constantly held on to it these days, and always seemed to know where it was. Mr. Goss was at first greatly worried about him handling it—until Mrs. Stone had a private word. Leera theorized she was hoping it would unlock some hidden potential in the boy, something Bridget found utterly preposterous, claiming such an ancient artifact needed no end of complex training to use.

Harvus frowned at the Agonex. Augum had overheard the man privately make his opinion clear to Mrs. Stone how inappropriate it was placing an artifact of such import in a "blind and unfortunately daft" boy's possession, but she had dismissed his worries with a terse but quiet reproval Augum wished he had heard.

Bridget smiled at Leland as he squealed from the bouncing he was receiving on her knee. "A quest?" she asked. "What kind of quest? Must be serious."

Augum turned over his wet shirt by the fire. "It is, but we can't go on it until she thinks we know what we're doing with the 4th degree."

"Not to mention the Reflect spell," Leera added with a tired groan.

Mr. Harvus straightened in his chair. "Why have I not been informed of any of this? What sort of quest?"

Augum ignored Harvus, well knowing how much it would infuriate him. "Nana wants the three of us to go to the library of Antioc," he said to Bridget. "We're to do it during the warlock tournament there, wearing a necrophyte disguise to blend in."

"Preposterous—surely that is not what she meant," Harvus said, looking to Mr. Goss and Mr. Okeke for support, but both were fixated on Augum.

Mr. Okeke rubbed his gray-streaked beard with a veined and bony hand. His dark skin tightened with each tug. "Mrs. Stone has a lot of faith in the three of you."

Mr. Goss pushed on his spectacles. "Oh my, this quest sounds frightfully dangerous."

Augum shrugged. "Can't be more dangerous than Occulus' castle."

"Mind your manners when speaking to an elder, Augum Stone," Harvus said.

"Yes, sir." Augum could barely conceal the contempt in his voice.

Leland moaned.

"I'm afraid you can't come along on this one," Bridget whispered into the boy's mangled ear, giving him a light cuddle.

"Well I insist on having a word on the matter with Mrs. Stone," Harvus said, standing. "Hardly a fitting venture for children."

Augum felt his blood quicken. He hated to be called a child. But he chose to ignore the remark. "Mrs. Stone says she failed to understand the Agonex," he said. The room stilled. He knew what they were thinking—if the legendary Anna Atticus Stone couldn't figure out how to use it, what hope had they?

"That's not all." Augum turned his wet trousers over on the mantle, keeping his back to them. "Sparkstone found the sixth scion."

There were audible gasps. He knew this news was almost graver than Dramask falling. Even Harvus took a seat again.

"Oh my." Mr. Goss absently took Leland from Bridget and began rocking him slowly on his lap. "Oh my …"

Bridget got up to pace, as was her habit. "What will Mrs. Stone do?"

Augum played with the golden rope around his waist. "Don't know. She seems pretty bent on learning … *that spell*." It also infuriated Harvus whenever they referred to Cron, the secret spell no one but the inner circle was to know about. Mr. Okeke, Mr. Goss—even Leland—knew about Annocronomus Tempusari. But not Harvus. Leera was particularly deft at torturing the man with this, sneaking in a reference to Cron whenever she thought she could get away with it. None of this has endeared them to Harvus. And lately, the rift has only been widening.

Bridget kept pacing. "They're going to throw everything at her now. She can't run forever. And with her pushing herself so hard lately …"

"That's why we *must* succeed," Augum said. Especially with training, if they were to have any hope of learning Cron later.

Mr. Harvus stood in a huff. "This is unacceptable. Children doing the work of soldiers. Where is the orb? I shall have a word with Mrs. Stone immediately." Before any of them could answer, Harvus' eyes found the basket and he strode over, picked up the Orb of Orion, and headed to Mr. Okeke's room, slamming the door behind him.

" 'Soldiers'?" Augum said to Leera. "From what army?" There was no organized resistance against the Legion, at least none that they knew of. Everyone's hopes pretty much rested on Mrs. Stone.

Leera acknowledged the point with a nod while sneaking over to the door. "This should be fun," she whispered.

"Leera Jones, get away from there," Bridget hissed.

Leera shrugged and stepped away. "Whatever, guess we'll know soon enough how it went down."

The door opened again. "Excuse me, how does one work this thing?"

"I'll help, Mr. Harvus," Bridget volunteered, and disappeared into the room with him.

Mr. Okeke filled a large copper kettle with water and placed it over the fire. "Mrs. Stone believes this … undead army … powerful enough to stop your father?"

"I guess so, Mr. Okeke," Augum replied.

"It's Occulus' army, Kwabe," Mr. Goss said, "armed with Dreadnought weapons and armor. From Augum's earlier descriptions, it sounds like there are thousands of them."

"Tens of thousands, Mr. Goss," Leera said. "If not more. Occulus used to teleport them right into the heart of a city, using the Agonex."

Mr. Goss swallowed. "Perhaps it would be best if we all hid in the country."

"I will not leave my son, Albert." Mr. Okeke removed his tunic and folded it onto a chair, straightening his silk shirt. "Jengo would never leave without Priya, and Priya would never leave without her mother."

"We all know what might happen if my father discovers us here," Augum said, referring to one of the darkest days in his life, the day his father slaughtered an entire village before his eyes. Leland and Mr. Goss were one of only a handful that had survived that day—and Leland only barely so. His father had murdered Mr. Goss' wife, Bridget and Leera's parents, and all their friends and relatives. That infamous day, Augum gained a great-grandmother and a father while his friends lost everyone.

Standing there in the Okeke home staring at the hearth, Augum once again saw the flames of Sparrow's Perch and Willowbrook leaping tall into the night sky. Then he saw Mya's throat being cut by his nemesis—a *boy his age!*—and had to shake the thoughts away. He could not change the past, though his worst nightmare now was the same thing happening to Leera or Bridget.

He glanced at Leera, only to find her gazing at him with—was it fear, bittersweet affection, or both? He broke the gaze, cursing himself for liking her so much, wanting to spend so much time with her. What kind of danger was he putting them all in? His father did not care one spit about anyone here—all he wanted was Augum, and that was only because through Augum, he could get the scion.

And who could save them? When not spending precious few moments with them training, Nana was constantly on the run. Now she was even asking the trio for help with a dangerous quest! And Sparkstone's armies surely were only increasing in strength. He had to agree with Mr. Goss. If he had it his way, he'd evacuate the entire village of Milham.

Feeling the world closing in on him, Augum had to take a breath.

After a hushed conversation, Bridget and Mr. Harvus emerged from the room, the latter as pale as a sheet.

"It seems there is no changing the great archmage's mind," Harvus said, numbly handing the orb over to Bridget. He slumped back into the armchair, hairpiece slightly askew.

"It's late, I know," Bridget said, placing the orb into the basket, "but I think we should study a bit. You two up to it?"

"Definitely," Augum replied.

Leera flashed Augum a mischievous smile. "It was polite of Mrs. Stone to stop practicing *the spell* to talk to you, Mr. Harvus. Guess we got some work to do now that the quest is on. "

A FOOLISH ATTEMPT

It was dusk when the trio set out.

"Shall we snag Haylee?" Leera said.

Augum nodded, admiring how far Leera and Haylee had come together since rescuing Haylee from the Legion. They weren't exactly best friends, but Leera no longer went out of her way to needle Haylee, an accomplishment in itself. Haylee, for her part, had developed a grudging respect for Leera, even occasionally asking for advice on arcane matters.

The Singh home was at the far end of the village, shaded under large pines. It was a two-story affair made of brick and mortar, with ornately carved shutters in the curving Tiberran style.

Bridget was about to knock on the door when they heard shouting from within.

"The one-legged witchling will not pick Panjita's flower petals while reciting some heathen verse!"

"Mother, stop it!" It was Panjita Singh's daughter, Priya, and she sounded exasperated. "That's a flower Chaska gave her. It's *her* flower."

"While things are inside this home, they belong to Panjita. Things will be respected, especially living things. And Priya will not speak to her own mother in such a scandalously callous way. This is Panjita's home, and if witless bags of earwax cannot fathom such a simple concept, they can find another home to drool in. And how many times must Panjita insist on not hearing that grotesquely inflated savage's name! They'll see him from Blackhaven if he gets any larger—"

"He is *not* a savage!" Haylee cried.

Leera snickered, whispering, "But he is kind of … fat."

"*Leera Jones*," Bridget said.

"That's two in the space of an hour. Come on, admit it, Bridge, Chaska's widened a step or two. It's not like it's hard to spot."

"You're incorrigible, Leera, really."

"That *was* pretty mean," Augum had to add.

Leera crossed her arms. "You two are no fun."

Augum sighed. Not too long ago, Chaska was beefy strong. Now, he had filled out, even grown a belly. Augum suspected it was a number of factors, not that they were any of his business—Chaska was struggling with the stress of living with his father even though Henawa culture dictated he should be living on his own now that he had completed his nemana, a spiritual quest signifying his ascent to adulthood. It did not help matters that his father did not approve of Haylee in the least, insisting Chaska find a proper Henawa woman.

For Chaska's part, it also wasn't easy being in love with someone like Haylee, who tended to go on about buying a giant house with servants, or dressing in fancy clothes, or obsessing about getting revenge on Robin, something she insisted a decent man would do for her. And then there was her leg, which she constantly complained about.

"Not true at all, Ms. Singh!" Haylee went on within the house. "He is a sweet, caring—"

"Maybe we should go," Bridget said.

Augum rapped at the door loudly. "Nonsense, we need to save her."

Leera rolled her eyes. "Here it comes."

"Who is the imbecile knocking at Panjita's door at this frightfully late hour! It better not be the son of that dastardly devil! WHY IS THAT GANGLY DEMON OF AN UNSUITABLE REACHING FOR THE DOOR AS IF HE OWNED THE PLACE—"

The door yanked open, revealing a flushed Jengo. "Uh, sorry, bit of, well, you know—"

"You two want to come train?" Augum asked as if nothing untoward was going on within. He had grown up with so much chaos at the Penderson farm this drama was minor in comparison.

"I'd love to, but, uh, I'm going to stay inside and try to comfort Ms. Singh. She's a little upset about Tiberra falling to the Legion."

"Good luck with that," Leera muttered.

"I'm game," Haylee said through gritted teeth, swiftly hobbling by with a cane, already wearing her burgundy apprentice robe. She was used to training late with them and had probably expected their arrival.

"Good luck, you four," Jengo said, gently closing the door as Ms. Singh began shouting about Jengo trying to engulf her house with his evil "unsuitable" presence.

"You all right?" Bridget asked as they walked.

"Believe her nerve," Haylee muttered to herself, sweeping aside long locks of blonde hair. "The stuff I have to put up with. And this stupid leg ... ugh." Her round face was chronically pale these days from trying to avoid the sun. Apparently she did not want it ruining her skin.

"Where's Chaska?" Augum asked.

"Probably getting yelled at by 'Achishi Zafu'." The last words—which meant "honored elder" in the Henawa tongue—were said with dripping sarcasm.

"For what this time?"

"Probably the usual. Not that it isn't all undeserved. He needs to get off his lazy butt and find work. I can't live with her much longer. I don't care if he builds us a hut with his bare hands."

"Sure you do," Leera chimed in.

"You're right, I do. Better be a grand hut."

"Do you think it's wise to move out so quickly?" Bridget asked delicately.

Haylee stared ahead as she hobbled with determination. "No choice. I'll kill her otherwise." She caught Bridget's mortified look and rolled her eyes. "I was obviously jesting."

The group strolled to a shallow valley in the woods where Mr. Okeke and Mr. Goss had built them a small plank cabin so the trio could have their own space. They often slept there, exhausted after a long evening's training session. It was protected by Mrs. Stone's enchantments, but best of all, was well away from Milham, serving as a nice getaway where they could focus on their training. It sat near a trickling stream surrounded by towering spruces, pines and firs. Patches of snow still sat in spots untouched by the sun's rays. Birds chirped during the day; at night, owls hooted and wolves howled. Since it was dusk, crickets sang in symphony.

Mr. Harvus of course disapproved of them staying there alone, but did not dare contravene Mrs. Stone's wishes. He did however routinely express how he thought she was far too liberal with them. Luckily, Mr. Harvus retired early tonight citing an upset stomach, though Augum thought the real reason was resentment for not being able to convince Mrs. Stone of abandoning the library quest she had in mind for the trio.

Mr. Goss and Leland also retired to the Miner's Mule Inn, having taken up residence there to give the Okekes space. Augum longed to live alone, or with Leera, but the latter just wasn't done until marriage.

Mrs. Stone had left a sum of coin with Mr. Harvus for lodging and expenses a while ago, though how much remained and when she paid him last was a mystery. When she teleported in, she could never stay long because the Legion warlocks were always teleporting after her, using Magua's divining rod to point them in the right direction. But the warlocks could only teleport to a location they had been to, and since apparently none of them had stepped foot in Milham before, Mrs. Stone guessed they initially appeared at the Legion constabulary in Eastspear, many leagues to the south. By the time they started on their journey to Milham, she would teleport away. The warlocks would then teleport to the next closest location they visited and the chase would start anew. But each time she came to Milham, they got a little closer, and so she stopped coming altogether of late. It was a dangerous game, one Augum knew had to come to an end one day, especially now that those warlocks had no other scion to track down.

As he watched Bridget and Leera practice dueling, he wondered if his father was part of that search party, or if he was in the bowels of Bahbell exploring its library or trying to figure out how to work the gate portal. Garryk surely would have told the Legion everything under duress, which meant they probably knew the trio had destroyed the recipe. That didn't stop Augum from entertaining the idea that his father frantically searched Bahbell's ancient library for a copy. Amusingly, he imagined the man throwing childish fits and tantrums as he repeatedly failed.

After ducking a stick Leera threw at her using Telekinesis, Bridget placed her hands on her hips, breath coming in short gasps, three ivy rings disappearing from her forearm. "More light, Aug."

"Right, sorry." The lightning rippling around his hand crackled brighter. He was so good with the Shine spell now he hardly gave much thought to brightening his palm.

Haylee, who was still struggling with her 2nd degree, angrily threw her cane. "I hate this thing! I *hate* this leg! Why couldn't they have done a better job healing it?"

"Just bad luck, Hayles," Augum said.

"Don't you call me that. *He* called me that."

"Of course. My apologies." He forgot Robin had a slew of nicknames for her. He could hardly blame her for being angry. Everything about Robin made Augum angry too. He often enjoyed remembering his fist slamming into that idiot's face in a most satisfying way.

Bridget turned to Leera. "Again?"

Leera, forehead beaded with sweat, nodded. She slapped her wrists together, three watery rings appearing around her arm. "Annihilo!" A jet of water shot forth, slamming into Bridget's shield of leaves and ivy.

Bridget grunted from the force of it. The moment the shield disappeared, she brought her own hands together. "Annihilo!" and a vine shot forward, the end a dull stump very much like a fist. It punched Leera's hastily summoned shield of pond leaves and driftwood, sending her tumbling backward.

Bridget's vine and Leera's shield disappeared, leaving no trace. The girls' shoulders heaved with exertion.

Leera brushed herself off. "Good one."

"Reflect," Bridget said, readying herself.

Leera groaned but withdrew the prism from her pocket.

Bridget slammed her hands together. "Annihilo!"

"Mimica!" Leera shouted, trying to catch Bridget's spell at the exact angle and reflect it back at her. Instead, the vine slammed into Leera's hands, bending them back. She yelped and fell to the ground, sucking air through her teeth from the pain.

"Sorry," Bridget said, hands on her knees as she breathed heavily. "I eased up on the hit too."

"Hate this dumb spell," Leera muttered, standing. "Never works ..."

Bridget jerked her chin, ponytail swinging. "Hit me back."

Leera slammed her wrists together. "Annihilo!"

"Mimi—" but Leera's jet of water bowled Bridget over before she could say the trigger word, which had to be spoken very quickly.

"Late," Leera said.

Bridget watched as the water disappeared from her robe. "I know," then slowly picked herself back up.

"Take a break, you two," Augum said, striding between them and extinguishing his palm. They both slumped onto a log bench around a dark fire pit, while Augum prepared to run through the spells he knew. Unconsciously, his three lightning rings flared to life around his arm.

"Haylee, want to join me doing a cycle?" It's what they called going through every spell they knew.

Haylee, who had been watching their jousting, picked up her thoroughly-dinged cane. She brushed aside her long golden hair, sighed, and nodded.

He started with Shine's extension, practicing shocking a stump. The lightning left a charred hole on the bark, but otherwise dissipated harmlessly. Haylee followed, temporarily icing the stump. He quickly moved on to Telekinesis, raising a log into the air before placing it a few feet away. Haylee moved the same log back to its original position. He then broke a stick over his knee, dropping the pieces to the ground. He splayed both hands over it. "Apreyo." The two parts came back together, light shining from the mending seam. Haylee took the stick from him and attempted to break it with one hand while holding the cane. Augum reached out to help.

"No! I need to be able to do stuff like this on my own." She placed the cane under her arm and strained to break the stick, but lost her balance and fell. She cursed and flung the stick into the stream, promptly doing the same with her cane. "I'm a cripple," she mumbled, weeping. "A useless cripple ..."

Bridget strode over and gave Haylee a gentle hug. "You're not a cripple. You've got a bad leg. Doesn't mean anything. Look at Leland. Little tyke is blind, mute and in constant pain, yet he is as happy as can be and never complains."

Augum took a seat beside Leera.

"Poor thing is really struggling," she said to him quietly, chin resting on her hands.

"She is." He watched Haylee retrieve her cane under Bridget's compassionate supervision. "Your friendship means a lot to her, you know."

Leera's brows rose. "Really?"

"Yup."

"Huh."

"I think it's helping her get past the murder of her parents. And ... maybe it's helping you too."

"Maybe." She idly kicked at the ground. "I've been thinking. Would you still ... you know, like me if I suddenly got older?"

"Where's this coming from?" but he knew exactly what she meant—he'd been thinking about it too. The side effect of Cron was instant aging. Every successful casting of the spell aged the caster. What did that mean for them? How much would they age? Would they suddenly turn old like Mrs. Stone? Would he miss out on the entirety of his life just to defeat his father? Was that really what all of this was coming down to?

"You've been thinking about it as much as I have," Leera said. "I know Bridget has. I can tell. You know she woke up the other night screaming?"

He glanced at Bridget, who was now whispering something to Haylee. The rings under her eyes looked darker. "Thought I dreamed that."

"Nope. That was Bridget. Fess up, you've been thinking about it, haven't you?"

He rubbed his face, ran both hands through his hair, and expelled a long breath. "I have."

Leera turned her head to watch him, chin still resting on her hands. "Could you imagine? What if we, you know, became old suddenly? Old like Mr. Goss. But we're still us. Fifteen-year-olds trapped in forty-year-old bodies."

She was a month away from turning fifteen, but correcting her right now, even jokingly, didn't feel right in this moment. But would they even get to her fifteenth? What if the Legion found them before that? And then, if all worked out and they learned Cron, they'd skip a whole bunch of birthdays all at once. Or is that even how it worked? What was the difference between getting captured and dying, and dying from old age very fast? What was the point?

He took his birthday necklace and absently placed it between his teeth, chewing on it in thought.

Leera returned to idly kicking at the dirt. "Feels like my dreams are dying. Like I have no future."

Augum's heart sank. That's the darkest Leera had ever sounded. Wait, did she mean no future with him, or no future in general? He shoved the thought away. He was being paranoid. Besides, it was best not to overthink it.

"Maybe the point is to …" He sighed, allowing the chain to fall from his lips. What was he trying to say?

What would Sir Westwood say? Or Mrs. Stone? "Maybe the point is we're to enjoy it while we have it."

She leaned her head on his shoulder. Suddenly she snorted. "That all you got?" She was smiling as their gazes met.

"You two make me want to puke sometimes," Haylee said, wiping her tears, voice full of envious affection. She had flung her cane to the stream once more after yet again failing at some spell Bridget was trying to teach.

Bridget patiently retrieved the cane. "You and Chaska are just as bad, and you know it. Now let's practice together."

"I wish we were," Haylee mumbled, accepting her cane and straining to stand.

Leera slapped Augum's knee. "Come on, I'll hide something for you." She jumped up, picked a rock from the ground and disappeared behind the cabin, soon returning and taking a seat. "Well?"

Augum strolled behind the cabin and extended his palm, concentrating on that subtle tug that told him something was purposefully hidden nearby.

"Un vun deo." Almost immediately, he found the stone buried under a branch. He brought it back to Leera, who gave a brief nod before standing apart from him. They were so practiced with their training regimen they hardly needed to speak.

Augum stood across from her, mentally readying for the Push spell. He shoved at the air before him. "Baka!"

She summoned her shield but was still knocked backwards a few paces.

Leera gave an almost imperceptible nod. "Now Slam."

Augum made to throw at the ground. "GRAU!" The sound of thunder ripped through the air, scattering birds from trees. Bridget, Haylee and Leera were so used to it they barely flinched. But the spell was more powerful during battle anyway, which they theorized happened from the excitement, giving spells that extra nudge.

Augum felt a minor throb begin in his brain—the side effects of depleting his arcane reserves. Grueling hours of training tended to do that, though these days it wasn't as big of a problem as it was at the beginning.

Leera strolled over and picked up the rock, tossing it to Augum's feet. "Object Alarm."

He dropped to his knees, gripping the rock with both hands. "Concutio del alarmo," and let go, closing his eyes. He heard Leera walk over. The moment a bell tolled in his mind, indicating someone touched his enchanted object, he raised his arm.

She gave a nod. "Good. Object Track."

Augum splayed out his hands over the stone. "Vestigio itemo discovaro," and once again closed his eyes while Leera took the rock and walked off to hide in the woods. He soon got up and followed the subtle arcane pull, finding her hiding behind a large spruce, where she immediately yanked him close and kissed him, sending a thrill through his spine.

"Cut it out, you two!" Bridget eventually called from the cabin. "We've got training to do."

Leera rolled her eyes and tugged on Augum's sleeve, dragging him back. "And you two could have made yourself useful and started a fire," she said to Bridget and Haylee. "It's getting cold." Dusk was quickly dimming to night.

"Grau!" Haylee yelled, but the noise generated was nothing more than that of a snow bank crumbling slightly. She flung her cane at the fire pit. "Use that damn thing for kindling."

Bridget sighed, recovered the cane and handed it back to her. "You're too hard on yourself. You're letting your emotions get in the way of concentration."

"Stop trying to be my big sister." Haylee's shoulders dropped. "I'm sorry, I didn't mean that. I'll try harder."

Bridget gave a proud nod, then smiled at Augum and Leera holding hands. "I'm amazed you're getting away with it so long. Just tell her."

"I don't want to add to Nana's worries," Augum said, though the truth was he was also scared of Mrs. Stone forbidding him and Leera from liking each other. Absurdly, he even feared her sending Leera away. She'd say it was for their safety, or whatever. "Everyone pretty much knows anyway." He grudgingly let go of Leera's hand and began scouring for dry branches.

"Everyone except your mentors."

Leera gave Bridget a sardonic look. "Harvus doesn't matter, nor is it any of his business."

"He is your mentor whether you like it or not."

"Mrs. Stone is our mentor." Leera shrugged. "And we'll tell her. Eventually. When we're ready."

"When we're ready," Augum agreed, thinking the best time would be when he turned sixteen and became a man in the eyes of the world. Could he hide their relationship for another year? He almost scoffed aloud—not a chance in Sithesia.

Haylee glanced behind her at the cabin. "Better keep your voice down if you don't want Mrs. Stone to hear."

Leera gestured dismissively. "I wrapped the orb in a couple blankets. She won't hear a thing."

Bridget frowned. "And what if we got into trouble? What if the Legion comes? How will she hear our calls for help? Really, Leera, sometimes I question where your head is at."

"That's what all her enchantments are for." Leera glanced from Bridget to Augum to Haylee. "By the Fates, between the three of you, I don't know who worries more."

Augum and Bridget shared a tolerant look. Haylee turned her back and used Telekinesis to repeatedly whack the cane against a rock until it broke. Then she repaired it, only to break it again, seeming to take great pleasure in the vicious act.

Bridget waved a hand and a branch floated over to the fire pit. "Never mind the fire. I'll take care of it. Keep training. Aug, I want to see you cast 4th degree spells on Leera while she practices Mind Armor."

"Yes, Mrs. Stone," Augum said with a wry smile. Ever since he and Leera admitted their affection for each other to her, Bridget went out of her way playing the protective big sister. It was as if she was afraid of something awful happening. It was an unspoken fear, sometimes showing itself in the way she watched Augum and Leera. Strangely, it made Augum respect and appreciate her that much more.

He and Leera stood to face each other. Leera winked and made to daintily adjust her hair like Harvus.

Augum cracked a grin. "Stop it, I need to concentrate."

She pursed her lips in a pout.

"Stop it already," he said, unable to cease smiling.

"You need to learn to concentrate through distractions," Bridget said absently, floating a small log to the pit.

Leera made a *See, how do you like that?* look and continued to make stupid faces.

Augum decided to start with the Deafness spell. He raised his arm at Leera, his three lightning rings leaping to life. "Voidus aurus."

Bridget arranged dry leaves into a clump in the fire pit. "Augum no longer likes you." When Leera kept making stupid faces but did not glance at her, she said, "Good job, Aug." Then she turned to Leera, pointing at her mouth and saying, "You've got to *concentrate*, Lee."

"HUH? WHAT? DAMN IT!" Leera made a looping gesture at her temple, speaking very loudly. "I could *sense* the spell working, just can't seem to get the hang of blocking it."

Augum pointed at his mouth. "Loud."

"WHAT?"

Augum spoke slower. "You're. Being. Loud. Again."

"OH. SORRY."

Behind Leera, Haylee snickered to herself. "Wish Chaska had the talent for arcanery, then we could banter on about spells too."

"Consistency and concentration, Lee." Bridget made a little house of sticks around the leaves. "Aug—try Confusion."

"Ready?" he asked Leera.

"Stop giving her warning," Bridget said. "She needs to be able to sense that initial arcane attack."

"Right." He raised his arm, barely noticing the throb in his head had developed into a pounding. "Flustrato!"

Leera immediately developed a dazed look.

"You're getting better, Aug, really well done. But Lee, seriously, what's going on?"

Leera looked around. "Wha …?"

"Give her a moment, Bridge."

Bridget crossed her arms as she waited for Leera to snap out of it. "I'm worried about her. She hasn't been able to defend herself very well with Mind Armor. Really hit or miss. I mean, she was able to do it fine with Mrs. Stone. It's like she can't concentrate—" She suddenly realized something and gave Augum a scolding look.

"It's not my fault! I try to get her to focus, you heard me earlier—"

"Well you need to do a better job. I'm *not* kidding, Aug." She gestured at him and Leera. "You two messing about together better not cost you your lives."

Augum knew she was right—one slip in concentration could easily get them killed. He needed to take this more seriously, before it was too late.

"What happened?" Leera suddenly said, glancing between the two of them. "Did I mess up again?" They avoided her gaze. "Bah, I knew it!"

Bridget strolled to the cabin. "Keep working at it."

Leera made to move to him as soon as Bridget disappeared inside. As much as he wanted her in his arms, he held her at bay. "No. Let's keep working." He opened his palm as disappointment showed on her face. "Dreadus terrablus."

This time she was ready and blocked it using Mind Armor, though she had always done better blocking this spell above the others—not that he was any good with it, making for a poor practice partner.

Haylee, who had been practicing in the background casting Shield over and over, lost her balance again and screamed in frustration. She took the cane and started beating a small boulder with it, cursing with each whack, until the cane shattered.

"The rock attack you or something?" Augum said gently.

"I'm going to bed. Sick of this. Head's killing me anyway." Haylee placed her hands over the cane. "Apreyo." It reformed. She picked it up and hobbled off without another word.

Bridget emerged with flint and steel and proceeded to light the fire. "Where's Haylee?"

Leera shrugged. "Had another fit."

"She all right?"

Leera shrugged again.

Bridget sighed, blew on a spark. "Don't forget Centarro."

"Oh yeah." It was his favorite spell.

"And do something different with it."

"Like what?"

"I don't know, try chronocasting or something."

"Dare you to try *simulcasting*," Leera said with a cheeky grin.

"We don't want him to hurt himself, Lee."

"I'll try chronocasting," Augum said, knowing casting one spell and then another while the original was still in effect was easier—after all, they had been doing it with Centarro for some time. Simulcasting on the other hand—casting one elemental spell and one standard spell in the same instance—was on the Mrs. Stone level of complexity.

Leera flicked her hand in a practiced movement. "Shyneo." It surged to life with a watery glow.

The fire finally caught and Bridget stopped blowing on it, joining Leera. The rule was when one of them cast Centarro, the other two would be there in support, as the side effects left the caster in a vulnerable and stupid state.

Augum rubbed his head, urging the dull thudding to die down. As rehearsed as he was with these spells, developing arcane stamina was a lifetime pursuit. He examined the area around him in thoughtful detail just as Thomas, his deceased Leyan great-grandfather, had taught him. He felt the cloth of his new royal blue apprentice robe between his fingers. He chased the smoothness of the golden silk rope around his waist. He listened to the quiet trickle of the stream; to a distant woodpecker tapping at a trunk; to the occasional clump of snow falling to the ground. He caught the attentive watchfulness of the girls—Leera's arched brows, her affectionate gaze, her slightly poor posture; Bridget's perpetually tired and worried face, the reflection of her palm in her hazel eyes, her soft and caring expression. He shut his eyes a moment before letting the words spill over his tongue.

"Centeratoraye xao xen."

The inner arcane energies instantly sharpened, as did the world when he opened his eyes. The first stars overhead became bubbling pricks of light, the evergreen canopy a blanket of green needles interacting in endless predictable patterns. He was aware of everything, from the blood rushing through his veins to the almost imperceptible pulse of the girls' lit palms, tied to the beat of their hearts.

First, he formulated a plan on how to deal with the side effects—he would lie down and watch the stars. Next, he ran through a mental list of spells, trying to figure out which two to cast. But as he looked past the girls into the dark forest, all thought of chronocasting and simulcasting disappeared from his mind. He recalled Occulus' silent undead army and envisioned it standing in the pitch darkness of Bahbell with such clarity that all he need do was reach out and touch their matte black Dreadnought armor.

Do something different, Bridget had said. Do something different …

A new thought occurred to him, an ordinarily impossible thought—*what if he could teleport?* After all, casting beyond one's level was possible and sometimes encouraged!

His mind raced under the influence of Centarro unlike ever before, applying the patterns he had learned from every single spell, as well as the gestures he had seen other warlocks perform. Like a word on the tip of his tongue, he knew there was something to it; all he needed to do was—

"Augum?" Bridget said, concern written on her face.

Too slow. They were too slow with their thoughts and he did not have the time to explain. Yes, he appeared to just be standing there, but his mind … his mind was *alive*.

The thoughts slammed on top of one another as his arcane energies built up with each new understanding, each new connection. Yes, it was wild casting. So what if he did not know the trigger word or the gesture or the exact series of cognitive functions? All he had to do was start *small*. The important thing was that he believed. That he knew it *was* possible!

Centarro would soon expire, but his arcane energies were peaking. He reached for a spot across the shallow stream, already envisioning himself there. The wild arcanery exploded over his senses like a wildfire, rupturing his very being. His vision and body suddenly yanked forward with such violence he instantly blacked out.

* * *

"Fates and damnation, Aug, what did you do?" Leera asked in a shaky voice when Augum opened his eyes. His throbbing head was in her lap, every part of him aching.

"Apreyo," a pale Bridget said, hands folded over his robe. He saw it stitch back together seamlessly—apparently he had torn it somehow.

Leera wiped his nose with a cloth. There was blood on it when she took it away.

"Augum, what did you do?" It was Bridget that asked this time. Her face looked as stern as Mrs. Stone's.

He sat up a little too quickly, wincing from the sharp stabbing in his head. When he saw where he was, his face lit up with a victorious grin. "I'm on the other side of the stream!" All right, maybe not at the exact spot where he had intended, but still—

Bridget's brows crossed. "Augum Stone, did you just try casting *Teleport*?"

He swallowed, suddenly realizing the absolute stupidity of it. "Um, seemed like a good idea at the time …"

Leera threw her hands up. "I can't believe how dumb that was! Teleport's a what—" and she looked to Bridget with exasperation.

"—a 9th degree spell, Augum Stone," Bridget said. "Let me repeat myself. That was a 9th. Degree. Spell. You could have ripped yourself to pieces, or appeared in a tree, or—"

"—I know, I know, I'm sorry. It was dumb. I … I don't know what I was thinking." It really did seem like a good idea at the time.

"Downright *stupid* is what it was." Bridget was glaring at him while stabbing a finger at his chest. "Stupid and unlike you. You should have known better. We've got enough on our plates with Reflect, Cron, and the entire 4th degree, and you go and do something so—"

"—stupid, I know. Sorry." She was right, as usual.

Leera dropped him to the ground like a sack of potatoes. "Sorry? *Sorry?* That's *instant* death, Aug. There's no coming back from that. Don't you ever—" She was punching him on the shoulder with each word. "Do. That. Again!"

"I won't, I won't!" He rubbed his battered arm. It hurt to see their scared faces. He felt his insides curdle with shame. It was the dumbest thing he had ever attempted.

Another punch. "Ever!" Leera shook her head at him, eyes moist. "No wonder you lightning warlocks die so much—you're all crazy, stupid fools." She jabbed at his chest, something that's been happening a lot lately. "Never. Again."

"All right, never again, I'm sorry!"

She gave him a sorrowful look before scoffing, flinging the cloth at his head, and stomping off to tend the fire.

Augum slumped, wincing from the drumming pain, and dabbed at his nose.

Bridget drew her legs in, watching him. "What were you thinking?" she asked quietly. "That was … unlike you."

"I don't know, I guess I … I guess I actually *believed* I could do it."

"You *did* do it, and yes it's impressive, but it was an extremely foolish risk. You can't just …" She flipped her hands. "… cast wild arcanery on whim, Augum." She sighed and glanced over at Leera, who stabbed the fire repeatedly with a stick. "We're all she has in this world now, you know that, right?"

Augum felt a queasy rush. He could deal with being hunted by his father, but hearing he was half of Leera's entire world sounded like a terrible amount of responsibility. And there he was being an utter idiot. What had he been thinking?

"I'm glad you two like each other in that way," Bridget said with a bittersweet smile, "I really am, but I'm worried. You can't let it distract you from your studies, either of you. Our lives depend on it."

There she went being right again. Truth was, he'd been thinking about it a lot—but he was not about to give up spending time with Leera or trying *not* to like her in that way. Every time her fingers curled around his, butterflies zoomed around in his stomach. When he felt her soft lips, looked into those dark eyes, or held her delicate hand … he felt *alive*. He could not put the feelings into words, but it was something he could not change.

"You need to focus, Augum, and prepare. Look at me."

He glanced into her eyes. The worry on her face was killing him.

"Focus and prepare," she repeated softly.

He nodded. "You mean prepare for …?"

"You *know* for what."

"Nana's never going to get caught." His thrumming heart said otherwise though. "She'd never let them win." But they might force it …

Bridget gently rested a hand on his forearm. "We must learn to become more independent. We must trust each other, train hard, and find a way to stop your father. I know we can do it. Mrs. Stone knows we can do it too, that's why she's trusting us with such a dangerous quest. I *know* we can figure out how to use the Agonex. I *know* we can learn Cron."

She's been very serious lately. "Hope so, Bridge." He thought about the bronze disk. Was it safe here? Mrs. Stone had left it with them, explaining she did not want it to fall into the enemy's hands should they finally catch up to her.

Bridget watched him a moment before getting up and dusting herself off. "Tomorrow we learn our 4th degree elemental spell with Mr. Harvus." She offered him a hand.

He took it and hoisted himself up. "Looking forward to it."

"At least *try* to sound more enthusiastic? Come on, I think we can still squeeze in another round of training before bed. We especially need to work on Reflect. All of us."

He groaned. "Hate that spell …"

UNEXPECTED ARRIVAL

The next morning brought heavy cloud cover. Augum, Bridget, Leera, Mr. Goss and his son, Leland, ate breakfast at the Okeke cabin, a daily ritual. Sometimes Haylee and Chaska joined them, but not today. Leera told Augum they probably got in another fight, but for all he knew, Ms. Singh could have drafted her to help around her scribe shop, as she oft tended to do.

"Pass the salt, please," Mr. Goss said with a smile.

Augum handed the saltcellar to Bridget, who handed it to Mr. Goss.

Jengo placed his fork on the plate. "Today's the day. Hardly slept. Can't even eat."

Leera tormented her eggs. "What doom awaits you today?"

"Is it Lover's Day already?" Mr. Okeke asked absently, pouring himself a steaming cup of tea with one hand while holding the Blackhaven Herald with the other.

"That's tomorrow, Father. Today ... today is more special—"

"Don't let Priya hear you say that," Bridget cut in.

"That's not what I meant—of course I love Priya, it's just that this has nothing to do with her."

Mr. Goss made sure his son—who was again playing with his favorite toy, the Agonex—found his eggs. "What is so special about today? Put that away, Leland, I do not want you playing with it at breakfast."

Jengo tapped the table with a flourish, making his father's cup dance in its saucer. "Today Augum, Bridget and Leera learn their first summoning spell!"

Mr. Okeke rescued the cup before it turned over. He sighed and resumed reading the crinkled parchment.

Leera tore her oatcake into manageable portions. "I'd be looking forward to it if we were learning the spell with Mrs. Stone instead of Harvus."

"Oh, come now, Leopold cannot be *that* bad," Mr. Goss said as he poured himself a cup of tea.

Mr. Okeke's skeptical eyes appeared from above the parchment for a moment, but he said nothing.

"Mr. Goss, I beg you, come to just *one* of our training sessions and you'll—"

"Stop exaggerating, Lee," Bridget cut in. "He really isn't that bad, Mr. Goss, he's just ... particular."

"You're only saying that because you're his favorite," Leera said, "and you even know what he thinks of women in general—"

While the girls argued, Augum glanced over at the Blackhaven Herald. He wondered if there was any news about the tournament, or his father, or especially, the search for Mrs. Stone.

Augum had learned that the Blackhaven Herald was crafted in the wee hours of each morning and hurriedly copied using arcane quills. Hired warlocks would then teleport to all the towns and constabularies, dropping off bundles. From there, couriers distributed them to the surrounding villages by horse. Apparently, being a warlock journalist used to be a fun job until the Legion started dictating what was written. Back in Willowbrook, the Herald was rarely seen, declared to be promoting witchery. Except, of course, when there was important news. Not that many of the villagers could read.

"... but I'm sure Mr. Harvus was only trying to teach you a lesson in concentration," Bridget said, referring to the time he made Leera write one thousand parchment lines saying *I will listen attentively while Mr. Harvus is speaking.*

Augum tried forcing himself to look forward to learning their first summoning spell with Harvus, but it was like looking forward to cleaning soiled laundry. Instead, he fantasized about getting Harvus fired somehow.

"—and why *can't* we hire someone else?" Leera said as if reading Augum's mind.

"Because Mrs. Stone approves of Mr. Harvus," Bridget said in a tone suggesting she was tired of repeating herself. "And besides, Mr. Harvus can keep our secrets."

Leera folded her arms across her chest, a sour expression on her face.

"Any news, Kwabe?" Mr. Goss asked, taking the Agonex away from a moaning Leland.

"A new decree, I am afraid."

"Another one?" Bridget asked. "What is it this time?"

Augum sat forward. The Legion had decreed a spate of new rules of late—no celebrating unsanctioned holidays; no gathering in groups of ten or more people without a permit from a Legion constable; no worshipping gods of any kind; no practicing arcanery without permission; and so on.

"No weapons of any kind are allowed," Mr. Okeke replied, "without written prior consent."

"I do believe we saw that one coming," Mr. Goss said. "They are afraid of opposition."

"I have to disagree, Albert." Mr. Okeke handed him the parchment. "I think they merely wish to control us. Read the last one, decree ninety-six."

Mr. Goss adjusted his spectacles. " 'Every hamlet, village and town in Solia will hereby host a Legion Constable who will collect taxes, keep the peace, and settle disputes'."

They all glanced at each other.

Suddenly there was a distant horn blast. For a moment no one moved. When the horn sounded again, everyone scrambled—Augum shot to a window; Mr. Goss picked up a fire poker and raced to the door; Leera scuttled over to the rucksack and dug out the orb; Mr. Okeke ran to his room; Bridget protected Leland from the scuffle; and Jengo grabbed his head, proclaiming their imminent death.

"I cannot see anything out of the ordinary," Augum whispered, prowling from window to window. The forest was silent.

Leera, who had been quietly trying to call Mrs. Stone through the Orb of Orion, raised her head. "Can't get a response."

Mr. Okeke finished putting on a crimson and gold tunic and strode to the door. "Please, everyone—do stay here, I shall return shortly."

"If we're not here, we'll probably be at the cabin, Mr. Okeke," Augum said. "The enchantments are stronger there."

"Father—" Jengo called. "Be careful."

Mr. Okeke gave a nod and carefully opened the door. Seeing nothing outside, he walked out, closing the door behind him.

Augum soon went for the door handle. "I have to see what's going on."

"I do not think that wise, Augum," Mr. Goss said, the fire poker trembling in his hand.

"I won't be long."

"Then we're coming with you." Bridget handed a moaning Leland over to his father, who hesitated, but put the fire poker down.

Jengo slithered to his room, voice low in defeat. "Then you'll get killed, all three of you."

"Don't be so dramatic," Leera said, "and Aug's right—we can't just sit here like trapped rats."

Augum grabbed the rucksack after Leera stuffed the orb back inside. Bridget snagged the Agonex and put it in too. They were practiced at being prepared, always ready to bolt should things suddenly go awry.

"Then be sure to stay safe, you three," Mr. Goss said, face scrunching with worry. Leland moaned his agreement.

Augum turned the handle. "We will, Mr. Goss."

The trio scampered through the door and into the woods behind the cabin. They ran amongst the soggy pines, circling the village. Only when they heard the sound of horses did they slow to a creep.

"There," Leera whispered, pulling aside a branch. Augum and Bridget crowded close. A few strides away stood a small procession—two black-armored soldiers on horseback and a covered wagon pulled by two oxen. The wagon was manned by a chunky boy their age and a squat man wearing ill-fitting black garments. He was so obese he almost lacked a neck.

There was no mistaking the burning sword of the Legion emblem on the soldiers' chests.

Augum shared a look with the girls—the Legion had come to Milham. This could mean a fight and an immediate evacuation.

Leera secretly found his hand and their fingers curled together.

The obese man reached for a cane. "Help me down please, Devon."

The boy dropped the reins he was holding. "Yes, Father."

A crowd gathered around the wagon, giving the pot-helmed soldiers a wide berth. Augum recognized Mr. Harvus; Panjita Singh and her daughter, Priya; Mr. Okeke; Huan, the innkeeper of the Miner's Mule Inn; and Chaska and his Henawa father, the storekeeper of the Good Medicine shop. Everyone wore an anxious expression.

As the obese man was helped to the ground, the soldiers scanned the crowd and the forest, forcing the trio to briefly duck.

"Who is in charge here, please?" the obese man asked the crowd, breath coming in short gasps. Stepping down from the wagon had evidently tired him.

"I am still." A dark-skinned old man with a pointy black beard and wearing a long robe stepped forward.

The obese man withdrew a cloth from his ill-fitting garments and dabbed at his chins. "Ah, Mr. Hanad Haroun. A pleasure to see you again."

Mr. Haroun gave a short bow. "Constable Clouds. I bid you welcome to Milham."

Augum remembered Mr. Haroun's rousing speech at Endyear, and how he swore opposition should the Legion attempt taking Milham's men. So far, Mr. Haroun appeared to be keeping his calm. Nonetheless, Augum was ready to plow through the brush should the call arise to take the soldiers down.

"Isn't that the supposedly corrupt constable?" Leera whispered.

"Shh," Bridget quickly said.

Augum did recall Jengo mentioning something on the subject, but then again, Jengo was quite prone to exaggeration.

Constable Clouds adjusted the grip on his cane with an arm that perpetually shook. "Mr. Haroun, I am sure you have already heard word from the Herald—"

"We have indeed. The news just reached us, in point of fact."

"I understand. The roads have been treacherous of late. Bandits, you see. Regardless, as before, I am here on behalf of the Legion. However, this time it is to stay."

The crowd stirred anxiously.

Clouds made a placating gesture with a meaty hand. "But I do not wish to cause any concern to you or to the villagers of Milham, Mr. Haroun. I am here to maintain order as per Legion decree number ninety-six. These are my trusted guards and enforcers of the law—Lieutenant Briggs and Sergeant Cobb. You will find them as just and fair as I."

That did not seem to quell the mutterings.

"What is it we can do for you, Constable?" Mr. Haroun asked.

Clouds coughed into the cloth. Augum noticed he wore a wedding ring. "Again, I do not wish to bestow alarm or fear in Milham. Like you all, I pray for peace. Let us ride out the war together without harm. All we require is a domicile. If none can be provided, we shall build one."

"But the war is over, is it not?" a woman called from the crowd. "Tiberra has fallen."

The constable dabbed at his sweaty face. He sounded tired. "Ah, if only it were so. I am afraid that for the Legion, the war is never over."

An odd thing to say, Augum thought to himself. Some in the Legion could even find that kind of talk treasonous.

"But I repeat, you yourselves need not fear," Clouds went on. "Milham is an isolated mining village. There shan't be armies marching through here."

"And what of our men?" called the same woman. "Are you here to take our men?"

Clouds glanced back at the pot-helmed soldiers, who sat silently on their stallions, before turning back to the anxious crowd. "Here me thus and hear me clear—as long as my commander has no reason to come to Milham, we will not take any men or confiscate property—except when absolutely necessary. Again, I repeat—we are not here to cause a disturbance. We wish you to go on about your business as before, without fear or worry." He took a moment to catch his breath before continuing. "We are family men who know the value of love and community. Please, do not be afraid to come to us with your concerns. I assure you, we will do our best to help everyone. I know you have heard stories of soldiers … taking advantage. We are not those kinds of soldiers. We are not spies. We are *not* your enemy."

"Must be some kind of trick," Bridget whispered as the crowd muttered amongst themselves, some in evident relief. "Isn't it?"

Augum only shook his head in bewilderment, mirroring the same slack look of disbelief as the crowd.

"That said," Clouds continued, "I am afraid I must confiscate *some* weapons. We should consider it a gesture of appeasement. Please place what you can spare into the wagon as soon as possible. Let us at least make a show of it. Further, I will be sending the wagon back to Eastspear on a regular basis with taxes and any necessary requests from command. Also, please refrain from speaking about the gods in public or gathering in groups of ten or more. I must stress that we must *appear* to be following the letter of all requests."

Augum shook his head slowly. What was going on here? This man wasn't like any Legion soldier he'd come across before …

Mr. Haroun raised his chin. "I hope you are truly sincere, good sir. Many here have endured enough grief for this lifetime."

"I assure you I am. As a token of our trust in each other, allow us to present our families." The constable tapped the wagon with his cane, and from the back emerged two women wearing peasant dress and country bonnets, holding hands with four children.

"These are the wives and children of my soldiers." Clouds rested a heavy arm on the chubby boy beside him. "And this is my very own son, Devon. We are not here to cause trouble. We have heard Milham is a town after our own hearts. I cannot express how sincere we are. Please accept us as one of your own."

For a long moment the crowd exchanged glances, until Mr. Haroun stepped forward. "Then on behalf of Milham, we wish you a pleasant stay. I insist you join my family for lunch. As for everyone else, please do as the constable says—bring any weapons you do not need and place them in the wagon. We must help our new neighbors follow regulations."

Augum kept shaking his head. This was baffling. Surely a real Legionnaire would have instantly demanded every weapon, followed by a thorough search of the town and most probably a questioning in some iron room.

The crowd closed in on Clouds, his son, and the soldiers. There were many handshakes, smiles, and even tentative hugs.

"I just can't believe it," Bridget said, slumping to the ground and looking between Augum and Leera. "Could it be they're actually on our side?"

Augum flipped his hand. "If so—and I'm not convinced they're for real yet—maybe we can work with them somehow. Find weaknesses in the Legion or something, I don't know."

Leera glanced past them at the procession. "I'm not convinced. What if it's a trick to disarm everyone before slaughtering them like lambs? Wouldn't put it past them, you know."

Augum watched as Devon shook hands with another boy, the pair smiling and nodding as they spoke. He noted how the children resembled the soldiers, who had taken off their pot helms and how everyone seemed at ease. They weren't checking the trees or communicating in secret. Their body language told him they were being open and sincere. "I don't think so. I think those are their real families. But we obviously shouldn't reveal ourselves just yet. Let's wait and see what happens."

"Agreed," the girls chorused.

Leera's eyes narrowed. "Harvus is heading to the cabin. Time to go."

MORAL GROUNDS

The trio made it back to the Okeke cabin in short order, passing on the unbelievable news to Mr. Goss, Leland and Jengo, though failing to raise Mrs. Stone on the orb. Harvus entered soon after.

"I still think it's a trap," Jengo said as Mr. Goss left to see for himself, leaving Leland in Jengo's care. His eyes wandered to the window. "There's probably thousands of soldiers surrounding the village as we speak. It's Clouds. He's taken bribes before. I'm certain he's corrupt."

Augum couldn't help but glance furtively out the window, recalling the raid on Sparrow's Perch. It did not escape his notice the girls did the same.

"Well, Mrs. Stone said she'd be here in a flash if any of her special enchantments are tripped," Leera said.

"Unless something happened to her," Mr. Harvus said without expression. "Let us hope that is not the case, of course." He brought his white-gloved hands together. "In the meantime, I absolutely forbid you three to show your faces in town until I deem it absolutely safe. And you are not to take any foolish risks like spying on the Legion or any other ill-advised behavior." He cupped his ear at them. "I am afraid I do not hear a 'Yes, Mr. Harvus'."

"Yes, Mr. Harvus," they chorused, Augum, Jengo and Leera lamely; Bridget with a firm nod.

"Jengo, you are to join us at the other cabin as soon as your father returns."

Leland moaned in protest.

"I am sorry, my dear child, but I am afraid today's training will be too dangerous for you." He adjusted his hairpiece, which immediately prompted Leera to elbow Augum.

Harvus' eyes flicked to her and she stopped grinning. "Do you have the blue book in your possession?"

Augum raised his shoulder. "Right here, in the rucksack."

"I say it again—please refer to me as Mr. Harvus, Augum."

"Mr. Harvus."

"And do not be clever with me. I am far smarter than you are. As it is, follow me, please."

"See you soon, Jengo," Leera muttered, following Harvus.

As they walked, Augum wondered what Harvus had meant by being "clever". Was he on to him and Leera? No, he was being paranoid, they've been so careful!

"Please fetch Haylee for me, will you, Bridget?"

"Yes, Mr. Harvus."

Augum glimpsed Leera silently mimicking Bridget.

When they reached the small cabin, a cool wind rustled the forest, pushing gray clouds overhead. The stream trickled on, joined by the perpetual drip of snowmelt.

"Let us wait for Bridget and Haylee to join us."

Augum raised an eyebrow. "Are we just to stand here? Why don't we practice some spells—" but he stopped himself from going on. Mr. Harvus had closed his eyes and pursed his lips, indicating he was in no mood to hear it. Augum sighed loudly in protest. He was getting sick of Harvus' stifling ways. His stupid mannerisms, which at first seemed trite and funny, now were irritating to no end.

Harvus picked a piece of lint from his robe. "Mind yourself, young Augum Stone. You are not the hero you think yourself to be."

Leera stayed Augum with a subtle pinch on his arm.

Bridget and a hobbling Haylee soon joined them. The latter had an impatient look on her face and rings around her eyes even darker than Bridget's.

"Haylee, I expect you to work harder today. You have been a disappointment thus far." He raised a hand when she opened her mouth to protest. "I do not want to hear it, young lady. You have had ample opportunity to study, yet your progress has been abysmal. In the academy, you would have had many more studies to worry about. Here, you have minimal responsibilities, yet you dawdle, throw tantrums, and cavort with that … savage."

Haylee was shaking her head throughout his speech, trying to keep tears from falling on her cheeks. "I don't need this," she finally blurted, lower lip quivering. "And I don't need you, you … pasty marmot. I'm done—" She began hobbling off.

Bridget took a step toward her. "Haylee, wait—"

"Nope, I'm done. Done!"

"But your training! You need to train with someone—"

She was still shaking her head while hobbling off. "Yes, I do, but I refuse to do it with him."

"We are indeed done, young lady. Do not seek my services again."

"Oh, don't worry about that, I won't."

"Mr. Harvus, please—" Bridget said.

"Back in line, Bridget. The young lady has insulted me and chosen the coward's path. So be it."

Haylee stopped as if to respond, fists balled. Instead, she shook her head a final time and hobbled off.

"Anyone else wish to cease lessons with me? You are absolutely free to do so." Harvus waited for a reply, but none came. Augum would have loved to tell him to shove his lessons, but too much rode on their studies, far too much. He felt terrible for Haylee though. What was she going to do now? He'd help train her on the side but there just wasn't time. They worked morning until night daily with Harvus, and if it wasn't with Harvus, it was for Mrs. Stone at the Trainer, or performing practice tasks either set forth for them.

"Good. Now then, I trust you to have diligently studied the chapter on today's lesson, as I assigned a tenday ago," Harvus began, gloved hands folded over his potbelly as he eyed Augum and Leera in particular.

Augum felt a pang of guilt, not because he was worried about letting Harvus down, but because by being behind in their studies, he and Leera, having spent nearly all their study time together, placed themselves and Bridget in danger.

"Bridget, what is today's lesson?"

Augum and Leera exchanged quick glances. Harvus had an agonizing way of asking the obvious.

"Today's lesson is on the 4th degree elemental spell Summon Minor Elemental, Mr. Harvus."

"That's a tongue twister if I ever heard one," Leera muttered under her breath.

"Excuse me, Miss Jones?"

Leera cleared her throat as Harvus stared her down.

"Very good, Bridget. Now, I am sure you three have diligently practiced your pronunciation, but just to make sure we are all on the same page, please speak the arcane words aloud. Augum, you first, please."

Great. Augum was really hoping for Bridget to go first—he could then have copied her pronunciation. "Uh, sorry, Mr. Harvus, with all this excitement in the air, it kind of slipped my mind." He tried to ignore Bridget's frown.

Mr. Harvus raised his eyes skyward in that begging-to-the-gods look he chronically gave when frustrated. "Augum Stone," he began slowly, still watching the heavens, "are you telling me that you do not even remember the simple words required to trigger the spell?"

Augum shrugged. "Sort of … I guess." Obviously, you fat nest-haired troll.

Harvus fixed him with a cold glare. "Your great-grandmother is paying me a small fortune to live here with this barbaric lot of fools. A small fortune, Augum." He shrugged. "Or at least she owes me that—but do not let that concern you."

So the money was running out, Augum thought with a sinking feeling.

"Anyhow," Harvus continued, "that is not the distressing part. The distressing part—no, the absolutely absurd part—is that an entire kingdom might depend on your actions, and yet you …" Harvus waved carelessly with a gloved hand, "do not even bother taking the time to learn your craft."

As the words hung in the air, Augum felt a prickle of shame. Harvus was right, as much as he hated to admit it.

Harvus placed his hands behind his back. "Pray tell me that you have not hit your ceiling, as I suspect Haylee has."

"What! No, of course not—!" Oh no … was that what was happening with Haylee?

" 'Of course not'. I see. Then why, my dear daft boy, do you neglect your studies? Do you think your father lopes around neglecting his studies?" Before Augum could reply, Harvus took a single step forward. "Let me tell you what your father is doing in this very moment. Murdering people." He accented the point with an exaggerated slow nod.

Augum had to stop himself from recoiling—Harvus' breath stank as if a rat had crawled down his throat and died some time ago.

"Murdering people," Harvus repeated with that annoying nod. "Or planning on murdering people. And you—you who may be one of only a handful of souls to possibly stop him one day—you traipse about like an idiot. An idiot."

"You shouldn't speak to us that way—" Leera began, but Harvus immediately turned on her.

"And you, my dear," he began in a deadly sweet voice, hands still behind his back, "do you happen to know the correct wordage and pronunciation to the 4th degree elemental spell?"

When Leera began mumbling something unintelligible, Harvus plowed right along. "How about its name then? All I require is the simple name of a simple spell, a name just mentioned a moment ago by your very peer. Oh for heaven's sakes, child, tell me you at least know the name of the spell!" His voice was a near shout by then, the first time he had truly lost his temper with them.

Leera seemed stuck on a word, a dumbstruck expression on her face. "I ... I ..."

Harvus slowly shook his head. "You stupid, stupid girl."

Augum's blood instantly boiled. "Don't you talk to—"

"Voidus lingua!" Harvus spat, flicking his wrist at Augum without taking his eyes off Leera.

Augum's throat immediately dried up and he choked on his words.

For once, Bridget's face registered shock. "Mr. Harvus, I don't think that's—"

Harvus raised a stern finger, still without looking away from Leera. "Do not test me, young lady. I am sick and tired of their deplorable conduct." The gloved fingers of one of his hands pronged between Augum and Leera. "Yes, that is right, you two—do you think me stupid? I know exactly why you have neglected your important studies. I know what it is you two little sinners have been up to, carousing about like two despicable little devils." He turned on Augum and jabbed him hard in the chest, speaking slowly as if to a dumb child. "You do not have the right to prance and cavort about wasting valuable time. Lives are at stake, do you understand me? Lives."

"Mrs. Stone will never allow you to get away with this," Leera finally blurted.

Harvus stepped back. "Is that so?" He raised a hand and beckoned at Augum's rucksack, which slipped off his shoulder and floated away before he could stop it. "Let us see exactly what the archmage thinks of your disgusting behavior."

Augum's fists curled—as much as he wanted to do something, Harvus was a far more powerful warlock.

"No, don't tell her!" Leera suddenly cried. She fell to her knees, hands together in prayer. "Please, Mr. Harvus, don't tell her. We'll do anything—"

Harvus adjusted his hairpiece. What was once an amusing gesture suddenly appeared malicious.

"Quite right that you beg, because we all know Mrs. Stone would not be pleased. In point of fact, I am confident she would separate you two far, far apart."

Leera whimpered.

"I know how you speak about me behind my back," Harvus went on, "I have excellent hearing and awareness and I am awfully cognizant of your witty little comments and cruel japes." He glanced skyward once more, one hand holding the rucksack, one over his heart. "The gods know how I put up with your cruel natures, they do. You are a wicked pair inciting nothing but more wickedness, and it must come to an end immediately."

He reached into the rucksack and withdrew the Orb of Orion, holding it before him like a prized hen.

"Mr. Harvus, please—" Leera was in tears now. "Don't tell her—"

Mr. Harvus' lips thinned. "Perhaps you should have thought of that first, my dear."

"Mr. Harvus," Bridget said, "we shouldn't trouble Mrs. Stone with this kind of news."

"I wholeheartedly agree, Bridget. I hate to do it, but it really is for their own good—"

"We'll stop!" Leera said. "We won't … look at each other that way."

Augum shook his head in protest, mouth still as silent as the grave. No way was he going to do what Harvus says. He wasn't that afraid of what Mrs. Stone would say on the matter either—in fact, he was sure she would accept it … at least, eventually.

"This is for your own good, Augum and Leera," Mr. Harvus repeated. "Mrs. Stone, are you there?" A moment of tense silence passed. "Mrs. Stone, do you hear me? This is Leopold Harvus."

A tinny voice sounded from within the orb. "Yes, I hear you," Mrs. Stone replied, huffing as if she was in a run. "Is something the matter? Now is not a good time."

"I am afraid there indeed is something the matter, Mrs. Stone. Leera Jones and Augum Stone are … how shall I put this delicately … frolicking in an untoward manner."

Leera placed a hand over her mouth, barely able to breathe. Bridget, looking pale, squeezed her shoulder.

"Is it affecting their studies?" Mrs. Stone asked between gasps.

Harvus' face lit up with victory. "Why, yes it is! Precisely that, Mrs. Stone! Do you give me the authority to discipline the pair—appropriately of course?"

"I must place my trust in you to do the right thing, Mr. Harvus, as I am in quite the predic—" Suddenly there was a tinny explosion and the orb fell silent.

"Mrs. Stone?" Leera cried out. "Mrs. Stone—!"

Augum felt a horrible tingle creep down his spine while Bridget's hand shot to her mouth.

Mr. Harvus' face went all sensible again as he carefully placed the orb back in the rucksack. "As you can plainly hear, the archmage is quite busy. There is a reason she has entrusted me with your care—my sound judgment." He used Telekinesis to float the rucksack back to Augum, who yanked it from the air.

Harvus dusted off his gloved hands. "You have another year before you may be allowed to ask for her hand in marriage, Augum Stone. Until then, you are not to look at each other that way. If I ever catch either of you cavorting in an unwholesome manner, you will be punished. And do not think for one moment I will not separate you entirely. Only Augum is essential to the quest. As such, from here on, Augum will be sleeping in separate accommodations with me, for clearly without supervision you two will run amok."

Augum could hardly believe what he was hearing. He shook his head in protest while mouthing the word "No!"

"You have not earned the right to speak yet, Augum. You are going to sit over there—" Harvus pointed at a log, "and read the appropriate chapter that you neglected thus far. As long as I am able, I will not let your youthful infatuations murder people through negligence of your duties. This frivolity ends now."

"Mr. Harvus," Bridget began softly, "do you not think you're being a touch unfair?"

"I am surprised to hear a word of protest from you, dear Bridget, seeing as he is placing you directly in the path of danger. I would think you to possess a sensible nature that sees how important Augum's place is, and how he is squandering opportunity after opportunity to take charge of his destiny, and most probably the destiny of so many others—all because some silly fling with nothing more than a common—" He stopped himself and cleared his throat authoritatively.

"The Arinthian line must be protected from itself," he said. " 'When thy fallen can't be slain, when lion children rise again, when fires burn from east to west, blood of kin can vanquish death'."

Augum remembered his great-grandfather's last words—identified by Mrs. Stone to be an ancient witch poem—all too well. But he'd be damned if anything or anyone would keep him away from Leera—prophecy or no prophecy. Stupid poem or not.

"If it was not for the Legion coming today," Harvus said, "I would parade you both through the town so everyone may see your shame." He smoothed his robe. "Now, Leera—since you have not bothered to study—and we plainly know why now—you will sit down with Bridget and learn the correct pronunciation. And just so both of you know how serious I am about you two not touching—" He placed his gloved hands on Leera's squirming shoulders. "Concutio del alarmo duo tactus dolor Augum Stone," then performed the same spell on Augum, replacing his name with Leera's. Augum could barely stand still with the loathing he felt for the man.

"That was an advanced off-the-book extension of the Object Alarm spell. When you two touch in any way, not only will I hear an alarm, but your touch will cause each other pain. It really is for your own good." Harvus stood back with a satisfied nod. "And now that that is over with and settled, let us return to your studies."

Augum and Leera locked gazes for a moment. Her eyes reflected the longing sorrow he felt.

HUMILIATION

Augum must have read the same paragraph a hundred times, yet nothing had sunk in—that is how clouded his thoughts were with anger. How *dare* Harvus stick his nose in their business! Who was he to tell him and Leera they were not to see each other in that way, or to touch! Yet every plan Augum formulated came up against the same obstacle—Mrs. Stone had given the man free reign, and regardless of what was happening, their studies were incredibly important.

When Jengo came to the cabin, his face contorted with a puzzled expression at their silent melancholy. Mr. Harvus acted as if nothing had happened at all—he was almost cheerful when he told Jengo to join Augum in study.

Jengo sat his tall frame on the log beside Augum, giving him a friendly elbow nudge. "How's it going? Saw Haylee. She's in a state. Wouldn't say what's bothering her though. Why's she not training anyway? Oh, and turns out we all get to live for now. Those Legionnaires are either crazy fools or really are on our side. Even sat for lunch with Mr. Haroun! Everyone is saying they're the real thing, all nice and stuff, though I still wouldn't trust them—" Jengo suddenly realized Augum was hardly paying any attention to him. He glanced to where Augum was staring—at Leera, who sat a distance away with Bridget, the pair being tutored by Harvus.

"What's going on?"

Augum pointed at his mouth and made a vague gesture.

Jengo's voice dropped to a scandalized whisper. "Did Harvus *mute* you? Really? Why in Sithesia would he do that? How are you supposed to study?"

Augum surrendered a bitter shrug.

Jengo glanced over at Harvus. "I hate that man," he said, before raising his voice. "Mr. Harvus! Sir, I can't study the book with Augum because he can't talk!"

Mr. Harvus sighed, gestured to the girls to wait, and paced over. Even the way his potbelly jiggled irritated Augum.

Harvus stopped before them. "Are you going to concentrate on Jengo for once and not just yourself, Augum, as you are want to selfishly do? The poor boy is still stuck on the 1st degree. I suppose it is not entirely your fault, for I fear him rather … slow."

Augum only glared.

"I see. I take umbrage at the fact that you do not realize I am doing all of this for your own good." He sighed. "You are a petulant brat. And I do not appreciate the black look, Augum Stone. Repair it immediately."

But Augum made his glare that much fiercer.

"As you wish. Then you will simply have to learn the hard way that I am not to be trifled with," and he turned his back, returning to the girls.

Jengo gaped. "I don't believe it, what a—I'm only stuck because he's an awful teacher. I mean, the worst. And what in the Unnameables happened before I got here, anyway?"

Augum took a deep breath and gestured for a quill.

Jengo felt his robe. "Hold on, isn't there one in your cabin?"

Augum nodded, making the shape of a table with his hands.

"All right, be right back—and don't you do anything, otherwise you'll just get into more trouble." When Harvus turned his back to make a particular point to Bridget and Leera, Jengo tiptoed to the cabin, quickly coming back with a quill and ink. "Here, use the back of the book or something."

Augum hesitated but opened the back cover to a white page and quickly started writing.

Jengo read what he wrote, finally blurting, "He *what*? He can't … he can't make you stop seeing each other. He just … he just can't do that!"

Augum placed a finger over his lips just as Harvus glanced at them. Augum quickly pretended to be studying, nodding his head sagely at Jengo. Soon as Harvus turned back to the girls, he continued scribbling.

Jengo's face fell. "Ah, so he also found out what you were saying behind his back. That explains a lot. He's really sensitive about that dead animal on his head."

Augum cracked a smile and nodded before continuing to write.

"Well we can try, but it's not going to be easy," Jengo said after reading Augum's writing. He glanced back. "Turn the page, quick—"

In his haste, Augum accidentally slammed the book closed. As he rifled through, searching for the right chapter, Harvus' shadow appeared.

"What are you two doing?" Harvus asked in an eerily calm tone.

Augum gestured between himself and Jengo, then at the book.

Jengo flashed a fraudulent smile. "We're studying, Mr. Harvus."

"Are you now? And why do you need a quill?"

Jengo picked up the quill from the ground. "Oh, this? Uh, we were going to write out the spell words."

Harvus' voice turned sweet. "Write out the spell words. Indeed. On what parchment, pray tell?"

When Jengo had no answer, Harvus held out his hand. "Hand me the book, please."

Augum glared at Harvus.

"Augum, are you refusing to hand over the book to your mentor?" The glint in Harvus' cold eyes was unmistakable. Seeing no choice in the matter, Augum surrendered the book.

Harvus idly flipped through the pages with his gloved hand, beady eyes occasionally flicking to them, while Augum and Jengo sat absolutely still.

Having gotten through halfway, Harvus stopped, gave them a certain look, and flipped to the back page. "Ah, here we are," and slowly began to read aloud so Bridget and Leera could hear. " 'Harvus won't let me and Leera like each other—' " He shook his head. "Poorly written at best, my dear boy. The correct word should be 'allow', as in, 'Mr. Harvus will not *allow* Leera and *I* to cavort improperly'."

His eyes flicked to Augum a moment before he continued, making each word sound as if it had been written by a dumb child. " 'He overheard us talking about him and is mad'." He chuckled to himself, a sound wholly unnatural. "Well I am not 'mad', as you put it, Augum, I am merely doing the right thing—preventing you from soiling yourself. Now let me see here, what else did you scrawl? Oh, yes. 'We have to find a way to fire that manure-eating squirrel-haired bastard as soon as possible'." Harvus' eyes swept to Augum like a spider descending on its web-bound prey.

Augum shrank a little, barely conscious of the girls watching.

"Not only did you ruin the back of a *very* expensive book, but you have slandered my good name, and—without cause, mind you—wish me fired." Harvus gently closed the book. "I see. After everything that I have done for you. After all the extra hours of training, the toil, the patience I have exhibited. After all the sacrifices I have made …" He held up the book with his gloved hand. "*This* is how you repay me?"

Augum pointed at his own mouth, wanting to tell Harvus he *did* want him fired, that he *did* think he was a manure-eating squirrel-haired bastard, and that he had no right whatsoever to treat them this way—

Harvus slowly drummed the book with two fingers. "I see we shall have to simplify things. A child is unable to learn at an advanced level when he lacks basic discipline. Augum Stone, you will not have the *privilege* of touching this book, since you obviously cannot help but desecrate it. And since you cannot seem to control that tongue of yours even when mute, you leave me but little choice."

Harvus held the book under the crook of one arm while digging into a pocket with the other, fishing out a bar of tallow soap.

Augum immediately got to his feet, but Harvus reached out, using Telekinesis to arcanely hold him.

"Open wide please, Augum, it is for your own good."

Augum's mouth was forced open with expert Telekinesis. He watched helpless as the soap floated over, jamming into his mouth. His lips closed around the bar and locked in place. His eyes watered from the strain of trying to force the bar of soap out. He wanted to gag but could not. He felt the bitter sting of humiliation, reminding him of being trapped with Erika in Evergray tower. The pair of them had to be cut from the same sadistic cloth.

Behind Harvus, Bridget grabbed Leera, preventing her from rushing over, something Augum was grateful for—she did not need to go through this agony again.

Harvus made a show of tearing out the last page of the book before handing the tome to Jengo. "I shall keep this as evidence. You may show Augum the pages, but he is not to touch the book itself. He has to earn that privilege back. Do I make myself clear, Jengo?"

Jengo would not look at Augum, his voice solemn. "Yes, Mr. Harvus."

Harvus hovered over Augum, watching him. "The less you struggle the better, my dear boy." He sighed. "See, what you need to realize, Augum, is that there is a high probability—and hopefully I am terribly wrong here for all our sakes—that Mrs. Stone may not come back. Let us be honest with ourselves, the Legion have all the scions but one, which therefore means they will have nothing better to do than hunt for her. I will thus be the only person able to teleport you to the library, or protect you from the Legion. You are the Lord of the Legion's son, which apparently gives you a chance to stop him." He leaned forward a little. "Or so I am told. Frankly, the more time I spend with you, the more I think you are just an ordinary, lazy, and wicked boy—a sinner of the worst kind. I can only hope you do not take after your father." He shook his head in that irritatingly slow way of his. "This I can only hope ..."

Harvus finally walked back to the girls, impatiently bidding them to continue training.

Augum glanced skyward, wishing Mrs. Stone would teleport back and have Harvus choke himself with his own gloved hands. How could she leave them with this twisted man? But was she in danger? What was that noise they heard from the orb?

Jengo glanced at Harvus before stealing a look at Augum's mouth. He quickly averted his eyes and began rifling through the book. "We, uh, we should really get going here, Augum. Don't want to, uh, upset Mr. Harvus anymore, you know?"

Augum slumped back on the log, defeated. Jengo was clearly afraid of the man, not that Augum could blame him. And as much as he loathed it, Harvus was right again—if something did happen to Nana, he would be the only one capable of teleporting them to Antioc, or protecting them. The thought whitened Augum's knuckles, but it was true. If it came down to it, he'd rather see Leera and Bridget safe, even if that meant keeping Harvus around and putting up with his revolting methods of teaching. At least for now …

His eyes wandered to Leera, sitting on the other side of the stream. She glanced up as if sensing his gaze, only to look away as Harvus made a gesture. Trapped, he leaned over the book and tried reading the same paragraph again.

***

It was well past suppertime when Mr. Okeke and Mr. Goss wandered down to the valley, Leland holding their hands.

"Ah, Mr. Okeke and Mr. Goss!" Mr. Harvus called in an unusually sprightly tone. "I suppose you have come to call us to supper, have you not?"

Mr. Goss flashed a brilliant smile as he hoisted his blind son. "We have, Leopold. How is the training going?"

When Mr. Goss glanced his way, Augum averted his face, feeling the awful prickle of shame. He prayed Mr. Goss had not seen the soap in his mouth.

"It is not going as well as I had hoped, Mr. Goss," Harvus replied in false sorrow-filled tones while rocking on his heels. "I am afraid we are behind a little and will be late for supper. There is, however, a small matter I wish to discuss. I need another cabin built immediately, one for myself and Augum, so that I may take a more direct hand in their studies and prevent any future transgressions."

"Transgressions, Leopold?" Mr. Goss' voice was suddenly full of concern. "What kind of transgressions?"

"I am afraid Augum and Leera have been ... acting inappropriately with each other. I am sure you know what I mean."

Augum caught Leera looking at him from across the stream. She was beet red.

Mr. Goss stiffened. "They have? Oh, dear me—"

"Yes, my sentiments exactly, Mr. Goss. They are placing everyone's lives at risk by neglecting their studies. Instead, they choose to focus their energies on ... idle, devilish fancies, if I may be so bold as to say."

Augum's chest tightened. The shame of it was unbearable. He stole a peek to witness Mr. Goss' mouth hang open a moment.

"Dear me," Mr. Goss said again. "But surely it has been perfectly youthful innocence, Leopold, nothing but a misunderstanding—"

"I am afraid it has not, Mr. Goss. I assure you there has *not* been a 'misunderstanding' of any kind. They have soiled themselves with each other's company—"

"But Mr. Harvus," Mr. Okeke interrupted, "they are almost man and woman grown—"

"Ah, but almost is not quite there now, is it, Mr. Okeke?"

Harvus rocked on his heels again in that disgustingly giddy manner, only stopping to adjust his hairpiece before resuming the motion.

"No, the gods have witnessed their indiscretion, as have I," Harvus continued. "Luckily I consulted Mrs. Stone on the matter and she agrees with me on a suitable punishment."

Mr. Goss put Leland down, his face unusually grave. "And that is—?"

"They are forbidden to look upon each other in that way, as they are forbidden to have physical contact."

"Oh. I see. Well, if Mrs. Stone thinks it appropriate—" He exchanged a bewildered look with Mr. Okeke.

"She has given me the authority to train the children as my conscience demands."

Augum couldn't take anymore. He narrowed his eyes, focused on Harvus' hairpiece and, summoning his arcane energies, flicked his wrist. The hairpiece was yanked off the stubby man's head, landing in a nearby puddle of mud. Harvus, his bald head revealed in all its wispy glory, immediately scrambled for it, while everyone—Mr. Goss and Mr. Okeke included—snickered. Leera fell to the ground rolling in laughter.

Harvus raised the soiled hairpiece using Telekinesis, nostrils flaring. When he slowly looked around, everyone clammed up.

"That was quite a gust there, Kwabe," Mr. Goss quickly said.

"Yes, yes it was, Albert," Mr. Okeke agreed with a grave nod of his head.

Leland moaned, even making a sweeping gesture with his arms and a garbled whistling to imitate the wind.

Harvus' cold stare landed on Augum.

Augum tried to act casual. Inside though, his stomach was buzzing. Great, now he'd done it …

"We can certainly build you another cabin, Leopold," Mr. Goss went on, as if nothing had happened. Augum knew otherwise—they were in serious trouble.

Mr. Goss hoisted his son up again. "The only question is, where?"

"Right here by this cabin would be most appropriate, I think," Harvus replied, voice ice cold, eyes still fixed on

Augum, corner of his mouth twitching dangerously. "That way I can be sure of everyone's safety."

"As you wish. We can begin right after supper."

"That would be fine."

There was an awkward silence.

"Well, goodbye then, Leopold."

"Mr. Goss. Mr. Okeke."

Augum felt Jengo's shaking knee accidentally bump into him. "We're goners," Jengo whispered, flipping through the book.

Augum made sure to keep his face slightly averted until Mr. Goss and Mr. Okeke were out of sight. Then he stole a glance back at Harvus, only to find the man still staring at Augum, hairpiece hovering and dripping mud, corner of his mouth still twitching.

Augum swallowed. He had a bad feeling, a really bad feeling …

THREATS

The wind picked up as the sun slowly reddened the sky, yet Augum, Bridget and Leera were still at the cabin, the girls separated from him across the stream. Jengo had been sent back home, but not before a stern and hushed conversation with Mr. Harvus. Jengo towered over the man but nodded again and again, eyes on his feet, until he was finally allowed to leave—and then he strode quickly, head bowed. If he had a tail, it would have been tucked between his knees.

Augum had abandoned trying to absorb a single word from the book—which he was not allowed to touch—choosing to pretend to study the open page before him. His lips had long gone numb from the soap Harvus was still arcanely forcing him to hold in his mouth. Its acidic taste made his stomach gurgle unpleasantly and he began to feel queasy. He longed to rebel, to lash out, to do something, *anything*. But part of him also realized he needed to control himself. It was like a test. Some sort of crazy, twisted test of his tolerance.

Harvus ignored him, spending time patiently training the girls. The hairpiece sat on the log beside Augum, dripping down the sides. Harvus had walked it over and ceremoniously dropped it there without a word before returning to the girls. Augum spent a good deal of time fantasizing about what he would do to the mangy lump. Current favorite was sticking it into cow dung then lighting it on fire.

Augum tried to catch Leera's eye, yet she seemed to be avoiding him now, though he guessed it was probably because Harvus was too close. Sighing, he looked away, trying to think of a way out of this mess. He knew the only real solution was to somehow reach Mrs. Stone—except they hadn't heard from her since her voice had been cut off by an explosion. It was also obvious she had not heard a word Harvus had since said to Augum, for if she had, she would have instantly teleported over to set the man straight.

Or would she? She *had* once spoken of older, harsher methods of training that were supposed to advance the arcane arts quicker. Was this all part of some lesson, some plan for him to ignore Leera and study really hard? Did Mrs. Stone already know they liked each other, and was in fact regretting being so liberal? The thought made his stomach plummet to his turnshoes.

After a while of what seemed like ordinary training, Harvus brought the girls close, placing a gloved hand on each of their shoulders. He smiled as he spoke to them. He gave a quiet speech and they actually began to nod along. After concluding, he politely gestured for them to depart. Bridget and Leera strode by without glancing Augum's way, no doubt to eat a hot supper.

Augum could not believe it—why had they not even looked at him? What had Harvus told them? He watched as the man dusted off his gloves and approached, careful to step well over the stream. All Augum could taste was the acid of the soap. His loathing increased with each of Harvus' measured steps.

Harvus stopped before him, glancing at the muddy hairpiece. Augum's stomach contracted and he felt bile crawl up his throat, only to jam in his mouth. The sensation was so vile he thought he might actually pass out. Harvus only watched, hands behind his back. Finally, Augum had enough and desperately pointed at his face, feeling himself turn purple. Infuriatingly, Harvus kept observing. At last, the pressure was too great and Augum vomited through his nose, choking and gagging and gasping to get his airway clear.

And still, Harvus only stood there, a smug expression on his face.

Augum fell to the ground, writhing, feeling the tunnel of darkness closing in on him, nausea overcoming every sense. The sheer texture of the soap mixing with vomit made his stomach roil with more heaves.

At last, just as the tunnel closed to a pinprick, he felt the soap yanked from his mouth. He instantly vomited the rest of the nasty bile.

Harvus brought him to his feet using Telekinesis and held him there, for Augum would otherwise collapse.

Harvus' voice was matter-of-fact. "You like humiliating people, do you?"

Augum could barely summon the strength to glare—and he still could not speak; Harvus' spell casting was indeed strong.

Harvus tilted his head slightly. "And you seem to have a liking for filthy thoughts. One day, should the gods deem you fit, they will purify you. Until then, we have to resort to such … crude means."

A rage began building within Augum, an old arcane rage he had not felt in some time. It was wild and provoked, dangerous and hungry. Cognizant of its potential, he decided to try to aim it—at the soap. He stiffened his body like a lion about to pounce and expelled the buildup of energy through his mouth. A lightning blast emerged, vaporizing the soap and boring into the ground.

Harvus was so surprised he lost his concentration, allowing Augum to fall to his knees, gasping for breath.

"Damn you," Augum said, surprised he could talk.

"Excuse me?" Harvus' voice was a deadly whisper.

"When Mrs. Stone hears—"

"Voidus lingua!"

Augum's voice again snuffed. He slammed his fist into the ground in frustration.

"Temper, temper," Harvus cooed. "And wild arcanery will not do, Augum Stone, it will not do at all. I have to be honest. I am very disappointed in you. You seem to lack the ability to follow common instructions. Further, you lack respect and discipline. An entire kingdom is relying on you to somehow defeat your father, perhaps by convincing him not to be evil—or some such nonsense, who truly knows—and yet you cavort with some stupid little harlot who should have been left back at the farm."

Augum stood up, spitting out the last of the bile. He snorted through one nostril and then the other, before suddenly shoving at the air before him, screaming "BAKA!"

Except he could make no sound so Harvus was unaffected. Instead, the man chortled to himself as Augum's arms dropped to his sides, hands balled into fists, chest heaving like a bull.

Harvus leaned in a little. "You are nothing more than a common brute, Augum, like those disgusting Sierrans back there that should have stayed in the desert; like those barbaric, filthy Henawa that should keep to the north; like everyone in this hovel of a village. And you know what? I no longer believe you are going to save us or anyone from your father's insanity. You are simply … how shall one put it … too stupid. Too stupid and too weak, and I think our time together is going to be rather short, yes. And I assure you, I would take far more pleasure sipping a delectable fine wine than wasting my precious time with the likes of you and that … little fiend of yours." Harvus straightened, examining his gloved fingers. "However, I am a man of my word, and since I have promised your esteemed great-grandmother that I will look after you, well, I suppose I must endure your ignorance and unruliness for a little while longer. Of course, she also owes me a lot of money, but between you and I, that will be remedied one way or another." He winked.

Augum froze, wondering what he meant by that. Then he firmly pointed at his mouth.

"Oh, you wish to speak? All right. Just be sure it is something worthy of discussion, else you will truly regret it." Harvus made an idle gesture and Augum felt his throat loosen.

"I won't let you get away with this—"

"Now that *is* worthy of discussion, my dear boy, for let me tell you precisely *why* nothing will come of this. You see—" Harvus placed his gloved hands on Augum's shoulders, breathing his rotten rat stench into Augum's face.

"If you do not behave yourself, my dear boy, I am going to take that Agonex and disappear. In fact—" He reached behind Augum with one arm and stripped him of his rucksack, maintaining his grip on Augum's shoulders. "I am going to keep both the Orb of Orion *and* the Agonex, at least until I get paid. Should I hear even a single word of complaint, I shall—" He made a small sweeping gesture here. "—*poof*, disappear, never to be heard from again, and not even your legendary great-grandmother can stop me, for I have learned long ago how to evade those searching for me."

Harvus let go of Augum's shoulders with a slight jerk, holding the rucksack with two fingers as if it had been fouled. He glanced over at his sodden hairpiece. "You are going to clean my hairpiece thoroughly. After, you may go to supper. Then you are going to help build us a new cabin. And you will do it obediently without uttering a single whining word of complaint. And tomorrow, you are going to happily study, for we must keep up appearances, is that not so?"

Harvus took a step closer as Augum glared at him mutinously. "If I discover any kind of … rebelliousness, or … filthiness … or anything of that nature, I assure you, I can be quite mean, and not just to you, but to that little disgusting harlot. Now get cleaning."

Augum did as he was told, seething all the while. As he washed the cursed hairpiece in the stream, fantasizing about setting it on fire and placing it in a dung catapult, he kept asking himself what they could do. Nothing came to mind, other than hoping for Mrs. Stone to return. Yet if she didn't return for some time? They still had to learn their first summoning spell, and they still had to get to the Antioc library and figure out a way to use the Agonex against his father.

The more he thought about it, the more absurd it all sounded. Harvus was right again—they stood no chance, none. It was obvious now that the man was in it for the money and that was all. If only they had found out sooner! He didn't care one lick about them or the quest or anything. All he wanted was gold—gold and some twisted sense of control …

Augum suddenly realized something—he had been in this position before. The Pendersons; Dap; Vion Rames; The Blade of Sorrows; Erika Scarson and her vile nephew, Robin Scarson; even his own father—all wanted something from him, and all had failed. He had never let anyone triumph over him.

And he was not about to start now. A plan began to form …

"Here you go, Mr. Harvus," Augum said, handing over the freshly-washed hairpiece. "I am sorry I did that. I regret it now."

Harvus frowned, no doubt suspecting some trick. "Well then I am most glad to hear it, my boy. An apology is the first step to redemption. Now run off to supper, there's a good lad."

Augum strode off, not looking back, feeling better for some reason. So what if he can't kiss Leera or hold her hand? So what if the loaf of a man had the Agonex and the Orb of Orion in his possession? So what if Mrs. Stone might not be able to come to their rescue?

None of that mattered, because he vowed to find a way to fix it all.

* * *

By the time Augum got to the Okeke cabin, everyone was gone except for Mr. Okeke, who kindly re-warmed a generous portion of stew. Augum sat at the table without a word, mind racing with ideas, none of which proved practical as of yet—retrieving the Orb of Orion and the Agonex without Mrs. Stone would be risky at best. And how were they to get to the Antioc library without Harvus? Horses could prove very dangerous in these times. What about appealing to a higher authority? No, there *was* no higher authority, except, ironically, the Legion here in town. Mr. Haroun was not a warlock, nor was anyone else in Milham—

"Augum?" Mr. Okeke was sitting across from him, hands folded neatly. He was wearing a linen long-sleeved shirt decorated with woodblock-printed Sierran desert animals.

"Yes, Mr. Okeke?"

"Your food."

"Oh. Right." Augum absently picked up the wooden spoon, slightly unnerved by the way Mr. Okeke was looking at him with those perpetually bloodshot eyes. He must think him a lecherous fiend now. How disappointed was he in him, and what other stories had Harvus concocted for the man?

Augum tentatively spooned some soup, quickly realizing how hungry he was. He resisted the urge to rush. "Where is everyone?" he asked between mouthfuls, glad to be tasting something other than tallow soap.

"There is a meeting in town between Mr. Haroun, the townsfolk, and the Legion. After which, we will go and hastily construct a cabin for you and Mr. Harvus, though I cannot fathom why it must be done in such short order."

Augum could think of a few reasons. He noticed Bridget and Leera's royal blue robes folded neatly on a chair in the living area. His heart panged. Suddenly he felt alone. He missed Leera terribly. He missed Bridget's smiling face, her level head, her friendship.

"Augum, is there perhaps something you would like to tell me?"

Augum felt the blood drain from his face. Great, Mr. Okeke *did* think the worst of him. "No, Mr. Okeke," he said meekly. He returned to his soup, keeping his eyes low, mind once again racing with ideas. They could tie Harvus down and run away with the artifacts. No, that would still leave them short of a library trip—

"Augum, is Mr. Harvus … is he mistreating you?"

Augum's spoon briefly froze in midair before continuing to his mouth. How was he supposed to answer that? And what could Mr. Okeke possibly do about it anyway? He had no arcane powers, and if he got involved, who knew what Harvus would do to him or Jengo in revenge? It was no secret the two quietly despised each other. Yet something about the way Mr. Okeke was looking at him told him he could trust the man with what he longed to tell him, to tell *someone*.

Augum quickly checked the windows, half expecting to find Harvus' pale pudgy face peering in. Seeing them dark and empty, he left the spoon in the bowl and sat up, jaw firm. "Harvus is keeping the Agonex and Orb of Orion hostage."

Mr. Okeke immediately slammed the table with his fist. "I knew it, that foul dog. If I had any arcane—"

"Mr. Okeke, I never did anything … *untoward* … with Leera—"

"Of *course* you did not! You have not done anything any of us have not done before manhood or womanhood, and although I was opposed to it at first, my own son is going to marry a young Tiberran woman when they turn of age next year. Young love is precious, especially in these dark times, and we as a community must nurture it. Although I urge strong caution with young love—there is no need to rush into marriage, for example, for you have your entire lives ahead of you—I do now recognize people *must* be allowed to make their own choices, their own mistakes, and choose their own paths."

"I … I can't tell you how much it means to hear you say that, Mr. Okeke."

"You are almost a man grown, Augum. You have a great deal of responsibility on your shoulders, far more than any youth I have ever met, or probably ever will. Far more than I think healthy for one so young. You *will* make mistakes. You *will* know failure. But I have no doubt—none whatsoever—that you will make the best of those situations, and learn from them." Mr. Okeke finished his speech with a slow, proud nod that lifted Augum's spirits even more.

Augum swallowed and nodded his thanks, not knowing what more to say. But a creep of shame still remained—he only hoped he could live up to Mr. Okeke's expectations.

Mr. Okeke glanced toward the door. "Mr. Harvus has to realize this is *not* Canterra. I have never liked the man. There is something ... not right with him."

"But without Nana, we'll need him to get to the library in Antioc." If he'd even take them there. Everything was in question at this point. They had to solve this Harvus problem, and soon.

"He is cunning. What does he want?"

"I think he's only waiting for Nana to pay him, then I think he'll quit. Or at least I hope he will."

Mr. Okeke pressed his hands together. "Augum, do you honestly believe he will give up the Agonex and the Orb of Orion even after he is paid?"

Augum bit his lip in thought. Harvus had to know the immeasurable value of both of the artifacts, yet who would buy them from him? Only the Legion, and the man hates the Legion. But surely even he wouldn't do such a thing ... would he?

"I guess not ... err ... I'm not sure."

Mr. Okeke nodded slowly. "Do you mind if I speak with Albert on the matter?"

"Of course not, Mr. Okeke." If only Harvus had a weakness—suddenly it occurred to Augum that he *did* have one—

"Wine," he blurted.

"I'm sorry?"

"Harvus likes wine."

There was the sound of footsteps and talking outside. Mr. Okeke gave a knowing nod and fell silent. Soon the door opened and in spilled the entire throng—Jengo, Mr. Goss, Leland, Bridget, Leera, and lastly, tight-lipped Mr. Harvus, whose beady eyes immediately found Augum. There was a victorious glint in them.

"Those Legion soldiers are taking a mighty risk indeed, Leopold," Mr. Goss said, continuing his conversation from outside. "I think them brave men. Perhaps we could all work together somehow."

Harvus cleared his throat in a reminding fashion when Mr. Goss had not placed his shoes in a straight manner, something the trio had long learned to do. For a moment, Mr. Goss was taken aback, but then happily arranged his shoes, chortling, "You are quite particular, Leopold, almost as particular as my dearly departed wife, bless her soul."

Augum noticed Leera staring at him, but when he turned in her direction, she looked away, cheeks reddening. His insides buzzed like a scion.

"Perhaps a quick nightcap?" Mr. Okeke offered with a smile.

"I am afraid we still have work to do," Mr. Harvus said. "The cabin for Augum and I needs to be built, and I simply cannot do it myself."

He *could* do it himself though, Augum thought venomously, for he was an *earth* Warlock. Only he didn't want to risk getting his hands dirty!

Mr. Okeke retrieved a bottle of wine, readying to uncork it. "Surely one drink will not slow us swarthy men down?"

Harvus' gaze fell greedily upon the bottle. "No, I … I better not. Perhaps another time, Mr. Okeke. But a piece of chocolate would be nice, thank you very much."

Mr. Okeke's face fell. His eyes met Augum's and they briefly shared a look. He put the bottle away and found some chocolate, passing it around to everyone. Augum used the opportunity to stand near Leera, who still refused to meet his gaze.

"So, uh, how is Haylee?"

Bridget flashed Augum a strange warning look. It suddenly occurred to him Harvus might have threatened them, and he moved away from the girls, not waiting for a reply.

They stood around eating chocolate in silence, the tension as thick as porridge. Mr. Harvus was the only one who seemed unconcerned, adjusting his hairpiece—now dry and properly combed—and glancing around the room. There certainly was no joking about that mop of fluff now. In fact, nothing about the man seemed remotely funny at the moment.

"I have never really noticed these before, Mr. Okeke," Harvus said, approaching the carved ebony figurines. "What are they, and why are they so … grotesquely malformed?"

"Sierran nightmare carvings. When a Sierran has a nightmare, he is supposed to carve it into a figurine. He will then not have the nightmare again."

"How … superstitious and utterly barbaric, I must say." Harvus turned. "And I mean no offense of course, Mr. Okeke, I am sure you yourself do not believe in such … peasant fancies."

Mr. Okeke's ebony face flushed. "But are you not a believer in the gods, Mr. Harvus?"

Harvus stiffened. "I am indeed, Mr. Okeke, but I hardly think believing in the gods is superstition. Such talk is considered heresy in Canterra, and is liable to result in the separation of one's head from one's body."

"But Canterrans consider warlocks heretics as well, do they not? Witches, in fact, if I am not mistaken."

The corner of Harvus' mouth twitched.

After an awful silence of the two men glaring at each other, Mr. Goss hoisted Leland with forced cheer. "Perhaps now would be a good time to build that cabin, would it not, everyone?"

Harvus caught himself. "It would indeed, Mr. Goss. Come, children, put on your shoes, change into your robes, and help your mentor and your elders build a cabin for Augum and I."

The group gathered themselves and left, sharing fleeting looks.

DISCOVERIES

They built the cabin on the other side of the stream. It had taken a lot longer because Harvus refused to use his arcane powers to help, except to fell some logs. He did not touch anything with his white gloves either, except his hairpiece of course. The trio and Jengo performed most of the labor using Telekinesis and saws Mr. Okeke had brought from his cabin. He and Mr. Goss did what they could, sawing and setting logs into place; even Leland helped, squishing mud between the cracks. It was a hard-won effort that took them past midnight, all to complete a crude one-room cabin with one shuttered window and one door.

Throughout, Augum had not exchanged a single word with the girls, other than giving them instructions or asking for help. It was as if they were meek servants suddenly, too shy to reply. Even Mr. Goss noticed, once asking Leera if anything was the matter. She immediately said, "Nothing at all, Mr. Goss," and hurried off to help Bridget.

At the end of the night, they were tired, sweaty and muddy. Augum's palm light had dulled with his exhaustion—all he wanted to do was go to bed.

After the trio mutedly bid Mr. Okeke, Mr. Goss, Leland and Jengo goodnight, Harvus had them wash up in the stream. He then made them watch as he cast a protective spell on their cabins, as well as one more spell on Augum and Leera. Augum thought it another touch alarm spell, except this time it had to do with the cabins somehow.

"Just in case you get any impure ideas," Mr. Harvus said with a cold smile. "Now off to bed with you. I will be back soon."

Augum retreated to the empty cabin. He watched Harvus depart, taking the Orb of Orion and the Agonex with him. As soon as he was gone, Augum opened the door, finding Leera and Bridget already standing in the doorway of the other cabin across the stream. Both girls placed a finger to their lips. Bridget glanced to the hill and quickly scurried over.

"Aug, we're in serious trouble—" she began in a frightened whisper.

"I know. Harvus took the Agonex and the Orb of Orion as hostage."

"That's not the worst of it," Bridget said. "I don't think he'll give them back even after he gets paid."

"What did he say to you?"

"He told us that if we don't start behaving he'll teleport both of us to a place no one will ever find us, and I *believe* him, Augum." She swept her long cinnamon hair out of her eyes and sighed. "Leera misses you terribly."

Hearing that filled his heart with bittersweet joy. "Tell her I miss her too—" He reached out to his friend for comfort but she recoiled.

"Better not, you know—"

"Yes, of course." He fidgeted. "I told Mr. Okeke about it all. He'll tell Mr. Goss. Not sure what they can do though."

"Good." She paused, glanced at the ground. "I've been a fool, Augum. I shouldn't have been so trusting—"

"Don't even mention it." He smiled.

She swallowed, nodded, and returned a half-hearted smile. "Listen, I was thinking you need to focus tomorrow, really learn Summon Minor Elemental. The words to the spell are 'summano elementus minimus'. Can you remember that?"

"I think so. Sunnamo elementus niminus."

"No, you're switching your n's and m's. Again—summano elementus minimus."

"Summano elementus minimus. And the spell name is Summon Minor Elemental."

"Good. Practice it just the way I said it—and make sure to hit the inflection on the last couple letters."

"Right. Still a mouthful." He glanced back at the dark hilltop. "You better go, don't want you to get in trouble too—oh, and Bridge, stay on his good side if you can. One of us has to."

"Good point. Good luck tomorrow," and she ran back to Leera, who gave Augum a forlorn look.

"Miss you," Augum mouthed.

"Miss you too," Leera mouthed back, before disappearing inside.

Soon the light in their cabin went dark and Augum was left alone again. He curled up on the floor and waited, reciting the name and words to the spell, being particularly sure to nail the inflection. Sometime later, Harvus returned with a cozy bedroll, a pillow, washbasin, and blankets, but none of them were for Augum. In fact, Harvus completely ignored him, which suited Augum just fine.

* * *

"Time to get up, young man," Harvus said in the morning. "We have a long day ahead."

Augum had slept terribly on the floor. It had been a cold and damp night and he shivered through most of it. His brain was addled with tiredness, something he knew might affect his spell casting—if there was one thing being a warlock demanded, it was getting a good night's sleep.

Harvus knocked on the girls' door while Augum washed up in the stream. At least it was a sunny day. Birds chirped merrily. A light wind stirred the treetops. The snow was almost completely gone, though the incessant drip of snowmelt continued on, mixing with the bubbling stream.

Soon they were on their way to the Okeke home for breakfast, something Augum was actually looking forward to since Harvus never took breakfast with them, preferring to eat at the inn. Maybe they could come up with a plan together. But when they arrived at the Okeke cabin, Augum was disappointed to see Harvus invite himself in.

Mr. Goss stood in greeting. "What a nice surprise, Mr. Harvus."

Augum exchanged a secret look with Bridget and Leera—that was the first time Mr. Goss had called Mr. Harvus by his proper title and not by his first name. Mr. Okeke had to have told Mr. Goss everything—but what were the two of them up to? They were smiling like a pair of conniving foxes.

There was a mild look of surprise on Harvus' face as he took off his boots.

"How did you sleep, Mr. Harvus?" Mr. Goss pressed, offering a seat to the man. Augum noticed an extra bowl had been laid out on the table—they had obviously expected Harvus to join them.

"Very well, thank you, Mr. Goss." Harvus picked some dirt off one of his white gloves. "Though I much prefer the privacy and comfort of the inn, of course. However, sacrifices have to be made for the good of all."

"Indeed, for the good of all," echoed Mr. Goss.

Jengo took his place at the table, shooting Augum a confused and frightened look. He had obviously not been told anything. Knowing Jengo, that was probably for the best.

Mr. Okeke poured Mr. Harvus a cup of steaming tea. "Any word from Mrs. Stone?"

Harvus withdrew an embroidered cloth and placed it on the table. He unfolded it to reveal a golden engraved fork, knife and spoon. "I am afraid not, Mr. Okeke. I truly hope she is all right." Though everything about his face said otherwise. He gave the already shining utensils a thorough polish.

Mr. Okeke inclined his head. "As do we all."

Augum noticed something peculiar about the flatware—it was engraved with someone else's initials. Maybe it was bought second hand?

Jengo helped his father serve breakfast, which consisted of eggs, sausage, potatoes and oatcake.

"Today is a special day," Mr. Goss said. "A day banned by the Legion, but we are lucky to have a constable willing to look the other way."

"Lover's Day is a peasant holiday advocating depravity and immorality, Mr. Goss," Mr. Harvus said, carefully cutting up his sausage. "And the children and I shall not be participating in any of the events."

"That is most unfortunate, Mr. Harvus," Mr. Goss replied cheerily, "because there is going to be a marvelous evening feast, with the finest wine. There will be a dance and games and singing and—" but when he saw the sour expression on Harvus' face, he quickly changed tact. "Oh but during the day there will be butter cookies, tart cakes, and Canterran chocolate—"

Mr. Harvus looked up. "Canterran chocolate, you say? I have not had the pleasure of—" He cleared his throat quickly. "Perhaps we can make a brief appearance, I suppose. If all precautions are taken, of course."

"Of course. The festivities begin at noon."

Augum stole a look at Leera—he had entirely forgotten it was Lover's Day, and it made not being able to hold her hand that much more agonizing. By the look she was giving him, he guessed she was thinking the exact same thing.

Harvus glanced up and they quickly looked away, but Augum knew, judging by the man's stupid micro frown, that he'd been caught, and cursed himself for being careless.

"Are you going to see Priya and her mother later, Jengo?" Mr. Okeke asked after taking a sip of tea.

Jengo's eyes briefly darted to Harvus. "Y-yes, if it's all right with you, Father."

"What kind of father would I be if I were to stand in the way of my own son, betrothed to such a beautiful young woman, on Lover's Day? Of course it is all right. In fact, I encourage it. Go see Priya and make sure to tell her we look forward to sitting with her and her mother at tonight's feast."

"Yes, Father." Jengo took a nervous sip of tea before rushing through his food.

One of Harvus' brows rose knowingly and the briefest smug expression flashed across his pudgy face, before once again going blank. Augum had the impression Harvus might have something to say on the matter later.

"Will Haylee be spending the day with Chaska?" Mr. Okeke pressed.

Jengo paused, fork shaking in his hand. "I … I'm not sure, Father."

Of course they were spending it together, Augum thought. It's just that poor Jengo didn't want to draw Harvus' wrath.

"Do you have any children, Mr. Harvus?" Mr. Okeke asked.

"I uh, I do not, no."

"Ah, that is most unfortunate, for children are the light of life."

"Yes, well, I have my duties, Mr. Okeke, and they suit me just fine."

"I see you do not wear a wedding ring. No wife either?"

Harvus froze as if recalling something long past. Then he caught himself and cleared his throat properly. "When I was younger I … but that is long past, I was a sinner then."

Bridget gave a warm smile. "How young, Mr. Harvus?"

"Too young, I am afraid. I was desperately poor and stupid. Now let us not discuss the matter, it is inappropriate for breakfast."

Mr. Okeke gathered a potato onto his fork. "Of course, Mr. Harvus, forgive us for our prying ways."

The tense meal concluded with honey-dipped almonds and milk, after which Augum, Bridget, Leera and Jengo quietly departed with Mr. Harvus to the cabins, where they resumed their training. Jengo, still working on his 1st degree, was made to study the blue book on arcaneology on his own. Augum now realized Harvus had always refused to give Jengo one-on-one training for one reason or another—even though that is what Mrs. Stone hired him for—and that's why Jengo was so far behind.

Augum was running through his spells as usual, slowly developing a minor headache, when Jengo called out.

"Mr. Harvus, sir! I need some help explaining this part about hand gestures for the Repair spell."

Harvus, who had been busy critiquing the way Bridget was forming her hands with the Repair spell—a spell she had long mastered—turned to Jengo with a distasteful look. "Augum, would you please take a moment and instruct the poor soul? Mind you are not to touch the book as you have not earned that privilege back yet."

"Yes, Mr. Harvus." Augum hated being so polite to him, but knew it was necessary for now. He strolled over to Jengo. "Which part do you need help with?"

"This part." Jengo slid over the book, tapping at a particular paragraph.

"But this chapter's on the 3rd degree, Jengo, you're only on the—" Augum froze, suddenly realizing what Jengo was indicating—*the counterspell to Object Alarm!*

"You're a genius," Augum whispered. "Think it'll work against an off-the-book extension though?"

Jengo stole a glance at Harvus before whispering, "I don't see why not. The counterspell *is* an extension in itself."

"Right. Keep nodding your head while I read the section." Augum pretended to point to a few things in the book for Jengo, who faked interest, while he absorbed every word as if his life depended on it.

" 'The counterspell to Object Alarm is far more complex than the average apprentice suspects'," Augum read under his breath, " 'for not only is it critical for the caster to arcanely reverse the spell in its entirety, but the hand motion must be reversed as well, with the caster placing his hands on the object and withdrawing them the moment the spell is triggered. The exact phraseology is equally as important and must be said in reverse, with a reverse inflection. Here below is the exact wordage—' "

Jengo suddenly flipped the book to the chapter on the 1st degree as Harvus strode toward them.

"How are things coming along, my apprentices?"

"Excellent, Mr. Harvus. Augum is being very helpful."

"Good." Harvus picked up a nearby branch using Telekinesis and floated it over. With a flick of both gloved hands, he snapped it in two, allowing the pieces to fall to the earth. "Please demonstrate the correct gesture for the Repair spell then, Jengo."

Augum felt a cold sweat—Harvus was on to them again. But Jengo surprised him by simply spreading his palms over the stick and saying, "Apreyo," his pronunciation perfect. The two stick ends joined seamlessly.

Harvus' thin brows rose up his forehead. "Are you telling me, son, that you have been having trouble with the gesture, yet you know the spell?"

"Well that's what Augum helped me fine tune, sir," Jengo quickly replied.

"I see." Harvus' eyes flicked between the two of them. He presented a gloved hand. "The book please, Jengo."

Jengo dutifully handed it over. Harvus immediately began scanning through it, looking for guilt. After a time, his lips thinned and he returned it to Jengo, evidently finding nothing. "You may continue, child. Augum, follow me please."

Augum thanked Jengo with his eyes before following Harvus to a spot away from everyone, catching a pensive look from the girls as they practiced shooting the First Offensive at a stump.

Harvus turned around. "Are you sorry for the way you acted yesterday?"

"Yes, Mr. Harvus." Lying with a straight face was hard.

"You are what, Augum?"

"I am sorry for the way I acted yesterday, Mr. Harvus." Really hard …

"Good, I am very happy to hear it. I trust in the future you will think twice before slandering my good name or cavorting in an unwholesome manner." He raised his chin, hands behind his back. "You have been making progress, Augum. Now, if you can tell me the name of the 4th degree elemental spell and correctly pronounce its verbiage, you may begin learning it."

"The name of the spell is Summon Minor Elemental, sir, and …" Augum formed his thoughts together—he had been practicing the pronunciation to himself half the night and morning. The problem was the trigger words were a tongue twister and despite Bridget's warning, he still kept accidentally switching the n's with m's. "And the trigger words are … summano elementus minimus."

Harvus' face slackened. Augum knew he had been expecting him to fail that little test. Probably had a fine punishment lined up too. It gave him satisfaction knowing he had foiled the mangy-head's petty plans.

Harvus' shoulders drooped. "Good," he said tonelessly, sighing. "I suppose it is a waste of time training each of you separately. Bridget, Leera—come here please, girls."

Bridget and Leera walked over, blue robes swinging.

"Everyone here has now earned the right to learn the 4th degree elemental spell."

When Harvus had his back turned, Augum mouthed "Thank you" to Bridget for helping him with the pronunciation the night before. When Harvus turned to Augum to make some boring point, the girls smiled proudly in response from behind the man's back.

"… and since everyone's pronunciation is passable," Harvus droned on, "let us begin with the gesture, which will be the most complex for you thus far." Harvus rubbed his white-gloved hands together. "Watch my hands now." He drew a five-pointed star in midair, his two hands precisely mirroring each other's movements, coming together at the top. "As you will note, I have just drawn the outline of a small man—"

Augum dared the quickest glance at Leera who, as he suspected, had a mischievous look in her eye. *Small man*. He wanted to guffaw with her but was careful to keep a straight face, as was she.

"—you start from the abdomen and draw the legs," Harvus continued, "being careful to keep your hands exactly mirrored. Once you have drawn the outline of the legs, you draw the arms and then the head. It is important to finish speaking the last syllable of the spell the moment your hands touch at the head. As well, your arcane energies must reach an apex at the *same time*. Understand?"

"Yes, Mr. Harvus," they chorused languidly.

"Now observe." Harvus started drawing, beginning the phrase "Summano elementus minimus" halfway through, and finishing the last syllable as his fingers touched at the head of the invisible drawing. An earthen elemental about the size of small child immediately ripped to life, landing on its feet between them and Harvus.

The trio took a couple steps back, wary of the strange creature made of rocks, twigs and earth.

Harvus pointed at Jengo. "Elementus—attack!" and the little monster sprinted at Jengo, who yelped, tossed his book aside and ran for his life.

"Elementus—halt!"

The creature stopped.

"Elementus—here!"

The small earth elemental strode back to them as fluidly as Fentwick, the animated ancient suit of armor from Castle Arinthian.

"The duration of the spell depends on your concentration and typically increases with every degree." Harvus casually paced around the tiny elemental as Jengo warily made his way back. "The real trick of the spell is doing it precisely in battle. It is difficult as is, but during the heat of combat—well, let me just say that many a warlock has hit their ceiling with this very spell."

There was a glint to Harvus' eyes, as if he was betting on just that happening to Augum.

Harvus waved idly and the elemental disappeared with a pop. "Now let us practice the gesture together. If you all do a good job, I may allow you to attend this evening's feast."

"But Mr. Harvus," Leera began, "what about the afternoon's festivities and games?"

"I do not want to hear any whining, my dear child. We have more important things to do. As I said, if you work hard and focus, I *may* allow you to attend this evening's feast."

The trio couldn't help but groan.

***

They trained and trained, yet the spell truly was difficult. As Harvus had said, it was particularly challenging drawing a precise gesture while timing the words of the spell *with* the arcane energies. Thus it was no surprise that when noon arrived, none of them had found success, for juggling three very different concepts all at once was simply beyond their current capabilities.

"I am disappointed," Harvus said as they lay around gasping, exhausted from their efforts. "I do not think you have won the privilege to attend lunch at a festivities table. I shall have Mr. Goss bring some sustenance here. Please sit in silent reflection while I am gone."

Harvus left them alone, glancing back once from the top of the valley. As soon as he was gone, Jengo hissed to get their attention.

"Harvus hasn't told you the entirety of the spell. I've been reading up on it, suspecting something like that."

"What? He would do that?" Bridget asked.

Leera sat up to glare at Bridget. "Are you kidding? Where have you been?"

"He's leaving out the part about visualization," Jengo continued. "You have to envision the elemental being alive and stuff."

Leera groaned and fell back to the ground. "Great, the spell's hard enough."

"Of course! All we had to do is remember Mrs. Stone's teachings," Bridget said. "The spell demands all five precepts of arcane competence—visualization, pronunciation, arcane manipulation, gestural precision, and timing."

Leera, splayed like a defeated warrior on the grass, stared skyward. "Well I wish *she* was teaching us the spell instead of Harvus."

"This spell is complex," Bridget admitted, "and I suspect it would usually take at least a month to learn at an academy—"

"But … we can learn it quickly, right?" Leera interrupted.

"There is no 'but'. We train with it all day, every day, until we get it. At the academy, we have other classes. At the academy a day ends in the afternoon. But here, we can focus."

"It's going to take a lot of practice obviously," Augum said, "but we can do it, I know we can. Oh and by the way, Jengo discovered something. Jengo, can you flip to that page again?"

Jengo gave a furtive glance over his shoulder. "All right, but make it quick, I don't want to get in trouble."

The trio hurried over, Augum and Leera careful not to touch each other accidentally lest they receive some kind of shock.

"The counterspell to Object Alarm," Bridget mumbled. "Can't believe I haven't thought of that before …"

"I'm not allowed to touch the book," Augum said, "but you are. Think you can learn the counterspell and teach it to me and Leera?"

"I'll try." Bridget looked to the forest. "We better break this up."

They scurried back to their places and lay down.

Mr. Harvus soon returned with Mr. Goss, who was holding a basket. Mr. Goss placed the basket before them and adjusted his spectacles. "I am sorry you are unable to join Leland and I for lunch, but I am sure we shall see you at tonight's feast. Good luck everyone! Work hard!"

They ate quietly, Augum and Jengo together, Bridget and Leera separately, and Mr. Harvus inside the cabin, swatting at flies.

"Look at him," Jengo said under his breath, "it's like he exists just to cause us misery."

"I don't want to look at him," Augum said. "Might not be able to finish my lunch." Mentor or no mentor, Harvus had a particularly punchable face, and Augum was not ashamed to think it.

Jengo smiled. "Where do you think he hid the Agonex and the Orb of Orion?"

"If we're lucky, in his room at the inn. If we're unlucky, well … I should've cast Object Track on both when I had the chance."

"Spell would have expired anyway—you're not practiced enough yet."

Augum ceded a grunt and took a bite of the sandwich Mr. Goss had provided. "You're really taking arcanery seriously, aren't you?" It was interesting to watch. He wished he took as much pleasure studying the yellow and blue books as Jengo did.

"I *dream* of it, Augum. All the complexities, the nuances. I dream of performing them precisely and successfully. But the healing element is *hard*. I have to memorize all these internal body functions and stuff, not to mention weird names. Tibia. Femur. Those are names of bones!"

"Huh."

"It's ridiculous. Though lightning is more dangerous, Bridget told me healing is three times harder to master than any of the other elements. And I love that book. I'd spend all my time reading it if I could. Can't actually put any of it into practice yet, but I'll get there."

"You'd make a great arcaneologist."

"You really think so?" Jengo brightened before suddenly lowering his head as Harvus peeked out of the cabin suspiciously. When he disappeared, Jengo, while pretending to fiddle with his burgundy robe, whispered, "By the way, I know you didn't get that far, but the counterspell verbiage to Object Alarm is just the reverse."

"What do you mean?"

"I mean, you literally say the words to Object Alarm backwards, inflection and all, every letter."

"Are you jesting? How am I—"

But Jengo shushed him as Harvus' face once again popped out from the cabin.

"No talking!" he snapped.

They finished in silence, Augum's mind racing for a way to learn the verbiage backwards. Yet his brain couldn't do it. Then it came to him rather suddenly—all he had to do was *write* the words out backwards and read them. The inflection was the tricky part though, and without someone trained telling him how to say it, he didn't even know where to start. Luckily, that was exactly the kind of thing Bridget was good at.

The afternoon was even more grueling, with Harvus demanding they cast all the 4th degree spells, even though the trio wanted to focus on the Summon Minor Elemental spell. He made Bridget and Leera square off, casting Confusion, Deafness, and Fear on each other, while Augum was made to cast the same spells on Jengo, who proved a most susceptible opponent. Augum felt so sorry for him constantly stumbling about blubbering like a fool, that he purposefully bungled the spell when Harvus wasn't looking.

Yet the more success they saw with the spells, the stricter Harvus became, until his twitch returned. What he failed to realize, Augum thought in satisfaction, was that he was their primary motivation to learn—they would succeed out of spite.

"Unacceptable, you sun-baked beanpole!" Harvus sniped when Jengo had failed to locate a stone Harvus hid halfway up a tree. "You must concentrate!"

Bridget had gasped and was about to say something but held herself in check at the last moment, probably remembering one of them should stay on the demented mentor's good side.

Jengo meekly stared at his feet.

"Jengo?" came a soft voice from the trees.

Jengo glanced between Harvus and the forest. "Priya! Ms. Singh! You should not be here, we are training—"

Priya, a thin, sienna-skinned woman with very long black hair, gracefully helped an old woman down the slope, who Augum recognized as Ms. Singh, Priya's temperamental and quirky mother. The old woman had gray hair wrapped in a tight bun and was hunched over a cane. Large clunky spectacles dangled off her nose. Both women wore ornate coral cloth wrapped around their waists and draped over their shoulders.

As the women shuffled forward, Harvus straightened.

"Jengo, why have you not come to the festivities?" Priya asked in hurt tones. "I have been waiting and waiting." Jeweled studs piercing her lips and nose caught glints from the sun.

Jengo cast a sidelong glance at Harvus. "Priya, my love, please—we have been training."

Harvus cleared his throat in a perfunctory manner. "It is rude not to introduce people, Jengo."

But Augum swore Harvus knew exactly who they were, as he had undoubtedly seen them in the village, not to mention heard talk of them numerous times.

Ms. Singh swung her cane Harvus' way. "Panjita certainly agrees with the pasty toad."

"Mother that is *very* rude—" Priya quickly turned to Mr. Harvus. "Do please forgive us, Mr.—?"

"—Harvus," the man said as his twitch renewed. "*Mr.* Harvus." He was glaring at Ms. Singh.

"Mr. Harvus, I am sorry, Mother has a way of—"

Ms. Singh smacked Priya's hand. "Daughter will not condescend Mother!" She turned her unruly gaze back to Harvus, who actually matched her height. "Is the pasty marmot from Canterra? Is that why he holds himself in such stiff bearing, as if a stick were jammed—"

"Mother, *please*!"

Jengo quickly cut in. "Mr. Harvus, this is my betrothed, Priya Singh, and her mother, Ms. Singh. And this is my—our—mentor, Mr. Harvus."

Ms. Singh turned to Jengo. "Will the tall brute who has stolen Panjita's daughter please explain why there is a dead animal on the pasty marmot's head?"

Harvus turned a dull shade of pink. A second twitch joined the first, the two firing off at different times and from opposite sides of his pudgy face.

"Uh, we really ought to get back to training, Ms. Singh," Jengo stammered, wringing his hands.

Ms. Singh glared at him. "As is right! Lazy dogs need to learn how to work hard! That is how Panjita has earned her way through life—with hard work! Now Panjita must put up with all these asinine Solian customs, and out of courtesy she is forced to escort her silly daughter every—"

"We'll be going now," Priya said, smiling lovingly at Jengo. "It *is* Lover's Day though, my love. I guess I'll see you at the feast? There is a dance after, and music."

"Y-yes, sure." Jengo did not dare to look at Harvus, who Augum suspected was concocting other plans for Jengo, if not for all of them.

They watched the two women amble back up the shallow valley. Augum chanced a glance at Leera, who was staring at him, expression full of sorrow. How he longed to hold her then. Above all, how he longed for them to be rid of this cursed man.

PLANS

After the Singhs left, Harvus snarled terse commands for Augum, Bridget, Leera and Jengo to sit apart in silent study, though what they were supposed to study was not clear as Harvus had forbidden them access to study material. Meanwhile, the man patrolled in a slow circle, muttering under his breath. The facial twitches worsened, with one of his eyes joining in now and then.

He's coming undone at the seams, Augum thought, watching the man snap at Jengo as he passed. Jengo immediately sat up straighter, back against the tree he had been assigned to—as they all had, in opposite corners of the small clearing. They were not to look at each other or communicate in any way. The whole encounter with Ms. Singh must have really set him off, though to be fair, she did have that effect on people.

Augum glanced at the clear sky, wondering how much of the feast they were going to miss. Probably the whole thing, he surmised, tearing a blade of grass and placing it in his mouth.

"Take that out of your mouth," Harvus barked when he strolled by. "You are not a cow."

Augum spat the grass out with a scowl.

Harvus stopped walking. "Correct your attitude, Augum, lest you find yourself without a mentor of any kind, trading stolen goods with bandits to get by."

Augum made his face blank but Harvus still stood there. What an odd thing to say. Then he recalled that golden flatware of his and how the initials did not match up to his name. Was it possible Harvus had stolen the items? No, couldn't be …

Harvus stared at him with his nasty little eyes. "You know, the more I look at you, the more I am convinced of your inevitable failure. You are a useless child with a banal talent. Maybe you should think about joining one of those bandit camps as an outlaw, the gods know you would certainly fit right in."

It took a lot of self-discipline for Augum to keep his face blank. It paid off though, for Harvus smacked his lips together before finally strolling away.

Augum leaned back against the tree. It was like being imprisoned all over again. He worried about Nana. She usually contacted them at least once a day to check in. Though without access to the Orb of Orion, there was no way for him to know if she had been trying to contact them.

The fact Harvus had claimed the Agonex and the orb made Augum's shoulders tense up. After catching a glimpse of Bridget, with her legs pulled in and head resting on her knees, he realized he was wasting time. He decided to mentally rehearse all his spells, especially the newer ones from the 4th degree. When Harvus was not looking, he even moved objects with Telekinesis, summoned his shield, or quietly repaired a stick. Before long, the others were doing it too, but always behind Harvus' back, playing a daring game of cat and mouse.

At one point, Leera floated over a small piece of bark. Augum turned it over to find a heart scratched into it. Using a sharp stone, he etched in a plus sign and another heart, and sent it back to her. Her face lit up after receiving it. Then an idea came to him. He surreptitiously tore a piece of bark off the tree behind him and began etching in the Object Alarm trigger phrase—*concutio del alarmo*. Then, painstakingly, he wrote it backwards underneath—*omrala led oitucnoc*.

As Harvus patrolled, Augum tried to make sense how in Sithesia he was supposed say it backwards *with* the right inflection. It sounded utterly ridiculous, especially the *oitucnoc* word. Then he had another idea, and wrote, "Help pronounce" on the bark, before stealthily sending it to Bridget. She caught it, examined it carefully, and immediately went to work practicing saying it to herself.

The sky steadily ripened from a gentle saffron to glowing amber, and finally to a dusty crimson. The feast had to be going strong, Augum thought, and they were still stuck here. Harvus had long stopped patrolling, instead sitting on one of the logs, studying Mrs. Stone's blue arcaneology book, the Orb of Orion by his side. He had evidently brought the orb with him last night, perhaps hiding it in a pillow or blanket. But where was the Agonex?

Augum watched as Harvus read a passage in the book before placing his hand on the orb, muttering something. He did this again and again, until Augum suddenly realized Harvus was trying to manipulate the orb. He quickly scratched out a bark note—*Harvus messing with orb*—and sent it flying to Bridget, who promptly passed it on to Leera.

"Mr. Harvus, sir," Bridget began in a polite tone, hand raised. "May I please borrow the book on arcaneology? I would like to better apply your teachings by reading on the 4th degree."

"Can you not see I am using it, girl?" Harvus snapped.

Bridget stared with an open mouth.

"Err, excuse me, dear child, I am quite busy at the moment." His attention returned to the book.

"Then perhaps you will allow me to borrow the book on elements, Mr. Harvus?"

Harvus looked up. "Book on elements? What book on elements?"

Bridget gave him a pleading smile. "Inside our rucksack you will find a book with the cover burnt off. It's a book on the elements, sir."

"Indeed? I thought that was mere refuse, having such a desecrated cover." He tapped his chin with a gloved hand, muttering, "Certainly could be useful." He closed the blue book and paced over to Bridget, handing it to her. "You have been a studious apprentice and have earned this." He turned to the rest of them. "As for you all, you are to sit in quiet and studious contemplation. I shall return shortly."

Jengo raised his hand. "Mr. Harvus, may I be excused? I would like to, uh, meet my betrothed—"

"Absolutely not, you have done very poorly today, boy."

Jengo's head fell as Harvus strode off, taking the Orb of Orion with him.

The moment Harvus disappeared over the valley lip, Augum and Leera raced to Bridget.

"Jengo, can you keep watch for us again?" Bridget asked.

"Sure, put my life in mortal danger," he muttered, assuming a lookout position just below the lip of the valley.

"I suspect Harvus stashed our rucksack and the Agonex at the inn," Augum blurted. "Must be where he's gone now."

"And I think I might have this counterspell almost figured out," Bridget said, quickly skipping to the appropriate page in the blue book. "The tricky part is obviously the pronunciation, but I'll work on that."

"By the way," Leera said, "can we not cast Object Track on a pinecone and drop it in Harvus' pocket? Then we know when he's near and stuff."

"He probably knows the 11th degree spell *Reveal,*" Bridget replied. "Which means if he casts it on himself, he'd be able to discover any enchantments."

"Wait, how do you know he's gotten to his 11th degree?" Augum asked.

They paused.

"Come to think of it," Bridget said slowly, "I've never seen him light up his rings."

"Well he's got to be at least 9th because he can teleport," Leera said.

Augum glanced over his shoulder. "We need to find out what degree he is for sure. If he doesn't know Reveal, we can track his movements."

"Psst—he's coming!" Jengo called, and everyone immediately scattered.

Harvus soon strolled into the valley holding the Orb of Orion and the burnt yellow book the trio had found in Evergray tower. He found them sitting in their places, with Bridget reading the blue book, brows crossed in deep concentration. He gave a brief nod and returned to the log bench, where he began flipping through the yellow book.

"Mr. Harvus, sir, what are you doing?" Leera asked.

"Trying to find another way to contact Mrs. Stone, child. Now sit and be quiet."

Augum shared a skeptical look with Leera. Harvus was definitely up to something. But what?

The sky steadily darkened to a deep shade of violet. Bridget diligently studied the arcaneology book, the others secretly casting spells behind Harvus' back. Augum's stomach began to growl just as someone came down the valley bank. Harvus closed the yellow book and stood up with an impatient sigh.

"What can I do for you, Mr. Okeke?"

Mr. Okeke's gaze was sharp. "Mr. Harvus, are you aware the feast has started?"

"I am."

"And may I ask why my son and his friends are not in attendance?"

"You may, Mr. Okeke, but the answer should not surprise you. Simply put, they have not comported themselves with enough skill. As you can see, they are studying at the moment."

Mr. Okeke gazed around with his bloodshot eyes. "All I see are youths sitting in detention."

"It is all part of their training."

"I cannot see how punishing them with boredom can be considered training—"

"Nor would I expect you to, seeing as you are an *Ordinary*. Now will that be all, Mr. Okeke? I have work to do."

"That will not be all. I am afraid I must insist on them being allowed to attend the feast."

"They are under my jurisdiction, Mr. Okeke, and I decline your … 'request'."

Mr. Okeke's jaw squared. "Although Mrs. Stone has left Augum, Bridget and Leera in your care, my son is still my son. Stand up, Jengo," he said without taking his eyes off Harvus.

"If you take my pupil, he will not be allowed to benefit from my services again."

"As far as I can tell, your services are hardly worth paying for, and when Mrs. Stone returns, I shall have a word with her on the matter."

"*If* she returns, I am sure you will."

"Father, please, I want to keep studying—"

"Hush, Jengo, and obey your father. Your betrothed is waiting. Come."

Mention of Priya spurred Jengo to stand. He cast the trio a forlorn look before wordlessly departing with his father, head bowed, an oddly mismatched pair height-wise.

Harvus watched them go. "Good riddance," he muttered, returning to studying the yellow book.

Bridget raised a meek hand. "Sir, is there something we can do to *earn* going to the feast?"

Harvus turned his gaze upon her. He strolled near. "So that you may desecrate yourselves again? I think *not*." He reached out. "The book please, Bridget."

"But sir, I haven't finished—"

"Now, young lady."

Bridget handed over the book, though as soon as he turned away from her, she began quietly practicing a spell incantation. Augum suspected it was the counterspell extension to Object Alarm, and wished her success.

Later, as the first stars began twinkling, another figure emerged from the forest.

Harvus, who had been busy flipping through both books while consulting the orb, sighed and stood. "Mr. Goss, what a pleasant surprise," he said in a tone suggesting it was anything but.

Mr. Goss ambled over, carrying a basket full of goodies—Augum could see a couple pastries and two bottles of wine peeking out.

After a quick glance at the trio, Mr. Goss smiled. "Mr. Harvus, you have been working very hard, and because you have not had the time to attend a most glorious feast, I decided to bring it to you."

Harvus' face was blank. "How thoughtful of you."

Mr. Goss placed the basket on one of the logs and began taking items out. "Let me see what we have here. Ah, yes, a bowl of fine Solian poached and caramelized pear; hot apple tart; honey-glazed cinnamon sticks; cream-dipped strawberries; and assorted Solian pastries. All very difficult to make and acquire in these hard times. As for wine, we have a bottle of stream-chilled Dramask spiced white and a bottle of Titan red."

Mr. Harvus' brows had been traveling ever higher up his pasty forehead with each description, until he licked his lips and picked up the bottle of white wine. "If there was one thing the Tiberrans mastered, it is spiced white."

"And lastly—" Mr. Goss raised a linen-wrapped parcel and dangled it before Harvus' nose. "We have the finest Canterran chocolate. A most … difficult acquisition."

Mr. Harvus' mouth parted slightly before he seemed to catch himself. He put the bottle of white back into the basket. "I really ought not to partake, Mr. Goss, there is much work to be done." His eyes flicked to the Orb of Orion.

"Nonsense, Mr. Harvus, you have worked too hard and deserve a break. Just one drink. Please. Consider it a special occasion." Mr. Goss uncorked the white wine with a pop. "The bottle is now open. Surely we cannot let such a fine wine go to waste, especially since Tiberran wine is going to become quite the rare and valuable commodity now that Dramask has fallen."

Mr. Harvus' gaze wandered to the bottle. "Valuable, you say? I suppose one glass cannot do any harm, though I must confess it has been some time."

Mr. Goss' face lit up and he immediately produced two crystal goblets, handing one to Harvus. "The finest hand-cut crystal, courtesy of the Harouns." Mr. Goss began pouring liberally.

"That is quite enough, thank you," Mr. Harvus said, but Mr. Goss filled the goblet more than halfway before ceasing.

"I really ought to get back to work. The children need much training—"

Mr. Goss waved nonchalantly. "The brats can wait." He raised his goblet. "Cheers."

Mr. Harvus' brows rose in surprise, while the trio exchanged curious glances. Mr. Goss never spoke that way. What was he up to?

Harvus raised his goblet slightly and took a sip. As soon as he swallowed, his face relaxed. "That is … that is quite refreshing, I must say. Delectable, even."

"It is, is it not?" Mr. Goss took a seat, offering Harvus the bowl of sugared pears.

Harvus, holding the stem of the goblet with two dainty fingers, took another sip of wine and helped himself to the bowl.

Mr. Goss glanced around uncertainly at the trio, as if forming his thoughts. "The young can be a touch lazy occasionally, can they not?"

"Oh, you have no idea, Mr. Goss. I am aghast that our future lies in the hands of these lethargic, inattentive miscreants." Harvus swallowed a pear slice whole. "Only discipline and solid training will rectify their errant ways." He took a third, longer swallow. His cheeks developed a rosy hue. "You know, I have not tasted a white in … well, in too long, if I may say so. I do believe, Mr. Goss, that an occasional glass of wine is said to be good for one's health."

Mr. Goss took a tiny sip. "The drink of the gods, as they say in Canterra."

"Yes, they do, they certainly do indeed. Speaking of which, let us pour to the earth in acknowledgment of our humility before the Unnameables." Harvus poured the last of his wine into the soil.

Mr. Goss hesitated but joined in. "To the gods," he said in a somber voice, upending his goblet.

The pair sat in silence a moment while the trio looked on with slack faces.

"The gods are merciful," Mr. Goss said at last. " 'For thine own sins, thy blessed believers'—"

"—'shall see thy divine mercy'," Mr. Harvus finished, looking at Mr. Goss as if seeing him for the first time. "I did not know you were a follower of the faith, Mr. Goss."

"I confess it has been some time, but my father was Canterran and observed the rituals. I only wish he included me more."

"I certainly miss the tenday services," Harvus said wistfully.

Mr. Goss carefully refilled Harvus' goblet. "I wish I had the opportunity to have gone."

Harvus gazed skyward, seemingly unaware of his goblet being refilled. "Solians really are heathens. One day I shall spread the word of the gods to this godless kingdom." He glanced down at his goblet. For a moment, Augum thought he was going to upend it again. Instead, he turned in his seat excitedly, taking a sip. "But I shall do it in a way that includes warlocks—"

"—of course." Mr. Goss was nodding along and smiling while pouring himself another glass. "Everyone shall have a chance to learn the true path—"

"—the *only* path."

The pair of them chuckled, Harvus looking heavenward with dreamy eyes. "I am going to build my own monastery one day, Albert, you mark my words."

"That is quite an expensive proposition, Leopold. And in these times, with such grave danger from the Legion—"

Harvus' face soured. "Yes, yes indeed, that will have to be rectified. First, the money, but that should not be entirely too difficult." His eyes flicked to the Orb of Orion, and in that moment, Augum knew Harvus' ambition—he was going to sell the orb, and maybe the Agonex too. The artifacts, to the right buyer, would be invaluable. Something was obviously stopping him from having done it already—but what?

Harvus took a liberal sip and helped himself to a strawberry. "I have to tell you, Albert, I came from nothing, less than nothing even. When my parents died of the necrotic plague—may the gods bless their souls—I saw it as a sign. They spared me. I was a beggar, you know, even ..." His voice lowered, but Augum nonetheless caught the word "thief" escape his lips.

Now Augum was convinced the man had stolen that golden flatware.

Mr. Goss gasped. "Oh my, that must have been awfully difficult."

"It was ... contemptible. I was captured by bandits and beaten cruelly ... enslaved, I dare say." He whispered the last part. "I got to know their ways all too well. But I persevered, learning to trade services with them ... bartering even. One might say I was ... quite observant." His voice developed a momentary twang. "I reckon I could always return to their midst and thrive if I ever needed to." He finished his goblet in one gulp. "Now that I am a force not to be trifled with, that is. They would respect me. They would have to, of course," and he chortled.

Mr. Goss chuckled supportively while refilling his glass. "Do go on, Leopold, dear me, do go on, my poor man."

Harvus watched the glass fill greedily. "I was a bright warlock, you know. Truly possessed the gift. After living a bandit life, I begged and sold myself to the lowest of masters, secretly saving enough for a mentor. But the gods were not done with teaching me humility, Albert. My mentor turned out to be a cruel, selfish and uncaring man. Can you fathom what his favorite punishment was?"

"My word, I can scarcely guess, Leopold."

"He enjoyed sticking my face into manure." Harvus carefully adjusted his hairpiece while nodding. "Manure, do you believe that? What kind of sick man sticks a fifteen-year-old's head into manure, all for mispronouncing a spell?"

The shock on Mr. Goss' face was genuine. "That is a reprehensible and revolting thing to do! Tell me he did not get away with it—"

"I am afraid he did get away with it … for years." Harvus suddenly smiled, a gesture that looked unpracticed and awkward. "But I got him in the end, Albert, I got him in the end. Once my studies with him had completed, I sent an anonymous note to the witch hunters."

"You did—?"

Harvus took a sip, smiling throughout. "One of the highest pleasures in life, Albert, is seeing your greatest foe's feet helplessly kick at the air as he dangles on the end of a noose."

Mr. Goss paled a little. "I … I am sure it was an important day for you."

"That it was, oh, that it was indeed. A sweet, sweet day. I fled of course, leaving my home forever. I truly became a man then. With my diligent attention to academic arcane detail, I ascended the degrees, and I ascend still." Harvus' eyes sparkled proudly as he took a sip. "I have yet to hit my ceiling."

"Really? Now that is very impressive, Leopold, very impressive indeed. I confess I have no arcane talent whatsoever. But you, you must be, what, on your sixth degree by now?"

Harvus cackled. "Oh, heavens no, my dear man, heavens no. I have earned my 9th degree."

Augum instantly shared an important look with the girls—Harvus was only 9th degree, and therefore probably did not know the 11th degree spell Reveal! This meant they could enchant a piece of his clothing with Object Track without him knowing! Or even his hairpiece—! The idea of it almost made Augum burst with laughter.

Mr. Goss' eyes flicked to the trio as if in acknowledgment of this fact, and it was then Augum knew that Jengo must have talked to Mr. Goss.

"That is very impressive," Mr. Goss said.

"Is it not?" Harvus replied while helping himself to a piece of chocolate. "I pride myself on having what few have achieved. I *am* somebody. I am even employed by the most powerful living archmage."

"Mrs. Stone is a legend."

"Of that there is no doubt. A historical figure of great import I pride myself to be associated with." Harvus took a sip of wine. "And she is quite clever, I must say. Did you know she enchanted the Orb of Orion with a powerful version of Object Track? She did the same to the Agonex. She also cast some kind of anti-teleport spell, giving permissions to certain people to bypass those protections. I have only heard tales of such rare off-the-book spells—and of course we know of the 15th degree spell Sanctuary—but still, it is quite something to see the practical application." He cackled.

Mr. Goss chuckled along. "I am sure I understand," though his perplexed face said otherwise. "But why the books, Leopold?"

"Oh, I was merely trying to understand how the spells functioned—for academic purposes of course—but have had little luck. Her level of knowledge is simply too great, her arcanery too complex. But what a wonderful challenge it is to … you know, attempt to understand them." Another sip.

"Well she *is* the only living master. She even has a statue at the top of the stairs at the Academy of Arcane Arts."

"I am sure the Legion has torn it down by now, Mr. Goss. And she perhaps *was* the only living master. We have not heard from her in a while. I fear the worst." He sighed. "We must be brave—for the sake of the children."

"For the sake of the children."

Augum hated the way Harvus spoke about Nana. Nonetheless, the man's plans were as clear as day now: he was trying to remove Nana's protective spells on the artifacts so he could sell them.

The two men sat on the log, chuckling in reflective mirth between sips of wine. Mr. Goss finally leaned over. "What are you going to do if Mrs. Stone does not return?"

Harvus stopped smiling. "Well, I am owed a great deal of coin, you see. My time is most precious these days, and it is not easy training such incompetent brats."

"I am sure it cannot be easy at all." Mr. Goss poured Harvus the last of the white wine, though Augum noted he himself was still on his second glass, which remained half-full.

Mr. Goss gestured at the Orb of Orion, nestled in the grass beside them. "These objects must surely be worth some coin."

Harvus smiled. "They are worth far more—" Suddenly he stopped smiling and sat back. He looked down at the basket and back at Mr. Goss, face contorted with suspicion. "Mr. Goss, are you trying to get me drunk?"

Mr. Goss swallowed while adjusting on the log bench. "Heavens no, Leopold, I—"

Harvus placed the glass back into the basket and hastily stood. "I do not know what I have been saying, Mr. Goss. I fear myself slightly inebriated. I do not have any intention of selling these precious artifacts. I am afraid I must ask you to take the basket and leave. The children and I have important training to do."

Augum thought that if Harvus kept calling them children, he would develop his own facial tick.

"But Leopold—"

"It is *Mr.* Harvus." There was no mistaking his tone now.

Mr. Goss pushed his spectacles back up his nose and nodded. "It was a pleasure, Mr. Harvus. I hope we can do it again sometime." He turned to leave, conveniently forgetting the basket full of treats and wine. He stopped halfway up the small forest valley. "Mr. Harvus, if I may, will you consider allowing the trio to have supper? It is getting late. Perhaps they may still be able to join the tail end of the feast—"

"Impossible, Mr. Goss, good evening to you."

Mr. Goss nodded somberly. "Good evening." He cast the trio a last pitiful glance and left.

BEATEN

It was dark and cloudy when Mr. Harvus watched Mr. Goss depart, shifting his weight from foot to foot while wringing his cotton-gloved hands. His beady eyes kept flicking between the pumpkin-sized Orb of Orion and the bottle of Titan wine sitting in the basket of sweets.

The trio watched him like hawks.

Choose the wine, Augum kept thinking, choose the damn wine!

At last, Mr. Harvus took a seat, mumbling to himself, and picked up the blue book.

Augum fell back against the tree trunk in defeat. If only he could get the man's attention back to the wine somehow … He bit his lip in thought, eventually deciding to try something simple. He subtly raised his hand and, concentrating on the wine bottle, made it move a little.

Harvus lowered the book ever so slightly to stare at the basket. After a moment of apparent indecision, he suddenly tossed the book aside and snatched the bottle of wine. He scrambled at the cork like a drowning rat, before using Telekinesis to pop it off. Then he tipped the bottle to his lips and sucked greedily.

Augum was leaning forward in gleeful disbelief, as were Bridget and Leera.

Harvus slowly put the bottle down, staring at it with invigorated eyes. He stood, cleared his throat, and said, "Shyneo." Glowing green vine wrapped itself around his palm. He placed the bottle and books into the basket, picked it up, and scooped up the Orb of Orion.

"You are not to move until I say so," he said, glaring at each of them in turn. "Focus on your studies."

Bridget raised her hand just as it began to rain a little. "But Mr. Harvus—"

Harvus made a bizarre barking sound like a tiny dog. He stared Bridget down before marching to the hastily erected cabin, where Augum heard another long gulp of wine.

The rain graduated to fat drops that lingered on the needle branches. Augum drew his hood, as did the girls. They sat in hopeful silence, listening to every sound from inside the cabin. Harvus' distrustful face repeatedly appeared in the window. His light pulsed and his face was as red as the wine. After the umpteenth appearance, he burped and fell back with a thud. The light inside the cabin instantly went out.

For a moment, the trio sat there, stunned. At last, they crept forward as if readying to commit some great robbery.

"I think he's out," Augum whispered, crowding around the window with Bridget and Leera.

"A bottle of Titan will do that," Leera said. "But there's only one way to find out for sure." Her large eyes bored into his. She held up her hand. Augum matched it with his own and they slowly closed the distance, until their hands touched. A burning sensation immediately emitted from

Augum's palm and he recoiled, Leera doing the same. Together, they checked on Harvus. He moaned and turned, snoring. The alarm that would have gone off in his head after they touched had not woken him.

Leera kept glancing between the loaf of a man on the dirty floor and Augum, her face wet with rain. "Screw it," she said, and drew Augum near. The burning was intense as they kissed, both wincing through the pain. They had to let go quickly after, both holding their lips but smiling.

Bridget's voice melted. "That … that was so romantic."

Leera smiled. "Missed you, Aug."

"Missed you too."

"Hurts like I'm on fire though."

"Maybe I can help." Bridget grabbed them both by the hands and marched them back to the girls' cabin across the stream. The rain plonked on the roof boards as she sat them down on the floor.

"I've been practicing the pronunciation and gesture almost the entire time. Wish me luck." She placed her hands on Augum first. He could just make out her form in the darkness of the cabin. "Omrala led oitucnoc," she said, removing her hands at the last moment. The inflection was perfect, as if she was actually speaking backwards.

"I didn't feel anything," Augum said, worried.

"Hold on, let me do Leera." There was a pause. "Omrala led oitucnoc."

"Did it work?" Leera asked.

"Shyneo." Augum's hand rippled to life with lightning, turning the cabin blue.

"Shyneo," Leera echoed, glowing water lapping around her palm, throwing a cooler blue light around the cabin.

She raised her palm, as did he, and they both winced as they drew them together. Their fingers intertwined without any pain. The two of them threw up a cheer and embraced, dragging poor Bridget into the hug as well. She protested that she could barely breathe and they were being too loud, but Augum and Leera did not seem to care. When they drew apart, their eyes were only for each other.

"Can't thank you enough, Bridge," Augum said, lit fingers still interwoven with Leera's.

Leera was all smiles. "You did it, Bridge, you really did it."

"I know it's Lover's Day, you two," Bridget began, "but we have some things to take care of first."

Augum nodded. "Right," but he could barely think. All he wanted to do was hold Leera in his arms and spend time with her.

Bridget rattled off what they needed to do on her fingers. "We need to get the Orb of Orion, we need to cast Object Track on Harvus so we can track him, we need to recover the Agonex, we need to get in contact with Mrs. Stone, and we need the blue book—oh and by the way, I think I can learn the counterspell to Object Track too."

"You're a marvel, Bridge," Leera said absently, though she was staring at Augum.

"Focus, you two! We don't have all night."

Augum reluctantly let go of Leera. "No, we don't. All right, let's do this."

They extinguished their palms and quietly filed out of the cabin. The rain pelted the forest in a great cacophonic symphony, plunking into the stream and deadening all other sound. The door to Harvus' cabin squeaked as Augum opened it. He paused, but the snoring continued unabated. He crept inside and kneeled by Harvus' feet. While the girls silently collected the books and the Orb of Orion, Augum placed his hands on Harvus' embroidered leather turnshoes. "Concutio del alarmo," he whispered.

"Wrong spell—" Bridget hissed.

"What?"

"You want to cast Object Track, not Object Alarm."

"Oh, right."

Leera helped herself to a pastry from the basket while Bridget wasn't looking.

Augum prepared himself before casting the spell. "Vestigio itemo discovaro."

"I'll cast it too," Bridget said, scooting over beside Augum. "Just in case."

When she accidentally touched the shoe, a loud alarm rang in Augum's head.

"Can you counterspell it first?" he asked. "Don't want my head ringing every time Harvus touches his shoe."

"Doesn't work that way—you only get one alarm. Watch." She touched the shoe again, but no alarm went off in his head. "You have to get better at the spell for it to ring more than once."

"Get on with it," Leera hissed, licking her fingers.

"Right," Bridget said. As she readied to cast Object Track, Augum spotted Leera carefully peeling Harvus' hairpiece off his head.

"What are you doing!" he mouthed.

Leera finished removing the hairpiece with a final yank, making sure Bridget had not seen, and stuffed it into her robe. She had a determined but mischievous look in her eye. "Revenge," she mouthed back with a wink.

Maybe not the best idea, but he'd be lying if he said he wouldn't have done it himself.

When Bridget finished, they grabbed their stuff and scrambled to the Okeke cabin, arriving soaked from the rain. There were unfamiliar voices inside, but the trio barged in, only to freeze.

There before them stood the obese Constable Clouds, leaning on his cane, flanked by his two guards dressed in shining black Legion plate, both holding their pot helms under their arms. A sword hung on one man's hip, a battleaxe on the other's. For a moment nobody moved.

Augum's mind buzzed with spell incantations, heart thundering in his chest.

Finally, Mr. Goss ran to the trio. "Dear me, I am so glad to see you! Is he out?'

"Sorry?" Augum managed to say, still eyeing the soldiers, who made no move.

"Harvus—has he passed out?"

Augum focused on Mr. Goss for the first time. He had a grave look on his face. "Yes," he blurted.

"Splendid." Mr. Goss paced back to the group. Augum was finally able to see who was in the room—Haylee leaned on her cane near Chaska, who held onto his war bow. His Henawa war shirt was tearing at the seams, revealing a snow-skinned belly. He was slowly growing his milky hair long in the Henawa way, and wore a necklace of harpy wing bones. Priya and Jengo held hands in the corner, Priya holding Leland protectively before her. Mr. Okeke was standing in a somber pose, absently rubbing his beard, Mr. Hanad Haroun—the town elder—beside him.

"What's going on?" Augum asked, ready to bolt or strike. "Why is the Legion here?"

Mr. Goss held up his hands. "It is all right, Augum. This is Constable Clouds and his guards, Lieutenant Briggs and Sergeant Cobb. They are on our side. I assure you."

Constable Clouds turned to face Augum. The effort made him wheeze. "It is an honor to meet you, Augum Stone. A great honor."

Augum gaped, not sure what to make of this. Leera's fingers secretly found his and their hands curled together with a squeeze.

Bridget finally strode forward. "It is nice to meet you, sir. I'm Bridget Burns and this is—"

"Leera Jones," Lieutenant Briggs finished for her. He had flaming red hair trimmed close to the scalp.

"Daughter to Oscar and Selma Jones," continued Sergeant Cobb. He had the same haircut, but as blonde as the sun.

"Do not be alarmed," Constable Clouds said. "We mean you no harm. We know much about you, as do all Legion officers, for we are taught every detail about your lives so that it may aid us in the hunt." He glanced over at Haylee, who had a determined look on her face. "We even know that that is Haylee Tennyson." Clouds fumbled for a cloth and dabbed at his sweaty forehead. "My men and I serve the Legion, but our hearts are in opposition."

"You're part of the Resistance!" Leera blurted, smiling. "It's not just us!"

"I am afraid there is no resistance, my dear young lady," Clouds huffed. "Not yet at least. The truth is we went in search of such a resistance. It seems that we have found it here, in a small, out-of-the-way mining town."

"Constable Clouds and his men put their lives and the lives of their families at great risk aiding us," Mr. Haroun said, striding forth. "We are grateful. It is invaluable to have men on active duty in the Legion ranks. And now we can indeed start a true resistance, with Anna Atticus Stone as our leader."

The trio exchanged disbelieving looks. It has begun!

"But Mrs. Stone has lost contact with us," Bridget said. "We don't know what's going on."

A grave look passed over Constable Clouds' wide face. "That is most disconcerting. I know Lord Sparkstone has stepped up efforts to track her down. He has three warlock squads who trade the divining rod off with each other, so there is always a squad hunting for her."

Augum felt queasy. If they were hunting her that relentlessly, how could she even sleep? She would have to go to opposite sides of the world to get away. Maybe that is why they had not heard from her—she was too busy evading. But what about the explosion they heard from the orb? Was that a squad getting close? He only hoped she had not already been captured and stripped of the scion, for it was keeping her alive.

"Without Mrs. Stone," Mr. Haroun began in a quiet voice, "I fear any resistance movement has little chance, not unless we somehow gather an army as powerful as the Legion."

A moment passed in which all that could be heard was the pelt of rain on the cabin roof.

"The Agonex," Augum said at last.

Mr. Haroun looked up. "The Agonex? What is that?"

Leera gripped Augum's hand tighter, whispering, "Can we trust them?"

"We have to," he replied. It was time to take a risk. He only hoped these men were genuine. He placed his gaze on Constable Clouds and Mr. Haroun. "We captured an ancient artifact that can control Occulus' undead army. The army is equipped with Dreadnought steel and stands waiting for command under Bahbell. There are tens of thousands of soldiers. I saw them for myself."

"You jest with us," Mr. Haroun said.

"No, it's true," Leera interjected. "It's a bronze disk engraved with skulls and stuff."

The constable nodded. "The Legion is looking for the Agonex. I must confess, we were not sure who had it. I am glad to hear it is in the right hands. Most glad indeed."

"The only thing is, we don't know how it works," Augum said.

"And it's in Harvus' room at the inn," Leera added. "We were just going to get it back. He's keeping it hostage, and we think he plans to sell it the moment he figures out how to break Mrs. Stone's protective enchantments."

Clouds immediately turned to his guards. "Get to the inn and find that artifact."

"I'll come with you," Bridget said, handing the Orb of Orion to Leera.

Both guards looked at her as if she had lost her mind, not realizing this was something the trio routinely did—danger was a constant in their lives and they were quite used to it.

Bridget glanced between the two of them. "Harvus probably enchanted the door handle with Object Alarm. Unless you know the counterspell, I'm coming along. It's best to disarm it, just in case."

"Neither of us are warlocks," Cobb confessed.

"What degree is this Harvus anyway?" Briggs asked.

Bridget's face was impassive. "9th."

The guards glanced at each other.

Bridget did not wait for them. "Come on then," and strode through the doorway, blue robe billowing.

Jengo began biting his nails. "If Harvus wakes up and finds the Agonex gone, he's going to kill us all. I mean it. It will be cold, ruthless murder."

"Who is this Harvus?" Clouds asked.

"A vile piece of useless dung," Haylee said.

"He's our mentor," Augum said. "Well, sort of. Nana—Mrs. Stone, that is—hired him to train us while she evades the Legion. Thing is, he hasn't been paid, so I think he wanted to sell the Orb of Orion and the Agonex."

"The man is a fool then," Clouds replied. "The greatest reward lay under his charge the entire time." He eyed Augum appraisingly. "But he is dangerous. If he figures out how much you are worth to the Legion, he might actually kidnap you and turn you in. We ought to tie him up and drug him immediately, while we still have the chance. He is drunk at this moment, is he not?"

Augum nodded. "Passed out cold on the floor of our cabin."

Mr. Okeke strode to a closet and dug out a coil of soot-stained rope. "I second the notion. He is too dangerous."

Clouds waved his cane. "Wait for my men to return."

Mr. Goss grabbed his woolen coat. "What if it is too late by then? I agree with Kwabe, it should be done immediately. Augum and Leera know a great deal of arcanery. I trust them to protect us more than swords."

"Is there an apothecary in town?" Clouds asked.

"There is." Haylee turned to Chaska. "Does your father have a sleeping draught in his shop?"

Chaska frowned in concentration. "I think so, yes."

"Then let's get it."

"Allow me to administer it," Constable Clouds said.

Haylee and Chaska exchanged a hesitant look but nodded.

"Meet you at the cabin in short order," Constable Clouds said to Mr. Okeke.

The three departed, Haylee hobbling as quickly as she could, Chaska and the Constable waddling along.

Leera tugged on Augum's sleeve. "Try to reach Mrs. Stone."

Augum put his ear to the orb. "Nana, can you hear me? Nana—" but there was no response. He did however hear something faint—"I hear voices," he blurted, and everyone froze. Multiple voices, all fading in and out, as if people were walking by. And there was a rustling of grass that came with their footsteps. Oddly, there was the sound of crickets too. It was almost as if—

"I think she lost it," Augum said, staring at each of them in turn. "Nana lost the pearl somewhere." But what that meant, he did not know.

"We'll have to worry about that later," Leera said. "Let's go and tie Harvus up now."

Mr. Okeke gathered his coat. "Jengo, stay here with Leland and Priya please."

"Yes, Father." Jengo exhaled as his body relaxed.

Augum handed Leland the orb. "Listen to this, Leland, and see if you can make anything out." The boy, happy to be given a mission, eagerly complied with a moan.

Mr. Okeke armed himself with a shovel, handing Mr. Goss the coil of rope.

"Can't believe we're really going to do this," Leera said as they exited the hut.

"I can't believe we're working with the Legion," Augum countered.

The dark forest was quiet other than the sound of steady rain dripping through the branches. Wet pine needles squished underneath their boots as they pressed on in single file. Soon they were slipping down the soggy bank of the valley, the two cabins materializing before them in the downpour.

Augum and Leera, holding hands, crept along in front, blue robes soaked through. Augum pointed at the hastily-erected cabin before tiptoeing to the door, which stood slightly ajar. He pushed and it opened with a squeak. When he spotted the interior, a terrible chill ran down his spine.

Harvus was gone!

Just as he turned to report that fact, someone slurred, "Flustrato!" and a dull look passed over Mr. Goss' face. He began to mumble while chewing on the end of the rope.

Augum, whose arm flared with three lightning rings, reflexively shoved at the air where he saw nine glowing green rings. "BAKA!" but Harvus summoned his shield—a hodgepodge of bark and twigs—and blocked the spell, stumbling a step back in the process.

"Shyneo!" Leera called, palm rippling to life with a cool watery glow, three rings appearing around her own arm.

Mr. Okeke, meanwhile, charged at Harvus with the shovel.

Harvus flicked his wrist. "Disablo!" and the shovel went flying from Mr. Okeke's hands.

Augum pointed at the shovel, which twirled in midair, and caught it with Telekinesis, shooting it at Harvus.

Harvus, wobbling from the wine, barely dodged the clumsy attempt, countering with a slurred, "Dreadus Terrablus!" Had Harvus not been so drunk, his spell might have been too strong, yet Augum blocked it with Mind Armor, though not before he lost a moment fighting the feeling that he was about to drown in the rain.

Mr. Okeke lunged for Harvus, yet the man jumped out of the way—and it was no ordinary jump, but an arcane one, high and unnatural looking. Unfortunately, Harvus had not orientated himself properly and slammed into the branches above, tumbling to the ground a moment later in a soggy heap.

"Summano elementus minimus!" Leera called as she finished drawing the shape of a small elemental, but the attempt garnered nothing more than a fizzling sound.

Harvus cackled, slurring, "A terrible effort, girl. You are a poor student!"

Mr. Okeke dove for Harvus once more only to end up slamming into Mr. Goss, who had absent-mindedly wandered across Mr. Okeke's path. The pair of them tumbled right into the stream with a splash.

Augum pointed at Harvus. "Flustrato!" but the man squinted as he used his Mind Armor to block the spell.

Harvus, now muddy as a hog, pointed at Augum's throat. "Voidus lingua!" and Augum felt his throat close. This time his Mind Armor had failed.

Leera shoved at the air before her. "BAKA!" but Harvus, lying on his back, still managed to summon his shield in time.

Augum charged. Harvus flicked his wrist at Augum's foot and he tripped, slamming into the sodden ground face first.

Harvus staggered to his feet. "Annihilo bato!" he shouted, slamming his wrists together. Two thick ropes of vine shot forth at Augum's head. Augum closed his fist over his reflection crystal, hoping to cast Reflect, when he remembered he had been muted. Luckily, "BAKA!" shouted a girl's voice from nearby, violently shoving Augum out of the way. He rolled into the stream with a splash. When he looked up, he saw Haylee raise her ice shield in time to block another of Harvus' vine attacks. The attack was so powerful she was sent tumbling out of sight. At the same time, Chaska fumbled trying to nock an arrow while Constable Clouds bravely tottered forward, dagger in one hand, a vial in the other, cheeks puffing with every breath.

Leera swept her arms out. "Centeratoraye xao xen!" and began half-tumbling and half-running at Harvus, who had gotten to his feet and was shoving at the air, shouting, "Baka!" between trying to spear her with shooting arcane sticks and vines that appeared out of nowhere. Leera deftly cartwheeled over the strikes before shoving at the air. "BAKA!" Harvus failed to raise his shield in time and was sent flying into the forest, landing in the bushes. An arrow from Chaska whizzed through the spot he had been standing, thwacking into a tree trunk.

"Effectus xadius!" Harvus shouted from the darkness. Leera immediately began to move in slow motion.

Augum and Mr. Okeke had risen by then and charged.

"Let me show you how it is done!" Harvus slurred from the forest. "Summano elementus minimus!" A moment later a small green elemental plowed awkwardly through the bush, its movements clumsy, as if it too was drunk. It tried to tackle Augum but he jumped over it, though it did manage to knock Mr. Okeke's legs out from under him.

Harvus leaped from the undergrowth straight at Augum, moving surprisingly quickly for his girth. He grabbed Augum in a bear hug and threw him against a tree, knocking the wind out of him. Augum, coughing and gasping for breath, realized the man had to have cast some kind of strength spell—his grip was like iron.

Mr. Goss, who had evidently recovered from the Confusion spell, grabbed Harvus' shoulders. Harvus spun around, casting, "Flustrato!" Mr. Goss, now drooling from being confounded a second time, stumbled off into the woods, mumbling gibberish.

Constable Clouds had finally reached Harvus and bravely jabbed at him with his Legion dagger. Harvus let go of Augum and weaved out of the way, scoffing at the large man. He let him take two more stabs, which he danced out of reach of, before yanking at the air. "Disablo." The dagger twirled out of Clouds' hand, jamming into the mud.

Chaska loosened another arrow, but Harvus saw the attack coming and did something Augum had never seen before—he pointed at the incoming arrow and *bent* its flight path with Telekinesis, striking a hapless Constable Clouds in the back of a shoulder. The large man grunted and fell to his knees, wheezing. Behind him, Chaska cried out in despair.

Augum slammed his wrists together, "Annihilo!" but nothing came out. He was still mute.

Leera aimed a kick at Harvus' chest, but she was way too slow. He dodged easily and punched her in the stomach with his arcanely-enhanced strength, sending her flying to the soggy grass, where she writhed in slow motion. Something fell out of her pocket and into the mud.

Harvus' nostrils flared when he saw what it was. "You filthy little witch …" He weaved over and picked up his hairpiece, face firing multiple twitches.

Augum frantically gestured at the dagger. It dug itself out of the ground and shot at Harvus. The warlock, who was glaring at Leera, did not see the attack coming and the dagger lodged into his side up to the hilt. Harvus gasped and whipped around.

Augum quickly waved at Chaska, who let another arrow fly. This time, it struck true, burying itself in Harvus' stomach almost to the feather.

"Ah," Harvus exclaimed, weaving, eyes on Chaska. Augum scrambled to his feet, but Harvus raised his arm and arcanely pinned him to the trunk, all the while staring down Chaska, who had another arrow nocked but did not let fly, perhaps fearing Harvus would perform the same telekinetic feat and hurt someone else.

The group was a mess. The minor elemental had disappeared, leaving behind Mr. Okeke, who lay in a heap, exhausted from wrestling with it. Mr. Goss was in an arcane stupor, lost somewhere in the forest. Constable Clouds was on his knees breathing heavily, a disbelieving look on his face and an arrow sticking from his shoulder. Haylee had crawled back over the crest of the shallow valley, gasping. She was missing her cane and had a defeated look on her face.

Harvus flashed Augum, still pinned and mute, a victorious look. "Lessons are done, my boy." He snatched Leera by the hair and yanked her up. She howled in pain, eyes unfocused in the deep confusion that came as a side effect to Centarro's expiration. "Say goodbye to this little harlot. She has offended me for the last time. Impetus peragro bato!" There was a reverse sucking sound and Harvus and Leera were gone, leaving Augum to scream silently in the downpour.

THE CHASE

Augum barely knew what he was doing as he stumbled back to the village, still trying to catch his breath, back aching. He had left everyone behind, thinking of one thing and one thing only—he needed to find a horse and rescue Leera. Luckily, the Object Track spell he had cast on Harvus' turnshoe was still in effect, ever so gently pointing him in the direction of the foul mentor. Unfortunately, Augum was not experienced enough to judge the distance of the enchanted object yet. For all he knew, Harvus could have teleported her to the other side of Sithesia.

The rain hammered at him, making loud plonking sounds against his skull and streaming down his face like tears. One foot after the other splashed into the soggy earth as he made his way along the dark and muddy path. It was Lover's Day and this was not supposed to happen. He and Leera were supposed to have spent the day together in each other's arms. Even the very idea of losing her made him want to retch.

He stumbled on, wincing from the pain in his back, a result of being slammed into the tree so hard. The battle replayed in his mind. He should have cast Centarro too, or even attempted Summon Minor Elemental. Then he recalled the fizzling sound of Leera's failed attempt at the spell. No, it would have only cost him time, just as it had Leera …

He didn't bother stopping by the Okeke home—Mrs. Stone couldn't be reached anyway and time was supremely precious. The only thing that was important was that he had to get to Harvus before the bastard did something awful to her.

Augum careened past a couple of unaware drunks—two burly miners holding each other by the shoulders and singing the dreamy *Lover's Lure*. He squinted past the rain, looking for a horse, finally spotting two tied at the front of the Miner's Mule Inn, and lumbered forth, each step slapping a puddle. People sang *A Farmer's Daughter and the Heir* from the balcony of the inn. Rain plonked and tinked off table after table of abandoned dishes and empty bottles, the detritus of the evening's feast, a feast he and Leera should have attended hand-in-hand.

"If I don't know none better," said a dark-skinned man in an ale-stained jerkin to a colleague, "I reckon that one there's a warlock. Look at them robes." He nodded at Augum's sodden attire.

"Muddy as a pig," replied his friend, a scruffy man as short as Harvus. "But why is he untying that there Legion horse?"

Augum didn't care whose horse it was and, despite whatever injury was plaguing his back, he managed to hoist himself on.

The door opened, allowing a brief glimpse into a packed tavern of rowdy people.

"Augum, what are you doing!" Bridget shouted.

"Harvus has Leera," he found himself saying, as if in a trance. "He has Leera and I have to go find her and—"

"Just slow down and think for a moment! Let me get the soldiers—"

"There's no time and they can't help anyway, they're not warlocks—" He began turning the horse.

"Damn it, Aug!" It was the first time he had ever heard Bridget swear. It was such a strange thing that Augum did a double take.

She grabbed the saddle. For a moment, he thought she was going to yank him off. Instead, she hoisted herself up and grabbed onto his waist. He immediately kicked the horse into a gallop, exiting Milham to the south, rain attacking his face and hands.

The night was thick, but the road was made visible by the slightest glimmer of a moon from behind dark clouds.

"I sense it too and was wondering if I had it wrong," Bridget said into his ear, the rain pelting them like small stones. "He's gone south. But this is madness, Aug, who knows how far he took her. We have to try to reach Mrs. Stone."

"Haven't heard from Nana in days, not going to waste more time trying!"

Bridget sighed and drew his hood for him, drawing her own after.

"Stop there," she said after a while. "Let's see if we can sense the spell better."

Augum stopped at a muddy fork surrounded by evergreens. Besides his ramming heart, all he heard was the steady quiet roar of rain falling on a vast forest. His skin and insides felt fire-hot from the battle and from the terror of losing Leera. Nonetheless, he searched for that fragile arcane trail that would get him to her.

Panic rose to his throat. "I sense nothing!"

"You're too upset, just listen to the ether. Concentrate."

Augum tried to still his nerves and capture those faint reverberations, but all he could see was that trapped look on Leera's face as Harvus yanked her up by her hair.

"If he does anything to her, I swear I'll—"

"Aug! Please, you're not helping. Let me try the spell."

He forced himself to sit and wait. Soon the sleeve of Bridget's blue robe appeared to his left, hand pointing into the rainy night. "That way!"

Augum rode the stallion hard, not caring about the pain in his back, the wet cold seeping into his undergarments, his hollow stomach, or the status of everyone back in Milham. Bridget forced him to stop at every fork so she could concentrate on the spell, saying nothing more about how dangerous and foolish this quest was.

Sometime in the depth of the night, the rain lessened to a drizzle and the clouds parted slightly. There was a horrible peace to it, a peace Augum couldn't listen to, as it didn't match up with the frantic thunderstorm in his heart.

They rode half the night, through thick forests, wide valleys, and raging rivers. The horse could barely keep up, gasping and neighing, eventually forcing Augum to slow to a canter lest they tire the animal out completely. They neither rested nor spoke, until Bridget told him to stop beside a lake surrounded by evergreens and an abandoned farm field. Nestled in a clearing past the field, under a clear starry night, was a camp. And at last Augum could clearly feel the pull—Leera was there!

"Slow and easy, Aug, we don't know what kind of camp this is."

Augum did not care. He was going to rescue Leera and no one was going to stop him.

As they rode closer, they could make out a white sack hanging from a post in the middle of the wheat field. As Augum was trying to figure out what it was, Bridget gasped and clenched his waist.

"Stop the horse."

"What?"

"Just stop the horse!" She pointed at the sack. He squinted and finally understood—it was a Henawa woman, hogtied and hung. Red tendrils hung off her where carrion birds had had a go. For a moment, the pair just gaped. A nauseous bile began rising in his stomach.

"Quietly, to the woods—" Bridget hissed.

Augum directed the horse to the forest, where he tied it under a stubby pine.

Bridget gripped him by the arms. "It's all right, Aug, we'll get her, just don't do anything foolish, all right?"

He could barely hear her beyond the roar of blood rushing through his ears.

"Take a few deep breaths with me." She breathed deeply, keeping eye contact, still holding his forearms. "In and out, in and out. Good, that's it. Now, let's form a plan."

"A plan, right." Storm in there and kill them all, he was thinking, recalling Robin slicing Mya's throat. They had to rescue Leera before that happened, before she too hung on a post in a field …

Bridget placed gentle hands on his cheeks. "Let's study and watch the camp, all right? We don't want to do anything rash, do we? Focus."

He swallowed, feeling his veins buzz.

"Augum? Focus."

He nodded sharply. "Focus, got it." He'd focus his First Offensive right through Harvus' brain.

Bridget's voice was soft. "Augum."

He took a deep breath and rubbed his eyes. She was right. He had to get a grip. He couldn't risk Bridget or Leera's lives with brash stupidity. They were alone in the middle of nowhere and there was no rescuing them should things go wrong. In fact, no one had a clue where they were.

"Let's list all the spells we can successfully cast," Bridget said calmly. "Shine, Telekinesis, Repair, Unconceal—" He joined in, feeling better with each word, "—Shield, Push, Disarm, Slam, Mind Armor, Object Alarm, Object Track, The First Offensive, Centarro, Fear, Deafness, and Confusion."

Repeating back the spells with her gave him strength. He was not a bystander here, he could make things happen—just as he *had* made things happen many times before.

"Aug," Bridget said, looking deep into him with caring eyes, "we *can* do this. No, we *will* do this." She took one last big breath and gave a firm nod. "Come on."

Damn right we will, he thought. He felt the stillness of a warrior as they prowled around the stubby trees. Thick in the air was the scent of freshly rained-upon pine. They soon reached a spot at the edge of the forest, from where they could observe the camp. Augum counted twenty tents, a log cabin at one end. Several oxen stood in a pen, along with stacks of hay and a dilapidated chicken coop. A low fire guttered in the center of the camp, with five or six men casually sitting and drinking around it. Most wore hunting attire—loose hide, some Henawa accouterments. The men had tanned bronze skin, dirty faces and hands. No women were present.

Augum closed his eyes and concentrated on the arcane pull of Object Track. It emanated from the cabin, he was sure of it. Bridget sensed it too and led him through the sparse forest, both being as quiet as deer. They heard music as they neared the cabin. Someone inside was playing a lute and singing in a country twang. The cabin's windows were lit with a warm glow. Traps hung on its exterior.

The pair skulked to an outside window that faced the forest, giving each other a grave glance before edging their faces over the windowsill to peek at the interior. A man with a cleaver in one hand and a half-empty bottle in the other was dancing around a chair. He was tanned bronze and heavily wrinkled, with a grizzled salt-and-pepper beard. Harvus sat in the chair, hands tied behind his back. He was slumped forward and wheezing, blood soaking his cream robe. The dagger and arrow still protruded from his body. His hairpiece sat limply on his head, looking like it had been run over by a cart.

Bridget ducked, both hands on her mouth, eyes as wide as plums.

Augum reached out to her before forcing himself to study the scene. There were three men inside—the crazed dancer with the salt-and-pepper beard, a haggard lute player, and a stick-thin younger man with close-set eyes, wearing a dented Legion breastplate. A bloodstained sickle hung at his belt.

But where was Leera? He strained to look around the cabin but couldn't locate her, yet the spell told him she was close by.

The man with the cleaver stopped dancing and took a swig. Harvus' hairpiece fell to the floor, much to the amusement of the others. The man picked it up and tried to arrange it nicely back onto Harvus' scalp, eliciting more laughter from his gang.

"All right, you mangy cur," the man said, "how's about you tells us where them treasures be."

Harvus only groaned.

"You done feed him too much of that draught, Sal," said the skinny young man.

"I done feed him enough. Trouble is he drunk and 'urt. Makes the brew stronger. But he a witch-man wizard and you best be ready to take off his head with that there sickle if he be dumb enough to do something."

"I is ready."

Sal pointed his cleaver, eyes coal black. "You is not. He can turn you into a toad in a dipity-nick of time. Now stand behind 'im, I says!"

The skinny boy grudgingly paced behind Harvus.

"And boy, you hear one word that sounds like magic, you take that sickle and you carve 'im a Nodian smile. This witch-man a stone killer, I knows it like I knows the smell of death."

Harvus moaned.

Sal put his hand to his ear. "What's that you says? You knows where the treasures be?"

Harvus mumbled something.

Sal raised Harvus' chin with the cleaver. "Can't hear you, speak up, piggy."

"Artifacts ... worth gold ... to Legion." Harvus' voice was very faint, his breath labored. "I can take you—"

Sal slapped Harvus. "I tells you before we ain't do no tradin' with the Legion! Look around you, witch-man, half these boys be deserters or runaways. And what else did I say the last time you is come here? Huh? What did I say? We needs to see the loot before we can hand over them gold." He laughed, looking around at his gang. "Is all wizards this stupid?"

Augum exchanged a look with Bridget. Harvus had been here before!

When the laughter died down, Sal crouched, using his cleaver for balance. He took a pull from the bottle and set it on the floor, grabbing the mangled hairpiece off Harvus' head. "I can be a witch-man too, you know," Sal said. He placed the hairpiece on his own scalp and did a little dance while his crew laughed. "Want to see my magic trick? Looksie, I can make this here turd of hair disappear."

The lute player began a dramatic tune, his hollow eyes dancing in rhythm.

"Want to see it disappear, witch-man?" Sal pressed. "Like them gold you took from us with your tricks the last time you was here?"

Harvus shook his head. "No, I did not—"

"Oh, yes, did you not think we was going to find out about that? Them fake gold coin you done switched for our real coin? You think givin' us that there girl make things right? You think us dumb as dirt, don't you, witch-man? Tell you what—" Sal dangled the hairpiece before Harvus. "I can do a magic trick too. Here now, watch it disappear—" and he stuffed it into Harvus' mouth.

Harvus weakly struggled, eyes rolling around wildly, but Sal gestured and the boy placed a hand over his mouth, preventing Harvus from spitting the hairpiece out.

Sal grabbed his drink and stood up with a snort. "Trade with the Legion. Dumb fool." He glanced between his roguish cohorts. "You know what me pappy always used to say to me? He say when a witch talks, best to cover your ears lest ye lose 'em. Heck, they is lyin' even when they ain't speakin'."

Sal pointed his cleaver at Harvus' pale forehead. "I be a thinkin' since you last come. Some years back, a witch-wizard done killed the guards. This be in the day when we is poachin' the caravans, way on down south. Beef done remember better than I."

The lute player stopped playing. "You think this be the witch-wizard that took all o' Beef's gold?"

"Aye, it could be this here vagrant. What you reckon, hand 'im over to Beef?"

Harvus, voice muffled from the hairpiece in his mouth, shook his head, moaning a denial.

"Kill him, Sal," said the boy. "I don't like the look he givin' you. He going to hex you."

"You is wanting to hex me, little pig of a witch-man?" Sal tapped Harvus' big belly with his cleaver. "You tryin' to hex old Sal, is you?"

"Stick 'im," the boy said. "He too dangerous. He want to hex us!"

"No, hand 'im over to Beef," the lute player said. "Beef'll want to have a word first."

Harvus' jerky movements began slowing. His eyes eventually wandered up into his head and he went limp.

The boy kept his hands over Harvus' mouth. "He pass out?"

Sal made an idle gesture and the boy removed his hand. Harvus' head fell limply forward. Sal withdrew the hairpiece from his mouth, placing it in Harvus' lap. "He done pass out, he did."

The lute player leisurely tweaked his strings, checking their tuning. "Might be from the fight he was in. I says someone done caught him thiefin'."

"Or he done fight that there Legion," said the boy. "Had a Legion dagger stuck in 'im, ain't he?"

Sal massaged his neck. He flicked the arrow stuck in Harvus' chest. "These here feathers say Henawa to me. They quarrel with the Legion nows and then. Fool done messed with the wrong savages. But it don't matter none, he dying now. Bleed out soon."

The lute player started a mournful tune before suddenly switching tact and playing something festive. Sal's boots scuffed the plank floor in time to the rhythm of the song. The boy clapped along, sickle bouncing on his hip.

"How much you think we can sell that witch girl for?" the boy asked over the music. "She be feisty. Tried to hex me, she did."

Augum briefly exchanged another look with Bridget.

Sal took a swig and threw the empty bottle aside. "She be a fiery one. Might be a good chunk o' gold to the right buyer."

"We is going to be rich," the lute player howled, making a song of it. "We is a rich men yes we is, rich men, I says, rich men …"

Sal stopped dancing. "Get me another bottle, boy."

Augum and Bridget ducked back down. "We have to do something," he whispered. "She must be inside." Yet the pair of them just stared at each other blankly. He had no idea how to go about this, especially with Harvus there. There were only two options—sit and wait to see where Leera was, possibly risking her life further, or attack and find out by questioning one of them.

"Attack them head on," he whispered.

Bridget gave him a hard, appraising look. "Agreed."

"Burn it?"

"Not enough time to get her. And she could get trapped."

Then it came to him. "Confusion—"

"That'll do it. Then Push, the First Offensive, Centarro if need be."

The pair of them peeked over the windowsill. Sal was doing a two-step dance that the lute player accented with a double twang of notes.

This was it. Augum surreptitiously opened the window. The bandits were too busy watching Sal dance to notice. He raised his hand, readying the correct arcane energy, focus, and phrase. "Flustrato." He felt the arcanery drain from him as his rings flared to life.

Sal, who was about to uncork the bottle the boy had given him, stumbled and fell, the bottle crashing to the floor. The lute player roared in laughter as Sal fumbled to get back up.

"The look on your face, Sal!" the lute player managed to gurgle between laughs. "You is looking like a hog in a trap! Woo-wee, look at you go!" He quickly cranked out a galloping melody on the lute.

Bridget raised her arm. "Flustrato," she whispered, and the lute player's hands jammed in the strings. He scratched at his head and glanced down at his instrument stupidly.

"What be the matter with you two, you done stiff drunk?" the boy asked.

Sal began licking the floorboards while the lute player tried to touch his nose with his tongue, making the boy snort with laughter.

"Flustrato!" Augum said, but he had mistimed his visualization with his arcane energy and the spell failed.

The boy seemed to feel something and whipped his head their way. He immediately drew his sickle. "We has intru—"

"Voidus aurus!" Bridget cut in and the boy furiously rubbed his ear with his free hand.

"I can't hear, I can't hear! They is hexin' me, Sal, do something!"

Augum jumped over the windowsill and raised his palm. "Dreadus terrablus!"

"Not that spell—" Bridget said, but it was too late. The boy dropped his sickle, eyes widening. His mouth slowly opened wide. In a delayed reaction, the scream finally followed. Then he scrambled frantically for the door, yanked it open, and shot outside, shrieking like a banshee.

"Shyneo!" Augum pointed his lit palm at Sal. "Where is she!" but the man had reverted to a fetal state, holding his toes while rocking back and forth.

"Shyneo." Bridget pointed her lit palm threateningly at the lute player. "Where is she!" but he only gaped stupidly at her.

Harvus suddenly moaned. Augum and Bridget immediately turned their attention to the man, hands forward, ready to cast a spell should they need to. But Harvus was as pale as parchment, and his lips were barely moving.

"Where is Leera?" Augum yelled, taking a step closer. "Where is she!"

Harvus' lips were moving, but no sound came out. His head hung limp.

Augum took a risk and leaned forward to hear better. "You try anything and I'll shock you. Now, where is she!" Outside, a commotion was beginning to stir up.

"Trap … door …" His breathing was slowing. He was staring at the hairpiece in his lap. "Under …"

Augum shook the man. "Under what …? Under what!" but Harvus let out a final wheezing breath before going still. For a moment, Augum only gaped. Their former mentor had died, and the last thing the man had seen was his own hairpiece in his lap.

Bridget suddenly began tearing at the place and Augum immediately joined her, the pair kicking and shoving everything on the floor in an effort to locate Leera, all while shouting her name. Then they froze, both spying the sack in the corner at the same moment, before using Telekinesis to shove it aside, revealing a trap door.

Augum made a yanking motion and the trap door flew open. He and Bridget dropped to their knees, searching the darkness with lit palms.

And there, lying at the bottom on a straw-covered floor, was Leera.

"Leera!" they yelled in unison, but she did not respond.

"She's unconscious," Bridget said.

"Telekinesis," Augum quickly countered, trying to ignore the voices outside that were rapidly getting closer. "Ready? One. Two. Three—!"

The pair of them concentrated on arcanely lifting her body. Despite their hunger and exhaustion, it worked—soon as she was in reaching distance, they stretched down and hauled her over the lip.

"Aug, that you?" Leera mumbled in a weak daze.

"I think she's been drugged—" Augum said, heart racing. How were they going to get her out of there now?

They hoisted her to their shoulders.

Leera's words slurred. "We going somewhere?"

"We are, Lee," Bridget said. "Hang in there—"

Suddenly the door flew open, revealing a huge man the size of a bear, wielding a spiked club. The bearded behemoth swept the scene with giant owl-like eyes, stopping to stare at Harvus' form.

"You!" he said in a deep guttural voice. His black eyes settled on Sal and the lute player. "What in damnation be goin' on here—?"

Sal and the lute player both squinted in concentration, the gesture taking some effort. If they had been warlocks, they probably would have fought off the spell effects by now.

"Stay back!" Augum warned, arm unconsciously rippling to life with three lightning rings. "Or we'll hex you! We're warlocks, and we're getting out of here whether you like it or not—"

The huge bearded man took a step forward. "You be nothing but young—"

Augum pointed at the sickle and it flew into the air, hovering dangerously between them. The man stopped, raising his club. Augum could see doubt and suspicion on his brutish face. Behind him, other men closed in, all brandishing weapons.

"We can do things you can't even dream of," Bridget said in the iciest tone Augum had ever heard her utter. To demonstrate, she threw at the ground with her free hand, the word out of her mouth barbaric. "GRAU!" The cabin shook with the sound of cracking trees and timber. All of the bandits flinched, most ducking to the ground or jumping aside. The rest took a few steps back—even the large man had exited the cabin, though his club was still raised before him.

Augum, well experienced in hearing and feeling her spell by now, did not even allow his sickle to drop. "Keep back, or I'll bury this between your eyes!"

As the bandits retreated, Augum and Bridget edged out of the cabin step by weary step, Leera between them. Suddenly there was a slicing sound and Augum felt hot fire in his back. The sickle dropped to the ground as he turned, reflexively summoning his shield just in time to block the second blow of a cleaver, this time meant to have removed his head from his neck. A third would certainly kill him. He instantly let go of Leera and slammed his wrists together.

"ANNIHILO!" A thick bolt of lightning connected between his hands and Sal's head, exploding it into a cloud of blood and brain matter.

Men cursed and screamed. All but a few backed away as the body fell in a heap. The lute player, who had obviously been thinking of charging next, dropped his knife and ran back inside the cabin, begging for mercy from the gods.

Augum winced, trying not to think of the painful wound in his back. He wrapped Leera's arm around his neck again, staring that giant mountain of a man dead in the eyes. "You will move or suffer the same fate," he spat, never meaning anything more.

The giant man's eyes flicked to Sal's body. His great club wavered only slightly before he slowly backed away, but he did not step aside, and behind him, some brave bandits gathered.

"They is only two of them, Beef!" called one. "We can take 'em!"

"Don't let no kids get the best of us, Beef!" called another. "Look what the demon witches done to Sal—"

"Hold on to her," Bridget said quickly, letting go of Leera. Augum brought Leera close as Bridget drew a five-pointed figure in midair.

"Summano elementus minimus." A chunky elemental made of rock and earthen debris crunched to life and jumped to the ground before them.

"Unholy gods, what is that—" a bandit squealed.

"It's a demon!" Bridget said. "And if you don't want to get dragged to hell with it, you best stand out of our way!"

Augum couldn't help but feel a surge of pride. Bridget was shaking, but it wasn't from fear, but rather *determination*. And she made their first successful casting of Summon Minor Elemental! A thought that seemed ludicrous considering the danger they were in.

They slowly moved along, careful to keep a lookout from all sides, as the men shadowed them with hesitant retreating steps, eyes firmly trained on the trio, weapons wavering in front. When one bandit got too close, Augum briefly let go of Leera to throw at the ground, shouting "GRAU!" and the loudest crack of thunder he had yet managed ripped through the camp, sending nearly everyone scampering for shelter.

"If any of you come too close, the next bolt will rip through you all!" Augum said, staring down every single man before him. When that still was not enough to move Beef from their path, Augum turned and pointed at Sal's dead body. He knew it was beyond his arcane limit, but he went for it nonetheless—a moment of epic concentration later, Sal's headless corpse rose into the air and began hovering forward, feet dragging along the dirt.

Men screamed and shouted for mercy and dove for cover. As soon as Beef realized the headless body was coming for him, he retreated so quickly he tripped and fell, rolling on the earth like a great log. That broke any remaining morale, and the trio was allowed to escape the bandit camp, leaving behind cries of anguish, prayers to the gods, and curses that the trio never return, damn witches that they be.

OLD JORY

Bridget had the reins on the ride back, with Leera sitting right behind, tenderly held by Augum, who sat in the rear. The horse cantered along, the trio bobbing to its rhythmic trot. Augum, head nuzzled into Leera's neck and arms wrapped around her torso, had a giant smile on his face. All was well again.

That is, all except for the stinging wound in his back from Sal's cleaver, which was becoming increasingly more difficult to ignore. Every bounce made him feel weaker, more light-headed, more thirsty. And wow did it sting!

Augum's smile faded. There was also the dark knowledge he had ended another life, and in such a violent way. The memory of the man's head exploding was seared into his brain forever. Just like the memory of killing Corrigus, back at Hangman's Rock. Taking life was such a difficult thing to fathom, and it bothered him on a level that subtly poisoned everything. He supposed his anxiety over the matter should be tempered by the knowledge they were at war with cruel people. But justifications only felt like he was lying to himself, and the memories of what he had done would haunt him like ghosts.

Life is cheap in war. That's what Sir Westwood had always said. Life is cheap in war.

His back suddenly twinged with searing pain after a particularly hard bounce. He winced and raised his head from Leera's shoulder, trying to will the pain to go away. High above the dark trees was a vast field of bright stars, and the largest, most beautiful silver moon he had ever seen. At least they were alive to witness it, to enjoy each other's company once more. At least she was safe in his arms. At least, that is, for a little while longer, for life to him now seemed a harrowing existence, a delicate dance on the sharpest blade, of which falling meant the nothingness that was death.

His head swam from staring at the heavens. He nuzzled his face again into Leera's raven hair and gently gave her a squeeze. Her hands closed over his. But he wasn't feeling that good now, what with the horse's canter. He might need to lie down soon, else throw up. He should have dressed the wound … or even told Bridget about it. What was the matter with him?

"We need to stop," he gurgled, feeling thoroughly queasy now, as if he was swimming through an ocean of bile.

"Huh?" Bridget said.

"We need to …" but then he felt all the fight go out of him. The long and stressful day, combined with lack of food and blood loss, had triumphed. He slipped from the horse and smashed into the soggy earth.

He woke up to Leera's panicked face staring at him. She was slowly stroking his forehead. "Oh, Aug … why didn't you say something?"

Bridget was kneeling beside her. "Augum Stone, you can be such a fool sometimes."

"Just a tiny cut …" he mumbled.

Bridget stared at him. "A tiny cut. *A tiny cut*. Augum, do you—"

"Spare him, Bridge," Leera said in exhausted tones, giving her a pleading look.

Bridget's countenance softened.

Leera sighed, returning her gaze to him. "Bridge bandaged you up with a small Legion banner we found in the horse's pack. I also repaired your robe." She reached behind her, retrieving a skin of water with the Legion emblem on it. It immediately made him aware how parched he was and how dry his lips felt. She placed it to his lips and he drank greedily.

"Not too much, not yet." Leera then passed it to Bridget, before taking a swig herself. "We've also got a bit of dried beef. But that's for tomorrow. Now rest …"

And rest he did, soon falling asleep in Leera's arms.

* * *

They resumed the journey the next morning, after Augum felt a little better. The water had helped, but his stomach still panged with hunger. The morning was misty, cool and quiet, the forest still wet from the recent rains. It was good to have slept. It was good knowing the girls were safe. And as far as hunger was concerned, after Bahbell, they certainly knew their limits and could endure far more.

"You should switch and let Augum take the reins, Bridge," Leera said. "Then you can rest your head on my shoulder." She turned her head to Augum. "She slept poorly again. Nightmares."

Bridget gave the reins a stern yank while giving the horse's flanks a kick, so he would go a little faster. "I don't want to talk about it."

Leera sighed. "You should. Might help."

Bridget said nothing. It wasn't long before she stopped the horse at a fork in the road. "Aug, you don't happen to remember which way it is?"

Augum glanced past both girls' shoulders. The forks looked unfamiliar. "No idea at all."

Bridget chose the path to the right, mumbling, "Should've enchanted something with Object Track before we left."

"But then it would have superseded the one you cast on Harvus, and we might not have found Leera."

"Good point."

Augum wasn't worried. They'd find their way back somehow, even if they had to stop to ask some farmer for directions—not that they saw any farms along the forest road.

"How's your back?" Leera asked.

"Fine," he lied. The cut hurt terribly. It was a deep, throbbing pain edged with a fiery stinging. And his bones still ached from being slammed against a tree by Harvus. He felt stiff and sore all over. Who knew how many bruises he had from that vicious tussle.

"We missed Lover's Day," Leera said, tracing over the scar from when he hastily sliced his own palm open to make life-saving golden vitae for Bridget.

"Could have been worse," he said.

"You two aren't making out back there, are you?" Bridget said.

"No," they chorused.

"Maybe later though," Leera added. She turned in the saddle. "How does it feel to rescue a fair maiden?"

Augum reddened. He kissed her cheek and smiled. "Pretty good, actually," and squeezed her waist gently.

Bridget stared at the forest and sighed. "We survived another one," she whispered.

"Another what?" Leera asked, turning back around.

"Another close call."

"What're you saying, that we got lucky?"

"Yes." Bridget turned her head in the saddle to face Leera a moment. "Just hoping our—"

"—it won't," Augum cut in.

Leera glanced between the two of them. "What won't?"

"Our luck. It won't run out." He had to stop this lying thing.

Bridget stared at him a moment before returning her gaze to the road. "What makes you so sure?"

"Because we won't let it." But he knew that one day, their luck would run out. It felt inevitable, like a cloud of doom hanging over their heads. How many times had they already escaped death's clutches? How many more times will they tempt the eternal abyss? It was a daring dance, one that felt ever more dangerous with each song.

"Well someone's luck ran out," Leera said.

Augum knew she was talking about Harvus, but he again became aware of the gut-wrenching rot he felt about killing a man. He had killed someone. A person. Someone's son. Even if it was in self-defense, *he had killed someone*.

Then he remembered Leera had killed Vion Rames in Augum's defense back at Castle Arinthian. What an awful thing to have in common. If Sir Westwood were still alive, he would look Augum in the eye and say, "But that is war, my boy, that is war."

"How'd you cast the elemental spell so soon after learning it, anyway?" Leera asked Bridget.

"While you two have been spending time getting all lovey-dovey, I've been reading up on the spell. Practiced it in my head for ages before Harvus taught the final portion. Been practicing it every moment of my spare time since."

"Why am I not surprised," Leera muttered.

"She's not perfect," Augum said.

Bridget scoffed.

"What do you mean?" Leera asked.

"She swore. Actually swore. For real. Said the words 'damn it' when we first rode off."

Leera sat up, dramatically gripping her head with her hands. "No! Not our sweet Bridgey-poo!"

"Look, she's blushing," he said.

Bridget was smiling. "Shut up, you two. And I don't remember swearing. Anyway, your boyfriend is getting braver."

Leera gave Bridget a playful but weak shove. "Stop embarrassing him."

Augum felt his cheeks tingle. "We did what we had to do."

"Though I could see you becoming a general or something one day," Leera said in afterthought.

Augum snorted. "About all I could lead is a cow to pasture."

"And you did once."

"It was a mule." He fondly remembered old Meli, her tail swatting tiredly. That felt forever ago, yet he still missed her companionship.

"I think Leera's on to something though," Bridget said in somber tones. "If Mrs. Stone doesn't come back—"

"Nana *will* come back," Augum said, a little harsher than he meant to.

Bridget stopped the horse. "I'm just *saying*, Augum, if she doesn't—" She paused and turned to look him in the eyes. "If she doesn't, I'd follow you, and I don't think I'd be the only one."

"What do you mean? You're a better leader than I! I'm just a dumb farm boy who happens to have a twisted father and a famous great-grandmother—"

"It's not who you're related to." Bridget placed a hand on her heart. "It's what's in here."

He pressed his lips together firmly and looked away. "Can we just talk about something else?" The leader of a resistance movement? How ridiculous was that? Might as well put Leland in charge. He'd be just as effective, if not more.

Bridget flicked the reins and kicked at the horse's flanks. "We got the Agonex back at least."

"You really think we can trust those guards and that constable?" Leera asked.

"Don't have a choice," Augum replied. "Have to trust someone along the way. Besides, if Mr. Goss and Mr. Okeke trust them enough to bring them into the home and tell them about us …"

"The soldiers brought their families too," Bridget added. "I haven't sensed any treachery from them yet."

"Just remember Canes," Leera said, referring to the man that betrayed them in Castle Arinthian. She leaned back against Augum. "If they did turn on us though, I mean, if they took the Agonex straight to your father, they'd be handsomely rewarded. Heck, their lives might even be extended arcanely."

"The only life-extending my father is doing is turning people into undead walkers."

"True."

Bridget adjusted her grip on the reins. "The guards were supposed to take the Agonex to Mr. Goss and Mr. Okeke. I trust them, so I'm sure that's exactly what they did. And Augum's right, we simply have to trust some people along the way."

"Who's going to train us now?" Leera asked after a pause. But no one had the answer to that.

They rode for the rest of the day, refilling the waterskin at a stream and snacking on berries and beef, eventually coming upon another fork.

"I really have no idea which way to go," Bridget said. "And I'm so hungry I can't think straight."

"Should have been there by now," Augum said. "Think we might be lost." His entire body throbbed from the pains in his back. It was worse than the hunger. "Let's just find a quiet place to sleep for the night."

The girls agreed and they soon found themselves a spot under a lonely birch amongst a sea of evergreens. After tying up the horse, they huddled closely, preserving their warmth. Augum fell asleep holding Leera, grateful to be able to do such a simple thing.

* * *

He was jerked awake by a sudden yelp from Bridget. He sat up, whispering, "Bad dream?"

She nodded, face mottled by moonlight shadows of evergreen branches. She glanced at a snoozing Leera.

"Want to talk about it?"

Bridget shook her head, lying back down.

Augum watched her fall asleep, worried.

They slept in, waking late morning. The day was cloudy, gray and damp, with a light wind from the south that gently swayed the trees.

Augum stretched and listened to the soft rustle of the forest. "Looks like it might rain again."

Leera yawned and gave Augum a peck on the cheek. "I could really go for some bread, eggs and bacon right about now. Maybe some buttered potatoes, then a slice of sugared blueberry pie. Mmm, pie ..."

"Stop it, you're making my stomach feel like a cavern," Bridget said, picking leaves out of her hair, before doing the same to Leera.

Leera watched the stallion graze. "If only we could get by eating grass like him."

Augum recalled the moss they ate in the labyrinthine cave system deep under Bahbell. "We did, remember?"

"Trying to forget."

Bridget nodded at his back. "Let me look at it before we go."

He groaned. "If you have to."

"I have to."

Leera helped her check the wound, the girls saying remarkably little, though Augum did catch them sharing a dark look.

"That bad, huh?" he said, gritting his teeth as Leera finished the new bandage, torn from the same Legion banner.

"Don't think about it," she replied.

"Easy for you to say."

After changing the dressing, they gathered themselves and mounted the horse. This time Augum took the reins, with Leera delicately holding his waist, Bridget in the rear.

It wasn't long before Augum halted the horse at a triple fork. "Bridge?"

"No, it's just a fork," Leera said.

"Very funny. Bridget—you remember this one?"

"Nope," Bridget said from the rear.

"They all look identical." Leera began pointing in a different direction with each syllable. "Sticks in the sand, sticks in the snow, re-veal a man, dead long a-go."

"Middle one it is," Augum said, gently prodding the horse's flanks.

Gray clouds steadily moved overhead as the day wore on. Low on energy from the lack of food, and out of water, the trio said little. Sometime in the afternoon, they stopped at a puddle-splattered road nestled in the woods, grooved with wagon wheel tracks. The stallion drank from one of those muddy puddles while the trio was more selective, choosing the clearest one. They soon resumed the trek, but after passing a bend in the road, Augum stopped the horse.

"Now *that* we definitely hadn't ridden through," he said, squinting to make out if there were guards manning the large wooden gates ahead. "Can't see anyone."

"Spooky quiet," Leera whispered.

Augum noticed it too—no sounds of children playing, no smith hammering at an anvil, nothing. He led the horse onward, carefully paying attention to how it reacted. If there were any walkers here, the stallion would probably not want to go in. Or so he hoped.

They passed through the gates, finding a small village surrounded by a twig wall. Thatch-roofed huts sat quiet, uprooted vegetable plots in front. There was not a person, chicken or hog in sight, only a bone-thin stray dog that watched them from afar between sniffs of the mud.

Augum kept the reins tight in his fist. "Looks abandoned."

"Well we need directions and food," Leera said. "Hello! Is there anyone here?" She waited before repeating the shout.

"No souls to be found," said a grizzled voice behind them, startling the trio. "At least none that matter."

Augum turned the horse to find an old man with a severe hunch, holding himself up with a gnarled stick. He wore a tattered shirt and muddy trousers. His shoes were farming slippers.

Augum raised a hand. "Hello. Are you alone?"

"You ain't no Legion."

"Oh, this—we borrowed the horse."

"Borrowed. You ain't bringing no more trouble here, is you?" The man revealed a single black tooth as he spoke.

"No, sir, we just need to find our way home to Milham."

The old man gave a grunt. "And yes, we is alone, just me and me wife. Last of Belham, we is." He examined them with a roving eye. "You look hungry."

"We very much are."

"And where did you say you were going?"

"Milham, sir."

"Well like I says, this is Belham. Milham a ways north-northeast. And I reckon we can spare some rice. Haven't had company in some time."

"We would be very grateful."

The man cocked his head at the stallion. "You sure you not Legion witches?"

"Definitely not, sir."

The man glanced at the gates. "And you sure they isn't on your tail?"

"They aren't, sir." At least not at the moment.

"Very well. Tie 'im out back." The man hobbled off, disappearing into a nearby hut. They tied the horse in back and walked around. A viciously rotten stench hit them the moment they stepped inside the hut, forcing them to cover their noses with their sleeves. It was a single room with two shuttered windows open to the air. The ground was barren dirt, barely covered by old straw. There was a rustic cedar trunk, trestle table, bench, bucket, and a cot, on which lay a sleeping figure covered by a blanket. A nest of gray hair peaked out the top.

The man opened the lid to the trunk, retrieving a sack of rice with a shaking hand. Augum immediately came in to help, trying to ignore that awful smell.

The man gestured at Leera with his stick. "Well's out back. Bucket's here."

Leera grabbed the filthy bucket and disappeared while the man set to making a fire with dried dung.

"We don't want to disturb your wife, sir," Bridget whispered.

"Woman's always sleeping. Some noise'll do her good, get her up and about." He lit the fire with flint and steel almost worn down to the nub, and placed a tired iron pot on the small black fire.

"Go on and sit and tell Old Jory abouts where you from and such."

Augum took a seat on the bench beside Bridget. "I'm from Willowbrook."

"Willowbrook. Never heard of it."

"It's a ways to the west."

"You look and sound like city kids. You look like privilege."

"Two of us are from Blackhaven," Bridget said. "And yes, we've been luckier than some, sir."

Only some, Augum thought with dark cynicism.

Leera came back in, holding the slopping bucket with both hands. Augum helped her pour water into the pot. "Had to wash it out first," she whispered from behind her sleeve before taking a seat beside Augum.

"What happened to everyone here?" Augum asked.

"Most up and died on the sword when the Legion took the able." He made a snatching gesture with a shaky hand. "Took women and men, they did. Just like that. Rest plain starved. No farmin' could get done by the old and folks ain't have no money. No food stores either—stolen, they be. Bandits." Old Jory gave a practiced nod while gumming his lips. "There be shallow graves all about, even in the huts."

The trio glanced at the uneven floor. Was there a grave underneath them? Certainly would explain the smell.

Old Jory poured a measured amount of rice in and stirred it with a grubby wooden spoon. "You be wearing warlock robes, yes?"

The trio exchanged glances. "Yes, sir," Augum replied.

Old Jory revealed his black tooth with a smile. "Do an old man a good and show me them stripes."

The trio summoned their respective rings for him. He gazed at their arms fondly. "Three is the witch's number." Then he stretched his own blotchy arm out and groaned from effort, but nothing came of it. "Ah, I be too old, she don't come back no more. Had me a single stripe. Could move things with me mind once. See, I stopped practicing a long time ago. Got tired. Kids took it up though. Couldn't be prouder."

Augum extinguished. "Your children are warlocks?"

"Oh yes, had ter join the Legion, they did. Haven't heard word since." The man kept stirring. "That's life, it is. She be a harsh mistress."

They watched the man patiently cook the rice, sleeves over their noses to block the stench. Augum was so hungry his eyes would not leave the pot as it boiled.

"You rich city folk not too high-minded to use your hands, be you?"

"Of course not, sir," Bridget replied with a smile. "And thank you."

They hardly let the rice cool before they were at it.

Old Jory gave a snicker. "Like a pack o' feastin' 'ungry dogs. By the looks of your faces, I'd say you 'aven't eaten in days. And you done look like you seen battle."

"Bandits," Leera managed to say between mouthfuls.

"Sal an' Beef an' their gang west o' here?"

The trio nodded.

"Aye. Sal don't come 'ere no more. Nothin' to steal."

Augum flinched as he remembered. And he never will again …

Leera gave him an *Are you all right?* look. He nodded that he was fine.

"Are you and your wife not going to have any?" Bridget asked.

"You is hungrier than I am. Go on an' 'ave your fill. I'm an old man. Hardly need none to get by." Old Jory adjusted his tattered shirt as if readying for a formal supper. "Nice to have decent company for a change, it is." He languidly chased away a fly that had settled on his knobby nose. "Nothing but famine here. Famine, death, an' Old Jory an' his old wife." He watched as they scraped out the last of the rice with their dirty nails. "I suppose you be wanting to know which way to Milham."

"We would be grateful, sir," Augum said, washing out the pot.

"Go on through town. Left at the fork. Right at the next one. A good ways on you'll cross a stream, and you're almost there."

"Thank you kindly."

The man used his stick to stand. "Like I says, nice to have company." He turned to his wife. "Ain't that right, my love?" but she did not move—nor had she moved since they had come … and suddenly Augum knew the awful truth of the smell. He squeezed Leera's hand in his own. She squeezed back. Her face was pale as she gave him a heartfelt look of sorrow. She had to know too. He glanced at Bridget. Her head was bowed, eyes closed, hands clasped in front. And so did she.

"Would you like to come with us?" Augum asked the old man. "To Milham? Start a new life?"

The man watched his unmoving wife, covered in a rotten wool blanket. "A new life." He glanced at Augum and Leera. "It's a precious thing to have a hand to hold. A precious thing, fleeting though it oft be."

Bridget gathered herself, eyes now lingering on the bed. Her voice was soft. "We'll send back supplies for you."

"Send nothin'. Forget this place. It don't exist no more." The man's face grew stern. "You hear? Send nothin'. " He glanced at his wife. "I wants nothin' from no one. I wants my peace. I can feel it comin' for me. I'm a waitin'." The man's voice dropped to a whisper. "Do you understand?"

Augum swallowed through the hard lump in his throat. "Yes, sir."

"You is them, ain't you, the ones they be lookin' for."

"How did—"

"I never forget no face. Not even a badly drawn one. You keep strong now, you hear? Plenty o' folk out there need you and that ol' warlock o' yours. Plenty of folk …" He shuffled past, pointing at the far gate. "Like I says, left, right, ride some, then over the river. Now go on home. Go on and do some good for this poor kingdom, for us wretched folk. Go on and make things right if you can. I be too old and too daft and my time done come and gone. But not yours, no, not yours." He closed his eyes and nodded. "It was right that you be the last I see. It was right. I am glad of it."

"Thank you for the directions and the rice, sir." Augum and the girls bowed their heads out of respect for a long moment. "Thank you again," he said, then retrieved the horse, helping the girls mount.

Old Jory raised his chin. "Who would'a reckoned. And so young. What a thing to see." He hobbled back to his doorway and stopped. "You be sure to keep well clear o' the black-armored. An' if you can, send some o' them to hell for me," and with that, he disappeared inside his hut.

EXPECTATIONS

The trio hardly spoke on the return journey. What was there to say after seeing such a thing? An old man robbed of everything, the last of a village stolen of its inhabitants. An old man and his deceased wife. An old man awaiting the loneliest of ends. There was an entire kingdom of that. Burned-out villages. Lonely, starving people. Wives awaiting husbands that would never return. Parents thinking of their children. Children missing departed parents. The whole of it made Augum's heart ache with heaviness, and made him that much more grateful he was being held by Leera just then.

They followed Old Jory's directions very carefully, until they heard a single horn blast. Soon they cantered by an old wooden sign carved with the words *Village of Milham*.

"Just in time for supper," Leera whispered, head resting on Augum's shoulders.

Soon as they entered town, a pudgy boy Augum recognized as Devon, Constable Clouds' son, threw up a shout of victory. With a wide smile on his face, he ran up to them, limbs flailing about as if he had never used them before.

"You made it! I don't believe it!" Devon turned his chubby-cheeked face back to the village, cupping his mouth. "And they brought Leera back! They rescued Leeraaaa!" He tromped over to the trio, wearing an ill-fitting mustard doublet, copper hair in a small ponytail. His smile was infectious.

Augum extended his hand. "You must be Devon."

Devon heartily shook it. "I can't believe I'm meeting you three. You don't understand!" He kept shaking Augum's hand. "When I heard the famous trio—the heroes and future saviors of Solia—were in town, I just … I can't believe I'm meeting you! Father and I are on your side! We're all on your side, you see—the whole village!"

Augum was nodding along, but he was thinking, oh great, how many others knew?

Devon finally let go, moving on to the girls. "And you must be Leera Jones and Bridget Burns—you're both so much prettier than the poster!" He hastily withdrew a well-worn parchment and unfolded it. It was a drawn poster of the trio, with Mrs. Stone's image looming largest of all in the background. Augum was drawn in front, Leera and Bridget flanking.

"Huh … 'Wanted. 5000 gold reward'," Leera read aloud. "Crazy. That's a fortune."

Augum glanced around at the crowd. There were more than a few soot-faced down-on-their-luck miners staring. What's to stop them trying to claim the 5000 gold reward?

"And you're not kidding, I look like some kind of evil freckled owl," Leera went on.

"They made me look like a squirrel," Bridget added, "and Mrs. Stone looks like some twisted hag."

"Aug got off easy though," Leera said. "Actually looks handsome."

Bridget frowned. "Hmm. I think I know who fed the details to the artist. Think about it—Freckles and Squirrel. Can only be—"

"Erika Scarson," the girls chorused.

"Who's that?" Devon asked.

"Long story," Leera said as a mass of people ascended upon them, including Constable Clouds (with a patched-up shoulder), his two soldiers, Priya, Jengo, Mr. Okeke, Mr. Goss, Haylee and Chaska and a slew of others.

"I'm too tired for this," Augum muttered.

"What, does the whole village know about us now?" Leera asked.

Devon splayed his palms at them. "Don't worry, as I said, everyone's completely behind you. I mean behind *us*. After all, we're the Resistance!"

Augum raised his brows. This was spiraling out of control. Were they all mad? Did they not realize there could be Legion spies in this very crowd? Did they not realize what the Legion did to towns harboring fugitives? When he saw the look on the girls' faces, he knew they were thinking the exact same thing.

Once the trio dismounted, the throng congratulated Augum and Bridget with handshakes and welcomed Leera back with hugs. It was bizarre and Augum did not know what to make of it. He remembered his great-grandmother swamped in the same way at Sparrow's Perch before his father ambushed them and razed the place to the ground. He couldn't help but look around at the trees, half-expecting to see deathly horses and armored men hiding there.

"... yes, my shoulder is just fine," Constable Clouds was saying to Bridget. "Merely a flesh wound, and I have a lot of flesh."

Mr. Goss wiped his tired eyes. "Dear me, I really did fear the worst. We spent half the night combing the woods for you three. I cannot tell you how overjoyed I am to see you safe and sound."

Leland groped his way to the trio, hugging each in turn and moaning happily.

"Any word from Nana?" Augum quietly asked Mr. Goss after pinching Leland's dimpled cheek.

"None, I am afraid, though Leland has listened carefully to the orb and has made notes."

"Notes?"

"His studies have not stopped just because he's blind and mute, Augum," Bridget said in an undertone. "He *can* write, you know."

"Right, of course."

"We considered holding the *other* artifact," Constable Clouds said in a whisper, "but realized we needed to foster trust. So we turned it back over to Mr. Goss."

Mr. Goss beamed. "The constable has proven himself time and again."

Augum had to grudgingly admit that if the Constable was an enemy, he would have confiscated the artifacts, not to mention the Legion would have swept through there by now.

"Some battle," Haylee said after finishing hugging the trio, cane in hand. "Glad you three are all right. I'm sorry I wasn't more help."

"What are you talking about?" Augum said. "You saved my hide."

"Owed you. Still do." She thumbed at Chaska. "Big lug felt so bad for not firing more arrows."

Chaska nervously glanced at the constable. "I could have done better."

The constable clapped Chaska on his meaty back. "Wasn't your fault, my dear boy. And one did strike true, did it not?"

Chaska let a smile slip. "It did."

Leland moaned sharply while searching his garments, finally finding a crumbled piece of parchment.

Augum took it, reading it aloud. " 'Pearl near Legion camp.' "

Leland nodded.

"Great work, Leland. Do you know which one?"

Leland fumbled for the small parchment and made Augum turn it over.

" 'Velmara'," Augum read. They were going to need a map. He frowned—the mystery of what had happened to Nana suddenly cut through the celebrations. Had she been captured already, or simply lost the pearl?

"Mr. Okeke, your arm—" Bridget exclaimed upon seeing it in a sling.

"I do believe now I know what my son felt like," Mr. Okeke said with a nodding smile, referring to their initial meeting when Mrs. Stone healed Jengo's broken arm in exchange for shelter. "Though it is only a muscle tear and not, thankfully, broken."

"Speaking of—" Augum said as Jengo finally managed to squeeze himself near. The towering Sierran immediately drew Augum, Bridget and Leera into a hug.

"Straight out of the grave, you three," he said. "A miracle you lived. Can't wait to hear the story."

At last, Mr. Hanad Haroun joined the fray and raised his hands to the assembled mass. "All right, everyone, remember what we discussed in sacred trust—not a word to outsiders! We must be strong and brave. Now, our heroic trio needs to rest and eat, so please allow them space. Once again—not a word!"

The throng allowed them to depart, though not without a sizeable following embroiled in animated discussion.

"I don't feel comfortable at all," Augum said to Leera, turning to glimpse a sea of smiling and chatty faces. "Not only are we vulnerable to being discovered if word leaked out, but it's like they expect something huge from us."

"They only hope for the Legion to fall," Bridget said, walking beside Leera, "and they believe we and Mrs. Stone are going to make that happen. But yes, I agree—we have to be very careful."

"Belief is enough to make reality," Constable Clouds threw in, waddling along behind with his cane, his son beside him. "If I am not mistaken, that is one of the foundations of arcanery."

"I don't mind being a *little* famous," Leera admitted with a roguish grin, "as long as there are plenty of sweets. But what if someone turns us in for the reward?"

"Do not concern yourselves with being found out," Mr. Okeke said, "we have taken careful and deliberate precautions."

"We also have a plan in place in case the Legion *do* arrive," Constable Clouds threw in.

Mr. Goss fell in line beside them. "We will distract them while you are secreted into the woods, away from harm. From here on, we will be organized and the village will be protected."

Augum was doubtful. Sparrow's Perch had been protected too, and by powerful arcanery no less. Made no difference whatsoever.

"Augum, are you all right?" Jengo asked. "You're walking funny and you're kind of pale."

"I'm fine." Fine except for the fact that he was hungry, exhausted, stiff, and in constant stinging pain—not to mention haunted by Sal's exploding head.

"It's his back," Leera said. "Harvus slammed him against a tree. Then he got sliced by a bandit."

"Can I try healing you later?" Jengo asked. "Been studying the yellow book like a madman. I'm going to become an excellent healer, you know. And I promise you won't die."

"Guess so." Augum wasn't entirely sure it was a good idea, seeing as Harvus barely trained Jengo, but what choice did he have? There weren't any healers about. And besides, maybe part of that trusting thing was putting faith in those close to him. Leera didn't help matters by giving him a look he interpreted as *It's your body, but I wouldn't*.

"What happened to Furhead anyway?" Jengo pressed.

"Bandits," Leera replied. "Bandits happened. He tried to sell me, then he tried to sell the artifacts. Funny thing is, he once stole from the bandits and somehow thought it was a good idea to return."

"So … he's strung up on a pole?"

"Not quite."

"But he's dead, right? Tell me that he at least met his end."

She surrendered a single nod.

Jengo's face went serious, but then he simply shrugged. "There's that then."

"A life is a life, Jengo Okeke," said his father. "Have respect for the dead."

"Yes, Father."

Augum swallowed. A life is a life. He had just taken a life. Will the Unnameables punish him later? Will karma find him and settle the score? Self-defense or not, a man was no longer alive because of his actions. *Two men now*.

Leera was watching him. "Something's troubling you."

He shrugged. What *wasn't* troubling him?

A dark look crossed her face. "We have *that* in common now too."

So she has also been thinking about it.

"What are you two talking about?" Devon asked, beaming.

"Nothing," they replied in unison.

Mr. Haroun led them to his home, a two-storied manor nestled in the forest like Mr. Okeke's cabin, in front of a small tree-clustered hill. Constable Clouds posted

Lieutenant Briggs and Sergeant Cobb outside the doors. The two Legion soldiers refused entry to a gaggle of people, most of whom Augum did not recognize.

The group allowed entry was herded into a high-ceilinged hall, where everyone began taking off their shoes and coats, still chattering excitedly.

"Augum Stone, wanted rebel hero," said a soft voice.

Augum turned. "Malaika," he managed to say. "Uh, hi."

Malaika Haroun curtsied. She had ebony skin and wore a spring-green dress. Her long, tightly-curled black hair was secured with a ribbon.

Augum felt his ears grow hot. Malaika had visited the trio with her father after their ordeal in Bahbell. She had this odd way of making him feel uncomfortable. "Malaika danced with me at the Star Feast," he blurted to Leera.

Leera gave him an odd look. "Uh, I know." She slipped her hand under his elbow. "He's an awful dancer, isn't he?"

Malaika giggled, eyes solely on him. "He is, yes, but I very much enjoyed teaching him."

"That's my job now." Leera looked around at the exquisitely carved doors, the octagon-patterned inlay work on almost every wooden surface, and at the fine tapestries hanging on the walls. "Place is a palace," she mumbled.

"It is true that Father has done well as a merchant, but his generosity has cost the estate a great deal. I fear him giving too much to charity while keeping little for his family."

Augum and Leera opened their mouths to speak when a pale man with pinkish eyes and wearing a black servant gown appeared. "Please follow me, everyone," he said stiffly, leading them into the parlor. He was middle-aged, with milk-white hair and a bearing that had him carry his hawkish nose high.

"She has no idea how much people are suffering in the countryside," Leera whispered to Augum, watching Malaika rush to speak with an auburn-haired girl. "We're all lucky not to be starving right now."

Augum caught Malaika and her friend watching him as they whispered to each other behind their hands. They immediately giggled, shoulders hunkering, but resumed whispering and exchanging wide-eyed and mischievous glances.

Leera's eyes narrowed, but she said nothing.

Haylee had a distant look on her face. "I lived in a place like this once …" She kept straightening her already rigid-straight blonde hair with her free hand. "I wish I was dressed for the occasion."

Chaska was glancing around with a sneer. "Looks like a bunch of flashy junk to me. Nothing useful for a warrior."

Haylee, using her cane as leverage, slowly turned to give him a scathing look that took in his new girth. "Warrior, huh?"

Chaska reddened and glanced down at his belly.

"Hey," Bridget said to Haylee and Chaska, glancing softly between the two of them. "Be kinder to each other, you two." The sorrow of what the trio had seen showed on her gaunt face, in the dark circles under her eyes, in the tightness of her pressed lips. Haylee and Chaska must have noticed because they dropped their heads, cheeks reddening from … was it shame, perhaps?

Suddenly there was a commotion at the entrance. Augum turned to see a cane fly at Briggs' head. The man caught it deftly, receiving a stubby kick to his armored shin instead.

"Unacceptable!" cried a voice. "Panjita will not be denied her right of entry as an elder of this village! The tall carrot-head shall stand aside, as will his banana-headed companion!"

"Mother, no—!" Priya said, running to the hall.

"Father, do something, it's that ghastly woman again!" Malaika called.

Mr. Haroun sighed before striding to the entrance, watched by a gaggle of snickering and gossiping faces.

"I am afraid Ms. Singh and Mr. Haroun have never quite seen eye to eye," Mr. Okeke explained to Mr. Goss. "Or rather Ms. Singh has not quite approved of Mr. Haroun's leadership. The last time Ms. Singh was allowed into his home, she denounced Mr. Haroun as a devil-worshipping ingrate who did not know his bottom from his ankle."

"Dear me," Mr. Goss only said.

"Though you can imagine her wording to have been a touch more … creative."

This came as no surprise to Augum. There was not a soul in all of Sithesia Ms. Singh seemed to approve of.

"The so-called 'town elder' believes himself superior to Panjita!" Ms. Singh spat after finally being allowed entry. "Perhaps Old Haroun might stoop himself to recall that Panjita is a valuable and necessary part of the elder council of Milham."

"Please forgive me, Ms. Singh," Mr. Haroun said in a voice straining for patience. "Follow me."

"Oh, so Haughty Haroun now thinks of Panjita as a follower, does he? Why is Panjita not surprised in the least?"

"Mother, *behave* yourself—" Priya hissed, leading a grumbling Ms. Singh to the parlor, where the elder Singh proceeded to give the servant a whack on the shins for not immediately offering her a glass of wine. Jengo could only sheepishly watch as his betrothed tried to exasperatedly manage the situation.

"… and the milky vermin will bring *red* wine, not wash water!"

"Ugh, why does she always have to come to our meetings?" Malaika loudly said to her auburn-haired friend, just as Priya drew near. "She's hardly fit to serve and should retire from the council."

Priya pretended to fiddle with her chartreuse shawl, though her cheeks reddened considerably.

"Try living with her," Haylee muttered.

Soon a servant boy and girl of about the trio's age or a bit younger appeared with trays of wine, both just as pale as the older servant and with the same milk-white hair. Their pinkish eyes would frequently land on the trio, though both looked away when caught. Augum wondered if they were related to Henawa.

"My lady," said the servant boy, appearing near Leera. "Would you care for a sweet?"

"Now you're talking." Leera snagged three sugared biscuits.

"Lee, don't be rude," Bridget whispered.

"Nonsense, we're the guests."

"I don't think—"

Leera frowned. "Let me ask then. Excuse me, uh—"

"—Gabe," the boy said with a hint of a smile. He had the same high cheekbones and hawk nose as the middle-aged servant.

"Right, Gabe, uh, all right if I have a bunch of these?"

"My lady may have as many as she pleases, for she is prettier than—" Suddenly his eyes grew wide as he spotted someone behind them.

Augum turned to find the older servant glaring at the boy.

"My apologies, my lady," Gabe quickly said, shuffling off.

"Please excuse my wayward son," the elder servant said. "He is still an apprentice to service. There is much he has yet to understand."

"Oh, it's no problem," Leera said, mouth full with a biscuit. She turned to Augum after the man left. "I feel bad for getting him into trouble."

"He likes you," Augum said, feeling an unfamiliar prickle in his chest.

Leera waved the matter aside dismissively, readying to stuff another treat in her mouth.

Haylee watched the boy and girl work the room with quiet, nostalgic fascination.

"Strange to see servants in times like these," Bridget said. "I wonder if they had aspirations beyond the service life."

"They are lucky to have steady employment," said a cool voice nearby. The trio turned to see an ebony-skinned woman wearing a maroon dress with a square-cut neckline. A brilliant ruby hung around her neck, catching the candlelight.

Malaika drifted to the woman's side, taking her bejeweled hand in both her own. "Mother, this is Augum Stone, the hero I was telling you about."

Mrs. Haroun extended a hand palm down. "Charmed."

Augum shook it awkwardly.

One of Mrs. Haroun's brows travelled far up her forehead and Augum already knew he had broken some stupid protocol.

"These are my friends," he quickly said. "Bridget Burns and Leera Jones."

"Indeed." Mrs. Haroun swept the girls up and down with her eyes. Bridget and Leera curtsied, though the latter barely so.

Malaika flashed Augum a fawning smile. "Augum is *famous,* Mother. His poster is everywhere."

"Uh, well, I'm not the only one on it," he said, searching his mind for an excuse to get out of there.

Mrs. Haroun's jowls hardened. "For all the wrong reasons, Daughter. His father is a prolific murderer, a monster of the first order."

"But Augum is nothing like his father. He comes from good breeding. And besides, his great-grandmother is Anna Atticus Stone."

Augum felt Leera tense up beside him.

"Indeed," Mrs. Haroun said.

"I have found breeding isn't everything," Haylee said. Chaska was beside her, absently eating a cake portion he had pilfered off a silver tray.

Malaika's eyes slowly travelled to Haylee, then to her cane. "And who might you be again?"

"Haylee Esmeralda-Ray Tennyson, of House Tennyson, the Rose Quarter, Blackhaven."

"Ah. Well, I am sorry, but breeding is *everything*. Always was, always will be." Malaika took a moment to inspect Chaska. "And he's with you?"

Haylee hesitated, but then she straightened. "He is."

"We've met plenty of times, remember?" Chaska said between mouthfuls. "Big place. Could house ten families."

Mrs. Haroun was glaring at Chaska's filthy hands. "Not as big as some of the people in here, it seems."

Haylee reddened, opened her mouth to speak, when Malaika's auburn haired friend appeared by her side.

"Malaika, you simply *must* introduce me," she gushed. Her sapphire necklace matched her embroidered blue dress, and she had very fair skin.

Malaika hooked her friend's elbow with a devilish smile. "Augum Stone, meet my very best friend, Charissa Graves. Charissa, this is *the* Augum Stone."

Charissa extended a pale hand in the same manner as Mrs. Haroun. "Charmed." She had a round simple face and wide-set eyes.

Augum took her hand and awkwardly gave it a tap with his lips, hoping it was the right protocol. He turned to present Bridget and Leera. "And these are my—"

"—he really *is* a warlock," Charissa said to Malaika. "And he's so …" She gave her a meaningful look.

"I *know*, right?" Malaika replied with a mischievous smile, before growing serious. "Now settle down, we don't want to appear rude before such distinguished company." Her eyes flicked to Chaska. "Well, mostly."

Bridget was staring at Malaika, Charissa and Mrs. Haroun with a mixture of horror and shock, but she said nothing.

Charissa gave Malaika's elbow a tug. "Are you going to have him recount some heroic tales? Bet you he gets into all sorts of trouble."

Leera turned to Augum and loudly declared, "Don't you love it when people talk about you as if you're not there?"

Bridget curtsied. "Forgive us, Mrs. Haroun, Miss Haroun and Miss Graves. We have had a very trying couple of days."

Mrs. Haroun, who had swelled to the size of a bull, nonetheless raised her chin a little. "I certainly hope you will recover your manners soon. Come, Malaika."

Malaika gave Augum a longing look but obeyed her mother. Charissa lingered only a moment before following.

"What was that?" Augum asked after the women left. He was more curious than offended.

Leera shoved a third biscuit into her mouth. "Welcome to high society."

Haylee watched them go. "My old haunt."

"Snobs," Chaska said. "I don't like them."

Haylee grabbed his elbow. "Agreed. Come, let us eat."

Augum raised a brow at Leera. "Why did Mrs. Haroun ignore you?"

Leera rolled her eyes. "You can be so daft sometimes."

"You'll get used to it, Aug," Bridget said with a sigh. "Lee, we're guests here. Can you at least *try* and be civil?"

"Forget it. I just survived hell like, a thousand times, so if any of those vipers so much as hiss, I'm going to cast Confusion on them all. Then I'm going to sit back and stuff my face while they make mules of themselves before the entire town."

"Ugh, please just don't make a scene again."

Augum flashed Bridget a wry smile. "What, you mean it's happened before?"

Bridget folded her arms. "Don't remind me."

"Long story short," Leera said, "bunch of snobby girls played head games I didn't like."

Bridget covered her mouth as she quietly spoke. "She poured stinkroot into the tea and the spirits at an academy supper party."

Leera chortled to herself. "It was worth it. Should have seen them all hurrying to the lavatory."

"You almost got expelled though."

"Then I would've learned wild and blown myself up."

A bell rang from the dining room.

"Please, everyone, do take your seats," said the head servant.

"Finally, I'm starved," Leera said, and dragged Augum and Bridget to the table.

SUPPER AT THE HAROUNS'

As guests of honor, Augum, Bridget and Leera were seated to the right of Mr. Haroun. His daughter Malaika and her friend Charissa sat to his left. Charissa kept giving Chaska, who sat beside her, horrified looks. Haylee, meanwhile, sat stiff as a board beside him. The table was long and covered with fine white cloth. Places were set with shiny silverware, fine porcelain, and crystal.

"What are all these knives for?" Augum whispered to Leera, feeling uncultured.

She shrugged. "Ask Bridge."

Bridget leaned in. "That one there is for cutting bread, that one for cutting meat, and that one is for oysters."

"Of course, oysters are very hard to come by this far from the ocean," Malaika said loudly, "but we do try. Only the best for the town hero."

"I, uh, I really haven't done much," Augum said. "Bridget and Leera though—"

"—would you like something to drink, Augum?" Malaika interrupted with a cheery smile. Before he could reply, she snapped her fingers at the servant girl. "Annelise, bring Augum and I some youngling ale, right away."

The pink-eyed girl curtsied. "Yes, my lady," but she flashed Malaika a hateful look soon as her back was turned, before disappearing to what Augum assumed to be the kitchen.

"Such a peculiar lot," Malaika said to Charissa.

"You are braver than I to hire such ... ghosts," her friend replied.

"Father insists on his charity, but I really don't care for the way they spook the guests."

"Do not be rude, my dear child," Mr. Haroun said after finishing a conversation with Constable Clouds. The latter was helped to a chair by his son Devon, who could not keep his eyes off the trio.

"We are extremely fortunate, Malaika," Mr. Haroun continued, washing his hands in a basin of warm water, "far more fortunate than most, especially in these times. And if it were not for the demands of your mother, I would have us live ... far more modestly."

Malaika rolled her eyes. "If you had your way, Father, we would be living in squalor. I would be wearing rags and *never* find a suitable match." Her eyes drifted to Augum with a flutter.

"Ugh, could she be any more obvious?" Leera muttered to the ceiling.

Ms. Singh picked up her bread and threw it at the elder servant. "Panjita is to be served the same bread as the host, not this peasant rat food older than she!"

Priya quickly glanced around the table before whispering, "Mother, if you do not behave, I will take you home."

"Daughter will not speak to Panjita in such a manner if she wants to survive this so-called 'feast'."

"Mother, *please—*"

The servant picked up the bread with two fingers. "I shall rectify the problem immediately, my lady."

"I hope Daughter hears how to properly address an elder," Ms. Singh said to the table as Priya shrank in her chair. "Priya should be very kind to Panjita, as Panjita is still recovering from the nearly mortal blow of hearing her daughter betrothed to an unsuitable. A tall-as-a-beanpole, dark-as-night unsuitable. Look at him." She waved a wild arm. *"Look!"*

"Really is quite the scandal," Malaika said to a nodding Charissa.

Jengo only smiled and nodded his hello to the table, apparently taking it all in stride.

Priya, on the other hand, suddenly stood up. "He is *not* an unsuitable!" She grabbed Jengo's hand. "Come, Jengo," and stormed out, taking the tall Sierran with her.

"How rude," Malaika said to her friend.

Ms. Singh adjusted her thick spectacles, chin held high. "Panjita's daughter is ungrateful and spoiled. Panjita has a good mind to cast her out of the house."

Mr. Haroun wearily rubbed his forehead as Gabe took the bowl of water from him, promptly returning with a fresh bowl and cloth, handing it to Augum.

"I am sure you find all this wealth … unnecessary, Augum," Mr. Haroun said, watching him awkwardly wash his hands and face. "I assure you I quite agree. People are dying across the kingdom while I play the rich merchant." He leaned closer to Augum. "I will give up my wealth—and there is a lot more of it than what you see here—the moment I see a worthwhile investment. Right now, the only thing I want to invest in is seeing the downfall of the Legion and the end of war."

It was a moment before Augum found his voice. "We have something in common then, sir. My father is …" In a flash he recalled an entire group of people lifted from the ground, feet twitching as they burned alive with lightning.

"Augum, are you all right?" Malaika asked with a look of fawning concern. "Please, may I get you something—where is that careless girl? Annelise!"

"I'm fine, thanks." He returned his attention to Mr. Haroun as Malaika kept snapping her fingers for Annelise. "My father *is* a murderer. He murdered Bridget and Leera's families. He murdered their friends. He even murdered my own mother. And he surrounds himself with murderers." Robin Scarson, for one …

Suddenly he saw an elderly warlock crumple to the ground, followed by a separate violent image of Sal's head exploding. The buzzing in his ears was so loud it took him a moment to realize Mr. Haroun was speaking to him.

"… has slaughtered many, and also risen many with his necromancy." Mr. Haroun accepted a glass of wine from the elder servant. "Thank you, Clayborne. Now as I was saying, Augum, I am a man of fortune, but even more importantly, I believe I can persuade other merchants to invest in a campaign to overthrow the Legion and return the rule of law. Secrecy would have to be paramount of course, as it would be quite dangerous."

Annelise placed a crystal glass of youngling ale before Augum as her brother took away the bowl of water. She kept standing there in profound paleness, staring at him with awe. She had large ears that made the rest of her mousey face look even smaller.

"Oh, thank you," Augum said, feeling uncomfortable with the staring.

Her milky cheeks reddened as her eyes fell to the polished floor. She quickly curtsied. "My lord," before scurrying away.

Gabe offered the bowl to Leera. "My lady, some water to wash your soft hands with."

"If I have to," Leera muttered.

Augum flashed Gabe a hard look, but the boy did not see it.

"I am sure there are many who would rather see their money go to a worthwhile cause," Constable Clouds announced as the table quieted to listen in. "They speak in whispers and tread on feathers for fear of having their fortunes confiscated and their daughters thrown into service."

"Or their sons turned into soldiers," Mr. Okeke added.

"This kingdom runs on gold," Mr. Haroun said. "As warlike as despots get, it has, does, and will continue to always run on gold." His eyes found Augum's. "Your father knows this, that is why he took Tiberra. It takes a great deal of money to run an army, even one aided by necromancy."

He took a small sip of wine. "We must all fight Lord Sparkstone in our own way, but united. Not everyone is a powerful archmage like your famous great-grandmother, Augum. Most, as you well know, are *Ordinaries* lacking the arcane talents. In fact, in this entire village, I do believe there are nine rings, and they are divided between the three of you."

"Ten rings," Haylee blurted, raising an arm and allowing a band of ice to flash to life around it.

Charissa made a *Well isn't she special* face at Malaika.

"They are only fifteen years old, Hanad," Mrs. Haroun said from the other end of the table. "What can fifteen-year-olds do in the face of such a monstrous army?"

Leera opened her mouth to speak, probably to say she and Bridget were not yet fifteen even, when she was silenced by an elbow jab from Bridget.

"Dear me, I too doubted their abilities once," Mr. Goss said with a sheepish smile. He accepted the bowl of water from Gabe with a grateful nod. "Let me tell those who are assembled today, that I have found nothing but courage in these young persons' hearts." He dried his hands while Gabe took the bowl. "But it is their friendship that has taught me true strength. They will speak of neither, but I can assure you, they have endured and accomplished a great deal."

He made sure everyone was paying attention as his gaze swept the table. "A *great* deal. The things they have survived are as harrowing as you can imagine. As to the things they have accomplished … well, let us say we stand a chance now. There is reason to hope." Mr. Goss stared at Leera, then Bridget, and finally Augum. "I have nothing but faith in them."

Augum felt his cheeks burn, acutely conscious of everyone staring at him and the girls.

"They might *look* fifteen," Mr. Goss added, eyeing the trio with a kind of fatherly pride, "but they have witnessed things and done things that have aged their souls. In my eyes, they are brave young warriors."

"Well, almost fifteen," Leera muttered. "And as far as aging, just wait till we learn Cron—" but Bridget gave her another elbow.

Leland slammed his hand onto the table, clattering the dishes. He let out a long series of angry moans.

Malaika startled. "How barbaric," she whispered to her friend, both girls clutching their chests.

"I am sorry, but what did the young unfortunate child say?" A portly woman with curly gray hair asked.

Everyone's eyes fell upon Mr. Goss.

"In essence, my son said that many of the trio's friends died, but no matter what the Legion threw at them, they are the ones who lived."

For a moment, the table was silent as everyone stared at mangled young Leland.

"How can his father understand him?" Charissa whispered to Malaika.

"My father did that to him," Augum blurted to the gathering. "His lightning melted his face and body like that. He lost his sight and his speech and he's constantly in pain." Under the table, Leera's fingers curled with his. She squeezed. It gave him strength.

"My father won't hesitate to do it to any of us," he continued, "even me. He's burned down two villages before my own eyes. I still hear those people screaming. I still see their feet kicking." He glanced around at the ironwork candelabras, the porcelain plates, and the stained glass windows. He only saw flames. "I know what he's capable of, and I know what his followers are capable of. What I don't know is … how to stop him."

Malaika clutched at her chest as she shared a fawning look with Charissa.

After a marked silence, Devon, sitting beside his father, leaned forward. "What about that Agonex thingy, Augum?"

"We don't know how to use it yet."

Leland made a series of quick moans while drawing a circle with his hand.

"What did the boy say, Mr. Goss?" Constable Clouds asked.

Mr. Goss hesitated. "My son thinks it could be a lot of, err … fun."

"They treat ancient artifacts like toys," Ms. Singh sang to the ceiling. "May the gods help these lost sheep, for they obviously lack the most basic competence. What sort of ill-advised resistance is this?" She turned to her daughter in search of the answer to that question before remembering Priya had stormed out with Jengo. She promptly sat up straighter, tersely clearing her throat.

"Did Mrs. Stone have a plan?" Mr. Haroun asked, ignoring Ms. Singh.

"My great-grandmother wanted Bridget, Leera and I to go the library in Antioc dressed as necrophytes, so that we could try to figure out how the Agonex works."

"Anna Atticus Stone charged you with such a quest?" Mrs. Haroun asked from the other end. "Preposterous."

"For once Panjita agrees with the fat hen," Ms. Singh said.

Mrs. Haroun looked Ms. Singh up and down. "How *dare* you speak to me in such a manner in my own house."

Mr. Haroun raised a hand. "Selma, please." His wife curled her lip but held her tongue. Mr. Haroun turned back to Augum. "If I may, can you tell us more about this army? How large is it?"

"It's Occulus' army," Leera said, turning her bread around and around on her plate, "and it's under Bahbell. Been there the entire time. Thing is, we couldn't exactly count how large it is because we were kind of running for our lives at the time."

"We estimate tens of thousands," Bridget added. "And the army is still equipped with Dreadnought weapons and armor."

Mutterings circled the table.

"That's not all," Augum said. "The entire army is undead."

The table immediately broke out into argumentative chatter. Ms. Singh pointed at the ceiling with one hand while gesticulating accusingly at the assembled throng with the other. Mrs. Haroun shook her head and loudly complained about the devilry of it all. Mr. Goss and Mr. Okeke exchanged quiet and quick words on what to do next. Mr. Haroun and Constable Clouds sat back with a sigh. Malaika stared intently at Augum.

"I thought Bahbell was a myth," Charissa said.

"I am afraid, young lady," Constable Clouds replied, adjusting his great girth in his chair so he may see her, "that it is quite real. The Legion revealed its existence to the public in yesterday's Blackhaven Herald. I confess, however, that I have known of its existence through my superiors for some time now."

"We are fortunate to have you on our side, Constable," Mr. Haroun said. "You are an invaluable asset to the Resistance."

Resistance indeed, Augum thought morosely. It made him nervous. One word of it to the Legion—one loose, gossipy word from anyone in the entire town—and the place burns.

"Where is this legendary Mrs. Stone?" Charissa pressed. "Why can't she just kill Lord Sparkstone?"

"She already tried," Augum replied.

"The Battle at Hangman's Rock," Bridget added.

"And because he's got six scions and she only one," Leera said, as if the answer should have been obvious. "Because he's got Dreadnoughts on his side making weapons and armor day and night. Because he's got an army and she doesn't. Because he's in charge of an entire kingdom and she isn't. Because he's a necromancer. Because, because, *because*." Her lip curled at Charissa and Malaika. "Not to mention he's got warlocks who track her day and night with some witch artifact, so she's always on the move. And somehow she's supposed to train us at the same time. It's not easy—"

"—enough, Lee," Bridget said, placing a gentle hand on her arm. She sighed and turned back to the table. "Thing is, we haven't heard from Mrs. Stone in days."

Mr. Haroun's face was grave. "So you are saying it could very well be just us."

Bridget hesitated, but surrendered a slight nod, enough to cast a pall over the table.

Constable Clouds accepted a glass of wine from Clayborne. "Anna Atticus Stone is a symbol of resistance to many out there. An important symbol." His eyes travelled the room, landing on the trio. "As are these three young people before us. Anna Stone has entrusted them with a quest. We must do everything we can to carry out her wishes."

Many at the table nodded.

"But without arcane support," Mr. Haroun countered, "it would be difficult for them to access the ancient library."

"Father can help," Devon said. "Can't you, Father?"

Clouds idly rubbed his triple chins. "What about sending them by horse with one of my men acting as their guide? For disguise, I may be able to acquire necrophyte robes through a formal requisition. Of course, a believable story would have to be contrived for the trip—though I imagine three necrophytes visiting the ancient library would not raise much concern." He raised his head. "It will all take time to organize, but it can be done."

Devon raised his palms dramatically. "Wait, the Herald said there's a warlock tournament!"

Haylee gave a brief nod. "The Antioc Classic." She noticed some blank faces. "It's a yearly warlock tournament, one I would have liked to participate in. As it is …" She glanced disdainfully at her cane.

"An ideal time to blend in then," Constable Clouds said.

Mr. Goss cleared his throat. "Forgive me, but, would the journey not be easier with the help of a high-degree warlock?"

"All warlocks who have not fled have been forced to serve the Legion," Clouds replied. "However, I am sure a small handful would risk everything to secretly help the

Resistance. In fact, some time ago a colleague stationed in Antioc told me about just such a warlock, a woman by the name of Miralda Jenkins—"

The trio exchanged a sudden look.

"Constable," Bridget began in somber tones, "Ms. Jenkins died helping us at the Battle at Hangman's Rock."

Clouds slowly exhaled. "I see."

Clayborne brought two plates out, his children in tow with more. He placed one before Mr. Haroun and the other before Augum, who stared dumbfounded at a single armored oval shell.

Leera leaned over, whispering, "What the hell is that?"

Augum, half expecting the object to sprout legs and scuttle away, was wondering the same thing.

Malaika giggled. "That's an oyster, Augum. They're really quite divine."

"We consider it an honor to shuck one's own oyster," Charissa threw in, picking hers up.

"Indeed," Malaika added. "It's just a shame we get so few. Keeping them cold and fresh is a tremendous challenge. Mother even had to pay for arcane delivery."

"Arcane delivery?" Augum asked. "How does that work?"

Malaika flushed from his gaze. "Oh, but you're a warlock, Augum, how do you not know this?" When he gave no response, she quickly continued. "All right, so you send a letter to an arcane delivery service and a warlock shows up. You tell him what you want, pay him, and he delivers your letter or fetches something for you. That kind of thing. Mind you it's very expensive, really only for the well-off. Of course, couriers are very difficult to acquire these days. Mother had to pay a fortune for the one that delivered these oysters."

"You mean bribe," Leera muttered under her breath.

Charissa leaned near Malaika. "I don't think they know anything about deliveries, they're all too poor."

Leera cocked her head and raised a finger. Charissa's oyster began moving toward her. The girl immediately recoiled with a squeal, nearly falling out of her chair.

"Young lady," Mr. Haroun said with the faintest smile, "please, no arcanery at the table."

"Sorry," Leera muttered.

"Well I never," Charissa said to Malaika, hand clutching her chest. "What an awful thing to do. She's utterly uncivilized."

"Really doesn't deserve him," Malaika said.

Leera's eyes narrowed dangerously. "What did you just say?"

"Ladies, please," Mr. Haroun said. "Daughter, mind your tongue, you forget yourself."

Malaika dropped her gaze. "Father."

"Wait, about that arcane delivery service," Augum cut in, not wanting to let the matter go. "How large can the object be?"

"As large as you like," Malaika replied.

"That might work," Bridget suddenly said, catching Leera's hand before she could cast any more arcanery.

Malaika raised her brows. "What might work?"

Bridget was staring at Augum. "It'll have to be a sealed crate of some kind."

"A large donation to the library, perhaps," Mr. Haroun said with a smile.

"Donation? What are you going on about, Father? Has everyone lost their minds?"

Haylee suddenly sat up straighter. "It should ideally be something the Legion confiscates."

"Something heavy," Devon threw in, grinning excitedly, "like books!"

"Yes, of course!" Constable Clouds said, catching wind of their conversation. "I can even arrange for it to be shipped officially by the Legion, ensuring there will be no tampering of the box."

"Will someone please explain to me what is going on?" Mrs. Haroun asked from across the table.

Mr. Haroun leaned forward. "Selma, my dear, we are going to arcanely deliver our heroic trio in a crate."

EBB AND FLOW

Augum finally got around to trying the oyster, something he found revolting but pretended to like. Leera, on the other hand, promptly declared it "armored snot," and shoved it away, drawing condemning whispers from Malaika and Charissa. Haylee grudgingly taught Chaska how to properly eat his, though he showed nothing but discomfort with the many protocols required in fine dining. Ms. Singh flung her oyster at the elder servant, declaring it too oval. Before the entire household came down on her for throwing yet another dish, Mr. Okeke diplomatically offered to take her home, which she—much to everyone's surprise and relief—accepted. She tottered out with him, grumbling all the while about poor food and worse service.

As the second round was served (brace of quail, spiced leek broth, and some kind of roasted small fish), the table was alight with ideas on just how to accomplish the task of mailing the trio using a Legion warlock courier. Everyone eagerly offered an opinion on the daring plot, though not all were supportive—Mrs. Haroun, sitting regally at the far end, repeatedly stated how foolish she thought such an endeavor was to anyone who would listen.

"Where do you think we can find a map?" Augum asked Leera amongst the gaggle of conversation.

Leera, who had her arms crossed and was glaring at Malaika, shrugged.

"Maybe I can be of service." Malaika, ignoring Leera, snapped her fingers. "Annelise, fetch my book on the kingdoms. You know the one."

Annelise curtsied. "My lady." She disappeared, soon returning burdened with a large leather-bound tome.

Malaika took it from her and opened it, receiving help with the oversized pages from Charissa. "There it is." She removed a folded parchment and handed it to Annelise. "Deliver this to Augum Stone." Malaika flashed Augum a fawning smile.

Annelise placed the parchment on a silver tray, tromped around the table, and extended the tray to Augum with downcast eyes. "My lord. From Miss Haroun."

Leera snatched the parchment from the tray, promptly unfolding it.

"How rude," Charissa said to Malaika, but Malaika merely held her head high, a slight smile curving her lips.

Leera grimaced, as if hoping she would have found something other than what was there. "It's a map," she said, handing it to Augum.

"A map, who would have dared to think," Malaika sang to Charissa. She then gave Annelise a sharp look and the girl promptly curtsied and walked off, taking the book with her.

"Uh, thank you, Annelise," Augum said, flattening the parchment on the table. The girls were playing mind games, that much he could tell. He hated mind games. He pored over the map of Sithesia, which depicted Solia and the surrounding kingdoms.

Malaika gently bit her lip. "What are you looking for, Augum?"

"Velmara," he replied absently.

"Is that some kind of lake, Mal?" Charissa whispered to Malaika.

"It is a town in south western Tiberra," Mr. Haroun said. "But what is the significance of it, Augum?"

Augum soon found it on the map. "That's where Nana lost the pearl, Mr. Haroun, which she uses to communicate with us."

Bridget leaned over to glance at it. "Why would she lose it there?"

"Velmara is a strategic location," Constable Clouds said. "It is situated at the meeting of three rivers, allowing for the easy movement of troops. The Legion uses it as an eastern base camp. Perhaps she was watching them, gathering information."

"Could be an undead spawning ground," Haylee said. The table fell silent.

"And how would you know this?" Malaika asked.

Haylee raised an eyebrow. "Because I was once a necrophyte."

There were some mutterings around the table, most notably from Mrs. Haroun, who was heard to hiss, "How demonic!"

Constable Clouds winced at his injured shoulder as he leaned forward. "Perhaps you can help me fill out my knowledge of the necrophyte ways, young lady."

Haylee gaped a moment. "I … I would be honored."

"Good, because I could certainly use it."

"What is a necromancer spawning ground?" Devon asked.

Haylee hesitated. "Perhaps it should not be discussed at the table."

"Please go on, dear child," Mr. Haroun said, "these are dark times needing the light of honesty."

Mrs. Haroun opened her mouth to protest only to be silenced by a hard look from her husband.

Haylee chose her words carefully. "Very well. Uh, a spawning ground is usually a cemetery."

There were gasps from the table.

"Well that certainly leaves little to the imagination," Malaika muttered to her friend.

"How ghastly," Mrs. Haroun whispered.

Augum held up the map. "May we have this?"

Malaika flashed Leera a smug smile. "Of course you may."

Augum folded and slipped the map into his robe. "Thanks."

Malaika turned to her friend, the two exchanging a blushing look. Meanwhile, Leera smoldered. Augum was just about to reach for her hand when Gabe appeared between him and Leera, offering something yellow on a silver platter.

"My lady, fine Canterran lemon tart garnished with a sprig of mint and powdered sugar. I made it myself." His voice, so soft yet controlled, infuriated Augum.

Leera's eyes briefly flicked to Augum. "Why, thank you, Gabe."

Augum made a show of leaning over, making the same face Leera made when she spotted the oyster. "Is something growing out of that?"

"Looks sweet." Leera snatched the tart, scarfing it down in one gulp, promptly choking on it. Malaika and Charissa broke into chuckles, hands hiding their mouths. Augum, for his part, cleared his throat, refusing to look at her. It was hard to hold back a smug grin.

"I'll fetch you some water, my lady," Gabe quickly said, gliding away. Augum tried not to glare at him as he gracefully poured a glass of water from a fine crystal pitcher. He tried not to watch, out of the corner of his eye, as Gabe returned to the table with a doting, smarmy smile. He also tried not to notice how Gabe made sure to place the water just so, and how he effortlessly rearranged Leera's plate and flatware to appear more tidy, and how he—Augum finally had to look away if he was to prevent himself from suddenly throttling the boy.

"Augum?" It was Malaika, and she was smiling pleasantly. "Would you like me to have Annelise prepare you my favorite sweet?"

"No—! I mean, no, thank you." Stupid mind games.

Malaika's face fell, but she braved a smile. "As you wish."

Soon a third course was brought out consisting of venison, hot buttered bread, and sweet potatoes.

"Finally, some real food," Leera said. Much to Bridget's chagrin, she dug in without waiting for the host.

Conversation ebbed and flowed. Devon managed to coax the story of what happened at the bandit camp from Bridget, though she only shared certain details, omitting the gruesome parts. Nonetheless, the table hung on to her every word. Soon Mr. Goss was sharing stories about their training. Before Augum knew it, the trio were once again the center of discussion, with tales about their supposed heroics gathering momentum like a boulder tumbling down a mountain, supposed heroics that sickened him with every fanciful retelling.

"Actually, it didn't happen that way," Augum finally had to say when Devon recounted how he heard Augum bested the Lord of the Legion in a long and grueling duel at the Battle of Hangman's Rock. "I used Nana's staff and the scion. It was really quick and I got lucky—"

"So you *did* best your father," Constable Clouds said. "Is that not so, young man?"

Augum shrugged. "Maybe just for that moment, I guess. But it was more like I caught him off guard—"

"I told you so!" Devon said to his father as the table broke into excited chatter.

Gabe offered Constable Clouds a second portion of venison, stealing a glance at Leera. Augum was caught between trying to ignore him and wanting to arcanely shove him through the wall.

Clouds waved Gabe off. "My dear boy, thank you for being thoughtful, but I did not get this large from eating. I have a condition, I am sorry to say."

The young servant hastily retreated, muttering apologies.

"Please forgive my son," Clayborne said, staring straight ahead. "I will speak with him later."

Clouds raised an arm with a wheeze. "That will not be necessary, my good man. He is a fine boy who could not possibly have known."

"As you say, my lord."

"Constable Clouds," Mr. Goss began, "may I ask you how you came to work for the Legion?"

"Certainly, Mr. Goss. I was raised in Blackhaven as one of three boys. I was the youngest and the only one suffering from this—" He paused to indicate at his girth, "—condition. Healers could do nothing for me. I was called 'Corpulent Clouds' by kids and family alike. I was bullied and beaten mercilessly, and so I promised myself that one day I would be in a position to prevent that from happening to others."

Devon helped him adjust in the too-small chair.

"Thank you, Son. Now, as it so happens, I proved myself able with numbers, diligently overseeing the estates of the wealthy. It was then I met a woman I fell in love with. She was as large as I, suffering from the same condition." He glanced at Devon, who gave him a bittersweet smile. "She died of that condition a few years ago, though I take great comfort when I look upon my boy and see her eyes in him."

The curly-haired older woman near Mrs. Haroun smiled warmly. "I can see your son's chubbiness is filled with nothing but love."

Devon shrank with embarrassment as his father ruffled his hair.

"When the Legion came to power, I saw my chance to contribute," Clouds continued, taking a sip of wine. "I saw the direction they were going and witnessed the rise of the greatest bully of our generation. With my sound judgment, it was not long until I had a senior position. In the meantime, I used numbers to mitigate the damage caused by the Legion, awarding wronged families proceeds to cover their burnt homes; allowances for widows and widowers; extra rations for the young, and so on. Unfortunately, my efforts caught the attention of a lieutenant by the name of Tridian, who would later go on to be known as—"

"—the Blade of Sorrows," Augum said, recalling that iron room where Commander Tridian put people to the question. "We know him."

"*Knew* him," Leera corrected, making oddly aggressive eye contact with Augum. "Mrs. Stone ended that soulless revenant."

"I am glad to hear that evil man cannot harm another person again," Clouds said. "Nonetheless, his meddling curiosity forced me to take greater care with my activities. I regret it now, but I neglected to help more people because of my paranoia. I later realized I needed a new location with a new title, where I could build a resistance to greater effect. I ascended rank and made it to Constable. Over time, I met a few others such as myself." He nodded toward the entrance. "Lieutenant Briggs and Sergeant Cobb, and there are a few others I would prefer not to name in public for their safety, as they are fixed in higher positions."

"Please do forgive me for interrupting," Mr. Goss said, pushing his spectacles back up his nose, "but how many rebels do you think there are in the Legion ranks?"

"I only know of half a dozen or so, but some are key personnel. What we really require is a way to communicate. The Legion uses speaking orbs, for example. Now, I have been looking into the matter but lack the arcane knowledge. Whatever means we use, the object needs to be easily hidden and only accessible by a chosen few. If even a single one of these objects fell into enemy hands …" His face darkened at the thought.

"Maybe that's something we can research in the library," Bridget said.

"A wise idea, young lady."

"Can I come?" Devon asked.

This drew many snickers from the table, much to Devon's displeasure.

"If he comes, *we* get to come," Malaika said to her father.

"Don't be absurd, child," Mrs. Haroun said with a chuckle. "No one should be going, if you ask me. It is too dangerous."

"No one will be going other than the trio," Mr. Haroun said, Constable Clouds nodding along. "That is Mrs. Stone's wish, and until we hear otherwise from her, it shall remain that way. She is still the leader of the Resistance."

"It really is for the best," Bridget said, giving Devon a sympathetic look. "We tend to get ourselves into trouble." She elbowed Leera with a smile. "At least this one regularly does."

"Hey, I'm not the one afraid of heights—"

Light ribbing banter ensued, though Augum's thoughts drifted back to his great-grandmother. Where was she? What had happened with the pearl? Had she left it there on purpose? He resolved to listen in through the Orb of Orion as soon as possible.

"Is there anything Charissa and I can do to help you prepare, Augum?" Malaika asked, watching him with grave concern. "I know we're not warlocks or anything like that, but we're quite able women."

"I can mend and wash your blue robe, if you like," Charissa said. After seeing the look on Leera's face, she quickly added, "All of your robes of course."

"Thank you, but we can manage," Augum replied, trying not to smile at the strange offer.

"Now let us discuss the defense of the town," Mr. Haroun said, "something Constable Clouds and I have already spoken about at length. Milham's defense will be comprised of pure deceit." He let those words linger a moment before continuing. "We cannot best the Legion with force at this time, so we shall pretend to be a supportive Legion community. We shall plant a Legion flag in the center of town. If Legion soldiers or officials come through—which, thankfully, will not be often due to Milham's isolation—we shall conduct gatherings of support. We shall hear out the Legion heralds with joy and enthusiasm, making sure to send them on their way believing we are rooting for Lord Sparkstone to succeed."

"We have already told everyone in town," Constable Clouds chimed in, "that those who reveal information always get tortured by the Legion, in case they know more. We have done this convincingly as only Legion soldiers can do. That is why not a soul has come forward to the Legion reporting on Augum's whereabouts—everyone here believes doing so would result in brutal torment."

Augum, recalling a certain iron room, was all too familiar with Legion questionings.

Mr. Haroun gave an appreciative nod at the constable. "And that was a brilliant idea, if I may be so bold as to say." He swept the crowd with determined eyes. "We will do more, of course. Meanwhile, we shall conduct a secret campaign of resistance. We will *be* the Resistance."

He stood and raised his glass. "To the Resistance."

Everyone stood, raising their own glass of wine, water or youngling ale. "To the Resistance," the throng repeated.

Mr. Haroun remained standing as everyone took their seats, watching his wife. "I know some of you are anxious, as you should be. This is a dangerous endeavor. Secrecy is paramount. You must be wary of who you trust. When strangers come through town, we must all mind our tongues and send them on their way as soon as possible. Now let us pore over the details."

The assembled gathering listened as Mr. Haroun traded off with Constable Clouds on the defense of the town, including guard postings and horn signals—one horn blast for a friend, two for a stranger, three for the Legion or bandits. Course after course came until Augum was feeling fuzzy and exhausted.

Just before dessert, Mr. Haroun noticed the trio's glazed faces and stopped mid-sentence. "Where is my consideration? You three have been through an awful ordeal. I apologize with all my heart. Please feel free to excuse yourselves."

"Thank you, I think we will," Augum said, feeling the sting in his back and the aching tiredness in his bones. "We do need to rest." He stood, Bridget and Leera joining him.

"It is getting late," Mr. Goss said. "I hope our esteemed hosts do not mind if I put my son to bed."

"Not at all," Mr. Haroun replied. "We thank you and your son for your company."

Mr. Goss and the trio said their thank-yous and goodbyes to the assembly, which began breaking up anyway.

"I shall see you to the door," Malaika said, Gabe following.

"That's the first time I've seen you pass up dessert," Augum said to a tired-looking Leera. She only grunted, leaning on his shoulder. He thought she might fall asleep then and there, and would have picked her up and carried her had his back not been screaming with pain.

"May we call on you tomorrow?" Malaika asked Augum, her eyes flicking to Leera. She bit her lower lip.

"Uh, sure I guess."

Malaika bowed her head slightly. "Good night then." Gabe bowed at the same time.

"Good night."

It was dusk when they departed the Haroun household. Lieutenant Briggs and Sergeant Cobb nodded to the group as they passed, black Legion armor shining in torchlight.

"To the Resistance," Briggs said.

"If you need anything, let us know," Cobb added.

"Thank you," Augum could only say.

"To the Resistance," Leera said sleepily as they walked off.

Augum was starting to like that word more and more. Resistance. Rebel. They were officially both now, part of a secret and dangerous club. Perhaps it was a stupid and reckless idea. Maybe the entire place would burn. They would have to be extremely cautious, for everyone's sake.

The village was quiet, other than a few stragglers who raised a warm greeting or a "Bless the Resistance" to the trio. It felt weird to Augum to hear it said so openly. Every look their way spelled danger, every word a giant beacon fire, screaming for the enemy to charge into town. It all felt reckless, like poking a sleeping bear with a stick.

Mr. Goss shortly said goodnight and left to his room at the inn, holding a sleeping Leland while singing *A Boy and his Cat*, a sweet and soft lullaby.

"Think it'll work?" Augum asked Bridget, his arm around Leera.

"What, you mean sending us by Legion courier?" She swept long cinnamon hair from her eyes. "I think it's a crazy plan—so crazy that it might actually work."

It put Augum at ease hearing that from Bridget, who was the most careful of the three of them.

They passed the *Good Medicine* shop.

"I think they're good for each other somehow," Bridget said.

"You mean Chaska and Haylee?" He wasn't so sure, but then he recalled the snow-skinned boy appearing at the Okeke house holding a bouquet of pine branches, looking more awkward than a hen in a fox den. "Maybe …"

Bridget glanced at him and Leera wistfully. "You are very lucky, the both of you."

Augum gave Leera a light squeeze. "Yes, we are … and like Leera once said, we'll find you a proper boy one day, don't worry."

"And like I told you two then, I don't want one right now," Bridget replied with a smile. "Certainly don't need yet *another* soul to worry about," she muttered before sighing. "We have a lot of training to do. Going to be hard without a mentor."

"You can serve as our mentor for now. You know the Summon Minor Elemental spell, not to mention the counterspell to Object Alarm."

"I can try, but it's not the same thing. Anyway, we'll start first thing in the morning; work as hard as possible in the days ahead until everything's ready and we can go to the Antioc library."

"Hey wait up—!" Jengo called, catching up to them. "Sorry about all that, Priya was quite upset with her mother. Then there was a big fight involving Ms. Singh and Father, then Haylee and Chaska, but things have finally calmed down. So how much danger are we in now?"

"Bridget, Leera and I are going to mail ourselves using an arcane Legion courier," Augum said.

Jengo stared at him as if he had completely lost his mind. "Why do you three want to die so quickly?" He gestured grandly. "Life is beautiful and fun, why do you want to throw it away?"

"The Agonex needs to be understood," Augum replied flatly. "We have to try."

Jengo pointed at each of them. "I think you three are completely crazy." He smiled though after glancing down at Augum holding Leera. "Just promise to be careful. You're too adorable together to die."

This elicited a snort from Leera, but nothing more.

"What was I going to say?" Jengo asked himself, rubbing the scar on his chin. "Right, two things—Father says you should keep the Agonex and the Orb of Orion near you at all times from now on, and also you should let me try and heal your back."

"Your father said for you to heal Augum's back?" Bridget asked with a raised brow.

"Sorry, I mean *I'd* like to try and heal your back. All right, if I have to be completely honest, Father told me *not* to try my arcanery on living people anytime in the next, oh, fifty years or so, but—"

"So dead people are all right?" Leera asked with a smirk, eyes closed sleepily.

"Hey, I'll have you know Mrs. Stone *had* trained me some before she let that nasty Harvus take over completely. Speaking of which, tell me what really happened, I don't believe your escape could have been *that* easy."

"It wasn't," Bridget said with a distant look.

Augum saw her commanding those bandits with a firm voice, the absolute determination in her eyes. Something about that encounter had changed her, though he did not know in what way.

Jengo stayed silent in hopes of hearing the tale, but neither Bridget nor Augum elaborated, both lost in thought. Augum kept reliving two events: Harvus' feet rabidly scratching at the floor, and Sal's head exploding into red mist after he hit it with his First Offensive.

Mr. Okeke had a steaming hot washbasin ready for them when they arrived, insisting they slept there in his cabin, not in the lonely woods. Augum was relieved, finding the Okeke home far more comfortable. The trio washed up and changed into their night linens. Mr. Okeke collected their mud-splattered robes and departed to have them washed. Augum took some time listening in to the Orb of Orion, but heard nothing but crickets and distant hushed voices around a fire. It was evident the controlling pearl had not moved from the last time he had listened in. Nonetheless, he found something comforting about the sound of those crickets.

"All right, Father's gone. Lie on your stomach and let me try this," Jengo said.

Augum did as he asked. "My life is in your hands."

Jengo spoke as he carefully washed his hands in a basin. "Trust me, I've been studying this in your yellow book until I can recite it in my sleep—and that's *all* aspects of the spell. I've also been referencing the blue arcaneology book often." He carefully unwrapped the bandage then pressed two hands on the wound, muttering, "Seems the majority of the puncture damage was made to the left of the central vertebral." Augum winced from the stinging but let him work. "With some fluid buildup to the upper lumbar region at the base of the cut. Most likely a minor edema."

"What language is that?" Leera asked, sitting near and squeezing Augum's hand in support.

"Just healing jargon." Jengo removed his hands a moment to inspect the wound further. "Whatever sliced you was quite unclean. Normally you'd expect a high probability of sepsis. Lucky you have me."

"Certainly sounds like you know what you're doing," Augum said, hoping it wasn't gibberish he was hearing.

"With this I do. The healing element requires a profound knowledge and understanding of the internal workings and humors of the body. Now lie still." Jengo replaced his hands on the wound and began a rather complex but short incantation. After some initial pain, there was a glow and a comfortable sensation, as if Augum was taking a warm bath. The pain dissipated with the glow.

"That looked just like Mrs. Stone would cast healing," Bridget said, sitting cross-legged by the fire. "I'm impressed. What degree was that spell?"

"Uh, it's probably a little higher than I should be working at, but—"

"Jengo, are you *already* casting beyond your degree?"

"Wait, he doesn't even have his 1st degree yet!" Leera threw in.

Jengo swallowed as he wrung his hands. "Uh …"

Augum sat up, stretching his back but feeling no pain other than a dull soreness. He extended his hand to Jengo with a smile. "Thank you so much, I think it worked."

Jengo shook it. "It did? I mean, of course it did!" He pressed a hand to his head. "But now my head is splitting. I haven't just afflicted myself with some kind of incurable arcane sickness, have I?"

"That's normal. It'll go away with practice."

"And practice is something I'm sure I'll have lots of seeing how often you three get injured. Oh, and before I forget—" Jengo retrieved their rucksack, hidden under some pillows, and reached inside. "The Agonex."

Augum took the cold bronze disk. He traced the raised skulls with his fingers. It was hard to believe this mythic artifact controlled an entire army of Dreadnought-equipped undead soldiers. The only question now was, how?

Leera laid her head in Augum's lap as he handed the Agonex over to Bridget to inspect.

Bridget traced her delicate fingers along the fine arcane metalwork. "Occulus once held this very same artifact. It's odd holding a piece of history. And who knows how old it really is …"

Augum nodded at the Orb of Orion. "We have two pieces of history."

"We've been so focused on figuring out how this thing works," Bridget continued, "but what we haven't done, is talk about what we're going to do if we *do* figure it out."

Jengo stirred the fire. "Attack the Lord of the Legion, of course."

"She means," Augum explained, "do we attack his armies in the field, or send the horde after him directly?"

Bridget placed the disk before her. "We don't even know how to get the army out of there."

"You can't just … march it out?" Jengo asked.

Augum idly stroked Leera's hair. "There was no way out, at least none that we saw. Occulus used to teleport the entire army right into the heart of a city."

"That's what made him so devastating," Bridget said. "That, and his necromantic powers of course."

Jengo sat back on his hands. "Ah, now I see why the Lord of the Legion wants it so badly."

Conversation petered out, replaced by yawns. Before long, Leera was asleep in Augum's lap. Back newly healed, he was finally able to gently pick her up and carry her to her bed.

A NEW DAY

The next morning, Bridget, already dressed in a freshly-washed blue robe and face edged with determination, shook Augum and Leera awake, declaring they had a very busy day ahead. Augum and Leera got dressed and the trio helped Jengo make breakfast. Mr. Goss and Leland soon showed up, with Leland immediately grabbing the Agonex and the Orb of Orion, placing his ear to the latter.

Mr. Goss shook his head. "Goodness me, he was at that for hours the other day."

Augum gently tussled what remained of Leland's hair. "He's trying to help the Resistance like a true rebel."

Leland pointed at the two artifacts and moaned a few times.

"Sure you can," Bridget replied, "but they can't leave our sight. Mr. Goss, can Leland come with us while we train? We promise to take good care of him."

"Perhaps that would be best indeed, seeing as I am going to work on the crate with Mr. Haroun this morning."

"The crate?" Jengo asked absently while stirring oatmeal into a pot of boiling water.

"The one Augum, Bridget and Leera are going to use to get to Antioc."

"Ah, the deathtrap."

"Jengo—!" Mr. Okeke stepped out of his room, smoothing a burgundy doublet fringed with gold.

"*Jesting*, Father."

"Regardless, we do not want to cast any ill-omens on Augum, Bridget and Leera, do we, Son?"

"Of course not, Father."

"A trusted courier brought today's Blackhaven Herald," Mr. Goss said with a secretive smile. "Care to see it?" He laid out the densely-scrawled single parchment on the trestle dining table. The trio immediately huddled around.

Leera snorted. "Look at that, there's something about Erika. 'The Herald has received word that Ms. Erika Scarson has been placed in charge of the heroic tracking party tasked with finding the villainous Anna Atticus Stone and her mongrel grovelers.' "

She glanced up. " 'Mongrel grovelers'? Really?" She shook her head. "And that crazy loon. I'd love to see her try to face Mrs. Stone." Leera straightened the parchment with a jerk. " 'Ms. Scarson declares her leadership will bring a "badly needed breath of fresh air" to the search. It is well known that the tracking party has been having a hard time catching up to the slippery insurgent leader. Sightings of Anna Atticus Stone have come from all over Sithesia, though she has returned to Solia often to cause trouble. Although there have been some recent close encounters—' They must mean Velmara—" Leera interjected, quickly reading on, " 'the wanted crone has managed to escape every time. Sources close to the regime say she is researching a new and powerful spell, though the Herald is unable to confirm the assertion officially.' "

"At least it means they haven't found Nana yet," Augum said, suddenly feeling lighter. He playfully elbowed his way into reading where Leera left off. " 'The Lord of the Legion's own son has been taken under her spell, for he has destroyed a precious recipe on behalf of the old crone. He has also stolen the Agonex, a powerful artifact belonging to the Legion. The boy is feared to be quickly corruptible and weak of heart, something Lord Sparkstone vows to reform once the boy is rescued from the crone's clutches. Many have been put to the question in search of his whereabouts, but no credible information has been forthcoming.' " Augum rubbed his face, suddenly feeling queasy. They were torturing people to find him. It just didn't end.

Leera placed a gentle hand on his shoulder. "Hey, look at it this way. No one's going to dare step forward now, not if the Herald says they'll be put to the question."

"There's more on Erika—" Bridget tapped another article at the bottom of the parchment and took over reading. " 'Ms. Scarson, freshly freed from what she reported as a harrowing and highly demeaning stay at a Tiberran prison, will be attending the coming Antioc Classic. "I will be there to proudly support my nephew," said a rosy-cheeked Ms. Scarson while sipping Titan wine. Her nephew, Robin Scarson, is a heavy favorite to win his degree. Some have taken issue with the fact Ms. Scarson will also be a judge at the prestigious event, but she insists on her impartiality, claiming, "I neither see it as here nor there that he is my nephew, thank you very much. I will be a model of fairness." ' "

Leera scoffed. "About as fair as loaded dice. Probably rigged the whole thing already."

Bridget went on. " 'Ms. Scarson then proved she had quite the sense of humor by tossing our faithful correspondent off her balcony, only to arrest his fall at the last moment.' "

"She hasn't changed a bit," Augum said.

Bridget turned the parchment over and continued to read. " ' "I'm going to smoke the competition," Robin Scarson was quoted as saying when the Herald caught up to him in Antioc, where the boy lounged in lush lodgings, expertly rolling a rock between his fingers. "Been practicing a bunch of awesome new spells. I'm the best in my degree in all of Sithesia." Scarson now sports a crooked nose, a badge of honor from a fight with the unfortunately brainwashed son of the Lord of the Legion, which Scarson handily bested in a duel—' "

"That's not true at all," Leera interrupted. "Augum beat the snot out of him. Literally. His nose—"

"What do you expect with a Legion-controlled paper," Bridget said, returning to the parchment. " 'When not commanding walkers and wraiths, Mr. Scarson is followed by his faithful friend and—hold your breath, girls, but dare we say it—possible companion, Temperance Butterwax—' "

Leera burst with laughter. "I don't know what's funnier, Temper and Robin together, or her last name—*Butterwax*! Think of it, *Butt*—"

"Lee, get a grip." Bridget tried not to smile as she read on. " 'Mr. Scarson is constantly followed by a crowd of starry-eyed necrophyte girls, though there are rumors the throng was bribed to adore the degree favorite throughout the tournament. Mr. Scarson has decried the rumors as traitorous, and vows to root out the source and put him or her to the question.' "

Leera slapped her knee, wiping away tears. "Oh, this is gold …"

Bridget read on. " 'The Herald queried Mr. Scarson about his recent ascent in military rank, as well as his plans for the future. "After I win the tournament, I'm going to command my first field army," Mr. Scarson declared. The Herald speculates Mr. Scarson refers to the rapid troop buildup along the Nodian border. There have been widespread reports of the Nodian savages slaughtering and then burning entire Solian villages. The Lord of the Legion has sworn to avenge the unfortunate souls—' "

Augum felt a chill down his spine. "They're going to war against Nodia."

"On a pretense of lies," Mr. Goss said quietly. "Everybody knows the only slaughtering and razing in the kingdom is being done by the Legion."

"Why isn't Canterra doing anything about it?" Jengo asked, slopping steaming oatmeal into wooden bowls. "Father?"

"History repeats itself and Sithesia stands by," Mr. Okeke said, prodding the fire with a distant look. "No one likes to get into a fight if they can help it."

"This might be why," Bridget said. " 'But take solace, faithful citizens, for this Herald correspondent has recently beheld the sight of a most fearsome Dreadnought-equipped army, in a secret location, ready to do the Lord of the Legion's bidding—' "

"Ha!" Leera exclaimed. "Not without the Agonex they're not."

Bridget grimaced. " 'Rumors of Dreadnoughts working night and day for the Legion continue to abound, but there have been no sightings of the legendary creatures yet. Meanwhile, the quest for the seventh and final scion continues. All hopes now rest on the tracking party charged with the formidable task of finding Anna Atticus Stone and the Lord of the Legion's brainwashed son, Augum Stone. The tracking party, aided by the use of a powerful artifact only known as the *divining rod,* are said to—' " Bridget dropped the parchment and expelled a long breath. "I can't read anymore."

They sat in thoughtful silence for a moment.

Augum idly played with his birthday necklace. "Notice what wasn't mentioned?"

Jengo shrugged his bony shoulders as he began distributing the bowls of oatmeal. "What kind of death we're all going to get?"

Bridget tapped her lips. "There's nothing about the Leyans and the Great Quest, or eternal life."

"Exactly," Augum said, accepting a bowl from Jengo with a grateful nod.

Mr. Goss paced the room. "Come to think of it, there has not been a mention in quite some time."

Augum smiled. "They don't have a way to get to Ley now. This proves it. They stopped promising eternal life because they can't get it anymore. There isn't a copy of the recipe, and all the gates are destroyed!"

"Don't count your father out just yet," Bridget said as everyone else exchanged victorious smiles with Augum. "He's got Magua on his side, after all. He's still making war and still searching for Mrs. Stone."

She was right of course. His father had six scions, the Dreadnoughts, the divining rod, his necromancy, and Magua … and who knew what or who else.

There came a knock at the door. Jengo skipped over and opened it, revealing Haylee, balancing on her cane. She had rings under her eyes but was smiling.

"Just in time for oatmeal," he said, gesturing for her to come in.

"Great, I'm starved," she replied, hobbling by. "Who's mentoring us now?"

Jengo closed the door. "Bridget. Where's Chaska?"

Haylee found a spot at the trestle table. "Sent him to Mr. Haroun and Constable Clouds to be placed on the town watch. Gives him something to do other than mope around all day." She spied the Herald on the table. "I read it too. Oh, I'd love to face Robin in that tournament, give him a good—" She made a strangling motion.

"You and everyone else in this room," Leera muttered.

Haylee glanced around at them all. "When are we training? Can't spend another moment with—" She gritted her teeth. "—Ms. Crazy."

Jengo placed a steaming bowl before her. "Ms. Singh isn't so bad, you just need to know how to talk to her, especially when to back off."

Haylee rolled her eyes.

"This I am learning," Mr. Okeke was heard to grumble. He cleared his throat and adjusted his doublet. "I have to go to the mine soon." He nodded at the Blackhaven Herald. "I am going to bring that to remind the miners what loose lips get one in this day and age."

"I am sure you will not have any problems, Kwabe," Mr. Goss said, taking over stirring the fire. "Those miners are loyal to you and to the town. Most are hiding to avoid being drafted anyhow."

"Forgive me, Mr. Okeke," Augum began, "but is it really necessary to say anything? Can't we just keep the Resistance between a few people?" It still bothered him the whole town knew about them.

Leland shook his head ferociously and moaned.

"Agreed, kind of defeats the point," Bridget said, blowing on a spoonful of steaming oatmeal. "The Resistance needs to be more than us, Aug. We need to learn to trust others."

"Worry not, Augum." Mr. Okeke gestured at the table as he took his seat. "One more there, Jengo, if you please." He gave Augum a firm nod. "Leave it to us, we will get the town in order."

Jengo set another place. "Expecting company, Father?"

"Constable Clouds' son, actually."

Leera crinkled her nose. "Devon?"

"Yes. His father asked me to expose him to more friends. He seems like an amiable but lonely young man, and was quite enamored by you all, if I remember correctly. I hope I have not overstepped my bounds."

"Of course not," Bridget said with a smile. "We would be happy to be his friends, as long as he knows training comes first."

"This I warned him about, as did his father—"

There was a knock at the door.

"Ah, this must be him now," Jengo said, giving the steaming pot another stir before running for the door.

"Hi!" Devon said the moment the door opened. "I know we're practically the same age, but ... wow, you really are so very tall!" He let himself in, flinging off his shoes. "I'm Devon, you met me yesterday," he said, wiping greasy fingers on an ill-fitting quilted vest. "You're Sierran, aren't you? I've always wanted to go to Sierra. I bet the place is a giant desert, isn't it?" He rushed over to the table, extending his hand across it, knocking over the salt cellar. "Thank you for inviting me to breakfast, Mr. Okeke, it really is an honor. Oh, sorry about that—"

"Yes, indeed, it is a pleasure, young man. Would you like to have a seat—" but Devon had already run to Augum.

"I heard you're training today so I hope you don't mind if I come," Devon said, shaking Augum's hand, stubby ponytail bouncing. "Did you read this morning's Herald? Did you? You three are really famous you know, like, *really* famous." He kept shaking Augum's hand while throwing a dismissive wave with his other one. "Though *infamous* might be a better word, if you know what I mean, seeing as the Lord of the Legion is painting you as an ungrateful and brainwashed son and all that now—wow, I still can't believe I'm in the presence of the Lord of the Legion's son! I feel like such a rebel—"

Leland made two succinct and angry moans while covering his ears.

"Devon, come have some oatmeal," Bridget said, gesturing at the empty place.

Devon finally let go of Augum's hand, nodding at Leland. "I'm sure I'll be able to eventually understand him better, but I'm afraid right now I'm going to have to rely on a translator."

Mr. Goss ran a hand over his balding and burn-scarred scalp. "Dear me, I think he said his, uh, his ears hurt."

"That really is awful, Mr. Goss," Devon said, "and I really am sorry about his pain. Have you tried a healer yet? I know the Legion stole them all but—"

"Yes, Mr. Goss tried a healer," Leera said, shoving a spoonful into her mouth.

"Leera, hi—" Devon extended his hand across the table, once again knocking over the salt. "Oops, sorry, I'm a bit clumsy, but Father says that's natural to a chub like me." Leera just stared at him. Devon finally withdrew his hand, fumbling for the salt.

"Never mind that," Bridget said with a smile, "I'll get it."

"Thank you, Bridget, thank you so much. WOW! YOU'RE USING MAGIC—!"

"We call it arcanery," Bridget said, wincing at his sudden outburst and clearing the rest of the salt using Telekinesis. Augum was impressed, actually—he'd never moved a pile of anything before, nor had he tried. Sure, stone by stone, maybe, but not a *pile*. Bridget's arcanery was definitely getting stronger.

"Sorry, uh, arcanery. Right, I should know that, being the son of a Legionnaire and all. You know I was really upset when I heard that foul Harvus took Leera, but wasn't surprised at all that you and Augum saved her—"

Augum watched as Devon prattled on and on, the boy's face steadily growing more and more purple. When will he take a breath? He could not recall ever meeting someone so … energetic.

"And you're Haylee Tennyson. I've heard about you and your family. You were really rich once, right? I mean, back before you changed sides and all. My, you're really pretty, you know that? Chaska is very lucky—"

"Oh no," Haylee said, staring at him with a slack expression. "You're not …"

Devon blinked. "What is it? Are you not feeling well? Is it the leg? I heard if you—"

"No, I mean, you're not coming today, are you—"

"What Haylee means," Bridget quickly began, "is, you know, you should really … just take a breath once in a while, Devon."

Jengo took a seat at the end, nodding gravely. "It's really bad on the humors to go on like that. Could even kill you." He opened and closed his hand. "Heart can suddenly … explode."

Devon's eyes grew wide. "Explode? I mean, I've been told I can talk the ears off a jester, but … hey, do you really think—"

"I ought to get going," Mr. Okeke suddenly said, standing. "Good luck with your training today, everyone—"

"But, Father, you haven't finished your oatmeal—"

"Yes, well, the men need me at the mine and time is short—" He slapped on his boots and hurried out the door.

Mr. Goss, who had been rushing to finish his oatmeal, stood in haste. "Dear me, I do believe Mr. Haroun is expecting me. I ought not to keep him waiting. That would be terribly rude, it would." He kissed his son on the forehead. "Behave yourself and be *very* careful with those artifacts, Leland. I shall expect you all to be training at the cabins. Good luck, everyone!"

He strode off just as Devon plowed into another dialogue on cabins and how wonderful this one was and how he couldn't wait to see theirs and—

Leera pushed her half-finished oatmeal away. "Kill me," she mouthed to Augum. He squeezed her hand under the table instead.

"Aww, you two really are adorable together," Devon said. "I mean, *really* adorable. And nobody even knows that the renowned Augum and Leera are boyfriend and girlfriend! I bet you two are going to be a famous warlock couple, aren't you? Like Matilda and Franco Viperborn, or Semma and Sinna Trailweaver, or even Sarah and Anna Burnfire. So when are you getting married? I mean, I know you're not old enough, but it must be less than a year—"

Bridget, who was sitting beside Devon, placed a hand on his shoulder. "Devon, we have a great deal to think about and do today. We need to focus." She gave him a kind smile. "I hope you do not mind me asking, but can you help us do that? Can you help us focus on training?"

Devon gaped at her a moment. "I would do *anything* to help you three. I mean, no offense, Haylee and Jengo and Leland, but Augum and Bridget and Leera are legends in every school, every academy and … oh, please, just tell me what I can do to be of service. I'll do *anything* you ask—"

"You can begin by starting on your oatmeal," Jengo said with a weary sigh.

MATTERS OF THE HEART

Somehow they made it through breakfast. Throughout, Devon offered countless ideas on ways he could help.

"I can also hold the book for you while you read," he said to Leera, completely oblivious to the expression on her face. "Maybe even give pointers on any administrative language. I sometimes help Father with official documents and stuff, so I'm sure I can be of service." He turned to Bridget. "Or fetch things for you. I mean, not like a dog and stuff, but do serious errands, like run secret messages back and forth for the Resistance—"

Bridget, packing a rucksack with the Agonex, Orb of Orion, and books, was reduced to the occasional nod by then. "Let's go," she finally said, and tromped out the door without waiting.

Devon scampered after her, talking all the while. Augum, Leera, Haylee, Jengo and Leland mutely followed.

It was a sunny morning, cool and still. The forest was wet with dew that glistened in the slanted rays of the sun. Birds warbled softly. Bridget marched in the front. Devon struggled to catch up, offering wacky training ideas, like sparring on their stomachs, or flinging pinecones at their heads while they were trying to cast a spell, or standing on one foot while blindfolded.

"… oh, and you could climb the trees and try blending in," Devon said as they reached the two cabins on opposite sides of the creek. He was panting. "Wow, so this is the hideout—it could be a painting! There's a creek, and some nice looking trees in a meadow. But where are the—"

Leera's face lit up. "It's not too late—" she whispered to Augum.

Bridget turned to Devon, face strained. "Devon Clouds, I want to formally invite you in to our training ground."

Leera's face fell. "Now it's too late."

"Oooooh, there they are!" Devon flashed a confused smile. "But … but I thought I was already invited …"

"She did that to bypass Mrs. Stone's enchantment," Jengo said, walking by, holding Leland's hand.

"Wow, I just passed one of *the* Anna Atticus Stone's enchantments? I mean, a real live one? What's it do? Why can't I see it? Hey, wait up—!"

Once they descended to the sunny glade, Leland moaned. Bridget dug out the Orb of Orion and the Agonex for him. He plopped down in a patch of sun and immediately placed his ear to the orb. She left the rucksack beside him.

"That's the cabin Mr. Harvus built, right? Oh, can I look inside? I know they'll write about it in the history books one day, or maybe someone will write a grand adventure detailing your heroic deeds—"

Bridget watched Devon waving his arms about while he yakked on. She kept moving her jaw from one side to the other, as if stretching it. Finally, perhaps realizing Devon wasn't going to let up, she turned her back on him.

"I want to start by going over all our spells," Bridget said, ignoring him. She held up her hand. "Shyneo." A glowing vine entwined around her palm and fingers.

Devon was as animated as ever. "—and they'd have to mention that I was here as a visitor, wouldn't they? I mean, this is real live history—"

"Shyneo," Augum, Leera, Haylee and Jengo echoed. Augum noted Jengo's was the weakest, eventually flickering out. At least he had been practicing. It was astounding the boy could cast a complicated healing spell but not even know Shine. How was that even possible?

"—and I bet they'd write about Milham too, how it supported the legendary trio and—"

Bridget, whose nostrils actually flared, made the glow of her hand fade then brighten, nodding at them to do the same.

"Think you can teach me that, Bridge?" Devon interrupted, standing right beside her, pudgy face glowing with wonder. "I mean, I've never been any good at arcanery, but I think I can get the hang of it if you teach me."

Augum shared a look with Leera, mouthing, " 'Bridge'?"

Bridget firmly shut her eyes and took a very deep breath.

"Here we go," Leera murmured. "We're about to see a murder."

Bridget suddenly thrust an open palm at Devon's face. "Devon, first of all, can you take a step back please? Thank you." She turned to him, jaw set. "Look, you're very nice, you really are, but you need to let us concentrate. We're about to do something very dangerous, maybe stupid even, and we need to be ready. We need to *focus*, Devon, and I don't have the time to teach you arcanery from scratch—"

Devon's chin trembled as he stood there for what seemed an eternity.

"Sweet, blissful silence at last," Leera whispered.

"You hate me …"

"No, Devon, of course we don't hate you—"

"You really hate me …"

"Devon, how could you even—"

"You hate me and think me fat and ugly and stupid."

"Devon, don't be silly, we just need—"

But Devon suddenly did something quite unexpected—he shoved Bridget. She fell to the ground, stunned.

"Don't bully me!" he yelled through tears, storming off.

The rest of them stood gaping, too shocked to react.

"Yeah, don't bully him, *Bridge*," Leera finally said with a smirk, giving Bridget a hand up.

"It's not funny, Lee, he's obviously very unhappy and lonely." Bridget dusted off her blue robe, watching the back of Devon as he struggled up the gentle valley incline. "I don't know, I guess I was being too harsh or something."

"Harsh would have been stuffing a sock in his mouth," Leera said. "Firmly, so that only high degree arcanery could dislodge it." She sighed. "All right, stop giving me that look. He had it coming. He's our age yet he acts like he's nine."

Leland gave a sharp moan.

"No offense, Leland."

Leland nodded stiffly and returned to listening to the orb.

"I'll talk to him," Augum said, turning to go, feeling bad for the boy.

"No," Bridget said, voice firmer than usual. "What we're doing is important, Aug. You need to focus. You're compassionate and you want to make sure he's all right, I get that, but we've got priorities."

Leera nodded along. "He'll just have to put on his big boy pants."

"He's got to learn to be independent," Haylee added. "Hmm, maybe I can get Chaska to spend time with him."

"All right," Augum finally said. Though Chaska might end up pummeling the poor boy if he gets too annoyed with him.

"I'll keep studying, I'm wretchedly behind." Jengo strode over to Leland, fetching the yellow book from the rucksack. "I want to be able to defend myself in battle, and I'm nowhere near that yet. But I also want to learn battle healing—"

Bridget placed her hands on her hips. "Jengo, you need to learn all the spells of the 1st degree, not just the elemental healing spells."

"I know, I was just—"

"Stop fooling around, Jengo, this is serious. Your Shine spell is weak and your—" Bridget stopped and rubbed her forehead. "I'm sorry …"

"You all right?" Augum asked softly.

"Fine. Just haven't been sleeping well."

"Same nightmare?" Augum pressed. It was a guess.

She surrendered a nod.

Augum watched her a moment, wondering if she was finally going to talk about it. She had deep circles under her eyes. Her cheekbones protruded a little as if she hadn't been eating much, and her long cinnamon hair was thin and stringy.

"You know you can talk to us," he said gently.

She gave him a tired look. "I keep dreaming the same stupid thing," she said at last. "Remember that moment on the cliff when the harpies attacked me?"

Augum's palm scar tingled. "How could we forget." He recalled her dangling below as one harpy after another swooped in. She had sustained serious injuries from the attack and nearly died. Luckily, Raptos the wolven allowed them to make a concoction using Augum's own blood to save her.

"Anyway," Bridget continued, "In the dream, I'm alone—none of you are there to help me—getting attacked by all these harpies, while I'm dangling and swinging on that rope. I always wake up at the same instant, when the rope breaks and I suddenly …"

"… fall," Augum said. She always had a horrible fear of heights.

She slowly nodded. "Look, we're all under a lot of pressure, let's not worry about it, all right?"

Leera placed a hand on her shoulder. "You sure you're fine?"

Bridget's gaze wandered to the forest where Devon had disappeared. "I wonder if it's right that we stay here. We're putting them all in danger. Maybe we should leave and train elsewhere. What if—"

"Bridge," Leera cut in. "You said it yourself plenty of times to me—we can't do this alone. It especially counts now that Mrs. Stone is missing." She nodded toward the village. "They know what they're getting into. We'll just have to …" She made a vague gesture with her hand. "… trust the Fates or something, I don't know."

Bridget gave her a funny look before finally surrendering a nod. "All right. Let's move on then. Repair?"

Haylee stepped away from them. "You know what? Why don't I help Jengo train in the 1st degree, that way you three can concentrate on what you need to do."

"You … you'd do that?" Bridget asked.

"Yes, of course I would." She made a derisive gesture at her cane. "Look, I'm not going with you, that much is plain. I'll stay, train Jengo, help Leland, help the Resistance in whatever way I can. Besides, now that you told me about that dream, I … well, I just didn't realize *how* much pressure you're all under."

Even Leera's brows travelled up her forehead. "Are you coming down with something?"

"I'm fine, that's the point." Haylee hobbled over to Jengo. "I've been resisting … everything. Holding too much in. Seeing Augum and Bridget go after you like that after Furhead kidnapped you … well, *I* want that in friendship too. I mean, yeah, I'm stuck with this stupid cane—" She gave it an angry shake. "But life goes on. We go on. *I* go on. And besides, I've taken so much. Now I want to give back … for a change. Or something. Anyway, stop gaping and get back to work, you bunch of … fools." She was smiling as she plopped down beside Jengo, who was staring at her with a perplexed expression.

"Hell has frozen over," Leera mumbled, giving Augum a stunned look.

Bridget smiled, nodded. "Right. Uh, let's get back to it, shall we? We'll begin by warming up with one cycle."

The trio began a challenging regimen, truly pushing themselves with every spell. Augum felt an underlying sense of urgency throughout, as if time was not on their side. In one very unique sense, it wasn't—at the back of his mind, he still thought about Cron. What would happen to them if they aged rapidly in a short period of time trying to learn the spell? And then to perform it in battle? How would that affect their—

"Concentrate!" Bridget said after knocking him down with the Push spell. "You didn't even raise your shield, Aug. What's the matter with you? Where's your head at?"

"Sorry," he said, allowing her to help him up. "Try it again. I'll be ready."

And the second time, he got it right.

They worked through the gamut of spells, focusing on the 4th degree, especially Summon Minor Elemental, though even after hours of practice, neither Augum nor

Leera were able to cast it successfully. They next tried the Reflect spell using the prisms, but failed at that too. Bridget, still uncharacteristically short-tempered, was about to move on to the counterspell for Object Alarm when four figures climbed down the valley slope—Malaika, Charissa, Annelise, and Gabe.

"Great, just what we need," Leera muttered.

Malaika frowned at the top of the valley. "I don't see anything."

"That's right, they can't hear or see us," Leera said. "This is fantastic, all we have to do is ignore them and they'll go away." She gave Bridget a hopeful but apprehensive sidelong glance.

"We can't do that," Bridget finally said with a sigh. She marched up the valley. The moment she crossed the invisible boundary of the spell, the newly arrived foursome startled.

"Oh my!" Charissa squealed, clutching her chest with one hand and Malaika's elbow with the other.

Bridget's voice was weary. "Malaika, Charissa, Annelise, Gabe—I formally invite you in to our training ground."

The looks on their faces said it all. Charissa in particular, who kept clapping her hands, tugged on Malaika's sleeve and whispered something into her ear, to which Malaika nodded her head, flashing a secret smile Augum's way.

"Here comes trouble," Jengo said to Haylee.

"Hello, Augum!" Malaika called with a wave, wearing a bright floral-embroidered spring dress, offset by her chocolate skin. "We've come to call as we promised!"

Charissa skipped along, wearing a tight dark brown dress that looked too hot for the weather. Her pale skin glistened with sweat as she wafted a hand at her face. Behind the girls walked Annelise, wearing a black servant outfit and carrying a basket, looking thoroughly miserable, and a smiling Gabe, also wearing a servant outfit and carrying a polished silver tray brimming with sweets.

"We brought you refreshments!" Malaika said, gracefully gesturing at the basket and tray.

"Think my headache just got worse," Leera muttered, plopping to the ground.

Bridget wiped her brow with her sleeve. "Let's take a break," and sat down beside Leera.

Malaika's hand drifted toward Augum. She wriggled her fingers. "Take this fair maiden's hand in greeting, good sir."

"Uh, all right." He took her soft hand and made a clumsy bow with it.

"No, you have to *kiss* it, silly," Charissa whispered.

Leera's eyes narrowed. "Yeah, kiss it," she goaded.

"Uh, what did you bring?" Augum asked in forced tones instead, allowing Malaika's hand to drop.

Malaika's face fell but she quickly recovered. "Annelise, what *did* we bring?"

But Annelise just stood there staring at Augum, looking like a pale, trembling leaf.

Gabe flashed Leera that stupid smarmy smile Augum hated. "Forgive my daft sister," he said, gliding over to Leera and placing the tray before her.

Leera, sitting cross-legged in her blue robe beside Bridget, immediately brightened. "Ooo, sweets!" and dove in.

Malaika lightly stroked her neck while staring at Augum. "I hope you do not mind us disturbing you …"

"We were just practicing and learning. I guess we could use a break."

"Tell them about that grotesquely fat creature," Charissa whispered.

Malaika straightened a little. "That boy, Devil I think his name was—"

"—Devon," Bridget corrected sharply. "And please do not call him fat."

Malaika's brows crossed at Bridget. "Anyway, he practically barreled into us. He was crying like a little baby, saying how you broke his heart and how you bullied him—"

Bridget's cheeks reddened. "But that's not what happened—"

"If you say so, but he was very upset. You really hurt his feelings." Malaika turned back to Augum and tilted her head with a smile. "We brought refreshments."

"You said that already," Leera said with a mouthful of colored jelly sweets.

Malaika ignored the remark. "Annelise, if you please."

Annelise's mouth thinned as she reached into the basket, retrieving a checkered blanket, which she spread on the ground. Then she removed a wheel of white cheese, a couple branches of dark coldland grapes, a bowl of olives, bread, pomegranates, honeyed waffles, and two skins of water, placing them neatly on the blanket.

Augum, glancing at the wide array of luxurious foods, could only think of Old Jory and his deceased wife and that dirty, scraped-out pot of rice.

Leera eyed the waffles but pretended to be looking elsewhere. Gabe quickly settled on the blanket, tapping at it for Leera. She gave Augum a *How do you like it?* look before crawling over to sit beside him.

Augum felt his jaw stiffen.

Malaika reached out for Annelise, allowing the girl to guide her to a spot on the blanket. Charissa did the same, sitting beside her friend. Annelise dropped to her knees, smoothing her servant gown underneath her, and began tearing the bread into chunks, keeping her gaze averted from Augum, though he swore she snuck glances when he wasn't looking.

"What a pleasant day," Malaika said, turning her face toward the azure sky. She patted the empty spot beside her. "Please join us, Augum."

Augum suddenly felt everyone's eyes on him. His stomach tightened. He would much rather sit with Leera … or punch Gabe in the face. "There's not enough room for Haylee and Jengo and Leland," he said instead.

Malaika swiveled her head to where the others were sitting and expelled a long breath. "Would you like some refreshments as well then?"

"We're good," Jengo immediately blurted, resting a hand on his chin as if he was watching a stage play. Haylee had the same look beside him, and was nodding along with Leland that they were fine.

"Well, uh, I really should be training," Augum said, taking a step away from them all.

"Nonsense, surely you deserve a break too, not just Bridget and Leera. Besides, you must be starved—"

Leera jumped to her feet. "No, we have to train." She grabbed Augum's hand and yanked him to the center of the clearing. She took a few paces back from him, three watery rings springing to life around her arm.

"Ready?" but before Augum could reply, she violently threw at the ground, shouting, "GRAU!" The air roared with the sound of crashing water. Malaika and Charissa screamed and grabbed each other, while Annelise and Gabe rolled away, knocking over the basket and tray.

Leera kept her gaze on Augum. "First Offensive." She smacked her wrists together before her. "ANNIHILO!"

Augum barely summoned his shield in time to block the sharp jet of water, strong enough to make him stumble backward a few steps.

"She's trying to kill him—!" Charissa shrieked. "Somebody do something!"

Bridget stood up. "No, she isn't," and joined Augum and Leera, running through a short cycle with them. At the end of it, Leera, forehead dotted with sweat, strode over to the blanket Gabe and Annelise hastily re-arranged, reached down into a bowl, and took two honeyed waffles, shoving one into her mouth. "Mmm, good," she toned while munching, her shadow falling on Malaika.

Charissa watched her while holding onto Malaika's arm. "How beastly."

Annelise looked up at Leera, hand shading her eyes from the sun. "You're awfully pretty. I can see why he likes you."

Leera's cheeks reddened.

Malaika whirled on her servant, voice a hiss. "Annelise! You will not talk unless addressed!"

Leera pointed a waffle at Malaika. "She's not your slave, you know."

"No, she is *not* my slave," Malaika replied, "but she *is* our paid servant, and if her family wants to continue to have employment in these difficult times, she will do as she is told."

Annelise stiffened at the mention of her family. "My apologies, Miss Haroun." She dropped her head and shakily began to spread cheese on some of the chunks of bread.

Malaika nodded. "That's better, and don't let me catch you stepping out of line ever again."

Annelise's ears reddened. "Yes, Miss Haroun."

Malaika turned on Gabe. "And you. Try *harder*," she hissed.

Gabe paled. "I will, my lady."

Augum wondered what that was all about.

Leera finished the second waffle. She gestured to a branch of grapes and it floated out of the bowl to her hand. Malaika and Charissa flinched, but Leera smirked, turning away to share the grapes with Augum and Bridget.

The trio shortly began a second round of training, this time focusing on the 4th degree. Despite Charissa's constant whisperings to Malaika, the trio lost themselves in the work. Malaika was leaning forward, lips slightly parted, mostly watching Augum, except to occasionally give Leera a foul look whenever Leera squeezed his hand or gave him a kiss, something she was suddenly doing a lot more of. Annelise watched too, but only when she thought Malaika and Charissa would not notice. Gabe tried all manner of doe-eyed looks to get Leera's attention, until Augum "accidentally" split a log with his lightning First Offensive very close to the boy.

After a while, Augum just hoped Malaika would go away. Her staring at him hardly helped his concentration, sometimes leading him to bungle a spell. Leera was just the opposite, performing the spells precisely, often flashing Malaika victorious looks. Her Mind Armor had improved rapidly. She even managed to cast Summon Minor Elemental, calling forth a watery creature that promptly trundled over to Malaika and Charissa. The latter shrieked, overturning the bowl of olives in her haste to crawl away.

"Lee, really, that's enough," Bridget finally said, though only after Malaika used Annelise as a human shield.

Leera, panting from all the arcane exertion, idly waved at the little monster. "Elementus, back." She smirked at Malaika. "Only kidding, you can relax."

Bridget ran her fingers through her hair, tying it up in a ponytail. "Let's work on the counterspell to Object Alarm. Jengo, can we snag the book?"

The tall Sierran rubbed his eyes. "Of course. I need to start practicing Telekinesis for real anyway, enough theory. I've been watching you all carefully and I think I can do it." He stood and strode over, handing the blue arcaneology book to Bridget. "Besides, I've got Haylee helping me now."

Gabe lightly cleared his throat. When he caught Augum's attention, he made a slight nod at Malaika, who extended her hand, palm down.

"Augum, will you please help a fair lady up?"

Augum hesitated, sighed, then paced over. He took her hand and brought her to her feet.

"Annelise, gather everything, will you?" Malaika turned to Augum with a smile and tucked one hand through his elbow, placing the other on his forearm. "Thank you, Augum. Walk with me a moment."

"Uh … okay." Augum glanced at Leera, feeling trapped. She was staring at them with crossed arms.

Malaika glanced at Leera and the two shared a hard look beyond Augum's comprehension. She slowly walked with Augum around the clearing while Bridget and Leera returned to practicing.

"I know you have an … *infatuation* with her," Malaika began in a silky and quiet voice, tapping his forearm with her free hand, "and I understand why, I really do, but you deserve someone of a more … *noble* bearing."

Augum stopped midstride. "What are you talking about?" These stupid mind games again.

Malaika looked into his eyes before closing her own, drawing in a deep breath. "You are a great figure in history who deserves an equally great partner. Think of it, together we can rule the kingdom once you return it to its former glory—"

Augum drew away. "What? I don't want you. I don't think of you that way—"

Malaika took a step closer, reaching out to him. "You don't *yet*, but you will."

Leera stopped what she was doing to look over.

Malaika giggled before speaking in a loud voice everyone could hear. "Thank you, no one ever called me pretty before—"

Augum felt a horrible flush. "What? I didn't—"

"—and I promise I'll see you in secret," Malaika added with a wink. "You're right, she's not good enough for you."

Augum felt lightheaded. His lips were suddenly drier than sand. "What … how …"

Malaika reached for her friend. "Come, Charissa, we must let our noble hero train. Annelise, Gabe—to me." Before Augum could find the words, they were already gone.

Leera suddenly marched over to him, eyes filled with tears. Just as he began to speak, she slapped him. Hard. "After everything that we've been through … how could you!"

Augum couldn't care less about his stinging cheek. "But I didn't say those things to her. I didn't do any—"

"You took her hand like some eager puppy; and I *saw* the way you were looking at her—"

"What! No, I—Lee, come back!" but she too was gone, gone over the valley hill, gone to who knew where.

He glanced to Bridget, hands cold and clammy, heart racing. "What … what just happened?"

Bridget bit her nail in thought. She looked to Jengo, who stood with wide eyes; to Haylee, leaning on her cane, frowning; to Leland, who sat quietly holding the Agonex; to the lonely valley hilltop—and back to Augum.

"Malaika. It was Malaika, wasn't it?"

Augum felt heat flash through his body. "Of course it was!" How could she even question it?

Bridget sighed. "I'll talk to Leera," and strode up the valley.

Augum felt a consoling pat on his shoulder. "Girls and their stupid mind games," Jengo said. "Maybe you can help Haylee train me. Might get your mind off things."

Augum was frantically going over what was said. Why hadn't Leera believed him? How could she have just *slapped* him like that?

"Augum?"

"Hmm? Oh, sure."

But his efforts with Jengo and Haylee were fruitless. He couldn't concentrate past his numb hands, past his racing thoughts, past the awful betrayal on Leera's face before the stinging slap. Not a single spell worked. Not a one, not even Shine.

Haylee's face softened with empathy. "Don't worry, it'll work out."

But Augum's thoughts raced on. Nothing they said helped in the least.

After a while, Jengo gave up trying to move a stick and picked up the blue book to continue his theoretical studies with Telekinesis. Haylee plopped down beside him, coaching him through some of the concepts, occasionally shooting Augum a worried look. Leland kept listening to the Orb of Orion, or idly traced the Agonex while moaning softly to himself.

Augum remained standing in the same spot, still puzzling things over. Should he have run after Leera? Should he have said something else to Malaika?

Eventually, someone appeared at the top of the valley. Augum felt his hopes surge before realizing it was Malaika, her ebony face streaked with tears. She was in a hurry, glancing over her shoulder.

"Augum, help!" She ran forward, tripped, and rolled down the small valley, gathering mud and grass on her dress.

Augum strode to her with gritted teeth, readying to yell at her for her treachery; but as soon as he got close, she threw her arms around his neck and held on, loudly weeping into his blue robe.

"She threatened to *kill* me, Augum. Please, save me—"

Just as he tried to pry her away, he spotted Leera at the top of the hill, face also streaked with tears. She took one look at him and Malaika embracing and closed her eyes. A shaking hand found its way to her chest, where she squeezed the fabric of her blue robe, as if trying to tear her heart out.

Augum still could not get Malaika off. "Leera, wait—"

But she was already gone.

SCORNED

"We belong together, Augum," Malaika whispered tenderly, sobbing into his chest, hands caressing his neck. "King and queen ..."

Augum stood completely numb, not even bothering to fight her off. What the hell was happening? Leera had slapped him before running off, Bridget had chased after her, and all he could do was stand there like a stupid, useless fool, allowing this girl to hang on to him like some needy puppy.

Bridget suddenly appeared at the top of the hill. "Where did Lee—" but stopped mid-sentence when she spotted Malaika embracing Augum.

Seeing Bridget's face gave him the courage to pry Malaika off and throw her to the ground. "What have you done!" he sputtered, backing away, hands on his head. "What have you done ..."

Bridget's eyes narrowed and she marched down to them. For a moment, Augum thought she was going to give him a tongue thrashing or slap him, only to witness her yank Malaika to her feet by the arm.

"You vile witch," Bridget hissed. "Why would you do that! Tell Leera the truth!"

"No!" Malaika's face suddenly hardened. "I mean, no, I won't let you manipulate me! We love each other. Augum is just too afraid to admit that he loves me—"

Bridget opened her mouth to say something else but stopped herself. She turned to Augum, head tilting. "Is that true?"

Augum had had enough. "No, of course it isn't! How could you even *think* that—!"

Bridget gave a brief nod and whipped back to Malaika. "I thought so. Get out of my sight, you evil—" She threw Malaika back with the strength of indignation.

Malaika fell to the earth, weeping. "No, my love, don't let them rip us apart!"

Charissa suddenly appeared at the top of the valley along with Mr. and Mrs. Haroun, the former grimacing in concern, the latter shaking with fury.

Charissa pointed at Bridget. "That one's trying to hurt her too!"

"Stay away from my precious baby, you nefarious little witch!" Mrs. Haroun shrieked, raising her skirts as she hurried down the slope, a giant hat bouncing on her head. "Stay away from her! Shoo—! Where is she! She's invisible, isn't she? She's using witchery to deceive us! Behold! We know what needs to be done with witches, do we not, Hanad!"

"Selma, you have to be invited—"

Mrs. Haroun's hands were searching for them blindly. "Where are the vile vermin? Reveal yourselves, witches!"

"You are being ridiculous, Selma. Oh for—" Mr. Haroun gave Augum a pleading look.

Augum grit his teeth. "Mrs. Haroun, I formally invite you to our training ground."

Mrs. Haroun suddenly yelped, grabbing onto her giant hat. "There! They're here! Hanad! Grab the misfits, will you! Husband, do your duty!"

"Wait, that's not what's happening—" Haylee tried to say. "Please, I saw the whole thing—"

"Stay back, you crippled wench!" Mrs. Haroun shrieked. "Stay back, or I shall have you lynched!"

Haylee's mouth dropped.

Malaika reached out with heaving sobs. "Mother, these nasty girls were trying to hurt me!"

Mrs. Haroun scooped Malaika into her arms. "Mother's here, sweet darling, Mother's here—" She whirled on Bridget. "WHAT IS THE MEANING OF THIS!"

"I am sure there is a perfectly good explanation, Selma," Mr. Haroun said in weary tones as he made his way down the slope.

"I saw her trying to hurt Malaika, Mr. Haroun!" Charissa said.

Bridget raised her palms defensively. "Mrs. Haroun, your daughter—"

Mrs. Haroun recoiled with Malaika. "She's going to cast a spell on us! Hanad, help! Hanaaaaad!"

Mr. Haroun saw Bridget's hands. "Young lady, what are you doing!"

Bridget hurriedly dropped them. "I'm only trying to explain—!"

"Then by all means, do so!"

"Your daughter, uh … your daughter, Malaika, she … she threw herself onto Augum and—"

Mrs. Haroun clutched at her chest. "Hanad, I think I am going to faint. I am going to faint, Hanad! She just called our daughter a wench, a common harlot—"

Mr. Haroun stiffened to his full height. "Young lady, are you really suggesting my daughter 'threw' herself at this young man?"

Bridget was shaking her head, eyes darting between the three family members. "No, I don't know, I mean … yes, she was trying to—"

Mrs. Haroun, still clutching her chest, wavered like a tree about to fall. "You heard it from the girl's own lips, Hanad. This supposed hero witch just called your daughter a harlot to your face. The family name has been defiled, our honor besmirched. What are you going to do about it?"

"Mr. Haroun," Augum began in the calmest tone he could, "Malaika tried to …" but he couldn't form the words. What words were there to describe what she had done? He had never heard of such a thing, let alone experienced it before.

The Harouns turned to him, waiting for what he was going to say next.

"She tried to deceive me," he blurted finally, unable to think past the fog of confusion surrounding every thought.

"But you said you loved me!" Malaika cried. "You said we were going to get married! You promised! Mother, Father … he promised me! I am ruined now!"

"What! I never said that! I never promised you a thing! You aren't ruined at all!"

Haylee hobbled forward, pointing an accusing finger in Malaika's face. "She lied," Haylee spat in a clear and firm voice. "She's a liar. I saw it with my own eyes. The whole thing. Theatre. Nothing but theatre."

Augum gaped a moment before taking hold of his wrangled nerves. "Yes! Yes, she *is* lying! I don't … *like* her like that at all, and I never promised anything to her, nor did I, I … *ruin* her, whatever that means!"

Mr. Haroun studied Haylee and Augum a moment before turning to his daughter with a granite look. "Malaika, did you make all of this up? Is that what is happening? *Again?* Did you lie to your father?"

Malaika's eyes darted about before settling on her father's cold gaze. "No, Father, we love each other and he promised to marry me—"

"Malaika Haroun, do you recall when we had that long conversation about telling the truth? Hmm?"

Malaika shrank, swallowing hard. "But … but … but I *love* him, Father, we're meant to be together …" Her lips began trembling.

Mr. Haroun's voice was steel. "You are coming home. This. Instant," and he began marching away. "THIS INSTANT!" he roared, ascending the bank.

Mrs. Haroun placed the back of her hand to her forehead as she threatened to wilt. "But, Hanad—"

"Oh, open your eyes, Selma! Enough is enough!" Mr. Haroun made a firm gesture to the town. "Home. Now!" He turned to Augum with an apologetic look, opened his mouth to say something, but only ended up shaking his head at his daughter in revulsion. "What a *disgrace*. A disgrace! You have shamed this house in a most unwholesome way, Daughter. I am … beyond disappointed. The house. NOW!"

Malaika gave Augum a bitter look before stomping past her father, hands in front, head hanging. Mrs. Haroun, suddenly not feeling faint anymore, raised her chin and rigidly followed without a word, holding her skirts above the grass.

Charissa shook her head at Augum. "You threw perfect happiness away as if it was worthless. Hope you're proud of yourself." She turned her back on him and marched after the others.

Augum was in such a state he plopped to the ground. "What … what was … what was that …?"

"That," Bridget said, watching them disappear over the valley edge, "is high society. At least, one version of it."

"The crazy version," Haylee added.

Jengo, who had been watching from beside Leland the entire time, fell back to lie on the grass. "How does Father survive such a thing?" he mumbled. "Oh, please, Unnameables, let me avoid *that*. Please …"

Bridget sat down beside Augum. "You were perceived to be a good match. Sadly, I've seen it before."

Haylee sat down beside them with a groan, holding the cane over her knees. "There's even a name for it—love trapping."

"Love trapping? A good match?" Augum rubbed his face. "*A good match?*" He had a good match already. Suddenly he recalled the way Leera clutched at her chest, the agonized expression on her face. He shot to his feet. "I've got to find her—"

Bridget stood as well. "All right, we'll go look for her. Haylee, Jengo, mind staying with Leland?"

"I'll keep working with him," Haylee said. "Good luck, and don't worry, if it comes down to it, *I'll* even talk to Leera." She flashed a wry smile.

Augum nodded at Haylee. "And thanks … for speaking up for me."

She gave a nod in return. "That's what friends do."

LOOKING FOR LEERA

As sunset neared, Augum and Bridget searched everywhere for Leera, splitting up to cover more ground. They even recruited Chaska, who had been patrolling the outskirts of town in his new role as watchman. He had an extra bounce in his step and proudly showed off the sword the Constable's guards had lent him. Luckily, there weren't many people about to impede their search—everyone was having supper, and soon it would be dark anyway.

As Chaska strode between houses, peeking behind barrels and wagons, Bridget met Augum by the well in the center of town.

"Anything?" she asked, eyes darting about as she fixed her ponytail.

Augum held his elbows, shifting his weight from foot to foot. "Nothing. I'm an idiot. I should have run after her immediately—"

"It's all right, it'll get sorted out. Besides, you didn't know what was happening, and honestly, I don't blame you. That was some serious trickery. Just imagine if Malaika had been a warlock."

The thought made Augum shudder. It also reminded him of Erika.

"Maybe she just needs some time to herself," Bridget said.

"Malaika needs more than time to herself," he muttered.

"No, I mean Leera."

"Oh."

Bridget looked him over. "You look terrible."

"You blame me?"

"Of course not. We haven't eaten much all day. Come on, let's have supper while we think about what to do next."

"I'm not hungry. I'd rather keep searching."

"I know, Aug, but once you smell the food, you'll see how hungry you really are. Besides, you'll be able to think straight."

"The letter was drafted and sent on its way this morning," interrupted a voice behind them. Augum and Bridget turned to find Constable Clouds standing on the other side of the well, leaning on his cane, his great girth spilling out of his black Legion garment.

"Oh, hello, Constable," Bridget said.

"Briggs is the courier, so we can be sure it will arrive in a speedy manner." Clouds studied them a moment. "Is everything all right?"

"Yes, Constable," Augum replied. "Err, mostly," he added in afterthought. Only his entire world was crashing.

"I see." Clouds dabbed at his face with a cloth. "These garments are quite hot, I have to say, but duty is duty." He sighed. "My son is in a state—"

"—I'm awfully sorry about that, Constable," Bridget blurted, "I didn't mean—"

"It is all right, my dear, I understand. Unfortunately, it has happened before. But …" He dabbed at his face again. "Do you suppose …"

"Yes, Constable?"

"Do you think you can forgive Devon and include him in your activities somehow? He is in great need of friendship. It pains me deeply to see him in such a state, so alone and miserable."

"Yes, of course, Constable, where is he? I'll talk to him right away and apologize."

"He's with Miss Jones."

Augum perked up. "With Leera?"

"Yes, I believe they went on a walk together—"

"A walk? Which way?" Augum pressed.

Clouds pointed with his cane in the direction of the Okeke home, where a path snaked well beyond the cabin and into the woods.

"Thank you, Constable," Bridget said, and immediately set off with Augum.

Augum's mind raced as they strode to the Okeke home. Leera found Devon annoying … why would she be with him right now?

"Hello, Mr. Okeke," Bridget said as they walked inside, encountering the aroma of roasted chicken and potatoes. "Is Leera here?"

Mr. Okeke looked up from tending the roasting fire. "No, I am afraid I have not seen her."

"Ready for supper, you two?" Mr. Goss asked with a smile from the table, reading a parchment.

Augum's stomach rumbled. Bridget was right—suddenly he was starving, or at least his body was. Last thing he cared about right now was food though.

"Almost," Bridget replied. "We'll bring Jengo and Leland."

"Thank you, that would be wonderful. Oh, and the letter was sent by courier this morning."

"We heard, thank you, Mr. Goss," Bridget said absently, readying to leave again.

"And the crate is coming along swimmingly!" Mr. Goss added, pushing on his spectacles. "Should have it done soon. We've already started soliciting for book donations to be … confiscated, so to speak."

Bridget forced a chuckle. "Yes, we can't wait. Uh, please excuse us—"

Augum and Bridget set off again into the woods, following the path that led to the hilltop glade where the Star Feast had been held. They caught glimpses of the distant Muranians through the trees, their great snow-capped peaks glinting in the sun. Augum recalled scaling those rocky behemoths, and for a moment, couldn't believe they had actually accomplished such a feat.

The path rose and fell as they walked through the peaceful forest, neither saying a word. Augum had difficulty swallowing. His mouth felt dry and his nerves tingled. He couldn't get his mind off the way Leera clutched at her heart.

At last, they came upon the glade, sitting high on a hill, surrounded by stubby evergreens that made visible a vast panorama of forest and distant mountains. In the center of the clearing, by three dark fire pits, sat Devon and Leera, facing away.

A shock ran through Augum, stiffening every muscle—Devon was *holding* Leera in his arms.

Bridget saw his reaction. "He's just comforting her, Aug, I'm sure—" but just as she turned back to the clearing, they both witnessed Devon kiss Leera's head, then stroke her hair.

Augum felt his breath bursting in and out. His stomach twisted and churned. He felt lightheaded and braced against a tree.

"Aug, I'm sure it's nothing—"

Augum shook his head and began stumbling back the way they had come, numb as ice.

"Aug, I'm certain it's not what it looks like! Where are you going—!"

He stumped along, barely conscious of what he was doing, leaving Bridget and the glade and Devon and Leera behind. At some point, he veered off the path, not wanting to go back to Milham, not wanting to see anyone. He slumped against a gnarled oak, hidden in the woods amongst a nest of pines and cedars. A stream trickled nearby as crickets chirped, yet all he heard was the resounding thrum of a shattered heart.

TENDER AGONY

Augum sat against that gnarled oak replaying what he had seen—Devon kissing Leera's head as he held her in his arms, each time feeling the stabbing pain anew. Those butterflies he felt every time he had seen Leera; held her hand, kissed her—those butterflies had had their wings ripped out, leaving behind a hollow, rotting buzz.

He hugged his legs and drew his hood, resting his head on his knees. How he missed her already. How could she have moved on so quickly like that? It stung like a thousand needles. Just as he had witnessed her clutch her heart and tear it out, he now felt like his own had been ripped out of his chest—ripped out and ground underfoot.

He heard quiet voices nearby on the path. It was Bridget, Leera and Devon, and they were walking back to Milham. There was a laugh, a laugh that penetrated his soul like the sharpest dagger. He imagined Devon holding hands with Leera, the pair chuckling happily, and felt a hot flush of shame cascade through his body. He pictured them kissing and holding each other and felt a queasy nausea that made him want to vomit.

It took all his strength to push those visions out of his mind.

What was he going to do now? Go back and pretend everything was rosy? How could he ever smile again? How could he sit near her or lay eyes on her without feeling a thousand swords slice into his chest?

He slammed the ground with his fists, angry with Leera, Devon, Malaika … and especially, himself.

"Fool," he said aloud. "Stupid, arrogant, lousy, idiotic fool—!" A hot rage began building as he stood. The rage made his muscles and soul vibrate. Three crackling rings unconsciously ruptured around his arm. The energy kept building, so quickly it made him dizzy. He slammed his wrists together.

"ANNIHILO!"

A searing heat ripped through his very being, exploding from his hands. A bolt of lightning as thick as a log connected with a pine, instantly snapping it. The tree collapsed on itself, mirroring Augum's fall to the ground.

The crash ripped through the forest.

He lay there, spent, head throbbing, barely conscious. Was that wild arcanery? He couldn't tell. Great, he was regressing, like some fearful animal. No, like some wounded animal, for that's how he felt—a deer speared with an arrow, twitching, ready for slaughter.

Time passed. The sky dimmed in hue as sunset came and went. The throbbing slowly went away. His arcane energies replenished, yet he still felt as hollow as an empty barrel.

He stared at the fallen pine before him. "I'm sorry," he whispered to it, but that did not make the tree better again. It lay as before, silent, dying.

He had done that. Killed something that had stood in untroubled peace for many more years than he had been alive.

He had killed two men too. Men who had also walked Sithesia far longer than he had been alive.

Is this how it happens? How people turn into an Erika? A Blade of Sorrows? A Robin? One awful moment of rage after another? Of forgetfulness?

Was he turning into his father?

At last, with the sky a fiery red, he dragged himself off the ground. No use sitting out here pouting all night. There were things to accomplish, important things, things that took precedence over such small concerns like relationships and … love.

That word made his heart constrict so tightly he actually put his hand to his chest, again remembering Leera do the same thing. He winced but quickly shook off the feeling.

No, there were things to do. He had to learn to deal with his emotions. He had to be as cold as ice, as hard as … as hard as stone.

Augum Stone.

"Fitting," he said aloud with a blubbery snort.

He shook out his limbs, trying to release the tension, the deep sorrow, and began the long walk back to Milham, careful not to drag his feet or slump his shoulders. He was conscious of everything he did, every minor movement, as if readying to cast Centarro.

When he spotted the windows of the Okeke cabin aglow with warmth, he paused, feeling that familiar tightness in his chest. A burst of laughter from inside the cabin cut through him like a jet of water shot out from Leera's palm. A vision of him walking right by, walking on and on forever, paraded before his mind. They all certainly thought of him in an awful light now; why should he foul their joy with his shame?

"Augum—?"

He turned to see Malaika step out from behind a tree, ebony face wet with tears, which she promptly brushed away with her sleeve.

Augum felt his muscles tighten. "You."

"Augum, I … I am so sorry for … for my deceit." She held herself, rubbing her own shoulders while staring at her feet. "I … I know it was wrong, but I just want you to understand that it came from … it came from love." She glanced up. "I love you, Augum Stone, I do. I loved you since the day we first met. Do you remember the dance?"

Augum glanced away. "I don't want to hear it." He needed his feet to move, yet he just stood there. Like a fool. Again.

Malaika began slowly walking toward him. "Augum, please, just hear me. I would take it all back if I could. I … I would do things differently." She stopped an arm's length away and reached out for him.

He could not keep the venom from his voice. "I don't ever want to see you or talk to you again."

Malaika's hand froze in midair, a finger-length from his arm. Suddenly she burst with a cry that came from some deep, lonely place. "You … you don't mean that."

He turned to face her, except all he saw was Leera symbolically tearing out her heart. "I *do* mean it."

Malaika's hands shook as they rose to her face. "I think I'm going to be sick—" and she stumbled away, muddy dress fluttering.

He did not watch her go. His gaze lingered on the trees. He exhaled, not realizing he had not breathed since seeing her.

Now what though?

He paced to the Okeke cabin, feeling a little lighter. He reached for the door handle. His palm hung in the air, sweaty.

Suddenly the door opened and there was Devon. As soon as he saw Augum, his pudgy face lit up with a wide smile. "Finally! She was *so* worried."

"Is it him?" asked a shaky voice from inside.

Devon turned. "Yes—!"

Augum caught a shadow as someone ran to the door, immediately bumping Devon out of the way. Suddenly there was Leera, looking as radiant as the moon. Her face had a pinched redness to it, as if she had been crying, yet her freckles were soft in the rapidly dimming light.

Devon tactfully shut the door, leaving them alone outside.

"Hi," Augum managed to finally blurt, feeling his stomach churn. He had not even practiced what he was going to say, or how he was going to explain everything.

Leera's arched brows softened as she looked him in the eye. "Bridget and Haylee told me everything. It was Malaika. I'm such a stupid fool."

A waterfall of cool relief swept over Augum. He felt his muscles relax, his breathing ease. He could have floated away right there.

She reached out to him but stopped herself. "I'm … I'm sorry for behaving so … so childishly. And I'm *really* sorry for slapping you. I … I don't deserve—"

He stopped her by sweeping her long raven hair from her forehead. He gently raised her chin, drew her near, and kissed her.

"I missed you," he whispered, looking into those voluminous dark eyes.

Her hands found their way around his neck as tears flowed down her cheeks. "I missed you too."

* * *

Augum had a delectable late supper of roast lamb, salted spinach, and potatoes. In attendance were Mr. Okeke, Jengo, Priya, Mr. Goss, Leland, Leera, Bridget, Devon, Haylee, Chaska, and Constable Clouds. There was hardly room for them all—some had to sit in the armchairs and on the couch and by the fireplace. And as it turned out, Devon really had just been very sympathetic to Leera and was comforting her. It had not been *that* kind of kiss. It was the type of kiss Devon's late mother used to give him when he was being bullied or made fun of.

Augum also heard news that Malaika had got into a lot of trouble for her deceit with her father, and was not to leave the house for a tenday. Devon reported he heard her crying in her room. Augum had already seen her outside the house. He suspected she sneaked out a window or something.

He and Leera exchanged secret smiles and hand squeezes as they ate. Bridget spoke of little but their training, her plans on how they were going to learn the counterspells to Object Alarm and Object Track, fine-tune Summon Minor Elemental, and above all, finally learn the Reflect spell.

But that would all be tomorrow. For now, Augum was content to enjoy peace, at least for one evening. Perhaps he had been a little melodramatic earlier. A lesson for the future, if anything—he shouldn't jump so quickly to conclusions.

He barely listened as Priya quietly spoke of Tiberrans struggling under Legion rule, or how the Solian countryside steadily starved, or how Chaska has been enjoying being a night watchman and how Haylee smiled at him, or Devon again apologizing to Bridget for shoving her. He had Leera, and that was all that mattered.

"Aug, are you listening?" Bridget asked, face grave.

"Huh?"

"Leland wrote a note."

"He did?"

"Yes," Mr. Goss interjected, making sure he had everyone else's attention too. "It is short." He cleared his throat and held up a crinkled parchment. " 'Big army getting …' " He squinted at a word.

Leland moaned.

"Ah, 'Dreadnought', of course. 'Big army getting Dreadnought weapons and armor in Velmara.' Very well written, Son." Mr. Goss returned the parchment to his son and patted his head.

Leland moaned appreciatively.

Constable Clouds slowly turned his teacup in its saucer. "The Dreadnought equipment being forged in Blackhaven seems to be making its way to the general army."

"How long before the attack on Nodia?" Augum asked.

"Hard to say. They will amass an army at the border first. Probably sooner if they get their hands on the Agonex or the last scion, and if they do, I expect many of the cities to fall rather quickly. Regardless, all of Sithesia is in grave danger, even if the other kingdoms are not aware of it yet."

The cabin went quiet.

Mr. Okeke picked up his teacup. "It is easy for us to forget the hardships that exist outside of this isolated village. Trade is dwindling and grain prices are soaring. I fear we shall have to start rationing."

"Agreed, Mr. Okeke," Constable Clouds said with a nod that bounced his triple chins. "Milham has had it better than most. Many a village has succumbed to starvation. The supposed prosperity of raiding Tiberra has not come. The Tiberrans have hidden much of their gold, or burned their fields. Corruption among the troops has further slowed down the promised redistribution of Tiberran wealth. Those who thought invading that kingdom would bring riches and prosperity were fools, yet it is the poor that suffer most. Only the top echelons truly do well. Lord Sparkstone and his minions, for example."

Clouds turned his gaze on Augum and Leera. "Think of all the lovers separated by conscription; the mothers who lost their sons and daughters to fire, famine, or war. Think of the lonely ones that await news that shall never come, for those they love are forever gone, perhaps lying in some bog, after some unknown battle, to be buried in some unmarked grave. Or worse, risen as the dead to serve the Legion anew."

Or like Old Jory. Augum glanced at Leera. He could not imagine being parted from her again. Priya and Jengo. Haylee and Chaska. What would happen to them? Constable Clouds was right. The reality is out there. He hoped it would never fully come to Milham.

Conversation splintered after that. After some peach sweet cake, which Leera had an extra helping of, Mr. Okeke asked Jengo to gather more wood for the fire from the stores.

"Oh, allow me to do it," Mr. Goss said, smiling at Jengo and Priya sitting arm-in-arm together. "Augum, would you mind giving me a hand?"

"Sure, Mr. Goss." Augum untwined himself from Leera and stepped outside into the cool night. The sky overhead was filled with fields of twinkling stars. The tree canopy rustled in a light wind.

"Augum, I have been meaning to speak with you about a small matter," Mr. Goss said as they slowly strode to the stacked pile of cut wood.

Augum crossed his brows, perplexed. "Yes, Mr. Goss?"

"It concerns you and Leera."

"Oh." Augum's stomach rolled.

"I understand how young love is, dear me I do, but I feel I must say something. None of you have parents to care for you and can give you guidance along this path in life. Therefore, I ask you this—do you believe it is wise to be sharing a cabin with Leera at this time?"

Augum gaped. "I … I don't know, Mr. Goss, I haven't thought about it." He curled his toes in his shoes as his cheeks burned. Was Mr. Goss really asking this question?

Mr. Goss smiled as he began loading Augum's arms with logs. "You are a touch unfamiliar with customs, Augum, and everyone is more than forgiving, but all three of you must take on responsibilities parents are normally burdened with. All I ask is that you think about it. You are not, after all, married yet."

"Right," was all Augum managed to mumble.

"And please do not worry, I will not mention any of this to the girls. This is for us men only."

"Right. Uh, thanks, Mr. Goss."

Mr. Goss pushed on his spectacles and gave him a firm nod. "I *am* very proud of you, Augum. Do not forget that."

"Yes, Mr. Goss."

"Good. Now let us nip back inside."

They carried the logs back to the fire, and although Augum sat back down beside Leera, he did not take her hand as before.

The supper dishes were cleared away amidst quiet conversation, and the evening passed by slowly. Bridget spent her time studying the blue book, Jengo the yellow, Priya resting her head on his shoulder. Augum rehearsed some of the lighter spells with Leera and Haylee. Chaska sat quietly speaking to the constable about matters of security. Leland listened to the Orb of Orion while clutching the Agonex, before being forced to give both up as his father took him to bed.

"The tournament begins in a tenday, I believe," Constable Clouds eventually said, readying to depart.

"We'll be studying hard," Bridget said, stuffing the Agonex and the Orb of Orion into a rucksack. "We'll be ready."

"Come, Son."

"I'm sorry for all the trouble I caused," Devon said sheepishly from the doorway.

Bridget smiled at him. "No trouble at all. Good night."

Devon's cheeks reddened. "Good night," and he departed, helping his father along.

"You are welcome to stay the night again," Mr. Okeke said as he washed his face in a basin.

"Thank you, but we need to allow you and Jengo your space too," Bridget replied.

"That really is not necessary—"

"We insist, Mr. Okeke."

Mr. Okeke smiled. "Very well. Then I bid everyone a sweet night."

"Good night, Mr. Okeke," they chorused.

"Priya and Jengo are adorable," Bridget said wistfully as the trio made their way through the dark woods, palms lit. "And Chaska and Haylee seem to be getting along better."

Leera gave her a light punch on the arm. "We'll find you a boy soon too."

Bridget scoffed, gripping her rucksack tighter. "How many times must I tell you, I don't need a boy right now. Too busy."

Leera brought her lit palm close to Bridget's face. "See that, Aug? She's blushing."

Bridget swatted it away. "Nonsense." Nonetheless, she averted her face. "And you're sleeping in the other cabin, Aug; don't want you two smooching and giggling all night. We have a long training day ahead and we need to seriously focus. We only have a tenday to get ready."

"We *do* need a good night's sleep," Augum said, consumed with Mr. Goss' speech. "And … we aren't married, so it's not appropriate."

Leera snorted. "Fine, but since when did you two turn into such prisses?"

Augum shrugged. "There's no rush, that's all."

"Yes, and we could be dead any day now."

There was resentment in Leera's voice, but Augum let it go. She was right, they could die any day from their adventures, and he wanted to be by her side forever, but Mr. Goss was right too—they were young and unmarried. As per custom, it was not appropriate.

At the cabins, Leera's resentment dissipated as she gave him a kiss goodnight. Augum settled himself into the hastily erected cabin across the stream, now furnished with a feathered mattress, twig nightstand, wash basin, a cedar trunk for clothes, and Dramask blanket, almost all provided by Mr. Okeke. He lay there smiling to himself about how crazy this day had been, and promptly fell asleep.

A LETTER

The trio began a grueling training regimen for that final tenday before the Antioc Library quest. They would rise at the crack of dawn in their respective cabins, eat a quick breakfast at the Okeke home, and begin training, often enduring headaches and nose bleeds as a side effect of the boundary-pushing regimen. They would usually start with a full cycle before concentrating on individual spells for hours at a time, repeating the same thing in the afternoon. Augum finally got a basic handle on Summon Minor Elemental, but they all still had trouble with the Reflect spell—only Bridget managed to reflect a Push spell once, sending a surprised Augum tumbling into the stream. At sunset, exhausted and spent, they would gather for supper at the Okeke cabin, where they quietly bantered with various village guests while catching up on news.

The trio slowly bronzed a bit more in the sun. Augum became even leaner, stronger, and walked a little taller. Leera and Bridget thinned a touch, Bridget more so than

Leera (who snuck sweets now and then). Bridget still did not sleep well and had semi-permanent rings under her eyes, and Leera would often be overheard telling her to lighten up. Some days they would all feel the strain, snapping at each other and going for long periods of practice without a word said. Generally, though, they got along as well as friends could under the circumstances. As the days passed, Bridget became more comfortable in her teaching role, but she was still unable to pass on the complex and subtle arcane insights only a high-degree mentor could impart. And as her confidence grew, her nightmares lessened a little.

Meanwhile, Haylee trained Jengo on his 1st degree, practicing her own arcanery when she could, striving for her 2nd. After arguing with Ms. Singh for the umpteenth time, she moved into the cabin with Bridget and Leera, promising not to get in the way of their training. She would often still get frustrated with Chaska or the cane, but put up with both. Augum marveled how much she had improved as a person since they had first met her, and how she constantly strove to become even better. He was glad of her friendship, and enjoyed watching Bridget and even Leera ever steadily warm up to her by exchanging stories, talking about boys, and grooming each other's hair while gossiping about nothing in particular.

Leland continued to quietly spend time with the Agonex and the Orb of Orion. Mr. Goss would often join his son to teach him the written word, history, or other subjects of note. Mr. Goss would also occasionally give Augum a subtle nod. That talk the two had outside the Okeke cabin had been embarrassing for Augum, but he came to understand why it had to happen. Mr. Goss felt responsible for them. He also had to feel like a hesitant father figure, someone who wanted to give them their freedom while being a gentle guide, especially to Augum. Augum did not mind. He could use some guidance in this world, though Mr. Goss had not approached him since, perhaps trusting him to do the right thing. It was something Augum very much appreciated and was conscious of, not wanting to let Mr. Goss down.

At Haylee's urging, Devon became friendlier with Chaska, even joining him on the town watch. The pair also undertook the task of soliciting book donations in their free time. Chaska was getting fitter from the work and seemed to enjoy Devon's friendship, though the occasional light-hearted reprimand for talking too much was not unheard of. As for Devon, he mostly left the trio alone—as did everyone else during the day, for they all understood how vital their training was to the Resistance. They saw nothing of Malaika, Charissa, Annelise or Gabe, though would hear rumors of tantrums and late night arguments.

The trio watched as their infamy steadily grew in the Herald; as armies continued to amass on the Nodian border; as excitement grew for the coming warlock tournament; and yet there still came no news of Mrs. Stone … until the morning of the tenth day, when a grizzled, mud-splattered courier arrived to hand Mr. Okeke a letter at his cabin.

Jengo did not even raise his head from eating his porridge. "Another demand from the Legion for tax moneys, Father?"

Mr. Okeke tipped the courier, thanked him, and closed the door. "Not sure," he said, breaking the wax seal on the weathered yellow parchment. He began pacing as he read. Suddenly, he froze. "It's from Mrs. Stone—"

The trio bolted from the table, knocking over dishes, scrambling to gather around the parchment.

Leera was breathless. "What's it say?"

Mr. Okeke cleared his throat and began reading aloud. His slight Sierran accent gave the words a distant slant. " 'My dears, I hope this letter finds you as I am very far away in a strange land I have never been to before, with even stranger people. Regretfully, I lost the pearl somewhere in southern Tiberra in a battle. I had forgotten to enchant it so I could find it again. Alas, my memory is not as it once was.' "

Bridget placed a hand over her mouth, eyes welling up. Leera laid her head on Bridget's shoulder while giving Augum's hand a tight squeeze. It was a difficult letter to listen to. Augum's heart ached. He missed Nana so much.

Mr. Okeke continued. " 'The spell has been an onerous undertaking under the circumstances, especially as I am already quite old. It is taking its toll. I have developed a bit of a cough, and my spectacles have become inadequate. I have eluded the Legion thus far, but there have been many close calls. The tracking party's prowess has made it impossible for me to visit you at this time. They have proved to be formidable opponents especially well-equipped to thwart me. My days are spent on the road. My feet and bones hurt and I am always tired. I fear I cannot keep this up for much longer. It feels as if there is never enough time now, for time has become a most precious thing indeed. It seems eons ago since I have laid eyes upon you. I yearn for the simple things most—clean linens, a quiet fire, a good book, a warm meal, pleasant company, and above all, watching you grow before my eyes.' "

Haylee gave a sniffle as she drew Leland close. "Oh, Mrs. Stone," she whispered.

Mr. Okeke swallowed and read on. " 'How are your studies coming along? I trust you have been working very hard and pushing yourselves. I trust Mr. Harvus has been a good and thoughtful mentor. Have you discovered anything about the artifact in question yet? Perhaps you will have received this letter before your departure.' "

Mr. Okeke took a deep breath before reading the last portion. " 'I sign off hoping you are all together, that you are warm, safe, in good health and high spirits. Please know that you are in my thoughts often. As for me, my greatest challenge awaits, and that is mastering this formidable spell, and somehow teaching it to you. I only hope to live long enough to accomplish this last act. Remember, my dears, that you are strongest together, that life is precious and short, and that all things must pass. With love and deep affection for you all, AAS.' "

Mr. Okeke stared at the parchment before gently folding it up and handing it to Augum, who held the wrinkled letter close, finger tracing over the broken wax seal. For a long time, nobody spoke.

After quietly settling back at the table, Augum could not resume eating. Nana was out there desperately trying to learn Cron while being chased by that vicious tracking party led by Erika Scarson. He glanced down at the parchment. How long had this letter been in transit? How many leagues had it travelled?

When he glanced up, he caught Bridget's eye, and there was a steely determination there. Leera had the same look. He gave them the subtlest nod, knowing that today was the last day they could prepare for what awaited them, for by tomorrow morning, they would be undertaking a dangerous new quest.

The meal concluded in thoughtful silence, with the trio quickly moving on to training at the grove. Haylee insisted on staying behind with Jengo, where she could continue training with him while minding over Leland. She did it so the trio could focus on what they needed to do, telling them she'd make sure no one unnecessary came to bother them. Augum was grateful. It was their last day and they needed the time together.

It was a sunny morning with not a cloud in sight—perfect training weather. They launched right into the 4th degree—Fear, Deafness, Confusion, Summon Minor Elemental, then worked backwards.

At lunch, Mr. Goss arrived with a basket of food and a sheaf of parchment. He made his presence known by gently clearing his throat.

Augum unclenched his fists, shoulders still tense from summoning Shield ten times in a row to block Bridget and Leera's First Offensive. "Mr. Goss?"

Mr. Goss' eyes travelled over the black pile of destroyed wood, a legacy of their many castings. "You would make for fearsome adversaries."

Leera was hunched over with her hands resting on her knees, a drop of sweat falling from her forehead. "Any news, Mr. Goss?"

"There is. The arrangements for crate teleportation are set. The Eastspear Legion warlock is expected tomorrow morning. We must be ready by then. We will test fit you with the crate before supper tonight. Oh, and I thought you might want to have a last read." He handed a panting Bridget the Blackhaven Herald.

"They still haven't captured Mrs. Stone," Bridget said, scanning the articles.

Mr. Goss smiled as he placed the basket on the ground before them. "I thought you would appreciate that bit of news. All right, I shall leave you to it. Good luck with training today."

"Thank you, Mr. Goss," Bridget replied absently, even though he had already departed. She chortled. "Hey, they supposedly found an Augum Stone only to discover it wasn't you after all. Poor boy went through quite a spectacle, it seems. Paraded him about before presenting him to the Lord of the Legion himself, who had to confirm it wasn't you."

"Embarrassing," Augum said while practicing moving two stones at the same time. "Anything about the tournament?"

Bridget sat down cross-legged, folding her blue robe underneath her, and resumed reading. "Just a bunch of bracket challenges."

Leera sat beside her and leaned over to look. "Two divisions—*Lesser* and *Mid-range*. Ten degrees are battling."

Augum let the rocks fall with a thud. "No *Advanced* or *Legendary*?"

"There never is," Bridget explained, eyes darting across the parchment. "It's considered beneath the dignity of the craft to have high-degree warlocks dueling each other for a silly trophy. Besides, there'd probably be too few combatants."

Leera shrugged while digging around the basket. "I think it'd be neat, but what do I know."

"Temper's dueling," Bridget said.

"Oh?" Leera toned between spoonfuls of potato stew. "Against who?"

"Don't know, some boy."

"Wish I was dueling her."

Augum finally took a seat beside them. "And Robin?"

"Also dueling." Bridget frowned.

Augum reached into the basket and pulled out a small bowl of hot soup. He undid the linen covering. "What is it?"

"He's attained his 4th degree."

Leera choked on her stew. "*What*? How?"

"This might explain it." Bridget began reading an excerpt. " 'Robin Scarson, considered the odds-on favorite in his degree, has recently revealed he has been training with the Lord of the Legion himself.' "

The girls glanced at Augum for his reaction.

"Great," Augum only mumbled. But he still couldn't understand how Robin, that lazy, spoiled brat of a donkey, was advancing so quickly, even with his father's help. No way was he working as hard as they were. It had to be the

Destiny Stone. Why in all of Sithesia had One Eye given it to him?

He dumped his spoon into his stew. "And why can't we have something other than bland, boring potatoes for a change?"

Bridget gave him a sympathetic look. "We're lucky to be eating at all."

He knew she was right. The food shortages were so severe of late that everybody had been reduced to the staples. Word reached them the other day that even the Harouns had to make cutbacks, though Augum suspected it was only because Mr. Haroun finally put his foot down.

Leera resumed eating her stew. "They deserve each other. And who cares who he trains under, we're there for other reasons."

Augum said nothing, forcing himself to eat the stew. He was hungry, after all. Training always demanded a lot of energy, something that showed in their toned bodies.

They soon resumed their grueling training, working non-stop for hours until Mr. Goss returned.

"You three look exhausted," he said, eyeing them as they sat gasping and sweaty. "Ready for the test-fitting?"

Augum stood and stretched out his sore limbs. "Ready." He was nervous about tomorrow, though he didn't want to admit it to the others. What would the ancient library of Antioc be like? Would it be dangerous? How was the Legion presence? Would someone recognize them? It was the last part that scared him most. They would have to take precautions. Keep their hoods up, that kind of thing.

Mr. Goss led them to the village. Bystanders gawked and smiled at the trio as they passed. Many said hello and bless you and good luck on your journey. There were lots of hands to shake, lots of sad but hopeful faces.

"Word sure gets around," Leera muttered, giving a half-hearted smile at a toothless old man that kept bowing and repeating, "Bless the Resistance!"

"I am certain you can rest easy," Mr. Goss said, waving at a middle-aged woman with a wide skirt and a wooden necklace. "Everyone here is on our side. This town has been mostly anti-Legion since the beginning."

"Mostly?" Leera mouthed to Augum.

"Now it's a bastion of resolve and community." Mr. Goss gave them a cheery smile as he walked. "A full third of the book donations must have come from the Harouns, bless their hearts."

Augum supposed that was why they built it in the Haroun cellar, that and the fact the cellar was probably the largest one in town. He glanced up at the house and spotted Malaika at the window. She ducked as soon as their eyes met. He shuddered. Hopefully he wouldn't have to see her inside.

Mr. Goss slowed, a finger over his lips. "Erm, just a word of warning—Mrs. Haroun is not in the best of spirits, so just, ah, stay away from her if you can."

When they came to the door, they heard shouting from within.

"… books! What of our daughter's learning? The one you seem to think is some degenerate liar."

"She takes after her mother, does she not? She lacks discipline."

"Oh, sure, disrespect your own wife, like you always do."

"That is not what I meant—"

"And discipline? Whose fault can that possibly be, Hanad? But by all means, give away our entire book collection, and while you are at it, donate our house too!"

There was an audible sigh. "It is not our entire book collection, and we can do with some charity in our lives.

And as I said before, it is for an important and good cause—"

"Dear me." Mr. Goss cleared his throat loudly before knocking on the door.

"Ah, this must be them. Clayborne—if you please."

There were footsteps before the door opened. Clayborne, the white-haired servant, glanced at their blue robes as if checking to make sure their attire was appropriate, before surrendering a stiff bow. "Please follow me."

Mr. and Mrs. Haroun stood in the parlor, avoiding each other's gaze.

Mr. Haroun greeted them with a strained smile. "Good afternoon. Please allow Clayborne to take you to the cellar. I shall join you in but a moment."

"Perhaps you should help yourself to whatever you like down there," Mrs. Haroun said in lofty tones. "The Unnameables know how much 'charity' is needed around here."

"Good afternoon, Mr. and Mrs. Haroun," Mr. Goss said with an awkward half-bow.

"Please, Albert, call me Hanad, we have worked on the crate too hard together to call each other by formal titles."

"Goodness, I certainly am honored, Hanad." Mr. Goss fumbled to push his spectacles up his nose as his eyes darted to Mrs. Haroun. "Uh, and what a splendid house this is indeed."

"Do you need any of its planks?" Mrs. Haroun asked, arms crossed across her chest. "Perhaps you can make a second crate for our valuables."

"Selma, that is enough—"

As the Harouns jabbed at each other, Augum spotted the head servant's children—Annelise and Gabe, both as pale as ghosts, watching them with those pinkish eyes from the dining room. Annelise quickly glanced down at her feet, cheeks reddening. Gabe was casually staring at them. He had circles under his eyes. Augum subconsciously tensed his forearms.

Clayborne grabbed a lit silver candelabra and opened a door, revealing steps leading down to the cellar. "This way."

"Shyneo," Augum said out of reflex.

Clayborne gasped.

Augum dimmed his palm. "Sorry, didn't mean to scare you."

Clayborne straightened his servant gown. "I was merely expecting … a warning."

Mr. Goss placed a hand on Clayborne's shoulder. "It takes a bit of getting used to, does it not?"

Clayborne gave the hand a sidelong look and Mr. Goss promptly withdrew it.

"Father, may we see them perform arcanery?" Gabe asked from the top of the stairs.

"I hardly think that is appropriate, Son, and mind your tongue unless you are spoken to." Clayborne turned to Mr. Goss. "Please forgive the outburst, Mr. Goss, the boy—"

"—but Father, I wanted to become a warlock, not a stupid servant! I can even cast a spell, watch—"

"Gabe, I said no—! Now attend to the Harouns, I have this under control."

But Gabe raised his hand in defiance of his father anyway, and with a mighty strain that plainly showed on his face, he managed to make it momentarily ripple to life with lightning.

"I am terribly sorry for that," Clayborne cut in, "he shall surely be punished later—"

"You're a lightning warlock!" Bridget said.

Gabe's angular face lit up with a glorious smile. "I am? Like the Lord of the Legion? I mean, of course I am! I have always known it!"

"Cease speaking immediately, Son, else you shall feel the back of my hand—"

"Mr. Clayborne, your son is training wild," Bridget went on, "and if he continues to do so, he may injure himself or even—"

"Then he shall deserve the injury!" Clayborne's face had reddened. He cleared his throat and lightly tapped at his cheeks. "Forgive me, I … I am quite bothered by his … *supernatural* … tendencies. It is the devil's doing, I am sure of it—all witchery is."

"But Mr. Clayborne," Leera interrupted, "arcanery has been around for thousands and thousands of years—"

"So has murder and theft. That does not make it right or holy. Unnameables forgive us for such heathenry. The devil will take us all for our sins and our lack of piety." He closed his eyes and sighed. "Please, this way." He turned his back and descended, indicating an end to the discussion.

Bridget gave Gabe a look but followed. The boy's face was crestfallen.

Augum lingered a moment while the others passed. Part of him wanted to give Gabe a few sharp words for his brazen attempts with Leera. "Be extremely careful casting wild arcanery," he said instead.

Gabe raised his hawk nose much like his father. "I won't stop, no matter what."

Augum shrugged. "Suit yourself," and caught up to the others.

"I wonder if his sister has the aptitude too," Leera whispered as they walked down a long corridor.

"Well they can't train on their own, they'll kill themselves," Bridget replied.

Clayborne brought them into a dusty room filled with furniture covered in white sheets. In the middle sat a gigantic wooden crate surrounded by piles of books.

Mr. Goss gave it a couple knocks with his knuckle. "What do you think?"

Leera cocked her head. "It's huge …"

"Oh dear, do you think it might be beyond the warlock's abilities? The constable requested a highly advanced warlock for the job."

Augum leaned over the neck-height edge of the crate. In the center was a low platform. "Could hide, like, ten people in here."

"Yes, well, the purpose of its size is to truly conceal you all in case someone gets suspicious. There may be an inspection. It is the Legion, after all."

"But only three are going," Mr. Haroun said, entering the room. "Please do climb in and lie down under the center platform."

The trio did as they were told. Mr. Haroun, Mr. Goss and Clayborne then began filling the space with books.

"This might just work," Augum heard Leera say from beside him, her voice muffled by the books.

"I only hope the warlock can manage the size of it," Bridget added from his other side.

"We can still hear you talk out here," Mr. Goss said, voice muted from the books. "You will have to stay absolutely silent."

They kept piling books on until Augum heard the stairs creak.

"I had Briggs acquire us extra Necrophyte robes," said a huffing voice, "in case some did not fit. Bring them here, Son."

"Ah, welcome, Constable Clouds and young Devon," Mr. Haroun said. "What do you think?"

"I do believe it will work," Clouds replied after a moment of inspection. "Can you hear me in there, you three?"

"Yes, Constable," Bridget replied.

"Good, now listen carefully. You will have to come back here in the early morning and be hidden well before the warlock courier comes. He or she has never been to Milham, so will be riding in by horse. You will then be teleported to the Antioc library and are to see Lien Ning immediately. She is the senior arcaneologist there. She's really old and more than a little … eccentric, but she's with the Resistance." He frowned, muttering, "At least, I'm pretty sure she is."

" 'Pretty sure'?" Augum muttered to Leera within the dark crate.

"Are not all arcaneologists eccentric?" Mr. Haroun asked.

"This one especially so," Clouds replied. "You'll see what I mean. Now, she does not expect you three, but I have written a detailed letter you are to give to her. I expect she would welcome the opportunity to help you. After you complete your research, return to her. She should be able to teleport you back somewhere near. Then the challenge will be to find your way back here."

"Great," Leera whispered, "he's not even sure the arcaneologist can teleport us back."

"Or is even on our side apparently," Augum muttered in reply. "We'll bring the map and figure it out." He was not about to abort the quest, regardless of what obstacles lay before them.

"All right, that should be everything," Clouds concluded.

"I'll help dig them out," Devon said giddily, and began taking books off, the others joining in.

"Any questions?" Mr. Haroun asked when they climbed out.

The trio shook their heads.

Clouds gestured at his son. "Good, try the robes."

Devon held a pile of necrophyte robes, each adorned with black and red vertical stripes. "You're supposed to see which fit. Oh, I'm so excited for you! I wish I was going. I bet there's all manner of neat stuff to see. You'll probably meet so many different kinds of warlocks from all over and—"

"Devon, the robes," Constable Clouds said.

"Right, sorry." He extended his arms and they each chose one.

Leera grimaced. "Can't believe I'm trying one of these on."

"Do you know any necromancer spells?" Devon asked as they tried on the variously sized robes.

"Not one," Augum replied, "but Haylee knows a couple."

"This one time," Devon began, "I saw one of the necrophytes actually bring a corpse to life from the ground! Mind you, it was from a distance, but it was horrible, I couldn't stop shaking. She even—"

"Devon, not now, my son."

"Of course. Sorry."

At last, they found the right sizes of robes, placing the remaining ones aside.

The constable turned to the trio, face grave. "Remember the following—don't look superiors in the eye. Don't ask too many questions. Play it meek and quiet. If challenged, say that you are from Blackhaven on a scholarly quest. It's common to have necrophytes go there for study. Go to bed early and get a good night's sleep."

The trio nodded.

"Good, any questions?"

They shook their heads.

"Then we'll see you in the wee hours of the morning."

They thanked Mr. Haroun before departing with Devon, who was joining them for supper, while Mr. Goss stayed behind to dine with the Constable and Mr. Haroun so they may speak more on town defense matters. Augum, who was the last to step through the door, heard a "Psst—

" from nearby. It was Annelise, and she was cringing, but waving him over.

"I'll catch up," he said to the others, receiving a questioning look from Leera.

Annelise shrank and swallowed as he approached. "Hi," she squeaked.

"Hello, Annelise. What is it?"

Annelise rubbed her arm. "It's about my brother ..." She glanced about timidly.

"Take your time."

"Malaika made my brother go after your girlfriend."

"Oh." Somehow, that didn't surprise Augum in the least. In fact, it made a lot of sense. Gabe hadn't even glanced at Leera since. Obviously Malaika had to have given up on that stupid plan.

"Thank you, Annelise."

Annelise nodded quickly. "I just ... I just wanted you to know the truth, that's all."

"You're a good person. And I'm sure so is your brother." Augum turned to leave.

"Good luck tomorrow!" she blurted, wringing her hands and avoiding eye contact.

Was it just him or did she have something more to say? He didn't want to press the poor girl though, and so he only smiled. "Thanks, going to need it," and strode off.

"What was that all about?" Leera asked back in the cabin.

"Nothing you probably didn't already suspect," and he filled her in on what Annelise had said.

"Guess I shouldn't be surprised, but it's amazing she thought something that stupid would work," Leera muttered with a chortle, entwining her fingers with Augum's.

Back at the Okeke home, they returned to planning. While receiving the usual earful of stories and questions from Devon, the trio soon decided that the Orb of Orion and the Agonex would stay with Leland and Mr. Goss, not that they could take them along anyway seeing as Mrs. Stone cast an anti-teleportation enchantment on the artifacts. They also decided on false names to use in front of people—Augustus for Augum, Brie for Bridget, and Leigh for Leera, just for easy memory sake. Last time Augum chose an odd public name he had forgotten it. Despite the fact he was not coming along, Devon thought of one for himself too—Derius, along with a detailed history of why he would be going and what he would get up to.

The potato-laden supper was a simple and nostalgic affair. Jengo, Priya, Chaska, Haylee, and Leland joined Augum, Bridget, Leera and Devon. They shared stories, jokes, and hopes. After a while, with their bellies full of a special carrot cake Haylee and Chaska prepared, they sat by the fire drinking sweet pine tea, saying little and watching the flames dance. Then the trio excused themselves for bed early. After washing up, they slept in the training cabins once again, the night cool and quiet. Augum had a hard time falling asleep, thoughts full of the tournament, the library, and the dangerous quest to come. Judging by the restless sounds in the other cabin, he suspected he wasn't the only one.

THE CRATE

Mr. Goss awoke the trio well before sunrise. Everyone had dark circles under their eyes. The morning quickly proved a flurry of activity, with numerous hands pitching in with a breakfast of potatoes and some specially procured bacon, leek soup, and raspberry pie, the last courtesy of Huan, the innkeeper at the Miner's Mule Inn. Blue robes were exchanged for black and red necrophyte ones. The map was folded neatly into a black reinforced snakeskin pouch—chosen to blend in with necromantic fashion—along with a generous 100 gold, 50 silver and 50 copper coins. Augum had never seen a gold coin before and had to take a moment to study it, only to receive quite a shock—on one side was the chiseled and skull-like face of his father wearing a crown, above which were the words *Eternal Service to our Esteemed Lord of the Legion*. On the other was the burning sword of the Legion and the words *Duty unto death*. He had heard Legion coinage was being used in the cities, but hadn't yet seen it in the countryside.

Of course, it made sense it would take time for the coins to filter out to the smaller towns and villages, replacing the old crowns of King Ridian.

"Do I pass as one of them?" Bridget asked, giving a twirl in her necrophyte robe after securing the snakeskin pouch to her waist.

"I could see you raising the dead already," Leera replied, shoveling the last of her bacon into her mouth.

"He's on a coin?" Augum asked, looking around at them all.

For a moment no one spoke.

"I thought you were aware," Mr. Okeke said. "It was in the Herald. All coins are to be exchanged at a constabulary for Legion versions."

"Oh." Augum gave Bridget the coin to put in her pouch.

Jengo barely touched his food. "I'm nervous for you three, but I'm sure you won't die a horrible death doing this crazy quest."

Leera stared at him. "Thanks … thanks for that vote of confidence, Jengo."

Leland moaned, hands firmly clutching the Agonex.

Augum couldn't recall the last time he had seen him play with anything else. He gave Leland a light elbow. "Our little general is going to coordinate the Resistance while we're gone."

Leland moaned again, this time louder and shorter.

Augum raised his hands in surrender. "All right, all right. We'll be careful, we promise."

Mr. Goss kept readjusting his spectacles. "In all seriousness though, please do be mindful of yourselves. You are going without Mrs. Stone's help, and your face is on every poster—"

"You mean that poorly drawn attempt depicting a squirrel and a blob of freckles, Mr. Goss?" Leera pointed out.

"Nonetheless, I must ask you to be conservative, thoughtful, pragmatic, cautious, safe, and take risks only when absolutely necessary—"

"—we will, Mr. Goss," Leera said with a quick eye-roll at Augum. "We've done crazier things before."

There was a knock at the door. When Mr. Okeke opened it, Devon spilled inside. Augum glimpsed a sea of faces behind him that began talking all at once.

"What, has the whole village come to see them off?" Jengo asked. "Great, word is definitely going to get out we've been harboring fugitives. I can just see the fires licking at the door."

"Son, please." Mr. Okeke gave Jengo a tired look. "You know we have been having regular town meetings. Everybody is firmly on board, I assure you. Do not underestimate how much thought the constable and Mr. Haroun and everyone else involved has put into this." He offered Devon a place at the table, along with some leek soup.

"Thank you, Mr. Okeke," Devon said, taking a seat beside Bridget. "I couldn't sleep I was so excited! Father says what you three are doing is going to be written into the history books along with tales of Codus Trazinius, Selma and Sinna Trailweaver, or even Atylla the Mighty! I think you're true heroes—and you're already quite famous, I know—but I think this is going to change the course of the war, I really do. I also think—"

Mr. Okeke leaned down beside the boy. "Devon."

"Yes, Mr. Okeke?"

Mr. Okeke smiled and patted Devon's shoulder. "Eat your breakfast."

Devon blushed. "Yes, Mr. Okeke."

Mr. Okeke began pouring everyone tea. "Our brave threesome is going to do the best they can. We must let them enjoy the journey, not worry over it."

"But Father, how are we going to control what everyone says? I'm starting to get quite concerned."

"Leave that to us, Jengo. We old folks know a thing or two about keeping people in line. Remember that the threat of a Legion questioning holds tremendous weight. Also, vows of secrecy matter when attached to loved ones, and not a soul remains in Milham that has *not* taken the vow. And since we no longer receive visitors into town like we used to, it is easier to keep everyone in line."

"Am I supposed to be reassured by that, Father? Because I don't feel any—"

"—Jengo—"

"—I mean, the chance of discovery and dying—"

"Jengo!" Mr. Okeke gave his son a meaningful but hard look.

Jengo' eyes flicked to the trio. "Sorry."

There was a double knock at the door.

Mr. Okeke's ebony face lit up. "Ah, that should be the constable and Mr. Haroun." He let them in.

Augum noticed Lieutenant Briggs and Sergeant Cobb stationed outside the door, controlling the crowd. The thought that this was getting out of hand returned. He had to agree with Jengo—how could word possibly *not* get out? It took a lot of restraint for him not to tell everyone in that room to get out of Milham as soon as he and the girls left for the library. He simply had to trust they knew what they were doing.

Clouds waddled in with his cane, Legion robe flowing around his bulk. "How do you three feel? Get a good night's sleep?"

"They're excited!" Devon said with a gigantic smile, "but super nervous too, I'm sure."

"Will the money be ample enough?" Mr. Haroun asked, hands behind his back. "Because I can bring more."

Bridget dropped her eyes. "Should be more than enough, Mr. Haroun, thank you, very generous of you."

"Good. I am going to instruct the villagers to go about their business in a quiet manner and to remember their vow of secrecy. We are a tight-knit community here though so I expect no trouble. In a moment, the constable is going to take you to the crate. You will climb in and await the arrival of the Legion warlock courier." He glanced between them while taking a breath. "Are you prepared for this quest?"

Augum's stomach buzzed with butterflies. "We are, Mr. Haroun."

"Then let us get to it. Excuse me." Mr. Haroun left the cabin, immediately greeted by the throng. He began speaking to them in a calm manner, voice muted through the door.

Bridget paced back and forth while Leera absently chewed on her fingernails. Haylee stared at the fire, repeatedly straightening a lock of long blonde hair between her fingers, cane by her side. Jengo kept fidgeting with the blue book, which he had vowed to study at length while they were gone. Devon kept rubbing his hands together, looking like he wanted to start conversation, but was held back by his father, who had a firm hand on his shoulder the entire time.

The noise outside eventually died down as people dispersed.

Constable Clouds used his son's shoulder to heave himself to a standing position, other hand shaking on his cane from the strain. "It is time. It would be best for you to say your goodbyes now. As discussed, we do not want to make the Legion warlock suspicious, do we?" And so everyone gathered before the fire where hugs and well wishes were exchanged.

"Find your way back to us," Haylee whispered as she finished hugging the trio, wiping her eyes. "And Chaska wishes you the best of course. I'd so be coming along to help, but a bunch of those necrophytes know me. I'd be recognized instantly." She gave her leg a rancid look. "Not to mention I'd only slow you down …"

"We understand," Bridget said with a compassionate smile. "And thank you."

"Don't die," Jengo said, swallowing hard as his towering, gangly frame wrapped all three of them in one big hug. "I'll be studying very hard and thinking of you all."

Mr. Okeke wrapped each of their hands in his, giving a firm shake. "Mind yourself and be careful," he said to each of them. "May the Fates guide your path."

And so it went. It was the longest goodbye Augum had ever experienced. It made his heart ache. It also made him realize he was not very fond of long goodbyes.

Leland was the last; he reluctantly let go of Bridget, still clutching the Agonex with tiny fingers. She whispered they would return and wiped his tear-stained cheeks. The trio then solemnly departed with Mr. Haroun, Constable Clouds, Devon, Lieutenant Briggs and Sergeant Cobb. Villagers kept a respectful distance, but all snuck peeks at the three hooded necrophytes quietly making their way to the Haroun home. Augum felt like it was some kind of strange procession, almost funereal. He could not help thinking that all it took was one of those people to inform the Legion and claim a great prize. He had a sour feeling about so many people knowing who they were, and had to keep telling himself to trust the constable and Mr. Haroun and everyone else involved with the town's defense.

Clayborne greeted them at the door with a stiff bow. "Follow me, please." He led them past a stone-faced Mrs. Haroun and a sullen Annelise, who gave Augum a meaningful look he did not understand, before taking them down to the cellar, where Gabe was placing books into the crate.

Clayborne stiffened. "Son, what are you doing here?"

"Just helping, Father. I shall see myself out."

"That you will, and immediately."

Gabe kept his head down while he shuffled by and zipped up the steps. How odd, Augum thought.

"A reminder that the Legion warlock has never been here before," Clouds said as they lined up before the crate. It was mostly full of books already, leaving a gap for them to climb into. "And has therefore had to ride here from Eastspear, departing before sunrise. I shall greet the person at the entrance to town. We expect the warlock soon, so it is best that you hurry. Devon will help hide you."

Clouds let go of his son's shoulder and reached out to each of them, shaking their hands. "May the Unnameables light your way," he said after letting go of Augum's hand. "And remember—do not speak of the Agonex or the scions to anyone. Do not reveal who you are; use disguises. Do not befriend lightly. Do not trust lightly."

"Thank you, Constable," Augum said. "We will be careful."

Devon could not look any of them in the eye. His lip trembled and he said nothing.

"Goodbye, Devon," Bridget said at last. "Wish us luck."

Devon sniffed and nodded. "I … I wish you all the luck in Sithesia. May the Unnameables watch over you … and stuff."

"I shall leave you to your brave quest," Clouds said, departing, cane prodding at the floor. He turned to look them over one last time from the staircase. "The kingdom needs you," and he left, muttering, "So brave for ones so young …"

Mr. Haroun stepped forward, shaking each of their hands. "I wish you nothing but success. Be careful, stay alert, and watch out for each other."

"We will, Mr. Haroun," Bridget replied.

Mr. Haroun reached into a pocket and withdrew a wax-sealed letter. "This is for the senior arcaneologist, Lien Ning."

Bridget received the letter. "Thank you."

Mr. Haroun smiled before gesturing welcomingly at the crate. One by one, the trio climbed in, settling at the bottom. Mr. Haroun and Devon, the latter sniffling throughout, began burying them with books.

Augum and Leera found each other's hand and squeezed. The candlelight steadily dimmed, finally obscured completely by books. The trio stayed silent throughout, breathing short bursts in the confined space, which quickly grew hot and dark.

"I'll come and give you a warning when the warlock is almost here," they heard Devon say, his voice muffled as it fought through the piles of books.

"He better arrive soon," Leera whispered after Devon departed. "Can barely breathe in here."

Augum tried to keep his breathing even, thinking this had to be the most uncomfortable space he had ever been in.

Bridget's breathing was the fastest though. "Can't stand cramped spaces," she muttered.

"Hang in there, Bridge," Augum said. He recalled the cave under Bahbell and how Bridget had struggled. Poor thing.

Finally, Devon's voice rang out. "She's coming, she's coming—! The Legion warlock is here! Good luck, you three!" His footsteps echoed in the cellar, muffled by the heaps of books the trio was buried under.

Soon there were more footsteps, and this time the trio held their breath.

"It is here, Ms. Terse," said the wheezing constable.

"What is this? Are you transporting an entire library?" came a piercing female voice. "A bit overzealous with the confiscations, were you not?"

"I find it is best to keep the villagers as ignorant as possible, Ms. Terse. It serves our Lordship's interests best. And not all are confiscations. Milham is a proud supporter of the Legion. Many of these books have been donated by the local populace who are eager to see the Legion succeed. They recognize sacrifices have to be made for future necrophytes."

Augum could almost feel Leera smirking. He squeezed her hand in acknowledgment of Constable Clouds' deft handling of the Legion warlock.

"That is all well and good, but the object is much larger than I usually teleport. It's going to cost you more."

There was the sound of a bag of coins clinking. "I believe you shall find this adequate compensation for your troubles," Mr. Haroun replied.

"Ah, that will indeed do."

"Now if you would be so kind, Ms. Terse," Clouds continued, "please teleport this crate to Lien Ning, the senior arcaneologist in the Antioc libr—"

"—I know who she is," Ms. Terse interrupted. "The old lunatic receives a parcel every tenday regarding some fine point in arcanery. I do believe chicken scratchings would shed more light on any subject than the ravings of that shriveled thing."

"Nonetheless, the Legion is grateful for your services."

"Is it now? And when am I going to attain this so-called 'eternal life' gratitude supposedly bestows?"

There was a marked pause. "I shall pretend I did not hear that, Ms. Terse."

Clouds was indeed skilled at this, Augum thought.

"Forgive me, Constable, I forget myself." There was the sound of swishing fabric as someone strolled near. "Stand back, please." After a moment of silence, "Impetus peragro obiectum massus!"

But nothing happened except a groan.

"It's too heavy. You're going to have to lose some books."

There was a marked silence.

"Of course," the constable eventually said. "Devon, give us a hand."

There was a stuttering sound and quick footsteps.

Augum swallowed. He could barely breathe as the sound of books thumping against the ground echoed in the cellar.

"Try now, Ms. Terse."

"Constable, I do not think that is enough—"

"Ms. Terse, every book removed is one fewer book for our young necrophytes, the very future of the Legion."

"As you wish." After another moment of concentrated silence, "Impetus peragro obiectum massus!" and Augum felt himself and the crate yank.

THE ANCIENT LIBRARY OF ANTIOC

Being pulled apart in all directions while tumbling end-over-end only to wake up in a tight, dark space was enough to make Augum nearly throw up. He had not prepared for teleporting in such a manner, and judging by their silent writhing, neither had Bridget and Leera. It was a hard struggle not to make any noise as they heard quick, clacking footsteps approach.

"Giant crate of books for the lunatic, Prudence," Ms. Terse said.

"Jezebel," replied a squeaky female voice. "Did not expect to see you back so soon."

There was a barely audible noise not unlike a shrug. "This one paid well. Some fat constable and his contribution to necrophyte knowledge. Bunch of confiscations, blah, blah, blah. The usual."

There was a small snort of laughter. "What, did he hide himself in it? It's huge."

A wave of fear rippled down Augum's spine, combining with the nausea from teleporting. Oh no, were they going to search the crate?

"My thoughts exactly," Ms. Terse replied. "I'm willing to bet not one of these books has anything to do with arcanery."

"I'm of the same mind. Every eager constable from here to Dramask seems to think they can curry favor by 'contributing to the pool of knowledge'. Fools. They must think we have an unlimited supply of attendants to catalog and sort it all, forgetting most had been snatched for the war effort. What a waste of talent, if you ask me."

Ms. Terse sighed. "I should see her and get this signed in."

"She's busy berating the head examiner for volunteering as a judge in the tournament."

"So she'll be a while."

"You know how she is. Tea?"

"You're a shining light in this dark dungeon, Prudence."

"If only everyone else thought so. Guards here are about as sharp as a cake knife. Speaking of which, how does a bite of candied Tiberran apple sound?"

"In these times? That would be marvelous ..." Ms. Terse's voice trailed as the two women departed, one set of footsteps soft and relaxed, the other quick and noisy.

Just as Augum was about to whisper if everyone was all right, there was the sound of vomiting—*except it did not come from the trio*.

"Who's there?" Leera hissed.

There was a whimper and a muffled gagging. Suddenly there was another vomiting noise, this time from a new source, just as close, but from a different corner of the crate.

"What's going on here, who is that—?" Bridget whispered.

A panting and groaning. "Gods, I'm covered in my own filth, someone help me."

Augum immediately recognized that voice. Bumps rose on his arms. "Malaika—?"

There was a cough and another groan. "Ugh, I'm not feeling well."

This time it was Leera's turn to be incredulous. "Charissa—?"

"I need to get out of here," Malaika said in a panicked voice. "I can't breathe, and the stench—Unnameables help me before I—"

"Shh, someone's coming!" Bridget hissed, and everyone inside the crate fell silent.

"... said to me, 'I can teleport too, you just watch!' and do you know what happened?" Ms. Terse asked.

"I could scarcely guess, but knowing your other stories, something gruesome," Jezebel replied.

"The poor boy teleported all right—they unearthed him two days later *underneath* the spot he tried to teleport from. I swear these necrophytes are dumber than beheaded chickens."

"They don't train warlocks like they used to."

"You're damn right they don't. All they care about is training them how to raise corpses and kill things; hardly room for minutia. No wonder most of the poor wretches don't make it past the second degree. And guess how many healers are being trained? That's right—*zero*. You believe that? Necromancy is apparently more important!"

"Not to mention all the good teachers have fled—"

"—or been murdered."

There was a dual sigh.

"Did ... did they raise the boy?" Prudence asked, taking a bite of what Augum could only assume was a candied apple.

"What do you think?"

"Unnameables ..."

"That's right, used as a *teaching* example on how to raise a freshly-killed seventeen-year-old boy from the grave."

"I think I'm going to be sick."

"Speaking of which, what's that smell?"

The two women sniffed at the air as Augum stiffened.

"Must be a dead rat in the crate or something," Ms. Terse said.

"You sure that fat constable isn't in there?"

The two women laughed.

"PRUDENCE!" roared an arcanely amplified voice that echoed off what sounded like stone walls.

There was a deep sigh. "Gods, what is it now ..."

"Probably wants you to change her floating chamber pot."

"Stop it, you'll get me in trouble again. And don't you even think about making it do tricks behind her back."

"Wouldn't dream of it."

"PRUDENCE—! HOW MANY TIMES MUST—"

"I should go. Why don't you just fly off, I'll sign the crate in for you."

"Thanks, Prudes, you're a soul."

"I hate that nickname."

"Comes from love, you little thing. See you."

"Bye, Jez. Oh, and let's have wine again at the Hilt next time."

"When I'm not working. Maybe we'll see if you can make it through a glass. Impetus peragro atto." There was a THWOMP sound.

"PRUDENCE—!"

There was a long sigh. "Coming, Senior Arcaneologist Ning!"

"What the heck are we going to do with them?" Leera asked.

"We have to send them back somehow," Bridget replied.

"You're not sending us anywhere!" Malaika said. "We've come for adventure. We've come to help—"

"—and we've come to see the tournament!" Charissa added.

Augum couldn't stop himself. "Are you mad? Have you two completely lost your minds? We're on a vital quest and you … you …"

"Isn't it marvelous?" Malaika said. "I had Gabe working on the crate all night, getting our places set up just right. We got in before you showed up. Thought we were done for when the books started coming off. I think I only have *one* layer left—"

Augum's fists clenched. "Do you realize how much danger you put us all in—"

"—shh! Someone's coming!"

"What is this?" barked a deep and wheezy voice.

"It's a crate, Your Brilliance."

Augum wondered how the other person got there as he only heard one pair of footsteps.

There was a pause. "How did you come to serve me?"

"My work ethic. My ability to catalogue effectively, organize efficiently, command—"

"Not your brains, you palpably obtuse shrunken beetle?"

There was a pause.

"It was not my brains, Your Brilliance. I apologize for stating the obvious." Prudence's voice was even, as if she was used to being insulted in such a manner. "Legion confiscations and contributions."

"You signed for it?"

"I did."

"Have the juniors catalogue it."

"I am afraid there is quite a backlog, Your Brilliance."

A marked silence.

"I'll have it done right away, Your Brilliance."

"And Secretary Klines?"

"Yes, Senior Arcaneologist Ning?"

Another pause. "That is all."

"Your Brilliance." There was the slightest whooshing sound. Augum wondered what it was.

A long sigh. Then the clacking footsteps started again. Augum suddenly realized this Prudence Klines was on her way to get the juniors, whoever they were, and they couldn't afford to be found this way by others. He made a snap judgment and called out. "Wait! Uh, Ms. Prudence Klines!"

The clacking footsteps immediately stopped.

"Don't be alarmed, Secretary Klines," Augum hastily said from within the book pile, fully realizing how ridiculous it sounded. "We're here to, uh, to see Lien Ning in secret."

"Damn it, Jez, I told you to inspect all the shipments," the Secretary Klines muttered to herself. "GUARDS—"

"NO—!" Augum immediately shouted. "I mean, please, don't get the guards. Trust us, you don't want to do that. We have to see Mrs. Ning immediately. Please, can you help us? It's urgent."

"We have a letter—" Bridget chimed in.

"There's more than one of you—?"

"Uh, yes, there's, uh, five of us," Augum said.

"Five?"

"Five."

There was a pause in which Augum could hear his heart hammering against his chest.

A sigh as the clacky footsteps drew near. "I don't know why I'm doing this." The books started coming off quickly, far quicker than if someone was doing it by hand—had to be Telekinesis.

"Oh, hi there," Charissa said nervously.

"Get out and sit where I can see you. And don't try anything."

"Yes, ma'am."

"Secretary Klines."

"I mean, Secretary Klines."

Soon they were all out of the crate, sitting in a tight, nervous bunch, hoods drawn. Augum had a quick look around. They were in a huge gently curving flagstone hallway lined with pedestals featuring marble busts. The ceiling was arched with massive beam supports. Ornate iron sconces jutted from the gray walls at even intervals, each lit with a fat candle. Great portrait paintings hung behind each bust, depicting that person in study, battle, or some other occupation. The occasional deep-ledged window let in bright morning light. The air smelled of cleaning mint and musty books.

Before them stood a tiny beetle-like woman dressed in a gray scholar's robe embroidered with a small crimson gargoyle. The gargoyle was surrounded by a crimson oval and appeared to be reading a book. The pages of the book turned now and then, reminding Augum of Mrs. Stone's embroidered robe and how the lightning used to flash.

Secretary Klines gave each of them a studied look with eyes greatly magnified by thick spectacles much too large for her face. "Necrophytes. Figures. Why would you bother coming in through a crate?" She glanced down the hall as if considering changing her mind about the guards.

Augum wondered how the stowaways got their hands on necrophyte robes. As much as he wanted to yell at them, now was not the time. And as far as the secretary's question was concerned, he thought it best to tell her right away. Something about her gave him a good feeling. He only hoped he was right. "We're not necrophytes," he said. "We're, uh—"

"On a quest," Bridget interrupted. "And it's urgent we see Arcaneologist Ning."

"*Senior* Arcaneologist Ning." Klines' dark hair was done up in a bun as tight as her face.

"Senior, right."

She glanced at Malaika and Charissa's soiled robes with a revolted expression and sighed. "Her Brilliance will never see you looking like that." She turned on her heel and clacked her way to a large black oak door. She waved impatiently and it sprang open. She made another gesture and a pitcher of water floated over, along with a rag. The items placed themselves at their feet. "Clean yourselves at once."

Malaika picked up the cloth with two fingers. "Don't … don't you have servants?"

"*Excuse me?*"

"Nothing, Secretary Klines," Malaika and Charissa mumbled, and they began cleaning their robes while Augum and Leera glared.

"Remove your hoods."

They exchanged glances but did as they were told.

Secretary Klines scanned their faces, doing a double-take on Augum. "Have we met before?"

"No."

"You look familiar."

"I …"

"We need to speak to Mrs. Ning," Bridget said.

"*Your Brilliance* or *Senior Arcaneologist Ning,* if you value your hides. And if you remind her of her husband …" She left the rest unsaid.

"Yes, Secretary Klines, and thank you," Bridget said.

"Don't thank me just yet. You may end up getting arrested and put to the question should Senior Arcaneologist Ning deem it so." Secretary Klines folded her arms, tapping at her elbow, waiting for Malaika and Charissa to finish cleaning themselves. Meanwhile a young man in a gray scholar robe appeared at one end of the corridor, slowly washing the flagstone floor with a mop. He glanced up. Soon as he saw Klines, he sped up his pace.

"Hurry up," Leera hissed at the stowaways. "And I can't *believe* you two."

"This better be important," Secretary Klines said, flicking her wrist at the water and cloth. They were yanked out of their hands and zoomed back into the room. The heavy oaken door closed with a light click.

"Get up." She gestured for them to go first. "This way."

They did as they were told, Augum leading. He drew his hood.

"Hoods stay down," Secretary Klines barked.

They walked along the corridor, coming to a finely carved and exquisitely painted pair of giant oak doors, depicting a wise-looking crimson gargoyle reading a book. Behind the gargoyle teetered piles of tomes and scrolls.

Klines made a gesture and the doors opened soundlessly. Beyond was a vast round room with a giant desk in the center, covered in scrolls, parchments and quills. The walls were completely covered by glass-front bookcase cabinets. The bookcases continued skyward along the wall, all the way to the glass-domed ceiling, which had to be a hundred feet above them. And there, high amongst the bookcase cabinets, drifted an ornate throne-like chair.

Augum barely noticed the great double doors close soundlessly behind him. He watched mesmerized as a cabinet door closed high above, only for another to open on the far opposite side. A book soundlessly floated out, opening in time to meet the figure in the chair, who had floated over to meet it. The person, unseen from below, scanned the page only a moment before the book closed itself and returned to the case.

"Can we talk to her?" Bridget whispered, cringing. Augum didn't blame her—place was so quiet even her whispering felt too loud.

Secretary Klines kept her neck craned and raised a single stubby finger, indicating for them to wait.

They watched as the chair floated noiselessly from one cabinet to the next, with not a sound uttered throughout. Augum took the time to marvel at the sheer size of the room. It was gargantuan. The flooring was smooth stone, depicting a coiling pattern that centered at the desk. Every bookcase was intricately carved, as was the ink-stained desk.

"Secretary Klines," a clear but wheezy voice from above at last rang out, echoing along the curved walls.

"Your Brilliance. You have visitors. Necrophytes, uh, without an appointment."

"They are not necrophytes."

"How did—" Leera began to say but was immediately stopped short by a warning look from Klines.

The chair slowly hovered down to them, revealing a withered old woman with a shriveled body, dressed in a faded gray robe similar to Secretary Klines'. Her throne-like chair was carved in the form of a miniature castle—the supports were battlements, the arms draw-bridges, the backrest a castle facade tapering to a series of minarets. Runes and depictions of gargoyles were strategically carved into the chair throughout.

Secretary Klines made a small but sharp gesture, hissing, "Bow!"

They immediately did as she ordered.

Senior Arcaneologist Lien Ning soundlessly floated before each of them in turn, settling on Augum last.

Augum studied her as much as she did him. Her skin was pockmarked and blotchy. There was only the barest tuft of hair left on an emaciated scalp. Her hands were completely closed in on themselves, veins black. Curled-back lips revealed rotten teeth, and her almond eyes were so dark they reminded Augum of the Leyan elders. There was also the faint scent of cloves.

"Augum Stone."

Augum suddenly realized her lips weren't moving. The voice came from her, but was spoken arcanely.

Secretary Klines gasped, then immediately caught herself. She studied Augum, glancing nervously at the door, but said nothing.

Bridget shakily raised the letter. "We have—" but it was arcanely yanked from her hand, opening itself in time to meet the ancient arcaneologist's glare.

"You are late, Mr. Stone," Arcaneologist Ning stated as the letter burst into flames, disappearing into nothing before their eyes.

"I … I am?"

Secretary Klines suddenly stiffened with understanding, but said nothing.

Arcaneologist Ning's crisp arcane voice echoed off the walls as well as in Augum's head. "I was expecting you yesterday. I was expecting you here in this room yesterday. You dawdle almost as much as my useless husband." Her black eyes flicked to Bridget and Leera. The action demanded she move her chair slightly, for her neck and body did not move. "There was to be a Mr. Augum Stone. There was to be a Miss Bridget Burns, and there was to be a Miss Leera Jones. But these others …"

Malaika curtsied with a simpering smile. "I am Miss Malaika Har—" but suddenly her voice was gone. Her lips moved but no sound came out. She felt her throat with a shaking hand, cheeks reddening.

Arcaneologist Ning's black eyes roved over their hastily washed necrophyte garments.

Malaika swallowed, tried to say something, and straightened herself when she realized it was fruitless.

Arcaneologist Ning floated before her. "A waste of time is who you two are. Direction—that is what you require, for you are lost."

A fine porcelain bowl lifted off the desk and floated over. It hovered before Leera.

Ning's chair adjusted so she faced Leera. "You strike me as someone who likes sweets."

Leera flinched in surprise. She opened her mouth to say something but, glancing at Malaika, instead took a mint and slowly placed it on her tongue.

A mint jumped out of the bowl and floated over to Arcaneologist Ning, forcing itself through her rotten teeth. "I like sweets too." The bowl then returned to the desk.

Leera forced a smile and dropped her eyes.

Arcaneologist Ning floated before Augum, staring at him too long for his comfort. She did not blink, just stared. "Do you believe yourself capable of this?" she finally asked, lips unmoving.

Augum hadn't the faintest idea what she was talking about. "Uh, I guess so."

"You guess so."

Secretary Klines gave him a pointed look.

"I'm capable of this," he corrected.

"Are you certain?"

"I am."

Ning studied him. "You might not be."

He did not reply. Did she mean he might not be certain or that he might not be capable of … whatever it was she was referring to?

The chair floated before Bridget. "The cliff awaits."

Bridget paled.

"Do you fear it?"

Bridget surrendered a slight nod. "I cannot sleep. I do fear it."

"Wise of you."

The chair floated before Leera. The voice was cold. "Graceless."

Leera stared into those black eyes and her lip trembled. Augum wanted to reach out and grab her hand, to tell her that she wasn't *hopelessly* graceless—

"I was once graceless," Arcaneologist Ning proclaimed. "I still am."

Leera swallowed, forcing a weak smile.

"You have heart, Miss Jones, but do you have too much?"

Leera's hands twisted before her. "I ... I don't think so."

"Hmm." She studied Leera a moment longer before floating back a little. The ancient arcaneologist glanced at Augum, Bridget and Leera once again. "A mischievous trio. Mischief is the root of adventure." The chair faced Secretary Klines. "No special privileges. Initiate for three, guest for two. Discretion, but as they please." Her chair turned to the trio. "This is a place of learning, all kinds of learning. But you will be challenged. Tradition demands it so."

Secretary Klines gave a short bow. "Your Brilliance. Excuse me but, about Mr. Stone, Miss Jones, and Miss Burns—"

The chair froze. "Do I enjoy repeating myself, Beetlebreath?"

"Of course not. My apologies, Your Brilliance."

The chair began floating upwards. "And remember—discretion, Secretary Klines. Discretion ..."

"Your Brilliance." Secretary Klines made a sharp gesture at the doors and they silently swung open. She gave them a pointed look and the lot of them filed out.

TOURNAMENT

"What's going on, who is she?" Malaika pleaded as the group made its way down the hall.

"A most frightening countenance," Charissa whispered, clutching Malaika's necrophyte robe.

Secretary Klines gave them a warning look. "Shh!" and gestured for them to raise their hoods. They did so just as they passed more gray-robed figures, all of whom glanced their way curiously. Augum had the impression this area was usually off-limits to necrophytes.

Secretary Klines arrived at a handle-less oaken door carved with a single oval. She waved idly and it opened inward, revealing a spacious black stone room with a high ceiling. It seemed to be completely barren, other than simple torch sconces that burned low, throwing countless fiery reflections along the polished mirror-like walls.

She led them to one of the walls. Augum saw a thinly-etched oval there beside which were the words *General*

Quarters. He noticed other ovals too, all spread evenly around the room. There had to be dozens.

"Shyneo," Secretary Klines said. Her hand coiled with gray, smoky light. She pressed her hand against the oval and said, "Secretary Klines." A much larger oval immediately ruptured to life beside her, able to fit a very tall person. A light wind sprang from it, blowing at their hair and robes.

"*Don't* get sick." Secretary Klines then gestured impatiently and they filed through, spilling out onto a red carpet in a castle hallway lined with countless doors. Malaika and Charissa moaned, clutching their stomachs, but kept control.

"Follow me." Secretary Klines' clacking disappeared into the high pile of the lush carpet. This hallway curved much like the other and was just as quiet, but was smaller, cozier. The sconces were hooded, casting a warm and dim glow. There were no windows. Each room had a number—1057, 1058 … Secretary Klines led them to room 1099, pressed her hand where there should have been a doorknob, and whispered, "Secretary Klines." The door soundlessly swung inwards, revealing a spacious room with a leaded-glass window at the far end. She herded them inside and gestured at the door, which closed silently.

The room was sparse with simple mahogany furnishings—a study table, three beds with three small foot boxes, and two folding wooden privacy screens between the beds. The large central carpet, on the other hand, was a rich and colorful tapestry depicting knights, gargoyles, demons, peasants, and even a dragon. They surrounded a towering castle as if defending it from an outside force. The edges of the carpet were filled with exquisitely ornate books and runes. There was one other door in the room, which led to an equally simple bathing room and privy.

Klines stood behind them, arms crossed. "You will note there are no sconces here. That is because you are warlocks and expected to light your own way."

Charissa hurried to the window. "Oh my," she said, hand over her mouth.

The five of them crowded near the deep window ledge and could not help but gasp at the view. They were so high up not a sound from below reached them. A sprawling, walled city lay before them, with its own divided districts, or perhaps quarters, Augum did not know. For a moment, he forgot why he was here and marveled at the sight, unable to contain his excitement at possibly being able to explore some of it later. He had never been to a city before. Sure, he was born in the Black Castle in Blackhaven, but he had been an infant!

Looking down, Augum saw that the face of the structure they were in loosely matched the castle-like carving of Senior Arcaneologist Ning's grand chair, as well as the carpet in this room. Was it a castle, library, or both? Far below was a high crenellated wall studded with torches and spiral minarets and staffed with patrolling guards. Beyond was a wide moat with brackish water. There was also a grand brazier-lit drawbridge with two giant winged statues guarding the entrance.

Leera stabbed the window. "That must be where the tournament's being held!"

Augum's heart leapt at seeing the streamers and banners surrounding a large wooden arena filled with stands. Flags of all sorts ruffled in the wind, the burning sword of the Legion most prominent of all. There were swarms of people everywhere. Suddenly he longed to be there, testing his mettle against the best in his degree. He imagined himself making it to the finals, facing Robin … and beating him.

It was only a shame Robin was 4th degree.

"Wait, the opening ceremonies are today!" Malaika squealed. "We have to go see them!"

Leera whipped around. "Are you *mad*? You're not even supposed to be here! You're going back right away—"

Malaika raised her chin. "We're not going anywhere. We came to have fun and see the show and help you. If you don't like it …" She shrugged. "Too bad. Guess we'll just have to have fun without you. Besides, I left a letter with Father explaining we've come along to help."

Leera ballooned. "After everything you put us through, you come up with *this*? Do you know what I want to do to you right now—" but she was interrupted by Secretary Klines.

"Quite the view, is it not?" Klines paced to the window, arms still folded across her tiny chest. "It was one of the largest castles in all of Sithesia, before it was converted into a library. As is tradition, the drawbridge rises two hours before midnight."

"It's beautiful and majestic," Bridget said, voice full of childlike wonder.

"One of the finest in Sithesia, perhaps only second to the one in Canterra. Its halls are steeped in history. I feel privileged to be here, as I am sure you do as well." She sighed. "I admit I am surprised that you, the most hunted trio in Solia, are why she had me prepare this room. Brazen of you to come here."

"How did she know we were coming?" Augum asked.

"And how did she know I like sweets?" Leera chimed in, still giving Malaika a hard look.

"And who *is* that … woman?" Charissa asked.

Secretary Klines stared out the window. "Imagine a young gifted warlock with a strong memory, but even stronger curiosity. Imagine that warlock using all her talents for study in the pursuit of knowledge. Now imagine that warlock aging, but learning to stave off death a little at a time using that knowledge."

"You're saying Senior Arcaneologist Lien Ning is … really old, is that right?" Augum asked. What a mouthful that title was.

"That she is. A wise, old soul, if not a bit cantankerous." Klines leveled her thickly-spectacled gaze at Augum. "So you're *him*."

"I'm the Lord of the Legion's son, yes."

"Not quite what I meant."

"I don't understand."

Klines rested a finger on her chin as she studied him. "Forgive me, but there's no way you have it in you."

"Have what in me?"

"Take her place. Beat him. No way. Look at you."

"Take whose place? Beat who? My father?"

"Your father. We are studied people here. Remember that. 'When thy fallen can't be slain, when lion children rise again, when fires burn from east to west, blood of kin can vanquish death.' "

"Oh, come on," Leera said, flipping her palms incredulously, "don't spew those stupid riddles at us, we've been through too much!"

"What I mean is two have come to pass."

"You know the poem," Augum said. "But, how?"

"They say it is from the time of Attyla the Mighty, but it is older. It actually originates from the Seers. Do you know who they are?"

"They can see the future and stuff," Leera said.

"A people from the north, from Ohm," Bridget added. "You're allowed to ask them one question per lifetime."

"A long, long time ago, well before the Founding, someone asked the Seers a question, and the answer was that poem. The person who asked the question is long lost to history, but the premonition has proved true time and again. The last time it proved true was when Occulus the Necromancer ascended to power."

"He became Lord of Death and the Lord of Dreadnoughts," Bridget whispered with a nod.

"Indeed. But as you probably have come to understand, when knowledge is suppressed, when the Leyans are—"

Malaika scoffed. "Leyans. No such thing."

Klines gave her a pointed look. "When the Leyans are not believed in or when they shut themselves from the world, chaos ensues." She glanced back at the trio. "If knowledge fails to be shared then it dies. What usually results is regression. Civilization takes a step back until fire consumes all. Those that survive live to tell what they can remember."

Klines allowed that thought to settle before making an idle gesture at the room. "All of this is possible because of the Leyans. Your rings are possible. All of the knowledge and gains we have made as a civilization—all possible because of the teachings and sharing of knowledge by the Leyans." Klines placed her hands on the window ledge and leaned forward, examining the city. "Yet how many times do you think these libraries have been burned down through history? How many times do you think we have had to start again? How many cycles of war, destruction, death? We are regressing right now."

"Why does it all happen?" Bridget asked after a thoughtful pause.

Klines shrugged, withdrawing from the ledge. "People are stupid. They believe in stupid things. They believe in things without proof. They believe in promises no one can possibly give them." She glanced at Augum. "Your father, for example, promises eternal life to those most loyal to him. He will never deliver that promise, for it is—"

"—impossible," Augum finished in a whisper.

"Except if he raises them as the undead," Bridget added, locking eyes with him.

Augum suddenly turned to Secretary Klines. "You're part of the Resistance!"

She smiled as she glanced between Augum and Bridget. "Perhaps we stand a chance after all."

DECISIONS

Secretary Klines raised a finger. "But remember that the Resistance does not exist without a core, and right now, that core is Anna Atticus Stone."

Augum couldn't keep the excitement from his voice. "Have you been in contact with her? Is that how you know all this stuff about us? Is she all right?"

"We have. Though we have not heard from her in some time. She has been organizing the Resistance for a while now." Klines leaned forward. "A secret network of key people waiting for the right moment to band together and stand against the mightiest foe the kingdoms have seen since the time of Occulus." She turned her back on them, dropping her head. "But I have to confess, we have little hope. Morale amongst this small handful of individuals is low. The Legion is awfully good at rooting us out. We hardly communicate, and when we do, it is in code or whispers." She examined her tiny hand, opening and closing it, whispering, "Not that there are many of us.

Such a precious, *precious* few ..." She closed her fist and glanced up at Augum. "Above all, we cannot see how Lord Sparkstone can be prevented from attaining the final scion."

"But he'll be destroyed if he acquires all seven—"

Klines shook her head. "Magua. Mark my words, Magua will find a way, if she has not already. He will be able to possess it. It is a Leyan construct, after all, subject to Leyan rules. He will possess it with her assistance. It is only a matter of time, or so I believe." She took a measured step in his direction. "And you, Augum Stone, are not strong enough to face him. Not even close. Not even with Anna Atticus Stone's help."

"Not yet," he said, feeling the steel in his voice. "But I will be." He did not know how, but he would find a way.

"It is said that in the old days all apprentice warlocks were told they had no talent, no capacity, no desire to learn the craft. They would be scolded as being worthless and stupid. Sometimes even beaten. Only if they persevered would they be rewarded with the higher teachings." She studied him carefully. "If you prove to possess such stubbornness, such resolve, then those few of us who are able, will help in whatever way we can, for only sheer persistence can stand a chance."

For a moment, Augum just stared at this tiny being with giant beetle eyes. "And we would be grateful for such help," he said at last.

"Please, we need access to the library," Bridget said. "It's very important. We have a lot of research to do."

Klines turned to face Bridget. "Senior Arcaneologist Lien Ning said 'No special privileges'. Which is not all too surprising, considering that is the tradition of the library—one must earn one's knowledge here. History demands greatness from those seeking glory."

"We do not seek glory."

"Is that so? If true, then we are all the better for it. But it changes nothing—you will still have to earn your way here. The library was founded on the principle of merit. No help. No special privileges. No favoritism. Omnio incipus equa liberatus corsisi mei. All begin equal but only the curious thrive. Repeat it with me."

"All begin equal but only the curious thrive," the group solemnly chorused, Malaika and Charissa mumbling the ancient phrase.

"Memorize it, for it will be your guide here."

"So does the no special privileges thing mean we can't visit certain places, or what?" Leera asked.

"Come." Klines led them to an etching of a gargoyle on the wall by the door. "This is the ancient library crest. It also doubles as a control rune. Shyneo." Her hand burst with bright gray smoke. She placed it against the symbol and the gargoyle lit up with a crimson glow. "Secretary Klines. Register Initiate—" She turned to look at Augum.

"Oh, uh, I'll be going under the name of Augustus Westwood here."

"Register Initiate Augustus Westwood." She took her hand away from the rune, which stayed lit. "Augum, if you please."

"Shyneo." Augum's hand rippled to life with lightning. He placed his palm against the rune. He felt a light shock and the rune darkened.

"You are now an Initiate. Any time you place your lit hand on a rune, you may speak your name and it will grant you entry, at least for some places. That means you have basic library access, but must pass all the tests required for more … privileged access, as is tradition."

"What does that mean?" Leera asked.

"You shall see. Next please," and she repeated the procedure with Leera and Bridget, who chose Sparrows as their last names, making them Leigh Sparrows and Brie Sparrows.

Leera gave Bridget a light punch on the shoulder. "We're sisters!"

Bridget was unimpressed. "I still think we should have chosen less obvious names."

"What about us?" Malaika asked. "We are not warlocks."

"You will be registered as guests," and Secretary Klines processed the stowaways with their real names, since no one knew them anyway, and as Ordinaries, meaning they only had access to the non-arcane library, this room, the portal room, and the supper hall.

"That's all right," Malaika said with a bob of her head, "we have a whole city to explore anyway, we don't need to read any stupid books."

Klines looked her and Charissa over with a spiteful glance. "Those that care little for books fall prey to shallow ideas."

Malaika and Charissa exchanged eye rolls.

Klines sighed. "I shall have two more beds brought in and two more screens. If you need to send a message, there are messengers on the first floor. There is a map of the library in a drawer of the desk. Do you have any questions?"

"Only about a bazillion," Leera muttered.

"Such as?"

"Well, how about, like, uh ..."

"As I said, there are messengers on the first floor. Be sure to address me directly, and use *discretion*."

"How is the Legion presence in the library?" Augum asked. "Will we be recognized?"

"It is heavy, and there are spies. Be wary. And yes, you might be recognized, but surely you have a plan against that?"

"Uh, sure we do," he lied.

"Oh, Secretary Klines, may we receive today's Herald?" Bridget asked.

"I'll have it sent to your room straight away. Now will that be all?" When they only stared at her, she inclined her head. "We shall see each other soon, no doubt. And remember—"

"—discretion, yes," Leera said. "Got it."

"And the library motto is—?"

"Omnio incipus equa liberatus corsisi mei," Bridget replied with raised chin.

"Which means?"

"All begin equal but only the curious thrive," the trio chorused.

"Excellent." Klines turned to depart only to stop at the door. "One more thing. Do not get caught roving the library grounds after hours, understand?"

They nodded gravely.

Klines swept them with those beetle eyes one last time. "Good luck," and left the room.

Augum immediately turned on Malaika and Charissa. "What are you doing! You're endangering the entire quest!"

"Don't you worry, we'll be well out of your way," Malaika replied in silky tones. She batted her lashes at him. "But I *was* hoping we could be of service in some … capacity."

Augum groaned. "You're impossible! Don't you understand how much danger you're in! How much danger you put *us* in?"

"We're not in any danger at all, and neither are you. At least not in any more danger because of us. We'll blend right in. Nothing but budding necrophytes merely enjoying the city." She dug in her robe and withdrew a large sack of coins, which she proudly held up. "And we're going shopping!"

Leera placed a hand over her eyes and dropped her head. "Are. You. Kidding. Me?" She raised her head. "There is all sorts of stupid wrong with that. And you don't even know any spells, or … or … what your story is, or—"

"We'll figure it out." Malaika smiled at Charissa, who nodded excitedly.

Leera stabbed a finger at Malaika. "We're *not* babysitting you. If you get caught, we're not going to—"

Bridget placed a hand on her arm, giving her a pointed look. "They're not going home. We have to work together, maybe we should *give* them something to do."

"What? Bridge, are you crazy? They'll screw it up and bring the whole city down on us!"

Malaika crossed her arms. "She's so *graceful*."

Leera's eyes narrowed as three watery rings rippled to life around her arm. "Let me show you the grace of my arcane fist—"

Charissa raised porcelain hands in squeamish defense. "What a brute—"

"Lee, please," Bridget said, stepping between them. "And you two—you've complicated everything. Look, why don't you stick with us for a little while? We'll even … go to the opening ceremony with you or something."

Augum and Leera jerked their heads at Bridget.

"We have to work together," Bridget said, her eyes imploring them to go along with it.

Augum rubbed his face, suddenly feeling weary. "Fine." But only for now, at least until they found a way to parcel them up and send them on some rickety wagon all the way back to Milham.

A gentle knock came at the door, startling everyone.

"Secretary Klines?" Augum asked tentatively, but there was no response.

"I'll get it," Malaika said.

Leera grabbed her arm. "Not you—"

"Let go of me, you feral—"

Leera let go with a jerk, but her hand curled into a tight fist as she glared at Malaika.

"Allow me," Charissa said, giving Leera a smarmy look. "Trust me, I know how to be cordial."

Leera hesitated but stepped out of her way as Charissa went to the door, only to stare at it. "Uh, how does this door work again?"

"Oh for the—" Leera drew her hood and marched over, "Shyneo," placed her hand where the door handle should be and said, "Leigh Sparrows." The door swung open. Leera immediately turned her head away. Augum also kept his face averted, but glimpsed gray robes.

"The Herald, as requested," said a man's silky voice. "Will that be all?"

"Yes, thank you."

The man cleared his throat lightly.

"Oh, right, uh, excuse me." Charissa hurried back to them. "He wants a tip."

"You have a giant sack of coins," Leera hissed through gritted teeth.

"Country bumpkin," Malaika muttered, but she made no effort to reach into her moneybag.

"I grew up in Blackhaven, if you ever dare call me a country—"

"Lee, not now." Bridget exasperatingly rooted in her snakeskin pouch, handing a copper over.

"Don't be cheap," Malaika said. "We don't want to look like peasants. Father always tips in silver."

Bridget hesitated but withdrew a silver instead.

Charissa snatched it and skipped back to the door. "Here you go."

"Most generous, thank you," said the man, before striding off.

Leera was seething, muttering things like, "Ridiculous," and "Not going to put up with this …"

Charissa brought Bridget the Herald, which Augum immediately noticed was the *Antioc Herald* as opposed to the *Blackhaven Herald,* which they were used to. He crowded Bridget to give it a read while Malaika went on about all the things she and Charissa were going to see, including the tournament, and how it was a shame the trio were going to be cooped up indoors with a bunch of stuffy old books. Leera glared at her, looking ready to explode. Augum had to place a hand on her right arm, in case it suddenly flared with rings.

There were three pages in this special edition, two of which were solely about the Antioc Classic. Depicted were fifteen tournament combat brackets, each with sixteen combatants fighting to be the winner for that degree.

"Opening ceremonies today, qualifiers tomorrow," Augum noted.

Leera finally took notice and placed her chin on his shoulder. "Wish I was competing. Then I'd be matched against Temper *Buttwax*."

Augum spied an etching of Erika Scarson standing beside two other warlocks. She held something close to her chest, a mace of some sort. He leaned closer and suddenly realized what it was. "She's holding it!"

"Holding what?" Bridget asked, searching the same etching.

"The divining rod! Look—"

Bridget squinted. "I think you're right …"

"That's it, I know it is. She's parading it for all to see, it's just like her. What's the description say?"

" 'Ms. Erika Scarson, seen here with the other two judges, will be chasing the villainous traitor Anna Atticus Stone when not presiding over the duels. As the honored judge of this year's tournament, she will also be presenting the trophy to each winner in their degree.' "

Augum felt all the blood rush to his head. Erika Scarson was presenting the winners with the trophy, and she held the divining rod. Suddenly he knew exactly what he needed to do.

"Aug? What is it?" Leera asked, brows furrowing with concern.

"I'm going to enter."

"Huh? Enter what?"

"I'm going to enter the tournament … and I have to win."

PERSUASION

When the cries declaring Augum completely mad for wanting to enter the tournament settled down a little, he tried to explain himself.

"It's our *only* chance to steal the divining rod—"

"No, uh-uh, no way, no how," Leera was saying, shaking her head and making disavowing gestures with her arms.

"Look, I know it sounds crazy, but I've beaten Robin before. I think I can do it again." Though truthfully, he knew the odds were stacked against him—Robin was 4th degree already, knew some necromancy, and his crazy aunt was a judge.

Bridget scowled. "Augum, do you realize what it is you would be up against? Every eyeball in the city will be watching you, and that's even *if* you somehow get in to the tournament, since it's already fully booked. Then, you have to somehow make it past four opponents—"

"—*and* not be recognized," Leera threw in.

"So? I'll wear a disguise or something—"

"Augum, you can't get in anyway, you don't have your 4th degree ring yet!" Bridget said.

"Well, there's that, but …" He rubbed his forehead. "What if we took the test today?"

"Do you know how much it even *costs* to take the test in a city like this?"

"We have gold. Lots of it. We can at least look into it, can't we?"

There was silence during which they all stared at him with slack looks of disbelief.

"I think he can do it," Malaika blurted.

"Stay out of this," Leera snapped, "you have no idea what you're talking about."

"I don't, do I? What if I told you I happen to know someone *in* the tournament battling in the 4th degree!"

"You … you do?" Augum asked.

"Yes! Jens Madis Bjornsson. Big blonde-haired fellow who is a friend of the family."

"I thought he never wants to see you again after you declared your love—" Charissa began but was silenced by a stern look from Malaika.

"And what, you think you can convince him to drop out or something?" Leera said sarcastically. "After no doubt having put him through hell?"

Malaika crossed her arms to mirror Leera. "I think I can."

"This is the dumbest idea ever. Augum's not going to—Bridge? I don't like the look on your face—"

Bridget had wandered to the window, chewing on her nail. "I just realized something …"

"How crazy the idea is? Good, because we have work to—"

"No, not that. It's crazy, yes, but if …" Bridget turned to face them. "The divining rod looks for scions, so if

Augum steals it, that would mean we could find his father anytime we wanted."

Augum gaped at her. "Bridget, you're a genius."

"It'd also mean Mrs. Stone could train us without anyone getting in our way," she added.

Which meant Cron, Augum thought uneasily. But he'd worry about that spell later. In fact, it would be a privilege to worry about Cron, for it would mean success in this crazy endeavor.

"Am I the only one who suddenly sees reason?" When no one replied, Leera threw her hands into the air. "Great, just great. Throw your life away on the craziest, stupidest—"

"It's a chance though," Augum said. "And I'm going to take it, Lee. *I'm going to take it.*" He took a step toward her. "But I ... I won't be able to do it without you."

Leera gave him a sorrowful, exasperated look. "Damn right you won't." She sighed. "You stupid fool, of course I'm going to help you, but—"

He scooped her up in his arms and twirled around.

"Let go of me, you dumb, stubborn—" but she was holding back a giggle.

Malaika sighed, turning her head away.

"If we're going to do this, we need to really think it through," Bridget said, grabbing the Herald and scanning the page. "We have five days until the finals. You have one duel a day, *and* we still have to do all that research."

"While not getting caught," Leera added through her teeth, giving Augum a hard punch on the shoulder after he let her go. "Fool."

"But first, of course, we need to get you to a high degree warlock to take the test." Bridget lowered the parchment. "Maybe there's a test room in the library."

Augum strode to the desk and opened a drawer, finding the map of the library. It was a gargantuan castle. He read out the names of some rooms. " '... Portal Room

A, Portal Room B, Steward's Office, Study Hall, Supper Hall, Training Room …' Hmm, no testing room."

"No examination room?"

He scrolled back up the list. "There are four! Examination Rooms A, B, C and D."

"Perfect." Bridget glanced to Malaika. "And you're sure you can talk to your friend and convince him to drop out?"

"And do you even know how to find him?" Leera asked.

"Yes, of course." Malaika looked longingly at Augum. "We'll leave right away."

"Do you remember our fake names if you have to send us a message?" Bridget pressed.

"Remind me."

"Bridget pointed at herself. "Brie Sparrows," she pointed at Leera, "Leigh Sparrows," lastly at Augum, "and Augustus Westwood."

Malaika gave a nod of her head. "Room 1099. Brie, Leigh, Augustus. Kind of similar to your real names a bit though, don't you think?"

"Just go already," Leera said. "We'll meet here later."

Malaika gave her a cold look and turned on her heel, Charissa following dutifully.

"And be discrete!" Leera shouted after her.

Malaika stopped at the door, but did not turn around. "Door please."

Leera rubbed her forehead. "Neither of them were paying attention. Unbelievable."

Augum strode over. "Shyneo. Augustus Westwood," and it opened for them. "You just have to place your hand on it and say your name, that's all."

"Right, thank you," Malaika replied. She stared at him a moment. "Augum—" and tried to get near him but he stepped away, keeping his face impassive and eyes averted.

"I see. Good luck then," she said in hurt tones, and disappeared down the hall with Charissa.

"The portal room—" Bridget suddenly said, striding for the door. "I have to show them how to work a portal, otherwise they'll search for stairs," and she ran after them.

Augum closed the door, turning to face Leera. She played with the cuff of her sleeve, refusing to meet his gaze.

"I know what you're thinking," he said. "Yes, it's crazy, but you know it's the best chance we've got at saving Nana." When she did not reply, he strode to her and embraced her in a gentle hug. Her arms wrapped around his waist.

"I'm ... nervous."

"I'll be fine."

"Promise?"

"Promise."

They held each other in dead silence until the door opened. They let go as Bridget strode into the room.

"Right. You two ready? Then get your hoods up, because we're about to walk amongst the enemy."

* * *

Using the map and a portal room, they made it to the outside of Examination Room A, in some curving hallway in the depths of the castle. A scrawny elderly dark-skinned woman with a face brimming with piercings stood behind an iron-studded desk.

Augum spied a name plate etched with the words *Secretary Sanjipta. Examination Office*. "Uh, excuse me, Mrs. Sanjipta—"

"—*Secretary* Sanjipta," the woman corrected without glancing up from her work.

"Right, Secretary Sanjipta—we'd like to inquire how much it costs to take a degree test."

"Show me your stripes."

Augum proudly flashed his three lightning rings. She finally deigned to briefly raise her eyes, but only momentarily.

"At ten per degree, testing for the 4th degree is forty gold," she said, returning to her work.

"*Each?*" That was a fortune!

"Each."

That made it 120 gold for all three of them, and they only had 100. "Is there maybe a group discount or something if we all took the test at the same time? Would you accept one hundred gold?"

Bridget leaned into his ear. "Aug, we can't afford—"

"Are all three of you doing the same test?" Secretary Sanjipta asked in a monotonous voice.

"Yes," he blurted, flashing his most endearing smile.

The way her eyes flicked over them told Augum she'd prefer nothing more than to see the backs of them. She sighed. "Very well then."

"Great!" Augum blurted. It was all of their gold, but he'd worry about that later.

Bridget grabbed his arm. "Are you sure about this, *Augustus*?"

"Not doing it without you two by my side. Besides, you know we're prepared."

"Let's do it, Bridge," Leera said, gleaming. "I mean, err, Brie."

The trio quickly glanced at the woman to see if she had noticed the mistake, but she was immersed in her paperwork.

Bridget sighed. "We should do one final practice round then. Can't afford to fail."

"No refunds once the gold is paid," the woman said.

"Then where's your Training Room?" Augum asked her.

"Do you have a map?"

"Yes."

"Try using it."

"Uh, right. Thanks."

They strode off.

"Great, now we'll be broke too," Leera said.

"We'll still have some coin left." Augum turned to Bridget inquiringly.

"After the test, we'll have forty-nine silver, fifty copper," she said.

Leera made a quick motion for them to keep their heads low as they passed a gray-robed woman. "If everything here costs something, we're not going to last."

"We'll beg if we have to," he said. "And don't forget to tuck your hair in, you two."

The girls hurriedly tucked their long hair into their hoods.

They soon found their way to a pair of very large doors exquisitely carved with a dragon battling a gargoyle. There was a flowing inscription below: *Thou shalt suffer this day to reap ye fruits of tomorrow.*

Bridget placed a hand on a well-worn spot on the door where there should have been a door handle. "Shyneo. Bridget—err, I mean Brie Sparrows." The massive doors opened, flooding the hallway with the echoes of warlocks practicing their craft. There were dozens of them, nearly all wearing necrophyte robes.

For a moment, the trio could only gape. Before them was a vast cavern-like room with all kinds of scenery—there was a towering jungle in one corner with vines and ropes and bamboo ladders leading to bamboo platforms, on top of which dueled two warlocks, one blocking a wind attack with his shield. There was a trio of small mountains in another corner, with great boulders two warlocks hid behind, obviously fighting on the same side in some kind of war game. Springy platforms were embedded into another wall, with warlocks jumping from one to another, a wide rope safety net below. There was a stone maze with what looked like traps sticking out of it. Nearby lay a giant pool on top of which floated huge and squishy pond leaves. A young female warlock in a necrophyte robe stood too long on one and sank with a sploosh. To the left stood an obstacle field of straw dummies and statues of beasts and men that fought back, reminding Augum of the Leyan log and stick figure his great-grandfather animated. There was a giant rickety-looking house with all kinds of exterior perches, as if for owls or something, but bigger. There was a massive tree, except the trunk was hollow with open holes for windows. A warlock practiced by himself somewhere in its thick canopy, for they could see palm-light flashing now and then.

"There's a castle even," Leera said, pointing giddily at a miniature multi-story castle complete with arched stained glass windows, a moat, and a drawbridge.

"And look up there," Bridget said, neck craning.

They glanced skyward to see a cloud near the rock ceiling, lit orange by braziers. Rope bridges crisscrossed rickety-looking platforms.

"You should see the secret dungeons," said an amused voice from their left. They turned to see a gray-robed middle-aged man standing amongst a stall brimming with wooden practice swords, staves, body padding, and all sorts of other training equipment. "If you're looking for a fright, that is, but we're not supposed to talk about it." He was bald with dark amber skin and an infectious smile.

"Never been here before," Leera said in wondrous tones.

"I gathered. You know those supposedly secret academy Trainers? Imagine putting them all in one room. That's what you have here."

"Wow."

The man's smile never wavered. "Three souls? Three will buy the day."

"*Three gold*?" Augum asked.

The man chuckled. "Let's go with three silver. It's tradition—toll to pass."

Bridget rooted around her pouch and handed over the coins.

"Looks like a fun job," Augum said.

"Best in the world. Especially in these times." The man nodded at the door. "I could be out there. Instead, sometimes, when the place is empty—like it will be soon when they all disappear to see the opening ceremonies—I go on and frolic amongst the obstacles. Still a kid inside."

"Are you a warlock?"

"Hit the ceiling at the 7th." He rubbed his bald head. "Started late, but proud of what I accomplished. What outfit are you three from?"

"Blackhaven," Augum blurted a little too quickly. "Uh, what's the neatest obstacle course here?"

The man gave them a quizzical look but nodded nonetheless. "Do you know your First Offensive?" The crow's feet around his eyes crinkled.

Augum nodded.

"Then for pure fun, I'd do the waterslide. There's a bunch of targets you'll be shooting at that shoot back, so you'll need to be good with your shield. You can also try the Mayhem course, which is basically just random spells thrown at you while you navigate holes that appear in the floor." He chuckled. "But I don't recommend that one until you see about six stripes on your arm. There's all kinds of fun to be had here, depending on your skill level. However, if you want more of a classical training experience, try the obstacle field, just behind. It's designed to test you on all of your spells, standard *and* elemental."

"We'll start with the obstacle field first, thank you," Bridget said, giving Leera a staying look just as she was about to protest.

"And don't be too ambitious. Some of those obstacles are old and can be downright dangerous, like the Memory Wiper, for example."

"Right, thank you."

"And feel free to borrow any of the equipment, it's included in the fee."

Augum glanced behind the man at the wide assortment of worn padding equipment. "Thank you, we should be fine."

"Good luck!"

They strode off toward the obstacle field, Leera complaining how they never got to have any fun, and if there was one place where fun was to be had, it was here, and if only Bridget would lighten—

"We're here to train, not play," Bridget finally said to her as they arrived. A fit older woman in a black robe happened to finish with the course just then. She strode past, not even giving them a second look, forehead beaded with sweat. Augum noticed a Legion flaming sword crest on her chest and was glad she had not made eye contact.

"We'll need to find disguises as soon as possible," Bridget said, watching the back of her.

Leera pinched her raised hood. "What do you call these?"

"Inadequate. And you know what I mean."

"Not really," Leera muttered, but let it go.

The course was set amongst a wheat field, with braziers burning all around, giving the place a nighttime feel. All the objects were well worn and dirty. They started on the first one, which was a bunch of different-shaped objects that had to be telekinetically moved through matching holes. The objects teleported back to their starting locations once they were successfully matched. Augum found it surprisingly fun but challenging. He could see how the obstacle taught precision though, and he wondered if they could build something like this back in Milham.

They spent a good deal of time training on it. Some of the objects had to be fitted so precisely, and so high off the ground, that it was obvious they were meant for higher degree warlocks. One of the hardest ones was threading a needle through a series of pinprick holes over fifty feet above ground.

The next obstacle was an array of broken objects they had to repair. Each object broke itself immediately after being repaired, a sign that the spell had been performed successfully. There was a satisfaction in hearing the bursting of a glass bottle, or the crack of a rock.

Leera pumped her fist after successfully repairing a delicate porcelain statue, only to see it shatter anew. "We need to get us some of these training toys back home."

Augum placed his hands over the remains of a crystal globe. "Apreyo." It reformed, then shattered. "Think we can purchase some of them in town?"

Leera scoffed. "Yeah, with what gold? And you know how expensive stuff like this is?"

Bridget finished repairing an iron gargoyle sculpture that then burst apart, nearly cutting her. "Maybe we *can* build our own obstacle course …"

"I doubt it'll put itself back together like this," Leera grumbled.

"That's true, this could be ancient arcanery."

"But if we save Nana—"

"Aug, she's not going to have time to make us practice toys," Bridget said, eyeing a necrophyte strolling by not too far away. "Besides, we have to get the you-know-what first."

They continued on along the course. Some obstacles were quite physical, like the Shield one, which required them to run through a bunch of statues that attacked them with blunted weapons; or the Disarm one, which required them to disarm a series of animated wooden opponents with painted scowling faces. Others were trickier, like the Mind Armor obstacle. There were a series of statues with a button that, once pressed, released a mind attack on the subject, with each statue clearly marked as to what kind of spell it was going to attack with. There was even a switch to set it to a degree—up to 10th. Leera braved setting the Confusion attack dummy to the 7th degree, which she promptly failed. Luckily, she stumbled out of its defined space, marked by a square on the ground, which immediately nullified the effects of the spell.

The trio challenged themselves with Fear, Mute, Deafness, Blind, Sleep, and Paralyze, the latter few much more difficult to defend against since they had so little training against them (and none against Paralyze). They spent an hour on this obstacle alone, until all three had to sit down and rest from the arcane side effects.

"I can see how someone could get really good just by training here," Augum said, massaging his temples.

Leera grunted in agreement. She sat with her head and arms on her knees, hood drawn.

Bridget kept a careful watch on who strolled by. "The course reminds me of the one at the Academy." She gave a wistful sigh.

After resting, they resumed training, moving on to a series of dummies that they attacked with their own mind-offensive spells. Leera always got a kick out of seeing a Fear-stricken wooden dummy pretend to be scared by moaning with a hollow sound. Augum, meanwhile, kept cranking the degree of his dummy up until his spells failed. His attacks almost always failed against 6th degree dummies, though on particularly strong castings he managed to best a dummy set to a defensive 7th degree. He wondered how the dummies worked, and just what kind of arcanery was involved. There was so much of the arcane world he did not know or understand, so much to explore. If only this stupid war wasn't going on, if only he was with Bridget and Leera at the Academy of Arcane Arts, quietly apprenticing under his great-grandmother, and attending these amazing tournaments every year …

After a grueling half day spent on the course, Leera plopped down on a battered stump. "Anyone else as exhausted and hungry as I am?"

Bridget dusted off her necrophyte robe before bending to rest her hands on her knees. "We should eat before attempting our 4th degree. Maybe we'll hear word from—"

"—those fool stowaways?" Leera interjected. "They *better* succeed if they value their hides."

Augum wiped the sweat from his brow, wincing at his headache. "Supper Hall for lunch?"

THE SUPPER HALL

"How much—?" Leera asked in scandalized tones, holding a tray at the concession stand.

"I said, five coppers," replied a bored attendant with a sweaty face. A giant cauldron of water boiled behind him.

"Better be fit for a queen." Leera took the five coins from Bridget and dumped them on the scuffed oaken counter. "We'll be broke by day's end at this rate," she muttered to Augum, making sure no one else in the line of mostly necrophytes and gray-robed figures had overheard.

Ahead, a large woman with angular spectacles and a tight bun doled out slopping ladles of some kind of mush. Augum suspected she woke up with that frown. He tightened his hood, aware that there were way too many people in the noisy hall for his comfort, especially since most of them were necrophytes. Not that he was comfortable anywhere in public nowadays, even Milham.

They collected their food—mushroom soup, mashed potatoes, lanky green beans, and a shriveled side of pork that looked like it had been run over by an ox cart. There was a crude iron pump that they used to pour water into battered tin cups. Then they made their way to a trestle table with fitted benches and lit by hanging iron candelabras. The room looked much like a vast barn, the floors covered with hay.

"It's like we're livestock," Leera muttered, taking a seat.

"Quaint and cozy," Augum replied, taking a seat opposite alongside Bridget, then promptly diving into his food.

"Farm boys," Leera mumbled.

"What?"

"Nothing."

"No way, she can't beat him!" a small necrophyte boy with a pimpled face and a squeaky voice finished saying to a necrophyte girl. The pair sat down at the same table as the trio, who stiffened and kept their faces averted.

Augum realized they stood out like beacon fires—in the whole place, they were the only necrophytes with their hoods drawn. He wearily watched the pair beside them out of the corner of his eye.

The boy plowed into his food. "That Nodian warlock, what's his name—"

"Nix, or Nex, or something like that," the girl replied, picking at her beans.

"Whatever, he knows his 4th but purposely didn't take his test so he could compete in a lower degree. *That's* why Temper's going to lose."

"Good, cause I hate her anyway. She's a stupid oaf. And she doesn't deserve Robin either."

The boy groaned. "I'm so *sick* of hearing about him. Almost as famous as the fugitives." He had a narrow nose, short black hair, and was about their age, or maybe a year younger.

The girl, who was as thin as parchment with long sienna hair, seemed to notice the trio because she stopped eating, throwing a questioning look at the boy.

"Hey," said the boy, putting down his spoon. "Hey, you three—why the hoods? You part of some warlock bandit gang or something?"

The girl chuckled.

"Oh, uh, we're just cold," Augum replied, fully realizing that was about the stupidest reply he could come up with—it was furnace hot in there from all the braziers.

"Were you in the training room?" the girl asked. "Let me guess—the ice bath."

Augum nodded without facing them. "Yep, that's it exactly."

"Hate that bath," the boy muttered. "So are you all going to see the opening ceremony?"

Augum nodded again, overly conscious of every movement of his body. "Probably, yeah."

" 'Probably'?"

"Yeah, we are."

"Of course you are, why would you miss it?"

Augum could think of a few reasons.

"Do you have a favorite?" the boy pressed.

Augum couldn't help but look up. "Favorite?"

The boy gave the girl an *Is he slow or something?* look. "Yeah, you know, a favorite in the tournament," he said to Augum.

"Uh ..." Oh no, he didn't know anyone other than Temper and that murdering mule! "Robin Scarson," he blurted, hating himself for saying it.

The boy gave him a revolted look.

"He's a dream, isn't he?" the girl said to Bridget and Leera.

"Oh, yeah," Leera said in flat tones. "A dream come true."

The boy leaned closer. "Anyone ever tell you that you three look like the three on the poster?"

Augum and Bridget froze.

Leera, on the other hand, waved idly. "Get it all the time."

The boy gave a short laugh. "Yeah, I can see why." He returned to his soup.

"Ooo, I'd *love* to see Augum Stone in the tournament!" the girl squealed.

Augum, who had finished breathing an immense sigh of relief, choked on a bean pod. "Excuse me," he managed to say wheezily while Bridget slapped his back.

"He's *so* handsome," the girl said with a dreamy sigh, quickly catching herself. "In a criminal kind of way of course. Anyway, I know *he'd* win."

"Not if he faced Robin," the boy said. "No chance." He counted on his fingers. "Kid knows more necromancy than any necrophyte I know, he's been trained by the Lord of the Legion personally, and his crooked aunt's a judge—the Unnameables themselves couldn't win with her in that booth."

The girl shrugged. "Guess so."

"Besides, isn't Augum, like, only 1st degree or something?"

How Augum wished he could prove the boy otherwise!

The boy lowered his voice. "Know who I have a *huge* crush on? Bridget Burns."

It was Bridget's turn to nearly choke.

The girl smirked at him. "Oh, are you a Bridget boy?"

"What do you mean?" the boy asked.

"Well, you're either a fan of Bridget or Leera."

"Hmm, they're both super cute, but I'm definitely a fan of Bridget."

Augum couldn't resist glancing at Bridget. She was scarlet, and suddenly quite preoccupied with her mashed potatoes.

"Which one would you take to the Star Feast?" the boy asked Augum.

Augum had a very hard time concealing his smile. "Oh, uh, Leera."

Leera had to pretend to wipe her mouth to prevent herself from bursting out in laughter.

The girl smacked the boy's hand. "Think Bridget's cuter than me?"

The boy sighed. He put down his spoon with a clatter and crossed his arms. "Think Augum or Robin is more handsome than I am?"

"Ugh." The girl returned to eating, as did the boy.

"So what outfit are you from?" he asked the trio without looking up.

"Blackhaven," Augum replied quickly.

The boy gave Augum a look. "Yeah, but which *outfit*?"

"Oh, uh …" They should have prepared better, asked Haylee more questions about this kind of stuff. He regretted not having her along. Instead, they got stuck with idiot stowaways.

The girl leveled her spoon at Augum. "Let me guess—Stone Quarter."

"How did you know?" Augum lied.

The girl gave a lofty head wag. "Cut of your robes."

Augum glanced around—all the necrophyte robes looked the same to him.

"All right, let's go get a good seat." The boy took the girl's empty plate and bowl, as well as his own. "See you later."

"Bye," Augum replied.

Soon as they were out of earshot, the trio broke out snickering.

"Now *that* was an odd conversation," Augum said, taking note how the girls sat a little straighter, cheeks rosy.

They quietly bantered a little more before going to their room to check for a message from Malaika, but there was none. They washed up instead and made their way down to Examination Room A, where the trio paid the one hundred gold fee to Secretary Sanjipta, the scrawny gray-robed woman behind the desk. She accepted it without glancing up from her work.

"The rules are simple," she began explaining in a memorized rapid-fire way. "No weapons, no food, no off-the-books spells, no necromancy or otherwise any spells outside of the tested degree. No hints, winks or high jinks of any kind. No passing of notes. Any form of cheating will result in a lifetime ban and an automatic constabulary report. The applicants are not to place their hands on each other or the examiner without permission. The applicants are not to address the examiner without being spoken to first."

She took a bored breath before charging on while shuffling parchment. "The applicants will not remove any property from within Examination Room A. If an applicant should permanently damage any of the obstacles or objects within Examination Room A, he or she will immediately pay for said obstacle or object in addition to a pre-determined fine. Should an applicant fail to make immediate payment, he or she will be remanded into Legion custody until such time as payment can be provided by the family, a benefactor, or mentor.

"The Institution, henceforth known only as *the Library*, shall not be held liable for any cuts, bruises, broken bones, or bodily harm of any kind sustained by applicants. If an applicants loses their life in the process of the testing, *the Library* will notify the proper authorities but not be held liable in any way. By signing this form, applicants agree to all terms and conditions of the test and acknowledge the heretofore risks." She fired off three parchment forms, handing over a well-used quill and ink bottle. "Sign here and here and here."

The trio exchanged looks before signing their fake names on the dotted lines.

Secretary Sanjipta snatched the forms as soon as they were signed. "Applicants may now enter Examination Room A. The examiner will be with you shortly. A reminder that applicants are not to speak to each other at any time while inside the examination room, unless specified to do so by the examiner."

The trio shuffled their way to the great double doors. They were carved from old, black oak and studded with iron. The carving depicted a warlock with his arms raised in triumph, hands glowing. Below was another inscription.

" 'Chance favors thee if thee be prepared'," Bridget read solemnly.

"Good luck, you two," Augum said, giving them each a firm nod.

Leera squeezed his hand. "You too." She raised her palm. "Shyneo. Leigh Sparrows."

The door opened and the trio walked inside.

MAKING HEADWAY

Late that afternoon, the doors of Examination Room A burst open and out spilled a laughing Augum, Bridget and Leera, hugging immediately.

"But did you see the look on his face when you blew the statue apart?" Leera finished saying to Augum, giving him a peck on the cheek before realizing Secretary Sanjipta was standing right there. The gray-robed woman glanced up to scowl at them for ruining the peace of the hallway. They quickly hurried off.

"We're lucky he chose to arcanely repair it instead of charging us," a rosy-cheeked Bridget said.

Leera cracked a grin. "Imagine being 'remanded into Legion custody' because we couldn't afford to pay for a stupid statue."

Bridget raised her brows at her. "You were listening to that spiel?"

"I have my moments."

Augum flexed his arm to marvel at the four majestic lightning rings, which he swore crackled a little louder and shone a touch brighter. "I would have … forcefully repaired it or something."

Leera gave him a light shove. "Yeah, I'm sure that would have gone over well."

Bridget flared her four shining ivy rings. "Honestly, I did not think it was going to be that easy."

"—or tedious," Leera said, flaring her own watery rings. "Why make us perform each spell from each degree *three* times? It was so … official."

"*Bureaucratic* is the word you're looking for," Bridget said.

"He was kind enough to allow us to take breaks at least," Augum said as they entered the dim portal room.

"Pre-scheduled," Bridget noted, frowning. "You sure he didn't recognize us?"

Leera waved the thought aside. "He was older than everyone I ever met put together. Like, Fentwick old."

"Oh, come on, he wasn't *that* old." Bridget placed her hand on the etched oval beside the words *General Quarters*. "Shyneo. Brie Sparrows." The windy portal ripped to life and the trio walked through it, continuing the conversation on the other side.

"I'm just glad the fake names worked for the ceremony," Bridget said. Then, as they paced the silent hallway, Bridget threw one arm around Augum's shoulder and the other around Leera's, squeezing them close. "I'm proud of us. Not *one* mistake. All our hard work paid off. Can you believe it? We're 4th degree!"

Augum and Leera exchanged awkward smiles—it was unlike Bridget to show so much affection, but very pleasant indeed.

"All thanks to your mentorship," Leera said. "And I love what you did with your SME." They had taken to abbreviating the *Summon Minor Elemental* spell to avoid the mouthful of its name.

"Which part?" Augum asked. "When she made it leap in the air and kick the dummy or when it tried to strangle it?"

"Mine just barreled into the dummy like a little drunken oaf. I mean, that was impressive, Bridge."

She shrugged, still holding onto their shoulders. "Practice makes perfect."

"Looks like everyone's at the opening ceremony," Augum said. They hadn't encountered a soul since the examination room.

"Wish we were going," Leera chimed in.

They stepped into their room but found no note from Malaika and Charissa. What they did find were two additional beds with two privacy screens in between.

"Not exactly looking forward to sleeping in the same room as them," Leera muttered. "Don't be surprised if you hear two people choking at night."

Bridget gave her a look.

"Are my jokes getting dark?"

"Little bit," Bridget replied.

"Well, tough. These are dark times."

Bridget sighed and strode to the window. "Sunset soon …"

"Don't worry, I'm sure they're fine," Leera said, though she winked at Augum, whispering, "If we're lucky they're rotting in a Legion prison by now."

Augum forced a smile, but sincerely hoped not. That would be a disaster. He doubted they'd survive much less resist a questioning. "So what do we do now?"

Bridget watched the city. "Well, regardless of what we do, we can't keep going out without better disguises. You heard what that boy said. We still look too much like the poster. Just too risky."

"Hey, we'll be able to see the night portion of the ceremony!" Leera said, walking to the window with Augum.

The trio looked on as a ring of large braziers burst to life at the tournament grounds.

"Ooo," Leera said, entwining her arm around Augum's elbow.

"It wouldn't be a bad idea to go down there," Bridget said.

Leera flashed her a surprised look. "What? I thought you didn't want to take any unnecessary risks—"

"I know, but I mean if we found the right disguises. I read the ceremony will go late. We probably want to investigate the grounds, how many guards there are, and so on, *before* Augum competes."

"*If* he competes. They still have to pull through for us."

Bridget suddenly turned to Augum, gazing at him searchingly.

"Why are you looking at me like that?"

A sly grin spread across her face. "I have an idea for the disguises." She shared a knowing look with Leera.

"That could work," Leera said, giggling. "Yes, that could definitely work. But we have to do all of us."

Augum wiggled a finger between the two of them. "I don't know if I like what you two are up to."

Leera positioned herself before him and grabbed his arms, announcing, "Augum, we're going to give you a makeover—don't give me that look! It'll work, it's perfect!"

Bridget was trying not to laugh at his attempts to squirm away. "We just have to … pluck your eyebrows a bit, change the shape of them—"

" '*Pluck*'?" Like a chicken?

Leera snorted. "They'll grow back, don't worry. We'll mash on a wee bit of make-up—"

" 'Mash on'?" What were these horrible words?

"Maybe some putty," Bridget added with a devilish smile.

"You two are having way too much fun with this."

Leera reached to his head. "Dye your hair, you know, that kind of thing."

Bridget was nodding. "Yes, it's perfect. And don't worry, we're going to work on each other as well."

"I'm worried. I'm nervous. I'm rethinking the entire quest—" but the girls were ignoring him completely.

"I always wanted blue hair," Leera was saying.

Bridget shook her head. "We can't stand out. Anyway, why don't you and I go find some makeup from a shop and leave Augum here to wait for the stowaways?"

"Works for me."

"Don't I get a say in this?" Augum said, finally managing to squirm away from Leera's grip. "I mean, I don't want to look like a … buffoon."

Leera smirked. "You're so silly, it's not like that at all."

Bridget was already striding to the door. "If we're going to do this, we should go right away."

"Absolutely. Going to be all right all by your lonesome, Aug?"

"But—"

"Great. See you later—" Leera gave him a peck on the cheek and took off with Bridget, the pair still giggling.

Augum watched them go and expelled a long breath. Girls …

MAKING PLANS

Augum sat on the deep ledge of the window, watching the colorful ceremony from a distance. Besides the countless other obstacles in his mind, he needed to figure out what to do with the stowaways. The problem turned itself over and over in his brain until he suddenly realized something—Malaika and Charissa wanted to help, didn't they? So why not let them? Why not *assign* them things that will help the Resistance?

He sat up, drew his knees in, and placed his necklace between his teeth, eyes trained on the silent celebrations but mind elsewhere making plans. Arcaneologist Ning's words floated through his thoughts much like her chair. *Direction—that is what you require, for you are lost,* he remembered her saying to Malaika and Charissa. And then he recalled her asking him, *Do you believe yourself capable of this?* Had she been hinting at what has been at the back of his brain for so long? That he needed to take charge of his life and … perhaps the Resistance itself? Was this also what Mrs. Stone had been hinting at so long ago, when she turned to him at Castle Arinthian and asked him if he needed to be as strong as his father to beat him? Was she alluding to the Resistance too?

He adjusted the necklace between his teeth. Well, if there ever was a time to step up, this was it. At least, he might as well try.

Time wore on. He focused on idea after idea, discounting the ones that didn't make sense, until he finally thought of how he could ask Malaika and Charissa for help.

As dusk slowly settled over the city, the door finally opened behind him. Augum turned, expecting to see the girls, only to be surprised by the sight of Malaika and Charissa, who carried a basket with something steaming in it. Both were grinning victoriously.

Augum jumped off the ledge. "You did it, didn't you? You got him to drop out of the tournament."

Malaika was nodding her head. "We left the ceremonies early even, just so we could tell you the news. Brought a feast to celebrate."

"At first she and Jens Madis whatever-that-weird-surname is got into a *huge* argument," Charissa said, one brow raised dramatically. "But then they made up—"

"I offered a stipend toward his education at the Academy," Malaika said, crossing her arms, a smug look on her face. "On behalf of the Harouns, which I shall have Father forward as soon as he receives the letter I sent explaining everything. And don't worry, I was *discrete*."

"Good, well done," Augum said guardedly. He could smell the scent of roast chicken and had to ignore his rumbling stomach.

Malaika's ebony features turned scarlet and she even gave a little curtsy. "Thank you, Mr. Westwood. Also, I took the liberty of bribing the registrar to make sure there weren't any questions about the switch."

"You did?"

Malaika shrugged. "You learn a thing or two living around merchants."

"You have to show up first thing in the morning to register," Charissa said. "And I mean, first thing. They'll be expecting you, *Augustus*."

"And you're dueling in the early afternoon," Malaika added.

Augum felt his heart skip a beat. Suddenly it all became real. He was actually in the tournament! He was going to duel someone before an entire crowd! In that giant arena! Then he felt a little weak. What had he been thinking? In front of all those *people*?

Malaika adjusted the cuffs of her necrophyte robe. "So … what did *you* get up to today, Augum?"

He shoved aside the idea of thousands of faces watching him and flexed proudly. Four lightning rings burst to life around his arm.

Charissa and Malaika squealed with delight, gripping each other.

"Wait," Charissa said. "You had three before, right?"

"Of *course* he had three," Malaika replied, smacking her arm lightly. "I swear, you can be so daft sometimes," but the pair giggled.

"Bridget and Leera passed the test too."

Malaika immediately made a foul face before quickly correcting herself. "Anyhow, this calls for a celebration."

"Maybe some other time. I have something important to ask of you." Now was the time to change things up. "Look, I know we haven't always been getting along," Augum began, choosing his words carefully and glancing between the two of them, confidence boosted by his recent success with the 4th degree, "but I think we have an opportunity here. You came to help the Resistance, right?" It was important he framed this correctly, otherwise it might not work.

Malaika brought her hands together pleadingly. "Of course, we only want to be of service!"

"Good, because we do need your help." Augum began pacing, channeling Bridget, and maybe a little of Mrs. Stone and Sir Westwood. He stopped briefly to lock eyes with Malaika and Charissa, who he noticed were paying rapt attention. "It's dangerous so you'll need to be careful. I need you two to watch the judges and the guards. We need to know what kind of force we're up against. I want to be fully informed of their number and strength. I also want you to find out who I'm going up against in the tournament—and I want a report every day, with plenty of time to prepare." He made a vague gesture. "Use your social skills … or something … to dig up what you can."

Malaika and Charissa wouldn't let go of each other now, dancing and singing, "We get to be spies! We get to be spies—!"

"Ooo, we'll watch them as they practice—" Malaika added, stopping the dance but still holding firmly onto Charissa's forearms. "And we'll listen in on their conversations! Oh, this will be *so* much fun!"

"I know!" Charissa squealed, flashing her a *Can you believe this is happening?* look. "And we'll get to do some …"

"*Shopping!*" the girls sang.

"I also want you to keep tabs on Robin Scarson," Augum continued, hands behind his back, feeling like a general commanding troops—albeit fickle and crazy ones. "I want to know how he's doing, how he's feeling, and especially—"

"—his weaknesses," Malaika finished. She brought her feet together and awkwardly saluted, voice comically deep. "We shall have it done, sir!"

Charissa giggled behind her pale hand. "You're so silly, Mal."

She turned to Charissa. "This is so perfect for us! And we get to see the tournament! How exciting!"

Augum smiled to himself. That's exactly why it was going to work. It was the only way to keep them in line, and who knows, maybe something would come of it. At the very least, it would keep them out of the trio's hair. And now to close the deal.

"We have to work together," he said, gesturing with a closed fist like how he envisioned a general would. "There will be dangers—neither of you can get caught, and you can't tell anyone who you're really with. No matter what. Even if you get captured." He took a step closer to them. "Even if they drag you into an iron room. Should you get captured, know that the lives of your families would be put at stake."

Malaika and Charissa swallowed but nodded gravely.

"We'll also have to come up with alibis, warning signals, the works."

"We'll get on that right away," Charissa said. "Promise. Ooo, this'll be so much fun! *We're spies!*"

"All right, enough silliness, let's eat!" Malaika declared. "We're starved—" but just as she finished speaking the door opened once again, and in walked Bridget and Leera, the former carrying a linen bag. Leera's mischievous smile curdled the moment she spotted Malaika, and vice versa.

"Good news," Augum immediately said, and explained Malaika's accomplishment of getting him into the tournament. Then he quickly changed tact and made a small speech about how they were going to work together from now on, and how he had given Malaika and Charissa a very special task. Bridget took to the plan immediately, flashing Augum a secret, disbelieving look he translated as *Great idea!* By the look on Leera's face, he could see she was going to need some convincing—but after everything that Malaika had done to them, he hardly blamed her.

"Uh, sorry we took so long," Leera managed to say to him. "Guess we missed the opening ceremonies." She held up the linen bag with a roguish grin. "But at least we got what we need for the makeovers!"

Malaika jerked her head back. "Makeovers?"

Augum groaned. "Yeah, they have a plan."

"That's nice and everything," Charissa whined, stomping her feet like a child, "but can we please talk it over while we eat? I'm starved."

Augum rubbed his hands together. "Definitely."

Supper included roast chicken, salted and buttered potatoes, carrots and bread. And as the five of them savored every bite, they used the rest of the dwindling evening to flesh out a detailed plan, expanding upon what Augum first laid out—scheduling meet times for reports, background stories, secret warning signals and code words, and so on. Even Leera had to admit the sense of it—making the two stowaways part of the Resistance would make everything easier, and might even be a help, though she was profoundly skeptical of their spying abilities.

They resolved to do the makeup at first light, before Augum had to register, and went to bed early.

Augum, tired from the long day, slept better than he had in some time.

ANTIOC, DAY TWO

The next day Augum and Leera were woken early by a yawning Bridget, who had once again slept poorly. The rings under her eyes had deepened and she mostly communicated in grunts.

"She's devolving," Leera whispered to Augum with a snicker, watching Bridget numbly prepare the makeup.

"Wake them," Bridget said, voice cracking from weariness.

Leera glanced over at the sleeping Malaika and Charissa and made a face like something stank. "I don't want to do it."

"Well neither do I," Augum said, mirroring her face because he thought it was funny.

"Oh for the love of—" Bridget threw down the linen bag and marched over to wake them.

"Let's not get on her bad side today," Leera whispered.

Augum fervently nodded in agreement.

There was a buzz in the air as everyone prepared for the day. Hot sunlight streamed in through the window. It was a cloudless and bright morning. After washing up, Malaika and Charissa quickly excused themselves, excited for their spy quests. Augum was up first for the makeover, followed by Leera, though the girls somehow managed to work on each other at the same time. To start, they dyed each other's hair—Bridget's long cinnamon hair was changed to black; Leera's raven hair to dark brown. Augum's umber was changed to black as well. He found the whole thing fascinating, especially the way the girls preened and hummed and hawed about finicky details he couldn't make sense of. At least Bridget lightened up a little, even giggling now and then at how they all looked.

When Augum checked himself in the mirror, he received quite the shock—his sharply-arched brows had been rounded a bit (that "plucking" thing), and dyed to match his hair, which had been cut by the girls. The makeup made his cheeks appear hollow, his skin darker, face a touch longer. Nonetheless, he smiled—he could barely recognize himself.

"Still handsome and cute," Leera whispered from the doorway.

"You too." She looked as radiant as ever, though peculiar with dark brown hair, almost as if she was a caricature of herself. Though the makeup did manage to enhance her adorable freckles.

"Just be sure Robin or Temper don't lay eyes on your face until they absolutely have to," Bridget said as they gathered to leave. "And I mean, at the very last moment, preferably when it's too late. I'm sure we'll have a plan for all that by then anyway."

They left in a hurry, necrophyte hoods raised and robes billowing in the frantic pace, soon making their way to the vast and bustling central hall, ornamented by the largest iron hanging candelabras Augum had ever seen—each one must have a hundred candles. The entrance to the library had no fewer than six sets of double-doors, each exquisitely carved. Legion guards stood at attention outside, black plate armor glistening in the early morning sun. The trio passed through the busy courtyard, through the spiked portcullis gate, and onto the ancient drawbridge. Augum could smell the history in the old stone and in the rank odor of the canal, which sparkled in the sun. He could see gray-robed attendants in the minarets and guards in the sentry towers. He noticed drainage spouts shaped like gargoyles. More winged demons oversaw ledges and windows and glared down from perches and spires and hooded lanterns. Two hulking stone gargoyles perched like dragons at the end of the drawbridge, mouths perpetually aflame.

Augum could spend all day exploring the visuals of this ancient castle-turned-library, but Leera yanked him by the sleeve before he got left behind.

"Forgot this is your first time in a city, country boy," she said with a crooked smile.

The cobbled streets were busy with vendors crying out their wares, women shopping, ox cart wagons rolling, and necrophytes hurrying to and fro. A wooden sign with the words *Hilt & Scabbard Inn & Tavern* swung on its chains. A distant bell sounded. A smith clanked at an anvil. Babies cried and dogs barked. Chickens squawked and hogs bawled, often butchered there on the street. Food stands were near empty though, and prices were ridiculously high, a symptom of the famine plaguing the countryside.

Young grimy heralds shouted the day's news, carrying the Blackhaven Herald in one hand, Antioc Herald in the other. Bridget snatched a copy on her way, paying the two coppers, and read it as she walked. The girls seemed quite at ease with city life, matching the frantic pace. To Augum, everything felt hurried and everyone looked so busy, so important. He craned his neck every which way, wondering where they were all heading, feeling foreign and lost and overwhelmed.

He spied groups of warlocks wearing more traditional robes, and guessed they were from other kingdoms, perhaps coming to compete in the tournament, or just to watch. He felt small and insignificant, but wanted to be part of it all, to explore and discover this world he had known so little about, for the true depth of his sheltered life was becoming startlingly apparent in the city.

He glanced back at the distant grand library—a massive, towering gray-stoned castle streaked with ivy and embedded with hundreds of iron-rimmed windows. At the very top was a glass dome that gleamed in the sun. He pictured Senior Arcaneologist Ning floating around in it, steeped in silence, streaks of sunlight piercing the glass-paned bookcases. What a contrast from the noise of this bustling city.

Leera had to march back and yank on his hand. "Like a baby," she muttered.

His blood raced as they neared the tournament grounds, for that was where his heart truly lay—in the arcane arts. The closer they came, the more they could hear the crowd swell with boos or cheers.

"Any news?" Leera asked Bridget, hand firmly gripping Augum's.

"Mentions Malaika's friend pulling out," Bridget replied, keeping one eye on the Antioc Herald and one on the busy street. "Augum's bracket hasn't been filled in yet."

They picked up the pace.

"Anything else?" Leera asked.

"Just the usual stuff about the famine. Tax demands on Tiberra—"

"—I meant about the tournament."

"Other than gossip, nothing we don't know. Oh, and it does mention the 'three fugitives' have been spotted near Southspear, on the Nodian border."

Another pretense for war, Augum was thinking. At least the sighting meant there was yet another reason no one would expect them to be in Antioc.

They heard the stands rattle with the stomping of feet in time to a drum. Augum got goose bumps as he glimpsed the giant iron portcullis, sitting raised, the bottom spikes sharp as knives. They pushed past an increasing crowd, finally making it to a payment booth.

"Spine a head," said a young but bored attendant to the people ahead in line.

" 'Spine'?" Augum whispered.

"That's slang for a silver piece," Leera replied. She open and closed her palm at Bridget. "Gimme, gimme, gimme."

Bridget dug out one of the new Legion silvers and handed it over. Leera then gave it to Augum to inspect. On the front was his father's crowned skull-like head, just like on the gold coin, but on the back, rather than a burning sword of the Legion, was the ancient Solian symbol of a great pine, and the words *Solia the free*.

Leera leaned in. "A silver pine. Get it?"

"Spine. Right." He traded a smiling Bridget the silver for a copper. On the front was once again his father's head, but on the back was the image of a castle, and underneath were the words *The Black Castle, Blackhaven.*

"So if the other one's called a 'spine', this one's called a 'castle'?" he asked, wincing.

Leera flashed Bridget a giggling look. "Now you're getting it."

Augum found all this fascinating. "Then a gold coin would obviously be a 'sword'."

Leera shook her head, now thoroughly amused. "A skull."

He thrust the copper back at Bridget and crossed his arms.

"A skull, a spine, a castle. Gold, silver, copper." Leera chuckled. "Look at you. Halfway to being a city dweller already."

"Shut up," he said, trying not to smile.

She gave him a roguish grin and squeezed his hand. "Just teasing."

The line shuffled along until the trio stood before the bored-looking boy.

"Where's the registration booth?" Bridget asked him over the noise.

The boy looked at her like she was stupid. "Registrations for the tournament closed a tenday ago."

"No, this is a special case—"

"Spine a head or get out of the way."

Bridget glanced at two nearby Legionnaires. "All right," and dug out the money from her pouch.

"Might have to confiscate some of Malaika's gold for the cause," Leera muttered as they received their wooden chits and lined up waiting to get in. Augum saw a Legion guard taking the chits ahead, and wondered if this was the best idea—maybe they should find some alternate route in. Then again, they needed to test their disguises, and the sooner the better. One way or another, guards were going to see them.

At last, Bridget handed her chit over. The guard's eyes flicked to her face briefly before waving her by, doing the same to Leera. Augum's heart stopped as the guard peered into his face, and for a moment, he thought for sure the game was up, but the guard snatched his chit before lazily waving him by as well.

"That was stressful," Leera said out of the corner of her mouth.

Augum expelled a breath he hadn't realized he'd been holding. The disguises were working … so far.

The trio searched for the registration booth. They soon got a glimpse of the sheer size of the arena—a great wooden oval packed with people. There was a judging booth before a towering row of flags, the largest and central one being the Legion's burning sword. In the center was a walled arena. A massive drum, pounded by four large men, led a triple-thrum chant the crowd sang in one voice, accented with stomping feet: "LO-SERS SHALL! BEND THE KNEE! WI-NNERS FIND! ETER-NI-TY!"

Augum's throat felt dry and butterflies buzzed in his stomach. What was he getting himself into? How could he just waltz into an arena and face thousands of people and expect to perform competitive arcanery? *What had he been thinking?*

"Catchy tune," Leera said, tapping her foot in time.

A nearby vendor yelled, "Place your bets here on who'll die in the qualifiers! Place your bets here—!"

"Think I'm going to be sick," Augum blurted.

Leera punched his shoulder. "You'll be fine, champ." Then, after seeing his pale face, gave him a warm hug, whispering, "Trust me, you *will* be fine."

Hearing her say those words lifted his spirits.

"Get a room," a snarky teen said nearby.

"How about I shove you through that wall instead," Leera snapped back, much to the boy's surprise.

"Here!" Bridget called from beyond a gaggle of people. "Augustus! Leigh!"

They made their way over to a large wooden booth with a roll-up shutter. Inside, robed officials scrambled to get paperwork in order and post large public brackets of combatants, which people pointed at and discussed.

They shoved their way through to a frazzled gray-robed attendant, frantically scribbling with a quill.

"Hi!" Bridget yelled over the chanting. "We're here to replace Jens Madis Bjornsson—"

Thank the Unnameables she remembered the boy's name, Augum was thinking, as he had completely forgotten it.

The scruffy attendant looked up, revealing a boyish face and cropped blonde hair. "You are?" he asked in a squeaky voice.

Bridget yanked Augum close. "This is Augustus Westwood, from Everscale. He's supposed to take Jens' place."

Augum nodded along. They had planned this all out the night before over supper—Augustus Westwood was from a little-known Legion outfit in Everscale, the most middle-of-nowhere Solian town they could think of. Sisters Brie and Leigh Sparrows were his cousins. It was a better story than the one Augum spontaneously concocted back at the Supper Hall. Being from Blackhaven carried too many risks, especially because those necrophyte outfits were actually in the city and would instantly know if he was part of them or not. Regardless, by the time anybody caught on, Augum will have hopefully gotten to the finals, beaten Robin, snatched the divining rod, and they will all have scampered out of there. That was something they still had to figure out of course—their exit strategy, but one thing at a time.

"I'll get the official registrar," and the attendant strode off, soon returning with a pot-bellied man with gray stubble.

"This him?" the man asked.

"Yes, sir."

The man turned bloodshot eyes on Augum. "Show me that you earned them."

Augum gawked a moment before realizing what he meant. He flared his four lightning rings.

"Not the sharpest sword in the armory," the man muttered, signing a parchment and handing it over. "Sign here and here stating that you understand the risks and that you do not hold the tournament liable in case—" but he cut himself off and made a lazy gesture. "Blah, blah, you get the rest," and promptly tottered off.

"You're only the second lightning warlock in your degree," the boy said, marveling at the rings. "And you're very lucky you don't have to prove yourself for the tournament like the others."

Thanks to Malaika's bribery. Augum signed the form and handed it over.

"And what will be your nickname, sir?"

It felt odd being called *sir* by someone near their age. "Oh, uh …" Augum shrugged. "The Hood, I guess." What did it matter?

The attendant looked Augum's necrophyte robe up and down. "The Hood. Very cool."

"Oh, yeah, the ice bath," Augum said reflexively.

The boy blinked. "What?"

Leera giggled, leaned in to his ear. "It's city talk, Aug—cool means trendy or stylish. Basically, he's saying it's a neat nickname."

"Ah, I get it." Augum winked and flashed a thumbs up at the attendant while Leera smacked her forehead.

"Forgive us, we're not from here," Bridget quickly said. "What next?"

"That's all right, we see all kinds here." The attendant got up to write Augum's fake name on a bracket chart. "He's fighting at … the first gong in the afternoon."

Augum opened his mouth to ask what the boy meant by "first gong" but was elbowed by both girls at the same time.

"Perfect, and who is he dueling?" Bridget pressed.

The attendant referenced the brackets, now completely filled in. It gave Augum great relief to see that Robin was on the opposite side of the tournament brackets. That meant that they wouldn't meet until the final round, assuming of course each won all their duels.

"He's dueling Alejandra 'Annihilator' Ramirez," the attendant said.

"Is … is she any good?" Leera asked.

The boy shrugged.

"Does he have to come early?" Bridget asked.

"He should be here to sign-in on the twelfth gong at the latest."

"Thank you." Bridget tapped her lip as she turned away. "That isn't much time. Oh well, should be enough anyway."

"Enough for what?" Augum asked.

"The *biscuit*, remember? And then the briefing?"

"Oh, right." The *biscuit* was their codeword for the Agonex. He had forgotten they were going to race back to the library to start researching it. Then they were to meet up just before noon for a quick briefing with Malaika and Charissa. Truth be told, there was so much going on he felt a little lost. And being amidst such a bustling crowd in a strange city certainly didn't help.

Bridget leaned close. "The gongs refer to the old monastery bell. They ring on the hour. Twelve gongs for noon, then one gong after the first hour, two after the second, and so on, all the way to twelve gongs at midnight. Keeps the city running."

He nodded his thanks. There was so much to learn!

Suddenly the chanting stopped and a smooth voice thundered over the crowd. "Ladies and lads, men and women, young girls and boys—welcome to the Antioc Classic, one of the oldest warlock tournaments still running!"

The crowd cheered as Augum craned his neck to spy a gangly olive-skinned man standing on a platform in the center of the arena. He wore a shimmering rainbow robe and made extravagant gestures.

"I'm Lucca Giovanni, your announcer and master of ceremonies!"

More cheering.

"Oh, we have to stay for the first fight, Brie!" Leera shouted.

Bridget glanced at Augum, who was nodding in agreement.

"All right, *one fight*," she said, "but that's it."

"As you all know," Giovanni boomed in a practiced, articulate manner, "the 1st to the 10th degrees shall be represented by warlocks from all the kingdoms of Sithesia! There will be sixteen combatants per degree battling for the coveted Antioc Classic trophy, in four nail-biting rounds—today we have the qualifiers, tomorrow, the quarter-finals, the day after will be the semi-finals, and then, on the last and most glorious day, the finals—!"

As the man spoke, a slender woman in a peacock-like outfit paraded a large silver trophy of a warlock with hands raised in triumph. There were whistles and catcalls amongst the cheers.

"As well, there will be a one hundred gold-per-degree prize presented to every winner! That means that a 1st degree winner will receive one hundred gold, but a 10th degree winner will receive *one thousand*!" The crowd cheered loudest thus far.

"Past winners include such legendary names as Occulus, The Canterran Cobra, Narsus the Necromancer, Trintus, Matilda Viperborn, and the villainous but infamous Anna Atticus Stone!"

There was a mixed chorus of boos and cheers as Augum exchanged looks with the girls—Nana had been a champion of the tournament once! Why hadn't she said anything?

"Now, for the rules of the tournament—points will be scored with hits to the body. First to five points claims victory, or whoever has the higher score when the hourglass runs out. Off-the-book spells are welcome and encouraged. A contestant may drop to one knee at any time, indicating immediate submission. And of course, a knockout always wins, regardless of score!"

The crowd roared as the drum pounded. "LO-SERS SHALL! BEND THE KNEE! WI-NNERS FIND! ETER-NI-TY!"

"No eye-gouging or use of weapons of any kind other than the ones provided. No teleporting outside of the arena floor. No artifacts and no outside help whatsoever. Cheating will result in immediate disqualification! And now allow me to introduce our illustrious judges—"

Cheers rang out as three figures waved from a booth at the foot of the flags.

"On the near end, standing in the emerald green robe, we have our very own Head Examiner of the Ancient Antioc Library, Vulica Vaneek!"

A distinguished-looking ebony-skinned women with long and curly flaming hair bowed deeply, to cheers from the crowd.

"On the other end, from the Canterran capital city of Iron Feather, please give a warm welcome to the Headmaster of the venerable Academy of Iron, Martus the Black!"

A stern-looking pale man with coal eyes inclined his bald head. There were some boos mixed with scattered supportive cheers.

"And lastly, we have the charming, the indomitable, the famous head of the tracking party always searching for the villainous Anna Atticus Stone—Erika Scarson!"

Even more people booed, much to Augum's pleasure. He wondered if it was Erika, or the fact that she was head of the tracking party. If it was the latter, maybe there were a lot of secret future Resistance supporters in the crowd …

Erika ignored the boos while waving with a giant fake smile, blowing kisses. She was wearing a flashy gold-fringed red robe and the largest earrings Augum had ever seen.

"Delusional as always," Leera whispered into Augum's ear.

But suddenly he realized something—*Erika wasn't carrying the divining rod!* Of course—the tracking party had to be using it! His instincts told him Erika would most likely parade it for the trophy presentation though … or so he sincerely hoped. It was a big gamble, but one worth taking. This also meant the tracking party was out there this very moment, hunting for Nana … she had to last, *had* to!

Giovanni's voice boomed on. "Please remember that at least two of the three judges must pull their judging lever for a point to be awarded. And now … what you've been patiently waiting all year for … the first event of this year's Antioc Classic!"

The crowd cheered loudly.

"We begin with the 1st degree. Since our young contenders have no arcane offensive capabilities, they will have to score points using other creative means. In this corner, representing the Academy of Arcane Arts and the Blackhaven Legion outfit of the Rose Quarter; she wields the air element like a whip and is known to topple block stones in her spare time, please put your hands together for … Maybelle 'Born Blustering' Jackson!"

The crowd cheered as a tiny ebony-skinned girl wearing a necrophyte robe pumped her fist and flashed a single barely visible ring of air.

"And in this corner, coming all the way from the Nodian capital—" Lucca Giovanni held an arm up waiting for the boos to calm down. "From the newly-built Heartfire Academy, wielding the water element like he's putting out a fire … he's known to scowl his opponents to submission … please welcome … Nadir 'The Frown' Nazz!" Giovanni stretched out the z's into a snake hiss as the crowd booed—Nodia was on the Legion's to-be-conquered list, and the necrophytes and supporters in the crowd were making sure the contenders knew it. A sun-bronzed boy with an overdramatic scowl sauntered forth, giving a brief nod and flashing a single watery ring.

Attendants carried the platform away as Giovanni brought the two opponents together to give a final quiet talking-to. More attendants wheeled in six wooden stands, each with a small assortment of wooden practice weapons.

"Now as the ancient tradition of arcane honor dictates … combatants, show your stripes and bow!"

One ring flared to life around each of the combatant's arms. Then they gracefully bowed to each other as the crowd applauded.

Giovanni gestured dramatically at the girl. "Are you ready?" She nodded. He gestured the other way at the boy. "And are *you* ready?" Soon as he nodded, Giovanni made a chopping gesture, shouting, "Fight!" while an attendant near the judges flipped a giant hourglass and rang a bell.

The two opponents wasted no time using Telekinesis to hurl dull wooden spears at each other. The crowd rooted for the ebony-skinned necrophyte, gasping as she ducked the projectile. The boy was not quick enough and got plonked in the shoulder.

The judges pulled their levers and an arcanely-modulated wooden scoreboard flipped one of two zeroes to the number one. Above the one was a sliding slat board painted with the name *Born Blustering*. Opposite, above the zero, was written *The Frown*.

Leera leaned closer to Augum with a giggle. "The Frown. It's like calling someone 'The Wink', or 'The Stare'."

But Augum barely paid any attention. His hands were clammy—this was going to be him in only a matter of hours! In front of a bazillion people—!

"Shyneo!" the Nodian boy shouted, voice arcanely amplified somehow, echoing among the stands. His palm lit up with a weak watery glow.

Leera flipped her hand questioningly. "What's he going to do with that, light up some water with the extension?"

"Born Blustering is not in the least intimidated, folks," Giovanni's voice boomed. "That may have been a mistake on The Frown's part."

The girl gestured at a wooden practice sword behind the boy. It flew toward him, smacking him in the back of the head. The sound of an "Oof!" reverberated through the arena and the crowd roared.

"Two-nothing!" Giovanni stated. "She's really laying it on him—"

Leera was shaking her head. "Why doesn't he do something?"

The boy charged at the girl but she shoved violently at the air, shouting, "BAKA!" and he was sent sprawling.

"Three-nothing!"

Leera scowled. "Come on, he should have seen that coming."

The boy gestured at a wooden club behind the girl and it shot at her. The crowd shouted a warning but she failed to dodge in time and was knocked to the ground. The scoreboard flipped to three-one. The crowd called for her to get up but she suddenly began rotting instead.

"It's a trick, a trick!" Leera was shouting, but the boy couldn't hear above the roar. He sauntered forth, nodding triumphantly and raising his arms in victory.

Leera cupped her hands around her mouth. "The hourglass hasn't run out yet, you fool! It's a trick—!"

As the boy neared, the girl swept a kick his way, tripping him. He fell to the ground with a thud and the scoreboard flipped 4-1.

"What a move!" Giovanni shouted.

"Idiot," Leera muttered as the girl used Telekinesis to shoot a wooden practice sword into her hand, which she promptly used to swing at the Nodian boy. But Nadir "The Frown" Nazz surprised everybody by summoning a shield that blocked the sword strike with a hodge-podge of leaves and sticks. Even the boy seemed surprised that he had achieved the feat—but he had little time to celebrate, because the girl aimed a second strike. This time his Shield spell failed and he cried out as the sword smacked his raised arm.

"Five to one!" Giovanni shouted as the crowd roared their pleasure. "It's over, folks!" He strolled onto the arena, bringing the two panting combatants together. "Please give a round of applause to our two contestants, Nadir 'The Frown' Nazz, and our victor, Maybelle 'Born Blustering' Jackson!" The crowd clapped politely.

Giovanni's hand remained on the contestants' shoulders, even though they looked like they very much wanted to leave the arena immediately. He leaned to the Nodian boy. "How did it feel, Nadir, when you got hit in the head that first time? Was it a surprise?"

The crowd tittered as the boy nervously twiddled his hands. "Uh ... ya, good it not," he said in a thick Nodian accent.

"I bet. Thank you for participating, and try not to get trampled when our valiant soldiers come marching through your town, will you?"

The crowd roared with laughter as the boy's head dropped.

"What a jerk!" Leera called. She cupped her hands, shouting, "Boo! It's you that sucks, Giovanni! Crawl back under the slimy rock you came from!"

Some in the nearby crowd glared at Leera, including one Legionnaire. Bridget gave her a stern look, mouthing, "Are you crazy?" but Leera merely dismissed everyone with a derisive wave of her hand.

Giovanni, meanwhile, turned to the young girl by his side. "Maybelle, what were you thinking when he cast his Shine spell?"

Maybelle was still breathing hard. "Uh … that he messed up, because, uh, there's no useful extension for Shine in his element." The crowd clapped their approval.

"You did extremely well, my dear. I am sure your outfit is very proud." A segment of the crowd composed of necrophytes cheered loudly in high-pitched tones.

"All right. Congratulations, Maybelle, you'll be moving on to the quarter-finals tomorrow. Good luck! Another round of applause, everyone!"

"Ugh, let's get out of here before I barf," Leera said.

BACK IN THE LIBRARY

Soon as they reached the entrance hall, Bridget dug out the library map and gave it a quick study. "This way," she said, leading them toward a hallway. They still had a couple hours before they had to meet Malaika and Charissa for their pre-noon spy report, plenty of time to get started on some Agonex research.

But Augum's mind was mostly on the tournament. How old had Nana been when she won in the tournament, and at what degree had she won? She had to have been young, and certainly still attending the academy at the time.

They strolled down a vast and ancient hallway made from crude stone blocks. Verdigris bronze sculptures of mythical figures sat on carved ebony stands along the walls, behind which hung old tapestries. A smattering of people came and went—Legion warlocks, Legionnaires, necrophytes, people in fancy garb, but very few common folk.

Augum stopped before a sculpture of a wolven flashing his armor. "People here know wolven exist, right?"

"Not really," Bridget replied. "Nobody goes that far north, it's forbidden. Some old pact from some old war. Now wolven are like Leyans—legend."

"I didn't know they existed either," Leera said, "till we bumped into one on that mountain, that is."

They moved on, passing gargoyles and dragons and hellhounds and other mythical creatures. Were they all real too? Hellhounds certainly were, he had fought them at Castle Arinthian. But dragons? There was that tooth he had smashed against Hangman's Rock, a tooth gifted to him by One Eye, a tooth supposedly from a dragon …

The corridor merged into a vast hall with a high, arched roof painted with ancient depictions of scholars, some of whom Augum swore were Leyans, as they were hairless and had black eyes. Thick stone pillars ran down both sides of the hall. Behind the pillars were rows of doors, each guarded by a bored-looking Legionnaire. Some were closed, some open. In the center was a great statue of a gargoyle sitting with its chin resting on its fist in thought, a loose book in the other hand, wings folded neatly behind. Below was an inscription.

The trio slowly approached, marveling at the statue.

"Wonder what the gargoyle represents," Leera said. "See it everywhere."

"Wisdom, inquisitiveness, and strength of character," replied a hoarse voice behind them. They turned to see a bespectacled old man bent over a cane, wearing a gray scholar's robe with an animated embroidered oval depicting a crimson gargoyle. The man had a silver beard that hung past his waist and a matching bush of unruly hair. His ears were as pointy as the gargoyle's.

The man prodded at the ground, wheezing as he strode near the statue, then raised his cane and asked, "Know what it says?"

"No, sir," Augum replied.

"You would if you were studied, yes you would. It translates to, 'Thee wisdom of thy ages be scratched in scroll and parchment. Woe be to those who let either wither'." Then he grunted, nodding to himself. "Know who wrote those words?"

"No, sir."

"No, you certainly do not. But you should. That was written by the library founder, Theodorus Winkfield. Now let me ask another. Know how old the statue is?"

Augum exchanged a bewildered look with Leera and Bridget. "I'm sure we don't, sir."

"Ah, I was hoping you'd tell me." The man wheezed a laugh. "I don't either, but much older than me, yes it is." He rubbed his heavily veined nose and turned to look at them. He squinted at their robes, blinking rapidly, and loosed a great big sigh. "They don't teach you kids proper history like they should, no they do not. Once was a time they did, but not anymore." He waved his cane in a tight circle. "Once was a time you young 'uns knew more than the old fools who prowl these here halls, yes siree, you can bet on that." He kept nodding as if his neck was a swing. After staring at the trio with those rapidly blinking eyes, he suddenly thrust his cane at one of the doors. "Necromancy's that door there, yes she is, though she be a harsh mistress, yes she be, a harsh mistress indeed."

"Uh, sorry, sir, but we're not here to look at necromancy," Augum replied, quickly adding, "Today, that is. Maybe tomorrow."

The man's bushy brows rose. "Well then, sonny, what, pray tell, are you here for?"

"Is there a section on artifacts?"

"Oh, aye, there's a section on artifacts." The man's head returned to bobbing along as if it was a cork in water.

"Can … can you tell us where it is?"

"Aye, I can." His eyes stayed even as his head went up and down and up and down, driving Augum nuts.

"So … where is it?"

"Somewhere in this library."

"Right … Should we just maybe poke around then?"

The man's head now started swinging the other way. "Nay, ye probably shouldn't do that, nope, no siree … but you could."

"I don't understand—"

The man turned on his heel, looked up at the gargoyle. "Do you want to know a secret?"

The trio exchanged looks. Was this man mad?

"Sure, I guess," Augum replied, hoping this was going somewhere soon.

The old man's hoarse voice dropped to a tremulous whisper as he nodded at the inscription. "There are words behind these words, yes there are indeed."

The trio came a little closer to inspect the words.

Augum frowned. "You mean, like, a double meaning?"

The man stood impassively watching them, head bouncing.

"I don't see anything," Leera replied.

"That's because ye ain't really lookin', is you now? What does that there gargoyle represent?"

Leera frowned. "You just told us."

"But were you listening, lass?"

Bridget tapped her chin. "Wisdom, inquisitiveness, and strength of character …"

"Ah, this one here has brains to go along with them little ears." He made an impatient gesture with his cane. "Now put two-and-two together, dear, come on now, lest these bones grow any more brittle."

Augum and Leera glanced at each other. What was he going on about?

Bridget's face suddenly lit up. She approached the inscription, reached out, and said, "Un vun deo." The words immediately morphed. " 'Thou canst find wisdom, if thou not searcheth for it first'," she read solemnly.

The man smiled, head wobbling. "Very good, young lass, very good. And what does that tell you about this here ancient institution?"

Bridget crossed her brows in concentration. "It says two things—that not all is as it first appears, and that things cannot be found without being searched for."

"Omnio incipus equa liberatus corsisi mei."

Bridget immediately replied with, "All begin equal but only the curious thrive."

The man's smile broadened as he gave her an appraising look. He opened his palms and glanced at the ornate ceiling. "Unnameables, there is hope for this lost generation yet. Have mercy on the few we have remaining. Keep them safe and guide them on the path of knowledge."

He returned his gaze to Bridget's robe and started shaking his head again. "A pity, my dear, a real pity, yes it is." His voice dropped. "Your time would be better served as a scholar within these here walls, yes it would. There are many, many secrets to be unlocked here, to be rediscovered even, I dare say, yes I do."

He raised a stern finger and went absolutely still. "But if you repeat it, I shall deny it, yes I will. And then I shall play the old fool, and no one will be the wiser." He winked and wheezily chuckled, head bob returning. "Did you know that sometimes you can tell the age of an idea just by the smell of the parchment? Did you know that? Yes you can indeed. One must take time in life to bend down and sniff the pages."

Suddenly he put on a stern mask, freezing once again while whispering, "But be on ye guard, for there be people …" His rapidly blinking eyes flicked to and fro. "That do not like their secrets being aired, no they do not. And then … and then there be ghosts, and ghosts are never to be trifled with, no, never trifle with a ghost." His voice dropped even lower, to a gravelly rumble, and his face darkened. "But then … then there are ghosts of ghosts … the past come to life … that go out of their way to harm the soul, yes they do." His head bobbed slowly. "They do indeed … sometimes with a puzzle. Sometimes with a gesture." He tapped the floor slowly with his cane. "Some of those ghosts of ghosts rest in this here very library, yes they do. In its five foot walls. In its statues. In the bowels of bowels, deep, deep beneath the shell that is what the unlearned peasant sees. Old, tired ghosts, whom you'll probably never even get to lay eyes upon …"

The trio exchanged wide-eyed looks. Augum felt goose bumps on his skin. Something about the way the old man spoke …

The man raised that bony finger again. "But you shouldn't ask too many questions either, no you should not, not around here. Not in this time. Especially not the right ones." His eyes bored into Bridget. "No, those questions can get a young lass put in the ground awful quick, oh yes, awful quick …" His voice dropped to a whisper. "Or worse … raise her after she be buried."

Bridget drew her hood a little tighter.

"Omnio incipus equa liberatus corsisi mei," the man repeated in that same spooky tone before suddenly brightening. "Why don't I leave you to it then, eh?" He chuckled to himself while wiping his veined nose. "Never too early for a whisky, no it ain't, I says, never too early," and he padded off, cane tapping on the floor. He sang to himself in a warbling tone, *"Too early or too late, it don't matter here nor hine, yet the library it doth open, and close at the strike of nine, yes it does, it does indeed ...*"

"Who in Sithesia was that?" Leera said.

"Wish we'd asked," Augum replied.

Bridget watched the man go before turning back to the statue. "Not sure he would have told you anyway."

Leera nodded at the inscription. "Words are back to that gibberish again."

Bridget glanced around as if seeing the library anew. Augum, too, suddenly saw things he had not noticed before—a small odd gargoyle, out of place amongst a family tapestry scene; a runic carving up high on one of the pillars, not repeated on any of the other pillars and far out of reach; how each of the doors had a different rune, subtly etched among a forest scene, or a castle scene, or some other scene; he even noticed an odd stone in the walls, discolored from the rest. Everything seemed to have meaning, layers, depth ... secrets. Yes, this place had secrets, many of them. He could smell it in the musty and ancient air.

A RIDDLE

"We're almost out of time," Bridget said as a crier proclaimed the 11th strike of the morning bell. They had walked all about the hall, searching for the section on artifacts. They did not dare ask anyone where it was, especially not any of the numerous Legion guards posted at each door. Instead, they read what signs were posted, finding rather mundane sections thus far: law, languages, economics, farming, music, poetry, history, the trades, heraldry, herbology, and so on. A watchful gray-robed attendant and a guard manned each room, and the trio saw everyone who entered had to sign a form.

"But where are all the rooms on arcanery?" Leera whispered. "I don't get it, all of those sections so far have been for *Ordinaries*."

"Some people find that word offensive," Bridget said.

"Only Ordinaries do. And the necromancy study room doesn't count—they didn't even have spell books in there, or anything interesting really."

"What about those at the front of the hall?" Augum nodded at a pair of massive black doors, guarded by two brutish-looking Legionnaires, their mailed hands resting on the pommels of two-handed swords.

"You want to be the one to ask them?" Leera asked.

"Think I'll pass."

"Thought so."

Bridget withdrew the library map. "Interesting … it's unmarked. The room is grayed out on here, with a dotted line."

"Something tells me we're not supposed to be going in there," Leera said.

"Which is exactly why we should find a way in," Augum whispered, grinning.

"Let's look around." Bridget moseyed by a guard, pretending to glance at the ancient artwork behind him, though she was really searching the walls. Augum and Leera did the same.

"Don't whistle," Leera said to him.

"Why?"

"It's suspicious, and you're a terrible whistler, like squeaky bellows or something."

They casually walked the room, but finding nothing particular, exited back the way they had come.

"Place is spooky now," Leera whispered as she eyed the statues in the arched hallway.

Augum absently nodded as he spotted another tapestry with a hidden gargoyle.

Bridget stopped before one of the tapestries. "Look." She subtly nodded her head at a figure in a tapestry.

Augum paced over to see a proud and stern looking man with a large group of people behind him. Everyone wore ancient clothing that had lots of ruffles, and stood on a wide marble staircase flanked by two smaller curving staircases. Stone globes marked the baluster endings. Near the back stood an empty suit of shining armor.

"Look familiar?" Bridget whispered.

The hairs on the back of Augum's neck stood on end. "Castle Arinthian … do you think that's *him*—?"

"Could be," Bridget said. She glanced at a patrolling Legionnaire. "We shouldn't stare at this too long, come on."

Augum spotted another gargoyle in the scene as he slowly strolled away. This one was tucked away in a corner, camouflaged by the checkered flooring, and held a candle.

"Is this library really that old?" Leera asked as they paced away.

Bridget's gaze fell upon a triple-headed dog as they passed. "Something tells me it is. At least the castle part."

Augum's ancestor, Atrius Arinthian, defeated Occulus after receiving a scion from the Leyans, but the tapestry looked like it was a scene before the war of the scions started. That would date the tapestry, at the very least, 1500 years …

"Since the Legion made spell scrolls illegal," Bridget muttered, studying the map, "they would have restricted access to them, not to mention spell books, or anything related to arcanery. There's a large room beside that grayed-out one on the map here. Maybe there's a way to sneak in."

" 'Hall of Ancestry'," Leera read. "There's no hallway leading to it though."

"Must mean we have to take a portal," Augum said.

They soon returned to the entrance hall of the library, then dipped into the main Portal Room.

Augum thought to try something. He found an etched oval with the words *Arcane Studies* next to it. *Restricted* had been chiseled in underneath. "Shyneo," he said after checking to make sure they were the only ones there.

"Aug, don't—" Bridget said as he placed his hand on the oval.

"Might be worth a shot," he said. "We can just say we're lost or something and play dumb." He turned back to the oval. "Augustus Westwood," but nothing happened.

"No surprise since we don't have access," Leera said, finding another oval. "This one leads to the Hall of Ancestry." She activated it and they stepped through.

The trio was spit out into a vast, dim room with a vaulted ceiling. There were great stone sculptures everywhere, depicting figures, battle scenes, miniature castles, towers, towns and villages. Someone was chiseling distantly, the sound echoing with every strike.

"State your business for visiting the Hall of Ancestry," said a snippy voice. They turned to see a bell-shaped woman behind a battered desk, flanked by two gruff-looking Legionnaires, their helms removed. A single candle sat before her, fluttering with every labored breath she expelled.

Augum blurted the first thing that came to mind. "We're here to see the statue of Occulus."

The woman, wearing draping gray attendant garb, glanced at their necrophyte robes before scribbling something down. "Sign and date this." She wore pointy spectacles that gave her the appearance of a cat. Her hair was pulled back in a bun so tight it was distorting her face.

The trio paced over. Augum was conscious of the guards watching him with grim eyes, and noted their hands rested on their sword pommels. He signed his name and dated it in the spaces provided, 17th day of the 3rd month, year 3341, 11th toll of the morning bell.

"You are from out of town."

"We are," Augum replied.

"That will be four silver a head."

"It costs *that much* just to come in here?" Leera said.

"My, aren't you precious. Why of course it does, silly dear," giving the guards an amused look. "There are a lot of administrative costs to cover in keeping this place running. Nothing in life is free now, is it?"

Bridget hesitated but handed over twelve silver coins.

The woman nodded at the hall. "Occulus is around the corner in the very back, and be mindful of the works. Just because you are necrophytes does not mean you get any leeway." She snorted at one of the guards. "Kids these days. Always acting above their station." Their lips curled with sneers.

The trio hurried off, trying not to appear too curious as they shuffled past assorted large scale dioramas carved out of marble and blackened with age.

"Pure robbery," Leera muttered. "Bet you she's gouging us. Probably pocketing the difference."

"Not everyone is a thief, Lee," Bridget remarked, eyes traveling over the many works.

The place smelled of oil and was poorly lit, with only a portion of the braziers burning. Many of the carvings were hidden in shadow and covered with a layer of dust. The sound of chiseling slowly got louder as they made their way to the back of the hall.

Augum suddenly did a double-take at a defaced statue. He stopped, grabbing Leera's arm.

She gave a yelp. "What the—" and then immediately saw what he was looking at. "Bridge, I think you need to see this."

They crowded near a roped-off, full-sized statue, arm detached, with part of the head chipped off.

" 'Anna Atticus Stone'," Augum began to read in a whisper, " 'depicted here on her 10th degree victory at the Antioc Classic Warlock Tournament, is one of the few to hold the distinction of achieving victory in every tournament battle she has fought. She is noted for many academic contributions to the arcane arts, and gained respect as a lethal battlefield warrior after defeating numerous warlock opponents, most notably the Desert

Destroyer, the Canterran Cobra, and Totillus the Turncoat Monk. Known as a true arcane artist, the distinguished warlock later went on to accept the position of Headmistress at the prestigious Academy of Arcane Arts in Blackhaven, where she continued contributing to academic arcane knowledge, only to disappear during her most famous duel against Narsus the Necromancer, whom she is credited with vanquishing. Her whereabouts are currently unknown.' " The words *thief*, *traitor*, and *villainous dog* were scratched on her face.

Augum stood gazing at it, trying to ignore the clipped and echoed chiseling. He felt his nails dig into his palms. He glanced back the way they had come and saw that the attendant was unable to see them.

"Aug, what are you doing—" Bridget hissed as he stepped over the rope.

"Fixing it." He placed his hands over the damaged statue and visualized it repaired, channeling the appropriate arcane energies. "Apreyo," he said, and the statue began to reform. The scratchings disappeared, replaced with fragments from the floor the attendants never bothered to sweep up. Soon Mrs. Stone stood in her original condition, staring straight ahead in determination, chin slightly raised, right arm rippling with ten carved lightning rings. Only one small piece from her cheek was missing, perhaps too far away to re-attach.

Bridget sighed as she helped him back over the rope.

"She looks so … young," Leera said.

"And beautiful," Bridget added.

"She must have been an awesome combatant to watch," Augum noted, suddenly feeling the ache of wondering where she was, and if she was all right.

"You three—what are you doing!" shouted the attendant. "Get away from there!"

"Nothing!" Leera replied. "Just looking at this traitor here," and they quickly sped off. Augum risked a glance back and was relieved to see the attendant return to her desk.

"You can't take chances like that, Aug," Bridget whispered. "What if they discover it's been repaired?"

"I don't care," he said. "Couldn't leave Nana like that."

Bridget's mouth thinned but she said nothing more on the subject. Instead, she subtly raised her hand and said, "Un vun deo." Augum and Leera promptly did the same. Augum recalled doing this in Castle Arinthian—searching for the eggs together, or pieces of that map. Now here they were, using the same spell in the real world looking for a way to get into a restricted section, albeit with severe consequences should they get caught.

They slowed their walk, faces tight with concentration. Suddenly all stopped before the same statue—that of a lion draped in ragged cloth, overseeing a large iron chest.

Bridget dropped her hand, nodding at the chest. "Leads to that," she whispered. "I think it might be a secret door."

The chiseling suddenly stopped and a dusty and sweaty-browed man appeared from around the corner. He was middle-aged and wore a soiled leather apron over his gray attendant robe. He looked past them at Anna Stone's statue, and flashed a roguish grin before glancing at the chest.

"Found it, did you?" He dabbed at his balding head with a dirty cloth, chisel and hammer clutched in the other hand. "That's one of the easy ones there."

"Uh, we're here to see Occulus' statue," Augum quickly said.

The man gave a grunt. "Secret passageway are more fun, but suit yourselves." He jerked his head behind him. "He's between His Lordship and the library founder."

"Who is?"

The man gave Augum a look like he was slow, something Augum was getting used to in the city. "Occulus. You know—that there statue you came to visit?"

"Oh, right."

"Where does the passageway lead?" Leera suddenly whispered, much to Bridget's alarm.

His lips curled mischievously. "You I like. You didn't hear this from me, but too many of you necrophytes don't have the courage the previous generations had, before they made you wear those silly costumes. What a nice thing it be to see some rule breakers."

His voice dropped. "Did you know in the old days in this here library, warlocks were made to earn their learning by solving puzzles? If they were too stupid to solve a puzzle, they didn't get to visit the section, or find the book. Did you know that? You had to be smart, that's right. Smart and clever and curious. That's what the library was founded upon, curiosity … and *mischief*." He winked before making a dismissive gesture, voice derisive. "Now you can't even visit a section without the appropriate authority's blessing or whatnot. They even banned spell scrolls. You believe that? I reckon they're more paranoid that a—" Suddenly his eyes flicked to a spot behind them and he quickly returned to work.

The trio turned to see the bell-shaped attendant striding their way, brows crossed like two swords.

"Uh oh," Bridget said as the trio hurried to Occulus' statue, which stood near the Lord of the Legion's effigy. The carver was already on his knees, chipping away at the boot of the statue.

"Why did you fix that traitor's statue?" the attendant asked in silky tones after arriving.

The trio, who had been pretending to be studying the statues, whirled to gape at her.

Augum could barely speak. Nothing was coming to mind. "We … uh, that is …"

"I had 'em fix it, Secretary Watts," the man said in a suddenly heavy commoner accent.

Secretary Watts pushed her spectacles back up her oily nose. "Why in the Lordship's name would you do that, you simple fool?"

He shrugged from his seated position. "I spend tendays, sometimes months carving these here works without arcanery. Months. Now, that might not mean nothin' to someone as advanced in spell casting as you, Secretary Watts, but it mean lots to me. She be a villain and all, I give you that, but it don't mean my work is to be disrespected." He pointed at the trio. "These three stood yonder laughing at there statue, and I dared them to do somethin' positive and try fixin' it instead. I dared them, told 'em they ain't smart enough to fix that there statue I done carved years ago. They sure proved me wrong, but I is a simple fool, as you say."

The woman's wide lips widened even further. "Basil, I think the only reason you haven't been sent to the mines is because you are too stupid to handle a pickax but just smart enough to wield that chisel." She glared at the trio. "And don't you touch anything again." She made an irritated noise and turned on her heel to waddle off.

Basil watched her go. "That's Secretary Grizelda Watts," he said, mostly dropping the commoner drawl. "She's only 4th degree but puts on airs. More sour than a bucket of limes. Stay away from her, she enjoys inflicting pain and misery into people's lives." He smiled and winked at the trio, then returned to work.

"Thank you, but why did you do that for us, sir?" Augum asked in a whisper.

"And why did your accent change?" Leera added.

"You know, I've been working here all my life. That statue that you repaired, that was one of my first commissions, back when I was a wee apprentice about your age. Ever since Anna Atticus Stone was branded a traitor, that statue has been subjected to nothing but vandalism. Now and then, I'd spot someone standing in front of it, looking at it differently, like you three. But not once had I seen anyone dare to fix it. Not once. I ain't going to ask you your reasons, but I just appreciate it, that's all. Oh, and—" He made sure they weren't being watched before flexing his arm, revealing two fiery stripes, before quickly disappearing them.

"You're a warlock—" Bridget said. "In secret though?"

"How do you think I wasn't conscripted? By lying. Nobody knows I'm a warlock, and I intend it to stay that way. That's why I never repaired the statue myself."

Augum frowned. "So you've been working here all your life, carving statues and stuff, but you could be using arcanery to do the work—"

The man shook his balding head. "There ain't no craft in chiseling telekinetically. Tried it at the beginning, ain't no fun at all and nowhere near as precise. Maybe if I was a 10th degree or something, I'd be a better and more efficient carver, but I hit my ceiling at the 2nd." He tapped at his temple. "It was Mind Armor. That was the end of it. The old noggin's just too feeble for the advanced stuff, and to be honest with you, that's just plenty fine with me."

Basil the chiseler leaned a little closer. "Anyhow, when the Legion took over, they changed most of the attendants. Took the warlocks for their cause. But I ain't no fighter. I don't have the courage or the skill or the desire to kill. And I certainly ain't smart enough." He shrugged. "So I decided to play dumb. I was born in the country and I just decided to sound that way again. And no one's been the wiser."

"How do you know we won't tell on you?" Leera asked.

"Because you repaired Anna Atticus Stone's statue. That rightly mean you're not true necrophytes, ain't that right?"

The trio did not reply and the man smiled. "Your secret's safe with me, as I know mine is safe with you. Oh, and speaking of secrets—" He nodded past them. "There are a whole bunch of secret entrances like that, hidden around the library, and almost all of them lead to the Labyrinth."

"The Labyrinth?" Augum asked.

Basil tapped at the floor, voice even quieter now. "It's called *The Dungeon,* and it's deep below the place. Back in the day, it used to be a trial warlocks passed with pride—getting through the labyrinth and earning g—whoa, almost gave it away for you there. Don't want to do that, do we? Ruins the fun. Anyway, the builders of the library rewarded cunning, daring, and curiosity. They rewarded it with knowledge. If you read your history, you'd know it was the way of the old world, before the Leyans withdrew."

"How do you know all this?" Leera whispered.

"This a library, ain't it? I may not be as quick with the smarts as some, but I love to sneak a book now and then, more than what's good for me I reckon, especially nowadays. I also met plenty of smart folks over the years. Smart and good of heart that told me lots of stories, mostly in whispers. Most of them are gone now. It's darn sad to watch the old traditions slowly die and be smothered and kept under lock and key. Reckon you shouldn't be limited to no necromancy and only what they teach you—which isn't much at all from what I hear, just enough to make you a good soldier. You should be allowed to study whatever you want. Did you know they're slowly killing off the elements? Have you not noticed that?"

"Wait, what do you mean by 'killing off the elements'?" Augum asked.

Basil listened for a moment and they could hear the attendant gossiping with her guards. "They have a plan with you young ones—do you know what happens when you study necromancy from the beginning, and then pass the *Torment Trial* at the 5th degree?"

"Torment Trial? What's that?"

Basil the carver gave them an odd look. "You should know what it is, supposedly being necrophytes and all—anyhow, if you pass, you graduate from a necrophyte to a full-fledged necromancer. You know how right now warlocks have all kinds of rings? Once you become a necromancer, you stop learning your natural element. You become corrupted and the like, and your rings ... they turn *black*. I know because I read about it, you see. You haven't seen any true 'born-from-the-cradle' necromancers yet because none of them have been studying necromancy that long, and not from the beginning. But you'll probably see one eventually if things go the way they're going, you mark my words. Probably see a great many of them, young and old alike. That academy has been corrupted. Turned into a mill that pumps them kids out all brainwashed and the like."

Bridget's gaze lingered on a nearby brazier. "That's perfectly horrible. I can't imagine a kingdom without any fire or earth or lightning degrees."

"Or healing," Basil said, wiping his hands. "All of it'll be gone, that's right, that's the plan. Corrupt the youth, turn them into slaves of the dark arts of necromancy. I know, it's crackpot talk, but I believe it, I do. In any case, you didn't hear any of this from me, did you?"

"No, sir," Bridget replied quietly.

"If you want to be one of the last to experience the old traditions of the library, then you'll have to take your chances now, before they seal it up for good. They're finding them all, one by one." He nodded again in the direction of the secret passageway. "Can't get in that way no more, for example. The Legion done sealed up all the easy ones. Real tough getting to the good parts of the library. Real tough if you want to see down below."

"So how do we get in?" Augum whispered.

The man grinned. "In the tradition of the library's builders, I'm not supposed to give you a hint of that kind."

Secretary Klines didn't want to give them hints either.

Basil twirled his cloth. "But tell you what, because the Legion done made the Labyrinth inaccessible, I don't see why you can't get *one* little hint, just to make things a bit fair and all. They've sealed off the secret doors they know of by using the Unconceal spell, but they missed one really well-hidden one, one that only becomes accessible after the ninth toll of the evening bell, one that takes curiosity to find and cannot be revealed by any ordinary spell. Now listen close, for your hint is in the form of a riddle—*tap into a part of ancestry*."

"Tap into a part of ancestry," the trio mumbled back.

Great, Augum was thinking—he wasn't particularly skilled at riddles. Tap into ancestry? Oh no—that meant doing a ton more research. And whose ancestry? There were so many great historical figures. He almost groaned.

"By the looks on your faces I'd say you might be thinking of literature. Well, you're in a library, it's got to be literal, ain't it?" He chortled. "You'll enjoy that one later," he muttered in afterthought, before growing serious. "But be warned—the Legion dumped a bunch of walkers and stuff down there as guards, mostly the experiments that didn't quite bear fruit, if you get my meaning. Some of them be twisted and the like, so it's dangerous—sometimes very dangerous. If you make it down there even."

The trio exchanged looks.

"And then there are the ancient library puzzles," Basil continued as he returned to chiseling. "Puzzles which, depending on what section you'll be trying to access, will give you quite the challenge—some of them are deadly though, so don't try any section above your skill level. Traditionally, those that you did beat gained you entry in the form of higher portal access and initiate rank increases. But as you probably guessed by now, the Legion done locked all that out too, to prevent warlocks from accessing the restricted books and stuff. Oh, and be warned—the Legion patrol the hallways after hours. No one unauthorized is supposed to be roaming about, so you'll have to be clever. How well do you work together?"

"Pretty well," Leera said with a smile.

"Good, because there's no help down there. If you get in trouble, you'll be on your own. Warlocks *have* gone down there never to be seen again. Sometimes, giggling groups of young 'uns just like yourselves. Understand?"

The trio nodded.

"You better, because it's serious down there, especially these dark days. Now you best run off before Watts comes back. Good luck."

"Thank you … for everything," Augum replied, and the trio left, each mulling the riddle over in their mind.

FIRST MATCH

The trio hurried back to the room to meet with Malaika and Charissa. Unfortunately, they had very little time before the noon gong, when Augum was supposed to sign in by for his first duel. Thankfully, Malaika and Charissa were already waiting for them. They were perched on the window ledge, watching the city, and sprang off when the trio entered.

"Can we talk while we walk?" Bridget said breathlessly. "Augum has to sign in for his duel really soon."

Malaika flashed a cheery smile at Augum. "Of course! We were going to go see him anyhow."

The five of them set off through the bustling streets, exchanging stories of what they had been up to, particularly the riddle, which neither Malaika or Charissa could make sense of.

"I'd delve into the ancestry of the founder of the library," Malaika offered, which actually made sense to Augum, and narrowed what they had to look for.

"Or it could be the ancestry of the Lord of the Legion," Charissa added, giving a withered beggar a revolted look.

"But that's silly," Leera said, "because then he'd be looking into his own family's history."

"Oh, guess so. Never mind then."

Malaika flashed a cheery smile at Augum. "Anyway, Augum—"

Leera suddenly made a hissing noise much like a viper and Malaika realized her mistake—she had accidentally used Augum's real name. Luckily, no one in the busy crowd had noticed. Leera held a single finger in warning at her, eyes dangerous slits. Malaika edged away from her.

"Let's grab a quick lunch," Bridget said, finding a stall with Antioc street food, consisting of boar meat, soggy leeks and bread. But at least it was hot food, which they ate as they walked.

"So about Robin," Malaika said a little quieter. "They still say he's the favorite by far, but we couldn't see his match because it started right before we were supposed to meet you. But we did learn about your opponent, Alejandra 'Annihilator' Ramirez. We asked the gamblers about her, who seem to know everyone's weaknesses and strengths."

Bridget's brows rose. "That's clever."

Malaika gave her a patronizing look before babbling on. "They said she's quick on her feet and throws a heck of a First Offensive, whatever that means."

"What element is she?" Bridget pressed.

"Earth."

"And she's sixteen years old," Charissa threw in.

"That means it'll be similar attacks to mine, Aug—vine. Remember that. And don't forget—you can't use Centarro at all in case Robin is watching, because he'll instantly know it's you."

He was nodding, trying to ignore the nervous buzzing in his stomach.

"You'll recognize her by the flowers in her hair," Malaika droned on. "They also said she hasn't trained as hard with Mind Armor as some of the other combatants. I suppose Mind Armor is some kind of mental—"

"Hit her with Fear or Confusion straight away then," Leera interrupted, punching at the air. "And it doesn't matter that she's older. Your spellcraft strength is still probably going to be way higher than hers, especially if she's undertrained."

"Why is that?" Charissa asked.

"Because he's been training in the field."

"Field? As in, a farming field?"

Leera gave her a look before shaking her head and rolling her eyes. "Never mind."

Malaika said a bunch of other stuff about Augum's opponent, but by then Augum had stopped listening because the thunderous sound of the crowd reached his ears and all he could think about was standing before that chanting throng, making a total fool of himself, or worse … being found out.

All four of the girls rambled on with assorted advice, yet all he could do was nod stupidly, until Leera noticed the look on his face and told them to quiet down and give him time to mentally prepare.

They soon reached the arena, paid again, and strode to the registration desk. Augum was promptly signed in and told to go to the dressing rooms.

"All right, good luck," Malaika said, trying to reach for his hand only to have her arm smacked away by a glaring Leera. Malaika flashed her a hateful look before smiling sweetly at Augum, "We'll be watching and rooting for you in the stands. A thousand good lucks!"

Bridget gave him a hug. "You'll do fine. Remember that she'll attack with vine. Pivot when you can, bring up your Shield and—"

"Enough," Leera said. "You're overdoing it."

"Right. Good luck."

Leera hugged him close and gave him a secret peck on the cheek. "Show her what you're made of."

Augum was in a daze as he made his way to the dressing rooms under the arena. The place stank of sweat and burning oil. Old hooded lanterns flicked against roughly-hewn rock walls. Dust fell from the ceiling as the crowd chanted, "LO-SERS SHALL! BEND THE KNEE! WI-NNERS FIND! ETER-NI-TY!"

Suddenly he heard a familiar voice that instantly made him curl his fists.

"No, but did you see the way I threw him against the wall?" Robin Scarson gloated. He was striding Augum's way, a towel around his neck. Bouncing on his chest was the Destiny Stone, clasped in a claw setting. Temper was beside him, a smug look on her face, head surrounded by a halo of curly red hair.

"You're going to win this competition, Robbie, I know it," she cooed.

Augum strode by, head down, trying to resist the urge to punch his face in. To them, he must have looked like just another necrophyte because they walked right by without noticing. Too bad he'd missed Robin's first match. Would have been smart to see him fight. He resolved to watch his duel tomorrow instead.

"Of course I'm going to win, have you any doubt?" Robin's voice echoed and died off as they disappeared down the tunnel.

Augum, blood still running quick from the close encounter, soon arrived at a dingy room with rows of well-worn trestle benches on which sat various combatants, almost all older than him. The foreign fighters seemed to wear extravagant garb while the necrophytes, who were forced to wear necrophyte robes, made up for it by having different colored hair, or even having their faces painted. One necrophyte girl near his age had long blue hair and was practicing incantations by herself in a corner. There was an older olive-skinned boy with almond eyes and snow-white hair making gestures at a scuffed wall. He wore a colorfully embroidered robe and a foreign crest Augum did not recognize.

But among all of the combatants, the one that drew his attention was his adversary, Alejandra 'Annihilator' Ramirez. He knew it was her because of the flowers in her long black hair. The sixteen-year-old had amber skin, green eyes and a round face, and wore a beautifully embroidered velvet robe depicting exotic flowers. She was murmuring to herself and pacing. Her hands were shaking slightly. Augum wondered if this was her first tournament as well.

A slender cocoa-skinned woman with a plaited ponytail and gray robe was referencing a parchment scroll and looking around the room. She spotted him and said, "Augustus Westwood?"

He nodded, careful to keep his face hidden within his hood.

"I figured it's you because of the hood. I'm Secretary Sharma. Have a seat please." She checked off her parchment, muttering, "The Hood. Excellent."

Alejandra, his opponent, immediately stopped what she was doing to stare at him. She nervously rubbed her hands together before returning to murmuring spells under her breath. Everyone seemed to be doing the same, filling the room with an unintelligible buzz. Augum did not want to tip his hand with what spells he knew, and thus went over everything in his mind. Or at least he tried—it was difficult concentrating, what with the stomping and chanting above shaking the walls, and the occasional sudden roar of the crowd as a combatant fell or scored a hit.

Secretary Sharma called name after name. New opponents wandered in as old ones left. Augum had mentally gone through all his spells three times before she suddenly called out his and his opponent's names. They were paired side-by-side and escorted down to the end of a long exit hall, which opened into the arena. The roar of the crowd suddenly sounded louder than a thunderstorm. The announcer, Lucca Giovanni, finished interviewing the last combatants in a smooth booming voice, then sent them on their way to polite applause.

"And now we move on to a 4th degree qualifying round match-up. Hailing from the Canterran capital and the Academy of Iron … she may look pretty but she can move mountains … introducing … a sixteen-year-old earth element warlock going by the name of … Alejandra 'Annihilator' Ramirez …!"

Alejandra gave Augum a sidelong look before jogging out into the arena, hair bouncing. The crowd, which at first began booing the foreigner, changed to mixed applause, perhaps after seeing her colorful attire.

"Her opponent, hailing from the obscure Solian village of Everscale, a younger necrophyte of fifteen practicing the always dangerous lightning element … the mysterious … the reclusive … Augustus 'The Hood' Westwooooood!"

Secretary Sharma gave him a push and Augum strode out. The crowd was cheering wildly, the noise deafening. Augum stole a glance at the judge's podium. Erika and library Head Examiner Vulica Vaneek were clapping, while the Canterran judge, Martus the Black, looked on with a dissatisfied scowl.

Augum frantically searched for Bridget and Leera, but was unable to see anything except a dizzying sea of faces. He stopped near Giovanni, whose glimmering robe was blinding up close. The man stank like some kind of pungent weed, making it even harder to concentrate. He was already giving final instructions while attendants wheeled in six wooden stands, each with a small assortment of wooden practice weapons. "… no biting, no eye-gouging, and no artifacts. Don't be alarmed, but I'm going to touch your throats now so your voices may be amplified."

Both Augum and his opponent flinched at the man's hot touch.

"Quick and painless," Giovanni said in a kind voice so quiet and different than his loud one. "I know you're nervous, and that's normal. Fight fair, fight clean and fight well. Good luck to both of you. Now nod that you each understand the rules."

Augum nodded reflexively, barely able to hear past the blood rushing through his ears, past the roar of the stands. His palms were super sweaty and he needed to breathe; everything was moving too quickly. Meanwhile, the crowd chanted, "LO-SERS SHALL! BEND THE KNEE! WI-NNERS FIND! ETER-NI-TY!" to the deep pounding of the drum.

"Now in the ancient tradition of arcane honor … combatants, show your stripes and bow to your opponent!"

Augum was so nervous he could barely get his rings to flare. Then he almost forgot to bow.

Giovanni took a step back and gestured theatrically at Alejandra. "Are you ready?"

She got into battle stance and nodded, the crowd beginning to holler.

Giovanni swung his arms the other way at Augum. "And are *you* ready …?"

Augum swallowed and hesitantly nodded.

Giovanni chopped at the air. "Fight!" and the bell rang.

Alejandra immediately shoved at the air before her, voice arcanely amplified. "BAKA!"

Augum, feeling completely overwhelmed and unprepared, was instantly sent flying, much to the chagrin of the crowd. He tumbled through the dirt as his hood flew off his head.

"That's one-nothing for The Annihilator!"

Augum scrambled to raise his hood, hearing, "ANNIHILO!" and instinctually rolled away, only to see a vine slam into the earth near him, sending a spider pattern of cracks from the point of impact.

Seeing that made it all so very real. His fighting instincts, the ones he had used many times over in many battles, instantly kicked in—he summoned his shield, curled with hard black lightning, and effortlessly blocked Alejandra's next vine attack. Of all the spells, this is the one he had probably practiced most, seeing as he already had some shield training with Sir Westwood. The Shield spell was becoming like Shine—an extension of him. He was so good with it now he was able to keep it cast before him as he marched toward his opponent, who was backing up.

"Look at him firmly hold that spell!" Giovanni was saying as the crowd roared its approval. But Augum was focused only on one thing—his opponent, who finally shouted, "DISABLO!" and Augum's arcane shield was yanked from his arm, disappearing instantly. That surprised him, for no one had done that before.

Giovanni was gesticulating wildly in the background. "Yet his inexperience is clearly showing because The Hood has yet to unleash a single attack—"

Alejandra used Augum's hesitation to raise an arm, shouting, "Dreadus terrablus!"

But Augum, well-prepared for the tingling that the Fear spell triggered, blocked it with his Mind Armor, immediately countering by slamming his fists together and shouting, "ANNIHILO!" The spell—the word itself amplified arcanely to thunder through the arena—felt even more powerful than usual—except he changed his aim at the last moment. A crackling bolt of lightning connected with the ground at her feet, instantly blowing a deep hole in the earth and making her yelp. One of the flowers in her hair loosened and fell to the ground as she stumbled.

Augum knew how powerful his First Offensive was and did not want to hurt her. His always-sharpening sense of battle told him she would not have raised her shield in time.

The crowd roared again as Giovanni's booming voice was yelling, "A massive shot of lightning that surely would have done heavy damage had it struck true! Superbly advanced for a 4th degree—"

Augum used the initiative he had gained to concentrate deeply while shooting an open palm forward, yelling, "FLUSTRATO!"

Alejandra, still bouncing on one foot as she scrambled to get away from the smoking hole, suddenly had her head snap back as if hit by a stone. The crowd, having heard the spell and understanding its effect, roared its approval as she fell to the ground like a sack of potatoes, where she slowly writhed about.

"It's one-one, but that surely must be it, folks, for she is as dull-witted as a newborn babe now! Was that not a powerful casting of Confusion? Oh boy, the others better watch out, we have a real arcane warrior here. Now all The Hood has to do is finish her off—"

But Augum just stood there, breathing deeply. Finish her off? How? She was defenseless! Was he supposed to run down the hourglass or something?

The crowd was getting louder and angrier—everyone seemed to have an opinion on what he should do, but it all sounded like one great cacophonous roar.

Augum looked around for support, still unable to find Bridget and Leera in the howling masses.

"He's hesitating, folks, and she's fighting it off!"

Alejandra weakly gestured at a weapon stand and a spear soon hurtled Augum's way. He easily blocked it with another summoning of his shield.

Alejandra weakly got up on her feet, knees wobbly. "Voidus aurus—" but Augum's Mind Armor was too strong for her weakened Deafness spell. He gestured at a club on her right and practice sword on her left.

"A dual telekinetic attack!" Giovanni was shouting. "An exquisitely rare feat for a 4th degree, one I am sure we have not seen in someone this young since the likes of the villainous Anna Atticus Stone—"

Alejandra summoned a small shield to block the sword, but failed to block the club, which thunked into her back.

"Two-one for The Hood!" Giovanni shouted as the crowd's cheers swelled.

The club strike seemed to jolt Alejandra. She drew a star shape in the air. "Summano elementus minimus!" and a tiny creature about the size of a puppy ripped into existence.

Augum immediately drew his own star-like shape, concentrating on the appropriate arcane energies and thoughts. A lightning elemental three times Alejandra's size—but still only about waist high—crackled to life. The crowd made an *Oooo* sound as Giovanni snorted a laugh at the size disparity. The crowd quickly chimed in with its own laughter.

Augum pointed at the tiny earth elemental. "Elementus, attack!" His elemental made a sizzling sound as it shot forth, obliterating Alejandra's elemental with one kick. She made a yelping sound and began to retreat.

"She's lost her composure! Will The Hood finish her off now?"

But Augum didn't give the command for his elemental to attack her. The poor girl was holding her hands up. "Bend the knee!" he shouted instead. When she hesitantly lowered her arms, he mouthed, "Please, I don't want to hurt you."

The crowd took up the chant, "BEND. THE. KNEE!" to the pounding of the drum.

Alejandra, breathing heavily, immediately dropped to one knee, bowing her head. "I surrender."

The crowd roared.

"And there we have it! Our first non-knock-out submission! A fine display of arcane skill! Simply superb!"

Augum strode over and helped her up. "Good duel," he said, smiling.

"And a fine display of chivalry as well!" Giovanni shouted as the crowd rose to their feet, clapping and whistling their approval.

Augum led the trembling girl to Giovanni, who promptly raised Augum's arm in triumph. "Our winner, in an illustrious display of arcane strength, reservation, and chivalry—Augustus 'The Hood' ... Westwoooooood!"

After the roar diminished a little, Giovanni leaned to Alejandra. "You fought valiantly, but it's obvious to everyone you were outclassed. Your thoughts, Alejandra?"

She smiled and began speaking in a lilting but flowery accent. "Eh, I thought I well prepared, but, um—" She inclined her head at Augum, "he definitely stronger in arts." She giggled while covering her mouth. "I not ... how you say ... good prepared."

"And at what moment did you realize you were vastly outmatched?"

She covered her mouth again as she blushed. "Oh, so many!" The crowd chortled along, clapping politely in approval.

"Well, you've nonetheless won over the crowd with that smile, Alejandra, thank you for competing."

Alejandra detached a flower from her hair and extended it to Augum. "In my culture, we give thank you to, how shall I say, brave kindness. Eh, thank you, Augustus Westwood."

Augum accepted the flower, feeling it would be horribly rude not to, as the crowd *Awwed* and clapped and whistled.

Giovanni rested a hand on Augum's shoulder. "And you've won over a girl's heart. Well done, good sir."

Alejandra blushed crimson as more whistles were heard.

"That was an unusual fight, Augustus," Giovanni went on, "but a joy to watch. You started off slow yet quickly displayed remarkable arcane strength for your degree, but also, I sense, great reservation. You did not want to hurt her, did you?"

"Uh … no, I didn't," Augum had to admit, feeling the slight tremor in his voice reverberate the earth beneath his feet.

"Were you aware that we have two Legion healers on standby?"

"Uh, no, I was not."

"Ah, then there shan't be any excuse next time, will there?"

The crowd chortled as Augum hesitated.

Giovanni calmed them with a hand. "Before I let you go, when are you going to reveal your face to us, or would you prefer to stay mysterious?"

"Mysterious."

Giovanni chuckled. "I thought so. Suits the name well, doesn't it folks? Well, you have honored Solian necrophytes with your chivalry and skill, Augustus, and we cannot wait to see how you fight from here on." He raised Augum's arm again. "Advancing to tomorrow's quarter-finals … the mysterious … the arcanely agile … Augustus 'The Hood' Westwooooood!"

TAP INTO A PART OF ANCESTRY

"My brave warrior," Leera whispered as Augum stuck the red flower in her hair. They were leaving the arena and everyone was patting his back as they strode by. He had already talked to the registration booth, finding out his next match was tomorrow at the third strike of the afternoon bell.

"Didn't know you could use Disarm on a Shield spell," Bridget said. "How come we hadn't thought of that?"

"Battle makes people creative," Augum said, glancing at the suddenly darkening sky. "Looks like rain's coming."

Leera craned her neck. "That came out of nowhere. Won't keep the crowds away though. You're lucky you didn't have to duel in the rain. Wish we were all competing ... but then, I guess we'd be competing against each other."

"You fought amazingly!" Malaika said from the rear, elbow interlocked with Charissa's. "So bravely, so gallantly, so beautifully—"

Leera rolled her eyes. "Cork it, will you?"

"I was just being polite."

Leera shook her head, muttering, "Spare me."

"In any case, Augum, we're going to further our quest," Malaika said. "We'll find out who you're fighting as soon as the combatants duel, and we'll spy on that person too. Come, Charissa, there is spying work to be done!"

Leera watched the pair skip off. "They better not wind up in an iron room, or I swear I'll ..." but she finished the rest under her breath.

"Did Robin watch the fight?" Augum asked.

"Don't think so," Bridget said. "I saw him strut off with Temper just after you entered the tunnel."

Augum was relieved—he was lucky Robin hadn't been watching. He had to be extra careful with his hood, even his voice. And he shouldn't say too much at a time. If anyone here would recognize him, it'd be that arrogant miscreant.

The trio quickly dove into a more detailed discussion on the match, with an animated play-by-play retelling courtesy of a glowing Leera, who accented the story with air punches and dramatic dodges. After lambasting Augum for not following any of her shouted instructions, he had to explain how he hadn't even seen where they sat in the stands, let alone heard them. Leera explained the girls had parked themselves in the very corner near the exit, and that next time she expected him to listen to her coaching.

"And don't be so chivalrous either," she said, smacking him on the shoulder. "This is a competition, not the Star Feast. And just what were you doing accepting a flower from such a pretty girl anyway!"

"He couldn't just turn it down," Bridget said with a chortle. "That would have been the height of rudeness. Besides, didn't he give that flower to the one he truly likes anyway?"

Leera twirled the flower in her hair. "That he did," she said in a mock snooty tone, and found Augum's hand. He was very happy to hold it and wished he could hug her and squeeze her in his arms for a while. It felt like it had been *so* long …

The first drops of rain splashed onto the cobbled streets. Soon they made their way over the drawbridge and past the entrance guards to the library.

"Have either of you given any thought to the riddle?" Bridget asked.

"In case you hadn't noticed, I was a bit busy," Augum replied with a smirk.

"And I was busy hollering at him," Leera added. "You know, from the stands?"

Bridget gave them both a look. "Get serious, you two, we have work to do."

"I *am* serious!" Leera said.

While the girls squabbled somewhat playfully, Augum glanced around the entrance hall, trying to draw inspiration to solve the riddle. Tap into a part of ancestry. Part of what ancestry though? It was something historical, wasn't it? It had to be the library's ancestry. It's the only thing that made sense.

Large ironwork braziers in the shape of gargoyles burned near mammoth pillars that smoothly joined an arched ceiling. Women and men in gray robes quietly shuffled this way and that. Nothing overt stood out though.

He hated riddles. They were always something stupidly simple, or way too complex, or—

Suddenly he spied a curious-looking fellow. The girls stopped their squawking to watch the man too. He wore a simple weather-worn tan robe, rope slippers, and had a shaved head tattooed with a single, thin stripe that ran from the back of his neck, over his head, down to his nose, and through his lips, before disappearing into his chest, essentially dividing him in two, or at least symbolically. He would take a step, pause, ring a small bell, take another measured step, pause, and ring it again. It was a soft sound that barely penetrated the bustle. Yet the entire hall seemed to slow to his pace, even the flames of the braziers. Attendants stopped to listen, not even watching him. Even the Legion guards seemed to relax their stiff stances.

"Mountain Monk of the North," Bridget whispered in reverent tones.

"What's the tattooed line mean?" Augum asked in hushed tones.

"If I remember correctly, it's the division between the past and future. The line represents the moment, 'the eternal moment in which we dwell', or so I read."

A man in a silver-embroidered coat dipped his head and brought over money, which he placed into the man's pocket, already brimming with coins, before quietly backing away.

Bridget dug out a silver coin from her pouch and brought it over, placing it in the man's pocket, before also backing away, head bowed slightly.

Augum watched the monk with a heavy heart, for the man suddenly brought into focus the great danger they were in, what they had overcome, and what still lay before them. The monk's tattooed line was a symbol of the razor edge they tiptoed, that fine balance between life and death. Here was this soul, walking through an occupied library and a conquered kingdom, appearing to be unaffected by its troubles, completely reliant on others' kindness, and accepting his fate.

The trio bowed their heads as he passed. Soon as he stepped through the doors, the bustle of the hall returned, though a little quieter, a little slower.

"Never seen one before," Leera said. "Kind of makes me sad."

Augum slowly nodded in agreement. After a long pause of them watching the rain turn to a downpour, Augum found Leera's hand, squeezed, and said, "I have an idea. We could return to the *Ordinaries* library—" Bridget gave him a disapproving look at that word, "—and study ancestry, specifically about the library itself."

"I was thinking the same thing," Bridget said, and she led them through the hall of bronze statues and on to the large hall of pillars and doors.

Bridget took a deep breath, adjusting her drawn hood. "All right, we sign in, talk as little as possible, and make everything about necromancy if anyone asks what we're doing."

Leera was nodding along. "Yeah, we can say it's a homework assignment or something."

And so they studied, and studied … *and studied,* going from ancient room to ancient room, section to section, signing one entrance parchment after another. Books were large, hand-written, and always chained to a shelf, forcing them to stand along a special podium for reading. A great many books were missing, and they only knew that because there were empty spaces with matching empty chains.

After a crier announced the toll of the seventh afternoon bell, Augum, too hungry and exhausted from the research, could barely keep his eyes on the page any longer. His thoughts meandered to the training room, wondering if there was a way for them to get some time there. Or maybe take 5th degree classes or something, if the Legion let them. But then he recalled how necrophytes take that special test, the Torment Trial, at the 5th degree …

not to mention they'd certainly be expected to perform *some* necromancy.

"We're being watched," Bridget whispered, jolting Augum from his stupor. "It's her again. *Don't* look now though."

Leera's head shot off the page of a book, leaving a small puddle of drool there. "Huh? Who? Are we under attack?" she nearly shouted, drawing condemning shushes from almost everyone in the section. "I hate herbology," she muttered, rubbing her eyes. "When are we getting some grub?"

"Don't look now, but we're being watched," Bridget repeated, calmly turning a page in the enormous tome she was reading.

Augum cleared his throat and then pretended to cough, stealing a glance. He saw a bell-shaped figure talking in a low voice with the attendant that admitted them.

"Watts," Augum whispered to Leera.

Leera blew her dyed hair away from her face. "Hate that woman and I don't even know her."

"Let's just leave," Bridget said. "If she stops us, tell her we've been studiously looking for information on the founders of the town, as a historical task given to us by our mentor from back home."

"From Everscale?" Leera asked.

Bridget gave her a *Well, obviously* look.

"All right," Augum said, slamming his book closed and making a show of yawning, then rubbing his stomach. "Mmm, I'm hungry," he said loudly, and immediately got shushed. "Sorry," he whispered. He pointed awkwardly at the door. "We're going to the Supper Hall," then, after getting shushed again, mouthed, "Sorry, we'll go now … because we're hungry, not because—"

"Shhh—!" This time, even the girls joined in.

Augum meekly led the way to the door, the girls trailing, both hiding their eyes behind their hands out of shame.

Secretary Watts suddenly placed an arm between Augum and the door frame. She had long and sharp red fingernails perfectly shaped to scratch a chalkboard. "Excuse me, but may I inquire as to what you three have been up to over the course of the afternoon?"

"Studying," Bridget said, giving her a blank look.

Watts gave her a simpering smile. "I see. And what exactly have you been studying?"

"We've been trying to find out about the history of Antioc for our mentor back home."

"And where is home, pray tell?"

"Everscale."

"And your mentor is ...?"

Bridget hesitated only a moment. "Sanyika Shaeek. Big fellow, very ill-tempered. Hates to be disturbed."

"Indeed. And he is a Legion—"

"—lieutenant. 14th degree fire element warlock."

"Interesting, that is most accomplished indeed." She made a warbling chortle, a sound akin to a choking frog. "Though I confess I have never heard of him. And you say he is stationed in Everscale?"

Bridget shrugged. "He was. Might be in southern Tiberra by now. His Lordship's commands take precedence."

Secretary Watts gave a sickly sweet smile. "Of course they do, dear. Forgive the questions, but security is a chief concern of ours here at the library. You understand of course—"

"Of course," Bridget said. "Maybe it would ease your mind if you wrote to him to confirm that everything is in order?"

Secretary Watts' knife-thin brows clambered up her oily forehead. "I ... I was going to do that very thing."

"Great." Bridget stood there, staring blankly.

Watts swallowed, licked her lips like a lizard, and flashed a wide-mouthed but insincere smile. "Very well then, as you will."

"Good day, Secretary Watts," Bridget said, and the trio strode off.

The voice was smooth as snake oil. "How did you know my name?"

They froze.

"That worker told us," Leera blurted. "The chiseler."

"Basil. Indeed ..."

The trio got out of there as fast as they dared.

"I can't stand her type," Bridget said through gritted teeth as soon as they were out of earshot. "The meddling, over-controlling—" She made a choking gesture. "Ugh, know-it-all!"

Augum exchanged a look with Leera. "Bridge?"

"Nothing, it's just I had a mentor like that once, for a very, *very* short time." She shivered. "Horrible, *horrible* person."

"Oh, you mean Harvus?" Leera joked, throwing a light elbow. "Or Erika Scarson?"

"*Not* funny."

"No, I suppose it isn't."

"We've had our share of bad mentors now," Augum added.

"At least Mophead taught us how to cast SME," Leera said.

"Not really," he replied. "Left out a bunch of stuff we needed to know, remember?"

"Oh, right." Leera gave Bridget a proud smile. "Didn't realize you're such a good liar."

"We had a story prepared ahead of time. You know, just for such an occurrence?"

Augum guiltily recalled the evening before and how they made all these plans, but he had gotten sleepy and stopped paying attention after a while.

"Besides," Bridget added, "hopefully we'll be long gone by the time anybody figures out that mentor doesn't exist, or that we're not really from Everscale."

They made their way into the hallway of bronze statues, slowing to a lazy stroll.

"Anybody learn anything back there with those books?" Augum asked, hoping Bridget had something juicy.

Leera stayed silent, flashing him a guilty look. He guessed she hadn't soaked much in either.

Bridget rubbed her eyes. "Not too much, unfortunately. Kind of feels like all the important books were missing. Read about some of the founders, all crotchety old men. Oh, but I did learn a lot about symbolism, which could be useful. For example, I learned that fire represents understanding, and that the original symbol of knowledge was a sword—the Sword of Knowledge, it was called. Anyway, the Sword of Knowledge represented light—" She stopped, narrowing her eyes at Leera, who was suddenly pointing at her yawning mouth.

"I should point at my ears too," Leera added, "because everything that you're saying is going in one and out the other. Come on, didn't you learn anything interesting?"

Bridget stopped and ballooned. "Interesting? *Interesting?* And what have *you* learned? I've been studying for five straight hours while you did nothing but drool and pretend to—"

Augum groaned, too tired to intervene. But he did notice they had stopped right in front of the giant embroidery of Atrius Arinthian and his family. "Tap into a part of ancestry," he muttered, examining the family portrait. This was his ancestry. Did it have anything to do with the riddle?

He rolled his eyes at himself. How self-centered. Not everything had to revolve around him …

"Bet you it's something stupid," he mumbled to the arguing girls, who ignored him completely. "Like literally adding a tap into—"

Suddenly he froze, took a step forward and placed his hand on the ancient fabric. Basil had even hinted at it! It was so simple—

The girls stopped arguing.

"Found something, Aug?" Leera asked.

He took a step back to admire the whole of it. "Tap into ancestry."

"Yep, that's the riddle," Leera said.

"Tap *into* ancestry—!"

"Uh, *yeah*."

He glanced between the girls. Each had one brow raised skeptically. "Don't you get it? It wasn't *tap into ancestry* like literature ancestry, it was *literal*, like, literally adding the word 'tap' into the word 'ancestry'. Now do you get it?"

Bridget smacked her forehead. "*Tapestry!* Of course it's something obvious!" She rocked back and forth on her heels giddily. "That's great, Aug, really great job. How did we not see it?"

Leera was staring at her. "All that studying sure came in useful, huh?" she said dryly.

Bridget stopped rocking. "Sorry, Lee, I haven't been getting much sleep. I apologize."

Leera smiled. "Don't you give it a second thought, *Sister*."

Augum returned to studying the tapestry, specifically the spot with the gargoyle holding the candle. "Have you noticed these, you two? There are gargoyles in some of the tapestries."

Leera blinked. "There are?"

Bridget paced over. "The gargoyle represents wisdom, integrity, and curiosity."

"It's not the only one I've seen either," he said, keeping his voice low as an initiate strode by. He led them to another tapestry further back in the hallway. "See, here's one too."

"This one's winking," Bridget said.

"But not all the tapestries have the gargoyles," Leera pointed out, glancing around at the others.

"Spread out," Augum said. "Let's see what else we can find. Meet back here at the cry of the eighth bell. And keep your eyes peeled for Watts."

The girls nodded and dispersed.

Augum had a very hard time finding another gargoyle, eventually glimpsing one high up a tall tapestry, hidden in a corner. It was sitting in a wheat field, all but invisible among the chaffs. He resumed searching, trying to be as inconspicuous as possible, but found no more of them.

When the cry of the eighth toll of the bell came, the trio once again assembled in the hallway, now deserted.

"Didn't find another one," Bridget confessed.

"I found one," Leera said. "A gargoyle, that is. It was camouflaged and held a skull, whatever that means."

"And I found one sitting in a wheat field," Augum said. "That makes, what, four?" He counted them on his fingers. "A gargoyle holding a candle, a gargoyle winking, a gargoyle sitting in a wheat field, and a gargoyle holding a skull."

Bridget ran her fingers through her dyed hair and expelled a tired breath. "I need food. Can't think straight."

"Then we better get going," Leera said. "Supper Hall closes in an hour."

"Good idea. We can discuss the riddle while we eat."

SNEAKING IN

"I can't help but feel there's some sort of connection," Bridget was saying over a nearly empty bowl of potato stew. They were in the Supper Hall and there was hardly anybody there. Rain beat against colorful stained glass windows. Braziers burned low. The library castle would close within the hour, which is when they had to be back in their rooms.

Leera dipped bread into her stew. "Between the gargoyles?"

"Yes. Well, I mean …" Bridget waved her spoon in the air. "There's something awfully familiar about the symbolism. I don't remember if I read it or heard it or …"

"We've got four of these symbolic hints." Augum counted them on his fingers once more. "A gargoyle holding a candle, a gargoyle winking, a gargoyle holding a skull, and a gargoyle sitting in a wheat field." But what did they *mean*?

Leera finished her bread and grimaced. "The skull symbolizes death, that one's obvious." She glanced tentatively at Bridget. "Right?"

"Yes, I agree. But I think it's a riddle, very much like the one that man gave us. And I suspect it has to do with ancestry." Suddenly she peered between the two of them. "What have we been trying to find information on all day?"

"Ancestry—?" Leera replied uncertainly.

"Exactly." She leaned a little closer. "Come on, help me here, you two, there's something *really* familiar about these symbols, I *know* it."

Augum scraped the last of his stew from his bowl. "Did we ever find out who the ancestor of the library was?"

Bridget opened her mouth to speak. "I ... I don't know."

Leera pointed at Augum with her spoon. "Didn't what's-his-face, the weird old geezer we met by the gargoyle, didn't he say something about the founder?"

Bridget's face lit up. "He did, didn't he? The arcane quote ... it was said by the founder. But what was his name again ... Theodorus ... Theodorus what?"

The trio murmured names to each other, feeling they were onto something.

"Wasn't it Winky or something?" Leera finally asked.

Bridget gaped at her. "Yes! It was wink-something ... wink what?"

Augum recounted the hints. "A gargoyle holding a candle, a gargoyle winking, a gargoyle holding a skull, and a gargoyle sitting in a wheat—" He froze for just a moment, and then the trio said it together.

"Field!"

"Theodorus Winkfield," Bridget said in a hushed voice. "That was the founder's name! That accounts for the wink and the field. Now we just have to figure out how the skull and candle factor in."

Leera's hands froze in midair. "A tomb." She glanced between them. "It's got to be his tomb. That's what the skull means—death. And we know where the tomb is, don't we?"

"The Hall of Ancestry," Augum whispered slowly. "Except that's Watts' domain."

"That's not the biggest challenge though, is it?" Bridget asked. "The man said this secret passage is only accessible after the ninth bell, when the library closes—but we're not supposed to be caught in the hallways. So how do we get in there?"

"We hide," Leera blurted. "We go there right now and hide before it closes."

Bridget scrambled for the map. "But there's only the portal entrance that we know of. How do we get by the guards and Watts at the same time?"

"We do it right at the cry of closing," Augum said. "I mean, there'll be a changing of the guard, right?" Or the guards might leave the place altogether.

"Risky, but it might work." Bridget pushed her empty bowl away. "It'll mean we won't get a chance to see Malaika and Charissa. They'll think something's happened to us. Wait, no—I'll send a message by attendant, tell him to leave it under the door."

"It'll also mean we might be stuck down there until morning," Augum added. "But if we can get into the part of the library that's forbidden, that holds information on how to use the *biscuit*—" using the codeword for the Agonex, "—then it'll be worth it." Not to mention they might be able to discover information on all the other stuff they've been meaning to research.

"I say we do it," Leera said. She tapped the table. "And I say we do it now."

The trio exchanged excited looks before scrambling out of the Supper Hall.

* * *

"Hear ye, hear ye! The ninth bell tolls! The library is closing!"

"There's the crier," Leera whispered from the entrance hall after Bridget had sent a message by courier up to their room.

"What did you say?" Augum asked Bridget, worried about discretion.

"For them not to worry and we'll see them soon, that's all."

They were watching the portal room from behind a pillar, blending in with the thinning crowd of people departing the library.

"The crier's entering the portal room," Leera said. "Come on."

"Hey, you're The Hood, ain't you?" said a boy their age wearing a necrophyte robe. He extended his hand to Augum, who was forced to shake it quickly. "I could tell it's you because no one else wears their hood up. I think it's a neat visual, to be honest, and definitely an appropriate nickname. I saw your fight! How did you get so good so quickly? Advanced training methods or something? Oh and when are you dueling tomorrow?"

Augum was trying to keep the crier in view. "Uh, don't remember."

"There's been a bit of talk about you, you know." The boy was attempting to not-so-subtly peek into Augum's hood, but Augum kept looking away. "Got some real talent."

"Great," Augum replied absently, seeing the crier disappear into the portal room. "Nice to meet you, but will you excuse us?"

"Oh. Sure, I guess. Nice to meet—" but Augum had already hurried away with Bridget and Leera, blending in with the crowd.

They passed the large double doors into the portal room as people exited one portal after another, nearly all of them attendants, necrophytes, or Legionnaires. Some of the attendants and necrophytes activated the portal to the General Quarters, disappearing a moment later in a whoosh of wind. The whole thing seemed chaotic yet ordered and routine at the same time. The crier appeared from one portal and smoothly summoned and ducked into another, spreading the news of the ninth bell and the closure of the library. But Augum realized something profound—there was little chance they were going to get by the perceptive Watts without her recognizing them, not in this open room.

He could think of only one thing he could do. "Psst, you two trust me?" he whispered quickly.

Bridget's face turned serious. "Of course, but—"

"Then just go along with it, all right?" He spent a few moments taking in the details of the room—the smooth and polished walls; the sound of feet padding along the floor; the semi-predictable patterns people wove as they meandered tiredly from one portal to the next. He imagined some going to a tavern, and some to their families. He recalled dancing rhythmically with Mya in time to the shadow of a pillar …

The girls watched him with anxious unease.

Augum lowered his head, timing the spell words to when a group of guards loudly chortled about some woman they had met.

"Centeratoraye xao xen."

Everything instantly sharpened—the hooded lanterns, hiding a dim but warm glow behind iron bars, seemed more angular, if not a bit more sinister; the arched ceiling, with its massive ancient beams, looked like a spiky spider web, ready to ensnare the hapless victims below.

Augum formulated a quick plan on how he was going to deal with the side effects of Centarro, then turned his attention to the crowd, watching their faces from within his dark hood. Watching and learning. At the opportune moment, he suddenly reached out and yanked Bridget and Leera's hoods, much to their surprise. He tussled their hair before removing his own hood, turning his head strategically at all the right moments away from prying eyes, making it as difficult as possible for anyone to recognize him.

He waited until the portal beside the one to the Hall of Ancestry was not active. "This way," he said, guiding Bridget and Leera to it, where he bid them stand and wait.

"Don't look anyone in the eyes," he whispered, tussling his own hair a bit more.

"Aug, what are we doing here," Leera whispered. "It's so exposed—"

"Just wait."

They did not have to wait long—Secretary Watts soon appeared, heaving her bell-shaped body through the portal with a sigh. Her eyes wandered lazily over Bridget and Leera, but she did not seem to recognize them. Augum used that moment to slowly wipe his forehead as if he was really tired. He tapped his foot on the polished floor, sending the signal he was waiting for people to get out of the way—and he knew, instinctively, that Watts had seen these subtle but small gestures, that they had registered in her frog brain as things to dismiss.

Her two Legion guards followed her. Amongst the hustle and bustle, Augum picked up one muttering to the other, "Hate it when it tries to attack us, what a pain."

"Thing is speedier than lightning," replied the second Legionnaire. "At least she holds it at bay." It was then Augum realized they left some other kind of guard behind, but what? He watched Secretary Watts waddle off and realized it had to be a walker. It's the only necromantic thing that was that fast.

"Prepare yourselves," he said to Bridget and Leera. "There's a walker in there."

The girls exchanged looks.

Bridget swallowed. "Maybe we shouldn't—"

"Just don't kill it," he cut in. "And watch out for me. Ready?" The spell was starting to fade. They had to go *now*. Just as the girls nodded, he placed his hand on the portal engraving. "Shyneo." His palm crackled to life. "Augustus Westwood." The portal activated with a burst of wind, but his awareness was dimming; he could no longer sense if people were looking at him. He yanked on Bridget and Leera's sleeves to quickly go first, and the three of them disappeared into the portal.

HALL OF ANCESTRY

There was a clacking hiss in the near total darkness, lit only by Augum's waning blue palm light. It was the sole warning they received before a thin skeleton wearing ragged armor and wielding a rusty sword launched a rabid attack.

"BAKA!" Leera shouted, violently shoving the thing into a fragile statue that immediately shattered.

Augum scrambled to get out of the way, trying to make sense of what was going on. Centarro was fading fast and everything was fogging up. "Don't kill it," he remembered to remind them, but he forgot why that had been important. He forgot his plan, too, of what he was supposed to do once the powerful side effects of Centarro kicked in. His palm blinked out, but Bridget cast hers, enveloping the ancient room in a greenish glow.

"How are we supposed to *not* kill it!" Leera yelled as the skeleton scrambled to stand amidst the rubble of the statue.

"Disablo!" Bridget said, pointing at the walker's sword. It twirled away, clanging to the stone ground. The sound hurt Augum's ears. He covered them, wincing, unable to think past the heavy fog that had descended on his reptile brain.

There were shots and cries and a lot of noise. At one point he was shoved, yet his childlike mind focused on simple things—the green light that faded in and out, eventually replaced by a watery one; the carved marble hoof of a horse; the dusty and cold stone floor.

When Augum finally started coming to, it was to the sound of the girls desperately calling for him. He was lying on the floor gazing at the statue of a horse.

"Get up, Aug, help us! We can't hold it much longer!" one of the girls was shouting, but he had a hard time figuring out what all the fuss was about—until he looked behind him and saw Bridget and Leera sitting on a block of stone, underneath which was the walker, flailing. One of its arms was tangled in a short vine attached to Bridget's glowing hand.

Augum scrambled to his feet. "What the—"

"Help, Aug!" Leera screamed, voice echoing throughout the hall. She had a bleeding cut on her forehead. Both girls were drenched in sweat and breathing hard.

Augum jolted into action—he quickly used every ounce of his telekinetic arcane strength to lift another nearby block of stone, which had been some kind of prop in a diorama, and strategically set it on top of the rest of the walker. The girls immediately rolled off, panting on the floor, their spells extinguished.

"Thank the Unnameables …" Bridget gasped.

"Thank the Fates too," Leera added, equally out of breath.

Jaw clacking, the walker rabidly struggled under the stone blocks, but was no match for their combined weight.

Augum stumbled over to the girls. "You two all right?"

They nodded.

He snagged a cloth from Secretary Watts' desk and dabbed at Leera's forehead. "Just a minor cut," he said, tenderly holding her head in his lap.

"Thanks for the help, doorknob," she said with a wry grin.

"But I was busy with the side effects of—"

"—I was jesting, silly."

Bridget eventually sat up. "We'll have to get back before the library opens to release that thing."

Augum placed his hands over the shattered remains of the delicate statue the walker had been shoved into. "Apreyo." The pieces reformed with a final glow. "Good as new." He then went on to repair other things damaged in the struggle. After finishing, he eyed the walker. "Let's find that tomb, we'll worry about this thing later."

Hand lit, he led the way past the dark and silent statues, dioramas, and old paintings. High above them, stained glass windows featuring historical scenes rattled in the wind and rain, occasionally flashing with lightning that would light up the entire room. Distant thunder shook the windows, a noise that combined oddly with the desperate scratching of the walker.

"Spookier without the braziers lit," Leera whispered from the rear.

They cautiously found their way to the tomb. It was beside Occulus and the incomplete statue of Augum's father, the Lord of the Legion, who stood proud and regal and strong. Even though the stance was exaggerated, Augum thought the statue a little too life-like, almost expecting it to move and attack them. He recognized the sleek contours of the sword by his father's side—Burden's Edge. How he missed that awesome Dreadnought blade.

Bridget, who was studying the founder's tomb, began reading the inscription. " 'Here lieth Theodorus Winkfield, founder of thy Antioc Library. In his hand he doth hold ye Sword of Knowledge.' "

They glanced up at the statue behind the tomb. It was of a bald, stern-faced man wearing a scholar's robe. Much like the attendants they had seen, there was a gargoyle emblem over his breast. His hand was raised, except where there should have been a sword, there was only empty air.

"Someone stole the Sword of Knowledge," Leera said in a deadpan manner. "Why am I not surprised ..." She hovered a hand over the stone sarcophagus. "Un vun deo," but soon dropped it. "Nothing."

Augum inspected the sides of the tomb, but found no gaps—by all appearances it looked like a solidly carved and unmovable block of stone.

"Hmm," Bridget toned, slowly tapping a thumb against her chin.

Leera crouched before the engraved words, smoothing her necrophyte robe beneath her. "What did you say about the Sword of Knowledge again?"

"Basically that it represents light."

Leera glanced between the outstretched arm and Bridget. "Light, huh? Could it be as simple as—"

"—a candle?" Bridget finished, grinning. "Brilliant."

"Like I said, I have my moments."

Augum gestured between them. "You two have, like, some kind of mind meld or something."

Leera flashed him a deviant smile. "You can call us The Sparrow Sisters."

"Witches to the core," Augum said, shaking his head but smiling. "Hey, wait, there was a candle on Watts' desk, wasn't there?" and they hurried back to retrieve it, finding a flint and steel in the drawer. They lit the candle, put back the flint and steel, and strode off, hardly paying attention to the struggling walker.

"Now what?" Leera asked after returning to the tomb.

"This, I think." Augum let go of the candle, using Telekinesis to float it up into the founder's outstretched fist. As soon as the candle settled, the tomb began to grind open, blowing a cold draft that smelled of ancient mildew. The trio instinctively stepped back.

"Cool," Augum whispered.

Leera glanced over at him and cracked a grin. "There you go."

Augum brightened his palm, revealing a tight-fitting spiral staircase. He hopped down, leading with outstretched palm.

"Wait." Bridget reached behind her and telekinetically removed the candle. She snatched it out of the air as the tomb began to close. The draft disappeared as it shut completely. She placed the candle on the steps, spotting a small gargoyle engraved into the stone wall, which she nodded at. "That must be how we open it if we come back this way."

The trio exchanged an adventurous look and continued down the steps, lit only by their palms.

"Reminds me of Castle Arinthian," Augum whispered, blood quickened by the excitement of solving such a complicated riddle, and being rewarded with this ancient secret passage. Not even the Legion had found it!

The spiral went on for what felt like ten floors. By the end of it, Augum was a little dizzy and had to sit down in a small cellar-like room. The walls were cracked masonry—ancient fitted stone, on which grew mildew and rugged moss. The floors were uneven flagstone. At the fore of the room was an iron-bound wooden door. A gargoyle crest was burned into it.

"No torch sconces," Leera remarked.

Bridget approached the large door. "I think they expect you to light your own way, seeing as this place is intended for warlocks. There's no handle here either." She placed her lit palm against the gargoyle but nothing happened.

Leera blew at a carved wooden plaque, generating a small cloud of dust. "Hey, we know this word—'Entarro'."

Bridget placed her hand over the gargoyle again. "Be ready, you two, we don't know what's behind here."

Augum got up off the steps and drew close, ready to cast his First Offensive.

Bridget locked eyes with each of them before placing her lit palm on the oval. "Entarro." The door unlocked and creaked open as if pulled by a ghost. The trio stood frozen, listening. And somewhere, in that deep darkness beyond, they could hear a hiss.

"It sees our light," Leera said in the barest of whispers as they prowled into the room.

Augum felt his heart ramming into his chest. He indicated for them to spread out a little to make room for spell casting. The girls fanned out. Whatever room they had stepped into was vast. Behind them, along the wall, were more doors similar to the one they had walked through. The wall gently curved inward, as if the room was round.

The hissing ceased and a single clack echoed, followed by another. The clacking increased in speed. Then came the sound of bony footsteps that quickly turned into a sprint.

"There!" Augum shouted, pointing. He slammed his wrists together. "ANNIHILO!" His body surged, releasing a massive bolt of lightning through his hands. The bolt smashed through the first walker, obliterating it into pieces of bone and rusted armor that tumbled across the uneven flagstone floor.

At the same moment, "ANNIHILO!" Leera shouted, slamming her wrists together into a different direction. A jet of water smashed into another walker, blowing it apart.

"ANNIHILO!" Bridget's log-sized vine smashed through a third walker like a giant's fist, shattering it into smithereens.

For a moment, they listened to the darkness, but there was no other sound.

Leera, breathing hard, hands ready in a combat pose, relaxed and cracked a grin. "We're getting good."

Bridget did not drop her stance. "Don't celebrate yet." Just as she finished speaking, the door they had walked through closed with a strained creak, making them jump.

"What did that crazy geezer say about ghosts?" Leera murmured.

"Wait." Augum walked up to the door frame, placing his hand on a gargoyle crest he had spotted. "Entarro." The door squeaked open again. "See? We can go back anytime."

Bridget slowly paced further into the room, brightening her palm light, until they could make out distant walls. The room was indeed round, the walls evenly fitted with doors.

Leera shone her palm light over the ground. "Look down."

In the center of the room, beneath their feet under a layer of dust and dirt, was a giant map carved into the flagstone.

Augum kicked some of the dirt away. "We're here, aren't we? Round room with doors?"

Leera kicked more dirt away. "Hmm. Not all of the rooms are mapped ..."

Augum stared at a gargoyle engraved into the map. On a hunch, he placed his lit palm on it. A ghostly man in a gray robe suddenly crackled to life in front of them, making the trio jump.

"Und hallo!" he said with a harsh but jolly accent, extending his hands in welcome and giving a bright smile.

Augum kept his own hands raised defensively. "Uh ... hello, who are y—" but the man started speaking over him.

"Greetings, varlock und varlocks! Behold, for ye art in zee secret room to ze library trial groundz. My name iz Zeodorus Vinkfield. I founded zis library on tree principles—vizdom, integrity, und curiosity. But zis is no ordinary library. It truly iz a place of learning …"

"He can't hear or see us, can he?" Leera said, waving a hand at the man, who now paced as he spoke.

Augum walked around the ghostly imprint, but the man's eyes remained on the spot where Augum had triggered the apparition.

"… for here ye shall be tested on ze knowledge, unlocking only zat vich ye endeavor to earn. Just as ye have earned zose stripes on ye arm, zo shall ye earn ze knowledge to unlock more. Ze Leyanz taught us zat knowledge iz free. Alzough zey have recently abandoned us to our knave savageries, I see no reason vy vee cannot continue zeir tradishions, tradishions zey have bequeathed us."

"Can barely understand a word through that accent," Leera said.

"Und as ye see, before ye are a seriez of doors. In true varlock scholarly tradition, some of zese doors vould be poor choices. Some lead to secret pazzages zroughout ze library complex. Und some … some vill give ye ze chance to unlock advanced knowledge. Zere vill be obshtacles in ze way. Some of zese obshtacles vill be very dangeroush. I beseech ze—knowledge comes viz a price. Ye ought not to undertake anyshing ye are not prepared for. Use ze map und ze clues provided to guide ye path. Omnio insipus equa liberatus korsisi mei. All begin eqval but only ze curioush shrive. Good luck, und I hopen to see ye again." The man smiled and disappeared.

"Vell zat vas very intereshting," Leera said with a crooked smile.

Augum joined in. "Let ush talk zis vay from now on."

"Shtop it, you two," Bridget said, flashing a brief but mischievous smile. "Focus and help me." She began studying the giant map, dusting, and clearing the bones of the walkers as she went. Augum and Leera giddily joined in, needling each other with phrases like, "Ya! Look at zis!" or randomly blurting, "Zoot! Zat iz not it!" until they had uncovered the entirety of the map.

Bridget tapped a large rectangular room at the other end of the map. "This is the secret hidden library of all things arcane. This is where we want to go." She strode to a massive circle in the middle. "This is the labyrinth, the obstacle." She gestured around at assorted rooms. "Crypts. Dungeons. Sewers. Don't know how to get into those, but we don't need to anyway. The trick will be—" and she strode from the room they were in all the way to the arcane library, "—how to get from there to here, and back again."

"And in one piece," Augum said, trying to switch his brain back around to stop hearing everything in that funny accent.

"And in one piece, right."

"Ya, und in vun piece," Leera said. "So vere do ve start?"

"Enough of that already." Bridget turned around, eyeing the doors. "With those. See, what I figure is, there are portals behind most of them, that's why the map isn't filled in. What we don't know is, which door to take and where it leads."

Leera shrugged. "Just open one."

"Not sure it's a good idea to just open a random one." Bridget paced up to the nearest door. "It's got a rune on it. Three wavy lines in a box."

"That's a heating rune!" Augum blurted, striding forth. "From Castle Arinthian, remember? Same thing." But what did heating an entire area have to do with a door?

Bridget pointed at it. "So that probably represents fire." She strode to the next door over. "This one, this jagged line, represents ice." She moved on, pointing at each door. "Air. Lightning. Earth. Healing. And this one with the skull—"

"Necromancy," Leera said. "Let's avoid that one."

"Right. Elements. But then there are other symbols—two crossed swords."

"Battle," Augum said. "Pretty sure that one means battle."

Bridget nodded. "Which is probably some kind of warrior test or something." She stepped before another door. "Three figures, all identical. Could mean doppelgangers. And this one over here is just a circle."

"That could mean anything." Leera snorted. "Marriage, for all we know."

"Why marriage?" Augum asked.

"Because it's a ring. Really? You didn't get that?"

He shrugged. "Just looks like a circle to me."

"That's my point—"

"Unnameables give me patience," Bridget muttered as she moved to yet another door. "This one shows an arrow bouncing off a line. I think that means mirror. And this one over here, with two interlocking symbols, might mean a puzzle. And over here a square, which could be a room of some kind. This one over here I don't understand, it's just gibberish—"

"That's just upside down writing," Leera said, tilting her head. "Look, it says, 'Opposite is illusion'. Ugh, that just sounds like it'll be super frustrating."

"The door we came from only has a rectangle," Augum noted. "Interesting. If a rectangle is a tomb, what would a circle be?"

Bridget took a moment to think about it. "Another secret passage I suspect, probably one the Legion found and locked up." She pointed at doors near the one they exited. "There's a triangle, and there's a diamond, a half-circle, and so on. Those must all be ways to get back upstairs."

Augum studied the map again. "So which door do we take?" he said more to himself than anyone else. Then it hit him. He spread his hand over the map. "Un vun deo," and immediately saw a bunch of symbols light up crimson that were invisible before.

The girls jubilantly raced over.

"Hold the spell, Aug," Bridget said, studying the map with furrowed brows.

"They're not elements necessarily," Leera muttered, tapping at a fire symbol. "They might be elemental tests of some kind, like this one is some sort of wavy fire river we'd have to cross or something, which—and I'm just guessing here—would mean we'd have to fight it with water."

"Look, the crypts join up with the maze, as do the dungeons and the sewers," Bridget said. "The arcane library also joins up with the maze, just at the very top. And every symbol matches up—either to the maze, the dungeons, the sewers, or the crypts. But which way will get us through to the library?"

Augum finally lost his concentration and the symbols disappeared. "Looks like wherever we go, there'll be a test of some kind. And maybe all of them will get us there."

"Or maybe just one," Leera said, glancing around at the doors. "Should we just choose then?"

Bridget stood up. "We could, but if some are indeed going to be dead ends, we could waste a lot of time, or worse … get lost."

"And we can't spend *too* long down here," Augum added.

"Well then it's simple," Leera said, "we choose the one that gets us closest to the library straight away."

Bridget shook her head. "No, that wouldn't work, it'd be too easy, and labyrinths penalize quick and easy solutions."

"So then we choose the … hardest path?"

"Not necessarily. Remember what the founder stood for— wisdom, integrity, and curiosity. Those three paths—any of those would be best, in my opinion."

"Works for me," Augum said. He paced around the room, glancing at all the runes, muttering the words, "wisdom, integrity, and curiosity" to himself over and over, until he stopped before a door with what they assumed was a puzzle symbol. "These two locking pieces—this is most like our experience here. Riddles and all that kind of stuff. What do you say?" He wasn't that great with riddles, but he'd rather go with something familiar.

The girls promptly agreed. They all gathered at the door as Augum lit up his palm. He gave them one last grave look before placing it on the gargoyle rune next to the door frame.

"Entarro."

The door blew open, instantly sucking them in with a windy roar.

A LAND OF NOTHING

The trio was roughly spit out onto a field. It was dusk, and they could just barely see from one flat horizon to another. Dark blue clouds raced overhead as a chill wind howled, rustling stubby dry grass. Other than the lonely leagues of grass, there was only one thing visible—a dilapidated wooden cabin. A loose shutter repeatedly creaked open before thunking closed.

Leera looked around, hair and robe blowing in the wind. "Where are we?"

The fields reminded Augum of the Tallows, except the grass was shorter and more rugged. "I have no idea. It's got to be some kind of—" but suddenly a dark shape stepped out of the cabin. The silhouette was tall and muscled. Two points protruded above a bald head.

Bridget squinted. "What the …"

The silhouette expanded, revealing massive claw-tipped wings.

The trio took a step back.

"I think it's a gargoyle," Augum said, throat feeling dry.

The wings began to rattle violently as the creature hissed. The display made them take a few more steps back. The hissing died, as did the rattling, and the creature folded its wings. It stood there a moment, the only sound the incessant howl of the cold wind and the banging of that shutter, before ducking back inside the cabin.

"I'm not going in there," Leera whispered.

Thunk went the shutter.

Augum wondered if the gargoyle was watching them from the dark window.

Thunk …

Thunk …

Bridget swallowed, kept shaking her head. "Not going in there either."

Augum gritted his teeth. "I am." It was some kind of test, it had to be. He took a step, but was grabbed by Leera.

"Aug, please, don't be a fool—"

"It's just a game," he said.

"Who're you trying to convince?"

"I'll run if something happens. We can't stay out here forever."

Bridget was pale. "We should walk away." She kept shaking her head. "I have a really bad feeling about this."

Augum glanced at the empty horizon. "There's nothing out there." He took hold of Leera's firm grip and gently squeezed. "It's all right." He embraced her. She gripped him tightly, her body shaking. "It's all right," he repeated. Then he gently pried her away, and turned to face the cabin.

"Aug …" but he did not look back. It was a test, it had to be …

Thunk …

Thunk …

"Come on, we have to help if we can," Bridget said with a shaky voice. They slowly followed at a distance, each crouched and ready to fight … or bolt.

Augum took one step at a time, yet the creature did not step out of the dark cabin. He expected it to suddenly jump out and charge.

Thunk …

Thunk …

He came to the rickety door and reached out to the crude wooden handle. He slowly pulled on it, breath coming in rapid bursts. As it creaked open, the door steadily revealed the hulking monster. Augum's hands shook. He let go of the door, but it continued to open, fully revealing the gargoyle in its muscled ferocity. It towered over him. Its wings began expanding in the cabin.

Thunk …

Thunk …

Augum stood frozen to the spot. Absurdly, he thought nothing would happen if he just stood there.

Thunk …

Thunk …

Its wings began rattling violently and the creature hissed. "Sssssssssssssss."

Augum's breath was that of a frantic mouse—rapid and shallow. The girls were screaming, but he could barely pay attention, all he saw was that giant and powerful head and those clawed arms, able to destroy him with one swipe.

The voice that came from the creature was deep and grinding, like a giant stone door opening. "I do not fear you …"

Augum stood rooted to the spot. It was going to strike any moment, he was going to die, and there was nothing he could do.

"I do not fear you …"

Fear. *Fear!* Suddenly he understood! Augum summoned all his courage and concentration. He raised his arm and shouted, "DREADUS TERRABLUS!"

The gargoyle reared up, but instead of attacking, it suddenly began to crack and crumble. There was a gasping hiss as pieces fell from the creature, until there was nothing but a pile of dust, blown about by the wind.

Thunk …

Thunk …

Leera grabbed onto him. "What … what did you do?"

Augum could barely speak. "I made it fear me."

The dust blew away, revealing a shiny gold coin. Augum picked it up and they examined it. On one side it had a gargoyle, and on the other, a book. Written under the book were the words *Omnio incipus equa liberates corsisi mei.*

There was a sudden crackling sound as a black portal ripped to life before them. They stepped through, soon finding themselves back in the round room of doors.

"Let's choose something a little … less scary next time," Leera said.

Bridget examined the rune on the door they had gone through, which was now closed. "I thought this was two interlocking puzzle pieces, but now I think they might be wings."

Augum found the corresponding symbol on the map—it was in a room in the dungeon, which made no sense at all unless the whole thing had been an illusion.

"We need to get to the maze," Leera said, peeking over Augum's shoulder.

Augum absently played with the coin. "These must buy something …"

Bridget glanced between the coin and the map. "That's brilliant."

"What is?" Leera said.

"Access. You buy access with the coins. I mean, it only makes sense, doesn't it? The founder said something about earning the knowledge. He must have meant it literally. That's how we'll get into the secret part of the library! But what I don't understand is—"

"—how many coins it'll take to get in there," Augum said, standing.

"Exactly."

"How do we find that out?" Leera asked.

Bridget studied the map in more detail. "Here, look." She brushed away a fine layer of dust, revealing tiny etched lines before each room in the library portion of the map. She tapped at an identical series of rooms. "These rooms here are all ordered by degrees. And this symbol here is the amount of coins needed. You pay one coin to get into the 1st degree library room, two for the 2nd degree, and so on. But then—" She tapped at a separate, larger room. "This one here has the symbol of a cup which, if I recall correctly, represents *artifacts*."

Leera craned her neck. "How much to get into that room?"

Bridget sighed. "Looks like five coins."

Leera groaned.

"In fact, all these other rooms are five coins. And again, recalling my studies from earlier, I think this tree represents ancestry, and this figure means that room is about historically distinguished individuals. The book symbol probably represents history—"

"It'd be kind of neat to study the 5th degree in there," Augum said. "Imagine what insights we could find."

Bridget smiled. "Glad you're changing your tune. Studying is essential."

"I've always loved studying! I just don't have the ability to concentrate for as long as you."

"And we needn't say anything about *my* studying abilities," Leera muttered. She tapped at a symbol inside the maze. "A bird doesn't sound too threatening. Let's get in there, see what happens."

Bridget stood, dusting her hands. "As good as any, I suppose."

They found the symbol on a corresponding door and were soon once again sucked in, this time tumbling out onto a flagstone floor in a curving corridor. The trio shone their palm lights, getting their bearing. The walls were ancient uneven masonry ascending at least fifty feet, with no ceiling, only inky blackness. A cold and clammy draft came from the walls, whistling now and then.

"The labyrinth," Augum whispered.

"Which way?" Leera asked.

Augum extended his palm, urging the arcane ether to help him find something purposefully hidden. "Un vun deo," and immediately felt a tug in several different directions. "Odd," he said, dropping his arm. "Getting lots of pulls."

They chose to go right and cautiously prowled forth. Suddenly one of the flagstones Augum stepped on lowered with a grinding noise, and part of the wall ahead opened, revealing three large birds with faces of haggard old women.

Bridget paled. "Harpies—"

The harpies' crooked black beaks clicked as they waddled out of their stone prison.

Bridget's face hardened. "I *hate* harpies!" She slammed her wrists together. "ANNIHILO!" A thick vine slammed into the first one, smashing it into a pulp against the wall. The other two spread their wings and took off. One of the harpies immediately dove.

"ANNIHILO!" Augum shouted, but his lightning missed, hitting a distant spot up one wall, sending flaky debris down. The trio ducked as the harpy raked at them with its claws, barely missing Bridget's back.

The other harpy was right behind the first. It was Leera's turn. "ANNIHILO!" A jet of water blasted right through its chest, blowing it apart in a cloud of feathers. The remaining one swooped high into the corridor and dove again.

Augum slammed his wrists together once more. "ANNIHILO!" This time his aim was true, and the thing slapped into the ground, a smoking mess. Soon all three were piles of dust.

Leera collected the coins. "And now we have four."

"I could use a nap," Augum mumbled, rubbing at his temple, feeling the slight onset of an arcanely induced headache.

Leera made a graceful gesture. "I have a nice pile of harpy you can use as a pillow."

Grinning, the trio quickly moved on. When they came upon a fork, Bridget said, "Wait." She placed her hands over a loose stone on the ground. "Vestigio itemo discovaro." She stood, dusting her hands. "There, now we can find our way back if we need to."

"Good idea, Leera said. "And Aug—maybe one of those Unconceal pulls you felt earlier pointed at that harpie trap back there." She raised her hand. "Un vun deo." She kept her palm extended as she investigated the floor, pointing out a slightly raised stone along their path. "I think that's another trap," she said, dropping her hand.

Augum spotted a series of holes along the walls. He got the impression something might shoot out of them should they trigger the trap.

They moved on, trading off on casting Unconceal, choosing to take a right and then a left at two forks, before arriving at an ornate stone door. Above the door was a stone gargoyle, glaring at them.

"No handle," Augum noted.

Bridget raised her palm at the door. "Un vun deo." Words slowly began to appear.

Leera read the arcane inscription. " 'If I art belong to thou, thou wouldst long to share me. But if thou share me, I no long belong to thee. What, say you, am I?' "

"What belongs to you that you want to share it?" Augum reiterated, "but doesn't belong to you when you finally do share it?"

"That's easy," Leera said. "A secret!"

The words instantly disappeared and the door rumbled open, revealing a wall, before which stood a stone dais. On top of the dais sat a single shiny gold gargoyle coin.

Leera snatched the coin. "That's five."

They retreated to the last fork and went in the other direction, eventually arriving at another stone door with another gargoyle. This one had four crude etchings on its face—a cup, a feather, sand, and a scroll.

"It's another puzzle," Bridget said. "Which one doesn't belong?"

"The feather," Leera replied. "It's the only thing that comes from a living creature."

Augum shrugged. "Sounds about right."

Leera reached up with her lit palm and pressed the feather etching. The etching flashed a green color and she recoiled. "Ouch! Something bit me!" Suddenly there was a ripping noise behind them as a portal opened up, instantly sucking them in.

CHOICES, CHOICES

"I must have picked the wrong one," Leera said groggily as she picked herself up off the floor, rubbing her hand. They were back in the round room of doors.

Augum was by her side. "You all right?"

"Just a pinprick. No big deal."

"Let me see." He took her squirming palm, spotted the pinprick—and saw the slightest shading of black under her skin. "Might be poison."

"I'll be dead within the hour then."

"Don't jest about things like that."

"You better say your goodbyes, Augum Stone."

Bridget strode over and snatched Leera's hand. "I agree, it could be poison."

Leera jerked her hand away with a laugh. "Don't be silly. The library wouldn't do that to us."

Bridget raised an eyebrow. "You sure? We were just attacked by a bunch of harpies."

"You two always overreact. I don't feel noth—" Suddenly Leera staggered, swallowing and blinking rapidly. "Uh oh," and just like that, she fainted into Augum's arms.

"Lee?" He shook her, but she did not wake up. "You better not be jesting—" He felt his heart thrum when she remained still. What if it *was* lethal? No, he was just being paranoid. "I don't think she's jesting with us."

"I'm sure it'll be fine, Aug, no need to panic," Bridget said as she ran to the doors.

"Who's panicking? You're the one running!"

"It was one of these, if I remember correctly ..." Bridget stopped before one of the doors. "This one. It has a potion as the symbol—"

Augum hesitated. What if she was wrong and they had to go through some stupid challenge, only to start again? "How sure are you?"

Bridget glanced his way with a serious look.

"All right, but help me with her—" and the two of them carried Leera to the door. Bridget placed her lit palm on the gargoyle rune. "Entarro." It opened and they were sucked inside, stumbling out on the other end.

Before them was a round room with countless shelves of colorful beakers. In the center stood a dais, on top of which rested a giant book and a wooden bowl.

Augum gently laid Leera down and joined Bridget at the book.

"Recipes," Bridget said as she turned the pages. "But they're in some language I don't understand. I'm going to search the room arcanely. Let's switch." She extinguished her palm while he lit his, flooding the room with a blue glow. She crossed her brows and splayed her palm. "Un vun deo." After a few moments of concentration, she whispered, "It's subtle, but I feel something," and followed the ethereal trail to a wall. Her hand kept rising.

She pointed at the highest shelf, a good twenty feet above them. "Up there."

Augum strode back until he could just make out something oddly-shaped resting near the paneled ceiling. He reached out, concentrating his Telekinesis. The object started moving slowly toward him, until it suddenly fell off the shelf. Bridget, who was standing just below, deftly caught it.

It was a pair of thin rose-colored spectacles. She strode to the book, putting them on.

Augum was right beside her, white-knuckling the dais. "Well?"

"Shh!" Her finger was streaming down page after page. "Here, this one might work—"

"Might?"

"It's an antidote that neutralizes poison, and it lists the right symptoms—small black sting, dizziness, sudden loss of consciousness. It should work. One part essence of mint, two parts powdered licorice root, one part powdered stinkroot, two parts water."

Augum was already searching the shelves. "Found one." He brought her a beaker labeled *Stinkroot*. Inside were the notoriously gross brown lumpy roots with red welts all over.

"No, it has to be powdered—"

Augum raced back to fetch the one beside it, which had the same label, except the contents were powdered. He placed it on the dais. Bridget helped him find the rest, and soon they had them all ready.

Augum was staring at the ingredients. What if he got it wrong? What if the poison was deadly?

"Your hands are shaking," Bridget said. "Bring her over, I'll do this."

"You sure?"

"Trust me."

Augum gently picked Leera up and brought her over, laying her head on his lap. He watched Bridget work while he unconsciously kept smoothing Leera's hair away from her face. His heart skipped a beat when he noticed her lips turning blue. But surely the library wouldn't *kill* warlocks … would it?

"Almost … ready … there!" Bridget brought the bowl to Leera's lips. He gently opened her mouth and she carefully poured the contents in. Leera gasped almost immediately. "That stinkroot," she gurgled. "Ugh … disgusting."

Augum, sighing in immense relief, was barely conscious of the bowl floating back to the dais, the spectacles back to their place on the shelf, and the ingredients refilling as they floated back to their places.

Leera sprang to her feet, shaking off her limbs. "Told you I was fine."

"Of course you were," Augum muttered, but he was smiling along with her.

Suddenly she grew serious. "But you did say your goodbyes, right?"

"Shtop it, you are ze vorst troublemaker."

Bridget exhaled. "I know that was a touch nerve-wracking, but if you two are up for it, there's still time enough to give one or two more obstacles a try, hopefully earn a few more coins. Then we should go and get some sleep. Big day ahead tomorrow."

"Fine," Leera said after punching Augum's shoulder. "But no more stinkroot. Next time, let me die." She caught the looks on their faces. "Oh, loosen up, you two."

They found the gargoyle emblem on an empty portion of wall, activated the portal, and returned to the round room of doors. From there they portaled to the maze again, slowly finding their way back to the door with four crude etchings—a cup, a feather, sand, and a scroll.

"That's why I got it wrong," Leera said, smacking her forehead. "That's not a feather—it's a quill! And that's drying sand. All three of those are scribe implements." She lit her palm and pressed the cup. The door immediately rumbled open, revealing another golden coin.

"Six," Leera said, flicking it over to Bridget, the designated coin holder.

They moved on, successfully tackling a *Spot the differences* challenge involving nearly identical tapestries; a battle challenge requiring them to use their minor elementals to defeat a small stone statue; and a Telekinesis challenge that required them to skillfully navigate different-shaped objects through holes matching them.

"Just like the Training Room," Leera said, flicking another gargoyle coin to Bridget.

Bridget counted the coins. "Puts us at nine. That'll buy us entry into the artifacts room. Of course, we still have to actually get *through* the maze to the arcane library portion."

"Let's get one more coin," Augum said. "That way we can at least maybe get into the 5th degree section. Then we head back and get some sleep." It was late, and he was so tired he could barely concentrate on his spells.

They pushed deeper into the labyrinth, casting Object Track at significant forks. Unconceal helped them avoid several traps, one of which triggered despite their caution, revealing a deep shaft.

"Maybe they really are trying to murder warlocks," Leera commented, glancing down into the darkness. "I think I see corpses."

Augum peeked into the bottomless shaft. "No you don't."

"All right, I don't."

At last, they stumbled into a ruined section of the labyrinth. Just as they stepped over a rubble wall, the smell hit them.

Leera gagged. "Ugh—! What died?"

Bridget held her nose. "I think we're at the sewers."

"Oh, we're so going back—"

"Wait." Augum saw something ahead catch his palm light. His hand was the only one that was lit—they had long resorted to taking turns to conserve their energies. "Let's just explore a little longer."

They crept forward, keeping their sleeves firmly over their noses, soon reaching the bank of a wide and fast-moving river of sludge. But that's not what caught their attention. On the other side, sitting on a dais, were *five* golden coins.

Augum searched the bank. "How do we get across?" There wasn't a boat or bridge to be seen.

Bridget gave them a grave look. "I know how to get across."

"You don't mean—"

"I do, and this time, it isn't going to be me."

"Nor me," Leera quickly added, giving the foul green waters a putrid look. She punched Augum's shoulder. "You're it."

Augum groaned. "Fine, but are you two sure you're up to the task? It's a bit of a distance, and I don't want to fall in just cause you two got tired."

"Ye vill 'ave to trust us, shpineless malingerer."

Augum sighed and readied himself while the girls took a moment to concentrate. Then they both slowly lifted him up using Telekinesis, and began floating him over the bank. His palm lit the brackish waters below, but he tried not to look, or imagine what would happen should he fall in.

"Almost there!" he called out. Only feet away from the bank, he felt a lurch and his foot skimmed the top of the water. Luckily, the girls caught him and set him down safely on the other side, before collapsing in a gasping heap.

After making sure it wasn't a trap, Augum recovered the coins, finding a portal etching on the wall. At least there was a way out of there if he needed it.

"Hey, are you two going to be able to bring me back?"

"Only if you want to go for a swim!" Leera called.

"Sorry, Aug, we're exhausted!"

Uh oh, now what? He didn't want to take the portal without them. Thankfully there was a tunnel a ways up the bank.

"Stay there, I'll see if there's a way around!" and he tore off up the bank, palm lit. The walls here were crude, as if he were in a mine, and the floor was covered in slime. "Great," he started muttering to himself. "Stuck in this filth with no—" Suddenly there was a spring sound and a sparkling cloud of powder blew into his face from a nearby wall. His light extinguished as he coughed, plunging him into total darkness. Oops, he had forgotten to check for traps.

And then something quite unexpected happened: iron candelabras gracefully descended from the ceiling, lighting a grand feast on a long table. There was roast duck, pheasant, loaves of fresh bread, all types of soups, fine silver plates and flatware and crystal goblets—

"Hello, Augum."

He turned around and saw two almond-shaped eyes staring at him. They were the color of brilliant emerald.

"Mya ..."

She wore a pristine white gown. A wreath of bright roses circled her long jet hair. She extended a porcelain hand. "Please have a seat with me."

"Oh, of course." It seemed perfectly natural that he should do just that. He accepted her hand and led her to one side of the table, which now had two finely ornate chairs on either side, and sat down across from her.

"Are you hungry?" she asked.

"Starving." He placed a cloth onto his lap, as seemed proper.

"What are you going to start on first?"

"Such a grand selection." He glanced up and down the table. Everything looked delicious and smelled *so* good. He'd eat here forever if he could.

"You could eat as long as you want," Mya whispered with a wink. "And stay as long as you'd like. Would you like to do that, Augum? Would you like to stay with me?"

He nodded like a simple child. "Very much so." She was as radiant as ever. But where had she been all this time? He couldn't recall losing her. His brain had a bit of a mist in it.

She smiled pleasantly. "What are you going to eat first?"

"Oh, I don't know, kind of hard to choose." Everything was just so … good-looking and tasty. He glanced at the iron candelabras. "Beautiful …"

She looked up as well, and that's when he spotted a line at her throat. It was bleeding. "Are you all right?" he asked, reaching across for her hand, which she promptly stole away to conceal the wound.

"Oh, yes, I'm fine, thank you," except the blood stained her sleeve.

"You're hurt."

"I am fine. Why don't you have a bite to eat, Augum?"

He stared at her. Something wasn't right, but he couldn't place his finger on it. "You shouldn't be here, should you?" he whispered.

"Augum, please, have a bite—"

"No." This wasn't right, none of it. Was he dreaming?

Mya giggled, the blood spreading on her sleeve. "Augum, you're being silly. Please, have some chicken—"

"I said, NO!" He stood up, toppling the chair. The candelabras instantly snuffed, plunging him back into darkness. Yet he still heard her breathing. She was sitting right there in front of him.

He slowly raised his hand. "Shyneo." His palm lit up a table of rotten food, behind which sat a woman in a white dress, except where he expected Mya's face, he only saw a wreath of roses encircling a skull.

The skeleton opened its palm, revealing a shiny gold coin. Augum did not take the chance—he used Telekinesis to retrieve it. The skeleton closed its palm and sat there as he slowly backed away. Part of him panicked for a moment, thinking he had left Mya behind again in the darkness, but he also knew it wasn't her, *couldn't* be her …

He turned his back and moved on, using the subtle pull of Object Track to loosely guide his path through fork after fork and tunnel after twisting tunnel, until arriving at a rope bridge that spanned the river below.

"Now what?" he muttered, seeing the hulking figure of a dark-skinned man standing in the middle. Some of his flesh had rotted away, partially revealing his skull. Augum, in no mood to waste more time, marched onto the bridge toward the man, who started to speak.

"As long as I am clear-minded, you shall not pass—" but he barely finished speaking before Augum, who had already faced a *Fear* challenge that was similar, said, "Flustrato!" and the man choked on his own tongue before tumbling over the rope and into the water below. Augum hardly broke his stride except to collect the golden coin waiting for him at the end. He then quietly followed the riverbank until he found the girls patiently waiting for him.

"We were starting to get worried," Leera said.

"How'd you acquire two extra coins though?" Bridget asked, accepting seven from Augum.

"Just a bit of trouble on the way, nothing major." He clapped each of them on the back. "Let's get out of here and catch some sleep, shall we? I'm exhausted."

* * *

The trio had little difficulty returning to the room of many doors—all they had to do was unleash a portal, accomplished by defeating a portcullis puzzle involving a series of levers. It also rewarded them with two more coins, which added up to eighteen.

They backtracked to the Hall of Ancestry. Along the way, Bridget picked up the candle and replaced it onto Watts' desk. Then they expertly freed the walker while one of them held a portal open.

The hallways of the great library were a little trickier in the wee hours of a stormy morning—a tired Legion guard spotted them immediately, and it took some agile lying to convince the man that they were just eager necrophytes looking for the Training Room, trying to get some extra early practicing in to impress their superiors. Luckily, the guard was a bit of a dimwit and never caught on, even escorting them personally to their room. There they found a sleeping Malaika and Charissa. Bridget left a note asking them not to wake the trio until the first strike of the afternoon bell.

As Augum lay in his bed listening to the tap of rain against the windows and the distant howl of the wind, he thought of that foggy moment supping with Mya, and truly hoped it had not been her.

ANTIOC, DAY THREE

As requested, the trio was woken up by Malaika and Charissa at the toll of the first afternoon bell. Actually, Malaika woke Augum, who then had to wake the girls, while she kept trying to convince him to come down and have lunch with her alone, something that only made him flash her a hard look.

"Fine, then we'll see you down there for the meeting," she finally conceded, and left with Charissa in tow.

The trio groggily began a whirlwind of activity. They did their makeup routine to look as far from the wanted poster as they could, raised their hoods, snagged a copy of the Antioc Herald, and raced to the lunch meeting with Malaika and Charissa in the Supper Hall.

After filling Malaika and Charissa in on *some* of the details of what had transpired below in the dungeons (the trio did not feel it safe to inform them of everything, such as the gargoyle coins they hid in their room), they caught up on the day's events.

"... and he's *really* quite a brute," Charissa added, referring to Augum's next opponent. "That's why his nickname works so well for him."

"So ... he's a bully?" Leera cracked a grin. "Aug's getting pretty good at defeating bullies."

"Just wait until you see him though," Malaika said. "He's much older. I think he was held back in school or something. Got a mean-looking face. But he's also another necrophyte with a bit of a following in the stands. We saw him fight yesterday."

"Can't wait to see you fight today, Hood!" someone shouted as they strolled nearby.

Other people, suddenly aware The Hood was in their presence, quickly took up the call.

Augum kept his head down and concentrated on his soup. "Great," he muttered.

"All right, people, settle down!" Leera finally had to shout. "Sheeze, you'd think Attyla the Mighty just waltzed in here. " She elbowed Augum. "And you—try to have a boring fight this time, would you?" Her voice dropped. "Don't need any more attention, do we?"

"Right." Maybe he'd try to make it so that he was losing for a while, before somehow striking a win. That should quiet things down.

"It's because he's in the Heralds," Malaika proudly said, extending a copy to Leera.

"You mean the Heral*d*," Leera replied, snagging it.

"No, I mean the Herald*s*—the Blackhaven has a snippet on him as well."

Leera skimmed the parchment. Her eyes widened. "Aug, do you want hear what they're writing about y—"

"Nope." He didn't need his head getting bigger, or worrying about what people were saying. He was here on a quest, and he had to focus. This fame business was all sheer nonsense anyway, as Nana would say.

"Not even the awesome part about how you—"

"Nope."

"Oh. Okay."

Malaika gave Charissa a snooty look. "Quite prudent, I must say."

Charissa gave a high-browed nod. "Indeed." Then she frowned, whispering, "By 'prudent', you mean smart, right?"

Malaika placed a hand to her forehead. "Oh for …"

Leera narrowed her eyes at them but said nothing. She went back to the Herald and snorted. "Temper's out. Defeated five-nothing. Wish I had seen that."

"We saw her duel," Charissa said. "She got slapped in the face for the final point. The whole crowd laughed, especially because she had a lot to say pre-match about how she was going to beat the snot out of the other girl."

Malaika's face tightened. "We also saw Robin duel."

Augum perked up. "Oh?" Unfortunately they had missed his morning duel, needing the sleep.

Malaika shared a look with Charissa. "He's, uh …"

"He's what—?"

"Quite advanced," Charissa blurted. "He cast all this weird magic—"

"Arcanery," Leera promptly corrected.

"Well, not exactly. It's kind of evil stuff."

"Necromancy is still arcanery."

"Whatever. Anyway, he cast a lot of it." She put a pale finger to her lips. "At least, I think it was necromancy, I'm not an expert or anything."

"No kidding," Leera muttered.

"He was showing off mostly," Malaika said. "And we were told he knows a 5th degree spell too, and some off-the-book ones, whatever that means."

Augum felt all the girls' eyes on him. "Interesting," he muttered. *Not good* is what he really wanted to say. Robin was already working on the 5th degree!

Leera nudged him with her shoulder. "That muttering of yours is becoming a habit."

He didn't reply.

"I've been thinking," Bridget said, finishing reading the Antioc Herald over Leera's shoulder. "We don't have time to learn 5th degree spells, but we *can* train. After Augum's match, I think that's what we should be doing until the eighth strike of the afternoon bell. Then we meet here for a late supper and discussion, before heading down to you-know-where." She gave the slightest nod at the floor, toward the dungeon labyrinth. "The only thing is getting back in there again."

Charissa shrugged. "Just go the same way you went last time." She frowned as if struggling with a complex idea. "How *did* you get in there?"

Leera made a *poof* gesture with her hands. "Magic."

"I thought you said—"

"Never mind."

Charissa folded her arms across her chest. "Wish you weren't here."

"I bet you do."

"Just ignore her," Malaika said, mirroring the arm-folding gesture. "She thinks she's so clever."

Charissa gave a little head bob, hair bouncing. "She's just jealous she can't be a spy like us."

Leera shook her head, not bothering to respond.

Bridget returned to spooning her soup. "Can we just … stop?"

They finished their lunch and parted ways, Malaika and Charissa giving Augum and Bridget a warm goodbye, while turning a cold shoulder to Leera, who merely rolled her eyes.

"You needn't press their buttons so much," Bridget said as they filed out of the Supper Hall.

"Can't help it. Those buttons are just so … big and pushable."

Bridget sighed but said no more on the subject.

As they paced the dimly-lit halls on their way to the portal room, they came across Secretary Klines. The gray-robed beetle-like woman glanced around to make sure they were alone before approaching them.

"How are you faring?" she asked in her squeaky voice. Her eyes, magnified to absurd proportions by her thick spectacles, traveled over their faces as if she was worried they may be coming down with something.

"Uh, fine, Secretary Klines," Augum replied. He had a thousand questions, but didn't want to voice any of them in such a public place.

Klines waited for a young gray-robed attendant to pass before quietly saying, "I hear word of a disturbance in the Hall of Ancestry. Secretary Watts is quite upset about a number of items being out of place. She seems to think three necrophytes, who she swears are 'up to no good' had something to do with it." There was a hint of a proud smile.

"She's a bit of a pest," Leera said.

"Indeed."

"Secretary Klines," Bridget interrupted. "Can … can we ask you a tiny favor?"

"Library tradition dictates that no hints be—"

"No, not that. Um, we were kind of hoping you could … remove Secretary Watts from her post a little early tonight."

Klines studied Bridget a moment before the corner of her tiny mouth curved with a smile. "I shall see what I can do." Her giant eyes flicked to a spot behind them. "Ah, Secretary Watts—"

Augum and the girls did not dare to turn around. They had not even heard her approach, as if she had been spying on them.

"Secretary Klines," Watts said in her gratingly snippy voice. "How do you do. I see you have found the troublemakers I have been searching for. I am sure you are aware of the disturbance in the Hall of Ancestry—?"

"I am."

"Further, I have discovered that my walker had damage to its chest. There were numerous scratch marks along the floor. I find this a most grievously disturbing occurrence, and I demand an immediate investigation by the head office, and these—" Augum saw a chubby hand with long sharp nails flick between himself, Bridget and Leera, "—be remanded into custody and questioned. I believe them to be—" She dropped her voice to a conspiratorial whisper. "—trying to get in to the you-know-what."

Secretary Klines placed her hands behind her back. "I see. I, too, have been informed of something interesting. It seems there have been reports of damage to some of the display pieces in the Hall of Ancestry—"

Augum could sense Watts ballooning. "Quite right! There was a statue of that villainous traitor—"

"I speak of a wide variety of statues and display pieces. I hear it on good authority that someone's walker may be damaging valuable property."

"But surely you do not—"

"There is a *rumor*, Secretary Watts."

"A … a rumor?" Watts sputtered.

"A rumor that a certain secretary has been experimenting with her walker in a certain very fragile and very valuable hall."

"Preposterous—"

"Necromantic experimentation is strictly restricted to the training grounds, Secretary Watts. Failure to abide by this rule will result in immediate expulsion from one's duties."

"This is absurd, I do not … 'experiment' with my walker! My administration of the walker is totally in accordance with Legion protocols."

"Shall I arrange for you to have a word with Senior Arcaneologist Ning again, perhaps?"

Watts was now speaking very fast. "Oh, no, Secretary Klines, that would be most unnecessary. Senior Arcaneologist Ning is a very, very busy woman and I wouldn't want to disturb her with such trivial matters. I'll … I'll investigate these rumors and make sure there will not be any more trouble in the, uh … the hall. Good day, Secretary Klines. Hail to the Legion."

"Secretary Watts." Klines watched her waddle off in a huff, whispering, "She will be doubly suspicious. I will not be able to help you with that favor now. I suggest you find alternative means to accomplish any … goals … you may have. Good day." She strode past them before they could even thank her.

Bridget tapped her lips. "We'll have to figure something out. Watts is going to be a thorn. She'll probably have extra guards and walkers there tonight."

"Lucky she didn't see my cut," Leera said, dabbing at her forehead. Augum agreed. It was small, but enough to warrant further suspicion from Watts, and that's the last thing they needed right now.

A gray-robed crier strode through the hall, calling out, "Hear ye, hear ye—the second afternoon bell tolls!"

"We're late for registration," Leera said. "Come on."

QUARTER-FINALS

It was a cloudy and windy day outside, the cobbled streets still wet from last night's thunderstorm. Due to the Heralds, people recognized The Hood even more now.

"Uh, thank you," Augum said to an elderly couple who had told him he was a stand-up fellow for fighting for the Legion.

"I'll try," he replied to a young girl who proudly flared her single ice ring after telling him to "Kick that mean jerkface in the bum."

"He's going to beat you to a pulp!" one older necrophyte boy shouted, obviously a fan of the other boy.

It was a tedious and odd situation—they couldn't risk lowering their hoods for fear of being recognized as the most wanted young warlocks in all of Solia, yet here Augum was being recognized for an altogether different reason—fighting in an arena under an assumed name.

The noise of a cheering crowd soon reached their ears as they hurried through the streets. Sudden shouts and swells indicated a match was underway. They paid the entrance fees (Bridget was looking worried now every time she rooted around her coin pouch), received their chit only to hand it to a bored-looking guard, and entered. Augum registered for his fight. Leera pointed out where they were going to sit. She gave him a tight hug and the girls both wished him luck before disappearing into the crowd.

Augum strode past another guard and on through the tunnel, feeling the energy of the crowd above. They were stamping their feet, chanting, "LO-SERS SHALL! BEND THE KNEE! WI-NNERS FIND! ETER-NI-TY!"

"You're late," Secretary Sharma said, checking off her parchment. "Have a seat."

A hulking necrophyte boy with a small mop of frizzy hair immediately strode over to Augum. He cracked his thick neck from left to right and flashed a gap-toothed smile. "You're The Hood, huh?" He made a snapping gesture. "Like a twig. That's going to be you."

Augum wanted to roll his eyes so hard. "What are you, like, thirty?"

"Nineteen."

"You look older."

"I told you I'm—"

"You should have a cane."

"You're mincemeat."

Augum was feeling immature. "And you're so old there's moss growing on your head."

The boy took a menacing step forward. "What'd you say about my hair?"

"Settle down, Brutus," Secretary Sharma said absently, ticking off her list as another competitor entered the room.

"He thinks he all bad because he beat some wimpy girl from Canterra. She don't even know any necromancy! Look at him. He's a gangly nobody from a nobody town, and by the time I'm through with him, *my* name will be in the Herald."

Augum couldn't help himself. He had no patience for this kind of stuff anymore. "You talk a big game. Let's see if you play one."

"I'm going to—"

"To what? Bore me to death with idle threats?"

The boy smashed a fist into an open palm. "You're *so* dead—"

"*Brutus!* Sit. Down." Secretary Sharma's hands were on her hips. After the boy reluctantly sat down, she muttered to herself while returning to her parchment, "The stuff I have to put up with."

The boy kept eyeing Augum, whispering insults and threats when Secretary Sharma was out of hearing range. "… destroy you like I did that other fool yesterday …"

Typical intimidation just to get him spooked before the fight. The boy was probably a spoiled brat who always got his way, someone who wasn't used to being stood up to. Augum couldn't wait to get in that arena. But he had to prepare first …

He refused to get distracted as the boy muttered on with inanities. Instead, he kept his head down, mentally going over his spells as well as strategizing his initial attack. The boy was twice his size but Augum knew that meant nothing in a warlock duel. The constant mutterings spurred him on.

They mutedly heard the crowd swell as Giovanni proclaimed yet another victor.

Secretary Sharma snapped her head at the exit. "Augustus, Brutus—you're up."

Augum strode down the tunnel leading to the arena, Brutus right beside him, scowling and still making threats. "Going to make you cry like a baby, crawl back to your mommy and—" Suddenly he stopped to listen to Giovanni's voice.

"… a nineteen-year-old 4th degree ice warlock from the Academy of Arcane Arts … representing the Legion outfit of the Stone Quarter … He's known to choke his opponents into submission … please welcome … Brutus 'The Brute' Johnson!"

The crowd roared as Brutus flashed Augum an arrogant *Yeah, you know what's coming* look. He then strutted out into the arena, waving at the crowd as if he'd already won.

"His opponent … hailing from the little known village of Everscale …" The crowd was on its feet. "A rare lightning necrophyte with impressive arcane dexterity … you've read about him in the Herald … the mysterious … the reclusive … Augustus 'The Hood' Westwoooooood!"

Augum strode out, heart pumping, head low. He stole a glance at Erika in the judge's booth, but still did not see the divining rod. He glanced the other way at Bridget and Leera, who cheered him on. Malaika and Charissa were in the stands too, but he didn't bother looking for them.

Augum faced Brutus as Giovanni went through the usual rule pronouncements.

Brutus, smirking and cracking his knuckles, nodded at the weapon racks. "Not going to need those."

The crowd tittered at his amplified joke.

"As per tradition, let the combatants give respect," Giovanni said.

Augum flexed his arm, allowing his four lightning rings to burst forth, then gave a slight bow, never taking his eyes off his meaty opponent.

Brutus, after seeing his lightning rings—and perhaps the look on Augum's face—hesitated, but flashed four rings of ice. He didn't bother bowing though.

Giovanni took a step back and gestured dramatically at the boy. "Are you ready?" Brutus nodded. He gestured the other way at Augum. "And are *you* ready?" Augum curled his fists and gave a slight nod. Giovanni made a chopping gesture. "Fight!" and the bell rang.

Augum quickly and violently shoved at the air. "BAKA!" completely catching Brutus off-guard with the force of the attack. Augum glimpsed a stupid look on the boy's face as he slammed into the stone wall, crumpling in a heap at its base.

He did not get back up.

The crowd fell totally silent for a moment before roaring.

"Aaand we have a knock-out!" Giovanni shouted, striding over and placing a hand on Augum's heaving shoulder. "That had to be one of the quickest knock-outs I have ever seen! A vicious shove attack. The Brute has been brutalized!"

The crowd laughed as two Legion healers jogged out to attend to the boy.

Augum was a little disappointed. He was looking forward to showing Brutus a little more of what he was made of.

"Congratulations, you continue to wow." Giovanni allowed the crowd to clap and cheer before continuing. "The Brute is known to be a difficult opponent on and off the arena floor. Did he have a lot to say to you in the dressing room?"

"He did some talking."

The crowd chortled.

"But you're standing here and he isn't." Giovanni waited for his reaction.

"I am," Augum finally said.

"Two more matches to go, think you can take the semis?"

"I'll try."

"Well there we have it, folks. A contestant of few words but quick off the draw." He lifted Augum's arm. "Advancing to tomorrow's semi-finals … the mysterious

… the arcanely agile … Augustus 'The Hood' Westwoooooood!"

BACK AT THE LIBRARY OF ANTIOC

"Weren't you supposed to *not* draw unnecessary attention?" Leera said once they had left the arena, leaving Malaika and Charissa behind to continue spying.

Augum shrugged. "I had a plan to start off losing, but it didn't quite work out that way."

"Well now the whole city will be talking about your super fast knock-out." She sighed. "As if they hadn't been going on enough about you already. Anyway, Robin was in the stands watching you fight. Saw him brush off the win to Temper Buttwax, that cow. I'm sure he thought you got lucky or something."

"Before we go to the Training Room," Bridget began, giving Leera a disapproving look for continually twisting Temper Butterwax's last name, "do you mind if we go to the library to do some more research? I'd like to study a bit more on symbolism."

Leera groaned, mumbling, "Only if I can bring a pillow this time ..."

They eventually crossed the drawbridge, passed through the bustling entrance hall, and on to the *Ordinaries* section of the library—the area with the large gargoyle statue. After a few mind-numbing hours of study in a room with a pile of dusty books, someone peeked into the room.

"You three—!"

They looked up from their desk to see a Legion guard striding toward them, helmet tucked under his arm. He possessed high cheekbones and a shaved head. Augum's stomach plummeted. This was it, they had been recognized. For a moment, he debated attacking him and just making a flat-out run for it—

"Why aren't you at the meeting?" the Legionnaire snapped.

"Meeting?" Bridget asked. "What meeting?"

"All out-of-town necrophytes are to report to the training grounds for an official Legion meeting. Why aren't you down there? Who is your commanding officer?"

"We just got back from the arena, sir, and he's in the field."

The guard stared at them with cool eyes that eventually settled on Augum. "You're The Hood."

"Yes, sir."

"Been hearing about you. You've been elevating the Legion's standing in the common folks' hearts. Sign-ups have increased. Well done, soldier. Now follow me, you're late."

They exchanged a brief look but followed. Augum's mind was in turmoil—the last thing he wanted to do was help the Legion. But then he smiled to himself—wait until they find out who he truly was! And if he could only somehow let people know a resistance existed, maybe it would spur others to join …

They soon arrived at the training grounds. A Legionnaire stood at the entrance, waving them along. Behind him sat the kind middle-aged attendant they previously met. But in place of his infectious smile was a face of melancholy. He did not raise his bald head, but instead quietly stitched a patch onto a padded practice vest.

They spotted a large crowd of necrophytes gathered in the obstacle field around a platform, on top of which stood a robed figure. Augum's immediate thought was Robin and Temper will probably be there, and tightened his hood.

The Legionnaire with the shaved pate led them to the crowd, where more than a few heads turned their way. Necrophytes started whispering to each other and pointing at Augum. Unlike the trio, none of them had their hoods up. A good many of them were their age or younger. The much older kids, usually sixteen or older, tended to already be in the field, training at the art of war.

"And speaking of winning over hearts and minds," said an ebony-skinned man with cropped gray hair and hawk-like eyes that immediately found Augum. He wore a shiny black robe fringed with crimson threading. The burning sword of the Legion was neatly embroidered over his heart. "We have been graced by The Hood."

The rest of the necrophytes turned to look Augum's way. Augum kept his face hidden in the shadowy folds of his hood.

"And I believe his cousins," the man continued in a penetrating voice, extending two wide-sleeved arms toward the girls. "As you can see, appearances are important. They show a united front by having their hoods raised together. As most of you know, The Hood won over the hearts and minds of the people with a simple public gesture of chivalry the other day in the arena. That is the essence of what we are trying to accomplish together as an army."

That's a steaming pile of dung, Augum was thinking as the necrophytes slowly turned back to the man, clapping politely.

The distinguished-looking warlock slowly paced the platform. "Some of you will soon be undertaking the Torment Trials. I know you are afraid, I do know that. And it is true that failure of the trial may result in death."

He let that thought sink in as he slowly eyed the crowd. "But that is why you shall work hard at impressing your commanders—at impressing me—with your diligence in studying the necromantic arts. You will be sacrificing your outdated pursuit of an element for the greater good of all. You will sacrifice for the security of a kingdom. You will sacrifice with the hopes of bringing glory to yourselves. And maybe, just maybe, you might find eternity along the way."

The necrophytes clapped while the Legion guard with the shaved head nodded, flexing his jaw. Augum and the girls had to clap along in order to avoid raising suspicion.

"One day necrophytes will be cultivated from birth," the man on the platform continued. "You are but the first generation. With starry eyes you stare into the horizon of destiny, awaiting the glory to come." He raised his arm and stared past them. "Somewhere out there lay great enemies. They are to the south and to the north and to the west. They will be conquered. And one day, we shall find those who dare to commit treason against the cause of the mighty Legion!"

The crowd roared and saluted, chanting, "Hail to the Legion!"

He raised a hand to silence them. "Yes, the traitor Anna Atticus Stone is strong—"

"Not as strong as you, Commander Jordan," one of the necrophytes piped in from somewhere up front, and the crowd chortled. Augum immediately recognized that grating voice.

The warlock commander smiled. "If only that were true, Robin," then raised a finger. "Never underestimate your enemy. Yes, she is strong, but together, we are stronger. Together, we will find her. Together, we shall complete the Great Quest. Together we will claim eternity. Every day brings us one step closer to that goal."

The necrophytes clapped and whistled.

"Yes, but my aunt really will find her, Commander. I guarantee it."

"I am sure she will indeed." Commander Jordan swept the crowd with his hawk eyes. "As you progress in your training, you will be drafted into the army. Some of you are already part of a company." He nodded at some of the older boys and girls in the crowd. "I know Malfease is represented, as well as Wolfpack—" A few of the necrophytes hooted their particular company call, "Comborai, Axon ... and so on. This is a time of celebration. You are here to watch the tournament, but also to continue your training. This is a special event, and many of you—those not drafted—will return to the Academy after it is over. But rest assured, the remainder will be placed when you are needed, and the time is coming. Train hard and earn your place in history. Duty unto death!"

"Duty unto death!" the crowd echoed as one. Augum pretended to say it, but no sound came from his lips.

"Now I have a special surprise for you all. Our Dreadnoughts, whom very few of you have seen thus far, have been hard at work indeed. You have all heard of speaking orbs, is that not so?"

The crowd nodded their heads in a vague fashion. Augum recalled his father using one of the palm-sized orbs to communicate with the Blade of Sorrows. Speaking orbs are similar in appearance to a scion at first glance.

"Well, for the first time in history, the Legion has developed a unique communication system. Each necrophyte will be receiving a special Dreadnought ring tuned to a specially-designed Dreadnought speaking orb, that only their commander will possess. This will allow direct communication between necrophytes and their superior officers."

The necrophytes clapped.

"When do we receive these rings, sir?" Robin asked.

"Your commanding officers will be receiving the packages as we speak. They are only for necrophytes, and only for those who have passed their 2nd degree."

There were some groans.

"Those who receive them will commence training with them immediately. The rings will be an incredible boon in battle, especially because you are warlocks. Imagine trying to conquer a city otherwise. No enemy will possess such a system of communication. That is why we will be victorious."

Augum exchanged a look with the girls. Not only were these orbs and rings bad news, but they were now talking about conquering cities …

"All right, let us do some training! Who would like to demonstrate how to properly summon a walker? How about … The Hood!"

The necrophytes all clapped and made an alley, but Augum did not step forward. He had to think fast.

"Uh, I'm sorry, sir, but I hurt my wrist today at the arena." Augum made a show of rubbing his wrist while Leera pointed to it, making exaggerated apologetic gestures. Augum thought it was overkill but luckily the commander nodded.

"Of course, I understand. We need you in top form tomorrow to face that Tiberran brat, to show the Tiberrans the might of the Legion, and to have them bend the knee not only on the battle field, but on the arena floor as well."

The crowd snickered and clapped as Augum mouthed "Tiberran brat?" at Leera. She only shrugged. For once, he looked forward to hearing a report from Malaika and Charissa on who he was facing next.

"I'll do it," Robin said, jumping onto the platform, slicking back his hair, pinched face glowing. "Where's the body?"

"Death is a natural part of life. We want you to be comfortable with death. Allow it to be a friend, not an enemy. Some of you have already taken life—"

Robin folded his arms and sneered while giving a proud nod.

"—others have yet to experience the honor of their first kill. A true necromancer will be as familiar with death as they are with their own rings. Look forward to that moment, for it is truly special. You must be cold. You must be pitiless. For that is how you conquer death."

The necrophytes clapped politely while bumps rose on Augum's arms. Oh no, they were planning on killing someone on that platform!

"I know you are excited, but we will not be taking a life today—" The crowd made a disappointed *aww* sound, and the commander raised a hand. "But rest assured, as we become more organized, every necrophyte will have ample opportunity to harden themselves and show their commitment to the Legion."

The necrophytes again clapped, some even whistling.

Augum glanced at the girls. Both looked pale. He subtly looked around at the crowd, noting the fervor on many of the faces, the absolute zeal and belief in the Legion. But he also spotted more than one anxious face. A young girl with olive skin and clumpy hair sniffed into her sleeve. A boy near her, maybe her brother, swallowed hard, and seemed to want to comfort her but was probably afraid of being called out as weak or afraid.

Augum felt terrible for them and couldn't imagine what they must be feeling. What were the odds of stopping the Legion before these young people were forced to do something that would haunt them forever? Every day that passed caused so much harm. How much of it was irreversible?

"We happen to have brought a few traitors who have not survived questioning." Commander Jordan opened his palm to an area behind the platform, and a wrapped-up body soon lifted into view, landing on the planks. The commander turned back to the assembled crowd. "Now let us go through the proper way to quickly and efficiently raise a walker."

The trio kept their gazes averted as Robin performed the ghastly ritual, transforming the body into a walker. Instead, Augum watched that unfortunate boy and girl as they obviously squirmed. When they tried to look away, the Legionnaire with the shaved head noticed, and stood close, glaring at them. The pair stiffened and watched the spectacle with wide eyes and colorless faces.

Augum felt his nails dig into his palms. This was indoctrination of the first order. This was how they won the young. It had to be stopped.

The commander thanked Robin as the crowd clapped, then proceeded to lecture them on the finer points of walker summoning. After every topic he would make a speech about the glory of the Legion and how important they all were and blah, blah, blah. The clapping tended to last longer than it should, and was usually followed by three successive chants of "Hail the Legion!" It was tedious and repetitive and eventually made Augum's eyes glaze over.

"Ugh, how much more of this do we have to put up with?" Leera whispered into his ear during the umpteenth clapping round. Although it was sort of interesting to see how they bullied and brainwashed necrophytes into obedience, he hoped it would end soon. They had things to do, namely to train on their own somewhere away from prying eyes, somewhere like … he craned his neck at the ceiling sky bridges … somewhere like up there.

Commander Jordan ended up going through a bunch of rudimentary necromancer spells, spending no time at all on standard spellcraft. He jabbered on about Feign Death, Rot, Pestilence, Ghost Light, and various other minor spells, like Raise Animal, which was supposed to be great practice for raising people. The trio wasted almost two hours listening to him, with no way to excuse themselves, until at last the man allowed them to go off on their own to train for the evening, as he had duties to attend to.

Augum tried to creep away with the girls but was immediately stopped by a gaggle of necrophytes, all his age or younger, and all trying to peek into his hood. Nearby hovered Robin and Temper, further complicating the situation. Robin seemed to enjoy the attention, making extravagant gestures and telling everyone how he was going to be the winner of his degree. He flashed superior looks toward Augum, who had to be very careful to keep his head averted and speak very little.

There was a barrage of questions.

"Can you teach me how to get a strong Push spell like that?"

"What's it feel like to compete in the arena?"

"How are you only fifteen yet already at the 4th degree?"

"How come you haven't cast any necromancy spells yet? Saving them for the finals against Robin?"

"He must be really good then."

Augum got away with nods or grunts mostly. When he did reply, it was in a whisper and with one-word answers.

When the crowd saw he was no fun, they migrated to Robin, who took particular pleasure in seeing himself as the more popular one.

Augum, meanwhile, skulked away with the girls, each breathing a massive sigh of relief when they finally got completely clear.

"That was disturbing on so many levels," Bridget whispered from behind her sleeve.

"That brainwashing though," Leera said with a shake of her head. "See the looks on their faces? They worship that fiendish commander."

Augum recalled the unfortunate boy and girl. "Not all of them, thankfully." But still far too many.

"Not to mention they're openly talking about conquering cities now," Bridget added. "Nodia's next. Then who knows what kingdom."

"Probably all of them." Leera cleared her throat in warning and they fell silent. A group of giggling necrophyte girls crossed their path, on their way to the pond leaf obstacle course. "Ugh, the Legion sure love making boring speeches," Leera muttered when they had gone.

Bridget pretended to scratch her nose as she spoke. "Those communication rings they're going to give out just made necrophytes infinitely more dangerous."

"Sure, they'll be dangerous," Augum said, wiping his mouth with his sleeve to hide what he was saying as there were way too many necrophytes milling about still, "but they'll also have a weakness—their commanding officers. Take them out, or steal the orbs, and they'll be like chickens running around with their heads cut off. You can even misdirect them or something."

"Except these chickens can still raise the dead," Leera added. "And that's not a bad idea—maybe we can steal an orb or two and a set of matching rings."

Bridget pretended to cough. "Agreed. Let's send a message right now to meet Klines, see if she can somehow get us a set."

They exited the Training Room and ported to the entrance hall, where Bridget left a message with an attendant at the front desk.

"What did you say to Klines?" Augum asked as he led them back after.

"Too dangerous to say anything specific," Bridge replied. "Just told her to find us as soon as she could, and that we'd be in the Training Room until the eighth bell. Then we'll be in the Supper Hall—"

"—meeting Malaika and Charissa," Leera said. "Always a treat."

They soon returned to the stand presided over by the bald attendant, who was waving at a small warlock boy after fitting him with a bulky set of training pads that made him look like a giant bale of hay.

"Hello again. Can you tell us how to get up there?"

The man followed Augum's gaze skyward. "Up there? You'll just have to figure that out, won't you?" His crow's feet crinkled as he smiled warmly.

"Right, the no hints thing."

The man only nodded. Something about his smile gave Augum the impression he was happy to see the Legion commander gone from his training grounds.

"Toll to pass."

"Excuse me?" Augum said.

The man kept his kind smile. "Earlier you came to a Legion meeting, but now you come to train. Toll to pass, I am afraid."

"Right." Bridget dug around and withdrew three silver coins.

"Good luck," the attendant said, accepting them.

The trio sauntered off, keeping a look out for other necrophytes, trying not to get too close. Everyone was diligently training, seemingly inspired by the commander's speeches.

"Imagine losing your element to necromancy," Leera said, watching a necrophyte practice making himself look undead in the wheat field. She shuddered. "So unnatural. I wonder how many of them would rather keep training in their chosen element."

"Hopefully a great many," Augum said, trying to imagine a way to build a secret resistance across the entire kingdom using those special Dreadnought rings.

They casually poked around the various obstacles and scenes, looking for a way to get up to the sky bridges, but then another obstacle course became free—the miniature mountains in a corner of the great cavern. The trio made their way over and climbed them, taking note of the various charred and beaten boulders; the tiny stream—

"What are you looking at, Bridge?" Leera asked as she started her spell casting warm up routine. "Bridge—?"

"Hmm?" Bridget was frowning at the stream. She tapped her chin. "Where do you suppose that goes?"

Leera shrugged. "Who knows, probably the sewer—" She froze. "Oh."

Augum saw where the stream ended—in a hole in the wall. "We can't fit through there." It reminded him of the cave below Bahbell, and how unnervingly tight some of its squeezes had been.

"Maybe not through there, but …" Bridget scanned the cavern. "What about that?" She nodded at a waterfall that started up high at the sky bridges and ended with a constant roar into a small pool.

"Where does the water go though?" Augum asked.

Leera flashed a mischievous grin. "That's what we're saying. Let's find out."

They went over to investigate.

Augum placed his hand in the crystal-clear pool. The water was surprisingly warm. He could see the rocky bottom, but no exit point for the water. "Maybe it's arcane. Maybe somehow it cycles the water back up top using a spell of some kind—"

"I'm not so sure." Bridget approached the waterfall from the side, placing a hand on the slick rock wall to stabilize herself. The roar was immense, and the wind that got whipped up from the falling water sent her hair and necrophyte robe fluttering. She poked her head into the waterfall, getting soaked in the process, before jumping out and jogging over.

"Just like I thought," she said, wringing out her hair. "There's a river behind the waterfall. It flows away into darkness."

"The water's warm enough that we could swim it," Augum said.

Leera tested the water and nodded. "That would bypass Watts and her stupid guards. I say we risk it. But we come back after supper just before the place closes."

"What do we do about the attendant though?" Bridget asked. "He'll know we haven't exited. Might send guards searching."

"Leave that to me," Augum said. He'd already been thinking about that part, and had some ideas.

They returned to the mountain scene and began training, this time surreptitiously focusing on the Reflect spell. Bridget was adamant they work on it, convinced it could save their lives at a crucial moment.

"I don't get the big deal!" Leera yelled after again failing to reflect Augum's Deafness casting.

Bridget waved at her. "Shh! You're yelling—"

"What—!"

Bridget made the gesture for her to tone it down, indicating at her ears.

"Oh, right. Sorry. But I don't get why this is such an important spell. We can only successfully cast it once a day anyway."

Bridget pointed at her mouth, over-annunciating the words. "Just keep trying."

Leera swatted at the air. "Bah."

They continued training. At long last, after the place had mostly cleared of people, and as they were expecting the cry that the eighth bell had rung, Augum finally managed to reflect Bridget's purposefully weakened First Offensive back at her. She was so stunned by the maneuver she only gaped as her own vine smacked her in the stomach, doubling her over. He pumped his fist, which clutched the crystal he had used in the process.

Bridget, who had already cast the spell successfully near the start of their session, picked herself off the ground, smiling proudly. "Well done. Remember exactly what you did there and how it felt. Now it's Leera's turn to succeed next."

"Maybe if it wasn't near impossible," Leera muttered.

They kept training, focusing on Leera, until the cry of the eighth bell. Then they hurried to the Supper Hall. As they turned a corner, a short and shadowy figure called out from behind a gargoyle statue.

"Who's there?" Augum asked.

The stunted figure stepped forward.

"Oh, hello, Secretary Klines."

The beetle-like woman looked around before hissing, "You ought not to send for me anymore, it's too risky."

"Yes, sorry, but we need your help with something non-library related," and Augum and Bridget took turns quickly explaining all about the new speaking orb sets they were giving out to necrophytes and their commanders.

Klines' giant eyes narrowed. "You want me to steal a set for you?"

"Yes, exactly—"

"You are out of your minds," and she began striding away.

Augum took one step after her. "Secretary Klines—please, it's really important. For the Resistance …"

Klines stopped, took a breath. "I promise nothing," and strode off.

"Well, that's a shame," Leera said.

Bridget frowned. "Come on, let's eat."

A WINDING RIVER

The trio met Malaika and Charissa in the Supper Hall, receiving the latest news about the tournament.

"Tomorrow you're going to face last year's 3rd degree champion," Malaika said as they hurried to finish their meals.

"Some sixteen-year-old Tiberran girl," Charissa added, mashing her last potato in her bowl. "Her name is …" She gave a vague glance at Malaika. "Um, I forget."

"Caireen Lavo."

"Oh, right. Anyway, apparently her town was razed by the Legion."

Then we have something in common, Augum thought.

Malaika was nodding along. "They mocked her victories, but there's revenge in those wild eyes of hers."

"What did she fight like?" Leera asked, shoving aside her lumpy soup and muttering, "Broccoli. Gross."

"We actually didn't see her fight."

"We went shopping!" Charissa added proudly while Malaika tried shushing her with a meaningful look. "I got myself a nice new pretty dress—"

Leera gaped. "You went shopping."

"Uh, *yeah*, that's what I just said—"

Leera rubbed her forehead with both hands and sighed heavily. "They went shopping."

"Yeah, *so*?"

"Ugh, what's the point?"

Bridget leaned forward. "Malaika, Charissa, I know you two can do better. Please, help us."

Malaika's eyes flicked to Augum before dropping. "Sorry. We'll … we'll try."

Bridget nodded. "All right then. I'm sure you'll work harder next time. Anything about the Legion?"

"Nothing you don't know," Malaika replied. "Except more rumors of war soon. Though we overheard two commanders talking about some kind of strange disturbance in Bahbell they're 'officially not supposed to acknowledge', whatever that meant. Had to do with soldiers moving about on their own."

Augum exchanged a look with Bridget and Leera. Had his father found a way to use Occulus' ancient army without the Agonex?

"Oh, and I received word from Father," Malaika went on in a singsong voice.

"You *wrote* to him?" Leera hissed.

Malaika's face was indignant. "Of course I did! And I already told you I left him a proper note before stealing away with the lot of you—"

"You wrote to him from here though."

"Obviously—"

"And he wrote you back. *Here*."

"Uh, *yes*. Where else would he send the letter?" Malaika gave Charissa a look saying *Is she slow or what?* before returning her attention to the trio. "He knows we're here to help you in your quest—and I have to admit, we're doing a wonderful job, aren't we?"

Leera's mouth hung open.

"Anyway, you'll be glad to know we shall have horses at the ready at the stables on the south side of town, anytime we need them." Malaika gave a satisfied nod. "Father will arrange everything."

Leera's eyes narrowed. "Oh, daddy will arrange everything. Well that's wonderful. I guess everyone can soon go home all happy and safe."

"I do not appreciate your tone."

"She doesn't appreciate my tone," Leera said to Augum, before dropping her voice even lower as she leaned toward Malaika. "Did you, on the off chance, ever stop to think what would happen if your correspondence was intercepted?"

"What does intercepted mean?" Charissa whispered.

"I took the proper precautions, thank you very much," Malaika replied, ignoring her friend. "No mention of names or anything like that."

"Indeed now? Nothing suspicious at all about horses waiting in a stable—"

"Don't be paranoid," Charissa said. "We sent the letter by courier and paid extra." She gave a firm nod. "Lots of extra."

Leera opened her palms to Augum. "They paid extra. Problem solved." She dusted her hands. "Nothing to worry about here because they paid extra. Ugh, only spoiled, bratty rich girls think—"

"Lee, enough," Bridget cut in with a deep sigh. "We have to trust they did it without tipping our hand. We're out of time, we have to go."

Leera smacked her bowl further away, sloshing goop onto the table, but said nothing more. The trio departed, leaving Malaika and Charissa to finish their meal with frowning faces. They retrieved the gargoyle coins and made their way to the Training Room just as the crier let everyone know the ninth evening bell had struck and the library was closing.

The middle-aged attendant gave them a kind smile. "Training Room's closed, sorry."

"Yeah, we know," Augum replied, giving the girls a reminding look to trust him, then made sure nobody was near. "Sir, we were hoping that, uh, well …" He cleared his throat lightly and dropped his voice to a whisper. "This library has a long and rich tradition of making warlocks earn their way into the, uh, labyrinth."

The man's brows rose up his forehead.

"And we can't get there because the Legion blocked all the entrance points. We want to explore the old traditions before it's too late."

"We're aware of the risks, sir," Leera added. "Please, let us stay. We can find our way down there and back without getting caught—"

"We've already done it once," Bridget piped in.

"You have?"

The trio gave fervent nods.

"We were in the round room with all those doors," Augum said, "and already passed a bunch of challenges."

"I see." The man glanced back at his stall of armor pads. "It would be against protocol—"

"We know that, sir," Augum whispered. "But we think it's important some of us learn about the old ways. We know the library was built on curiosity and mischief and stuff. Shouldn't all be necromancy now, should it?"

"We promise we won't tell anyone you let us stay," Leera said.

"And we promise to be *very* careful," Bridget added.

The man studied them a moment more before the crow's feet returned around his eyes along with his smile. "You remind me of myself. You better hurry then. They're going to bring in the walkers soon."

"Thank you *so* much, sir," Augum said, shaking his hand.

The man stopped Augum at the last moment. "But you'll still have to pay the evening toll, I'm afraid. It's tradition—toll to pass. Otherwise you'll incur very bad luck."

"Of course. How much is it?"

"Same as the day—spine a head."

Bridget handed over three silver coins.

"Good luck and be careful."

They scurried to the pool, jumped in, and swam toward the waterfall. Augum stole a glimpse of the distant entrance to the Training Room, just in time to witness walkers being ported in, escorted by Legion warlocks. He wondered how they were going to get past them on the way back and exactly how many they would face.

The river moved slowly through a rocky cave with a low ceiling. The trio lit up their palms. Leera used her Shine extension to make the water ahead visible, something that seemed to give her great pleasure.

"And look, I can make it blink too!" she said, flickering her pale blue underwater light. "Ooo, let me try something—" She concentrated for a moment as they bobbed along, then she made a small portion of the water rise, forming it into a crude figurine. "I knew it! I can manipulate water!"

"That's just Telekinesis," Bridget said, but when she and Augum tried the same trick, nothing happened.

Leera raised a sharp brow that paired nicely with the smug expression on her face. To her credit, she did not rub it in their faces. Instead, she dove. After surfacing, she said, "Huh, I swear I can see better underwater than above it."

"Water's moving fast," Bridget said, getting increasingly nervous as the ceiling dipped lower and lower. "Maybe this wasn't such a good idea …"

The ceiling ahead dropped suddenly to the water, and Bridget got a panicked look on her face.

Leera dipped her head below water and shone her light ahead. "There's a perch just on the other side," she said after rising. "Get ready to get out on the left."

They swam over and, due to her good spotting, were able to catch the ledge and climb out onto a small alcove with drawings on the wall.

"Look at that, it's a map!" Leera said, dripping water everywhere.

Augum brushed her wet hair away from her face so she could see better. She smiled at him. Unlike back at Milham, they had hardly spent any time alone together, and he missed that.

"Focus, you two," Bridget said absently, holding her greenish glowing palm closer. "There's a fork up ahead. River to the right looks like a dead end. Leads to some sort of large pool that feeds the other water sources in the Training Room. That's my interpretation of these markings, at least."

"And the path to the left?" Augum asked.

"Goes down. But this … this doesn't make sense."

Leera spotted something else on the wall. "Hey, there's old graffiti here. 'Sepitus Ptelmus, 3241, water, 3rd'. That's a hundred years ago! And there's more—'Grazilda Cunningsworth, 3101, water, 5th'. That's even older!" She scanned the walls reading out the names and the dates. "Huh, they're all water warlocks … why do you suppose that is?"

Bridget was frowning at the map while biting a nail. "Because I think this is a water Trainer."

Leera exploded in a giant smile. "It *is*? Awesome!" She smacked Augum and Bridget's arms. "That means there's got to be a secret lightning and a secret earth Trainer somewhere around here!"

"Maybe." Bridget stabbed a tunnel with her finger, on the other end of which was a fountain within a maze. "This is where we need to go. I remember that fountain from the map in the round room of doors."

Augum tapped at the room adjacent to the tunnel, scratched with four marks. "In order to get to the tunnel, we'll need to get into this room."

Bridget traced the scratches. "Four marks. Four degrees?"

"I think so. All the rooms are scratched with marks, starting with one. Looks like they go all the way up to ten. Ten degrees, wow."

"We've gone blind into rooms before," Leera said. "Hasn't stopped us yet. Besides, it's part of the castle. Can't be *that* dangerous."

"Well, technically," Bridget replied, "we've never been to rooms that demanded a certain degree of skill."

Leera's head bobbed as she playfully but silently mimicked, " 'Technically' " behind Bridget's back.

"First up is a distance swim," Bridget said. "Underwater. Hold your breath for …" She traced a finger across a long tunnel up ahead. "A while."

"Hmm, they didn't mess around back then," Augum said. "Wonder how many drowned trying this."

"From what I remember reading," Bridget replied, "people did die on the obstacles. Back then, they were more about weeding out the weak than being safe." She gestured at the fast-moving river. "I mean, look, there isn't even a way to get back if you wanted to with that current. And imagine if some poor warlock who couldn't swim accidentally stumbled in here."

"Maybe they shouldn't have then," Leera muttered. "Stumbled in here that is."

"Don't be insensitive. Imagine your child dying from some stupid obstacle course—"

Leera placed her hands on her hips. "Arcanery isn't a safe discipline, you know that. Never was, never has been, never will be."

Augum glanced between their reddened faces. "What's with you two? You've been squabbling a lot lately. Can we just work together?"

Bridget rubbed her forehead. "I'm sorry, it's my fault. All this worry and planning and … combined with those stupid nightmares …" She sighed. "I just … I just need a good night's sleep, that's all."

"We all do," Leera said. She turned toward the water and rubbed her hands together. "All right, you two ready for a long dip? Catch your breath, because this one's going to be a long one. And watch your heads!"

They took a series of deep breaths together before holding the last one and jumping in.

WATER OBSTACLES

The supposedly long underwater tunnel passed rather quickly, for the water sped up in the tight rocky space. It was the part after that was a surprise—the trio didn't even get a chance to catch their breath before being dumped over a high waterfall, splashing into a deep pool thirty feet below.

They clambered out over the edge and collapsed, panting, necrophyte robes suddenly twice as heavy from being water laden. When Augum finally caught his breath and re-lit his palm, he took a good look around, spotting a great many slides and a bunch of harmless looking water specific obstacles.

"It's some sort of 1st degree fun room," Bridget said, getting up to examine a water wheel that slowly revolved, dumping water into a basin, which then dumped water over a series of old chimes that no longer worked. "Doesn't appear to have been cleaned in ages though."

"I guess people don't come down here as much as they used to," Leera said, flaking rust off a windmill painted with faded targets. "Not since they've switched to necromancy. Kind of sad, seeing as it's a 1st degree warlock's paradise." She used Telekinesis to zoom a crude miniature wooden boat around the pool.

Augum could almost hear the echo of young warlocks laughing and playing here in ages past. Some of the obstacles were ancient, so caked with rust they probably stopped working hundreds of years ago. Others looked like they had been installed more recently, but before the Legion took power.

"There's a portal etching here that looks like it will take us back to the Training Room," Bridget noted. "I guess this is an official secret Trainer, even though it looks like it was unsupervised."

Augum strode to one of the rock walls. "Found another map. Next room is down the river." He nodded at a portion of the wall. "Got to dive for it though. Says it's the 2nd degree room."

"Relax a little, you two. Let's have some fun!" Leera went down one of the slides, hands raised. "Weee!" She splashed into the pool, surfaced, and slicked back her hair. "I feel like a kid again. Wish I'd discovered this place when I first began arcanery."

"How *did* you begin arcanery?" Augum found it surprising he had never asked either of them that question before.

Leera swam over, placing her chin on her arms at the edge of the pool. "Took an aptitude test when I was thirteen. Showed some promise, so Mum and Dad put me through basic lessons. Only theory kind of stuff. Hated it, don't think I remembered a single thing. Everything was so repetitive. Oh but I did *finally* manage to move something telekinetically—"

"—cause *someone* helped you with the training," Bridget said with a wink. "And it was a feather which I blew. Remember? You thought you did it yourself, and that gave you the belief you needed to actually perform the spell."

"What? You never told me that!" Leera slapped water her way.

Bridget reddened. "I didn't? Oops." She shrugged and smiled. "Surprise, I guess."

Leera rolled her eyes, but was smiling. "Anyway, went to the academy a year later, after summer. But then we had to flee because the Legion did this whole purge and forceful recruitment thing. The parents built a village in the middle of nowhere. Almost got killed, like, a bazillion times after meeting you. Rest is history."

"A bazillion?" Augum brushed that aside. "'Tis but a trifle."

Bridget chuckled. "You wanted to be a knight. I still remember that. Both of you, actually."

Leera slapped water her way again. "And I would have been a fine one too!" Then she grumbled, "Or a blacksmith. I'd have been good at that. I like working with my hands. Besides swords, I'd have made, like, stupid iron baskets, or coat hooks or something. You know, useful stuff."

Augum raised a brow. "Baskets—?"

Now it was his turn to get splashed. "Shut up. I happen to like certain girlie things, all right?"

"An iron basket isn't very girlie," Bridget remarked.

Leera shrugged. "I'd have started there. Then, I don't know, made iron barrel straps … or something."

Bridget snickered. "You would've been a terrible blacksmith."

"Yes, yes I would have."

"I still remember when you told me about the sword your father gave you," Augum said wistfully, thinking

back to what felt like a more innocent time, even though they had probably been in as much danger then as now. "It was named Careena, because it careened into things."
He smiled. "Cute."

"Cute? You don't describe a sword as cute—"

"I was talking about you."

"Oh." She snorted, wagging a finger at him. "You." She raised one of her sharp eyebrows. "Bridge ever tell you how *she* started arcanery?"

Bridget instantly stopped snickering. "Not this story again."

"Why? He's never heard it—"

"Please no."

"She's embarrassed. Look at her cheeks!"

Bridget hid her face behind her soggy sleeve.

"Tell me," Augum said, amused.

"A boy who had a massive crush kept teasing her, until she had some kind of fit and used wild arcanery to shove him down an outhouse."

"It wasn't like that!" Bridget said, still hiding her face. "I shoved him *against* the wall of the outhouse."

"But he still fell in, didn't he?"

"Wait, our Bridget used *wild arcanery*?" Augum pointed at her. "This Bridget here? This very one?" He folded his arms. "I refuse to believe it. She's incapable of doing anything that breaks rules, let alone such barbarity."

"I didn't *know* better back then, all right? I was only twelve! And I got into *so* much trouble for it."

"She started arcanery young," Leera said. "But parents forbade her from doing anything for ages."

Bridget raised her head, and she was actually smiling, even though her cheeks were the color of autumn apples. "Only after I turned fourteen was I allowed to learn arcane theory and history and everything else. Still wasn't allowed to cast a single spell until I attended the academy."

"She would have been a genius if they had let her study early. Too bad she shoved a boy down an outhouse—"

"Stop already," but Bridget was giggling along with Leera, who suddenly started in with, "Shtop! Shtop zis zilliness!"

"Unnameables, no, not that again!" Bridget said, covering her ears.

All right, all right, I'll stop." Leera's chortling settled down as her chin returned to her arms. She gazed at Augum, her legs kicking the water lazily behind her. "You ever had any clues about your talents?"

"Not that I recall. Didn't even know warlocks existed. Always assumed people were telling tales."

"Oh, right, the farm boy thing. Yeah, them country folk can be dumb an' ignorant as dirt."

Bridget made a noise with her teeth. "Leera, not everyone can grow up in a city or be surrounded by books."

"I know, look, he turned out all right. And handsome to boot—"

"I was talking about regular country folk. You shouldn't make fun of them. Most are very poor, and are not doing so well, especially in this day and age."

Leera sighed. "I was talking about the ones that *suppress* arcanery. But yeah, I know I can be crass sometimes." She let go of the edge and gracefully dove. Augum watched as her light swam searchingly around in the dark pool like an underwater firefly.

"Have you noticed how long she can hold her breath?" he asked Bridget. "I think she might be turning into a fish."

"What do you expect, she's a water warlock. You just wait until she gets higher in degree." She thumbed at the wall. "We'll see her swim to the bottom of the ocean."

"That's … that's a joke, right?"

Bridget snickered as Leera finally resurfaced.

"Can you show me your neck?" Augum asked.

Leera gave him a suspicious look. "What? Why?"

"I think there might be gills there."

"Eww, that's just … ugh, eww!" She shook the idea off, rubbing her neck, then brightened. "Hey, did you two know there are a whole bunch of mini Trainers at the bottom of the pool?" She dove again, resurfacing quickly this time. "There's broken stuff down there that you can fix with Repair, stuff that reforms itself! Oh and guess what! I can cast spells underwater! Watch—" She dove again and a jet of water burst out of the pool.

Augum, after enjoying watching her in her natural element, could no longer resist the fun and dove in. "Let me try," he said after surfacing. He dipped down and slammed his fists together underwater, gurgling, "Annihilo!" but the spell didn't work.

Leera, who had been watching him underwater, surfaced alongside. "Maybe you'll be able to get it after a bit of practicing."

Augum doubted it though. He suspected complex underwater spell casting came easily to a water warlock, and was one of the perks of her discipline. It was interesting to see their arcane differences slowly start to take shape.

He punched her lightly on the shoulder. "And you cried about how useless your element was."

"I did *not*!"

Bridget strode to the edge of the pool, arms folded across her chest. "I remember that, Aug. 'My Shine extension sucks!' " she mimicked in a pretty good impression of Leera, doing the nose crinkle.

"I don't sound like that—!"

Bridget didn't let up, accenting with a classic Leera eye roll. " 'You guys get all the good stuff and I just get to light up stupid puddles!' "

"And I don't do that … eye roll thing … do I?"

"We don't get to tease you often," Augum said, playfully splashing her face.

"Oh you—" She dove and went after him underwater, and soon the two of them were play wrestling. Except Augum quickly found himself scrambling out of the pool—she was an exceptionally better swimmer and could have easily pinned him if she wanted to. Not to mention she could cast spells underwater.

"That little cheat, did you see that—?" he said to Bridget as Leera patrolled the edge of the pool like a shark. "Shoved me underwater like a rag doll."

Bridget had a hand on her chin and a big smile on her face, seeming to take great pleasure in watching them. But then she heaved a big sigh and returned to the map.

"Loser," Leera sniped with a grin. "Anyway, going to sniff around down there some more with Unconceal." As she dove down, Augum strode over to Bridget.

"You're doing that frown thingy again. What kind of trouble should we expect?"

Bridget tapped the room after the next one. "The 3rd degree room worries me. We'll be using our First Offensive. Look at all these carved figures. We might be in for a fight."

Augum examined the figural etchings. They were plain except for lines radiating from their heads, and they looked like they were standing in water. "Yeah, maybe, but they'll be dummies or something. I wouldn't worry about it too much."

"Unless we have to fight them underwater."

"Oh. You have a point." He slapped her back. "Come on, we'll worry about it when we get there."

It took a bit of convincing to get Leera to stop playing. She whined like an eight-year-old, only relenting when Bridget said, "Shtop horshing around already, ve have vork to do."

The next obstacle was a dive straight down into murky and freezing water—a deep one, so deep Augum's ears felt like they were going to burst. Except at the bottom they swam up against a gate and had to immediately resurface.

"I think that's an arcane portcullis," Bridget said, gasping. "But I couldn't see anything down there, even with my lit palm. Water's too murky."

Augum unsuccessfully tried to stop his teeth from chattering. "There might be a secret lever."

"It's a pass gate of some kind," Leera said. "I have an idea. Be right back." She took a deep breath and dove.

Meanwhile, Bridget and Augum exchanged a worried look, each trying to stay warm in the frigid water by rubbing their shoulders.

"Just like I thought," Leera said after surfacing some time later. "Have to cast all the 1st degree spells to get by. Give me a moment," and she dove again, but this time she took so long Augum had to dive after her, meeting her on the way back up. She was pale when she broke the surface, gasping for breath.

"Gate's up, but that was hard. We have to go, don't know how long it'll stay open."

They took a deep breath and dove. Barely visible at the bottom were a series of sharp iron spikes Augum recognized as the lowered top of the gate. Leera allowed him and Bridget to pass first. As soon as she swam through, the gate slammed shut behind her with a dull clang. Augum realized the horror of it—if Leera had passed through first, he or Bridget would have been impaled. It was enough for him to lose a breath underwater, making the swim all the way up on the other side quite the chest-burning exercise. The last few feet were especially agonizing—Augum and Bridget both ended up choking on water.

"This is getting harder," Bridget gasped after they surfaced. "And more dangerous."

Leera scoffed as she hauled herself out of the pool. "Lightning one is probably much worse. Bet you that's where the deaths really mounted."

"After seeing this, I don't think I'd want to go through it," Augum said, noticing something shiny on the ground behind Leera. He hauled himself out and grabbed it. "Look at that, a gargoyle coin."

"Must be for successfully passing through the portcullis," Bridget said, taking the coin and stuffing it in the snakeskin money pouch tied to her waist. "Now we know this part is tied to the arcane library and the labyrinth. No wonder there's a secret passage to the maze later."

Augum glanced around the room, using his lit palm for light. He saw the silhouettes of dark braziers, probably unlit for some time, as well as a series of black pools. He got up and strode over to one of the iron receptacles. Nearby on the wall, he spotted an etching of a miniature brazier inside a square.

"Anyone remember the runeword for a brazier rune?"

"I think it's the same as for a torch or fireplace," Bridget replied.

"Which is?"

"*Firemente*. And don't forget to visualize the flame."

He placed his lit palm over the rune, visualizing the flames roaring. "Firemente." The brazier burst to life. The girls scampered over to warm themselves.

After they were sufficiently warmed, they explored more of the cold and damp cavern-like room, discovering that each of the dark pools had a submerged statue, the stone heads just barely visible below the surface. The last pool, the one abutting the wall, was too deep and dark to see into.

"Well, here goes nothing," Leera said, jumping in before Augum could tell her to be careful. He watched as her palm light faded, finally disappearing altogether in the black depths. He swallowed, wondering if he should go after her to make sure she was all right. What if something attacked her down there?

Time passed and he and Bridget exchanged anxious glances. Suddenly there came a deep thrumming sound as if someone cast Slam underwater, followed by bubbles. He was about to jump in when he saw Leera's pale light. She soon surfaced, gasping.

"Had to fight some stupid fish while using all my 2nd degree spells." She rubbed her ears. "You should hear how loud my Slam is underwater. *Unbelievable.* Anyway, gate's open now. This one's an even longer dive, so prepare yourselves. There's some writing on the wall I have to read first though. Just need to … catch my breath."

She soon dove again while Augum wondered what she had fought down there. Something told him it was more than just "some stupid fish".

Leera resurfaced a while later. "All right, here's the thing—the underwater area ahead is some kind of maze. I have to use Unconceal to get us through it. But it's *really* dark down there so you'll have to stay close. Oh, and I don't know how far it is, so conserve your breath."

Great, Augum thought. They were already burdened by these heavy necrophyte robes which acted like sails underwater. Now it sounded like they would be blind too.

"Maybe we should take a portal back," Bridget said in a weak voice.

"Bah, it'll be fine, just stay close to me. All right, hop in and get ready."

Augum and Bridget slowly got in the ice-cold water. It didn't seem to bother Leera, but Augum and Bridget's teeth instantly began to chatter.

"One final thing," Leera said. "Whatever you do, don't panic."

Bridget made a small cringing noise.

"You'll be fine, it's not *that* scary. All right, deep breaths now—!"

Bridget and Augum exchanged a last worried look before taking deep breaths and diving, palms lit.

It wasn't long until the ear pressure was unbearable. Augum almost lost his breath when he glimpsed a giant fish with rows and rows of sharp teeth, impaled by a spear. The fish floated upside down amidst the inky darkness, staring at them with dead saucer-like eyes. He and Bridget quickly swam past, then through the sharp portcullis that slammed shut behind them the moment Leera swam through.

Before them were the dim outlines of three small tunnels. Leera extended her hand and said in a surprisingly clear voice, "Un vun deo." Augum noticed her palm stayed lit—she was chronocasting underwater, an impressive feat. After a moment of concentration, she began to swim down the central tunnel, Bridget and Augum following closely.

The tunnel swerved before coming to a fork. Leera chose the left one. Suddenly she spotted something ahead and gestured for them to swim back and take the other tunnel. Augum glimpsed a set of black spikes before turning around, trying not to panic about the fact he was quickly running out of breath.

Back at the fork, Augum and Bridget allowed Leera to go first. She zoomed ahead, pausing at something that had flashed. She swam through then indicated for them to advance slowly. Bridget scooted through the obstacle next. Augum felt his insides go even colder when he spotted the flash of a blade swish through the water. He noticed a bone on the tunnel floor and let loose a bubble of air. Bridget was frantically waving for him to hurry. He timed his move and shot through successfully, but felt himself turning purple as they swam on through the ever-tightening tunnel.

This was it, he wasn't going to make it out of there alive. He started frantically pawing at the tunnel, feeling a flesh-withering panic take hold.

Suddenly his light flickered out.

Bridget turned around, her eyes magnifying when she saw him. She scrambled his way, grabbing his sleeve and yanking him along, desperate to catch up to Leera, whose light seemed far ahead now.

Augum's vision began to darken. He felt a black tunnel of unconsciousness closing in as his heart thundered in his chest. There was nowhere to go, no way to breathe. He was suffocating and panicking.

Bridget kept tight hold of him. She grabbed something ahead. Whatever it was jerked them along so abruptly Augum expelled the remainder of his breath, instantly inhaling water.

The last thing he saw before losing consciousness was a distant light blinking out.

INCREASING DIFFICULTIES

Augum jerked awake gasping and choking out water. Leera and Bridget were holding him. His chest felt as tight as a drum and he could barely breathe.

"Oh, Aug, I'm so sorry," Leera was saying over and over, clutching him close.

"He's all right," Bridget repeated, letting go, herself gasping for breath. "He's all right, Lee. Shh, it's fine."

Leera gently kissed his forehead before squeezing him tight. "Thought I lost you. I'm so sorry."

"I'm fine," he said in a weak voice. "Just need … a moment. What … happened?"

Bridget thumbed back at a dark pool. "Leera saw that we were in trouble. She swam ahead and found an arcane underwater winch. She sent the chain back to me using Telekinesis."

"We're … lucky …"

"At least we got two more coins," Bridget added with a pained smile.

Leera brushed wet hair aside from his forehead. They sat there catching their breath and getting their bearings. They were in a low-ceilinged cavern. Sharp stalactites dripped water into puddles on the pockmarked ground. There were no braziers to warm up beside, but there was a small area of the wall carved with a portal rune.

"Spooky," Leera whispered. "Wonder how long it's been since anyone's been here."

"Historically, fewer and fewer would make it to the next room." Bridget squinted at the distant dark walls. "This is the 3rd degree room, isn't it?"

"I think so," Leera replied.

"Then where are those figures that were on the map?"

"Must be hidden or something. Or maybe they attack us after."

Bridget stood. "Keep your wits about you." She took a few steps and froze, shaking a feeling off. "Just got attacked by a Fear spell. Prepare your Mind Armor." She raised her foot. "There must be hidden invisible traps." She took another few measured steps before suddenly stopping and wincing again. "Yup, there goes another one. A Confusion attack. Don't know where it's coming from."

Leera was still holding onto Augum. "You fighting them off easily? How's the strength of the attack?"

"I'd guess it's 5th degree." Bridget took another few steps, once again stopping and wincing. "6th degree Deafness. Close one. I'm going to see if I can make it to a wall." She jumped from puddle to puddle, suddenly dropping to her knees and screaming.

Augum and Leera scrambled to their feet and raced over, dodging the stalactites, and immediately encountering numerous mind attacks. Augum successfully warded off Confusion, Fear, and Deafness with his Mind Armor, but failed against a strong Blindness attack that instantly blacked out his vision. He froze in place, lest he compound his misfortune with other failures.

Leera reached a whimpering Bridget. "I got you, Bridge, I got you ..."

"That was a *very* high degree Fear attack," Bridget finally said in a quivering voice. "It was a cliff. I ... fell. *I fell!*" Her whole body was shaking. "Horrifying, just ... horrifying."

They waited a bit to calm down and recuperate.

At last, Augum's blindness dissipated. "All right, we're supposed to cast Object Alarm, Object Track, and our First Offensive to get by this room, right?"

"But on what?" Bridget craned her neck without walking anywhere.

"I see a gargoyle rune on that wall there." Leera jumped over the puddles all the way to a distant wall, wincing when one of her feet touched the edge of a puddle.

"It's the puddles!" Augum said. "I saw your foot touch that one. That's what's triggering the attacks." He tested the theory by carefully walking over without touching a single puddle, and had nothing attack him. Bridget promptly did the same, meeting them at the inscription.

Augum placed his shining palm against the gargoyle rune. It did not light up.

"Let me try." Leera placed her hand and the rune lit up crimson, along with an inscription which she read aloud. ' "Object thy will track. Wrong thou shalt be not'." Soon as she finished reading, a wooden ball popped into a small hidden cavity in the wall. Below it was another hole, this one empty. Leera placed her hands over the ball. "Vestigio itemo discovaro." Then she placed it into the other hole, where it rolled away. A moment later, five balls rolled out of nearby holes, each plopping into a puddle.

Leera breathed a sigh of relief. "Something easy for once." She used her hand to guide her to the correct ball. As soon as she picked it up, she winced. "Ah."

"Mind attack?" Augum asked.

"Strong one. That actually stung."

"Looks like you beat it though." All the balls had disappeared and a new inscription lit up on the wall, along with a fresh ball in the top hole. Further, a new hole appeared where there was none before. Leera carefully returned, navigating the puddles, to read the new inscription. " 'Thither this here ball, alarmed it thus be, finds itself, thitherto thou goest, and open thine door, but before thy bell in thee head ringeth true. Hearken thy spirit, for thenceforth through thy door a most wicked fiend awaits'."

Leera grimaced. "What gibberish did I just read?"

Even Bridget had to re-read the inscription to herself several times. "I think you enchant the ball with Object Alarm, then a door will appear. As soon as the alarm goes off in your head, you're supposed to open the door."

"Which means something will have picked it up," Augum said.

"And we're supposed to fight it." Leera sighed. "Hence the First Offensive use. Fine." She placed her hands over the new ball. "Concutio del alarmo." She took a breath. "Might as well see if I can follow it too." She concentrated another moment. "Vestigio itemo discovaro," before releasing it into the new hole. They followed the sound as the ball slowly rolled along inside the walls, being sure to avoid the puddles. At last, it thunked against the foot of a particularly flat area.

"It's just behind here," Leera whispered, inspecting the wall. "I see grooves."

"There's the handle." Augum pointed at a jutting rock. "Don't pull on it yet though, wait for the alarm." He braced himself, ready to cast his First Offensive. Bridget joined him in an attack posture.

"I smell smoke," Leera whispered, hand pressed against the rock. "And the wall's getting hot."

"Look at the seams," Augum said, watching as a red glow formed the outline of a door.

"Getting hotter," Leera said after placing her palm on the handle. "Get ready …"

There was a flaming groan from the other side.

"Now!" she shouted, and flung the door open. The trio was immediately greeted by what appeared to be a wall of fire, except it *moved*! The thing roared flame that nipped at their sodden robes.

They stumbled backwards from the heat of the fire. Augum immediately felt his mind under attack as he stepped into puddle after puddle. He had to be sharp to ward off the multiple mental incursions. Bridget, who had struck her head on a stalactite, was not so fortunate—she suddenly stretched out her arms. "NO! I'm blind—!"

"Don't move, Bridge!" Augum slammed his wrists together. "ANNIHILO!" A thick bolt of lightning struck the towering inferno creature, but it seemed to do no damage at all. The beast started coming for them, each step evaporating puddles with a hiss.

Leera slammed her wrists together. "ANNIHILO!" A jet of water shot at the thing, snuffing one of its arms with a loud hiss. Embers and coals fell to the ground as it roared, a guttural sound that sent licks of flame shooting out of its black soot mouth.

Augum shoved at the air before him. "BAKA!" but the fire beast took only a small step back. "Leera—hit its legs!" he shouted as he made his way to Bridget.

Leera slammed her wrists together. "ANNIHILO!" The fierce water blast instantly snuffed out one of its legs with a hiss. The thing toppled to the ground with a guttural roar, but continued to crawl forward. "ANNIHILO!" but she happened to have stepped into a puddle resulting in a wild miss that nearly took Augum's head off. Wincing from a mind attack, she backtracked to avoid the creature's fiery swipe—right into another puddle. "Gah!" she said, holding her head with one hand.

"I gotcha, Bridge!" Augum said before grabbing her. She had been hunkering in her blind state, arms sweeping like insect antennae.

The fiery beast tried to lunge but slipped, unsteady with one leg missing.

Leera slammed her wrists together once more. "ANNIHILO!" but nothing happened—she had run out of arcane stamina.

"I can see, I can see!" Bridget hollered in Augum's arms. "What can I do?"

"Telekinesis—" Augum said. "All three of us—we drag it over the puddles!"

They extended their palms and began dragging the beast. While the smaller puddles evaporated, the larger ones snuffed out more and more flame.

"It's working!" Augum called through gritted teeth, watching the beast hit a particularly large puddle and wither in a hissing roar, until it was nothing but smoking coals and embers. Amidst the pile were three shining gold coins.

The trio collapsed against each other.

"Bet you the fire Trainer has a water elemental," Leera blurted with a laugh.

"Your nose is bleeding," Augum said.

She wiped it with her sleeve. Her accumulated arcanery was taking its toll.

"Let's go before the door shuts," Bridget said, scooping up the coins before suddenly jerking on Leera's sleeve, stopping her from going first.

"Oh, right." Leera waved them by. "Now that would have sucked." The door shut the moment she stepped through.

Augum could still smell acrid smoke. "Hey, at least we're a little drier."

"All right, it doesn't matter what's in this fourth room, we have to find the passage to the fountain," Bridget said as they walked the narrow rock tunnel.

"Can you two believe these dumb rooms go all the way to the 10th degree?" Leera said. "Why would anyone risk their lives for them?"

"There's probably some kind of reward at the end," Bridget replied, navigating a series of boulders that had come loose from the ceiling. "Besides the gargoyle coins that is. Maybe an artifact that compliments your element, or an ancient tome detailing a rare off-the-book spell."

"Or maybe you get to join an elite warlock club," Augum said, giving Leera a mischievous look.

Leera stopped, eyes magnifying. "Ooo, and you learn a secret handshake that identifies you to other members, or you have a secret mark only they know about, or you get new awesome robes." She resumed walking, an extra bounce in her step. "Well … I guess those *would* be worth it. Hate these stupid necrophyte rags."

They stopped before a granite door with a gargoyle emblem and four etched strikes.

"The fourth room." Leera placed her lit palm over it. "Entarro," and the door swung inwards.

It was a damp and dark room with an arched masonry ceiling, from which hung ancient rusted iron candelabras. Three simple tombs sat in the center, each overgrown with tendrils of ivy and moss.

"Hmm, could be more of the founders," Leera said, pacing over to the stone tombs.

"Let's stay focused," Bridget said, searching the walls, "we need to find the passage to the fountain—" but she was cut off by an alarmed squeak from Leera, who was suddenly backing away from the tombs.

"What is it?" Augum asked, hurrying to her.

Leera nodded at the sarcophagi. "Look."

Augum glanced over and what he saw made the hairs on the back of his neck rise. *His* name was etched into one!

"These are our tombs—" Leera blurted to Bridget.

Bridget gave the tombs a nervous glance. "It's just arcane trickery, never mind them, come help me look for the secret passage—"

But Augum had to take a second look. He got on his knees and brushed aside the ivy, reading the inscription aloud. " 'Augum Stone, of the Arinthian line, died fighting the Lord of the Legion, Lividius Stone, while trying to save Leera Jones'."

"What—?" Leera shot over. "I'm confused … how can it …" She frantically brushed aside the ivy on her tomb. " 'Leera Jones, of the Artemesia line, died of ineptitude while facing the Lord of the Legion, Lividius Stone'." She stared at it, hands covering her mouth, before suddenly beating her fists on the stone. "No, no, no, no …!"

Augum slumped onto his tomb, suddenly nauseous. He knew he'd save Leera at the cost of his own life without even a second thought. The only other option would be to never face his father.

He slowly ran his fingers tightly through his hair. The blood in his ears was a raging torrent. But it was his destiny to face his father. He had even convinced himself that's what he wanted!

He shivered, feeling cold and alone. His throat felt dry and his head swam in confusion. He hadn't even heard Bridget speaking until she angrily waved a hand before his face.

"Aug! Stop it!" Bridget grabbed him and Leera by the wrist. "Both of you, stop it. It's your *fears*, get it?"

Leera jerked from her grip and slowly backed away. One of her hands was bleeding from pounding on the stone, but she did not seem to notice. Her face was contorted in utter agony, and she, too, began running her hands through her hair, slowly shaking her head.

Bridget tilted her head and sighed. "Lee, you're being silly—"

Leera stopped her by raising an open palm. "Don't. Just … don't." She backed into a wall and slumped down against it, drawing her knees in and burying her head, shoulders heaving as she wept quietly. "I don't want him to die …"

Bridget sighed. "Augum's not going to die." She gave Augum a meaningful look to help her with the situation, but he only stared back, mouth slack.

They were going to die facing his father.

Bridget pursed her lips. "Look, you two are both being utterly ridiculous, and to prove it—" She marched over to her tomb and jerked at the ivy, muttering, "Completely absurd … like children sometimes …" She sighed loudly and quickly read the inscription. ' "Bridget Burns, of the Demeteria line, died—' " but suddenly she too froze, face going ashen.

Leera's head slowly rose. "Died from what? Died from *what*, Bridge—!"

Bridget slumped against her tomb. " 'Died from falling off a cliff in the Library of Antioc …' "

PROPHECIES AND PREDICTIONS

For a while, the trio just sat there in the room housing their three tombs, tombs that were inscribed with predictions of their deaths. At last, Leera schlepped over on wobbly legs to stand at the end of her sarcophagus, staring at it.

"I'm not going to let Augum sacrifice himself for me."

Bridget glanced up, face pale. Her hazel eyes were dark and unfocused, as if she was reliving a nightmare.

Leera turned to Augum, lower lip trembling. "Do you hear me? I'm not going to let you do that, and I *know* you would in a heartbeat."

Augum's mouth was too dry to speak.

"We're through, you hear me?" Tears trickled down her cheeks.

Augum had to steady himself on his tomb.

"Through," Leera repeated softly, chin quivering. She was breathing rapidly while staring at Augum. "Well aren't you going to say anything—?"

Augum's head was swimming. He felt bile rising in his throat and a vertigo-like nausea in his stomach that forced him to shakily lie back on top of his own sarcophagus. He wished he was inside it already, gone and done and unable to feel anymore. Feeling hurt too much. So very, very much …

It was Bridget's voice that broke the icy silence. "You don't mean that, Lee. I know you don't."

But Leera said nothing, and neither did Augum.

Bridget glanced between the two of them, wiped her eyes, and marched to the wall.

"What are you doing?" Leera asked in a shaky voice.

Bridget angrily turned over an earthen pot, accidentally smashing it in the process. "What does it *look* like I'm doing?" She searched behind it. Finding nothing, she moved on along the wall.

Augum sat up, body as numb as if he had been swimming in an ice bath. Leera would not look at him. He would not look at her.

Leera took a step toward her. "Bridge, now you're the one being—"

Bridget whirled, pointing a stern finger at Leera, as if to say something. Instead, she returned to violently searching.

Leera's head dropped. For a moment, she just stood there. Augum was painfully aware, with every fiber of his being, of her proximity to him. He missed her so much already it hurt.

After a while, Leera walked over to a portal etching on the wall. "Shyneo," she said in a quivering voice. Her palm flickered to life with a weak watery glow. She placed it against the etching. "Leigh Sparrows." The portal burst to life, blowing wind at her soggy hair and necrophyte robe.

Bridget ceased what she was doing while Augum stepped down from the tomb.

Leera stared into the black abyss of the portal. Somehow, Augum knew if she went through it, he would never see her again. Never. She would hide from him, and she would do it to save him.

Bridget, who at first wavered and looked like she was going to collapse, took a firm step forward and balled her fists. "Leera Jones, don't you *dare* go through that portal. My destiny is *not* to die in some stupid, dark dungeon falling off some ridiculous cliff. My destiny is to die old, maybe a little fat, and surrounded by family. Do you understand? And I'm going to *prove* it to you. I'm going to survive that damn cliff, with or without you!" She glared at Augum. "With or without *both* of you!"

Leera whirled on her, the portal still howling with wind. "You're not going near that cliff!"

Bridget stood as strong as iron. "I. Am. And I am *not* going to die."

Augum glanced between his two very best friends, one of whom meant even more in so many ways. Each had her strengths and weaknesses, her tempers and desires and pains and fears. Each had lost her family, murdered by his father. Yet each, against all rational odds, had come along with him, to help him, on probably the most foolhardy and idiotic, the most dangerous and impossible quest in the history of quests.

And there Bridget proudly stood, even having dyed her hair black so that she wouldn't be recognized; having sacrificed her sleep, possibly her sanity, and now threatening to *once again* put her life on the line to keep this impossible quest alive.

And opposite stood Leera, having sacrificed just as much, her raven hair now dark brown, her cheeks wet with tears. And how she suffered …

Even *if* somehow everything worked out; *if* Bridget didn't die in this hovel of a dungeon; *if* Leera came back to him, it guaranteed nothing, for they might grow very old in a short period of time from an ancient spell, all just to defeat his father.

It was ridiculous, and perhaps in another life, Augum would have laughed, called them both fools, and walked away from the whole absurd mess. But walk away to what? What life was there beyond chasing one's dreams, beyond chasing one's perceived destiny? Dreams which, after some thought, he realized he desired more than anything. If he gave up, how would he ever be able to look back with dignity, with pride? How would he be able to live with himself knowing he turned his back on a slim hope, a hope an entire kingdom seemed to be resting its future upon? How many lives could be saved if he could indeed—*dare to*—defeat his own father, the Lord of the Legion, the Lord of Death, and the Lord of Dreadnoughts—?

Augum clenched his jaw, straightened, and strode toward Bridget. "And I'm coming with you."

Bridget, who had been in a staring showdown with Leera, glanced at him as if seeing him for the first time. She finally nodded, the color returning to her cheeks. "Right. Help me find the secret passage."

The two of them set to searching, both ignoring Leera.

The portal howled for a little while longer before suddenly going silent.

Augum froze, unable to peek. Had Leera just gone through it? Had she deserted them? Would he ever see her again?

But then he heard the most comforting sound in the world—that of a third person rummaging, helping with the search.

THE CLIFF

At long last, they found what they had been looking for—a secret door, hidden behind a ragged old tapestry depicting a bunch of people merrily enjoying an ancient dinner party. Interestingly, behind them sat a spiral fountain.

He almost turned to Leera to say, "Huh, look at that," before realizing they hadn't looked at each other or spoken a word the entire time they had been searching for the secret entrance. What was there to say? She was coming along for now, but that only meant she was doing it to stop Bridget. And he couldn't speak to her either. It felt impossible, not to mention it would be fake and painful. Suddenly his birthday necklace felt awfully heavy around his neck.

Insides roiling, he forced himself to concentrate on the task at hand.

Bridget, whose jaw was firmly clenched, cast Unconceal to find a crude handle, which she used to open the secret door. Augum stepped inside the musty passage first, palm lit, trying not to think or feel. Bridget told him to focus, and that's what he was going to do. He was going to ignore Leera; ignore the cacophonous turmoil in his very being.

Bridget followed, Leera close behind in the rear. They said nothing as they traversed the tight passage that forced them to duck. It smelled of old earth and possessed a faint scent of death, reminding Augum of the crypts in Castle Arinthian. Part of him was curious what was inside them, but no way in all of Sithesia would he have dared open his own sarcophagus. For all he knew, he'd be attacked by an undead version of himself.

The passage meandered down crude rock steps, all the while constricting until they were hunched over. At long last, Augum pushed on a rocky door that opened into a vast cavern. The air smelled of sewage and musty old rock. Tall masonry walls surrounded them with passages scattered about.

They had reached the maze.

Before them stood a magnificent spiral fountain. It was made of marble, its sides elaborately decorated with figural depictions. At the very top was a gargoyle holding a staff with a coiled snake around it, its other hand pointing a single raised finger. It stared proudly ahead, chin high, wings folded smartly behind. Water had long stopped trickling from its mouth, leaving a dark stain. Once upon a time, that water would have traversed the spirals like a miniature waterfall, perhaps making the marble glitter.

Beyond the fountain was a marble staircase flanked by towering walls and two mighty pillars carved with neatly stacked books and scrolls. Augum knew that was the way because the breeze blew toward it. He strode over to the staircase. The workmanship was so intricate it appeared the shelves had once been made of real books and had simply petrified over eons of time.

Or maybe he was over-thinking things just to keep his mind off what had happened in the previous room. He refused to glance behind him at the girls. He refused to look at Leera. Instead, he climbed and climbed. It seemed to go on forever, so much so that he was gasping by the end of it, when the staircase abruptly stopped at a great set of double doors made of black oak and studded with massive strips of iron. There were no handles, only an inscription.

Bridget, huffing, finally caught up to him. She began reading in a solemn voice. " 'Horror, horror of horrors, hailed from a hallowed hamlet known thus as Hyona. Begat she Hal and Heather and Heath and Haleema, but what, hearty human, was *her* name?' "

She glanced between Augum and Leera, who stood apart. "So, uh, any thoughts, you two?"

Neither of them replied, keeping their eyes averted. Last thing Augum was in the mood for was another stupid riddle.

Bridget sighed, thought about it some more, then tilted her head up to the doors, proclaiming in a clear voice, "Her name was Horror."

The doors groaned open. The wind immediately increased to a howl and was sucked down, for directly before the doors was a drop-off into nothing, as if the staircase and doors floated above a gaping abyss. Far, far on the other side was a small perch and another set of doors just like this one.

Bridget began breathing rapidly, backed away, and dropped to her knees. She had turned ashen and was shaking like a leaf. Her dyed black hair whipped her face in the wind.

Leera grabbed her firmly by the forearms. "You're *not* doing this."

Bridget's voice was faint. "I dreamed this. This is my nightmare. This is where I fall again and again—"

Leera shook her. "That's exactly why you're *not* doing this."

For the first time Augum glimpsed a haunting sight—he saw a shivering young girl mocked for being broken. *Broken Bridget*. That was the nickname other kids had teased her with. He glanced over the cliff. It seemed to have no bottom, no sides, and no end. There was no way to get across. "She's right," he said, feeling hollow. "It's over."

There was a moment during which the only sound was the howl of the wind.

"Like hell it is—" Bridget suddenly jerked away from Leera, stood and thrust her hand out. "Un vun deo," she spat. A stone block at the very edge of the cliff lit up with a crimson inscription.

" 'Believe in thyself'," Augum read in a whisper.

Bridget clenched her teeth ... and marched straight for the edge.

Augum grabbed her right arm, Leera her left.

"What are you doing—" Augum said while Leera cried out with, "Are you *mad*?"

Bridget glanced between the two of them. "What, you think I'm going to let our own stupid fears get in the way of our quest, a quest more important than either of you realize?" She was practically shrieking, an unnerving sight to behold. "You think I'm going to let our fears ruin what you two have together!"

Augum and Leera held firm. For a moment they shared a fleeting look before glancing away.

Bridget stared ahead. "I love you two both so much, but you have to let go."

"No way—"

"Forget it—"

"Please. I *have* to do this. I won't live the rest of my life with that nightmare. I won't live knowing I never *tried*, that I let myself down, that I let *us* down. That is not life. That is death—"

"Don't you remember the tower—?" Augum pressed in a panicked voice.

"Evergray Tower," Leera added. "You're terrified of heights, you'll fall—"

Augum squeezed her arm firmer. "There's nothing bridging the gap! It's a one-way trip to the bottom!"

On the other side, Leera shook Bridget's shoulder, tears falling freely now. "Bridge, you're being stubborn and stupid and—"

Augum saw Bridget's jaw flex before she suddenly did something she had never done before—lash out arcanely at them. She made a savage throwing gesture at the ground, shouting "GRAU!" The air tore with the sound of a massive tree splintering, the loudest she had ever cast the spell, so loud that, even though Augum and Leera were used to her training with it, they flinched. Bridget used that flinch to twirl away from them, shoving violently at the air and shouting, "BAKA!" Augum and Leera were *both* sent flying.

Augum got up just in time to see Bridget staring at them, before taking a step backward into the abyss.

IN THYSELF

Bridget's face registered the shock Augum felt rippling through his body, for the step she had taken over a fathomless abyss did not see her plummet. Instead, she seemed to have stepped onto an invisible bridge! She took another step back, chest heaving, face ashen but firm. She didn't look down. Her night-black hair and matching robe whipped around her, wind threatening to throw her into the depths of nothing. Yet she continued to walk backward, step by measured step.

Augum and Leera watched speechless. Somewhere in the middle of the yawning abyss, Bridget turned around with a yelp, steadying herself, arms jutting out for balance.

"Come on, Bridge, you can do it," Augum whispered. He hurried over and felt for the bridge—but his hand fell right through—there was nothing there! Her sheer will, sheer *belief* was holding her up!

Leera quickly joined him. "I don't believe it," she mumbled in a voice full of awe.

Soon both of them were shouting encouragements at her, tears running down their faces.

"Eyes straight and level!"

"That's it, Bridge, you're doing it, you're doing it—!"

Bridget Burns strode confidently over the last few steps, making a final hop to the perch on the other side. She turned, raised her arms, and let out the most joyous, triumphant cry Augum had ever heard a person utter, before dropping to her knees and sobbing.

Augum and Leera instantly hugged, jumping up and down and shouting celebratory cries. Bridget hadn't died from that stupid tomb prophecy after all ... which could only mean—

Suddenly the pair stopped dancing and stared at each other's eyes.

"It didn't come true," Leera said, sniffing.

"No, it didn't."

She grabbed the back of his head and brought his lips to hers.

Augum's heart exploded with joy. They were back together. All was well again. The world had not ended. Their quest continues. But for now, he allowed himself the sweet pleasure of kissing the girl of his dreams.

Bridget must have been feeling particularly generous, for she let them snog for some time before finally shouting, "Oh for the love of—anytime now, you two!" but she was smiling throughout.

Augum and Leera stopped to giggle. He hugged her gently, wiped the tears from her freckled cheeks, and kissed her forehead, before turning toward the abyss.

"Together?" he said.

She nodded and smiled.

They took a moment to harden themselves with belief. Then their hands clasped and they took the first heart-leaping step—and found solid, albeit invisible, ground. And while Bridget shouted encouragements from the other side, they walked hand-in-hand, together, over a black abyss. They did it confidently, without wavering, without falling, and without fear.

Though, truth be told, Augum dared not look down, and he noticed neither did Leera; and his legs trembled and his stomach fluttered, though that might have been from regaining her once again.

By the time the pair stepped onto the perch on the other side, Bridget was clapping and shouting. She enveloped them in a great big jumping hug, until she almost lost balance and took them all over the edge.

When she let go, it was to wipe her face. She was staring into the black abyss, standing close to it.

"I do believe Bridget may have conquered her fear of heights," Leera said to Augum.

"I'm going to sleep like a baby too," Bridget said. "I know it."

"That's great and all, but you're kind of close to the edge. I mean, even *I* wouldn't stand that close."

Augum agreed and gently grabbed Bridget's sleeve, tugging her back toward the doors while keeping a hesitant eye on the chasm. "Enough staring down the abyss. You done beat it good," he added in a country twang.

Bridget placed her hands on each of their shoulders. She glanced between the two of them and gave a firm nod. "I'm proud of us. And, uh, sorry about that back there—"

"It's fine," Augum and Leera blurted simultaneously, laughing.

"We deserved it," Augum said.

"For not believing in you," Leera added. She looked at Augum. "For not believing in each other."

He nodded in agreement, never feeling so happy to have these two wonderful people as friends.

But boy was he glad to be with Leera again!

"Stop grinning like that," she said. "You look like a fool."

"What, I'm grinning cause you're grinning!"

"Pshaw."

They turned toward the massive doors. Bridget placed her lit palm on a gargoyle etching. "Entarro." The door swung inwards, revealing a dark and spacious hall with a dusty marble floor.

Bridget's arms shot out, blocking Augum and Leera from stepping in too far. "Something's over there," she whispered.

"What? I don't—" but Augum was cut off by a loud hiss, followed by a series of all too familiar clacking noises.

"Shyneo," Augum and Leera said at the same time, adding their lights to Bridget's.

Up ahead in the hall stood a looming wraith encircled by six walkers. Every one of the walkers was clacking its jaws. They held rusty swords and wore old beaten chest plates. But it was the wraith that made the trio freeze—a monstrously disfigured giant skeleton stinking of rot and decay. Wet rags hung in strips from gnarled limbs too large for its body. Black goop drooled from its gaping and hissing maw.

The wraith inclined its head and made a single loud clack. The walkers immediately bolted at the trio, who instantaneously slammed their wrists together, shouting, "ANNIHILO!"

Unfortunately, they all aimed at the same walker, blowing it into thousands of bony pieces that slid across the polished floor.

The other five charged on.

Augum shoved the air before him. "BAKA!" sending one flying back toward the wraith that was now advancing.

Leera made a rapid twisting gesture with her palm. "Disablo!" One of the walker's swords spun out of its hands.

Bridget carefully drew the figure of a small creature. "Summano elementus minimus—" and a waist-high earth elemental rumbled to life. She pointed at the walkers. "Elementus, attack!" The creature charged ahead, bowling over one of the walkers with its small but mighty bulk.

Three walkers rabidly charged on, and there was only enough time to make one more attack before they would be upon them.

Augum slammed his wrists together. "ANNIHILO!" obliterating one in a lightning crackle.

Leera shoved at the air before her. "BAKA!" Another walker was sent flying back to the wraith, which finally began making its way toward them.

Bridget summoned her leaf and twig shield and ducked as the walker that had been disarmed slammed into her. It twirled right over her shield, through the gaping door, and into the abyss, clacking the entire way. Augum barely had time to note that it did not hit the invisible bridge, but rather fell through it.

There was a crunch as Bridget's elemental smashed its powerful little fist through a walker's skull. The walker feebly fought on, but its rabid attacks were no match for the elemental's supernatural strength. Meanwhile, the walker Augum first shoved back was almost upon them again. This time, Leera made a low yanking gesture and its leg flipped out from under it. It slammed into the ground and slid. The trio just managed to jump out of the way as it careened through the door and fell into the abyss.

The last intact walker sprang to its feet after being shoved, but instead of charging again, merely skulked near the wraith like a chick around its mother hen. Meanwhile, the wraith had slowed to a hissing prowl, maintaining a low attack profile, its oversized limbs sweeping back and forth.

Augum, who had jumped left of the door, was forced to back away along the wall, while the girls, who had jumped right, backed away on the other side.

"We've got to send it into the abyss!" Augum shouted, taking measured steps, arms poised. He estimated he could only use his First Offensive once more, twice if he needed to stretch it, but the latter would mean he'd drain the rest of his arcane stamina. Problem was he didn't know if the spell would even be effective against such a monstrosity.

He began distancing himself from the wall, luring the walker while the wraith stalked the girls. He kept circling around, until the walker was lined up with the giant open doors, then he shoved at the air as hard as he could. "BAKA!" The walker flew through the doors. There was a sickening crack as its skull smacked the door frame, silencing its clacking whilst twirling its body into the abyss.

The wraith looked back and hissed its discontent. Behind it, Bridget's elemental disappeared, leaving a walker with a mangled skull to feebly crawl toward Augum.

Augum concentrated and began drawing a shape, envisioning his own lightning elemental while following the proper mental procedures. "Summano elementus minimus." A lightning elemental crackled to life. It was not as powerful as a first-of-the-day casting, but would certainly finish off the last walker. As the elemental ran at the slithering skeleton, the wraith charged at the girls who simultaneously summoned their shields, barely blocking a wide swipe that sent them reeling across the polished floor in a cloud of dust.

Augum considered casting Centarro, but worried his arcane stamina would limit the spell strength. Instead, he picked up a bone and chucked it, making sure to guide the bone with Telekinesis, until it clonked off the wraith's head. The monster hissed, turning its attention on him.

Augum waved his arms. "That's it, you stupid bag of bones, this way—!" Now for the tricky part. He needed to position himself in a spot where he and the girls could shove it into the chasm. An idea came to him—he ran for the open doors, shouting, "Get ready to shove it—!" but the wraith, which began charging at him, stopped short, somehow able to sense his plan, perhaps because it had seen its children flung into the gaping maw.

"We have to blow its head off!" Leera shouted. "It has to be at the same time!"

That meant Augum had to get to the girls. He'd have to try something crazy, something he only saw Leera do under the influence of Centarro. He sprinted at the beast, and it sprinted for him, roaring with a wide swipe of its giant clawed hand. Augum summoned his hard lightning shield while dropping to his knees. The blow glanced off as he slid through its legs.

"Baka!" the girls shouted at the same time, knocking the wraith off balance long enough for Augum to scramble to them.

"On the count of three we hit its head," he said, panting. "Ready?" They nodded. But the wraith began to charge and Augum had to hurry the count. "One two three—!" He and the girls slammed their wrists together. "ANNIHILO!" A fat vine combined with a bolt of lightning and a sharp jet of water smashed into the monster's head, obliterating it into mush. It slammed into the ground, bowling them over in the process.

"Ewwww," Leera moaned, untangling herself from the goopy wreckage.

Bridget rolled clear but remained on the ground, prostrate and gasping. "Close one. Good teamwork."

"And a good fight," Augum said, slowly freeing himself of the corpse. He went over and closed the doors to the abyss, plunging the hall into silence. Then the girls joined him in exploring the vast hall, one end of which seemed to go on and on. The walls were the same as before the abyss—exquisitely carved marble shelves, complete with carved-in books and scrolls. The marble here was blacker and shinier, but still caked with dust and mildew. The occasional tapestry hung in framed squares.

They soon discovered polished marble steps as wide as the hall, steps that climbed for many stories. They climbed them just to see what they led to. At the end loomed two familiar massive black doors.

"These are the ones in the library hall," Bridget said. "Where we met that weird old man by the gargoyle statue."

"We got through then," Augum said with a proud nod.

"I'm surprised the guards on the other side didn't hear the fight," Leera added. "Then again, since it's the middle of the night, there's probably a wraith there instead, or walkers."

Augum placed a hand on the massive doors. They were bound with ornate strips of iron and studded with giant bolts. "They're way too thick anyway. Probably arcanely sealed too."

They descended the stairs, returning to the hall where they had battled the wraith and walkers.

"And here are the doors we want." Bridget led them to the wall opposite the doors to the abyss, embedded with sets of towering doors, doors so tall they went all the way to the distant ceiling, making them appear stretched. They were carved with minutely detailed scrollwork and had no handles. Before each set of doors stood a muscled statue of a gargoyle with its palm outstretched, wings folded neatly behind. They numbered on into the darkness identically, as if mirrored. Above each gargoyle was an inscription.

" 'Pay thy toll of five and gain entry forever thus'," Augum read. "Guess we give it the gargoyle gold to get in."

"Well spotted, Captain Obvious," Leera said with a wry grin. She craned her neck at the oaken doors and stretched out her palm. Her light barely made it to the ceiling. "But what's inside this room?"

Bridget was about to place her shining palm on the statue when a crimson inscription and a coiled symbol appeared on its chest, one that seemed sensitive to her palm light being near. " 'Healing arts'," she read. "And that coiled snake symbol means healing venom, which corresponds with the art." She paced over to another gargoyle statue. The inscription and a lightning symbol lit up for her as she drew her palm close. " 'Lightning arts'." Augum and Leera followed as she read out all the main elements. The hall seemed to stretch on forever. Then came the degrees—the 1st all the way to the 10th, a room for each, followed by History, Archives, Philosophy, Cartography, Kingdoms, Luminaries, Folklore, Planes, Monstrosities, Restricted (which made them share curious looks, especially because it appeared that the sign had been recently changed), Tongues (which they guessed meant languages), and at long last—

" 'Artifacts'," Bridget read with a nod. "Finally. This is what we came to Antioc for." She withdrew five golden coins from her pouch and placed them in the gargoyle's palm. It closed its fist, inclined its head, and stepped aside, its great stone bulk making a grinding noise as it moved. Bridget pushed hard on the doors and they slowly opened. "They're heavy," she said.

"Let us help." Augum came near but was suddenly blocked by a muscled arm. The gargoyle was looking at him with blank stone eyes.

"It's just as I feared," Bridget said. "We *each* have to pay five gold for entry. That means—"

"We'll have to be picky," Leera concluded.

Bridget rooted through her pouch. "Now that I paid, we have nineteen coins left, which will get us into three other rooms."

"I need to find information on my father," Augum blurted. As much as he wanted to read up on the Agonex, he needed to know about his father, needed to find a weakness. Besides, Bridget was more than capable of researching the Agonex on her own.

The girls stared at him.

"Right, of course." Bridget handed him five gold. "Then you want to go to the room marked 'Luminaries'." She turned to Leera. "Did you want to come help me or—"

"Restricted—" Leera immediately said. "I want to see what's in there. What, don't look at me like that, you know I find this research stuff about as exciting as taking a nap."

"You *like* napping," Augum said.

"Shush, you!"

Bridget held back the coins. "I don't think going to the Restricted Room on your own is a good idea. There could be an arcane guard in there or something, or a trap."

"I agree," Augum said. "It's too risky. Either we all go in or no one does."

Leera flipped her palms. "There could be a guard inside every room though—"

"That's why I'll check mine first and report back," Bridget said. "But still, restricted means *restricted,* so I don't want you going in there."

Leera crossed her arms. "You two are infinitely fun. Fine, I'll explore my element then." She stuck out an open palm. "Gimme, gimme."

Bridget handed her five coins. "We meet out here in about two hours, all right? That should give us enough time to get out of here. Now wait for me while I check to make sure there aren't any nasty surprises inside." She slipped into the room as they waited, peeking out a short time later.

"Everything all right?" Augum asked.

"All clear. Good luck, you two," and disappeared back inside. The gargoyle soon resumed its post before the door, a silent stone sentinel.

Leera followed Augum to the Luminaries room. He paid the toll, watched the gargoyle step aside, and entered through the heavy doors, soon poking back out to let her know all was well.

"You going to be all right?" he asked.

"I can handle myself. Go on, have fun and good luck," she said, waving and winking as he slipped inside.

LIVIDIUS STONE

The first room beyond the towering doors was a vestibule, with another smaller set of golden doors ahead. Augum shone his blue light around, taking everything in. Marble statues of historical figures marked the corners. The walls were lined with tapestries reaching all the way to the high vaulted ceiling. There were hooks for coats and a clean brass tray for boots. A small empty booth sat near the doors. He imagined past attendants greeting visitors with a smile.

He stepped before the golden doors and pushed on them. They swung inward soundlessly and he immediately caught the heavy scent of ancient musty books. Before him was a vast, long room in which everything seemed to glimmer and glint in his blue light. The walls were lined with the most ornate bookshelves he'd ever laid eyes upon—scrolling works of art in their own right, with motifs of ivy intertwining with gargoyles and cherubs. Gold was everywhere, even worked into the fine masonry between shelves of books. Scattered about were gilded claw-foot study tables.

But it was the center corridor that was of most interest to the eye—oversized statue after statue stood on a long and ornate runner carpet, each posing with books before it, except the books *hovered* in mid-air. Some statues only had a few books, whereas others had dozens.

One thing stood out—the absolute silence. It was as if he was inside a tomb, frozen in time. Nothing moved here. Nothing made noise. It was so quiet he swore he could hear his own thoughts crashing about in his head.

He stepped before the first statue, depicting the founder of the library, Theodorus Winkfield. Everything on him was gilded, with accents of silver and bronze. His robe was gold and had a glittering gargoyle over the breast. The fringe was tarnished silver. Even his bald head had a sparkle to it. His hands were splayed in a gesture of welcome, with no less than twenty books floating between them, each on a different subject: *Formative Years*; *Elementary Teachings*; *Accomplishments*; *Institutional Biography*; and so on.

Augum moved on, admiring the workmanship of intricately inlaid wooden pedestals, twisting ornate obelisks, and fine silk carpets. He passed many statues of historical figures, including Attyla the Mighty, Occulus, Atrius Arinthian, and even his great-grandmother, Anna Atticus Stone. She was portrayed, as in the Hall of Ancestry, in her prime. Although the statue was undefiled, not a single book floated before her, which was terribly disappointing for Augum. Perhaps they were hidden somewhere in the library …

He strode on to the end, where a somewhat newly-erected statue stood looming over all the others. This one wore great golden full plate with the Legion burning sword engraved into the chest. His fists were at his hips, one arm crooked over a plumed helm, iron gaze fixed ahead. Seven clear orbs hovered around his head—they were absolutely still, eerie replicas of the real things. Inscribed into the base in golden lettering was the name *Sparkstone*. Underneath was written *Lividius Stone, of the Arinthian line,* followed by a series of titles that included *King of Solia, Lord of Death, Lord of Dreadnoughts, Lord of Scions,* and *Lord of the Legion.* A set of ornate golden-covered books floated in front of the man.

Standing there before his father, Augum felt small and insignificant, especially unworthy of the task of defeating him. But the Legion blocked access to this part of the library, so why bother putting a statue of him here? He noted how the man presumed he'd acquire all seven scions. Typical and arrogant.

He picked out the first book, titled *Formative Years,* and carried the heavy tome to a nearby table. He sat down at a fancy chair with crimson padding and cracked the book open. Each phrase was written in a neatly scrolling hand that was so even it gave the impression it was done arcanely.

After some initial browsing, it seemed to Augum that every detail of his father's life had been catalogued, as if there had been a scribe there the entirety of the man's life. Nearly every day described what he had eaten, where he had gone, what he had done, what he had said, even how he slept. The writing was cold and without judgment, stating only the facts, such as one passage he found when his father was a young boy of eight.

Young Lividius slept soundly. Ate stew for breakfast. Played with a squirrel in his room. Strangled the squirrel. Carried it to Anna Stone.

He asked her thus, "Why is it not moving?"

"It is dead," replied she after inspecting it. "You strangled it."

"Can I have another one? I want to strangle another one!"

Augum had to take a breath. This was difficult reading, yet only the beginning. Remarkably, it appeared to be an honest retelling, which he hadn't expected.

He skipped ahead, looking for something—anything—to give him a clue as to how to defeat his father, but all he found thus far was how brutal a child the man had been. The pattern started with lies. The boy lied a lot.

"Did you clean your room?" Anna Stone thus asked.

"Yes."

Young Lividius watched as she checked and returned.

"You lied, Lividius. How many times have we discussed that lying is wrong?"

Lividius merely shrugged so. "Can I go play now?"

Later, he would boast, taunt, and needle.

"You're a stupid old hag!"

"You do not call people names, Lividius, especially your elders," replied Anna Stone whilst peeling an egg.

"Why are you so stupid? Why don't you die!"

The boy quickly moved on to theft, then the torture of insects, then animals. Augum skimmed over callous act after callous act, even finding the part about him poisoning two of his bullies at ten years of age, which Mrs. Stone told him about back in her cave.

Lividius stole into the boy's home through a window. He tiptoed into the mother and father's room. He watched them from the doorway. He moved on through the corridor, feeling at home in the darkness, until stepping into the room of the boy who dared to bully him.

What the passage described Lividius doing next curdled Augum's blood. It was so cold he skimmed through it quickly, whispering aloud only the last line, disbelieving the nature of the man. " 'He calmly strode out in search of the girl's home next.' "

His father's actions reminded him of the monsters under his cot he had feared as a boy, except his own father was one of those monsters, a monster that now ruled two kingdoms. It was difficult reading, but he forced himself to go on.

As the boy aged, there were mentions of Lividius pestering Mrs. Stone about the scion.

"Give it to me, it's mine!" thus spoke eleven-year-old Lividius.

"I should not have told you about it. You need to forget it exists."

"It's mine, you stupid crone, and one day I'm going to take it from you!"

Poor Mrs. Stone appeared unable to control the child, as if she didn't know what to do with him. Neither did she discipline him in a way Augum would have liked to see, or, for that matter, seek help for him.

How he wanted to read it all! Especially the part about when Lividius took the bird test, but there just wasn't time. And so he skimmed on, stumbling across a bit about how Lividius came across a crowd of people gathered around a man. This was later that year, in the streets of Blackhaven. The man told the crowd he could bring back the dead, for a gold coin price. A curious onlooker eventually promised to pay this steep price, if the man could bring back his father first. The whole crowd followed the man to a cemetery, where he miraculously raised the onlooker's father—except the raised creature then proceeded to attack his own son. The horrified crowd declared the raiser a necromancer and summoned the watch. Meanwhile, Lividius watched from behind a tombstone as the dead creature mercilessly beat his son to death. He watched with a smile on his face, taking peculiar delight in what he saw. Internal emotional description entered the text here, as if it was a significant moment.

Lividius was flush with excitement. For the first time in his life, he wanted to be someone, someone who held that much power over life and death, a man who everyone feared and paid attention to—a man who could raise the dead. Lividius wondered if he could prevent his own demise. He wondered if he could raise his own father and mother, so that he may kill them for leaving him alone.

"Huh," Augum said to himself after reading this passage. He sat back to think. So the necromantic desires started early. Lividius later *did* raise someone from the family only to kill him—an ancestor, Atrius Arinthian. But that had served a purpose, and that was so he could gain control of the Dreadnoughts.

Augum flipped ahead, discovering Lividius had sought out that man from the cemetery, later becoming his secret apprentice. The man's name turned out to be—

"Narsus the Necromancer," he whispered, remembering how Mrs. Stone would later defeat the infamous man in a legendary duel under the Academy of Arcane Arts.

He skipped ahead again, this time to the areas that discussed his mother. Lividius met her in his seventh year at the academy. The pair would marry in his eighth and final year. Except the entire relationship seemed based on lies and control, as exampled in the following passage near the beginning of their marriage.

At the toll of the eleventh bell, Lividius, contented from the murder of the old woman, returned home to Terra Titan.

"Where have you been, dear?" Terra thus asked.

"Helping a neighbor with chores. I told you not to ask me questions like that. I am the man of this household, I do as I please." He kissed Terra on the forehead. "Supper ready?"

"Yes, but I burnt the pork—" Terra suddenly thus cried out as Lividius slapped her.

"Why must you be so damn clumsy? Do you think I arcane money into existence?"

Terra fell to her knees crying, holding her cheek. "Why, Livie? Why do you treat me this way?"

Lividius watched her. He hated how she had a hold of him. This was one of those times he wished her dead.

"Livie ..."

He sighed and paced over. "I'm sorry. It won't happen again. I'll change."

"Promise?"

"Promise, Tee."

Tee had to be her nickname. Augum noticed the only time Lividius used it was when he was trying to apologize while promising to change. Yet Augum, skimming the pages, saw that Lividius never did change. In fact, the pattern seemed to repeat itself—the man would abuse her time and again, and each time she would seem weaker, more cowed by his ways, and he would apologize less and less, just as she used her arcanery less and less.

"Did you just move it telekinetically?"

"Livie, I was just trying to—"

"What, is my arcanery not good enough for the household? I told you, you don't need to perform it anymore! I'll do it enough for the both of us. You know better. And stop looking at me like that unless you want a smack."

She did, however, once seek advice from her only friend regarding her troubled life with her husband. Except the woman mysteriously disappeared not long after. Augum could have probably found what happened to her, but he did not have the time. Lividius was questioned in the disappearance by the town watch, but by then he had become superbly adept at hiding his true self from people, becoming popular and very persuasive.

"I'll bring you that fire drink I promised, Captain Scott," Lividius thus spoke to the head watchman.

"Good, and let us have another merry game of chance. I enjoy taking your gold."

But Lividius was calculating—he purposefully lost at gambling with the night watch, playing the fool, secretly keeping a close ear on what was going on in town, particularly the details of any ongoing investigations. He also learned who controlled what, how strong they were, and what secret lives they held.

Lividius kept doing dark things, brazen things, especially at night. He once even got a beggar to burn himself alive for a sum of gold, promising immediate healer attention. Instead of calling the healer, however, he watched the man expire in front of him—he did this right outside a watchtower, knowing they were gambling inside.

And it kept going and going, dark deed after dark deed, everything in secret.

"Can't read this," Augum muttered, angrily shoving the book away. There were acts in there no one should have endured. Unspeakable, unthinkable things he wouldn't repeat to anyone, not even Leera, for they were too dark.

Augum rubbed his head in frustration. No, he needed to read on. In particular, he needed to read about his mother. He had this deep sense that somehow she was the key. There was something he had seen in his father's eyes the first time he met him in Sparrow's Perch, when Mrs. Stone mentioned Terra—real pain, authentic sorrow. Something was there and it needed exploring.

Then he recalled Mrs. Stone telling him about nineteen years during which Lividius had disappeared with Terra, at the end of which Augum had been born.

He yanked the book back over and flipped ahead to that time, reading about how his father had travelled all over Sithesia with his wife, searching for famous necromantic landmarks of old while trying to learn the dark craft. And as Augum skimmed along the pages with a finger, he saw signs of frustration and anger, which Lividius took out on Terra. One particular day deep in a southern jungle, Lividius and Terra were sleeping in the ruins of an ancient sacrificial pyramid.

Terra pointed at Lividius. "I'm sick of this place! I'm sick of your stupid rituals! I'm sick of you! I want to go home! I don't want to travel anymore!"

Lividius stormed at her and she cried out, backing into a wall. But he froze before reaching her, suddenly realizing the ritual in the other room needed immediate attention. Sierran stinkroot needed to be mixed with the bones before they boiled, otherwise the spell would fail.

He spoke through clamped teeth. "If you move, I'll kill you." He thus spun on his heel and returned to the room. But no matter how hard he tried, he could not muster the concentration, and the angrier he became the more he lost focus, until the boiling pot made a fizzling sound, and Lividius screamed in anger.

Augum did not want to read what happened next, though realized it was some kind of dark life-extension ritual. He skipped ahead, coming across another instance of Lividius losing his focus due to anger. It was during a duel in the Canterran countryside, when a giddy warlock had telekinetically thrown dung at Lividius' head. Even though he missed, and it was supposed to be a somewhat friendly duel to show skill, Lividius became so angry at the affront he charged the man and tackled him, instead of simply using his arcanery.

Lividius also grew in power, for he studied diligently, even allowing himself to be mentored by masters, which he of course killed and robbed after he was done with them. Terra knew nothing. She was there in the background, a shadow of her former self, quiet, broken, distant. This seemed to be perfectly acceptable to Lividius, for he could then concentrate on what he needed to do.

Augum soon ran across a particularly insightful passage.

The spell failed and Lividius scurried to a corner, shaking. He had seen his own death. He did not want to die. It was the only thing he truly feared. He enjoyed seeing others perish instead, for then he had beaten them; become victorious. Killing was, in a way, a form of extending life to him, for by taking it, he consumed it.

Augum reread that last part aloud. " 'Killing was, in a way, a form of extending life to him, for by taking it, he consumed it.' " A telling passage. He returned to the book, finding more.

Lividius at last successfully cast the spell. He raised his fists in triumph as the three bodies dug their way out of the graves, limbs merging and enlarging with every passing moment. Soon the head became misshapen as the limbs outgrew the skeletal body. Flesh tore in strips as the thing hissed. It kept growing bigger and bigger, until it towered over Lividius.

"You are … beautiful," he thus said. "And mine. You are a part of me forever. My first wraith. I shall call you— "

But then the wraith struck him with its talons, ripping open his chest. He was flung against a tomb. He inspected his gored chest and began shaking. The wraith quickly closed in on him.

"Adai!" he thus shouted at it, but it kept coming. "ADAI!" he shouted again, this time with an arcanely amplified voice. The wraith stopped, tilted its head at him, watching. Lividius began sobbing and shaking as he inspected his wound. "I can't die … not now, not like this …" He glanced up at the wraith and his face contorted in fury. "You dare betray me?"

Lividius violently brought his wrists together. "ANNIHILO DIO!" A four-pronged bolt of lightning crumpled the monster.

Augum skipped ahead—Lividius had destroyed that wraith, but he made others, stronger ones, and became better at controlling them. And he searched for deadlier spells and more astute mentors.

But that's not all he searched for—he also sought the scions.

"But you didn't have one with you when you came back," Augum said to his father, glancing up at the statue standing nearby, bathed in the blue light of his palm. "So you started the quest for the other scions during that time

… but why? Why get greedy?" Then he thought about it. "You wanted to use them to defeat Nana, didn't you? You wanted to take the scion from her, and the only way to do that was to get much stronger, isn't that right?"

The statue of the Lord of the Legion stared menacingly ahead, unmoving, stone silent.

Or he could have done it to extend his life. He was, after all, afraid of death. But then, he had been gone for quite some time studying necromancy, hadn't he?

"You did all that for so long," Augum went on in a wondrous whisper. "Nineteen years. What does that tell me about you?" He drummed the book with his fingers, imagining Nana sitting across from him, waiting for him to put it all together. "It tells me you had far-reaching plans for some time. It tells me you are persistent. It tells me you're spiteful. It tells me …" He groaned. "It tells me I enjoy talking to myself—" He expelled a long breath while running fingers through his hair, muttering, "This is driving me crazy."

Augum eventually returned to the text, finding another revealing passage.

Lividius pointed a finger in Terra's face. "You need to be with child."

"Why do you keep insisting? Our lives are … so dark. A child should not be born into such an existence."

"You need to be with child. I do not expect you to understand."

For a time, Terra searched her husband's face. "Gods, I think I do understand. I think I finally do. You want the scion—"

Lividius thus lashed out. "Come here—"

Augum had to stop reading that part. He swallowed, but his throat was suddenly so dry it hurt. The passage had confirmed his worst fears. He had been born so that Lividius could use him to gain the scion through inheritance. That was the sole purpose of his coming into existence.

For a while, Augum could only sit, numb, hands shaking. It took courage to regain some semblance of self-control and return to the cursed book.

He skimmed quickly, trying to avoid more grisly details, until he came across another interesting portion—sometime after his birth, Lividius had cast an Object Track spell on one of Terra's most prized possessions, a locket given to her by her mother. He had done this without her knowledge, when she was asleep.

Augum jerked his head up at the statue of his father. "That's how you tracked her down, didn't you, you fiend?" Even whispering, the sound carried greatly. The room was dead silent, so silent it was unnerving. "You found her using Object Track, interrogated her trying to find out where she hid me, and then killed her out of a jealous rage when she said she was finally leaving you." When Mother finally had had enough. *Mother* … he was not used to that word.

Augum riffled pages forward again until he came across something unexpected—a letter. He carefully opened the yellowed and crinkled parchment. Some of the writing was blurred, as if splattered with water.

Even after everything that you did to me, I still love you, Liv, I do. I love you for the little things of the past. Memories that keep me company in the darkness. Picking me up and twirling me after we were married. Calling me "My sweet Tee". Kissing my forehead after you had come home. Holding my hand briefly after I gave birth to our precious boy.

But your ever-growing ambition and callousness scares me. Did you have anything to do with Harisha's disappearance? She was my best friend. She was my only friend. Or that kind old woman neighbor who offered to help me relearn arcanery? What happened to her? How is it that I am even asking these … horrible things of my husband?

I know you have secrets, Liv, I do. I wish you'd let me in, share some of them with me. Yet I fear what they are. I fear them as much as I fear you.

I do not want to live forever. I want to grow old. I want to die a natural death. That which you demand of me is the work of darkness, and what terrifies me is that you know it. I never asked anything of you, but this I must ask you—do not make me take this path with you.

When my time comes, I wish to be mourned in the old way. I wish for a memorial ceremony attended by loved ones, with my body in the arcane sapphire flames that have enveloped my ancestors.

I do not want eternity. I want us to live a quiet life raising our son. I want peace.

Your loving wife,

Terra

Augum reread the letter twice more before slowly putting it down, realizing it wasn't water that had splashed the parchment. He brushed the words with his fingertips, feeling connected to the mother he had never known. Here she was in these words, perhaps in anguish and sorrow, but here she was nonetheless.

So his father had asked her to try something necromantic, something involving living longer. Perhaps an experiment of some sort. And she did not want to join him …

After staring at the letter for a while, he gently folded it and placed it back in the book, for that is where it belonged. A piece in a puzzle.

It took some willpower to read on, for he next sought out that which haunted him most—the night his father murdered his mother.

He needed to know.

Yet upon coming to the right section, he found the page torn from the book. He placed his hands over it. "Un vun deo," but nothing happened. Not a shred remained, at least nearby.

He dropped his hands in frustration and threw a furious look at the statue. "You were ashamed of what you had done to her, weren't you? It's the one thing that's ever bothered you about yourself, that you murdered the only person you cared about, the only person that cared about you." Talking aloud seemed to help his thought process. "That's why you left the letter in there. This is your way of making amends—by keeping an official record of it all. Except you don't actually intend on people reading it, do you?"

One day, this story would come out. It had to, for the kingdom's sake. He contemplated secreting the book away but realized there were likely countless arcane wards against that. It would probably set off an alarm, and that's the last thing they needed right now. He even feared his father knowing the book was open in that moment.

"But why did you have this written?" Augum asked his father's statue. "Why, if everything in the Herald is twisted lies, why did you write such an honest account?"

"Because your father believes everything he has done is a part of his glory," said a hoarse voice nearby. "Yes he does indeed."

Augum was so startled he fell off his chair. He had not heard a soul enter.

Nearby stood a familiar gray-robed old man with pointy ears.

"You!" Augum said, picking himself up, along with the chair. "So *you're* the historian."

The man the trio had met at the gargoyle statue gave a slight bow. "Rafael Herzog, lad, at your service, that I am." The man blinked constantly behind his oily spectacles, hand perpetually shaking as it clung to his cane.

Augum smoothed his necrophyte robe. "I did not hear you enter."

Herzog's unruly-haired head bobbed. "I still have the knack then, that I do."

"So you know who I am."

"Aye, lad. But you be a darn fool for comin' into the wolf den, yes you be, a darn fool."

"I need information on my father, sir. Please, if you know something …"

Herzog shuffled over to the statue, glanced up at it. "I sat with this man for many days as his scribe, using the ancient crafts to complete the memories, that I did. I sat with him, listening to the errors of his ways, without judgment, minding my tongue, oh yes, minding my tongue."

"Why?"

"The task needed completion in a thorough manner, indeed it did. And I ask you, lad, would it serve the kingdoms if the story had been told falsely? For I, *and only I*, was able to persuade this—" Herzog thrust his cane in the direction of the statue, "—monster that his story was important enough to tell truthfully. I told the fool what he wanted to hear, and so he dictated and I transcribed. A dangerous game I played, indeed I did, but he is not as smart as he thinks himself to be, no he is not."

Augum spun the tome on the desk to face the man. "Where is this page then?" There was no time to mess about.

"He tore it out, did he? I suppose that should not surprise me, no it should not." Herzog hobbled over and slumped into a nearby chair, wheezing a great sigh. He massaged his veined nose. "She don't work right. Can hardly smell them books like I used to."

Augum wouldn't let the man get distracted. He stabbed the tome with a finger. "But you remember what this page said, don't you?"

"'course I remember, you think me daft like some peasant scribe?"

"Then tell me—!" Augum caught himself. "Sorry, sir, this has been a difficult—"

"As it should be, lad! All you younglings think is everything be coming easy to you, but the world is complex, oh yes it is. Stories have facets, facets and angles and all kinds of intricacies, that they do."

Augum sat down. "Look, Mr. Herzog—"

"Call me Rafael."

"Uh, Rafael—I know my father regrets murdering my mother. And I know he tried to involve her in some sort of necromantic experiment before she ran away with me. I know that he—"

"Loved her, that he did." The man stared at Augum with bloodshot eyes as he let that thought settle. "He loved her, in his own way, yes he did. Possessive kind of love and all that, poison kind, but something was there, that we can be sure of, yes."

"I … I need to know what happened after he—"

"Murdered her?"

Augum swallowed. "Yes."

"But you already know, yes you do."

"No, I don't, I—" Augum froze. He did know. He had subconsciously known it all along. He had *feared* it. He glanced at the torn page from the book, then at the statue of his father. He allowed the silence to amplify the blood rushing through his head until it was unbearable. He pried the words from his tongue.

"He tried to raise her. He tried to raise my mother."

Herzog leaned forward in his chair. "Based on what you know about him, lad, do you think he succeeded?"

Augum stared with a blank look. "I … I …"

"Why did he want to become a necromancer in the first place?"

Augum recalled the story. "Power, attention, control over life and death—" There's one other thing he'd been quietly ruminating. "And fear of death." It was almost like

Augum was talking to himself now. "But his rings aren't black, so he isn't a full-fledged necromancer yet, is he? And he wasn't then."

"What are his defining traits?"

Augum did not need long to think it over. "He's manipulative, brutal, cold, selfish, and arrogant."

"And his primary battle weakness?"

"Arrogance."

"NO!" The outburst was sudden, startling Augum. "It is not. You must think clearly, lad, yes you must."

Augum slowly ran a thumb across his forehead before looking up. "He loses concentration when he's angry."

Herzog watched him with rapidly blinking eyes. "And so …"

"And so …" Augum continued, choosing his words carefully, "as he was training himself in necromancy, he was experimenting, and that's when he asked my mother to get involved. But because he was frustrated that his experiments were failing—"

"Vagueness! Vagueness does no one any good, no it does not. Leaders think clearly, decisively. Now I ask you again. Based on what you know, do you think he succeeded?"

Augum swallowed. "No. He failed raising her."

"Which means?"

"It means he's holding her body in the Black Castle, training himself until the right time when he's powerful enough to raise her."

"Deduction is a powerful mechanism of the mind." Herzog stood with a groan. He glanced over at the statue of the Lord of the Legion. "All winners of wars took the fight to the enemy, yes they did. As they say, 'Ye don't win a battle sitting in ye castle', lad, no you certainly do not."

Augum slowly closed the book.

"Tell it to return," Herzog said without looking over.

"Sorry?"

Herzog nodded at the book.

"Oh." Augum envisioned it returning and said, "Return." The book lifted off the desk and returned to its hovering position. Neat.

He stood, marveling at this strange and ancient place so full of history and arcanery. "I wish I could spend a tenday here." He wished he could find those missing books about Mrs. Stone; or read about his ancestor, Atrius Arinthian; or learn about the Dreadnoughts; but it was getting very late and he needed to get some sleep before his duel.

He faced the curious old historian before him. "Thank you, sir, you've helped me put a few things together in my head." The pieces to the puzzle were taking shape. A plan was slowly forming.

Herzog continued to stare at the statue of the Lord of the Legion. "Thank yourself, lad, for you have come here at great risk, searching for answers, yes you have. And that is the spirit of this ancient place. Omnio incipus equa liberatus corsisi mei."

"All begin equal but only the curious thrive," Augum whispered. "Sir, will you join the Resistance?"

Herzog's turned to give Augum a smile. "A good general will strike at the right moment, when his opponent is weakest, yes he will indeed. Timing is everything. 'When thy fallen can't be slain, when lion children rise again, when fires burn from east to west, blood of kin can vanquish death'."

"Does that mean you *will* join us?"

The man smiled mysteriously. "I do believe your friends are waiting for you, yes they are."

They made their way through the silent room. Herzog spoke quietly as they passed the many historical statues.

"When your ancestor Atrius Arinthian defeated Occulus, besides being allowed to keep the scion as a gift, the Leyans also gave him one other, yes they did. Can you guess what that gift was?"

"Are you talking about Burden's Edge?"

"Ah, I am afraid I am not, lad. Burden's Edge was a thank you gift from the Dreadnoughts for allowing them to sleep instead of serving as slaves. No, this gift was in his blood, given by the Leyans, and he would pass it on to *some* of his children. It is a gift that would sometimes skip entire generations before re-appearing in his distant progeny, a gift known to appear only in a rare few." His bushy brow rose at Augum. "I wonder if you have it."

"What is the gift, sir?"

The historian's face registered disappointment. "Ah, I dare say you would know if you had it, yes you would indeed. A shame, yes, for it would have helped."

"Oh." Well, there was nothing special about him at all, so whatever that gift was, he certainly didn't have it. He spotted Mrs. Stone's statue. "Sir, where are the books that belong with my great-grandmother's statue?"

"That, my dear lad, I do not know. I suspect your father confiscated them, or worse … had them destroyed."

They passed through the vestibule and on into the library hall, where they were greeted by a grinning Bridget and a bedraggled Leera, whose hair was disheveled and robe ruffled.

"Oh—" Bridget said when she saw Herzog exit the room behind Augum.

"This is Rafael Herzog," Augum said. "The library historian. Mr. Herzog, this is—"

"Bridget Burns and Leera Jones," Herzog interjected. "Though you lasses don't look much like the poster, no you do not." He waved vaguely at Bridget with his cane. "Err, I expected more of a … squirrel-like appearance—"

"Yes, well, someone we don't get along with had that drawn," Bridget said quickly, brushing dyed black hair out of her eyes.

"In any case," Herzog continued, teetering on his feet, "no one would expect to see the most wanted younglings in all of Solia in Antioc, no they would not. I'll give you points for courage, that I will."

"Mr. Herzog was kind enough to help me think a few things through," Augum continued. "I learned quite a bit about my father. Gave me some ideas." He nudged Leera, who was holding her stomach and wincing. "Looking a little worse for wear. You all right?"

"Peachy," she blurted, suppressing a hiccup. "Juuust peachy."

Bridget tried to keep a straight face. "She kept trying to get past the Restricted Room guards and somehow ingested stinkroot—"

"We won't be discussing what I may or may not have ingested, thank you very much." She elbowed Augum. "And you can avert them judging eyes."

"I didn't say anything!"

"Spent the whole time out here sick," Bridget added in a snickering whisper.

Leera only moaned.

Bridget cleared her throat politely. "Mr. Herzog, sir, we'd like to safely return to our quarters, but the Legion guards are an unnatural presence, not to mention they blocked most of the secret entrances. Surely the founders never intended for warlocks to face outside obstacles ..." She twiddled her fingers innocently as she glanced at the nearby remains of the wraith.

Herzog rubbed his shaggy beard. "I have a better idea."

The trio beamed as Herzog led them to the distant end of the hall, opposite the great black doors, where there were a series of portal etchings, along with a gargoyle rune.

"Shyneo." Herzog's palm lit up with an icy glow that gently radiated fog. He placed it over the gargoyle rune, which lit crimson. He gave Augum a side look. "Initiates, I presume, lad?"

"Yes, sir."

"And you are here under false names, is that not so?"

"Augustus Westwood. Bridget and Leera are under Leigh and Brie Sparrows."

"Let us do your real names as well, that way, if you survive your grand quest, you may one day return to explore and learn as yourselves. Consider it a reward you can look forward to, as well as a gift to the Resistance." He winked at them.

The trio exchanged mystified but excited looks.

Herzog frowned at the rune and raised his chin. "Arch Historian Rafael Herzog. Promote Augustus Westwood, Brie Sparrows, Leigh Sparrows, Augum Stone, Bridget Burns, and Leera Jones to cloaked administrative access. Full privileges." Herzog let go and dusted his hands. "There we are."

"But sir, don't we have to place our palms on the rune or something?" Augum asked, referring to the time Klines had signed them in as initiates.

"Not for promotions, lad. The library already remembers you. Make sense?"

"I think so. But what does 'cloaked' access mean?"

"You're still initiates, just with full access. It's an ancient secret that administrators may bestow upon those found to be worthy. You need only say your name and destination as per usual. Not even the Legion know about cloaked access, and I dare say they would not take too kindly if they found out, but then we shan't tell them, will we now?" He frowned. "Come to think of it, my wife would not be too pleased, so you best not tell her either."

"Wait, sir ... is your wife Senior Arcaneologist Ning?" Bridget asked.

Herzog groaned. "Woman is the bane of my existence, that she is. Won't even admit to the Herzog name. Bah, off you run, and do watch out for them guards."

ANTIOC, DAY FOUR

The trio slept in late the next day, once again waking past noon. Malaika and Charissa were already gone, leaving a note to meet them in the Supper Hall around the first afternoon bell. As the girls got ready while sitting in bed, Augum told them about his father, including the kind of child he was, how he had tried to raise Augum's mother, and his weakness—that he lost concentration when he became really angry.

"We could definitely use that to our advantage," Bridget said, a comb gripped between her teeth while she fixed Leera's hair, which was unusually tangled. Bridget had been quite energetic since she got up, smiling and talking more in the last hour than Augum remembered her doing so in a tenday, all courtesy of having slept well for a change.

Leera, still a bit pale from the night before, winced from a hard jerk of her hair. "We'd need something big to make him angry. Like, really big."

Augum finished washing his hands in the washbasin and sat down on the bed across them, placing his chin on his fingertips. "I have … an idea. But don't immediately jump down my throat about it, all right?"

"Oh no," Leera muttered. "Ouch, Bridge—!"

"Sorry! Hold still, would you? It's like an owl's nest back here."

"Anyway," Augum went on, choosing his words carefully. "I think I know how to make my father angry enough to lose focus, enough to help even the odds a little bit in a major battle. But we'd have to tell him at the right moment."

"You going to say it or tip-toe around it all day?" Leera said.

Augum hesitated. "We rescue my mother's body from the Black Castle."

The comb fell from Bridget's mouth as the girls gaped at him.

"I know, I know, it's crazy—"

"Crazy?" Leera raised a finger to make some other point, but instead scoffed. "Ugh, crazy. Yeah, it's crazy all right. I'm not interested in suicide."

"No, but, wait—I can finally give my mother a proper funeral. It's what she wanted. There's a locket and stuff too, um, and we don't have to do anything stupid, we just have to be smart about it. All we need is a way to covertly get in the Black Castle."

Bridget picked up the comb and accented what she said with it. "Augum Stone you have completely. Lost. Your. Mind. The Black Castle is probably even more arcanely protected than Castle Arinthian. It's the lion's den—"

"Look, I've been thinking it through. Trust me, after what I read, I know it would utterly—" Augum made a loopy gesture at his head here, "—unhinge him."

Leera made the same gesture, but in a mocking way. "Oh, unhinge him? Unhinge *him*. Not you? You're not unhinged at all? Are the stairs not reaching the top floor here? Did the wraith chuck your brain into the abyss when you weren't looking? Nuttier than a squirrel turd, you are."

"Just ... just imagine us with an Agonex Dreadnought-equipped army at our back, using Cron or whatever at the same time—"

"NO, AUGUM!" the girls chorused.

"I mean, I know it's a gamble, and it sounds completely and utterly mad, I get that, but it's what we need to do—take the fight to the enemy and all that, like a smart general would."

Their eyes narrowed simultaneously.

He raised his palms. "All right, all right," muttering, "just think about it then," before quickly moving on. "Anyway, uh, what did you learn about the Agonex?"

The girls switched places as Bridget told them what she learned, which turned out to be a lot. There were challenges ahead, most notably tuning to the artifact, which apparently took quite some time. Then, once tuned, the controller had to somehow mentally defeat the undead commander in charge of the Agonex army. Bend him to his will or whatever. Augum imagined this commander standing amongst his troops in the deep darkness of Bahbell, one of the many faceless undead.

"The artifact is Teleport-infused," Bridget explained as Leera fixed her hair, face cross with concentration. "Which means it can teleport an entire company all at once. I forget how many soldiers a company is, but—"

"Two hundred," Augum said, chin resting on his hands as he sat cross-legged on the bed.

"Right. And we think there are tens of thousands of them. Now, how many companies can be teleported in a day is apparently dependent on the skill of the possessor of the artifact, or at least that's what the history book says.

Speaking of which, the history of the Agonex is simply fascinating—"

Leera gave Augum a *Kill me* look. Bridget had been rambling for a while now.

"—for example, did you know the Agonex was forged with all the souls of those soldiers? And did you know they *volunteered* for it? Yeah, Occulus told them they'd be immortal. Sound familiar? The poor things were duped. Killed in sacrifice and risen as the undead. Anyway it's important to know because you can't add more soldiers to the army—" Bridget made a snatching gesture, "—but you can take them away, like when they fall in the battlefield. Once a soldier is destroyed, he can't be risen again. The army is destined to be whittled down to nothing in combat. So if—and that's a big *if* as the artifact has layers of complexity—we somehow get control of the Agonex, we'll have to use it very carefully and time our strikes, not only because it doesn't replenish, but because we probably won't be able to teleport more than a company at a time. And I suspect the army is so large still because it wasn't used to full effect—scion-endowed warlocks took the fight to Occulus before he could conquer all of Sithesia. Interesting, isn't it?"

"Huh." The whole thing seemed rather convoluted to Augum.

"Oh and guess what happens to your brain if you enter into a mental battle with the commander and lose?"

"Your brain melts?" Leera said in a deadpan voice, comb between her teeth.

"Actually, yes. No, seriously, it actually melts. That's what the text says."

Leera made a face. "My brain is melting right now. Can we hurry this along and get some food? I'm starving."

"This is important stuff, Lee—"

"Of course it is, but—" Leera stepped before Bridget. "You know, *priorities*!" She pointed at her stomach with the comb. "Do you hear that pathetic tiny crying? Hear that? That's my poor tummy squealing and pleading for mercy. It's saying, 'I surrender, gods, I surrender, aaaaah!'—"

Bridget snorted a laugh and smacked Leera's wildly gesticulating arm with the back of her hand. "Oh, hush already. We'll go after we work on Augum." She shook her head, muttering, "Water warlock. Pfft. Should have been an actor. Ridiculous …"

After the girls finished applying their makeup tricks on Augum, the trio raised their hoods and joined Malaika and Charissa in the bustling Supper Hall for their daily midday meeting.

"Like a necrophyte beehive in here," Leera muttered, grabbing a tray full of food after Augum. Semi-finals were happening today and every necrophyte who was from out of town seemed to be congregating in there for lunch.

Augum kept his head low, painfully conscious of many eyes on him. Whispers about The Hood abounded.

"You're in the Herald again," Malaika proudly said to him after the trio joined them at a table in a corner. "Want to hear what they're saying about you?"

"Definitely not. Any news?"

Malaika's face fell.

"Robin's dueling soon," Charissa said.

Augum dug into his gravy and potatoes, famished. "Right, we need to watch that fight."

"We also need to discuss our exit strategy," Bridget said in a whisper, mindful of nearby necrophytes, who would glance over now and then.

Malaika was curling her hair around her finger. "I told you, we have horses any time we need them at the edge of town."

"I don't feel comfortable with that," Bridget said. "We need to talk to Senior Arcaneologist Lien Ning about a safer way out, that's what Constable Clouds said—"

"You worry too much." Malaika exchanged a *She's such a goodie-goodie* look with Charissa.

Bridget's voice dropped even lower. "And we also have to plan for tomorrow, Aug. You know about what."

He nodded. He was quickly losing his appetite even thinking about it. Tomorrow was the day. The crazy day. His plan, should it work, would bring the entire city down on them. Bridget was right, they needed an alternate escape plan, a safer one, and they needed to formulate one sooner than later. Above all, he hoped his gamble that Erika would possess the divining rod paid off. Of course, that all hinged on him beating his next two opponents …

"He's got a duel today," Leera said, scarfing down a second apple tart. "Let him concentrate, will you?"

Bridget raised a corner of the Antioc Herald. "Can I see this?"

Charissa shrugged. "I don't care."

Bridget dragged it over and began studying it with furrowed brows.

"Oh did we tell you we went shopping yesterday!" Malaika said, her and Charissa giggling. "I bought this fabulous pink dress that will be ready today—"

Charissa placed a hand on Malaika's arm as she joined in. "And I bought a new blue one. The fashion for the nobles here is just *divine*—"

"You two got any useful information for us about The Hood's opponent?" Leera asked, waving her spoon around. "Or maybe about the Legion, you know, the kind of stuff you're supposedly here for?"

Malaika flashed her a hateful look. "Just because you have the fashion sensibilities of a blunt tool doesn't mean—"

"Leera, *no*—" Bridget caught Leera's arm before she did something stupid, then promptly placed a hand over her own mouth, realizing she had used her real name.

The trio glanced about but luckily none of the other tables had noticed in all the loud bustle.

"Anyway," Malaika went on in a supercilious tone, "to answer your oafish question, actually, yes, we do have some information. His opponent is named Caireen Lavo. She's sixteen and from Tiberra. We get a sense she's here for revenge. An honor kind of thing."

"You told us all this yesterday!" Leera said.

"Yeah, well, she's also really pretty, in a wild kind of way."

Leera spoke through gritted teeth. "We don't care how pretty she is, we need to know how she fights—"

"That's because she's prettier than you—"

"Please stop playing games," Bridget said in a weary voice, still holding onto Leera's arm, which now had four watery rings circling it.

Malaika smirked. "Oh, going to attack me?"

"You keep talking nonsense and I'll shove your bosom buddy through that pie hole of yours!"

Charissa cringed. "How beastly …"

"Can we please hear how she fights?" Augum asked impatiently.

Malaika smiled at him. "Certainly. You'll be interested to know she's a lightning warlock, and her style is … well, she's into using Shove—"

"You mean *Push,*" Leera said.

"Whatever. Anyway, she's also really good with those—" She gestured at her temple, "—mind thingy spells."

Right, the only other lightning warlock in his tournament bracket! Augum had forgotten about that. This will be interesting …

Charissa made a show of glancing around as if readying to impart a scandalous secret. "And as far as the Legion, we've got an *exact* count of how many guards there are, where they go—and, get this—what entrances and exits there are from the arena."

"That's … that's actually useful," Bridget said. "Can you see if you can find out how tomorrow's trophy ceremony is going to go? We need as much information as possible—"

"Especially anything about Erika," Augum chimed in.

Malaika and Charissa nodded gravely.

"We'll be excellent spies, promise," Malaika whispered. "You'll see."

"We're *very* good at it," Charissa added, holding onto Malaika's elbow.

"Oh, before we forget," Malaika said, "there was a woman who came looking for you in the morning."

Augum gestured at his eyes. "Did she have really pointed spectacles and look like a toad?"

"And a really annoying voice? Yeah, that's her."

"What did she want?" Leera asked.

Malaika shrugged. "Just asked where you three were."

"That's it?"

"That's it."

The trio exchanged looks. Great, Watts was after them. What was it this time?

Bridget suddenly spied something in the back of the Antioc Herald. "Listen to this. 'Rumors abound of strange goings on in Bahbell. One particularly stubborn rumor—which the Antioc Herald unequivocally decries as false—is that the Lord of the Legion has been frustrated in certain endeavors in Bahbell. Legion authorities are refusing to comment on the subject, however, perhaps further inflaming gossip. Meanwhile, the search for the stolen Agonex and scion continues. The good citizens of Solia are asked to keep a wary eye out for the villainous Anna Atticus Stone and her young brainwashed cohorts, including Augum Stone, the Lord of the Legion's own son. "The Great Quest lives on," Commander Jordan has been quoted as saying, "and there shall be eternal glory and life bestowed upon any soul capturing Anna Stone or her insurgent gang." Commander Jordan has declined to comment further, citing his eagerness to watch today's tournament semi-finals. Word has it he will be recruiting some of this year's crop of winners …' "

Bridget stopped reading there. "We need to find out what's going on in Bahbell. Someone's got to know something around here."

"Hear ye, hear ye!" shouted a crier's voice in the hall. "The first afternoon bell tolls!"

"We should go soon if we want to catch Robin's fight," Malaika said.

They finished lunch and cleaned up after themselves. Just as Augum turned away from the table, he bumped into a hulking boy. He looked up to see a wide neck and a gap-toothed smirk.

"Ain't going to weasel your way out of this again," Brutus said.

Nearby tables began to gape and people stopped eating.

Brutus' voice got louder. "This here's The Hood, everyone. He caught me off-guard at the arena. Ain't going to happen again though."

A hush fell over the hall.

Whispers of "Fight!" began circling.

"We don't have time for this," Augum said. He tried to get by but Brutus stepped in his way.

Augum sighed. "Fine, you really want to do this here?"

"You bet—" Brutus shot a hammy arm out, quickly saying, "Dreadus Terrablus!" but his Fear spell was the weakest Augum had faced—he barely had to give it any energy to block, and so was doubly fast on the reply.

"BAKA!" Augum said as he shoved violently at the boy. Brutus was once again sent flying, slamming into a wall.

Leera took a step forward. "Did … did you just knock him out a second time?"

Laughter began in the hall as people realized what had happened.

"Hood just knocked him out again!" a giddy necrophyte girl squealed nearby.

Augum saw a gray-robed official hurrying in their direction.

"Let's get out of here," Leera said, yanking on Augum's sleeve. They scurried out of the hall amidst all the energetic chatter and clapping.

ROBIN'S SEMI-FINAL

"I'll be glad to be out of here tomorrow," Augum said as they quickly strode through the busy streets of Antioc. The sun shone from behind a bank of clouds, occasionally peeking through with its warm brilliance.

"Too many close calls," Bridget said.

They soon arrived at the arena, which had a line trying to get in.

"Oh, forget this, we're not waiting," Leera said, and began shoving through the crowd. "Contender here, move aside! Contender coming through, got a match to fight—"

Surprisingly, people allowed them to pass, though Augum suspected it was more the necrophyte robes than anything else. The common folk had an obvious fear of necrophytes. It showed in the anxious looks they gave and how they quickly glanced away when noticed. More than once the trio had heard someone anonymously whisper, "Demon worshipers" in the bustling crowd, or

"Brainwashed hellspawn." It was good to hear there were secret pockets of resistance.

Bridget rooted through her snakeskin pouch. "Slowly running out of money."

"Need to borrow some?" Malaika asked, stopping and making a show of reaching into her pouch.

"Actually, yes, thank you."

"You … you do?"

"Just a few silver should get us by, yes."

"What, Father's money wasn't enough?"

Bridget gave her a surprised look.

"Fine, here." Malaika thrust a handful of coin into Bridget's hand. "There, happy?"

Bridget sighed. "Thank you."

"We'll find our own way in," Charissa said with a smug smile, taking Malaika's elbow and guiding her away.

"Snobs," Leera muttered, watching them go. "Did you really have to do that? We could have earned it."

"Don't have the time."

"I suppose you're right."

They paid the entrance fee and Augum signed in at the registration booth. They told him to report to the dressing room after the next fight. The trio then began the arduous search for empty seats. In the arena, a troupe of actors mimed out King Brimal Pradeep's final moments, much to the amusement of those in attendance.

Augum recognized a hawk-like face in the crowd—an ebony-skinned man with gray hair and a shiny black robe fringed with crimson. "Look, it's the commander we saw in the Training Room, the one quoted in the Herald today." He was with that shaved Legion guardsman, the fanatical-looking one.

"Let's follow him, see where he sits," Bridget said.

They cautiously made their way after the pair, shoving through the throng, getting lucky and settling just behind them in the stands. Augum leaned forward to listen, pretending to be watching the actors.

"... received it today," the Legionnaire with the shaved head was saying. "We *Ordinaries* finally have something to be proud of. Have you seen it?"

"I'm sure it's a fine blade, Lieutenant," Commander Jordan replied in bored tones.

"A fine blade? It can slice through the edge of parchment." The lieutenant appeared to wait for a better reaction, but the commander was busy watching the troupe. He demonstrated with his hands. "That means that when you hold the parchment this way, the blade could slice—"

"—thank you, Lieutenant, I think I understand how sharp a Dreadnought blade is."

The lieutenant scratched his nose. Augum had the impression he was trying to find a new way to tell the commander how sharp his blade was. "When will we be receiving the armor?" the lieutenant asked instead, proud shoulders drooping.

"Dreadnought armor takes time to forge," Commander Jordan replied distractedly, chortling at the stunted actor playing the Tiberran king, who had taken a dramatic tumble. "Relax and enjoy the show, Lieutenant, there will be time enough for battle."

"Yes sir, it's just ... it's hard to relax when there's so much going on." He seemed to make an attempt at watching the show, but after a pause, leaned over to the commander again. "What do you think is going on with that army?"

"What do you mean, Lieutenant?"

"Well I keep hearing it's been behaving real odd. Not taking his Lordship's commands and all that. Do you think those criminals have figured out how to use it?"

"Just part of gaining control, that's all, Lieutenant. Let's not give it anymore—"

"—but it's killed a bunch of our men. That doesn't sound like—"

"—*enough,* Lieutenant." The commander had turned his hawk-like gaze on the man, before steadily returning his attention to the performance. The stunted King Pradeep was squirming in his death throes.

The Lieutenant flexed his sharp jaw. "So is he coming?"

"Tomorrow." The commander suddenly stood, clapping along with the rest of the crowd.

"And wasn't that a fantastic performance?" Giovanni boomed with his arcanely amplified voice, striding into the arena, arms spread wide. He was wearing a shimmering multi-colored robe and his hair was slicked back. "Give it up for the Blackhaven acting troupe, *The Tumbling Rapscallions*!"

As the crowd clapped politely and the troupe bowed, Bridget whispered into Augum's ear, "I think I know what's going on with *that* army. I'll explain it to you later."

"And now, let us get to what you've been waiting for … the first of two semi-final matches in the 4th degree!"

The crowd clapped louder as gray-robed attendants pushed forward six wheeled stands brimming with practice weapons.

"A reminder there are several ways to claim victory—have the most points when the hourglass runs out—" He pointed at an attendant manning a giant swiveling hourglass. "Or be the first to five points—" He pointed at the wooden scoreboard above the judges. Augum saw Erika's overly-painted brows rise in smug satisfaction. "And of course, an automatic victory is scored with a knockout or when the opponent is forced to—" He cupped his ears with his hands and the crowd shouted, "BEND THE KNEE!" An attendant began banging a giant drum and the crowd took up the chant, "LO-SERS SHALL! BEND THE KNEE! WI-NNERS FIND! ETER-NI-TY!"

Giovanni was nodding his head theatrically with the beat until the chant devolved into cheering and whistles. Then he raised his arms indicating the moment had arrived.

"Allow me to introduce our valiant combatants! First, hailing from the cold northern kingdom of Ohm … this seventeen-year-old trained in the scenic Semadon Academy at the top of the world … representing the air element … she runs up and down the Cloud Scrapers for fun and could blow your shack down with a single puff … introducing … Fung 'The Hurricane' Zheng—!"

There was a mix of cheers and boos as a light-skinned girl with almond eyes trotted out. She wore a turquoise robe embroidered with birds and snow-covered mountains. Her long black hair was tied in a ponytail with a colorful ribbon. She bowed to the judges, the crowd, and lastly to a small segment within the crowd that Augum guessed, judging by the traditional look of their colorful robes, were her relatives and friends from Ohm, at least one of whom was a monk. Then she resumed bouncing and stretching.

"What are the Cloud Scrapers?" Augum asked Leera, who sat to his right. She only shrugged as she clapped for the girl.

"That's the name of the tallest mountain range in Ohm," Bridget said from his left while clapping.

Giovanni raised his arms indicating he was about to say something important. The crowd, including the lieutenant and the commander, got to their feet and began cheering loudly.

"The next opponent hardly needs an introduction … he trained in the Academy of Arcane Arts and mentored under Lord Sparkstone himself … representing the fire element as well as the future heart and soul of the Legion—"

"I love you, Robin Scarson!" screamed a girl not too far behind them.

"Marry me—!" screamed another.

Leera made a face like she was going to vomit.

"That's right, girls," Giovanni said with a chortle, "not only is he a dream, but he can raise grandma from the grave as a wraith … soon to join our brave troops in the field … stand up and give a bow to … Robin 'The Tormentor' Scarsoooooooooon—!"

The drum pounded and the mob roared as Robin swaggered out, nodding his head in a *Yeah, you know who it is* style. His necrophyte robe swayed as he played up the crowd with beckoning hand gestures. Girls hollered as boys gave throaty academy chants. Robin stopped to theatrically point at his opponent before giving two thumbs down. The crowd cheered even louder.

"Hope you lose, you pathetic evil little—" Leera shouted but Augum immediately clamped her mouth just as the commander and lieutenant in front of them turned to look at her with deadly serious expressions.

"She meant the girl," Augum blurted. Much to his relief, the two Legion soldiers returned to cheering for Robin.

Giovanni brought the two opponents together to quietly go over the rules, a hand on each of their shoulders. Fung Zheng was bouncing, trying to stay loose, while Robin glared at her with a menacing expression. Giovanni had each of them confirm they understood with a nod before giving them space.

"In the ancient Arcaner traditions … opponents … bow and show your stripes!"

Robin snarled and four fiery rings burst around his arm, while Fung bowed politely, calling forth four barely visible rings of air.

Giovanni pointed at Fung Zheng. "Are you ready?" When she nodded, he pointed the other way. "And are you ready?" Robin's mouth curled as he gave a slight nod. Giovanni chopped the air. "Fight!" and backed off as the hourglass flipped over.

Robin, instead of attacking right away, took a few steps back, grinning. Meanwhile, Fung slammed her wrists together, shouting with an amplified voice, "ANNIHILO!" A super-concentrated sharp tunnel of wind thwacked into a shield made of hot coals, which Robin had summoned with plenty of time to spare. The crowd cheered.

"The Tormentor easily blocks The Hurricane's first attack!" Giovanni shouted.

"Flustrato!" Fung shouted, pointing at Robin's head, but Robin merely shrugged off the spell, much to the disappointment of the trio and amusement of the crowd.

Giovanni nimbly danced around the combatants. "She'll have to do better than that, won't she now?"

Fung shoved at the air before her. "BAKA!" but Robin again summoned his shield, leaning into the strike to avoid even having to take a step back. He grinned. "That all you got?"

"He's toying with her," Augum said.

Fung curled her fists before drawing a shape. "Summano elementus minimus." A waist-high air elemental whirled into existence and charged at Robin.

"Summano arma," Robin said, flexing his right arm. A flaming short sword appeared in his hand and the crowd roared. Augum instantly understood the significance—the symbol of the Legion was a burning sword.

"That's a 5th degree elemental spell!" Bridget said. "He should have taken the 5th degree test! Ugh, that's just unfair—" But Augum could barely hear her over the crowd, not to mention his own thoughts—how had Robin advanced so quickly?

Robin swung his burning blade and instantly cut the air elemental in half. It fizzled and squirmed on the ground before disappearing in a puff of smoke. Again the crowd roared its approval.

"The Tormentor is flexing his confidence now!" Giovanni sang.

Robin took a moment to soak in his glory before turning on his opponent. "You get one more free one. Make it good."

Fung was breathing heavily. She narrowed her eyes and raised her palm. "Voidus vis!" The area Robin stood in instantly went black. An opaque cloud had appeared, consuming everything. The crowd murmured worryingly.

"Shouldn't that be a point?" Leera asked.

Giovanni placed his hands on his knees as he studied the situation with a serious expression. "The Hurricane is taking a different approach. Let's see if it pays off."

Fung took a step forward, again slamming her wrists together, voice booming over the arena. "ANNIHILO!" A spiky wind attack shot through the cloud but seemed to miss, gouging the arena wall with a dull thwacking sound.

Giovanni glanced up at the scoreboard. "We have yet to see a point here, folks."

"My turn," Robin's voice echoed from within the black cloud.

The crowd cheered with calls of "Attack!" "Get her!" and even "Kill the gutterborn, Robbie!" The last was shouted by Temper, who stood a few rows over from the trio.

"Closs pesti!" A swarm of bees buzzed out of the black cloud.

"Here we go—" Giovanni chirped.

Fung seemed ready, throwing at the ground. "GRAU!" A loud hurricane roar confused the bees, but only for a moment—they regrouped and kept on. Fung stumbled backward, bringing her hands together. "ANNIHILO!" A jet of sharp wind plowed through the swarm and half of the bees disappeared. She shoved at the air. "BAKA!" and the rest of the bees vanished.

Meanwhile, Robin still had not exited the black cloud.

Fung held her head, wincing. Augum recognized the sign—she was suffering from the side effects of too much arcanery too quickly.

"Dreadus terrablus," Robin said from within the darkness, voice cool and calm.

Fung's mouth fell open before she began a slow, horrified scream. The crowd's cheering died as people became unnerved by the blood-curdling sound. Augum felt goose bumps rise on his arms from her amplified voice, a voice filled with a mix of sorrow and horror.

"Point for The Tormentor!" Giovanni shouted. Augum caught a glimpse of Erika watching with a malevolent gleam as the scoreboard flipped to 1-0.

"Itak oos iu azim!"

Those words sent another chill down Augum's spine. He remembered facing the vicious little spell in Bahbell.

"One of The Tormentor's specialties!" Giovanni shouted as a small specter wielding a dagger zoomed out of the cloud straight at Fung. The crowd hollered for her to jump out of the way, but she was still struggling with the Fear spell and the first pass struck true.

"Urgh—" Fung gasped, clutching her cheek. Blood appeared between her fingers.

"Two-nothing!" Giovanni boomed.

Fung, eyes still wide and terrified, began wildly swatting at the air. The second pass also struck, opening a gash in her arm.

"That's three-nothing! And now four!" Giovanni said as the specter finished a third pass that had sliced Fung's back. "This is almost over, folks!"

But the specter disappeared mid-dive, before it could score a final point. Augum instantly knew what had happened—Robin had called it off so he could make the final blow himself.

"Bend the knee!" people began calling out. "Submit!" Even some of the necrophytes got in on it. "Give up, you fool!" "Kneel, gutterborn!"

"Stop the fight!" Bridget was calling. "It's over, stop the fight—!"

Temper egged Robin on in her screeching voice. "Smack her in the face, Robbie! Finish her good!"

The black cloud finally evaporated, revealing a grinning Robin. He opened his palms to the crowd in an *Aren't you impressed?* gesture. Many of the necrophytes cheered, but the common folk started booing. Robin scowled at them. "Only gutterborns think that way," he said in his amplified voice. He turned toward his opponent, who dropped down to one knee.

"There! It's over!" Bridget was shouting along with Leera. "Stop the fight!"

Giovanni was already striding over to Robin. "Ah, we have a bent knee—"

But Robin bared his teeth and raised his arm, voice deadly soft. "Vikari vikarei." Fung began choking as her throat blackened. She grabbed it with her hands, eyes bulging.

Giovanni called, rushing over to Robin. "That's enough now—" but Robin kept his arm up, face twisted with malevolence.

Fung choked, gave a jerky spasm … and fell to the ground in a heap.

The crowd gasped and fell silent. For a moment, Giovanni just gaped.

"Get the healers!" Augum shouted, the only one in the arena to make a sound.

Giovanni quickly took up the call. "The healers, the healers!" making quick gestures at the sidelines while running to Fung.

But by the time the healers came out, it was already too late. Augum was barely conscious of the score flipping to show five points to zero for Robin, and his aunt smiling proudly.

AUGUM'S SEMI-FINAL

"Aww, didn't even get to cast the good spells," was the last thing Robin Scarson said before being led away by a gray-robed attendant.

The crowd was muttering angrily, a few calling for Robin's expulsion from the tournament, others his arrest. Only some necrophytes were cheering, one of whom was of course Temper, who shouted, "Woo! Way to go, Robbie! Good fight!"

Augum had to watch Leera in case she shot over to pound the snot out of her. Instead, Leera grabbed his arm and gave him a pointed look he interpreted as, *Tomorrow, you beat him. You beat him and make him pay*. It was quite the contrast to Bridget, who looked pale and worried.

"I have to report to the dressing room for my fight," Augum said.

Bridget gaped at him a moment before realizing what he had said. She furrowed her brow and nodded. "Right, uh, remember to keep your hood up. Watch her gestures, anticipate her moves." She lunged forward and hugged him tight, whispering, "Good luck."

Leera hugged him next, squeezing him harder. She gave him a secret peck on the cheek, met his gaze and nodded firmly.

He hurried past the crowd, ignoring the whispers and attempts to get his attention, mind busy running through spells. As he made his way down the tunnel, he passed Robin, who was on his way out, a towel wrapped loosely around his shoulders. The Destiny Stone hung around his neck, clasped in a claw pendant. His nose bulged in the middle and was as crooked as ever, a memento from meeting Augum's fist.

"You!" Robin said.

Augum stopped but kept his back to him.

"You're next. Try not to piss yourself."

Augum felt his nails dig into his palms. It took every measure of self-control to keep his mouth shut and keep walking.

"That's right, you better slink away," Robin said with a cackle.

Tomorrow, Augum was thinking. Tomorrow we fight, and I won't go easy on you, no I will not.

In the dressing room, the pall of a combatant's death hung as heavy as a funeral curtain. Secretary Sharma chewed on the end of her quill with a distant expression. A few older combatants Augum didn't recognize stood in thoughtful reflection. It was silent, the air musty and stifling. Above, a troupe sang overly cheery songs which the crowd did not respond to, muttering restlessly instead.

Secretary Sharma finally noticed him. "Oh," she said, and checked off his name.

It seemed his opponent had not arrived yet. He took a seat and mentally went over his spells as well as possible moves and tactics, until a girl sauntered in. She wore a cerulean garment consisting of a long cloth wrapped around her body and tucked at the waist. It was embroidered with a stormy country scene. The lightning bolts flashed now and then.

"Caireen Lavo," Secretary Sharma said in a lost voice. "Have a seat please. And you're late. Try not to be late."

Caireen gave the woman a pitied expression before taking a seat beside Augum, which surprised him. "Mother made it for me," she said in a quiet voice. "Father enchanted it." She had a wild bush of orange hair with matching wild orange eyes, offset by dark skin.

"Your robe?"

"Yes. Before they …" She swallowed, unable to finish. The sorrow of the occasion had slipped into her voice too.

He gave her a moment before replying quietly. "The Legion?"

She nodded, staring absently at the wall, reliving something in her mind's eye.

He stared at the same spot. "You see flames. The sky black and red. You hear the echoes. You smell the thatch burning."

She slowly nodded. "Is that what you're going to do when you become a necromancer? Raze villages?" She paused, sniffing. "Will you take pleasure in it?"

Augum glanced around to make sure no one was listening, but the other competitors were now too busy mumbling practice incantations, and Secretary Sharma had gone somewhere. He leaned closer to her and whispered, "No, I'm going to fight them." He shouldn't have told her this, yet he knew in the bottom of his heart that she would never reveal that secret, not after witnessing the Legion raze her village. They shared that horror in common.

She slowly glanced at him. He allowed her to see his face within his hood, see that he was genuine about what he had said. Her wild eyes narrowed slightly and her mouth opened as she examined his face closely. Suddenly she jerked her head away.

"You're ... you're *him*," she whispered. "Augum S—"

"Shh," he said gently. "Please. I trust you not to say anything." He had just let his opponent know who he was. Was he out of his mind? He could practically see Bridget and Leera's visceral reaction.

Her voice was barely audible it was so quiet. "Back in Tiberra, we had better drawings of you in our Herald. You were a hero there, standing up against the Legion. All three of you, and of course, Anna Stone. They wrote ... stories, fantastical stories of your adventures. Now it's the opposite. Now the Legion spins lies and cruelties about you."

Augum did not know what to say. Being talked about, fame, infamy—none of that mattered to him. What mattered was the downfall of the Legion. What mattered were his friends.

"I came here for vengeance," Caireen went on. "To make Mother and Father proud of me ... but it's just a dumb tournament. My kingdom burns as we speak. You don't ... you don't know what they're doing. They're raising the dead ... they burn the villages but *raise* the dead—"

He made a quick gesture for her to stop—she was getting too loud. But that was an interesting point. Raiding kingdoms and making troops—of course! Now it all made sense. And the more necromancers, the more troops raised. Walkers, wraiths, they all needed *bodies*. How come he hadn't realized that before? The war effort would self-perpetuate. Every enemy slain is another added to Sparkstone's ranks ...

It was diabolically genius, and just like his father.

"Sorry," Caireen mumbled. "But tell me you're doing something about it. Tell me *someone* is. Tell me there's something beyond this stupid tournament—"

He made the slightest nod. "There is … a secret resistance."

Her face lit up with a glimmer of joy.

"Where are you staying?"

"The library. Room 1478. Send me a note after the fight. Don't worry, no one enters my room. I'm supposed to report to a Legion constabulary after the tournament is over and sign up as a necrophyte." She shuddered at the thought. "I'd rather die." She paused, gave a furtive glance around before smoothing her robe. "You're here for something important, aren't you?"

He gave the slightest nod.

She looked at him searchingly with those wild orange eyes. "You're here to get to the end of the tournament—"

He nodded again.

Caireen's wild eyes turned to steel. "Let us make that happen."

"Get ready, you two," Secretary Sharma said, striding into the room.

"Run the glass," Caireen blurted, getting up.

"What?" Augum was trying to process what she had just said.

Secretary Sharma made a jerky wave. "Over here, you two. You're about to be introduced. Move it—"

Augum and Caireen followed Secretary Sharma down the exit tunnel, lining up at the mouth to the arena. The noise from the crowd here was loud and oppressive.

Augum's blood raced. He was going to face Robin. Caireen was going to throw the match and he was going to face Robin! But what had she meant by *run the glass*?

"And now, a very special and rare battle," Giovanni was saying as attendants once again wheeled out stands filled with practice weapons. "Folks, for the first time this year, we're about to see two lightning warlocks duel." The crowd clapped and cheered. "May I introduce, from the newly-liberated Kingdom of Tiberra … a sixteen-year-old who learned her 1st degree wild before finding a mentor … you've seen her speed, witnessed her arcane intelligence … she can split stones with a flash of her hand … Caireen 'Blitz Bolt' Lavo—!"

Caireen furtively glanced over her shoulder at Secretary Sharma, then at Augum. "Run the glass," she mouthed, before a push sent her jogging out of the tunnel.

"What?" he mouthed with a shake of his head. Then it occurred to him. *The hourglass!* He wanted to smack his forehead. He could be so daft sometimes.

"The next opponent you've already come to know as an inventive, strong warlock … possessing a heart almost too big for his fifteen years … they write about him in the Herald … a necrophyte hailing from the tiny town of Everscale … the elusive … the mysterious … Augustus 'The Hood' Westwoooooood!"

Augum strode out to a chorus of cheers. He caught a glimpse of a clapping Bridget and Leera, and not too far away, a sneering Robin and Temper.

Giovanni pulled the two combatants close to face each other before running through the usual set of rules. Caireen wore an expression of … was it peace? It was hard to say. As Giovanni pulled away, she gave Augum a secret wink. He gave her a grateful smile in return.

"Combatants please observe the ancient battlefield tradition!"

Augum and Caireen's arms flared with four lightning rings each as they bowed deeply to each other, except Caireen's were on her left arm, meaning she was left-handed.

Giovanni pointed at Caireen. "Are you ready?" She nodded. He pointed at Augum. "And are you ready?" As soon as he nodded, Giovanni chopped at the air. "Fight!"

Caireen slammed her wrists together, her voice amplified. "Annihilo!" Augum noticed she had done it a bit slowly, giving him ample time to raise his shield and block the bolt, which packed an arcane punch that made him take a step back from the force of the blow.

He did the same spell and she blocked it too.

"A bit of a slow start," Giovanni was saying in the background, "they're obviously feeling each other out, testing for strengths and weaknesses … now they're circling, trying to decide how to attack. Meanwhile, the hourglass is trickling …"

Augum used Telekinesis to throw wooden practice weapons at her from both sides. She saw them and made a limp effort to dodge, stepping aside from one but taking the other in the back, making a theatrical "Ow!" gesture.

"One point for The Hood!" The crowd clapped, but was already starting to shout for them to go at it harder.

Caireen gave Augum a meaningful look he interpreted as *Attack me already!* But how was he to attack her in a way that didn't hurt? Arcanery was combat-oriented, offensive and painful and—

Exasperated, she shoved at the air. "Baka!" but he again raised his shield. She gave him that same look.

All right already, might as well give the crowd a show. Augum traced the air with a finger and Caireen promptly did the same. "Summano elementus minimus!" Two lightning elementals sizzled into existence before the combatants, Augum's slightly larger.

"Elementus, attack!" Caireen and Augum chorused, and the two elementals charged at each other. The crowd loved this and began cheering.

Meanwhile, Augum made a gesture aimed at Caireen's ears. "Voidus Aurus!" He wasn't sure the Deafness spell worked until she suddenly blurted, "WHAT?"

The crowd laughed at the unusual outburst.

"Looks like a successful Deafness casting," Giovanni said. "Kind of useless if you ask me, but it counts as a point. That's two-nothing. What an odd fight. Not much imagination here."

Yeah well pretending to win fairly was harder than it looked, Augum wanted to say. He grit his teeth and slammed his wrists together again. "Annihilo!" but, seeing Caireen was distracted by the elementals, purposefully missed. Even knowing there were healers present didn't help, it seemed. He just couldn't knowingly hurt her.

"A poor attempt at best," Giovanni narrated as the crowd began to hiss and boo. "And that hourglass trickles on … are we going to see a fight here?"

Caireen threw at the ground. "GRAU!" and the crack of thunder boomed over the arena, wowing the audience.

"Another impressive but useless gesture," Giovanni said, frowning. "And the judges agree, refusing to award a point."

Caireen pointed at a spear and flung her arm at Augum. The spear hurtled toward him, barely missing his head as the crowd gasped.

"That's a little better!" Giovanni said.

She and Augum threw various weapons at each other, all either missing or lamely plonking off their summoned shields. Augum felt a prickle of embarrassment. Their fake attacks must be so obvious that the fight was going to be stopped soon. He had to change tact. Maybe arcanery wasn't the way to go …

He summoned a wooden practice mace to his hand and charged. Luckily, Caireen took up the challenge, grabbing a short sword.

"Look at that, we have some hand-to-hand combat here, folks! How unusual!" But after a while of watching, Giovanni added, "Maybe I'm being silly, but they seem to mostly be aiming at each other's shields—" The crowd went from semi-enthusiastic cheering to booing and hissing again.

Augum let a sword strike hit his shoulder, just to liven things up a little. They had listlessly been draining the hourglass.

"A point for Blitz Bolt, but the Hood is still in the lead at two-one—"

Caireen followed up with another strike that Augum accidentally forgot to block. It hit him on the other shoulder.

"Two-two, we have a tie, folks!"

Caireen gave Augum a frustrated look before shoving at the air, shouting, "BAKA!" Augum did not expect it and was sent flying back.

"It's three-two for the Tiberran! And the hourglass is almost done—" The crowd was on its feet now, booing and urging Augum to do something, anything.

Oh no, Augum realized, still lying on the ground—he only had moments to score two points. Caireen must have realized the same thing because she stood there awkwardly, giving him an important look. He knew what she wanted but he was terribly afraid of hurting her.

But he had no choice now, and he only hoped the healers would help her in time. He saw the hourglass finish just as he slammed his wrists together. "ANNIHILO!" concentrating on purposefully weakening the strike. Unfortunately, weakening his First Offensive was something he hadn't practiced much. The powerful bolt struck her in the stomach and she was blown back with a horrifying scream.

"Get the healers!" Augum immediately shouted, before she even hit the ground.

"A knock-out, the fight's over—" Giovanni was saying as black-robed warlocks rushed into the arena. "But did the hourglass run out before the blow was struck—what do our illustrious judges say on the matter … will it be the Tiberran or the Legion necrophyte?"

Giovanni glanced to the judge's booth, where the bald Martus the Black argued vociferously with a smug Erika and a sneering Vulica. "It appears we have quite the deliberation going on—"

At last, Martus the Black threw his hands up in the air in exasperation before punching his voting lever.

"And there we have it, folks, by a vote of two-to-one, with Vulica Vaneek and Erika Scarson voting for and our guest judge from Canterra voting against, our winner … Augustus 'The Hood' Westwoooood—!"

Giovanni strode over to raise Augum's arm in victory, but Augum ran to Caireen instead, asking the two healers, "Is she all right?" forgetting his voice was amplified still.

"He's an honorable fellow, isn't he, folks?" Giovanni said as he followed Augum. The crowd agreed with polite clapping. "And there we have the signal from the healers that Miss Lavo will survive." Giovanni had a firm hand on Augum's shoulder as the healers carried her off. "Come, my boy, and let us discuss this odd—but in the end, somewhat satisfying—victory. Now, it certainly wasn't the best or most interesting fight. It seemed you two were testing each other throughout most of it. What was the strategy there?"

"Uh, yeah." Augum cringed. He wanted nothing more than to get out of there. He had nothing to say.

"Almost seemed like the match was a fix, wouldn't you say?" Giovanni chortled along with the crowd. "I jest, I jest, you can relax, my boy. But seriously, we need to see a better performance. You can't compete like that in tomorrow's finals now, can you, son?"

"No."

"Because as Mr. Scarson aptly demonstrated for us, he can be a deadly foe."

Augum only nodded.

"Well there we have it, folks, a man of few words. Our winner, advancing on to tomorrow's historic finals … Augustus 'The Hood' Westwoooooood!"

SUSPICIONS

Augum had a lot of explaining to do to Bridget and Leera on the way back, both of whom were mystified by the performance, as was the crowd, for they had lots of colorful things to say on his way out—

"Loser—!"

"It was a fix!"

"You suck, Hood!"

"What happened out there, you piss yourself?"

"My grandma could've fought better, and she don't even know arcanery!"

"Ouch," Leera said after the last one.

"Tell us what happened," Bridget said after they finally broke free of the arena and made their way through the bustling cobbled streets of Antioc.

Augum explained everything, even including how the Legion was raising troops in Tiberra.

"Why didn't you come up with a better plan at least?" Leera asked, fending off an exuberant beggar promising to allow them to raise him as the undead in exchange for meat. "You know, one with a bit more … theatricality?"

He shrugged. "Didn't have time. It all sort of … happened so fast."

"That's true, you weren't supposed to fight so quickly," Leera said. "They rushed the singers from the arena after the crowd started throwing food. You know you're doing badly when you get a face full of tomato during a famine."

But as expected, Bridget and Leera mostly gave him a hard time about letting a stranger know his true identity.

"You two need to trust me a bit more," he said. "Besides, I think Caireen could help us. And you *know* we need all the help we can get."

"She's a *stranger*," Leera said for the umpteenth time.

He stopped replying after that, instead grabbing her hand and squeezing. She shook her head at him but at least said nothing more on the subject.

"You two have got to stop doing that, you're cousins here."

Leera shrugged, smirking. "So what? Isn't that typical of the rural villages?"

"Leigh Sparrows—"

"Hey, points for proper full name usage there."

"Ugh. Incorrigible."

Augum had to interject, using the codeword for the Agonex. "What were you saying about the biscuit before my match, Brie?"

"Oh, right—" Bridget glanced around to make sure no one was within earshot. "You two aren't going to believe this, but I think I know what's been going on in Bahbell. It's *Leland*! Leland's figuring out how to use the biscuit—"

Leera stopped, placed both hands on Bridget's shoulders. "I know you've been under a lot of stress, but there's no reason to make stuff up. If you need attention, we're here for you."

Bridget slapped her hands away. "Stop it. You need to take things more seriously. Look," she went on as they continued walking, "I've been thinking it over and it all makes sense. It's actually the *only* thing that makes sense when you factor in the requirements and complexities of the—" She froze. "Stop. Giving. Him. That. Look."

"What look?"

"That look suggesting I'm sleep deprived and going crazy again. You give it to him way too often and I'm sick of it. Worse, you know I'm *not* sleep deprived!"

Leera held her palms up. "All right, I'm sorry." She paused. "I'm *sorry,* all right? I'll stop being such a dork."

Bridget took an exasperated breath but continued walking. "I did the research and I'm telling you, Leland's figuring the biscuit out."

"All right, he's figuring the biscuit out."

Bridget stopped. "Argh! You're doing it again!"

"Doing what—!"

This time, Augum got between them. "Stop it, both of you. Look, I get it, we've been doing crazy stuff together for so long we're getting on each other's nerves for dumb things." He'd been wanting to say that for a while, jus hadn't had the chance to properly articulate it. "But w still have a lot of work to do so you two need to st stepping on each other's toes for stupid little things l that and learn to—" He brought his hands together, loss for words. "You know, like—"

"Harmonize?" Bridget said.

"Yes, exactly. I mean, you're *best friends,* for m sake! That means you need to harmonize and, ul well together!"

Leera grinned at him. "Nice speech."

"And you do need to take her a bit more seri said, adding in a whisper, "just a smidge."

Bridget sighed and he whirled on her. "An to stop snapping so quickly."

"You're right, I'm sorry," Bridget said. "I'm just really worried about Leland. If he fails …"

"I'm sorry too," Leera said in honest tones. "I make light of everything almost all the time. Not always appropriate. And don't worry about Leland. Something tells me he might actually be perfect for the biscuit."

Augum nodded. "And if Leland really *is* figuring it out—which I'm sure is true, by the way—then maybe that's a good thing. We need all the help we can get. Besides, I agree with Leigh—bet you he'd be better with it than all of us put together."

Bridget strode purposefully on. "That's why it's a thousand times easier to start arcanery young than it is to start it old. Still, I think Mr. Goss might kill us when he finds out—"

"Do we have to tell him, like, right away though?" Leera said. "Maybe we should let him get accustomed to it a little. You know, have Leland kill off some—" She checked to make sure no one was listening, but the streets were packed with busy and chatty people, "—baddies and stuff first."

"We're going to tell Mr. Goss everything right away," Bridget said.

"Of course we are, that's what I meant." Leera secretly rolled her eyes at Augum, but this time he forced himself to ignore it.

As soon as they made their way through the library entrance, they were accosted by a young gray-robed attendant. "You're The Hood, right?" When Augum nodded, the boy handed over a note. "It's urgent." The boy strode away. Augum unfolded the small parchment as Bridget and Leera crowded near.

See me in my office immediately.

Secretary Prudence Klines

They exchanged a look before hurrying to the portal room, where they immediately bumped into Grizelda Watts and two Legion guards. "Ah, just the three I've been looking for." She gave them a toady smile, simpering, "This way, dears."

"We have to see Secretary Klines," Augum said, holding out the note.

"I am sure you do, but we shall be seeing Senior Arcaneologist Ning first."

"Why?"

Watts opened a portal as she adjusted her sharp spectacles. "You shall address me as Secretary Watts. I am certain I have earned the title. In you go."

Augum rephrased the question. "Why must we see Senior Arcaneologist Ning, Secretary Watts?"

"Ask me again on the other side."

The trio glanced at the two guards before hopping into the portal.

On the other side, Augum again asked the question. "You shall see," was the infuriating response.

Watts led them down the hall, the two Legionnaires stumping along in the rear. Watts had a self-satisfied look on her face that worried Augum. He wondered if she had figured out what they were up to.

Watts stopped before the hulking oak doors that led to Senior Arcaneologist Ning's chamber. She gestured idly at them but they refused to open. She swatted but they still refused to budge. "Oh for—" She strode up to a small gargoyle engraving. "Shyneo," and placed her icily-lit palm on it. No sooner had she opened her mouth to speak when a voice barked, "Who is it!"

Watts, startled, clutched at her chest. "Dear me! You gave me quite the fright—"

"Stop wasting my time—" There was a fizzling sound.

"Yes, of course, Senior Arcaneologist Ning," Watts replied in a sing-song voice. "May I please enter? There is a grave matter to be discussed immediately. Uh, hello? Senior Arcaneologist Ning? It's Secretary Watts—"

Leera tried to keep a straight face as she made a tiny gesture at the etching. "I think you, uh, have to call her again."

Watts flushed. "Hush, girl!" She cleared her throat loftily. Then cleared it again. She pressed her lit palm to the etching. "Secretary Watts here requesting—"

"WHAT!"

"Your Brilliance, we need to discuss—"

"Oh for the sake of the ancients, get in and stop sniveling." The doors began to open before Ning even finished speaking.

Watts waved briskly at them to enter first. "Get in! Shoo! And keep quiet." She and the soldiers followed on their heels.

Senior Arcaneologist Lien Ning was once again floating amongst her books in the vast chamber, enveloped in silence. "What is it now, Watts?"

"An urgent matter, Senior Arcaneologist Ning."

The trio exchanged looks. She must know something that would get them into serious trouble.

The chair floated down, revealing the grotesquely malformed person sitting in it. Ning's black eyes flicked to the trio before settling on Watts. "You dare waste my time again with nonsense." The voice was arcanely projected, for Ning's curled-back lips did not move.

Watts' knife-thin brows came together as she made a face that Augum thought looked like feigned hurt. "I do believe I have uncovered a startling truth, Senior Arcaneologist Ning. I caught these three supposed necrophytes snooping. I questioned them on the matter and they told me they belonged to a Commander Sanyika Shaeek, who is supposedly in the field. Naturally, as a good and loyal citizen of the Legion, I took it upon myself to make inquiries. I wrote the Blackhaven Constabulary and they insisted there was no such active duty commander."

"Indeed," Senior Arcaneologist Ning said. "How peculiar, because as it so happens, I believe Secretary Klines received a parcel from Commander Sanyika Shaeek just this afternoon."

Watts' mouth fell open. "She … she did?"

"I have summoned her. She will be here momentarily."

"Even so, I … I am certain these three here are *the* three we're all looking for—Augum Stone, Bridget Burns, and Leera Jones. They are merely in disguise."

The trio froze. Augum thought his chest would explode.

"I confess the image of the poster is not *that* close," Watts prattled on, "but even their fake names! I dare say there is no *way* they could be necrophytes." When Ning merely floated there, unimpressed, Watts blurted, "and I can prove it! Only an ordained necrophyte can possibly cast necromancy spells."

There was a sigh from the floating chair. "I believe Feign Death is one of the first spells taught, am I not correct?"

"Yes, but they can't possibly—"

"Miss Leigh Sparrows, please demonstrate a proper casting of the spell."

Leera swallowed.

"Go ahead, do not be nervous, child."

Leera lay on the ground and played dead. Augum could barely breathe. As expected, nothing happened. Suddenly, just as Secretary Watts' stupid face exploded with a triumphant grin, Leera's own face began to decompose. It was so real and frightful Augum had to avert his eyes.

Watts' forehead shone with sweat. "But … but I was certain—"

Leera was soon up on her feet, confused. She mouthed at Augum, "Did it work—?"

He replied with the slightest of nods.

The doors silently opened and in clacked the tiny beetle-like Secretary Klines, carrying a parchment-wrapped parcel stamped with a burning sword and the written words *From CSS*.

"Ah, just the three I was looking for," she said, handing the parcel over to Bridget. "This is for you, from Commander Sanyika Shaeek."

"Impossible!" Watts said in her snippy voice. "Which company does he belong to?"

Klines glanced questioningly at Ning. "I am not at liberty to say."

"What do you mean? I knew it! This is all a sham—"

"—because it's a shadow company," Klines blurted.

"A what now?"

"A shadow company. That means it's a secret company under the direct command of Lord Sparkstone. Those who inquire about the company are to be reported and questioned."

Watts nervously glanced at the Legion guards, who looked at each other.

"I … I did not realize—but I was so sure these were the three villainous traitors—"

Klines folded her hands before her. "This is the second time you have accused someone of being Augum Stone, is that not correct?"

Watts was stammering now. "That was a simple and unfortunate misunder—"

"A misunderstanding. You declared the boy to be Augum Stone and paraded him about the library, then to the constabulary. Except when they finally took him to the Lord of the Legion himself, it turned out to be some poor farm boy. The story even made the Herald. An embarrassment to the institution."

"I … I …"

"You were 'absolutely certain' then too, were you not? Those were your exact words, is that not correct?"

Watts' mouth opened and closed like a fish.

"I am afraid Lord Sparkstone will have to be informed immediately. He will be told exactly who is responsible, and I am sure his Lordship will not be as amused a second time."

Watts went beet red. "That … that surely will not be necessary, Secretary Klines. Senior Arcaneologist Ning, have mercy, I see no reason to escalate a minor blunder—"

Augum enjoyed watching her squirm, and by the look on Leera's face, so did she.

"Please, I'll do anything."

Senor Arcaneologist Ning stared from her chair. Watts shriveled under her expressionless gaze.

Klines took a step forward. "Very few souls have been entrusted with the information of the existence of shadow companies. Do you believe yourself worthy of this information?"

Watts' thin brows bounced around as she struggled with the question. "N-no, I do not, I suppose."

"Then, if we never hear an inquiry from you or these guards—I'm sorry, what were your names again?"

"Private Ribbons, m'lady," stammered one in a commoner accent, snapping to attention. "Private Matthews, m'lady," squeaked the other.

"As I was saying, if we never hear of an inquiry about shadow companies from any of the three of you, I do not see why a questioning would be necessary. It seems this was indeed but a minor misunderstanding."

Watts and the two guards visibly relaxed.

Klines nodded at the guards. "You are dismissed." They snapped to attention before hurrying out of the hall.

Ning's chair floated closer. "If so much as a sneeze of this reaches the Herald and embarrasses this institution once again—"

"It w-won't, Your Brilliance!"

Ning glared with her black gaze. "I know about the overcharging as well."

"I … I …"

"Do you deny charging four silvers a head to out-of-towners when the entry fee is only one?"

Watts gave a toady swallow and shook her head.

"I am placing you on administrative leave. Consider yourself lucky not to be dismissed and put to the question."

Watts curtsied awkwardly. "Very fair, Your Brilliance."

"But I do have a task for you to complete in your absence."

"A task?"

"A penance for your repeated indiscretions. You are to take a horse and deliver a message to the senior arcaneologist at the library in the city of Ironfeather."

"But that's … that's so far! It'll take me a month to—"

"Indeed. It is a trusted mission. And you have much trust to earn back, I dare say. See me in one hour and I shall give you the message. You will depart immediately. Am I understood?"

"Yes, of course, Senior Arcaneologist Ning. I shall not fail."

"And Secretary Watts—I wouldn't mention the shadow companies to anyone if I were you, not if you do not want to be made example of."

"Y-yes, Your Brilliance."

"You are dismissed."

"Thank you, Senior Arcaneologist Ning." Watts turned on her heel and quickly waddled through the open doors.

EXPLANATIONS

Secretary Klines waved at the doors. Once they closed, she expelled a long breath. "We're lucky she's as daft as she is naive."

"There's no such thing as a shadow company, is there?" Augum asked.

Klines waved the matter aside. "Utter fiction. Came up with it on the fly. Wish the story was stronger, but there was little time."

"How did you know about our fake commander?"

She calmly strode over. "Do not look so surprised. Senior Arcaneologist Ning is one of the few warlocks able to cast a rare off-the-books spell known as Telepathy. She gave me all the details of the accusations as she heard them. I came as quick as I could, labeling the box as I walked."

"Pardon me, Senior Arcaneologist Ning," Bridget said, "but how did you make Leera appear undead like that?"

"Genius has its privileges," Ning replied. "But to answer your question, it was mere illusion." She floated before Bridget. "The fear is gone from your eyes. You have conquered the cliff, I see."

"I … I did, Senior Arcaneologist Ning."

Her chair swiveled to Augum then Leera, but only a grunt was emitted. "You three have found what you were looking for, I presume? Good," she said before they could reply to the contrary, "then we shan't have any more trouble, shall we? I expect a quiet and hasty departure. You will, seeing as it will be unnecessary, not attend the tournament, of course. A most pointless and vain idea in the first place, entering a tournament to show one's arcane prowess …"

Augum opened his mouth to say that that wasn't why he had entered the tournament at all, and how they could use their help in the coming attempt to steal the divining rod, but instead found himself staring at the bottom of the chair as it floated up and away.

"Give Anna Stone my regards," Ning's voice rang out. "Dismissed."

Klines followed them out of the chamber.

"Uh, Secretary Klines," Augum began as she escorted them along in the hall, "if we get in a bit of trouble tomorrow—"

"—you won't," Klines said, coming to a halt, her giant spectacled eyes focusing on him. "We have taken great risks on your behalf. Do not disappoint us with careless traipsing. You will leave quietly, the sooner the better. Tonight would be best, but if you stay until morning, make sure it is in your quarters, and depart first thing."

"Right …"

She strode into the portal room. "Be sure not to show anyone that package. It was *extremely* difficult to acquire. I even had to disenchant the powerful Object Track incantation placed upon it. They should not notice it missing until you are gone, by which time it will of course be too late to do anything." She summoned a portal. "In you go, straight to your room, no dawdling. Goodbye and good luck."

They meekly went through the portal. As with Ning, Klines' brisk manner heavily discouraged rebuttal.

"Great, now what are we going to do?" Leera said as they traipsed along the lush carpet in the dimly-lit hall. "If we go through with it tomorrow, how are we going to get away safely without Klines' and Ning's help? Maybe we should just leave now—"

"No," Augum replied. "We stay. We just need a good plan, that's all." A *really* good plan.

"We'll have to give this serious thought," Bridget said. "Though I can't help but think we should have told them of our intentions."

"What, so they could call us fools and stop us?" Leera said. "No thank you."

They entered their room, nearly tripping over a giant pile of clothes.

Leera picked up a frilly dress. "You've got to be kidding me. These are all clothes those two stupid stowaways bought!"

"Never mind all this right now, we'll talk to them later." Bridget placed the parcel on the desk and unwrapped it, revealing a fine pine box intricately carved with the burning sword of the Legion, along with the words, *Duty unto death*. The number *005* was engraved into one of the corners. She opened the lid and they gasped in wonder. Fitted snugly into the wood were ten steel rings and a small steel orb. All were uniquely patterned with black swirls.

Bridget picked up a vellum parchment and began reading. " 'Congratulations, Commander Emmett Jordan'—"

"—that's the gray-haired commander who gave that long speech in the Training Room!" Augum said. The hawk-eyed one who sat in front of them at the arena.

" 'Enclosed within is your very own Exot set. The communication orb, which you will refer to in the field as an *Exot orb,* is arcanely connected to ten rings, referred to as *Exot rings*. The Dreadnought-forged steel artifacts are the first of their kind and strategically invaluable. Your name is associated with this particular set. Do not under any circumstances allow it to fall into enemy hands.' "

Augum imagined the reaction of the ebony-skinned commander when he discovered his set had mysteriously gone missing. He wondered how Klines came to acquire it, and suddenly appreciated the risk she and Ning had taken on their behalf. No wonder they didn't want more trouble from them …

Bridget read on, using a raised finger to accent the important parts. " 'Merely a night of sleep with the orb will tune you to its arcanery. Possessing the 5th degree is strongly suggested but not required to wield the Exot orb. The possessor of each Exot ring, however, must be 2nd degree at minimum. You will only hand out the rings to those necrophytes under your *direct command*. As with the old speaking orbs, in order to reach the recipient, the Exot ring or Exot orb bearer must think of the subject's appearance and speak the word "contact", followed by the recipient's name. The possessor of the Exot ring or Exot orb will hear a voice inside their head and may reply verbally into the ring or orb. Contact may be ceased by either party with the words "cease contact", or by removing the ring or letting go of the orb. *Communication between rings is not possible*. Distance may be a factor in voice clarity. As a secondary quality, the orb may be used to *track* the rings at a 7th degree Object Track proficiency.' "

Leera elbowed Augum. "Now *this* is a cool toy. Let's try them on."

"Excuse me, but this is *not* a toy." Bridget gingerly withdrew three rings, handing Augum and Leera one each. "We'll wear them after one of us tunes to the orb."

"These are huge, no way are they going to—" but Leera's brows arched after slipping hers on. "Neat, it's sizing itself!"

Augum watched as his ring shrank to fit his finger. "Am I supposed to feel different though?"

Leera examined hers, wrinkling her nose at it. "Don't think you're supposed to feel anything."

Augum gave his back to Bridget. "Which one of us should tune to the orb?"

"Let's come up with a plan for tomorrow first." Bridget took the ring from Leera, returned all three to the box, and closed the lid. She placed her hands on her hips. "So, what do we do about tomorrow if—"

"—*when* Augum beats Robin," Leera corrected.

"Of course. When Augum beats Robin."

Augum paced to the window to watch the arena grounds, its flags fluttering in the breeze. "We need to talk to Malaika and Charissa, hear what kind of guards are going to be posted, where the trophy ceremony is to take place, and whatever else they have to say about tomorrow."

"*If* they follow through," Leera muttered. "Anyway, we've got a few hours before we have to meet them in the Supper Hall."

"Oh, I almost forgot," Augum said, striding to the desk and fetching a scrap of parchment. "I'm supposed to send Caireen a note. She's joining the Resistance and I want to give her one of the rings. We're going to need all the help we can get tomorrow."

"Good idea." Bridget withdrew a ring from the box, tossing it to him.

He caught it, dipped a quill into an ink bottle, and wrote a quick note, saying: *Put this on, it will come in handy.*

—*A.* He sprinkled some drying sand on the parchment and gently blew on the ink.

Bridget bit her lip. "Do you not think it's a bit risky just … slipping that under her door?"

"She's expecting a note and told me no one enters her room. She'll be back from the healers soon anyway." He placed the Exot ring into the parchment, folded it up, and stuck it in a pocket.

"I suppose." Bridget nodded at the pine box. "We need to hide that until tomorrow."

The trio glanced about the room, but there were precious few options.

Bridget winced. "I hate it, but under the bed?"

"Doesn't look like we have much of a choice," Leera replied.

Bridget placed her hands over the pine box. "Concutio del alarmo," then she carefully hid it under her bed. "Hopefully no one sees it here." She stood up, dusting her hands. "Right, hoods up, let's go."

They made their way to room 1478, which was a long ways down the curving corridor. Augum knocked but, as expected, received no reply. He pulled the folded note from his pocket and slipped it deep under the door.

Leera stuck her hands in the pockets of her necrophyte robe. "Now what?"

Bridget expelled a long breath. "Now we train. It's important Augum is as prepared as possible for tomorrow's duel."

"What about the exit plan?"

"We'll come up with a detailed one tonight after supper."

They strolled to the portal room. Bridget placed her palm on an oval etching, but then paused. "Hmm."

"What is it?" Augum asked.

"It just occurred to me that we have access to the entire library now."

Leera shrugged. "Yeah, so?"

"So, what if we found the room that held all the arcane scrolls? The Legion has forbidden them, right? There must be a giant stash somewhere."

"What do we need a scroll for—" Leera paused. "Ooooh. Group Teleport. We can use one to escape after the tournament!"

"*Exactly*."

"There *is* a scroll room," Leera said. "I've been in it. Well, sort of."

"What do you mean you've—" but it was Bridget's turn to pause. "The Restricted Room."

Leera nodded. "It won't be easy. There's guards and stuff. Though, if all three of us got in, we might get by them."

Bridget rooted around in her pouch but stopped as an attendant strode by, giving them a curious look before stepping through a portal. Bridget resumed searching her pouch. "Nine gargoyle coins left. That means we'll need another six to get all three of us in there."

Leera smirked. "Whoa, Bridget Burns is wrong about something for once." Augum could tell she enjoyed using Bridget's full name for a change.

Bridget's head swung faster than a scythe. "What do you mean I'm wrong? I'm not wrong—"

"Oh, really?" Leera's sharply arched brows rose smugly as she crossed her arms. "You forgot I *already* got into the room, which means I have access and we only need *one* more coin. I'll accept your apology now, thank you very much."

Bridget's cheeks flushed. "You're right. I apologize."

"Apology accepted."

Augum summoned a portal. "A single coin shouldn't be hard to get. Let's go train."

DISCOVERED

After paying the toll, the trio found a secluded spot in the jungle behind a hill, then spent two grueling hours preparing Augum for his fight with Robin. The girls eventually exhausted themselves by mostly attacking him with the First Offensive, which he repeatedly defended against with his Shield spell. He was getting better at angling his weight forward with the shield, preventing himself from getting thrown back.

They strategized on Robin's most likely attacks, almost all necromancy-related; how he might cheat, especially with his aunt being one of the judges; and how it was important for Augum to keep his hood up at all times.

"Augum!" a boy suddenly shouted in a squeaky voice. Augum reflexively turned, immediately realizing the mistake—*he had answered to his real name!* For a moment, he just gaped at a small necrophyte boy with a pimpled face and short black hair, standing on the hill behind them. It was the boy from the Supper Hall, the one who had asked him if he was a Bridget or Leera fan.

"I knew it—" the boy said, and ran. The trio immediately bolted after him. Augum, heart punching his chest, stopped on top of the hill and telekinetically yanked at the boy's foot. The boy tripped, careening into a bush of pink grass. Augum focused and kept pulling, the girls quickly joining in. The boy struggled but was no match against their combined telekinetic pull. He was dragged back along the grass, shouting, "I found them! They're here—mlrph!" Bridget clamped her hand over the boy's mouth. He was tiny enough she had no problem handling him.

Leera waved at a necrophyte who had taken notice. "Just our friend playing hide and seek!"

They half-dragged, half-walked the boy back out of sight.

"Great, now what do we do?" Leera said, panting. "He's going to blab as soon as we let him go."

Bridget held the boy firm. "We're not going to hurt you, promise. I'm going to remove my hand now. Please, don't yell out. We just want to talk to you, all right?" She slowly withdrew her hand from the boy's mouth.

His pimpled face was pale, eyes darting about. "What are you doing here?"

"We're on an important quest," Augum replied. "How did you know it was me?"

"You told me you were from Blackhaven, but then I heard the arena announcer say you were from Everscale. Then I was in the Hall of the Ancients and I overheard a fat attendant saying to her guards that she swore you three were the fugitives—"

"Watts," Leera muttered. "Figures."

"Then I watched you and checked a Tiberran poster, which had a better drawing of you all, and you were near identical. I'm going to tell on you as soon as I—" but Bridget clamped a hand over his mouth again.

Leera sighed. "What a mess. What do we do with him?"

"Hold on." Augum raised a hand, concentrating. "Flustrato."

The boy's eyes instantly crossed. He moaned, then whined, "But Ma, I don't *want* to do my homework right now …"

"We have to get him to Secretary Klines' office," Bridget said as the boy rambled on. "She'll know what to do with him."

"What if we take him to our room?" Leera asked. "Have Malaika and Charissa watch over him, then let him go tomorrow?"

"Too risky," Augum said. "Besides, he might be tiny, but I'd guess he's also a 1st or 2nd degree necrophyte. He knows arcanery—they don't. He'd get free in no time."

"I'll take him up to Klines' office," Bridget said, giving them a serious look. "With my hood *down*. It'll be less suspicious."

"On your own?" Augum asked.

"It'll be safest that way. Let's all cast Confusion on him at once. If it wears off too soon, I'll cast it on him again. If anyone asks what's going on with him, I'll just tell them he got in over his head in the Training Room."

"No, it's too dangerous—" Leera said, and the trio argued the point, until the boy mumbled, "Augum Stone … Hood …"

"He's coming out of it, we've got to do this quickly," Bridget said.

"Fine, but I still don't like the plan," Leera said.

The trio lined up before the drooling boy and stretched out their hands, chorusing, "Flustrato." The boy dropped like a sack of spuds.

"Is … is he sleeping?" Leera said.

Bridget ran her fingers through her hair in exasperation. "Looks like the combined effects were too strong for him."

"Jonathan—!" called a girl's voice nearby. "Jonathan, where are you?"

"It's that girl that was with him back in the Supper Hall," Augum whispered, grabbing the boy's feet. "Quick, help me carry him into the bushes before she sees us."

They grabbed the boy and hurriedly carried him to a thick bush underneath a tall palm tree, just as the girl appeared over the hill.

"This is a disaster," Leera whispered, craning her neck. "A complete disaster."

Augum watched the sienna-haired girl grimace and turn around, complaining loudly how he was standing her up again for supper, before disappearing back over the hill.

"Maybe Senior Arcaneologist Ning will have a spell that will erase his memory or something," Augum said.

Bridget grabbed his arm. "That's it—the obstacle field!"

"What about it?"

"Remember when we first got here and the attendant warned us about the *memory wiper* obstacle? All we have to do is set it to a high-enough degree that erases a couple days of memory, that's all."

Leera snorted. "Oh, nothing could possibly go wrong there."

"Look, I agree with you about how risky it is trying to drag him to Klines' office. This is the better option."

"Don't get me wrong, I'm all for it, I just think ... wow, Bridge, that's kind of cold."

"Would you rather have Mrs. Stone back or be in an iron room with a questioner?"

"I see your point. Besides, you're right, it's only a couple days of lost memory."

"Hear ye, hear ye!" called out an arcanely amplified voice from afar. "The eighth evening bell tolls!"

"Great, we were supposed to be in the supper hall by now to meet Miss Jealous and Miss Annoying," Leera muttered.

"We're going to have to skip supper altogether," Augum said.

Leera made a face at him as if *his* brain had been wiped.

"He's right," Bridget said. "We have to skip supper. We have to do this as close to closing as possible, that way almost all the necrophytes will be gone."

Leera sighed but nodded. Then she grimaced. "No, forget that. We've almost got a full hour. I'm going to the Supper Hall, talk to Dim and Dimmer, then bring us back some food."

"All right, but maybe I should go instead," Bridget said.

Leera gave Augum a quirky smile, which Bridget caught.

"Never mind," Bridget quickly said. "You go, otherwise you two will just make eyes at each other the entire time and the boy will run free."

"Pfft," Leera said. "All right, I'll meet you two back here in a bit. Oh, and—" She thrust out her palm at Bridget and wiggled her fingers. "Gimme, gimme."

Bridget withdrew fifteen coppers and handed them over.

"We're not that bad, are we?" Augum said, watching her go.

"I was just teasing." Bridget shrugged. "But still …"

"I do miss spending time with her."

"I know you do."

He and Bridget took turns keeping the boy under the Confusion spell. At last, Leera returned carrying a small potato sack stuffed with supper.

"What did Malaika and Charissa have to say?" Bridget asked.

"They're so useless."

"You argued, didn't you?"

"Let's just say we're not going to be best friends anytime soon, but then we all knew that anyway. I mean, one spent all the coin daddy sent on a mountain of stupid clothes she can't *possibly* take back without an army of warlocks helping, and the other one is a complete airhead." Leera made a circular motion around her head. "I swear you can hear things echo around in there when she walks."

"To be fair, I'd have said something too, Bridge," Augum said. He turned to Leera. "They're going to leave all those clothes behind, right?"

"They're still deluded into thinking they can bring the entire pile."

Augum shrugged. "Fine, let's burn their stuff then."

Bridget gave him a look.

"I was jesting." Sort of.

Leera waved dismissively. "I told them they can take their stupid horses and we'll take the arcane route." She bit her lip. "Except I guess that's when the argument really got heated." She added in an undertone, "There was some food thrown … and stuff …"

Bridget ballooned. *"What?"*

"Nothing to worry about, uh, I just won't be allowed back into the Supper Hall again, but that won't matter because we can catch some street food tomorrow—"

"Leera Jones—"

"I was merely *escorted* out of there by an attendant, it wasn't like, you know, the Legion was called in or anything. But look—" She flashed a cheery smile while raising the sack of food. "I brought supper!"

Bridget placed her head into her hands. Augum gave Leera a *You've done it now* look.

Leera lowered the sack. "It's really no big deal, Bridge." She paused, awkwardly placing a hand on her shoulder. "Uh … I'm sorry."

Bridget's shoulders shook.

Leera gave Augum a horrified look he interpreted as *Is she crying?* He nodded somberly in response. Leera plopped down beside Bridget and wrapped an arm around her. She placed her head on Bridget's shoulder. Augum did the same from the other side, and the trio just sat there a little while … until the boy beside them gave a drooling moan.

Augum casually reached over. "Flustrato," he said, and the boy resumed his stupor, which by then had devolved to staring at the exotic tree canopy with glazed eyes.

Bridget raised her head. "I'm … I'm sorry, it's all the stress. Everything's falling apart, and it just feels like we're juggling too much. I feel like I'm coming undone at the seams or something. We've still got so much to do—find one more coin, get past those gargoyles without getting killed, find a Group Teleport scroll, make a detailed escape plan, then Augum's got to *beat* Robin—"

"Which he will, handily," Leera said with a firm nod.

"—then he has to somehow snatch the divining rod from Earring Head—"

Leera snorted a laugh at that one.

"—amongst the most powerful warlocks in the kingdom, and *then* somehow escape without being caught."

Leera crinkled her nose. "Ehh, you put it like that and it *does* sound … completely crazy, yeah, but that's why we're going to plan it really well, right?"

Bridget nodded her head, wiping her eyes.

"You just needed a good cry," Augum said in a soft voice. "You're frazzled. It's all right. This isn't easy for any of us. I'm amazed we made it this far, if you think about it. I mean, we've kind of gone through a lot."

"You win the understatement of the year award with that one," Leera muttered with a gentle smile. "Oh, I guess I should also mention that they found the wraith and walkers we killed in that closed-off part of the library."

Augum and Bridget stared at her.

"When … when were you going to tell us that little, you know, kind of important piece of news?" Augum asked.

Leera shrugged. "When the opportunity presented itself. And now seemed like a good time."

Bridget was ballooning again. "Not earlier, when we were talking about—"

"Now don't get upset again, Bridge—"

"Hear ye, hear ye!" an attendant's amplified voice called out. "The ninth bell tolls! The library is closed. All warlocks are to vacate library premises or see themselves to their rooms. Hear ye, hear ye—"

Bridget threw up her hands. "Great, just great. There's no chance of getting back now without being caught."

"So are they doing anything different with the guards?" Augum asked.

Leera opened the bag and doled out some bread. "Don't know, but there were way more guards in the halls as I walked here." She glanced at the sleeping boy nearby. "That memory wiper obstacle is close to the doors. We should wait and hide until we see how many walkers we're going to have to deal with. Anyway, I'm starved. Let's eat."

Bridget stared at the chunk of bread. "After we deal with him, we might as well use our cloaked access to get into the labyrinth directly."

"Either that or we take the waterfall route again," Augum said.

Leera dug through the sack once more. "No thanks." She withdrew linen-wrapped chunks of beef, pieces of cheese, some carrots, and doled them out. They ate in silence, watching the arcane braziers steadily dim. The vast cavern would soon go dark.

A TALK WITH THE ENEMY

The necrophyte stirred and Augum raised his arm to cast Confusion again, but then dropped it. "No point, is there?"

"Not if his mind's going to get wiped, no," Bridget said, taking a swig from a waterskin.

"I'm amazed the attendant doesn't come around to check if there are any lingering trainees," Leera said with a mouthful of food. "They just dump undead guards in here and leave."

"I read that Library policies have changed significantly since the Legion took over," Bridget replied.

They ate in watchful silence until the boy, Jonathan, opened his eyes. He watched them for a while before weakly asking, "How old are you?"

"Augum's fifteen," Bridget replied. "And Leera and I will be fifteen very soon. Why do you ask? And how old are you?"

"Thirteen." He paused. "For your crimes, you'll be the youngest to see the public gallows in years."

"So we're going to hang," Augum said. "For what crimes?" What was the Legion telling necrophytes nowadays?

"You won't hang because you're the Lord of the Legion's son." Jonathan eyed the girls. "Them. They'll hang."

Leera put down the chunk of cheese she had been nibbling on. "What are *our* crimes?"

"Theft. Helping to brainwash the Lord of the Legion's son. Murder … and worse stuff."

Leera resumed her nibbling. "Really now?"

"You stole the scion and the Agonex." Jonathan's eyes briefly flicked to Augum. "The crone has put a spell on him. You murdered all those people in Sparrow's Perch and Tornvale—"

Leera froze. "How *dare* you—"

"My father murdered everyone in Sparrow's Perch," Augum said. "*Including* Bridget and Leera's families. We saw it with our own eyes." The memory of dangling feet flitted through his mind before he pushed it away.

"You *think* you saw it. It's a spell the crone cast to make you believe that. False memories."

Leera looked like she was about to say something vile but instead took a breath.

Augum gave the boy a pitying look. "Clever, but in my heart, I know that's not true." He leaned forward. "My father has managed to convince a lot of people of a lot of things that are not true. And he *did* murder and burn down those villages. It was no illusion, that I guarantee you."

"The Lord of the Legion is a just and fair man. He does not kill innocents. He's not a murderer."

"You don't know him," Leera said in exasperated tones. "And it's you that's brainwashed. The entire kingdom is."

The boy lay there a moment before replying. "What's more likely, that an entire kingdom is brainwashed … or just you three?"

"The bigger the lie the more people believe it," Bridget said quietly. "My father told me that."

The boy shook his head sadly at them. "A shame. You will be dead and I will live forever."

Leera snorted. "What, through Ley?" She pointed her cheese at him. "You can't take eternal life back with you. Besides, Leyan lives are ridiculously boring. Picture standing in a windy desert for, like, a hundred years, staring at nothing. The most exciting thing you see is sunrise. That's the only way to live for a long time, by reaching some dull nirvana or something."

"We watched someone return from Ley," Augum said. He recalled holding his great-grandfather in his arms, feeling the breath leave his body. "He aged before our eyes, dying within days. You really can't take that lifespan back with you."

Jonathan kept shaking his head. "False memories. Lies. You know not what you speak. And why should eternity only belong to a few?"

"This is pointless," Leera said, extending her hand in readiness to cast another spell.

The boy closed his eyes. "Do what you must, but my family is starving in Blackhaven because of you."

Leera curled her hand into a fist. "Ugh, seriously?"

"The Lord of the Legion cannot elevate his followers until he completes the Great Quest. When you return the last scion and the Agonex, he will open a portal to Ley. Only then will he be able to reward those most loyal to him."

"Your family is starving because he's been robbing the kingdom to fund his wars," Bridget said. "He's taken the fieldworkers for his armies. He's wiped out *entire villages*!"

The boy's head never stopped shaking. "You are so lost and brainwashed, I almost feel sorry for you."

"The only eternal life you'll be allowed is as an undead minion," Augum said. "Serving 'His Lordship'." He said the last words in a mocking tone. "It's *necromancy.* Think about it."

"Necromancy is nothing more than mastery over death. His Lordship has taught us that only when you conquer your fear of death do you open your heart to the possibility of eternal life."

Augum's muscles tightened. "At the sacrifice of everybody else!"

"Sacrifices have to be made in great pursuits." Jonathan, this small necrophyte boy they had heard casually kidding around in the Supper Hall, turned his flat gaze upon Augum. "You three and the crone *will* be captured or killed. It's only a matter of time."

Bridget's hand shot out. "Flustrato—" and the boy went dumb again. "Sorry, couldn't take it anymore."

Augum rubbed his face, suddenly feeling tired. "Well that was depressing."

"I saw all three of them in the library," the boy mumbled. "Oh, eternity? I would be most grateful, Your Esteemed Lordship ..."

"Father told me that an idea could be completely made up of absurd nonsense, but as long as it's popular and repeated often enough, people will believe it," Bridget said, watching as he rolled around in the grass, mumbling to himself.

"They're called *fanatics*, aren't they?" Leera threw away the stub of her carrot in aggravation. "I'd just call them loons seeing as no amount of proof will change their minds."

The trio sat in contemplative silence for a bit before gathering themselves in readiness for the memory wipe quest. Bridget cast Confusion one more time on the boy before Augum and Leera lugged him up, placing his arms around their necks. They dragged him to the top of the hill where they stopped to survey the ever-dimming cavern.

"You wanted to know about the guard situation?" Leera said, nodding at the distant entrance. "Well, there it is."

Before the great double doors were the dim outlines of two wraiths and five walkers. The obstacle course was nearby and it was going to take some sneaky prowling to get there without being noticed.

"Guess they didn't appreciate having one of their wraiths and a bunch of walkers taken out," Augum noted. He nodded at the giant rickety-looking house with exterior perches. "If we get to the back of that house, we can skip across to the stone maze."

"And behind the maze is the obstacle field," Bridget said. "I'll lead." Ducking, she slipped behind an exotic multi-colored bush. She peeked out and beckoned them over. She repeated this pattern from bush to tree, tree to ruined pillar, pillar to a cobble bridge, and then to the back of the old house.

"Flustrato," Augum said after laying the boy down. Jonathan gave a grunt, eyes wandering.

"I think there's some kind of cumulative effect happening to him," Bridget whispered.

"Huh?" Leera said.

Augum had noticed it too. "Spell is more effective with each casting."

"Oh." Leera frowned. "Right, look at how his tongue is lolling about."

Yet another one of the many peculiarities of arcanery Augum did not understand.

They hauled the boy up. Bridget peeked around the corner and soon zipped across to the maze. She looked again, holding her palm up to stop them. Suddenly she waved furiously and Augum and Leera ran with Jonathan flopping between them. One of the boy's legs suddenly caught between Augum's. They stumbled and fell the last few strides, rolling into Bridget. Augum's hand clamped across the boy's mouth just as a distant squeal echoed, followed by furious clacking.

Bridget dared a peek and instantly paled. She glanced around, finally gesturing behind them and hissing, "The maze! Go, go, go!"

They scrambled into the dim entrance, choosing to go right. The maze had tall crude masonry covered with moss and lichen. The torches had gone out, forcing them to light their palms. As they chose random passages, they could hear the frantic sprinting of the walkers.

"They're inside," Bridget whispered. "Let's try this way." She led them into a wide but straight corridor, at the end of which was a section of charred tiles. Each of the tiles had a letter and was just large enough for a single person to step on. On the other side was an old plank door with the symbol of a broken cup.

"Take him, I know this one," Leera said, leaving Augum to hold up Jonathan on his own. "It's the name of the Repair spell," and she stepped on the letter *R*, only to receive a nasty shock that made her recoil.

"Try the trigger word—" Bridget said, glancing over her shoulder.

Wincing, Leera hopped onto the letter *A*. When nothing happened, she hopped to *P*, then *R*, *E*, *Y*, and finally *O*. A latch sprung and the door opened with a creak.

"Hurry—fly him across with Telekinesis," Augum said. They concentrated, hands out. Augum quickly felt the boy's weight leave his shoulders. Jonathan gurgled a moan as his limp body floated across the tiles. Just as he floated through the open door, Leera slammed her wrists together, shouting, "ANNIHILO!" A sharp jet of water shot past Augum and Bridget's heads, slamming into a clacking walker. The undead creature smashed into the floor, skidding onto the tiles. Augum and Bridget had to jump to let it sweep underneath. It immediately began flopping around and smoking as miniature lightning bolts attacked it. Black smoke began to bellow out as if from a giant steaming kettle, along with a horrible smell that immediately took Augum back to that harrowing episode in Sparrow's Perch.

"You go," Augum said between coughs, sleeve over his mouth. Bridget nodded behind her own sleeve, eyes watering from the acrid smoke. Meanwhile, he turned to face the corridor entrance, hands in attack formation, trying to ignore the pain in his head. After training all evening, he had finally strained his arcane stamina with that last Telekinesis casting. His head now felt like there was a miniature demon inside it clawing at his brain. Behind him, he could hear Bridget yelp as she jumped from tile to tile while trying to avoid the burning bones.

A walker shot around the corner. "ANNIHILO!" Augum shouted, but it moved so quick he missed. He barely had time to raise his hard lightning shield as it slammed into him. Luckily his training paid off—he leaned into the hit and prevented the walker from bowling him over. The stabbing in his brain quickly sharpened as the walker beat on the shield with rabid ferocity. Augum refused to allow his shield to fail, grunting with the strain of arcane concentration combined with the physical effort of pushing against something with supernatural strength.

"Duck on two!" Bridget yelled. "One, two, ANNIHILO!"

Augum ducked just as his shield failed, but not before the walker caught him with a ferocious hook to the jaw, breaking it. Its skull exploded an instant later and the creature fell to the ground in a heap.

Augum couldn't help dropping to a knee, eyes welling with tears of pain, a grating sound coming from his jaw. Come on, seriously? This couldn't have happened at a worse time. He wanted to scream from the frustration of it but was prevented by the grating sharpness.

A hiss came from the corridor, quickly growing louder.

"Wraith behind you!" Leera screamed.

Augum stood, trying to focus on the tiles, but his eyes were so watery he could barely see. There—there was the *A*! He jumped and wobbled, arms flailing for balance.

"What's the matter with you, hurry—!" Leera shouted.

Augum found the next one, *P*. Behind him came the sound of thudding steps. He skipped from the R to the *E* as the hiss quickly approached, finally the *Y* and on to the other side where the girls yanked him through the door, slamming it shut. It immediately received a hard thwack, but held. Bridget and Leera slid to the floor, wincing and panting. There were repeated squeals and an angry hiss from behind the door. It sounded like the tiles were attacking the wraith. The hiss soon faded.

"It's going to look for another way around," Leera said.

Meanwhile, Augum groaned beside Jonathan, who was coming to. He raised his arm to cast Confusion on him again, but decided against it. He supposed it wouldn't have helped—he had already pushed his arcane stamina to a dangerous degree.

Bridget's hand shot to her mouth. "Aug, your face!"

"Runshed me!"

"What?"

Augum made a punching gesture at his own jaw. "Droken."

Leera shot to his side. "It's broken? No!"

"I're bre fine. Ret's go." His jaw felt like it was made of a bunch of sharp rocks, and the area was swollen and tender. Breathing was difficult and he tasted blood in his mouth, but he'd work through it and find a way to heal it later.

"We got him, you lead," Leera said, grabbing the boy with Bridget.

Thoroughly lost, Augum led them through a series of random twists and forks in the maze, until coming up to a corridor carved with three separate runic bands that ran along the floor and up the walls, each band separated by about four strides. He tentatively stepped over the first one, instantly feeling a tingling sensation in his brain he recognized as a Fear attack. He estimated the strength to be about 5th degree. Strong, but not unmanageable. He opened his jaw to warn the girls but gasped at the intense pain. Leaning against the wall for support, he gestured weakly at the ribbon, then at his own head.

"Brace for mind attack spells," Bridget said.

The girls made it over the first band okay, but Jonathan's eyes widened and he started screaming. From various nearby places in the maze came the sound of hissing and clacking, combining into a gruesome symphony. The girls jumped as they heard a frantic scratching at the wall just beside them.

Augum couldn't read the runes of the next band through his tears of pain. His hands were curled so tightly into fists that his nails were drawing blood. He steeled himself and passed through, feeling another familiar 5th degree attack, except this time his weakened arcanery failed and he instantly went deaf. He gestured at his ears to warn the girls before waving them over. The girls carried a shrieking Jonathan through.

Augum turned his attention to the final band, already suspecting the spell that awaited him. He steeled himself once more and stepped over the band. His thoughts immediately jumbled as if someone had picked up the lot and smashed them against a wall. There were somewhat familiar faces nearby, but why were they there? Their mouths were moving, yet for some reason, he couldn't hear anything. His vision was blurry and the lower part of his head felt like a bag of hot coals.

Right—they were supposed to be moving! He should nod and smile that he understood that. Don't want to look stupid, do we?

As soon as he did so, however, an excruciating heat flashed through his jaw, forcing him to lean against the wall. All right, bad idea. He twisted around on his heel. The girls had moved ahead, gesturing for him to follow. Was that the right way? Maybe they should have gone the other way. Why was it so hard to make sense of everything? Maybe he was supposed to go through those bands. Or had he already crossed them? It would be wise to test one, just in case.

His sleeve was yanked by that familiar pretty girl with a smattering of freckles. Why was she scared? Maybe if they went back she wouldn't be scared. He stopped her, hoping to somehow communicate they should go back. Instead, she grabbed him and dragged him along. Ahead, two people looked like they were playing some kind of wrestling game.

SCHWOOM.

Suddenly sound and logic hit him like a boulder. The sensation was so powerful he flinched, sending a stab of pain through his jaw and down his spine. What in Sithesia had he been doing? Leera was holding onto him as if he had lost his mind and Bridget was *fighting* Jonathan! He also realized both of them had likely reached their arcane stamina limits.

"BAKA!" the boy shouted, slamming Bridget against the wall. She hit her head and fell to the ground, clutching it.

"Ram frine, herp her—" There was little he could do without speaking properly, but he was confident Leera could handle Jonathan. She nodded and shot off, quickly tackling the small boy in a whirl of necrophyte robes.

Augum ran to Bridget. "Rou rokay?"

She took her hand away from the top of her head. There was blood on her fingers. They locked eyes, conveying the seriousness of the moment. She swallowed but signaled she was all right. "Come on," she said, allowing him to help her up.

They ran to the struggling pair, and soon the girls had a hold on the boy again. Augum focused through the stabbing pain and once more led the group. The passages snaked this way and that. He avoided one with an obvious floor trap composed of rusted iron stakes, and another with a water pit and a golem. Last thing they needed was more underwater fighting. Finally, he spied a giant slab pierced with holes. It blocked a dimly lit wheat field. Carved into the wall beside the slab was a crude depiction of a warlock making a shoving gesture at the slab.

Augum knew he and Leera did not have the strength to do it, but Bridget, having rested just long enough, might. He pointed at the carving and jerked on her sleeve.

"I'll try," she said. A sliver of blood had run down her forehead and dripped from her nose. She did not seem to notice, and let Leera and Augum handle the boy, who struggled in their grip.

"Let go of me, you brainwashed gutterborn scum!" the boy cried, aiming a punch for Augum's jaw. Luckily Augum caught it and bent his arm back. If the punch had connected …

"Vikari vika—" but the boy wasn't allowed to finish the vicious little necromantic spell as Leera's hand clamped over his mouth.

"BAKA!" Bridget shouted and the slab bounced a little out into the field, leaving a gap the width of a hand.

"Again, Bridge!" Leera said. Behind them, a hiss echoed off the walls, closing in fast.

"BAKA!" Bridget shouted again, screaming after and clutching her head. "Can't … do … more …"

The slab had bounced another couple finger lengths, but not enough for any of them to squeeze through. Augum let Jonathan go, hoping Leera could handle him alone, and raced to it and pushed, but it was like trying to move a mountain. He suspected only arcanery could actually have any effect, and specifically only the Push spell.

Bridget, who had been on her knees, suddenly made a squeak and frantically crawled toward the slab. An oversized claw emerged from around the corner. Soon a massive warped skull with vacant holes for eyes peeked into the passage. When the wraith saw them, it assumed a low attack profile. Its jaw opened and it hissed. Black goop dripped onto the flagstone.

Leera, who had her arm around Jonathan's neck, whipped him around. "Tell it to go away!"

"NO!"

"Tell it to go away or I throw you at it!" She gave him a sharp jerk, fear cracking her voice. "NOW—!"

"All right, all right!"

The wraith bolted forward.

"ADAI!" Jonathan shouted just in time, and the wraith halted mere feet away, its body wavering menacingly over them.

"Necro dodai!" Jonathan pointed firmly. "Onto! Necro onto!"

The wraith watched him with the malevolent expression of something that had been denied a meal, but it steadily retreated, soon disappearing around the corner.

"Take him," Leera said. Bridget and Augum grabbed the boy. Leera stared the slab down, blood dripping from her nose. "This is going to suck." Her shoulders heaved a few times before she shoved at the air before her. "BAKA!" The giant stone slab bounced a few more finger lengths as she collapsed onto Augum's other arm, whimpering and clutching her head.

"I got him, go!" Bridget said.

Augum squeezed through the gap with a groan, then helped a writhing Leera do the same. He had to lay her down so he could help Bridget, who awkwardly slithered through the gap while holding onto Jonathan's torso. But the boy had found a grip—his hands curled around the edge of the slab, forcing them to pull on his legs in a tug of war.

"Let go!" Bridget shrieked.

"NO!"

Suddenly the slab started to return to its position with a grinding sound.

"Let go or it'll squish you!"

"NO—!"

Augum winced as he forced himself to help the situation with Telekinesis. The boy screamed from the strain but finally let go. The three of them collapsed in a gasping heap beside Leera as the slab shut. Augum could hear the wraiths and walkers roving about in the maze, clacking, he assumed, with frustration.

Eventually, after hearing a hiss come a little close for comfort, they got up and trundled along the field, the girls firmly holding the struggling boy's arms. Augum was constantly fighting back the grinding pain of his jaw, which dwarfed the arcane-induced headache. Soon they were in the dimly lit obstacle field. Bridget eyed each obstacle carefully, mumbling to herself.

"Where are you taking me?" Jonathan asked.

No one replied as they hurried along.

"They'll hang you. No, *flay* you alive. Especially you two gutterborn wenches—"

Bridget flinched. "Don't use those horrible words."

"You're not my mother. You're an enemy of the kingdom. Brainwashed villains of the first order—"

"There, that looks like it," Bridget said, nodding at a black pillar on top of which sat a carved stone head with a shaved pate. Before the pillar was a large crimson circle.

"Looks right," Leera said, and they went over to it, half-dragging and half-walking the boy.

"No, you can't—" the boy said, struggling anew.

"I'm sorry but we don't have a choice," Bridget said. "Hold him, Aug."

Augum grabbed the boy as Bridget read the inscription on the pillar.

" 'Memory Wipe. Warning: this obstacle is for advanced warlock use only. Warlocks are advised to be proficient with Mind Armor at the 10th degree or higher. Rune one casts the spell at the 8th degree. Rune two casts the spell at the 10th degree. Rune three casts the spell at the 12th degree'."

There were three gargoyle runes below the inscription.

"It should only wipe out your time here in Antioc," Bridget said.

The boy increased his struggling. "Wait … I'll never tell! Promise!"

Bridget closed her eyes. "I'm so sorry, but we cannot take the risk. There is too much at stake."

"No! I'll hex you, I will!"

She rested a gentle hand on his arm. "Please don't or we'll cast Confusion on you, and the effects might make it much worse. *Please*."

The boy collapsed, exhausted. He gave them each a venomous look. "You're going to hell anyway. All of you. And you'll hang and I'll watch you choke and kick until you are dead."

"Shyneo," Bridget said, lightning up her palm with glowing green ivy as Augum and Leera placed him in the crimson circle. She sniffed but clenched her teeth. "I'm so sorry, Jonathan." She gave Augum and Leera a sorrowful look. "May the Unnameables forgive us," and placed her lit palm over the first rune. It glowed crimson, as did the circle. The boy made a kind of hiccup noise before collapsing.

"Is … is he all right?" Leera asked.

Bridget placed a hand on his neck. "Let's take him to the entrance before the wraiths return," she said, face as troubled as Augum had ever seen it. She and Leera placed his arms around their necks and they dragged Jonathan between them, hurrying as fast as they dared.

"Don't let him see our faces once he wakes up."

The boy woke with a groan not long after Leera said those words. "What … where am I?" His voice sounded even squeakier, and more innocent. "Why am I wearing a necrophyte robe? I'm not a necrophyte yet."

"What's your name and how old are you?" Bridget asked, huffing.

"Jonathan, and I'm twelve, but … how did I get here?"

Augum exchanged a look with the girls. It had worked, although maybe a bit too well. Before, the boy had been thirteen and a necrophyte zealot.

"What's going on? Who are you?"

"I'll explain in a moment," Bridget replied.

They brought him to the large entrance doors just as one of the wraiths found an exit from the maze. It spotted them and began galloping over.

"Hurry," Leera said.

Augum quietly opened one of the doors and peeked through, but there was no one on the other side. He waved them in, then closed the door behind them. They hurried to the nearby portal room, where Bridget lit up the portal to the General Quarters, still keeping her face averted.

"You weren't supposed to be here, Jonathan," she said. "You played around in the obstacle field past closing because you wanted to do more training. You challenged yourself by trying an obstacle too powerful for your degree level."

"I ... I don't understand ... I'm a warlock? So I *did* become a necrophyte—?"

"Tell anyone who finds you that the obstacle you tried is called the Memory Wiper. Goodbye and good luck."

"What? Wait—" but the girls pushed him through the portal.

The story probably wouldn't hold up, Augum realized, but it didn't really matter as long as it gave them enough time to conclude their quest in Antioc.

Bridget staggered away. "What ... what have we done to the poor boy?"

"We'll beat ourselves up after," Leera said, placing her palm on an unmarked portal etching. "Shyneo. Leigh Sparrows. The fountain inside the labyrinth." The portal flared to life. "Well will you look at that, it worked. Come on, you two."

THE LABYRINTH FOUNTAIN

"There are holes in our story so large you can fit a wraith through," Leera muttered to Augum, a sentiment he shared. She was leaning against a wall beside Bridget, comforting her with an arm around her shoulders, her palm lit with a dim watery glow. Augum sat beside Leera, holding hands with her, trying to ignore the throbbing in his head. His jaw had gone numb and his face felt as swollen as an overripe pumpkin.

He curled his fingers tighter around hers. It was small comfort. This whole venture was a complete mess now—who knew what sort of trouble awaited them when they returned to their room to grab the Exot set. And what about Commander Jordan? What if the boy ended up identifying them after all? Could they not have thought of a better solution than wiping his memory?

And then there was tomorrow's duel with Robin, all in the hopes of getting one precious chance to steal the divining rod from Erika. Assuming she would even have it in her possession, of course. And even *if* they were somehow successful, they still needed to make an escape …

He would have laughed at the utter ridiculousness of it all if it weren't for the pain laughing would cause. Unnameables, his broken jaw alone would probably prevent anything from succeeding.

Suddenly he just wanted to go to sleep. The harrowing excitement from the battle had worn off and he felt as drained as a squeezed lemon.

"What have we become?" Bridget gurgled between sobs, head in her hands.

"Probably for the best, if you think about it," Leera replied after a pause. "Honestly? I think you just did him a massive favor. Maybe the boy won't become a necrophyte now."

Bridget sniffed. "I still wiped an *entire year* from a boy's memory. I'll never forgive myself."

Leera sighed. "Yes you will. When Mrs. Stone is standing before us with a smile, you'll forgive yourself. We had no choice. Even trying to get to Klines would have gotten us caught with all those extra guards prowling the halls. No way you could have known the spell would be that strong. Give yourself a break, Bridge."

Bridget scoffed. She looked up at Leera with a red face and wet cheeks. "Stop trying to make me feel better! I took a year's worth of memory away from a thirteen-year-old boy!"

Leera's voice was a whisper. "We *all* did it, Bridge, not just you."

Augum would have chimed in supportively if he could speak, but it wouldn't do much good beating themselves up over it now, not with so much to do, or rather, so much to attempt. His eyes wandered to the fountain before him. He was thirsty and wished it worked. All they needed was one more stupid coin, then they could get inside the Restricted Room. Hopefully there weren't too many guards in there. He wasn't sure he could handle any serious arcanery right now beyond Telekinesis.

"How's your jaw?" Leera asked softly, concern in her eyes.

He shrugged, then wiped the blood from her nose.

She gave a pained smile. "Thanks. You look how I feel."

He smiled reflexively which instantly gave him a bolt of pain. Instead, he smiled with his eyes. His jaw had long swelled past the point of being able to make any intelligible sounds other than moans and grunts.

She leaned her head on his shoulder. "We're a right mess. There better be a healing scroll of some kind in that Restricted Room."

Augum was counting on it. He placed his arm around her shoulders and gave her a light squeeze. He missed her. It was strange, here she was in his arms, but he genuinely missed her. He longed for a quiet fire, doing nothing but reading, his head on her belly as she napped. Maybe there would be the patter of rain on the roof. Maybe he'd have a steaming cup of tea beside him. Maybe Nana would be in the next room studying an ancient scroll. Maybe Bridget too.

He felt old. So much was happening, and it was all so dangerous. How many moments would they have together still? Will they survive this experience? Will he defeat Robin tomorrow, then snatch the divining rod? And for what, so that he may face his father one day, maybe even growing old in the process via the Cron spell? That boy had lost a year of his life, but Augum felt like he and the girls were on the cusp of losing more … a *lot* more.

Never had he wanted to give up more than in that moment, while Bridget quietly wept, and Leera's head was on his shoulder, and his jaw throbbed with every beat of his heart, and the odds so against them. If someone with the power suddenly walked in offering a quiet life in the middle of nowhere for them, he would instantly accept. Why *should* they throw their lives away for a kingdom as brainwashed as that boy?

The answer was hard to hear, but it came nonetheless.

Because others had given their lives in the hopes of the trio vanquishing his father.

And that made him mull things over for some time. Upon further reflection, sure, they might not be perfect, or even close to perfect, or even that intelligent, but they were doing the best with what they had.

Fifteen years old … more like fifty. He snorted, causing blinding, tear-inducing pain.

"You okay?" Leera murmured in sleepy tones, gently squeezing his hand, eyes closed. "Should rest a little while …"

Augum watched as her palm steadily dimmed until going out altogether; listened as Bridget's sniffing slowed; to the low howl of the wind … and rested his eyes, just for a little while …

* * *

It took some time for Augum to wake up. He opened his eyes to see Bridget kneeling before him, shaking him gently, her face long and slightly gaunt.

"Hey," she whispered. "We should go."

He nodded, suddenly aware of the throbbing pain in his jaw again. He would have preferred to keep sleeping. He gently shook Leera awake, who had nuzzled into his side.

"Hmm—? What hour of night is it?" she asked groggily.

"Don't know," Bridget said. "No idea how long we napped for. Maybe a few hours."

"Great," Leera muttered, giving Augum's hand a final squeeze before letting go and glancing around. "One more coin. One more stupid coin. Let's just find the dumbest and easiest puzzle we can." She placed her hands on the edge of the fountain and stretched her calves. Then she froze. "Hey, look at this—" She nodded at the gargoyle on top with its staff and pointing finger. "That coiled snake around the staff, doesn't that mean something?" she asked Bridget. "We saw that somewhere—"

"Healing," Bridget blurted. "The coiled snake, or serpent, is the symbol for healing venom." She pointed at the bald figural pictorials that decorated the sides of the fountain. "And we already know these symbolize the Leyans. Remember the fountain back in Castle Arinthian?" She glanced between them meaningfully. "You know, I do believe this is a healing fountain!"

"Of course!" Leera said, beaming.

Bridget began pacing. "I can't believe we never thought of it—there *had* to be something like that down here, some way for warlocks to be able to heal without seeking out a healer. I mean, look at how dangerous this place is—" She froze and stared at the fountain, tapping her chin. "But how to make it work?"

Augum was already on it, studying the pictorials. Every single one was different, much like the Leyans he had seen in Ley. But they were just standing there, not making any gestures or symbols or anything. No, there had to be something more … He studied the gargoyle, with its staff and outstretched finger. He followed where the finger pointed, but it was only the distant cave-like ceiling. Then he noticed the fingertip itself was dark and blotchy, as if smeared with black oil. He pressed on the tip, but nothing happened. Soon he came across other splotches, also black, but some a very dark brown.

And then it hit him. Blood. They were blood! He gestured at his jaw, making a moaning noise.

"What is it?" Leera asked.

"What are you trying to say, Augum?"

He gestured more firmly, glancing between the two of them. Surely one of them would guess right!

"We have to break the finger?" Leera said with a skeptical look.

He shook his head gently to avoid causing himself pain. He made another noise, gesturing at her nose.

"You have to break my nose? No thanks."

"What do nose and jaw have in common?" Bridget asked herself, frowning. "They're both parts of the body—"

He rolled his eyes. Come on, you two, it's blood! He made slashing gestures at his arms and then made wild indications they simply *had* to interpret as blood spraying.

Leera's face contorted with further confusion. "We hack its head off to make the water flow—? That doesn't sound right at all."

Augum threw up his hands in surrender. He crossed his arms, tapping his foot as he glared at the girls. They exchanged mystified looks.

Suddenly an idea occurred to him. He strode over to Bridget and grabbed her head, finding the wound she had incurred in the maze above.

"Aug, what are you—OW!" She smacked him on the arm. "What'd you do that for!"

Augum wanted to smile—she sounded just like Leera. Instead, he made an apologetic gesture but showed them his bloody finger.

"Ohhhhh," the girls toned at the same time.

He marched to the fountain and touched the gargoyle's finger with the blood. But nothing happened.

This time it was Leera that smacked him. "Jerk—" but then there was a blurp and a gurgle and the fountain spurted to life. Soon clear water trickled down the spiral.

"You're a genius," Leera mumbled.

"I forgive you," Bridget quickly added.

He cupped his hands, scooped up some cold water, and carefully poured it into his mouth and over his face. The effect began immediately. It started with a warm tingling sensation that progressed to a prickling, as if a thousand ants were in his jaw. After a while, it became soothing.

He took a long, satisfied breath, feeling refreshed and energized, then turned to the girls with a grin. "Breaking the finger? Really? You two can be so daft."

They chortled. Soon all three of them were washing like cats. All the cuts, the bangs and bumps and bruises healed.

"Whatever house I end up living in," Leera said, repeatedly smoothing back her wet dyed hair, "has got to have one of these."

Bridget raised a finger. "Actually, healing fountains are some of the rarest—"

"Oh hush, you."

"All right then," Augum said with a smile, feeling more refreshed than he could remember. "You two ready? One last coin."

"One last coin," the girls chorused.

RESTRICTED

The trio found the easiest puzzle they had come across yet—a bunch of randomized sliding stone pieces on a wall that, once put together, formed a gargoyle.

Augum flicked the last coin to Bridget with his thumb. She caught it deftly.

"Look at that," Leera said as they strolled back to the fountain. "Didn't even have to risk our lives for once."

Bridget stopped at the fountain, which had gone dry once more. She nodded at the marble staircase that led to the abyss. Over that abyss was the invisible bridge that led to the secret arcane library. "All right, let's assume the Legion put quite a few new guards in that hall. I'm talking about wraiths, walkers, Legionnaires and maybe even warlocks." She looked them in the eyes. "How do we get past them?"

Leera raised a finger and her mouth opened but then she frowned. "No … never mind, that would definitely get us killed."

Augum flipped his palm casually. "What if we—" but then he frowned too.

"What?" Leera said. "Spit it out. Will it get us killed?"

"I was just thinking we could do some kind of distraction. Lead them into a portal," but he was shaking his head. "It'd never work, I know. They're not dumb enough to leave the entire hall unguarded."

"So it'll get us killed."

He nodded. How in all of Sithesia were they supposed to get past them? Even if all three of them cast Centarro, the odds were still almost remote. That hall was huge and had a lot of ground to cover with nothing to hide behind.

Bridget splayed her hands, one of which was lit with a bright green glow, demanding their attention. "What if one of us fought them from one end of the hall while the other two snuck in behind?" She grimaced, scratched at her nose. "That'll probably get the person killed, won't it?"

"Definitely."

"Yup."

They tossed around a few more ideas, but every single one seemed to end in gruesome death or a capture, which probably also ended in a gruesome death.

Augum stretched his arms, curling his fingers, his wrists, and bending back his shoulders. It felt good, helped clear his head.

"This boring you, Mr. Stone?" Leera asked with an impish grin.

He dismissed her with an idle swat and looked around. "Hey, where's the portal rune that got us here?"

Leera pointed. "It's—" Her finger waved about in the air before dropping. "You know, I have no idea."

"Huh." Augum searched the walls, finally finding an etched oval obscured behind some ivy. "Found it."

"Thought of something?" Bridget asked. She was sitting on the edge of the fountain, elbows on her knees, head resting on her hands.

Augum tapped at the oval, thinking aloud. "What do you suppose cloaked access means?"

"Means we can get in to places without anyone knowing," Leera said. "Obviously."

Bridget jumped off and strode over. "You think that would work? Bypass payment?" She was gazing searchingly at him.

"Just might."

"Worth a try, isn't it?"

Leera elbowed in between them. "Did you two form some kind of secret club you forgot to invite me to?" She waved her hands before their faces. "Hello? Team member asking to be involved here. Anyone want to fill me in?"

Augum had to force himself not to snort a laugh. Instead, he maintained a serious expression, hand on his chin as he stared at the oval. "We'd have to be quiet, just in case."

Bridget followed his lead, maintaining the same thinking posture, complete with hand on her chin. "Yes, and one of us would need to go first." Both of them were doing a superb job of ignoring Leera.

Meanwhile, Leera was giving them serious nods. "Oh, yeah, that would work. I love this plan. WHAT ARE YOU TWO TALKING ABOUT!"

Augum grabbed her and yanked her off her feet, twirling her about while she giggled and laughed.

"Let me go, you dumb brute!"

He kissed her cheek while she struggled in his arms. "We're going to see if the portal will take us right into the Restricted Room, bypassing the Legion *and* having to pay the gargoyle coins."

"Ooooh," she said, still pretending to struggle. "I get it. All right, let go of me, you silly fool." She punched his shoulder. "I hate you."

"No you don't."

"All right, maybe I don't, but that's only because you're so good-looking."

"You two are cute," Bridget said, placing her lit palm over the oval, "but even I sometimes want to gag."

Leera smirked. "Don't worry, Bridgey-poo, we'll find you some handsome necrophyte to convert."

Bridget gnashed her teeth at her. "*Don't* call me that."

"Sorry, you're right, that's reserved for your mystery future boy." She quickly raised her hands. "Only kidding! Don't turn me into cat food."

Bridget, who had taken a stern attack-like posture, kept her eyes narrowed while she turned back to the oval.

"Sheeze," Leera muttered to Augum, "we really *do* have to find her someone just so she can lighten up."

"Here goes. Brie Sparrows. Restricted Room." The portal instantly flared to life, whipping their robes and hair with wind.

"Well I'll be ..." Augum said. "All right, let me go first—"

Bridget shot out her arm. "No. If any one of us is going to get caught or captured, I want it to be me." She gave them a sorrowful smile. "As much as you two make me want to tear my hair out sometimes, I'd never live with myself seeing you torn apart."

Leera's face softened. "Oh, Bridge ..."

"Just be sure to follow right after," Bridget added with a wink. "Here goes nothing—"

"Wait," Leera said. "If it goes where I think it goes, you're going to end up in the vestibule of the Restricted Room. There's a bunch of ... tiny stupid dwarves there, and if they ask you a question and you get it wrong, well, don't be surprised if they make you eat, uh—"

"—stinkroot?"

"Yeah."

"I won't reply until you two come then."

They nodded and readied to leap through the portal after her. Except as soon as Bridget jumped through, the portal closed and Augum only managed to slam into the wall with a grunt.

They had forgotten a simple rule of portal use—*the person that opened the portal goes last.*

Leera scrambled for the oval. "Leigh Sparrows. Restricted Room—"

"Light your palm!"

"Right—shyneo. Leigh Sparrows, Restricted Room."

The portal burst open again and Augum launched himself through. He tumbled to the ground on the other side, Leera rolling into him a moment later.

Bridget was standing before them, a finger over her lips. "Only whisper."

"Hwat si het neacra drow rof larpot?" said a shrill voice that bounced against the marble walls of the vestibule.

Augum glanced up from the dusty floor to see a bunch of small bearded creatures. They were rotund little fellows with old faces and a waxy look to their skin. Each held one kind of root or another. A particularly fat one stood out front, still as a statue except for his moving lips.

"Hwat rea het neacra sdrow rof larpot?"

At least their plan had worked—it appears they had bypassed the gargoyle coin fee, not to mention the Legion.

"That's the kind of gibberish they were spewing last time too," Leera whispered as Augum helped her up. "I think it's some ancient language." She gave the dwarves a wide berth. "Let me tell you, they're vicious little things that won't hesitate to throw you out on your butt after making you eat—"

"We get it, Lee," Bridget said, brows crossed in concentration.

"What a room," Augum whispered. It was different from the others—older, mustier, more menacing. Stone gargoyles perched in the corners, watching with black eyes. Random spikes jutted from the crude masonry walls, as if the whole place was a pit trap.

He glanced at the tall doors behind them. He hoped no one could hear them on the other side, for that is where the guards would be at this very moment. Thankfully, it appears they had a way out—there was a hidden portal rune somewhere here, and all they had to do was find it.

"Hwat rea het neacra sdrow rof larpot?"

"I'm not sure it's a language," Bridget whispered, pacing over to an ancient stone table. Using a finger, she wrote the words into the dusty top.

Augum and Leera came over to study the phrase.

Hwat rea het neacra sdrow rof larpot.

Bridget wrote the word *What* under the first word. "It's an anagram." She paused, then wrote the words *are the*. Leera reached over and added *arcane words for*.

"Portal," Augum whispered, adding in the last word.

" 'What are the arcane words for Portal?' " they quietly read in unison.

"We know this one," Augum said, searching Bridget and Leera's faces. "It's the same words for the portal pillar we used in the Muranians. Starts with ... *portus*, I think?"

Leera squinted. "Yeah ... *portues ea* something ..."

"Portus ea ire itum!" Bridget blurted, and the dwarves shuffled aside, allowing free passage to the door behind them. "Portal is a 17th degree spell," she said to Augum and Leera. "This is going to be interesting," and she cautiously led the way.

Beyond was a cave-like room that smelled of ancient dirt and decaying parchment. It was exceptionally dark, forcing Augum and Leera to light their palms. The shelves were all crudely hewn rock, with books unevenly distributed among them, each spine chained to a ring mooring. The jagged ceiling hung low. Tables were carved right into the rock walls. The whole place almost reminded Augum of a giant termite nest.

"Anyone want to make a bet those come alive?" Leera whispered, shining her palm light at an armored stone golem standing before a shelving unit. There was one before each shelf set, hands splayed in an attack pose.

"I don't think these are training dummies," Augum said, noting the massive stone arms and the blank and angular expressions.

"They look immune to arcanery." Leera kept her distance. "Hope this place comes with instructions because I don't even want to attempt walking by one of those."

Bridget quietly paced from wall to wall, surveying each shelf section. "We need to find the section on scrolls."

Leera froze. "What's that noise?"

"What noise?" Bridget whispered in an urgent tone.

But soon Augum could hear it too—it was a distant clanking and shuffling noise, steadily coming closer. The girls began backing away, but he raised his hand and smiled. "Just wait. I think I know what that is."

A rusted suit of armor soon emerged at the edge of their light. It was full-sized and had a faded gargoyle crest over its heart. A withered blade hung at its hip, and its joints squeaked so loudly Augum was worried it would have the Legion rushing in there any moment.

The suit of armor stopped between two golems. "Guinevere at thy service, mine elegant lord and charmed ladies," it said in an echoing voice. "Librarian and minder to thee Restricted portion of thy ancient library."

"It's like a tall Fentwick, but a woman!" Leera said, approaching cautiously. "I *love* these things." She peeked into the visor. "Yup, nothing in the helmet!"

Guinevere rattled to life and Leera sprang away like a cat. Her voice was sharp and fast. "Hark! I beseech thee to neither tarry nor jest, give airs nor huzzahs, and I prithee thou taketh naught without just payment given in coin."

Augum blinked. "Uh … what?"

"Not quite sure," Bridget replied slowly. "Something about not disturbing others, but also giving payment for … what though?" She raised her voice a little. "How does this all work, Guinevere?"

"Thy voice shall be kept to a licking flame!" Guinevere roared, and the trio took a step back.

Then why are you yelling, Augum wanted to ask, but decided better of it.

"How does this all work, Guinevere?" A cringing Bridget asked in the barest of whispers.

" 'Work', m'lady?"

"Right," Bridget mumbled. "Has to be a simple question. How about this—where is the scroll section?"

"Bequeath I a path, quoth I. Follow me thus, mine esteemed young lord of autumn and divine ladies of spring."

"Aww, how adorable," Leera said, skipping along as Guinevere set a rapid gait. Augum exchanged a brief amused look with Bridget before following, palms lit. Leera accidentally dislodged a book during her jovial bouncing and Guinevere whirled on her, voice an echoing shriek. "Thou durst not disturb thee peace of thine most precious tomes! Warning has thence been given, foul little mischief maker."

Leera, who had shrunk away in alarm, carefully placed the book back on the shelf. "Uh, sorry … sorry about that. Won't do it again, promise." She turned to Augum and Bridget, muttering, "Seems Guinevere's got a bit of a temper."

Bridget gave her a *Just be careful then* look and they resumed following the squeaky suit of ancient animated armor. They passed section after section of large chained books, almost all marked with runic symbols along the spines or written in some archaic tongue.

"I suspect most of these are off-the-book," Bridget whispered to Augum. "The ones that are spells at least."

Augum managed to decipher one thick spine. It was written in an ancient version of the common tongue and labeled with the word *Doppelganger*. The runic symbol for 19 was underneath. "Did you see that—" he said to Bridget, but she was busy scanning the other side of the shelves.

"These are way beyond our degree," she whispered in awed tones, shaking her head. "So advanced …"

"I bet you Mrs. Stone has been here before," Leera said.

Augum pictured Nana spending hours and hours studying these ancient works. He wondered how she was faring. Was she all right? Was she sleeping at this hour of night? Or was she awake, running from the squad of warlocks tasked with chasing after her? He couldn't wait to see her again. The thought made him more determined than ever to succeed tomorrow, which meant they had to get the *right* scroll for the job.

At last they entered a new section of thousands of cubbyholes, each packed with a yellowed parchment scroll and labeled underneath.

Guinevere stopped and creakingly turned to face them. "Mine exquisite young lord and refined budding ladies—thee section on scrolls lies before thee. Henceforth thou shall be mindful of thy wickedness. And worry thou shall not, for each work shall be restored. Thou may unfurl and study at thine will. But hark, for thou shall cast none, but bring with payment thus to Guinevere. So quoth I." She trundled off back the way they had come.

"Did anyone get that?" Augum whispered.

Leera made a face that expressed the same confusion he felt. "Not a word."

"I *think* I understood," Bridget said, watching the armor rattle and disappear into the darkness. "We choose the scroll, bring it to her, and pay for it. We're not allowed to cast them, but we can study them. Oh, and they get replaced eventually, I'm assuming by library warlocks, hence the payment. Maybe this place doubles as some kind of ancient shop, I don't know."

"She'll take gargoyle coins though, right?" Leera asked.

"Not sure." Bridget began scanning the shelves.

Augum saw neatly-written labels, each with two numbers, one in the bottom left corner and the other in the bottom right. But none of the spells looked familiar, until he ran across one he finally recognized.

"Found Slam," he said. "Left number is two—"

"Corresponding to the degree," Bridget said.

"And the right number is twenty."

"That … that can't mean we have to pay *twenty gargoyle coins*, can it?" Leera asked.

"Let's find out." Augum carefully removed the scroll and marched it back down the aisle, the girls following.

"How much for this scroll?" he asked upon finding Guinevere micro-adjusting the books they had walked by earlier.

"For thee 2nd degree spell of Slam thou shalt pay twenty coin of the gargoyle."

The trio groaned.

"Wait, this is a library," Bridget whispered.

Leera flashed her an acerbic look. "A library? Really?" She glanced around theatrically. "What in Sithesia gave you that idea?"

Bridget ignored her. "Guinevere, what are the borrow rates for study?"

"Thy 1st to thy 5th degrees beg one gargoyle coin. Thy 6th to thy 10th degrees beg three gargoyle coins. Thy 11th to thy 15th degrees beg seven gargoyle coins. Thy 16th to thy 20th degrees beg ten gargoyle coins. Thou may borrow up to a tenday and must theretofore return thy scroll with nary blight to condition."

Leera idly drew at the ground with a toe. "And … what happens if we, you know, *accidentally* use one?"

"A most witless reckoning thee caster shalt behold!"

The trio exchanged dark looks.

"Thanks, Guinevere," Augum said.

"At your service, mine youthful lord and fledgling ladies."

They made their way back to the scroll section.

Leera sighed. "What are we looking for again?"

Bridget was already tracing the labels with a finger. "Group Teleport. It's 17th degree so it'll cost all ten coin."

"Lucky we didn't have to pay the entrance fee," Augum said, scanning the labels. He couldn't imagine trying to labor over finding ten more coins … or attempting to steal the scroll. Who knew what might happen then.

The shelves were long and went from floor to ceiling, taking quite some time to navigate.

"Found something similar to Group Teleport," Augum said at last, tapping a cubby near the ceiling. "Portal. 17th degree."

Bridget strode over. "That might actually work better."

"One hundred and seventy coins," Leera said. "Imagine spending a month getting that coin together? Assuming you even survived down there …"

Augum slowly withdrew the scroll. "Now we need a plan."

"I'll cast it if I have to," Leera said. "I don't care what happens."

Bridget took the scroll from him. "No, I'm going to cast it, and I don't want to hear a single word otherwise."

"What if, you know …" Leera left the rest unsaid.

"I'll risk it. Now sit, we have a lot to discuss and plan."

"Here? Now?"

Bridget shrugged. "Might as well."

PREPARATIONS

Sometime in the wee hours of the morning, as the trio sat cross-legged on the dusty floor, Augum ran his fingers through his hair and expelled a tired breath.

"Sounds crazier than ever," he muttered.

They had spent countless hours studying the scroll and coming up with a detailed plan. They were going to head back to their room to get some sleep, during which Bridget would tune to the Exot orb. Then the trio would have a final meeting with Malaika and Charissa; contact Caireen Lavo using the Exot orb; get to the tournament in time, where the girls would strategically position themselves in the arena tunnel; Augum would defeat Robin; Bridget would cast the Portal spell in a timely manner; and most daringly, as the trophy was being presented to Augum by Erika Scarson, he was to steal the divining rod. All this assumed they got out of the Arcane library undiscovered, that Bridget was successful in casting the Portal spell, and that Augum could beat Robin and snatch the divining rod before somehow getting to the portal, avoiding, of course, getting blown to smithereens by every warlock in the entire arena.

"Just toss me into a pit with every wraith in the kingdom," Augum added. "I think I'd stand better odds."

"We take it one step at a time," Bridget said.

He raised a finger. "No, wait, I have a better idea. You two shove me into the abyss." He dropped his finger, nodding in a satisfied manner.

The girls stared at him blankly, before Leera cracked up giggling.

"All right, Aug," Bridget said, "I think everyone here understands how daring this plan is. Just remember, we'll have the Exot orb and rings, so we'll be able to communicate. If circumstances change, we change with them."

Augum rubbed his face, something he'd been doing a lot lately. "I can write the headline in the Herald for you now. 'Idiot tries to be hero. Gets slaughtered.' "

Leera placed her arm around his neck and dragged him over with an elbow, so that he lay in her lap. "Since when did you become so cynical?"

"Since the odds went from *improbable* to *impossible*." He idly played with her hand. "How am I going to prevent Robin from recognizing me?" Let alone defeat the murdering knave …

Bridget, whose head was resting on her hands, suddenly brightened. "You don't."

Augum sat up as he and Leera stared at her with identical dumbfounded expressions.

Bridget continued smiling. "Hear me out." She accented her points with open palms. "You *reveal* to everyone in that arena that you are Augum Stone, and you're there to claim the honor of the kingdom.

Leera reached over to her. "Let me feel your forehead, I think you're coming down with a vicious fever—"

Bridget swatted her off. "I'm serious here! Think about it—they're going to find out anyway. They *won't* stop Augum, not unless they want to look weak in front of the whole kingdom." She paused to look between them. "This is the final of the most prestigious warlock tournament in Solia, maybe all of Sithesia. Robin Scarson, the most famous necrophyte in the kingdom versus Augum Stone, the *infamous* villain, and the Lord of the Legion's own wayward son. The Legion will want to prove their necromancy could best the old arcanery. It would send a strong message to everyone if Augum lost publicly, that's why they will let him fight—!"

Bridget leaned forward. "But here's the trick. If Augum wins, they'd also *have* to let him claim his prize, because there's one thing about the crowd—they want to see an honorable end. They want order. Most importantly, the Legion will want to look legitimate." She took a long breath. "You can stop looking at me like I've lost my mind."

Leera blinked. "I foresee a future in politics for you."

Bridget wrinkled her nose as if a rotten stench had entered the room. "Euch."

Augum resumed rubbing his face, which seemed to help him think.

Bridget prodded him with a finger. "Thoughts?"

"I don't know … I just don't know."

"Tell you what. See how you feel in the moment."

Augum's brows rose. " 'In the moment'?"

"Yeah." Bridget stood, dusted herself off. She extended her hands to them both, hauling them up. Then she fixed her gaze firmly on Augum. "You stood before the entire Henawa tribe and spoke out to save a man who once repeatedly beat you with his belt, giving you all those scars." She picked up the Portal scroll. "Now replace that tribe with an entire kingdom," and she padded off.

Augum and Leera gaped.

"I swear she has, like, Attyla the Mighty blood in her or something," Leera muttered.

"That wouldn't surprise me in the least. But ... I'm worried about her."

"The scroll?"

He nodded. What if it killed her? Even the thought of it made him want to throw up.

"I'm worried too." Her hand found his, squeezing tightly. "Come on."

* * *

"A tenday thou shalt have, not a moment more," Guinevere finished saying to Bridget after she was paid all ten of their gargoyle coins.

"Right," Bridget said, scroll tucked under her arm. "Let's get back to our room."

They returned to the vestibule. The dwarves allowed them passage by shuffling aside.

"You'd think they'd have something more menacing guarding the Restricted Room," Leera said, skipping by the lead dwarf holding the stinkroot. "Not going to get me a second time, you little fiend," she hissed at it.

"Hoods up." Bridget awkwardly stuffed the scroll under her robe then placed her lit hand on the etched oval. "Brie Sparrows. General Quarters." The portal ripped to life. She gestured grandly. "After you."

Augum went first. He came out on the other side—and slammed right into the back of a Legion soldier with a shaved head.

"What the—" The soldier turned in surprise and Augum instantly recognized him—he was the lieutenant that had led them to that necrophyte meeting in the Training Room.

"The Hood—" the lieutenant said in surprise, high cheekbones hardening. "Why are you up and about? You know there's a curfew, Necrophyte!"

A moment later, Leera and Bridget stumbled out of the portal, which closed behind them.

"Three of you—? Where did you come—" The lieutenant froze as he spotted something at Bridget's feet. Augum saw what he was looking at—the scroll had fallen out of her robe and was lying on the floor.

"It was you—" The soldier glanced at the three of them as if seeing them anew. "It was you who slew the wraiths …!" He drew his Dreadnought long sword, which immediately burst with flame. "Don't you try anything, this is a brand new—"

Augum felt his four rings flare around his arm. "Disablo!" and the sword twirled out of the man's hand, clanging to the ground and instantly snuffing out.

The lieutenant stared at it dumbly.

"Shyneo!" Augum called, slapping the oval engraving, speaking quickly. "Augustus Westwood. Labyrinth." The portal opened. He shot a look at the girls, who had already positioned themselves on the other side of the Legionnaire.

The lieutenant retrieved his blade. "You'll never get away—"

"BAKA!" the girls chorused, and the man was sent flying through the portal. Augum let go of the oval and a moment later it disappeared.

They froze, listening, but no other sound came, no portal opened.

"He's not a warlock," Augum whispered. "I remember in the arena—he described himself as an *Ordinary*."

"Then he'll have a hard time finding his way out of the labyrinth," Leera said.

Augum gave her a grave look. "Unless he knows how to use portals and actually manages to find a portal rune."

"Not in total darkness he won't," Leera said. "He can't cast Shine, remember?"

Bridget secured the scroll. "It's too dangerous for us to sleep here. We should evacuate as soon as the drawbridge is raised."

Leera shook her head. "But if Augum doesn't get sleep—if none of us do—we've got no chance. *None*. You know that."

"Not to mention I won't be tuned to the Exot orb," Bridget muttered. "You're right."

"Well we can't stay here," Augum said. "Let's get the Exot orb and make a decision then." What if it had been discovered? But hadn't Bridget cast Object Alarm on it? Regardless, he tried not to think about the consequences of walking into a trap. It was a pattern of late, trying not to think about stuff that *might* happen.

They walked as fast as they dared down the dimly lit corridor, passing room after room.

"Heads up," Leera whispered, tightening her hood. A patrolling gray-robed attendant strode their way.

The man stopped in front of them. "And why might you be out of your rooms? Surely you are aware of the strict curfew."

"We wanted to squeeze in some training," Leera blurted. "This is 'The Hood' and he has the finals coming up against Robin Scarson. Some grumpy lieutenant told us to turn right around and go back to our room, so that's where we're going."

The attendant glanced at Augum. "Ah, that explains the hoods. Well as much as I dislike that lieutenant fellow, I dare say he was right—you cannot train at this hour." He gave a wistful sigh. "At one time the library was open to such things. That time has passed. Protocol demands I march you straight to the constabulary." He dropped his voice to a whisper and leaned forward. "But I would much rather see you beat that … evil snob."

Augum gave a firm nod. "I'm certainly going to try, sir."

"Come, I shall escort you to your room."

"Thank you, sir."

"Most welcome, just do not let me or anyone catch you about before the seventh morning bell, as there have been … mishaps. Anyhow, that is only three hours away. Then you can train your hearts out."

"Yes, sir."

The attendant followed them to their room. "Good luck tomorrow."

"Thank you," Leera said, quietly closing the door after him.

The trio exhaled. The torchlight of the city filtered through the dark window, throwing dim light against the ceiling.

Charissa sat up in bed. "Who is it?"

"Just us," Augum said.

Bridget withdrew the scroll, placed it on a table, and kneeled beside the bed. "Still here," she said in a relieved voice, carefully dragging the pine box out from under the bed.

Malaika got up and rushed over to Augum, trailing the blanket she had wrapped herself in. "Where have you been—? We were so worried! The guards are like bees in the corridors—" She reached out to him, only to have her hand smacked away by Leera.

Malaika recoiled. "I was just—"

"You were just nothing," Leera snapped, glaring.

Augum forgot they had a fight earlier that evening, resulting in Leera getting banned from the Supper Hall. Last thing he wanted was drama at this point. There were important issues to discuss.

"We have to talk," he said.

Malaika swallowed. "What about?"

"We're all in a lot of danger," Bridget said, striding over with the box.

"What's that?" Charissa asked.

"Soon as they raise the drawbridge, you need to flee the city," Augum said, hoping to distract her. The less she knew the better. "It's urgent."

Malaika crossed her arms. "Excuse me, but we're not going anywhere."

"Excuse *me*," Leera said, crossing her arms too, "but you're leaving first thing."

Malaika narrowed her eyes. "You don't have the right to boss us around. We do and go where we please."

Charissa joined her friend by her side, wrapped in a blanket too. "Just because you're a warlock doesn't give you the right to bully us!"

"I wasn't—"

A tired-looking Bridget stepped between them. "Please, Malaika, you're in great danger. Both of you are. You need to leave as soon as possible."

"What about our clothes?" Charissa asked, gesturing at the giant pile. "You're going to—" She made an awkward waving gesture. "—magic them back to Milham for us, right?"

"We're not going to 'magic' anything for you," Leera said through gritted teeth.

Bridget shifted the box under her arm so she could place a gentle hand on Leera's shoulder. "Give us a moment, Lee."

Leera threw up her hands. "Ugh," and marched to the window, muttering to herself.

Bridget gave Augum a look that meant he should join her.

"Excuse me," he said, and strode to Leera, necrophyte robe rustling softly along the carpet.

"If anyone's going to get us killed," Leera grumbled, staring out at the twinkling city, "it's those two morons."

He placed his arm around her waist. "Just take it easy. We'll get through this."

She leaned against him, whispering, "I'm so tired."

"I know. So am I."

They listened as Bridget quietly spoke with Malaika and Charissa.

"That's. Not. Fair!" Charissa said, accenting each word with a stomp of her foot.

"Please, it's for everyone's good," Augum overheard Bridget saying.

Leera was about to turn to say something, but Augum stopped her. "Leave them to it."

"Fine, I'll let Attyla handle this one," she muttered.

The corner of Augum's mouth curved upward. Behind them, the argument continued, until—

"All right, we get it!" Malaika finally said.

"Yeah, shut up already—" Charissa added.

Leera grumbled she was about to summon her elemental. It took a lot to keep her from whipping around and following through on the threat.

"I'm sorry you feel that way," Bridget said. "Will you at least tell us about what you've learned—"

"Are you kidding?" Charissa turned her back on Bridget and jumped into her bed. "Leave us alone."

Malaika scoffed. "You want us to help you, after all this? You don't even appreciate what we've done for you! You have *no idea* how hard we've worked to get you information!"

"Yeah!" Charissa added from the bed. "No appreciation!"

Malaika flicked her wrist at the clothes. "Look at all of Daddy's money that you're wasting! Do you know how hard he worked for it?"

Leera broke free of Augum's embrace. "No one asked you to buy clothes, you stupid—"

"SHUT UP!" Malaika yelled at Leera. "I'm so *sick* of you!" She flashed Augum a mournful look. "All of you."

Bridget pinched the bridge of her nose and closed her eyes. "I'm sorry, I can't handle this, I'm just too tired. Can we talk about it tomorrow?"

Malaika stabbed at Bridget's chest with a finger. "You can go to hell for all I care," and she twirled away and stomped to bed.

Bridget stood there, barely visible in the dim light. Eventually she padded over to the window, clutching the box as if it was all she had left in the world. She glanced past Augum and Leera at the silent city.

"They said they'd leave," she murmured, "but I don't believe them. I have a bad feeling they'll get caught after the reveal. They've been seen with us in the Supper Hall and on the streets. Even *if* they don't get caught, someone might figure out where they're from. We're in trouble."

"They're not going to do anything of the sort—" Leera said through gritted teeth, but Augum and Bridget stopped her from starting the argument anew, or turning them into Leera's personal practice dummies.

"Let him talk to her," Bridget said, still holding her and nodding at Augum. "He's the only one they'll listen to."

Leera's jaw flexed.

Bridget drew Leera a little closer, voice a bare whisper. "We *need* to know about that trophy presentation. We *need* to know as much as possible. Lee, it's important."

Leera's shoulders slumped. She nodded at Augum. "See what you can do."

Augum sighed heavily. He didn't want to talk to Malaika or Charissa. He'd prefer to have nothing to do with them. Ever. Not after all those ridiculous, manipulative antics. But he straightened his robe and paced over, taking a seat cross-legged on the floor between Malaika and Charissa's beds. They had removed the folding divider between them, as best friends do.

"Can I talk to you a moment?" he asked Malaika softly. He chanced a peek at Bridget and Leera, but they were talking to each other in low tones by the windowsill, ignoring them.

"What do you want?" Malaika blurted in a shaky voice, back turned away. It was then Augum realized she was crying, and his stomach sank. Great, this is the last thing he wanted to deal with right now. Stupid, pointless drama …

"Hey, it'll be all right," he said. "We *do* appreciate what you've done for us, we really do, we're just … really, *really* tired."

Malaika was shaking her head. "You have no idea how much we've learned, the risks we took."

"Then … can you give me an idea?"

She turned to face him, ebony face wet with tears. "Why, so you can tell us to go away after? And just … *throw* those clothes out? So what if we don't want to look poor—?"

Augum rubbed his face. Clothes. Stupid. Clothes. The kingdom was in peril, they were about to risk their lives in the most foolhardy plan ever concocted in Sithesia's history, and they were discussing a pile of clothes. He wanted to keep rubbing his face until sleep came. He wished he could just rub all this craziness away.

"I'm going to be in the biggest fight of my life tomorrow," he said through his hands. "I don't know how it's going to go. Probably not well, to be honest." He glanced up at her. "But if I win … there's a four hundred gold coin prize. If you leave first thing, and *if* I win, I'll give all the money to your father."

Malaika opened her mouth to say something but just froze. Finally, "You'd … you'd do that?"

"Of course." *If* he lived.

She sat up, whispering, "Give me your hand."

He almost groaned—he didn't want her touching him. But he knew that if he didn't play along, she might not tell him what they so desperately needed to know. He tentatively gave her his hand, and she clasped it between her own.

"Brave Augum Stone. Know this—Erika Scarson is going to have the divining rod tomorrow—"

His heart did that excited flip thing. Thank the Unnameables!

"—and the trophy ceremony is going to be held right after your fight on the judge's platform, *with the loser in attendance*."

That meant he could lose the fight and still snatch the divining rod! Yes! There was a chance now!

Malaika sighed, closed her eyes. "One last thing. Your father—"

"—is going to be there," he finished, slipping his hand from hers. His mouth went sand dry. Somehow he knew it, but didn't want to admit the possibility to himself.

Malaika bit her lip. "He'll be the one presenting the trophy. He'll be surrounded by something called the 'Red Guard' or whatever, not to mention a whole bunch of warlocks." Her hands went to his shoulders and she squeezed. "Don't go. Don't do it. *Please*. You'll die, I know you will—"

He took her hands off his shoulders. "Thank you for everything." He stood up. "Will you leave first thing? Please?"

She withdrew from him, stared at the floor. "I … I wish you'd let us watch …"

"*Please* …"

She wiped her eyes with a finger. At last, she nodded. "I'll go."

"Promise?"

"Promise."

"Thank you," he whispered. "Thank you …" and quietly paced away.

ANTIOC, DAY FIVE

It was a tremendous risk sleeping in their room, yet they were simply too tired to do otherwise. Augum was the first to wake. Malaika and Charissa were gone, but most of their clothing pile remained. He noticed they also left their necrophyte robes behind—a smart move, all things considering. They would be safer looking like normal people.

He quietly padded over to the washbasin and splashed cold water on his face. Then he strode to the window as Bridget and Leera slept on, entangled in blankets.

The biggest day in his life to date was windy and dark. The clouds hung low, brooding. He could feel the tension of the city below in the common folk as they hurried this way and that, busy ants trying to avoid their doom. Or maybe that's how he felt about himself …

His eyes flicked to the arena. Crowds clapped to a performance brimming with fire dancers. That meant it was past the first afternoon bell. Soon the finals of the 1st degree would begin. There would be ten duels today. Ten trophies. Ten degrees. He was fourth up, and his heart was already buzzing in that nervous and all-too-familiar way. They would have to get going soon.

But not just yet …

Augum sat on the window ledge, back against the thick wall. He removed his birthday chain and placed it between his teeth. It grounded him, made him remember people cared about him.

Malaika was right. He should turn away. The odds of snatching the divining rod—let alone getting out of there without being captured or killed—were remote at best. He knew that. The girls knew it.

He sighed and drew his legs in, placing his chin on his knees. Yet so much rode on this day, so very much. And he dared to hope, for it might—just *might*—turn the tide. If he could only beat Robin somehow, then … yes, what happened next, how he behaved himself, how he reacted, would give him that precious chance he needed to do one desperate maneuver, the one maneuver he was truly banking on.

But would it work …?

Of course, now that he knew the loser stood on the platform as well, as long as he survived the duel, he should have a chance, no matter how remote. Although what it meant for the Resistance was another matter. And then there was the *other* question … should he reveal his identity? And if so, when? See how you feel in the moment, Bridget had said … see how you feel in the moment.

"Hey," came a whisper.

Augum turned to see Bridget sleepily shuffle over, clutching the Exot orb. He adjusted to sit cross-legged again. She slumped across from him in the windowsill, eyes puffy.

"You like chewing on that thing, huh?" she said, rubbing her face with the back of her wrist.

"Helps me think." He tucked the necklace away, whispering, "She still asleep?"

Bridget nodded, swallowed, pulled her legs in. "I slept terribly."

"Me too." More like tossed and turned. How he longed for an uninterrupted night's sleep without worry or fear …

She placed her chin on her knees. "I dreamed I lived in the gargoyle hut on some empty prairie. I was alone. So terribly alone. Missed you guys so much."

Augum shuddered recalling that experience. "We're right here."

"I can still hear the shutter thunking …" She turned her head toward the dark window. "I know you'll take care of her if something happened to me."

"Nothing will happen to you a healer won't be able to fix."

She patronized him with a half-smile. She was right of course—there were no available healers. Any healing counted on Mrs. Stone.

"It's just a scroll from a library," he added. An ancient library with dangerous obstacles that sometimes killed young warlocks.

She said nothing.

He gently drew her in for a hug. "It'll be fine, Attyla."

"Hmm?"

"Oh, Lee and I think you might have Attyla the Mighty blood in you."

She snorted. "Shut up," and sat back. She took a long breath and exhaled slowly. He had never seen her look as tired and worn out as she did then—her dyed black hair was tangled and frizzy, eyes half closed, face pale.

"Promise me something," she whispered.

"Anything."

"I know you can be proud. I know you can be angry. I know that you still want vengeance for Mya, for the iron room, for Hangman's Rock—and everything else. And I know you want to beat Robin for the kingdom's sake." She brushed aside a lock of hair, curling it around her ear like she used to back when she cared more about how she looked. "But, if you don't think you can beat him—" She leaned forward, placing a hand on his right knee. "*Bend the knee*. You'll still get up on that platform. You'll still have your shot at the rod."

This time it was him that did not reply.

"You promise me that, Aug."

He watched her a moment, but eventually nodded. "I promise."

She sat back, glanced out the window. "I guess we both know the odds anyway."

He nodded again. It's all he thought about. Their odds and how to improve them.

"We've been through a lot together, haven't we?"

He smiled. "That's an understatement."

A thoughtful silence passed between them.

Leera suddenly sat up in bed with a yelp.

"You all right?" Bridget asked.

Leera glanced over with a puzzled look as if she didn't know who they were. "Nightmare. You don't want to know." She dragged herself out of bed and thumped over, melting into Augum's arms. "Can we just stay here forever?" she mumbled sleepily.

He smiled as he stroked her dyed brown hair. It will be nice to see it raven again, but then, she looked beautiful to him regardless.

"Think the tuning worked?" he asked, nodding at the small Exot orb.

The Dreadnought steel orb lifted telekinetically from Bridget's hand to float before her face. She raised an eyebrow. "Let's find out." She snatched it and jumped off the windowsill, grabbed the finely carved pine box, and withdrew two rings, tossing them to Augum. He put his on first, then, with an amused grin, took Leera's hand and slipped the other on her finger.

Leera placed her arm on her forehead. "Oh, fairest Augum Stone," she said in a ridiculous misty accent, "however could I thank thee? You ought not to have, for I am nothing but an innocent—"

"Shut up—" he said, laughing while gently shoving her off him.

"Well, I never," she tutted, hands on her hips.

"All right, hit us with it," Augum said to Bridget.

"Here goes nothing." Bridget lifted the small orb to her lips. "Contact Augum Stone."

He frowned as there was a momentary fizzing buzz in his head.

"Did it work?" she asked. Her voice came from her lips but also sounded in his head. It made him jump.

"Seems it worked," Leera said, watching his reaction. "Let me try—contact Bridget Burns. Hi, Bridget!"

The fuzzy hum in Augum's brain disappeared. "Transmission ends when someone else cuts in."

"Makes sense." Bridget turned to Leera. "And you have to speak *into* the ring."

Leera placed her lips close to the Dreadnought steel ring. "Contact Bridget Burns. Hi, Bridget."

"There you go."

Leera startled. "Whoa, I heard you in my head at the same time! Neat, it's like an upgraded Orb of Orion."

"Cease contact," Bridget said into the orb, and she went on to remind them of some of the other qualities of the Exot set.

"Oh, almost forgot," Augum said, placing the ring to his lips. "Contact Caireen Lavo—Caireen, it's Augum," but there was no response.

"Only the orb bearer can contact other rings," Bridget said. She put her lips to the orb. "Contact Caireen Lavo. Hello, Caireen, can you hear me? It's a friend of Augum's. Reply into the ring." She smiled, took her lips away from the orb, whispering, "She's quite startled."

"I can imagine," Leera muttered. "Hearing a voice suddenly pop into your head might make you think you'd gone mad."

"No, the other one—Bridget," Bridget said into the orb. "Can you come to room 1099?" She nodded. "Good, see you soon. Oh—you wouldn't happen to have a rucksack, would you? Great—cease contact," and put down the orb. "Caireen's on her way. She was getting worried something happened to us. Sounds excited to help."

Soon a soft knock came at the door. Augum strode over as the girls stood. He opened the door and his former opponent skirted inside, giant bush of orange hair bouncing. She wore a tan cloth garment that wrapped around one shoulder.

"Hi," she said sheepishly, giving them all a small wave.

"Caireen, meet Bridget and Leera."

Caireen extended a slender dark-skinned hand and smiled. "I am very honored. You have no idea."

"Pleasure," Bridget and Leera said, taking her hand.

"Oh, here—" Caireen handed Bridget an empty rucksack. "As requested." Her orange eyes flicked between the girls. "My parents died the same way as yours. I just want to say that you three are heroes in my homeland. And I can see why. You are very brave. It means more to people than you can possibly know." She adjusted her wild orange hair while the trio exchanged awkward and shy looks. "I'll do anything to help the Resistance. Anything."

"Thank you, your help means a lot to us and is badly needed," Bridget said, taking Caireen by the elbow and walking her to the window. "We don't have much time until we have to go. This is what we're going to need from you …"

THE ROAR OF THE ARENA

Caireen left first as they did not want her to be seen with them. Not long after, Bridget stuffed the Portal scroll and the Exot box (minus the orb and the three rings of course) into the rucksack, and the trio departed, leaving the pile of clothes where it lay. They kept silent in the corridor, their hoods drawn, as attendants and necrophytes alike hurried to the portal room, eager to catch the finals.

"D'you hear a Legion lieutenant went missing too?" a pale necrophyte girl asked an ebony-skinned boy as they stood in line waiting to use a portal. The line was so long it snaked out into the corridor.

"Whatever's been going on is giving me the heebies," the boy answered. "And that kid who had his mind wiped?"

"He was just being dumb, I don't think that had anything to do with it. That wraith getting slaughtered in the restricted area though … now *that's* creepy. Maybe it was the gargoyle ghosts of the library."

The boy shrugged. "They're saying it could be insurgents. Either that or it's sabotage or something. I'll ask Commander Jordan."

"I wouldn't talk to him right now, he's mad as a walker."

"Oh, right, the orb set. He's in trouble."

"You know what I think?"

"What?"

The girl leaned closer to whisper. "I think it's *her*."

"No way, the tracking party would've found her."

"Maybe, maybe not. Maybe she found a way around it, who knows." She gave a mysterious smile. "Or maybe Augum Stone was here last night."

"Pfft." The boy shook his head. "Besides, I hear they've caught her already down south."

"Caught who?" Augum blurted, unable to help himself.

The boy and girl turned and their eyes went wide. "The Hood!" they chorused.

The whole line turned to gawk and murmur excitedly, but Augum didn't care. Had Nana been captured? No, it couldn't be.

"Who—?" he repeated urgently.

"The crone of course," the boy said. "Heard she got captured."

Augum exchanged looks with Bridget and Leera.

"Ain't true," said the girl, "heard she got captured *but escaped*. She's a wily one."

"Yup, she escaped," said an older boy further up the line. He casually wiggled his fingers in the air, one of which had an Exot ring on it. "Just got word from my commander."

"Oh," the boy said. "Too bad."

Augum breathed a quiet sigh of relief.

"Can I have your autograph?" the girl asked, digging in her rucksack and retrieving a colorful quill and ink bottle.

The boy rolled his eyes. "Lines moving, you ain't got time."

She used Telekinesis to hover the ink bottle while she dipped the quill into it. She thrust a little book at Augum. "Right here, in my journal please."

Augum awkwardly took the quill. "Here?"

"Yes, right there. My name is Maggie."

"Uh, okay …" He scribbled something and signed underneath.

She yanked it from him and read it. " 'Hi Maggie'? Couldn't have written something more—" She frowned. "Hey, you signed it as Augum Stone! What in the—" but she was suddenly yanked by the boy into the portal, held open by a bored-looking attendant.

Augum felt a cold flush. Oops. There was no time to do anything about it as they were next in line and the attendant was waving them through. The trio jumped in.

"He likes to jest like that," Leera said quickly on the other side, shoving Augum past the boy and girl and out into the library entrance hall. "Nice one," she muttered.

Bridget gave him a *Be more careful* look as they strode as fast as they dared out of the library and over the drawbridge. Augum took one last glance back at the majestic converted castle, wondering if he'd live to see it again.

Commoners milled in the streets. Bridget stopped at a stall and grabbed some food with the last dregs of her money—stringy hot beef on bread and a skin of water, but Augum could barely eat. His whole body buzzed nervously. It was like he was a swarm of bees.

After eating, "Contact Caireen Lavo," Bridget whispered into her sleeve, in which she clutched the Exot orb. "Are you in position yet?" She paused to listen to the reply. "How's it looking?" Another pause. "All right, we'll talk soon. Cease contact." She glanced about as they marched on. "Place is brimming with guards," she said in an undertone.

"Good luck, Hood!" someone nearby called, one of many shout-outs Augum received as they walked the cobbled streets.

"Avenge the girl!"

"Kill that swine!"

And so on. Augum tilted his head in acknowledgment of each one, but his thoughts were already focusing on the battle. He mentally ran through his spells, his tactics, everything they had practiced the night before in the Training Cavern, and of course, *the plan*.

They heard the great arena before seeing it. The people stomped in the stands to the pounding of a drum. A chant boomed over the city. "LO-SERS SHALL! BEND THE KNEE! WI-NNERS FIND! ETER-NI-TY!"

Soon they were at the entrance where a burly attendant shouted, "That's The Hood! Let him by, you hear!" He gestured with giant hairy hands. "I said, move aside, you peasant loaves, he has to fight soon—"

The crowd slowly parted for them to pass.

"So sorry," Bridget kept saying. "Excuse us. Sorry. Hi, sorry."

Leera just plowed forward with elbows out, declaring, "Coming through! Move it, people—"

Augum followed in a daze, still trying to go over his spells. Yet it was difficult to focus. Nearby, the stands shook as the crowd roared. Combat was underway. He could barely breathe. His hands shook.

Bridget paid the three silvers and they were admitted inside.

"He's late, bring him here!" a stubby gray-robed attendant called, which was convenient because the guards waved the trio by without searching them. Everyone else was searched for some reason.

"Get to the dressing room as soon as you can, I'll sign you in."

"What fight is this?" Bridget asked the attendant as Giovanni's smooth voice echoed over the arena, commentating on the fight in sharp bursts.

"3rd degree finals." The attendant nodded at Augum. "He's fighting next. Why in Sithesia did you not come earlier?"

"Sorry, we slept in."

The man snorted as he impatiently waved them along.

The trio shuffled by the stands but as planned, stopped to study the situation. The arena was decorated with colorful streamers and banners that fluttered in the chill wind alongside countless Legion flags. Dark and brooding clouds slid by silently overhead. The judge's platform had been extended, and a small podium added for presentations. Eight trophies were left, each a golden warlock figure reaching skyward. Legion guards were posted everywhere, including longbow archers with sharp crested helms.

Bridget was surreptitiously talking into her sleeve, inaudible over the roaring crowd. In the center, two combatants tussled, each attack met with a wave of boos or cheers. Giovanni fluttered around them like a hummingbird, commenting on the battle. The arena was one great living entity, moving with the flow of combat.

Augum studied the judge's podium. There were a number of people standing on it watching the fight, only three of whom he could make out properly: Erika Scarson, wearing a red velvet robe and oversized earrings, a patronizing smirk on her heavily painted face; Vulica Vaneek, the ebony-skinned head examiner at the Antioc library, wearing a satin green robe and standing with arms crossed; and Martus the Black, Headmaster of the

Canterran Academy of Iron, glaring with his coal eyes, bald pate reflecting torchlight. Not far behind them, Augum could make out towering figures wearing crimson armor, and his hands went clammy.

The Red Guard. His father, the Lord of the Legion, was here somewhere. Part of him suddenly feared his father knew he was here. Maybe he was watching him in that moment, studying him. He knew it was irrational, but couldn't help the thought from making him shudder.

Bridget tugged on Augum's sleeve and gave him a meaningful look before gesturing to follow. He nervously played with the reflecting prism in his pocket as they made their way down some steps, past a Legion guard who nodded at The Hood, through a doorway, and on into a dingy hall that would eventually lead them to the dressing room.

They stopped a little ways down the dim and deserted corridor. Dust fell from the ceiling as the stands shook with muted roars.

"Now remember," Bridget whispered, "only reach for the rod once we have the portal up, and not until then. Leave the guards to us."

"Bridget will be in your head coaching," Leera added, squeezing his hand. "While Caireen and I watch your back."

"And don't use up all your arcane stamina either," Bridget added. "Save some of it for after." The girls were practically talking over each other by that point.

"And no Centarro unless—"

"And remember your promise—"

"—all right already." Augum sighed, placing a hand on each of their shoulders. "I got it, you two." He couldn't show them how truly scared he was though, how heavy his insides felt.

They swallowed but nodded. He could see the fear in their eyes. He could feel it in the slight trembling of their bodies. He forced a smile. "This is the craziest and probably stupidest thing we've ever attempted." And probably the last.

They each smiled tentatively. Above, the crowd gave a roar. Muted announcements were made declaring a winner.

"Hold on," Bridget said, a finger raised, the other hand in her pocket clutching the Exot orb. "Trophy ceremony commencing …" She listened for a while, nodding subtly. Her eyes found Augum's. "Caireen reports the Lord of the Legion is presenting the winner a trophy …" She nodded. "Erika Scarson is handing over a bag of coin." Suddenly she pumped her fist. "She has the divining rod!"

Augum and Leera exchanged relieved looks. The gamble had paid off. Above, the crowd whistled and cheered as a patriotic Legion song began.

Bridget withdrew her hand from her pocket and brought it to her lips, the Exot orb hidden in her sleeve. "All right, thanks, Caireen. Cease contact." She brought her hands together, face flushed. "I suppose it's time."

Indeed. Augum gave them meaningful glances. "Let's do this. Keep your hoods low and faces hidden," and he led them to the deserted dressing room. He was immediately greeted by the cocoa-skinned Secretary Sharma, who was mumbling to herself and pacing to and fro.

"Thank the Unnameables, you made it," she said upon spotting them, but Augum was barely listening, for behind her stood two figures in necrophyte robes.

"Thought you might have weaseled out," Robin Scarson said with a sneer. He looked bigger, stronger. The veins were popping in his neck. His face was pointier, mottled hair a touch darker. But the nose was as crooked and broken as ever.

Temper cracked her hammy knuckles, watching them with that same stupid sneer. She made a sucking sound through her teeth.

Above, the song reached a wavering high note. Augum could make out the words. *And so we battle for the glory of our Lord … Lord Sparkstone … for so he shall deliver us into … into eternity …*

"Today I unleash my full potential," Robin said quietly, playing with the Destiny Stone around his neck. "Today I become a legend."

Augum glared from within the darkness of his hood. A small and crazy part of him wanted to attack there and then.

Robin chuckled. "Yeah, you clench your fists, kid. 'The Hood'. What a joke. I'm going to rip that thing off your head and smash your face in. Then everybody can have a good look at the new you. I guarantee the Heralds are only going to write about *me* after that."

Outside, the singing concluded on a somber note and Giovanni's smooth voice took over. "Is everyone as excited as I am for the next match?"

The crowd cheered wildly. The ceiling shook from the stomping. Red clay dust settled on their black necrophyte robes.

"It's time," Secretary Sharma said, voice edged with tension.

Augum swallowed. Everything was moving too quickly.

The trio followed Secretary Sharma, taking up a position on one side halfway down the tunnel, Robin and Temper on the other. Augum spotted two Legion guards standing sentinel at the end of the tunnel, facing the crowd. The girls would have to deal with them, and Temper too. But they had discussed all that. What mattered now was the fight and the aftermath.

Especially the aftermath.

Giovanni's voice boomed louder than ever, expertly drawing out the tension from the cheering crowd. "… widely considered the match of the tournament … are you ready … for the historical finals … of the 4th degree!" The crowd cheered and whistled.

Augum felt his whole body vibrate. He shook out his hands and bounced on the balls of his feet, channeling the gladiatorial mood of this dingy hall and an arena floor soaked with generations of warrior blood. Robin, seeing him do it, did the same, adding a twisting neck flex.

"These two contenders are well matched," Giovanni continued. "You've read all about them in the Herald. You've seen them vanquish their foes. The first needs no introduction. He has knocked out three of the four contestants he has faced, and you all know what happened to the fourth—" The crowd was a mix of boos and cheers.

"Easy peasy, baby," Temper said, massaging Robin's shoulders.

"He comes all the way from Blackhaven, and is surely destined for greatness. Mentored by none other than the Lord of the Legion himself, who graces us today with his presence—" The crowd cheered and saluted with cries of, "Hail the Legion!" Augum pictured his demented father nodding his head in acknowledgment.

"They fear his name … they fear his face and his arcane strength … he wields the fire element as sharply as he does necromancy … please give a hearty welcome to the one, the only … Robin … 'The Tormentor' … Scarsoooooon—!"

The crowd was on its feet as Robin jogged out. Temper followed him to the edge of the tunnel, where she remained.

Bridget grabbed Augum's arm and made him face her. "Remember your promise."

"I will."

Giovanni's voice returned. "And now for his opponent …"

Bridget grabbed Augum's other arm and gave him a firm shake. "You *can* do this. I *know* you can. Concentrate. Take it to the next level." She drew him into a tight hug. "I'll be out there with you in your head," she whispered into his ear. "Follow your instincts and … good luck."

He could barely talk, his throat had suddenly closed up. "You too." He squeezed her tighter before letting go. What kind of penalty will the library inflict upon her for casting a borrowed scroll? He was terrified for her, but also awed by her bravery and sacrifice.

"… representing the Lightning element …"

Augum turned to face Leera as Bridget stepped away to give them space. For a moment they just stared at each other, until Leera suddenly drew him close. Her fingers dug into him as she squeezed. They held one another, each nuzzling into the other's neck.

"… Augustus … 'The Hood' … Westwooooood—!"

"I love you," she whispered into his ear.

"I love you too," he instantly replied. He had wanted to say it for so long, before it was too late. If he was going to leave this life, it was going to be with her hearing him say it. They were young, so wretchedly and inadequately young. But it mattered not, for he loved her with every ounce of his being, and that love made him want to survive more than anything else.

The crowd was roaring. He gently kissed her on the lips before slowly letting her go, feeling her slip through his fingers as he walked backward.

There they stood, Bridget and Leera, watching him with proud and fearful tear-stained faces. Behind him, the crowd chanted, "HOOD! HOOD! HOOD!"

He gave a final firm nod to the girls, turned, and jogged out to meet his destiny.

IN THE MOMENT

The arena crackled with energy, the crowd a beast with thousands of faces, its roar deafening and constant. Giovanni brought Augum and Robin close, a hand on each of their shoulders. He carefully explained the rules, but Augum could barely hear anything past the blood rushing through his head, past the thunder of the crowd, past the fear of the unknown. He kept his hood hanging low as his body swayed to the rhythm of coming battle.

"Remember, these are the finals, folks," Giovanni said, straightening, "which means live weapons and no time limit—"

Augum was so focused on Robin he was barely aware as two sharp-edged weapon racks were wheeled out.

"A win can only be achieved by knockout, first-to-five points, or a bent knee—" Giovanni wanted to say more, but there was no stopping the crowd. "LO-SERS SHALL! BEND THE KNEE! WI-NNERS FIND! ETER-NI-TY!" The chant was the loudest thing Augum had ever heard. It thrummed in time to his own heart hammering against his anvil chest.

"Watch for any dirty tricks," Bridget coached into his mind. He could see her and Leera in his peripheral vision on one side of the tunnel, Temper on the other. Bridget's sleeve covered her mouth. "Use your Shield as much as you can, it's your best defense."

Robin was glaring at him, mouthing silent threats, but Augum was too focused to care. He did not hear the crowd anymore. He swayed from foot to foot, hands clenching and unclenching, barely conscious of his arm rings flaring and disappearing with each fist that he made. The whole arena seemed to sway with him. His whole *life* swayed with him.

"Robin Scarson ... any last words for your opponent?"

"He's so scared he can't even look me in the eye—" Robin said in an arcanely amplified voice. The crowd was a mix of boos and sniggers.

"And Augustus Westwood ... any final words for *your* opponent?"

Augum stopped swaying. The moment he had been envisioning in his mind's eye countless times had arrived. Without hesitation, he reached up and slowly pulled his hood back, raising his chin to meet Robin's shocked gaze.

"That's not my name."

The crowd suddenly hushed.

"My name is Augum Stone."

The noise of the crowd erupted into a cacophonous mix of outrage, hysteria, and wild cheering. It gave Augum courage, made his muscles tighten, the blood race hot through his veins. It made him feel strong.

Augum glanced up to see a figure shove past others on the judge's podium—a tall and hulking figure in matte black Dreadnought armor adorned with skulls and spikes. A heavy cloak hung from his back, held together by a golden chain in front. The helm was sharp, a towering crimson plume jutting from it. Six globes of various colors floated around him, sparkling in the torchlight.

He could feel the power of the scions all the way from the arena floor. It was a subtle pull, warping the space around his father, the Lord of the Legion.

Giovanni looked around, unsure what to make of this development.

Augum stole his gaze from his father to stare Robin Scarson down. There was the slightest trace of fear in the murderer's eyes. Perhaps a memory of their last fight. But then those eyes—full of malice and arrogance—narrowed, and Robin Scarson smiled.

"You've made my dreams come true," he whispered. Then he raised his fist and boomed, "Now they will write about me, for I'll show you the might of the *Legion*!"

When the roar died down, Augum turned to the crowd, channeling his ancestor, Atrius Arinthian. "The Resistance is real, but my father's golden promises are not." He could hardly believe he had said it. "Eternal life cannot be brought back from Ley—I have seen it with my own eyes! What my father means is he'll turn you into the undead, as he is already doing in the field!"

The crowd was a confused roar. Augum felt his chest heave. He expected to be struck down any moment, but his father only stood there, watching … *hesitating*! Augum turned round slowly as he faced down the crowd. "Help the Resistance overcome the evil that you know in your hearts has plagued this kingdom. Help us bring justice and peace to Solia!" He did not sound like himself. He sounded confident, strong … like a leader. It was an unfamiliar feeling. As a final gesture, he tore off the necrophyte robe, leaving him in simple linen pants and shirt. Leaving him, appropriately, he thought, in peasant garb. He tossed the robe aside like a rag and raised a fist, roaring the last words. "Join us … join THE RESISTANCE!"

The crowd was on its feet, the vast majority shouting in praise. Some were crying, a few pointing and cursing menacingly. Augum suddenly realized something—together they were strong. Together they could cheer. Together they could make their voices heard. And there they were, the people, *resisting*. The crowd roared in response.

"Well done," Bridget said into his head. "We're proud of you over here. You can do this, Aug. *You can do this!*"

Giovanni glanced up at the Lord of the Legion, who was now flanked by his Red Guards, the plume on his helm swaying in the wind along with the mammoth flag behind him. Soon the crowd watched their lord, as did his own soldiers. Even the judges faced him—everyone waited to see his reaction.

Black clouds trawled silently overhead, amplifying the quiet heaviness of the moment.

The Lord of the Legion clenched his fists as he swept his subjects with eyes hidden behind a thin helm slit. "My son is a fool," he said in a deep and booming voice louder than Giovanni's. "A fool misguided by the crone. A brainwashed fool cajoled into lying on behalf of the crone."

"Let him fight!" someone called from the stands.

"Yes, let him fight!" someone else said. Soon the whole crowd was chanting, "LET HIM FIGHT! LET HIM FIGHT!"

The Lord of the Legion raised his chin slightly as he held up a steel-gloved hand, and the crowd went silent. The space around him shifted subtly. He held their attention before ceremoniously inclining his head once … and the crowd cheered.

The fight was on.

Augum narrowed his eyes at Robin, more ready than he had ever been. His battle stance and sway unconsciously returned.

Giovanni cleared his throat, the first hint of nervousness Augum had heard from the man. "We are witnessing living history before our eyes, folks." He ceremoniously gestured at Robin with both hands. "The young and future heart of the Legion." He swung his arms the other way. "Versus the heart of the Resistance." The crowd cheered wildly. "Now as the ancient Arcaner tradition of honorable combat demands, combatants … bow and show your stripes!"

Augum allowed his four lightning rings to flare brightly, and maintained them. He enjoyed hearing them crackle menacingly. He inclined his head only slightly, keeping his eyes fixed on Robin.

Robin's four fiery rings burst to life. "You end here and now," and scowled without bowing.

Giovanni pointed at Augum. "Are you ready?"

Augum flexed his jaw and gave a single nod.

Giovanni pointed the other way. "And are you—" but Robin's eyes twinkled as he shoved at the air, shouting, "BAKA!"

Yet Augum had been ready, already suspecting Robin might try something like that. He instantly summoned his hard lightning shield and leaned in. Robin's Push spell was strong, making a deep thunk sound, but Augum held firm.

The crowd came alive as Giovanni hollered, "And they're off—!"

"Side attack!" Bridget said in his head.

Augum pivoted as a spear streaked from one of the racks, bouncing off his shield with a dull clang.

"Disablo!" Robin shouted, adding a dramatic flick of his wrist.

Augum's shield disappeared. Without missing a beat, he countered by pointing at Robin's head. "FLUSTRATO!" Robin gasped and took a step back, face registering shock from the strength of the Confusion attack. He fought it off, but doing so gave Augum time to draw a precise outline in the air.

"Summano elementus minimus!" A lightning elemental crackled into existence before him. Augum pointed at Robin. "Elementus—ATTACK!" The waist-high elemental charged.

"DUCK!" Bridget's voice shouted in Augum's mind. He ducked just as another spear whistled by his head. He had not seen Robin make any gesture.

"Someone else made that attack—!" Bridget said.

"ANNIHILO!" Robin shouted, obliterating the elemental with an explosive fireball that singed the dirt and sent a wave of heat Augum's way.

"A smoldering start!" Giovanni said in rapid tones as the crowd roared in agreement. "Still zero-zero, but we're seeing rabid attacks from both sides—!"

Augum thought to try his newest trick—he used both arms to point at two short swords from the two opposing racks and had them zip at Robin. One thunked off his shield, the other grazed his shoulder, slicing the robe but, apparently, not his skin.

"Oh that would have been a point under any other circumstances!" Giovanni boomed. "But these are the finals, folks, and the judges are not going to give points out lightly—"

Robin pointed at Augum's throat. "Vikari vikarei!"

Augum felt his throat burning. "BAKA!" he shouted, spoiling the spell by forcing Robin to raise his fire shield. Augum followed up with a combo—first he flicked his wrist, snapping, "Disablo!" and Robin's shield flamed out, then he quickly slammed his wrists together. "ANNIHILO!" A jagged blast of lightning cracked into Robin's torso and slammed him against the arena wall. He slithered to the dirt with a groan, grabbing his stomach. Yet Augum was amazed to see him slowly return to his feet. Any other person would have been terribly wounded from such a powerful strike, or at least winded!

"Surely that should be a point—" Giovanni said, but the board still showed zero-zero. "There seems to be some disagreement with the judges—"

Both Augum and Robin briefly looked up to see Erika Scarson and Vulika Vaneek smirking with crossed arms as Martus the Black yelled at them, apparently to no avail. The crowd showed its disdain with a chorus of boos. Some necrophytes though, the Legion diehards, cheered wildly.

"Looks like you're going to have to go for a knock-out," Bridget said into his mind.

Augum wasn't surprised, he just hadn't thought the cheating would be so obvious.

Robin, whose robe was charred and smoking in the area of his stomach, made a grand sweeping gesture at Augum, shouting, "CLOSS PESTI!" summoning a swarm of wasps.

Augum, seeing Robin's vision was blocked, sprinted at him. He shoved at the air twice. "Baka! BAKA!" and the swarm was blown apart just as Augum launched himself into the air with a flying leap kick, reappearing beyond the bees. There was an instant in which Augum saw a stupid, incredulous look on Robin's face before Augum's boot smashed into it. Robin had taken it square in the chin. His head smacked the wall with a thunk while Augum rebounded to the dirt, rolled, and jumped to his feet.

"A surprise physical attack! This is personal, folks—and *still* no points!"

"Ridiculous—!" Bridget shouted.

Augum had wasted no time at all though, lunging right at Robin with a sharply raised fist. It connected with his nose, re-breaking it instantly and splashing his face with blood. Robin made a pathetic moaning sound while he grabbed his face, the bottom half of which had a red boot print.

"That's for the iron room!" Augum spat, his words reverberating through the arena and over the shouting crowd.

"A savage punch to the head that did serious damage!" Giovanni hollered. "Yet the judges simply *refuse* to reward a point!"

Augum was rearing back for another vicious punch, but Robin somehow managed to recover just enough to shove at the air. "BAKA—!" sending Augum flying across half the arena. It was a very strong attack. As Augum hit the dirt, rolling with the impact, Robin, nose bleeding profusely, used the time to make elaborately demonic gestures at the ground, finally evoking, "Summano valkus skeletus!"

Augum spotted a mound of freshly disturbed earth move nearby.

"The Tormentor is summoning a walker, folks!" Giovanni shouted, dancing around the spot. "Things just got interesting!"

"That's cheating!" Bridget shouted. "He buried bodies ahead of time—!"

Augum, panting, sprinted for the walker, expertly summoning one of the racked swords into his hand. The walker got free of the ground just as Augum sliced off the balding head of a man recently buried.

Robin wasted no time. "Itak oos iu azim!" and a small specter wielding a ghostly dagger swooped at Augum.

"Incoming!" Bridget shouted, quickly adding, "But watch for secondary attacks—"

Augum used his shield to block the specter, then had to swivel to block two thrown weapons—a spiked mace and a knife, the latter making a glancing blow off his back that did no damage.

"One-nothing for The Tormentor!" Giovanni said.

"What? There was no hit!" Bridget said as the crowd booed in agreement. Suddenly she made a sharp noise.

"Watch it—!" and Augum was forced to repeat the whole double blocking procedure, except this time against a scythe and a war hammer. Luckily, after repeated misses, the specter fizzled out.

Augum slammed his wrists together. "ANNIHILO!" but Robin blocked it with his fire shield, immediately casting his own First Offensive, which Augum in turn blocked. The two of them traded three volleys like this, each hoping to break the other's defenses, until Augum felt the beginning head pains of arcane stamina loss.

Too soon, *too soon*!

Robin, on the other hand, despite a bloody face and a mangled nose, was grinning, seemingly enjoying himself. He changed tact, pointing at weapon after weapon and hurling them at Augum, who had to keep his shield up longer than ever before, because in addition to what Robin pointed at, other weapons were flung his way. They *had* to be thrown by someone else, because Augum was sure Robin did not know how to telekinetically throw more than one item at a time. Each thunked off as Augum danced about like a crazed actor, the crowd gasping with every dodge or shield block. How was Robin maintaining this kind of arcane stamina? It seemed impossible relative to their ages and arcane knowledge—

"A fierce barrage now from the Legion's finest!" Giovanni said. "A hit! And it's two-nothing, folks!"

Yet once more, nothing had struck Augum—he had successfully blocked that last spear attack with his shield. Bridget shouted something into Augum's mind about Erika being a vicious cheater. Giovanni was giving the judge's podium hesitant looks, but seemed unwilling to say anything. The crowd, on the other hand, wasn't afraid to make itself heard. A resounding chorus of boos filled the arena.

Augum pointed at the latest weapon being thrown his way—a curved short blade of some kind—and used

Telekinesis to twirl it back at Robin, who took another slice, this time to the leg.

Robin gave him a surprised look, as if he expected Augum's spell casting to be subpar.

But of course, no point was awarded. Instead, "Oh, a near miss!" Giovanni said in a voice that wavered.

"Unbelievable, Giovanni's now scared to tell the truth—!" Bridget said.

Robin winked at Augum. His voice boomed. "Now let's have some real fun!" He began making orchestrated demonic gestures at the ground.

"Hit him now—!" Bridget said. "While he's casting—!"

Augum shoved at the air. "BAKA!" but he felt his spell hit something invisible—he was being blocked, and Robin was allowed to keep working the spell!

Robin's elaborate gestures concluded as he shouted, "Summano wraithius skeletus!" Three nearby mounds began moving at once. Three disfigured bodies were soon exhumed, then started to quiver before the horrified crowd. Each body was arcanely torn apart to join anew, forming a massive beast.

Augum slammed his wrists together at Robin. "ANNIHILO!" but his lightning struck an invisible barrier. His head began pounding. He glanced up and saw Erika holding out her hands, face hard with concentration. It infuriated Augum that she was being allowed to get away with something so obvious. He turned to the tunnel, mouthing, "Erika—" at Bridget. It did not escape his notice that the girls were shaking with fury.

"Caireen's on it!" Bridget said into her sleeve, which he heard in his mind.

Augum whirled about and raced toward Robin, hoping to summon a sword along the way—only to suddenly trip. Someone had telekinetically yanked at his ankle. He glanced up to see Erika smirking. Suddenly she tripped too—and almost fell off the platform. She glanced around with a furious gaze, looking for the perpetrator.

"Way to go, Caireen!" Bridget said, quickly blurting, "Behind you—!" but Augum had already seen the shadow. He rolled aside as a clawed fist punched a hole in the ground where he had been a moment before.

"The Hood has his hands full now—!"

"DREADUS TERRABLUS!" Robin shouted, and Augum had to suddenly focus on two attacks at the same time—the wraith, which was swiping at him as he rolled around on the ground, and Robin's vicious mind attack.

Augum witnessed the wraith's great arms split into a thousand tiny spiked demons. They jumped off the monster and charged at him. There was a small ocean of them, dropping in waves. He desperately tried to roll away, but they sped over quick as rats, overcoming him in a deluge. He screamed as he saw them gnaw into his flesh. He was being eaten alive, and everyone was watching.

"Three-nothing!" Giovanni shouted as the crowd roared.

"It's an illusion!" Bridget shouted. "*Quick, roll—!*"

Augum rolled aside as a monstrous fist slammed into the ground, leaving a small crater while dislodging more of the demons.

"It isn't real!" Bridget said. "It's only a Fear attack! Fight it—!"

Augum, skin falling off and entire body stinging with bites from these vicious little monsters, somehow got to his feet and ran. He gnashed his teeth, demanding his mind do a better job of fighting the illusion off. Finally, the demons and wounds faded and disappeared.

Robin slammed his wrists together. "ANNIHILO!"

"DUCK!" came the voice inside Augum's head, but Augum had an idea—he wanted to explore that other trick he had learned, and used both hands to point at the fireball with open palms. He exerted all his arcane might, telekinetically curving the path of attack right into the charging wraith. The fireball slammed into it and the monstrous thing tripped, squealing and hissing as it skidded in the dirt, consumed by fire.

"NO—!" Robin shouted, face twisted with fury.

"Incredible arcanery, folks!" Giovanni shouted, the crowd roaring in approval.

Robin slammed his wrists together once more. "ANNIHILO!" and another fireball swooped at Augum.

"No you don't—" Augum shouted, and he channeled his arcane strength almost to the point of overdraw, once again curving the path of the fireball at the wraith, which was already trying to stand. It gave a quick squeal before being smashed into fiery pieces.

Giovanni was grabbing his hair. "An unparalleled feat of arcanery not seen since the likes of Anna Atticus Stone! This is history, folks! You'll be telling your grandkids what you saw here today—"

Robin repeatedly slammed two fists into his thighs. "No, no, NO! YOU CHEATED!"

Meanwhile, Augum felt a trickle of blood from his nose. He tasted the salty coppery tang as it dribbled over his lips. His bones vibrated from the double overdraw. Even his teeth buzzed. His stomach roiled with nausea, and he had to hold himself steady against the head-hammering dizziness.

"Focus, Aug!" Bridget shouted.

Augum, chest heaving, squinted at Robin. His nemesis had a furious look on his bloody face. His necrophyte robe was torn and charred. The Destiny Stone gleamed on his chest.

And that's when an idea came to Augum. Now only to—

But Robin's face twisted with malice as he made a squiggly gesture at Augum's head. "FLUSTRATO!"

Augum winced—he stumbled about and fell to the ground near a hammer, drooling and blubbering, "Uh ... we there yet—?"

The crowd gasped and hushed.

Giovanni, who had been dancing around the melee, abruptly froze, voice somber. "A successful Confusion casting makes it four-nothing. Looks like it's over, folks ..."

The arena went as silent as the grave.

"No ..." Bridget whispered. "Aug? Aug, please, do something ..."

But Augum only looked about dully, a simple look on his face.

Robin dusted off his hands. "Ah," he said with a twisted smile, summoning a nearby sword to his hand. He strode to Augum, raised the blade, and glanced up at the Lord of the Legion, who stood staring down at the arena, plume swaying gently in the wind.

"With your permission, Sire," Robin said, blood dripping from his chin. "For the glory of the Legion."

Augum wavered as every soul awaited the verdict.

At last, the Lord of the Legion inclined his head before booming, "Kill the traitor!"

The crowd gasped. Every soul was on their feet. Every mouth gaped.

"His own son ..." a spectator said in a quivering voice.

"Snap out of it!" Bridget screamed. "AUG—!"

The sword hissed neatly through the air.

But Augum was more than ready. He had fought off the initial Confusion attack and had been faking the symptoms. He rolled aside at the last moment, simultaneously snatching the Destiny Stone from Robin's neck while summoning the nearby hammer into his hand. In one swift movement, he smashed the stone into smithereens with the hammer.

Robin stumbled back, gasping and writhing, sword falling from his clutches. "No … no …" He rapidly turned pale. His stripes flared out, one after another—from four to three; from three to two; from two to one; and then disappeared altogether.

The crowd was a frozen painting of surprise. Every eyeball focused on the center of the arena. Giovanni held his cheeks, mouth gaping.

Robin's eyes swiveled around as ghostly figures appeared from the ether, surrounding him. Each stood firm, holding a dagger. Each glared with vengeance. Augum instantly knew who they were—his victims, those he had murdered. The Destiny Stone was karma-balanced, and now it was plain exactly what that meant.

One by one, Robin's victims calmly stepped before him and jabbed him with their dagger. He tried to twist away from each sting, but his body had shriveled and gone stiff. The wounds bled with green poisonous-looking blood. Meanwhile, each ghost disappeared soon after performing its final duty.

Above, Erika was shrieking, "KILL HIM!" but no one was doing anything. She slammed her wrists together. "ANNIHILO!" but mysteriously nothing happened. She repeatedly tried to cast spells which did not work. Someone was blocking her!

Augum returned his attention to the scene before him. One last ghost remained. She had porcelain, waxy skin, long jet black hair, and almond eyes. She was tall and slender and, even in death, beautiful. There was a gaping wound on her throat that did not bleed. Her cold gaze was solely reserved for Robin.

"You …" Robin hissed through clenched teeth. His whole body had tensed up, as if every muscle was overloaded. His hands were shriveled inwards like claws. He was shaking, small, and unable to move.

Mya strode forth and in one graceful movement sliced his throat. She watched her gurgling murderer before glancing at Augum with a final mournful look. Then she lowered her head, slowly disappearing into nothingness.

Robin spasmed and gasped, unable to even grab his throat. His eyes had magnified to great black orbs. The bleeding from the last wound was profuse, making his robe slick like the rags of a wraith. He fell to his knees, shaking violently. Above, Erika was screaming and cursing uncontrollably. Beside her, the Lord of the Legion watched with what, to Augum, appeared to be morbid fascination. Meanwhile, Bridget and Leera wrestled with a frantic Temper.

Robin Scarson, bloody face as white as snow and lips as blue as death, gave Augum a final look. There, in those tired and defeated eyes of his longtime nemesis, Augum saw something he did not expect.

As Robin fell forward, dead; as Giovanni kept jumping around grasping his head and wildly declaring victory; as the crowd roared in crazed abandon; as Erika slumped to her knees with an agonized wail; as the Lord of the Legion tilted his head in that strangely curious way of his; as Temper passed out cold at the girls' feet; and as Bridget and Leera suddenly hugged … Augum could only think of what he saw in those eyes …

Regret.

FACE TO FACE

The long and slow walk up those steps to the judge's podium was like walking up a volcano to his doom. Yet the crowd was still cheering madly, chanting his name. "AU-GUM! AU-GUM!" Even the drum took up the double beat. Boom, boom! Boom, boom! It was a symphony, a glorious symphony of resistance and victory.

"He won't strike you down," Bridget was saying in rapid tones. "Not unless he wants to lose control of the whole kingdom. And be prepared to execute the plan. I'll have the scroll ready—"

Augum, chest still heaving from the battle, kept focus, preparing himself for the casting of the one spell he hoped would give him a chance. He wiped the blood from his face with his linen shirtsleeve. The vicious throbbing in his head from the battle with Robin remained, but was slowly ebbing. If only he could pace himself and renew his arcane strength. He was desperately going to need it for what he intended to do next.

And so he slowed his ascent even more as he readied himself for the most powerful and ancient spell in his arsenal. He paid attention to the rugged wood of the steps; to the square heads of the iron nails, unevenly distributed across the planks; to the traces of mud and dust and dirt; to the cold wind on his face; to the sharp flap of flags …

At last he stepped onto the platform, a platform swarming with people—warlocks, judges, attendants, soldiers, archers, and the Lord of the Legion and his Red Guard—towering crimson-armored undead warriors, flaming swords hissing by their sides. The Red Guard glanced at Augum through slit helms and he immediately felt their natural Confusion and Fear attacks. But unlike before, he was now strong enough to block them.

Augum paced to stand at the edge of the platform, placing himself between the arena floor and the assembled throng of enemies. Below, the audience buzzed nervously. His eyes fell upon a sobbing Erika, who was being comforted by Vulika Vaneek.

"He murdered my nephew," she kept gurgling. She wavered in Vulika's arms, clutching the divining rod to her bosom as if it was her baby. The rod was black and embedded with seven polished stones, each a different color, each dimly aglow.

The third judge, Martus the Black, watched with coal eyes. Surprisingly, he gave Augum the slightest nod. Suddenly Augum realized it was he that had prevented Erika from casting those spells earlier! Was he part of the Resistance then? Or was it revenge?

The Lord of the Legion took a measured step forward. The scions buzzed menacingly around his head, warping the space around him. He reached up and slowly removed his helm, revealing a face that had changed drastically since Augum saw him last—it was skeletal in appearance, the skin so stretched and thin that white bone showed in places. His hair was reedy and unkempt. Those now deep-set eyes, blacker and colder than when Augum had seen them last, still crackled with lightning, but less so than before. They bore into Augum as if the man knew what his plans were. They seemed to say to him, *You are weak and pathetic and I shall smite you from my kingdom when it suits me*.

The Lord of the Legion's voice flooded the arena. "A noble but useless gesture." The buzz of the scions momentarily increased with the words, as if tuned to his thoughts.

"As tradition demands, I have come for the prize," Augum said, voice still amplified and echoing through the stands.

The Lord of the Legion smirked, as if to say, *I know exactly what prize you have come for*. But Augum kept a straight face, until the Lord of the Legion glanced over to a table. A single trophy lifted and hovered over, placing itself at Augum's feet.

The Lord of the Legion smiled, showing rotten teeth. "To the winner indeed go the spoils." He gave a lazy glance at Erika Scarson. A gray-robed attendant scampered to her side holding a coin pouch. Erika gritted her teeth and snatched it from him.

A flash rippled through the scions as the Lord of the Legion said, "He shall attempt to steal the divining rod."

The crowd gasped. Augum's hopes crashed into his stomach. Suddenly he felt as cold as death itself. His hands went clammy and his throat dried.

"Oh no," Bridget whispered in his mind. "No, no, no, no …"

His father patronized him with a crooked smile. "Give him the gold."

Erika marched over to stand before Augum, earrings jingling. She stared at him, makeup running from her tears, cold murder in her eyes. He caught the strong scent of wild rose as she lobbed the pouch at him. He numbly caught it. After just standing there stupidly, he placed it into his pocket. His eyes wandered briefly over the divining rod, clutched in her white-knuckled hands.

"Cast the spell," Sparkstone said.

His father knew everything. The whole plan. Somehow, Augum should have known. The man was not stupid, and looking back, this whole attempt now seemed as idiotic as it was clumsy.

"Cast the spell," Sparkstone repeated, eyes narrowing ever slightly.

"Don't, Aug," Bridget said in a horrified whisper. "He wants to kill you—"

Augum could barely breathe. She was right—he could see it in his father's demon eyes. There was anger there, but now he knew what that anger wanted—by killing Augum, not only would the kingdom lose faith in the Resistance, but Nana would lose all hope—and therefore her strength—and be found quicker!

Augum's head swam. He almost passed out. How could he have been so utterly stupid! So utterly naive! So—

The Lord of the Legion's skeletal smile widened, as if he could read Augum's thoughts.

Erika Scarson's nostrils flared. "Your Lordship, he has murdered my nephew in cold blood. I request vengeance."

The answer was swift. "And you may have it!"

The crowd yelped. Some cried out in horror, others in disbelief.

"Aug—" Bridget's voice wavered. She was weeping. "Aug …"

Augum closed his eyes, summoning every bit of courage he could muster. "You want to kill me?" His fist closed around the Reflecting crystal as his voice echoed through the stands. He spoke through his teeth, preparing himself. "Do it then. DO IT!"

Erika did not hesitate. She slammed her wrists together, screeching, "ANNIHILO!"

Augum reacted instantly, meeting her extended palms with the tip of the crystal, being sure to angle it just right and framing his thoughts perfectly. "MIMICA!" he shouted, feeling a massive pull on his arcane stamina. The mammoth fireball made a reverse sucking sound as it was suddenly shot back at her. She burst into flames with a gut-wrenching scream. But he did not stop there, quickly and eloquently evoking, "Centeratoraye xao xen!"

His thoughts instantly sharpened. The first thing he became crisply conscious of was the warping effect from the scions. It was like looking through a great fishbowl. He simultaneously became aware of the clammy sweat on his palms; the face-burning heat from the fireball; the raucous roar from the stands; the pebbles bouncing on the oaken platform.

All became one.

This was it. The true fight of his life had come, except now he faced the most powerful man in Solia—perhaps all of Sithesia. Not to mention the multitude of other foes on that platform.

Under the influence of Centarro, some things became as clear as a mountain stream. The Lord of the Legion knew Augum was going to cast that spell, and he knew it because he had heard him use it to save Nana back at the battle at Hangman's Rock. He probably did some research on it, but Augum guessed he did not know how to learn it, for each spell had secrets only mentors could pass along. He also knew Augum was going to attempt to steal the divining rod. He knew and expected these things.

So what would he *not* expect Augum to be able to do?

Augum's heart raced along with his thoughts, instantaneously quantifying the scene before him. The platform rumbled as the heavy boots of the Red Guard charged, flaming swords raised. Erika Scarson thrashed in a burning heap, the divining rod still clutched in her hand. The Lord of the Legion, Vulica Vaneek, and a bunch of Legion warlocks were all casting an offensive spell. Martus the Black was pointing at the platform, also casting a spell, but Augum sensed it was in aid of the Resistance.

He understood all of this in the blink of an eye, and he did so by channeling all his arcane energies into Centarro, the one spell that allowed him to tap into his arcane and strategic genius—a general organizing cerebral troops. It was his finest casting, a casting so acute it intuitively gave him a powerful ally—*overdraw*. Specifically, wild arcanery *and* overdraw. It was madness and the most dangerous thing a warlock could do, but it was the only thing that gave him a chance, the only thing the Lord of the Legion did not expect.

Before anyone actually completed a spell, the entire platform vanished with a *whoosh*. All on it were sent into free fall, interrupting everyone's spells—except for the Lord of the Legion's. The man fell as if he had not noticed the platform disappear—his concentration was *that* potent.

And he was about to cast a murderous mid-air lightning attack.

In the same moment came Bridget's frantic voice. "Casting scroll now—"

Heart in his throat and body falling, Augum focused his over-burdened mind on the flaming and writhing Erika, plummeting just feet away from him. He yanked sharply on the black rod while simultaneously summoning his shield with his other arm, concentrating on reinforcing it, sensing his father's attack by the rising hairs on his arms. The lightning strike happened a split moment later. It was so strong it plowed through his shield, blasted into his chest, and sent him cart-wheeling toward the opposite side of the arena.

He experienced a jolt and his entire body was seized with an excruciating pain that felt like he was being stung by a thousand wasps from the inside. An instantaneous memory overcame his senses, that of a searing flash he had once felt flying high above the yellow grass of the Tallows.

Except this one was much, *much* stronger.

Luckily, it was only momentary, and in the next twirling instance, under the focus-enhancing effects of Centarro, Augum made a connection, and an old mystery abruptly became clear.

The bolt of lightning from his father should have immediately killed him, for unlike natural lightning, his father's was arcanely amplified to the 20th degree. Yet in that tumbling mayhem, when Augum was able to glimpse his chest, the area had a gaping hole that went through his robe and undergarments. The edges of the cloth were on fire, but his skin was unbroken.

The lightning had done no damage!

Now, in centarric perfection, he knew why. Herzog the historian had asked Augum if Atrius Arinthian passed down a gift in the blood. At the time, Augum thought surely not, but now it dawned on him he had been wrong—and it should have been clear from the very beginning, for after being struck above the Tallows, Mrs. Stone had noted that the lightning had *not left a mark on him*. Atrius Arinthian had passed down to him one crucial advantage …

Lightning immunity.

It was as if the legend was reaching through the eons with an ancestral echo, giving Augum a fighting chance against his greatest foe.

As he cartwheeled through the air before thousands of screaming spectators, Augum took a quick moment to acknowledge how amazing Centarro was. Only this spell allowed simultaneous understanding on multiple levels. Only this spell allowed him to appreciate simplicity during the most harrowing of moments. The somber and brooding clouds above, laden with eager rain. The wind whistling in his ears. The bulbous throb in his head exacerbated by spinning force. The oozing of blood from his nose and ears. The multitude of battle cuts stinging sharply. Everything was greatly amplified by Centarro.

As long as it lasted, of course. And he was acutely conscious of the fact he had not planned for the side effects.

This was all or nothing.

His body was slowing—there was a force pulling on it, willing it to reach the ground safely. Caireen and Leera had come through in their crucial part! The initial plan had called for him to jump off the platform, his fall halted by their combined telekinetic efforts. Luckily, they adjusted, though it had to be testing their range.

But something else flew through the air beside him, and it was that which he needed to retrieve most. Soon as his feet hit the arena floor, he reached out telekinetically to the spinning rod. But, hearing a massive *whoosh* approach, he purposefully overextended. The rod snapped over so quickly it knocked him back—just as a giant rock slammed into the spot where he had been standing.

Augum stopped rolling in time to see the Legion warlocks were regrouping at the base of the platform, amongst a pile of writhing bodies. One of those warlocks was the Lord of the Legion, and he had just finished casting a spell Augum had feared from the beginning—it was the one that made him move so fast he was a blur.

It gave Augum a final moment to act, a moment he would once again use to dangerously overdraw wild arcanery. There was only one spell that would get him from the far side of the arena to the portal which Bridget had cast inside the tunnel to the dressing room. But this time, he knew the words, and he had already cast it once, albeit clumsily. Unfortunately, Centarro's power was already beginning to ebb. He could feel it draining like a pierced waterskin.

Not yet … not yet!

Augum focused every morsel of his throbbing concentration, pushing his arcane boundaries beyond all his known limits. He ignored the massive volley of arrows, fireballs, mini tornadoes, and vine attacks hurtling toward him. He ignored the blur that was his father, who would most probably arrive before he could utter the words. He ignored the chaos of the crowd, shouting and running and panicking. He ignored the vibrant rumble of the ground, the way the rocks and dust danced on the ancient arena floor, soaked with generations of warrior blood. He ignored everything, instead focusing on the complex arcanery involved in making the spell work while envisioning the spot he had to end up in. Just before casting, he glimpsed something eternal and dark. Centarro allowed him a brief moment of understanding. He was looking at the great arcane abyss, the eternal ether from which arcanery manifested. It was black and cold and so very, very lonely.

The moment of the spell arrived in blinding fury. "IMPETUS PERAGRO!"

Yet just as the ripping arcane forces began tearing him away, an arrow struck him in the back with a sickening squish. His body yanked a split moment later as the rest of the barrage destroyed the arena floor. Almost instantly, he smashed into the wall of the tunnel, feeling multiple teeth come loose and who knew how many bones break. His blood splattered the stone as he bounced off, crumpling in a jagged heap on the ground, vision obscured by something hot and sticky. But physical injuries aside, he knew something deep in his core was very wrong. Arcane overdraw had snapped something in his being, something crucial.

Leera loosed a frightened shriek upon seeing him. She grabbed him with both hands and yanked him to his feet. He was a loose puddle of bones and blood and flesh. Nothing worked right. Everything was filled with searing and grinding pain. The expression on her face when she grabbed him said it all.

It was sheer horror.

Past the blood that dripped from his brows, Augum saw that two Legion soldiers lay in a heap behind her. At the far end of the tunnel, Temper stumped about in a haze of confusion. Bridget wobbled near a portal, eyes unfocused, hair and robe blowing from its wind. She had successfully cast it and apparently suffered from the curse of breaking library rules.

He also noticed one other thing, clutched in his numb paw—the divining rod. Somehow, miraculously, he had maintained his grip on it.

"Help me, Aug—" Leera said with gritted teeth as she heaved him toward the portal. He stumbled and heard multiple bones cracking and scraping together. His entire body was an acutely throbbing mass. It was so intense he would have rather died, as if a thousand knives were stabbing him at once.

But the look in her eyes kept him going. It was a look of love and terror. He forced his legs, which barely worked, to move. But it was difficult, very difficult to get anything to work right. And Centarro was fading fast, quickly jumbling his thoughts. The glass of clarity was slowly shattering.

"Get Bridge," he mumbled, though what actually came out was a sickening gurgle. Somehow though, Leera understood. She shoved him toward the portal and reached for Bridget.

And all that remained between safety and death was the few short paces to the roaring black oval, versus the blistering speed of his father's blurred form.

He took one bone-cracking step and saw the hissing form take ten. A second crunching step and the form took another ten.

One … last … step …

The hiss was now so loud it was almost all he could hear, except for Leera's screaming battle cry from a final heaving effort—she plowed into him, Bridget clutched in her arms, careening the three of them into the portal.

AFTERMATH

Silence. Long, cold, quiet silence. In time, that silence gave way to a gentle sound—that of soft rain splashing a nearby stream. Soon, the rain could be felt dully and subtly on his body. And as feeling returned, so too did pain. Searing, throbbing, excruciating pain.

Augum finally opened his eyes. The sky was cloudy and dark. Drops gently splashed on his cheeks. A grove of trees surrounded his blurry vision, the canopy swaying in a stormy wind.

Someone was weeping nearby. He tried to move his neck but couldn't without experience a grating jolt.

Leera's blurry face appeared over his. "Aug—? Say something—"

He tried to speak but all that came out was a gurgle. He tasted the coppery tang of blood in his mouth. It was a pool of blood. He gasped and choked, exploding it over his face.

"Don't you die on me—" she said in a shaky voice. Her face disappeared out of sight. "Bridge, stay here, all right? Look at me. Stay. Here. I'm going to get help. I'll be right back—"

He could hear her run off, sobbing, footsteps splashing puddles in the soggy grass. He lay there, body throbbing sickeningly, wanting to throw up. He listened to the rain plink off a wooden roof, to the sound of a dribbling nearby stream. He tried to move again but only felt the jarring of bone-on-bone, and couldn't help but let out a gurgling yelp. His body simply did not work. He kept seeing momentary flashes of something eternally ancient and dark and cold. It beckoned to him in tendril whispers.

A face appeared above his. "Hi," Bridget said, examining him curiously. She covered her mouth and burst into a giggle, before her face changed to a look of child-like curiosity. She waved at him with floppy fingers and gave a silly smile. "Hi."

Augum wheezed. Oh, Bridget …

"Hi," she repeated. Her head tilted left as she kept looking at him. Then it tilted right as she began rocking, playing with something on his chest. His heart ached. The repercussions of casting a borrowed library scroll. Poor, brave Bridget …

She picked up the object on his chest to examine it closer. He saw that it was black and studded with seven polished stones.

The divining rod. Thank the Unnameables …

Nana, can you hear my thoughts? It's safe to return now. Nana, we need you more than ever. Please, *please,* if you can somehow hear me, come to us. We need you so much, so very, very much …

The rain continued unabated. There was no teleportation noise. Instead, there came the sound of rushing feet. Soon familiar faces appeared—Mr. Goss and Mr. Okeke and Jengo, and even Haylee. All went ashen upon seeing Augum. Haylee burst out a horror-stricken cry, a shaking hand over her mouth.

"How bad is it?" Leera asked in a weak whisper.

Mr. Goss placed a gentle hand on Augum's neck. He gave her a dark look and did not reply. But Augum's consciousness was rapidly slipping away. He felt weak, weaker than he had ever felt before. His vision shrank and shrank, until it was nothing, and he was nothing.

* * *

Augum woke in a small and dim candle-lit room. A fire crackled gently in the next room. The window above the bed showed that it was night. Wind howled overhead. He could hear the trees rustling outside, and rain pelting the roof. It was a comforting sound.

His body was on fire, like a thousand needles were pricking him. He felt light and nauseous, as if he was swimming upside down. His breaths came out as shallow wheezes. Unable to move, he moaned.

Bridget's face quickly appeared above him. Her hair had been washed and tied back in a ponytail. She was wearing a nightgown.

"Hi," she blurted, drooling. "Hi."

A door squeaked open and feet padded in. Jengo's smiling ebony face soon appeared above Augum. He lifted a tray of steaming soup. "You've been out for a long while," he whispered. "Day and a half. Been storming the entire time. And Leera hasn't left your side even once. She's quite distraught, let me tell you. I've been trying to get her to sleep, and here she is finally catching a snooze."

He put the tray down. "Easy, Bridge, you'll have some." Augum heard her trying to reach for it, but each time Jengo had to gently pry her away. Jengo then shook someone nearby. "Augum's awake."

Leera immediately snapped into his vision. She wore a traditional blue robe, their favorite. The numerous tiny cuts on her soft cheeks had scabbed over. She was also clean-looking, hair washed and shiny and hanging around her face. But there were purple bags under her bloodshot eyes.

"Oh, Aug …" She leaned down and gently kissed his forehead. "You're a mess."

He moaned, smiling with his eyes, though all he felt was a horrible grating and throbbing pain.

"Mrs. Stone hasn't returned, no," she said. "We think she doesn't know it's safe to come back yet. Who knows how long it'll be." She glanced at Bridget. "And … and Bridget's kind of … gone simple. From casting that scroll, that is. I … I don't know what to do. Nobody does." She sniffed as a tear rolled down her cheek. Augum wished he could wipe it away. He wished he could gently hold her in his arms, cradle her close.

Jengo placed a slender ebony hand on Augum's forehead. "Still hot," he said to Leera, before turning his attention back to him. "Father, Mr. Goss, and a whole bunch of others are on a quest to find medicine. Your whole body is in a splint, basically." He smiled. "I think you broke every bone possible." His hands twisted. "Err, everyone's very concerned, but we're keeping visitors down to a minimum. The village is basically on lockdown. The Legion's in a right state, yes they are. A right state. And the kingdom …" He leaned closer, voice conspiratorial. "There've been riots, Augum, *riots*. And the Legion are using a heavy hand to quell—"

"Not now, Jengo," Leera snapped.

"Right, of course, that can all wait." Jengo bit his lip. "Say, I wanted to try something. I've been studying up on healing and—"

"I told you, no, Jengo—"

"But if you'll just let me—"

"I *said*, NO!"

"Of course, my apologies," he mumbled. "Uh, why don't I leave you to it then." Jengo quietly excused himself from the room, which Augum finally recognized as Mr. Okeke's. It had a nice spruce truss above that reminded him of Sir Westwood's thatched house.

Leera rubbed her face. "I've been short lately. Patience ain't exactly my strength as you know." She lifted a bowl of potato and leek soup and dipped a spoon in. Despite the many pains, the smell made Augum realize just how hungry he was. He couldn't even recall the last time he ate.

Leera gave the first spoonful to Bridget, then had to wipe her mouth. She sighed and brought Bridget to sit in her lap. "Poor girl, what are we going to do with you?" She fed her another spoonful of soup. Bridget made a yucky face.

Leera brushed hair aside from Bridget's cheeks. "You have to, I know you're hungry."

Bridget shook her head. "Nuh-uh."

Leera sighed again. "Fine, let's feed Augum." She gave him a wry grin. "Like two babies over here."

He tried to smile but it hurt too much.

"We're all hoping Mrs. Stone comes back soon." Leera held onto Bridget while carefully pouring a spoonful into his parched mouth. It tasted divine. "Maybe she can heal you. It has to happen soon though, before the damage sets, or whatever. You remember Haylee ..."

Augum thought of Haylee and how she still limped even after receiving arcane healing. It was an imperfect art. He wondered if he would have to resort to flying around in a chair like Lien Ning.

"I tuned to the Exot Orb," Leera continued, feeding him another spoonful. "I've been in touch with Caireen in Antioc. City's a mess. Even the constabulary went up in flames." She froze thoughtfully, spoon hanging in mid-air, while Bridget squirmed in her grip. "I can't believe we survived," she whispered, shaking her head. "Your father ... I *saw* him. He arrived the moment I shoved us into that portal. It was a giant roaring blast." She chuckled nervously. "Pretty sure the tunnel came down behind us."

Augum moaned—all he wanted was that spoonful. He hated being immobile and useless. He hated the pain, the discomfort.

"Right, sorry." Leera fed it to him. Then she went on to tell him how everyone was doing. Malaika and Charissa still had not returned. Mr. and Mrs. Haroun were worried sick of course, the latter irate. Mrs. Haroun had even accused Leera of withholding information, and had to be led away sobbing by Mr. Haroun. Leland was with the Agonex all the time now, and he was acting strangely, though Leera didn't clarify, and Augum couldn't exactly follow up with questions. Haylee and Chaska were doing all right, though they still argued now and then. Apparently Chaska was taking his town watch thing very seriously, patrolling every moment of his spare time. Devon was with him every step of the way. He and his father were also busy making evacuation plans in case the Legion arrived, though she thought that was a waste of energy, as the kind of warlocks they'd face would quickly overcome any local resistance. And of course, everyone was dreadfully worried about him and Bridget, and hoped Mrs. Stone would return soon.

After feeding him, Leera put the bowl away and had Bridget lie on the floor, telling her, "Go to sleep, okay? Bridget? Go to sleep." She made a head-on-pillow gesture. "You know—sleep," and soon Bridget was snoozing peacefully.

Leera appeared by his side again, face troubled. "I miss holding you," she whispered, stroking his neck.

I miss you too, he wanted to say.

She sighed and curled up beside him on the bed, still stroking his neck, and soon both of them fell asleep again.

THE ABYSS

Augum was startled awake, thinking he had heard a familiar reverse-sucking sound—that of someone teleporting. The Legion were here! Someone do something! But he couldn't move or make a sound. He was deteriorating, he could sense it. His body felt hot and shaky. A flu was coming on, a strong one.

The candles had all gone out during the night. The room was as dark as the window. Rain pelted the glass. It plonked against the roof. Wind whistled through the cracks in the beams. Outside, trees swayed and rustled. Leera snoozed away peacefully by his side, nuzzled into his flank and covered by a blanket, while Bridget's slow breathing could be heard nearby.

The floorboards creaked.

That wasn't the Legion! Mrs. Stone had come! Finally! Now all that had to—

But it was Jengo's face that appeared silhouetted in the starlight. A finger was over his mouth in a *Shhh* gesture.

He gave a furtive glance at Leera before whispering, "Will you let me try healing you?"

Augum's hopes crashed like waves against a rocky shore. Where was she? Why hadn't she come yet?

Jengo nodded, imploring Augum to trust him with those caring eyes of his. At last, Augum blinked once, fearing a moan would wake Leera. He hoped Jengo knew what he was doing.

Jengo placed a gentle hand on Augum's jaw, making him wince. He closed his eyes in concentration, then began mumbling an arcane phrase. A soft light shone from his palm and Augum felt a warmth slowly spread from his jaw through his face.

It was working! He could feel that wonderful buzzing, akin to a thousand ants working away, on his jaw and face, and then his chest and back. Jengo's brow began to sweat and he winced, abruptly stopping the spell. He collapsed immediately with a painful moan. In the same moment, Leera jolted awake.

"What are you—" She paused when she saw Jengo, and immediately launched a verbal barrage. "How *dare* you, I told you not to—"

"Stop," Augum said, placing a weak hand on her arm as Jengo writhed on the floor, clutching his head. He could talk! It was a miracle! And his arm moved!

She gasped. "Aug—" and threw her arms around him, drawing him close.

"Careful, legs are still broken," Jengo said. His nose was bleeding.

She withdrew, sniffing. "Jengo …"

"Thank you, Jengo," Augum said, seeing she was speechless. "But are you all right?"

Jengo sat up to lean his tall frame against the wall, hands still clutching his head. "Is it supposed to hurt like this?" he asked through gritted teeth.

"At the beginning, yeah," Augum replied, enjoying holding Leera, something he feared he would never be able to do again. "And especially when you push yourself. You cast wild, didn't you?"

"I … maybe I did, I don't know. Hard to tell."

"You need a mentor."

"We all do," Leera whispered, face pressed into Augum's neck.

Augum gently felt his arms and neck and jaw, impressed with how well Jengo had done. A serious stiffness remained in his left arm, but still … multiple breaks arcanely healed with one casting. Not bad at all. There was no doubt that was advanced healing for someone who hadn't even achieved their 1st degree. It seems Jengo had been training and studying diligently. Augum was looking forward to giving him one of the Exot rings, but that would have to wait until he achieved his 2nd degree.

Jengo moaned as he dabbed at his bloody nose with a cloth. "Been secretly practicing on local volunteers. But the book doesn't quite prepare you for the real thing when you cast wild. I have a theory too. I think apprentices learn better when they're self-motivated. As much as I wanted to go to an academy, I don't think I would have come this far in so short a time there."

"How far ahead did you study?" Augum asked. Jengo's words were familiar. Nana had said something akin to it, something about them learning in the field, which advances arcanery faster. It was the ancient way of learning.

"Just kept reading and reading, oh and practicing everything I learned from you lot." Jengo sucked in a breath through clenched teeth, making a hissing noise. "Feels like someone's smashing my brains in with a hammer. Am I going to—"

"—no, you're not going to die," Augum replied with a smile. "Just don't push yourself so hard next—" He winced from the sudden and powerful flash of an eternal black void that momentarily blackened his vision and took his soul to a very cold place. He shivered violently for a few heartbeats.

Leera watched him with deep concern. "Aug?"

"It's nothing." Nothing except something fundamentally wrong in his very being. And the chill had returned. He was coming down with something very strong.

Jengo looked up from his seated position, ebony face framed in dim starlight. "I need your permission. You have to let me keep working on you. Especially your legs."

"You have it. Thank—" but a gut-wrenching wave of cold nausea made Augum shiver violently again, forcing him to fumble for the blanket.

"Oh, Aug, you don't look too good," Leera whispered, stroking his head.

Jengo gave a firm nod. "I promise I'll do better. I will work harder at healing than I have ever worked before. I mean, I know I originally thought you might die a screaming death in the process, but I really believed—"

"Jengo—" Leera said with an imploring look. "He's not feeling too well."

"Right, uh, why don't I let you all get some sleep." He stood with a groan, a hand still pressed to his temple, muttering, "I'm certainly going to need it."

After Jengo stumbled out, Leera pressed the back of her hand to Augum's forehead. "You're burning up," she whispered, drawing blankets over him. There was fear in her eyes. "Go to sleep, it looks like you've got another fight ahead."

***

Augum's fever worsened over the next several days. Jengo kept healing his body—and doing a great job of it too—but he could do nothing against the fever's potency. People came and went, some administering medicine, some to pay their respects to "the hero of heroes", as someone put it, which meant nothing to Augum. In fact, he repeatedly cut people off if they even hinted at anything so absurd as that. Others just stopped by to quietly say hello and wish him well.

But Augum slipped further and further away, soon thinking he was dreaming each visit. Faces blurred, voices echoed. After a while, he could no longer tell what was real and what was delusion.

And the eternal and shivering darkness returned more and more, until he felt like he was living in it half the time. It was a dreary and lonely place of vast nothingness, a place where he always thought there was something deep underneath him, as if he was treading on the surface of an infinitely black ocean, awaiting a monster to swim up and snatch him. The darkness frightened him. He was a child in a living nightmare.

"It's arcane fever," he heard someone whisper at one point, the voice bouncing in his brain. "He overdrew." But when he looked over, there was nobody there.

"I couldn't fully heal his left arm that well," he heard someone else say another time. "Too many fractures. I'm sorry. But ... but his legs seem to work fine, as evidenced by his frantic kicking ..."

"Hi," another person kept saying again and again. Some girl with a simple look on her face. He vaguely recognized her, but his thoughts had become so jumbled, so distant, that nothing quite made sense.

He had lengthy conversations with faceless people, only to blink and realize he had been talking to a fluttering candle. He caught himself mumbling often, until he was too tired to speak. The void enveloped him in cold waves. Tendril whispers tortured his existence. They spoke of the peace of death, of letting go. Light, when it came from that other world, a world of warmth and tenderness, was a blessing. Light was life, darkness death.

Sad faces came and went. Voices echoed on and on, getting quieter and quieter, further and further away. The sun dreamily rose and set in the window; the stars left streaks across the sky. Rain, fog, wind. Sometimes a girl held him close. Sometimes she quietly cried. Sometimes she was gone. Shapes blurred. His body trembled constantly, or sweat, or went numb. Eventually he lost track of time, of night and day, of people. He didn't remember eating. Existence became a quagmire of impressions. He felt himself growing thinner and weaker and ever more distant …

And then he slipped into the abyss, perpetually haunted by those tendril whispers. Like a shivering child clutching a blanket, he tried to hold on to them, for those whispers were all that remained of existence. Beyond was the silent unknown. The eternal cold. The great beyond, ever calling, ever waiting …

An arc of time passed, an abstract flow like that of molasses, yet he stubbornly hung on to a hairsbreadth of conscience. Somehow, he hung on.

Then, all of a sudden, he saw a glimmer of light in the far distance. It was but a pinprick. He was shivering violently, barely hanging on.

The time to choose had come.

But was it too late? There was a noise that he could hear—a wind—and behind that wind was chanting. There was a struggle. Something beastly roared. A battle was taking place … a battle for Augum's soul. He was vaguely aware of it, but also knew he had a choice. Was he that tired of shivering that he'd willingly step beyond the abyss, to the silent unknown? Or did he want to experience again? Breathe and live and laugh and love?

The more he thought about it, the more came back to him. Memories. Voices. Faces. One face in particular called to him stronger than the others. Sharp brows. Raven hair. Freckles. Beauty.

The moment he remembered her name, he made his choice, and just like that, the sound grew to a full windy roar before abruptly disappearing.

He opened his eyes to see Leera directly over him, looking into his face—and smiling. She drew him close in a gentle embrace, weeping softly. And suddenly many others were hugging him and congratulating him for beating the arcane fever. They were so happy—unnecessarily so, in his opinion—that they heaved him onto their shoulders. He almost cracked his head on the spruce beam. What if it had knocked him unconscious? The thought made him roar with laughter. He briefly caught sight of a smoking mortar and pestle before they carried him out into the Okeke living room on their shoulders, singing *Champions of the Robe*, an old tune from the gladiatorial warlock days. Someone even pressed the pouch of coins he had won into his hands.

Almost everyone he knew in Milham was there—Mr. Goss and a happily moaning Leland, who of course held onto the Agonex; a clapping and smiling Constable Clouds and his son, Devon, who was one of the people helping Augum remain aloft; the constable's guards—the red-haired Lieutenant Briggs and his blonde stoic companion, Sergeant Cobb; Panjita Singh was there, grumbling to her daughter Priya about the noise; Haylee and a fit Chaska, smiling and dancing together; Mr. Haroun and Malaika and Charissa, singing and clapping along; even the beetle-like Prudence Klines, which was a pleasant surprise!

"… and guess who brought you back," Bridget finished saying as the crowd put him down on his feet. She took one of his arms to keep him steady lest his weak body collapse. But Augum could scarcely talk, so shocked was he that Bridget was her old self again, and looking so well-rested! And her hair was back to its cinnamon glory.

"Well guess!" Leera said, taking his other arm around her neck. She looked marvelous, face glowing, with her raven hair returned to its original state and as shiny as it had ever been.

Mouth hanging open, Augum confusingly glanced around at the jubilant faces, many wet with tears of joy; at the celebratory mead in their hands; at their expectation of him to put it all together.

"He's still in a bit of confusion," Mr. Goss said, taking a step closer. "You're very weak from the ordeal. Take your time."

"All right, enough games," Mr. Okeke said with a smile. "Let him see for himself."

The crowd parted so he could see a small and withered figure in a chair.

What was Senior Arcaneologist Lien Ning doing there—!

Then Augum felt his face go slack as it dawned on him who it was. "Nana," he blurted, stumbling as he tried to walk.

"Easy there, warrior," Leera whispered, holding onto him tightly. "You haven't got out of bed in over a tenday."

He gave her a blank look. A tenday? It had only been *that* long? He felt like he had lived a lifetime in that eternal black abyss, a lifetime of shivering and loneliness. Now here he was surrounded by warmth, light, and life! And Leera and Bridget were all right! And Nana was back! It was so overwhelming he could not help the tears from flowing freely down his cheeks.

Leera nodded as if reading his thoughts. She gently wiped his tears with her hands before kissing his cheek, whispering, "Go say hi to your great-grandmother," and the crowd went *Aww*. "Shut up," she muttered with a smiling but suddenly crimson face, helping him walk and adding, "Weak as a kitten …"

Mrs. Stone wore a white robe that flashed silver bolts of lightning, similar to the one she had worn when Augum first laid eyes on her. But other than that, she was barely recognizable. Her hands were curled inward and she looked no larger than a child. Her face was as wrinkled and shriveled as an old apple. Gone was the long silver braid—all that remained was a wispy scalp. The crowd went silent as she glanced up at him with a perpetually shaking head. Those eyes, once as clear and blue as the sky, were as distant and foggy as a rain cloud.

"Come close, my dear child," she croaked in a bare whisper. "I can hardly see you."

The girls brought him nearer, setting him down on a chair.

"My vision is not as it once was," Mrs. Stone said, staff clutched between her body and one arm. She squinted at him. "Ah, Augum … how good it is to see you, my foolishly brave great-grandson. You have grown since last we saw each other."

The crowd chuckled.

"Mrs. Stone cast Abbagarro on you," Bridget explained in a soft voice. "Remember that vortex spell Mr. Ordrid cast on her when she had arcane sickness?"

Augum nodded, still trying to wrap his head around all this. He had survived the abyss, but only barely. And Nana was back! She was back and unafraid and not running for her life!

"She also healed the rest of you," Bridget added. "But your arm was too far gone."

Augum awkwardly bent his left elbow a little. It wouldn't go all the way yet, but maybe with time … It hardly mattered. He was just happy to be alive. "And how are you feeling, Nana?" he asked.

"As well as can be expected. I am most happy to be off the road, I must say. Most happy indeed." Her face creased in a smile. "You have made me proud, Great-grandson. Mighty proud."

"We told Mrs. Stone everything," Leera said. "She's been back for a day now and made us get the ingredients for Abbagarro while she gathered her strength. It's been an exciting day."

"I was only made better yesterday," Bridget said, glancing over at Prudence Klines. "Thanks to Ms. Klines."

Mrs. Stone wheezed a chuckle. "There's a reason historically few people steal a scroll from the Antioc Library. Though I should not be one to talk, for I myself tried to get around that very limitation when I was young. But that is a story for another time."

Augum gently drew her into a hug, whispering, "It's good to see you again, Nana ..." She felt so small and fragile in his arms. Her poor body would not stop shaking. He could distinctly make out a quiet hum, emanating from the scion on top of her staff. It was right by his ear, and reminded him of the great dangers that were out there, waiting for him, for there was one battle left, a final battle for the kingdom, a battle between him and his father, a battle that he now understood he had to face.

She patted him on the back. "And you, Great-grandson. Now come, there is much to discuss."

Yes, there was, Augum thought. The legendary off-the-books spell, Annocronomus Tempusari—Cron—had aged her significantly. And she was going to teach it to them next, so they may face his father.

Mr. Okeke raised his glass. "But first we properly celebrate our brave trio. A toast to the heroes of the Resistance!"

Augum and Mrs. Stone were each given a tankard of apple mead as the crowd raised their glasses, chorusing, "A toast to the heroes of the Resistance!"

Augum found Leera's loving gaze and raised his glass as they smiled at each other. "To the Resistance."

SNUG AND SECURE

As the merry celebration got under way, with much feasting and singing, Mrs. Stone regaled them with some of her travels. She had been to every kingdom in Sithesia, as well as some well beyond the continent, unknown and unheard of by Sithesians.

"Mercy, there are some savage lands out there," she said at one point to a crowd of listeners, shaking her head. "Be that as it may, no kingdom feels like my Solia."

She also spoke about Cron. She had carried that heavy golden book the entire time, studying and practicing it when able. As Augum suspected, it was that spell that was responsible for her rapid aging. It scared him how much it had affected her, how shriveled she had become. It didn't help that throughout her recitation, she kept looking at him with sad and knowing eyes. It made him wonder what she knew, what she was not telling him, and above all, what kind of effect it was going to have on him and the girls.

"It is a most dangerous and difficult spell," Mrs. Stone said, pausing to cough. "There are complexities and subtleties you will have to learn before even attempting Annocronomus Tempusari. Even I had trouble with it." She leaned closer. "But after hearing about your adventures and your ability to self-learn, I firmly believe that you are capable of mastering it. All three of you."

"What degree is the spell, Mrs. Stone?" Bridget asked.

"Let us not worry what degree the spell is. That is not what matters. Sometimes sheer diligence gets better results than traditional constraints and requirements. However, I can say you will be studying well beyond your capabilities. It will be … arduous."

Augum swallowed. He recalled all too well the grueling times spent at the academy Trainers, especially the ones among the Spikes.

Mrs. Stone sighed. "And of course, you are aware of the sacrifices involved, which we shall discuss in greater detail when your training begins, as soon as Augum regains his strength."

"Will we be training in the 5th degree too, Mrs. Stone?" Leera asked. She was sitting beside Augum, his arm draped around her waist. They no longer hid their affection for each other. Somehow, both felt as if they had earned the right to enjoy what love they could before they died, for both feared their lives might be quite short.

"Indeed, you shall also be learning the 5th degree with me." She glanced beyond them at Jengo and Haylee. "I shall train anyone who deigns to learn the arts on behalf of the Resistance."

Augum smiled. The Resistance was now a movement even spoken of in both Heralds. But nothing felt as legitimate as hearing Mrs. Stone say it.

Ms. Singh, sitting on the other armchair nearby, shook her cane. "Panjita does not believe it is safe for ones so young to learn a spell so complex and so dangerous. They shall surely fail or die—"

Priya gasped. "*Mother,* how could you say such a thing?"

Mrs. Stone sighed a rattling breath. "I am afraid Ms. Singh is most correct. The spell is indeed dangerous. There are no guarantees. I may not live to see the end of the training even." Her cloudy gaze fell on Augum. "A dark time is coming. The Lord of the Legion has not taken your victory well. He will unleash his armies upon the innocent. Time, as always, is against us."

"Did you know about my … immunity?" Augum asked.

"I suspected it, yes, but such matters are best discovered by the bearer, I find. It is called an *ancestral gift,* and it might be one of the few advantages you possess. Your father might not know that you possess it—" She stopped to cough violently. It bent her over. People exchanged worried looks. She held up a staying hand. "I am fine, though I fear myself quite exhausted."

"Let me take you to your room, Mrs. Stone," Bridget quickly said, and helped her stand.

Mrs. Stone patted Augum's shoulder with a veined and spotted hand. "We shall begin when you have regained your strength," and shuffled by, one arm leaning on Bridget. Then she stopped, turning to look at Augum, Bridget and Leera. "I dare say the Legion are arrogant fools."

"Why is that, Nana?"

"They could have discovered us with the most elementary spell—Object Track." She smiled. "The fools never fathomed anyone would dare to steal the divining rod." She shook her head, smiling throughout, and shuffled off to bed.

Augum exchanged a smiling and relieved look with Leera. They hadn't even thought of that possibility. He didn't want to think of what might have happened if the Legion *had* tracked the powerful artifact.

The celebration went on well into the evening. During that time, Augum caught up on some news. Apparently, Mrs. Stone only teleported to Milham once she had confirmation Augum indeed snagged the divining rod from the Legion, for she had suspected a trick. Then, upon arrival—and Leera's insistence—she immediately arranged to teleport Secretary Klines over so that she may heal Bridget, for only a secretary of the library could dispel the curse with a nullification ceremony.

"After hearing about what we did, Klines is now firmly part of the Resistance," Bridget explained, taking a sip of mead.

"She and that floating chair—"

"*Senior Arcaneologist Ning*, Lee."

"Whatever, anyway, they had to answer some questions after we took off."

"As you can imagine," Bridget continued, "they handled themselves admirably, though they are under suspicion and have to be very careful."

"Still, good to have them on our side," Augum said, glancing over at Klines and raising his glass to her. Klines raised her glass in return and inclined her head, before resuming a conversation with Mr. Goss, who seemed to be badgering her with a barrage of questions.

"Oh, that reminds me," Bridget said, searching the pockets of her blue robe. "I'm going to give her an Exot ring before she teleports back," and she sped off, leaving Augum to sit with Leera.

Augum's gaze shifted to Malaika and Charissa, who hovered near Mr. Haroun, conversing with a bored-looking Haylee. "And when did they get back?" he asked.

"Took them like four days," Leera replied with a snort. "And you'll never guess—they actually returned with a mule full of clothes! You believe that? Haven't learned a thing. Almost got robbed too."

Augum waved at Mr. Haroun, who seemed all too happy to break free of the chatter of the teenage girls. He strolled over and clinked Augum's glass.

"What a pleasure to have you back, young man, and congratulations on a legendary feat. They shall talk of you in Antioc for years to come, though from what I hear, that arena fight will be talked about for as long as people have tongues."

"Thank you, sir," Augum replied, reaching into his robe and withdrawing the pouch of four hundred gold coins he had won. He handed them over. "This is for you. It's a promise I made to your daughter."

"Oh, indeed, Malaika told me about this." Mr. Haroun placed a hand on Augum's shoulder. "Every copper of this money will go to the Resistance, I assure you of that. We are all very proud of you—"

"Speaking of the Resistance, Hanad," Mr. Okeke said, drawing near with a glass of wine. "I've been meaning to talk to you about some of the evacuation plans."

Mr. Haroun nodded. "Indeed. Then let us confer with the constable. Excuse us, Augum."

As the hour grew late and Mr. Goss and Mr. Okeke sang *For Those Who Return*—a war anthem lamenting the heavy hearts of the ones that made it back with nothing but memories of those that did not—Leera turned to Augum with a sly grin.

"Guess what day tomorrow is?"

Augum barely had an idea of what month it was, let alone what day. He shrugged. "Don't know, what?"

"My *birthday*, silly!"

"Oh, right!" She'll be fifteen years old, how exciting! "What do you want for your birthday?"

She pressed his nose. "Already got it."

He gave her a wry smile. He wasn't *that* daft. "No, really—" and the pair of them bantered back and forth before melting into each other's arms in front of the fire. And that's how they sat, talking in low voices while curled up in blankets and pillows, until the celebration petered out, and candles snuffed one by one, and everyone slowly trickled off to bed, and the fire dimmed. Yet they whispered on in hushed tones, wrapped around each other, never letting go.

Augum's thoughts drifted to the days and months ahead. To the final task. He imagined himself facing his father, a man who might not underestimate them again, a man who was probably quite aware of Centarro. He wondered what that battle would look like. He knew now that it was his destiny to face him. Son against father. How many legends told of such things? And what would learning Cron be like? And then there was Leland and the Agonex. Could they somehow muster that army in a way that made a difference? So many other variables too—the Dreadnoughts; his mother's body; the Exot rings; the people joining the Resistance in droves, waiting to be led, waiting for the right moment to strike …

"Hey," Augum whispered, holding a sleepy Leera in his arms. They were the last ones awake. The fire was but coals before them.

She squirmed in his soft embrace. "Hmm?"

"Love you."

"Love you too."

FOR FANS OF THE ARINTHIAN LINE

Thank you for reading! Are you excited for more? Sign up to my newsletter for news about future releases: severbronny.com/contact

Also, honest reviews play a vital part in readers discovering new books. Please consider taking a quick moment to leave one on Amazon.com and/or Goodreads.com for *Clash*. Thank you so much, it means a lot to me :)

Fifth book

The final book in *The Arinthian Line* is titled *Legend*, which you can find on Amazon.

Advance Review Team

Want a chance to read my next book before its retail release? Consider joining my Advance Reader Team at severbronny.com/team

Contest winner

A while back I held a character naming contest exclusively for my mailing list subscribers. The winner was Michael Wigham from the UK. Michael cleverly came up with the name Caireen Lavo, but he went above and beyond by making the name an anagram. Can *you* figure out what *Caireen Lavo* rearranges to say?

Michael will be receiving a signed first edition copy of

Clash. And if anyone wants to enter future contests, just sign up to my newsletter above :)

Connect

I love hearing from readers. Want to say hello, ask a question, or report an issue? Email me anytime at severbronny@gmail.com

Or find me here:

severbronny.com
facebook.com/authorseverbronny
twitter.com/SeverBronny
goodreads.com/severbronny

My other passion: **Tribal Machine**
www.tribalmachine.com

Acknowledgments

The Arinthian Line has been in the making for years, and I couldn't have done it without the loving support of my amazing wife and editor, Tansy.

As well, a special thank you to my family, friends, my ART team, and my loyal readers for supporting my work.

Thank you for reading, and I can't wait to continue Augum, Bridget and Leera's adventures!

All my best to you and those you love,

Sever Bronny

ABOUT THE AUTHOR

Sever Bronny is a musician and full-time author living in Victoria, British Columbia. *The Arinthian Line* is his first series and an Amazon best seller. He has also released three albums with his industrial-rock music project Tribal Machine, including the full-length concept album *The Orwellian Night*. One of his songs can be heard in the feature-length film *The Gene Generation*. Connect with him at his website severbronny.com.

Made in the USA
San Bernardino, CA
15 February 2019